CHRONICLES OF TARC

546–1

SUPPORT AND SISTER

Jiryü Räsen

FIRST EDITION

PUBLISHED BY J. KASSEBAUM

This novel is entirely a work of fiction. The names, characters and incidents portrayed in it are the product of the author's imagination. Any resemblance to actual persons, living or dead, or events or localities is entirely coincidental.

February 6, 2026 First Edition.
Paperback ISBN 978-1-949359-22-0
eBook ISBN 978-1-949359-23-7
© **Jiryü Räsen**. All rights reserved.
Published by J. Kassebaum, Indianapolis.
Cover background ©Sumners Graphics via Canva.com.
#NaNoWinner2023, #CampNaNoWinner2024

CONTENTS

Travelogue

When one enters a new nation, one always comes with eyes bright to see new landscapes, tongues salivating to taste new flavors, and minds keen to learn new things undiscovered until then. Entering Ryokudo from the south by ship traveling on the Inner Sea, one begins in the bustling capital city, Ichijoutsu. Captains sigh in relief to be coming into a port that welcomes them without extra heavy fees or taxes. That makes most passengers happy as well, since it costs them less coin to travel to that city than most others on the Inner Sea coast.

The first thing one sees upon sailing up to the port are the large warehouses spread along the wharf. Well built and maintained, they show any visitor from the beginning just how booming the industry of the nation is. Not to be missed is the unique Welcome Warehouse that is full of local flavors from the many restaurants and shopping booths that fill the main level. The second and third levels are sleeping rooms, from singles to large suites, for visitors to begin their stay in Ryokudo in restful style.

Two other beautiful landmarks are seen from the Sea: the majestic mountain that stands guard over the east side of Ichijoutsu and the equally majestic white–stone castle Ichijou that sits at its feet, above the city. The castle of the king of Ryokudo is the gem of the city and nation as a whole. It rises five stories tall on average and houses all of the national administrative offices and the staff to manage them. Once–per–month tours are available to those who wish to see the inside and the many national treasures held within.

Upon entering Ichijoutsu, the city is full of happy smiles and busy citizens happy to talk to neighbor, friend, or visitor. When one sits to eat at any restaurant table, citizens can be invited over to answer any questions one may have of the city or nation. They will happily tell one that crime is low, business is booming, and they're content with life. Invariably the visitor will be regaled with stories about the beautiful Touka monarch that sits on the throne of the nation. Pale blonde hair and piercing blue eyes unlike any other mark the rulers of the nation.

In the current reign, any mention of King Sasou will have the national talking to the visitor drooling. As a young monarch still in the prime of his life many are pleased to have him on the throne. They'll eventually remember to add that Queen Aryana is just as beautiful, if not quite so pale of hair and eye. The nationals aren't any less starry–eyed for her and they highly recommend that any visitor go on the castle tour just for an opportunity to perhaps catch sight of either royal.

For an even better opportunity to see the King and Queen of Ryokudo, one could visit during the annual spring People's Day festival held on the castle grounds. The royals open up the castle for all of the citizens to freely view their own national treasures. Entertainers and food vendors are invited to set up in the Grand Promenade. The crowning event is when the royal family welcomes the visitors personally to the castle, happy to see their citizens smiling and enjoying their hospitality. Castle guards stand watch over it all to see that everyone continues to remain safe.

During the tour of the castle, one thing that stands out from all of the wondrous treasures held within is what the nation considers it's greatest treasure. Taking up the whole of the center of the edifice is the largest library in all of this part of the world. Knowledge is very obviously enshrined within the people's hearts, as it is within the capital castle. Scholars from most nations visit the Ichijou library on a regular basis to research esoteric topics. On the rare occasions something isn't known in that library, those same researchers are sent northwest to Kouzanshi university. If something hasn't been discovered there, then the researcher has perhaps found a home in which they can discover it for themselves, enriching the world as a whole themselves.

Traveling north from Ichijoutsu along the well–maintained royal highways is a joy for any traveler. The nation has made sure that there are inns at every lunch hour and every dinner hour after a comfortable travel by carriage. Private carriages can be rented in Ichijoutsu, or there are public carriages that have regular routes from main city to main city that can be used for a reasonable fee. For the budget–conscious traveler those are most useful. One can get off at any village, town, or city, visit for as long as one wishes, then one can get on the next public carriage to come through to go to the next place one wishes to visit. Schedules can be picked up at the Ichijoutsu visitors center or any town garrison along the routes.

The pastoral views as one travels north to Nijoushi or northwest to Kouzanshi calm one's mind and soul. The southern portion of Ryokudo is rolling hills of green grasses divided by small streams and a few stands of woods. Woolly sheep and horses graze in the fields. Goats and pigs are herded from woodlot to woodlot so that they're kept pristine of undergrowth and hidden herbal treasures can be found and added to the local cuisine or medical bags of the well–trained medics of the nation.

Roughly two–thirds of the way through the nation to the north runs a road that crosses the whole of the nation, from the mountains that border Brulac on the east to the deep Gash of Altherly to the west. That road is one to travel on if one wishes to see the full beauty of the natural sights of Ryokudo. On the south of that road are the pastoral farms. To the north of that road are the wild forests of the Region of Suiran. The trees swallow up the whole of the nation north of that road and boast some of the best wood for working furniture, common tools, and transportation (wagons and the like).

As one travels from the east to west along South Suiran Road, one leaves the mountains of eastern Ryokudo behind but mountains never leave one's sight. The high rugged mountains to the far north can be seen just as far hazy grey peaks from the road. When the traveler reaches the rushing Urakawa river, travel along the road is nearly complete. Only a few more days and one reaches the far West road that travels north and south along the Gash of Altherly. That natural wonder can be viewed from any village or city along West road, but the best view is just south of Kouzanshi, where the width of the Gash of Altherly is narrow enough to allow for the Grand Bridge to cross over it. A secondary foot bridge has been built attached to the Grand Bridge to allow visitors to walk over the deep ravine and look down into it safely. The Kaikawa river at the bottom of it can only be seen as glints of light in the middle of the day. The rest of the time only the roar of its passage over the boulders it holds can be heard.

There are two cities to explore in northern Ryokudo. To the east is the seat of Suiran: Nijoushi. As one travels up Castle road, the city arrives to view first. Like Ichijoutsu, it's a busy city with many contented citizens happy to welcome the visitor to the region. Some of the best artisans of the nation call that city home. Crafter's Row is not to be missed, even if the visitor only window shops.

The flavors of Suiran are different than the light delectables in Ichijoutsu, where fish is plentiful. Rather, the rugged wooded land lends to a more robust palate of flavors. Those who enjoy heartier meals will find many dishes to delight in Nijoushi. If one samples the wares of all of the restaurants of the city, the visitor will come to learn that they all compete to have the best hearty soup to beat back winter's chill with.

The region's castle, Nijou, east of the city is the seat of the Regent. Usually that throne is held by the First Prince of Ryokudo, or some other Touka relation to the King. While this sprawling castle complex doesn't have a Spring People's Day, it is open to guided pre–arranged tours. The event to see the royal Regent at is the Spring Exhibition, a week–long martial event hosted by the castle garrison. The excitement of getting to watch the graduating class of the renowned Kishi Knight's school face off against the crown's trained soldiers in their final exams is not to be missed.

Neither is the newly crowned Regent and his wife, in this current era. The young couple are just as popular with the people of the nation as the King and Queen. Young and full of energy, care, and concern for their people, Prince Rei and Princess Mizi are even more delights on the eye, according to those who've seen them. Prince Rei's Touka looks are handsome and Princess Mizi's red hair and bright green eyes make for a brilliant contrast that keep one's eyes on them longer than would be normally polite. Their long romance kept the gossips of the nation happily engaged in their work for many years before their wedding, which is still talked about by the people in the taverns and inns.

In the current era, Prince Rei is assisted at Nijou by the royal brothers' sister, Princess Ilena and her husband, Prince Ore. With Selician blood in them both, they can be missed as anything but other visitors to the nation and castle if one is looking for the Touka blonde and blue. However, one can't miss their bearing and devotion to their nation. If a visitor should chance to see them and then recognize them from their black hair and golden eyes, that visitor can count themselves very fortunate to have then seen all six young royals of the nation. Seeing the Queen Mother in her regal Touka beauty is a rarity that even the most aspiring visitor will find difficult to obtain, as she greatly enjoys her retirement in Nijou.

The northern mountains begin to loom over Nijoushi, their rugged grey rock the main skyscape of the norther border. They hold on to the winter snows at their peaks, even in the middle of summer. For those who love winter sports, this is a region to not miss during that season. Guides should be taken when exploring the mountains. The citizens will happily house you in their homes along the road if the snows should be heavier than a carriage horse can pull the carriage through in half a day. Summer travel is, again, simple with the same easy travel distances between inns, villages, and towns.

Traveling west from Nijoushi on North road, one won't see the rivers. They remain under the feet of the mountains this far north, coming out to the surface partially down in the forest of Suiran for Urakawa river. That hidden wonder of nature can be found if one travels down south along River road and then one asks a local for where to find it. That is a journey best taken by foot, as the public carriage doesn't go down that road and the river head is hidden deeply in the woods.

Kouzanshi in the far northwest is built into the rocky mountains for a simpler visit to that natural view than trying to climb their steep sides closer to Nijoushi. The seat sometimes of any tertiary royal family member, the main attraction of the city is the university. Housed in beautifully carved buildings that still maintain the dignity of scholars, this busy place of learning is well worth touring for the visitor to Ryokudo. For the scholar, it's well worth staying for the two years it takes to get a diploma. Any topic can be researched, with guidance from at least three professors who stay to continue their own work.

The library of Kouzanshi university rivals that of Ichijou castle. Copies of completed diploma dissertations are kept at both libraries so that the research of the serious student can be used to better the lives of all peoples. The stews and soups of the restaurants of Kouzanshi rival those in Nijoushi, with at least one restaurant serving them exclusively. They are a favorite of students who come out of the university only to eat and then rush back to their research. But if a visitor manages to catch one before they do, plan on being regaled with what they're researching until midnight. At which point the student will fall asleep on the table until morning, making the owner of the establishment laugh and shake their head as they cover them with a blanket, apologizing for their enthusiasm and lack of self care. For the shopping visitor, the city boasts the warmest and best made winter gear: from boots to gloves to cloaks or coats.

On the return to the warmer southern coast of Ryokudo, the visitor can stop near the southwest corner of the nation. In the main it is marshy swampland: the delta for both rivers as they leave the land for the Inner Sea. While an intriguing natural area to explore, it is the least developed area of the nation. Visitors should hire experienced guides to explore the area or risk being lost to sudden quagmire traps. The hidden thing to visit there is the "Lost" or "Forgotten" castle. It's a rugged castle near the coast used in less kind times past as a place to put wayward or unwanted royals. For a small fee, it can be toured with a staff member as a guide.

As the visitor to Ryokudo steps back onto their ship to return home, it would prove fruitful to ask the captain to make one last stop. The islands off the coast boast some of the most beautiful landscape and wildlife. While the islands can be viewed from the deck of the ship, stopping at the main city for a lunch of unique seafood and views of the birds, followed by a short visit at the artisan booths, is well worth being the final goodbye to the nation of Ryokudo: the home to knowledge, beauty, and craftsmanship.

-o-o-o-

Handwritten notes on the draft travelogue:

1) *It definitely focuses on what the nation looks like in natural wonders — even the descriptions of the royals shoves them into that bucket. Do you really want to all be considered "natural wonders" on top of "national treasures"?*

2) *FYI: I've told the west side nightwalkers to put down any rumors that hurt Nijoushi, Suiran, or Ryokudo and to butter up any visitors to the city that aren't from Brulac or Gael. When you get the final version of the travelogue finished, let me have a million copies. I'll have those that can read let everyone (nightwalker, innkeeper, and tavern keep alike) know just how "nice and friendly" they're supposed to be, and then have them hand them out to every visitor they come across. Though, they'll likely try to sell them for minimal coin. I'm about done letting all the regular businesspersons know I'm not here to extort, only pressure them to see they stick to the plan to keep visitor business booming and coin coming into the city. They haven't been upset with that at all, by the way.*

Oh, and the next meeting of the Big Four will be at the Wooden Shoe Inn. Usual time.

- The Black Ram

Princess Ilena,

I've let Russel review it. He had a lot of snide comments, not surprisingly. I think it's about as good as I can get it based on what your requirements are. I'm sure it will need plenty of editing. I'd be happy to review the final, if you wish.

- Raine Marciel

Question to ask the Department of Scribes: Does this need to be approved by Ichijou before it can be published to the public? (It is assumed this was added by Princess Ilena herself.)

1-3 Ante-Cold Solstice: Moving Forward in the New Year

First Princess Mizi sat down on the couch in her place closest to the head chair in the Lower office of Intelligence. Ilena was waiting for her in the head seat of the seating around the short but long table in the center of the room. The seating area was closer to the fireplace side of the common room of the suite. That kept it a little warmer for them in the wintertime. The coals glowed warmly red and gold. It smelled like oak was burning this morning.

Mizi took a deep breath and placed both hands on the folder in her lap. Normally she'd take the time to ask after Ilena, but this time she merely observed her until Ilena raised an eyebrow. Mizi smiled a small smile. "I've finally received a positive answer from the lord I've been communicating with. He'll grant the hospital enough land for the facilities and garden space around it, enough for two greenhouses as well. He's also allowed for well rights so that water won't be a problem. However," she swallowed, "he's asking for a higher percentage than the financial advisors have estimated for us to be able to get the loans we need to begin construction."

Ilena's expression went to sympathetic understanding. Mizi also hadn't been too surprised. "I've been asked to ask you if it would be better to send him the next letter after the Court of Ministers meeting. If I present the proposal to them and they have comments, particularly that affect financing, then I'll have to negotiate further with him anyway at that time."

Ilena considered that point. "Well, actually, yes. It very well might be good to wait until after that. Even if they don't have any financial comments, you can still use them and that meeting as an excuse to bargain with. Having the approval of a place to build is the most important thing to set up ahead of time." Her expression went wry. "They'll want to tell you which of *their* holdings you get to build on, and argue that for hours otherwise."

Mizi couldn't help the slump of her shoulders and the roll of her green eyes. "Yes. I don't need that sort of interference at all." She looked at the folder in her lap again and patted it once. "I've got the construction estimates, the location, the names of interested investors — none of them are committed yet — and the other details.

"What I need to know next is how to write up the proposal to the ministers so they'll be at least somewhat favorable to it." She sighed as she looked back up at Ilena somewhat helplessly. "I'm not sure they'll be favorable at all, and I really don't want them to just summarily ignore it, reject me, and have all of this work wasted and the facility not happen. The last time I faced them they were rather angry with me, after all."

Ilena smiled kindly. "I've received several good proposals that have gone over well in the meeting generally. I'll let you have them to review for format, organization, and depth they're wanting. Too deep is too much. Not enough information and they'll reject it on that alone." Mizi understood that.

"It's true that if they reject it merely because of who you are, they'll be rejecting you yet again personally, for all we'll hope they don't. If that does happen, you still have the option of having Ryan presenting it in three months." Mizi could feel her face fall. "It would need to be that long to make it look like Ryan had been convinced through his own research that the idea had potential, was necessary to this part of the Region, and so forth."

Mizi furrowed her brow. "If I include his opinions in those matters at the beginning, would that help?"

Ilena clasped her hands together and looked off into the distance for a little. Her tawny eyes glinted gold in the lighting of the room, like Mizi's red hair would glisten with gold in the summertime sun. "Well, yes, it might. If that part comes fairly early in the proposal, they'll get the idea that you're working under his direction. They know he has little time for such things. He might want to be there with you, then, so they can question him directly, but you don't want them to shift their whole focus to him to sideline you. You'll both want to plan that so he defers to you in almost every case except where his recommendations are in question."

Mizi nodded thoughtfully. "That sounds like that could help a lot, so we don't waste the time if they think they'll push me that direction anyway." She pondered on that, then asked, "Are there any other ways they'd try to block me that I could set preventions in place ahead of time?"

Ilena counted them slowly as she considered it. "You've got the financial, construction, site, reason. If Ryan is there to back up the reason with his professional opinion that helps there." She pulled slowly on her long black braid as she thought. "You've already got people you're thinking of placing in the important positions?"

Mizi hesitated. "I have some people's names, but I haven't asked anyone yet. Many are in Kouzanshi and Rei has yet to decide when we can go."

Ilena gave a nod. "That's something you'll need to have comments on. Names, when you're expecting to have them accept, and alternatives. If you want, setting that part up so that they tell you by when you need to have the answer to that issue is the way to go there. Giving them slight holds of power like that one helps to settle them quite a lot. If you have all of the answers and they just get to say yes or no, you'll often get a no because they want to have more say than that. That would be a good place to let them. You don't have to hire the people they offer as suggestions, but you do have to honestly interview them, or have Ryan do it as a more neutral person, or they'll cry foul."

Mizi understood that. She'd already been in a few meetings like that. Rei always allowed for some wiggle room in the things he presented as well. Ilena continued, "I think if you read the example proposals, you'll see the other things that they look for. You can decide which ones you can leave somewhat open for them to poke at to feel important and which ones you'd rather close up tight so they don't take over in places they shouldn't." She turned to Leah and named three projects. Leah reached for a stack of folders on her secretary's desk and hunted until she'd found them. Tanner took them from her to hold for Mizi until she had time to review them.

Mizi turned to her next topic. "It's been suggested that it's time for me to face off against opponents when I'm practicing my hand–to–hand self defense. Justinian was suggested and he thought he might be able to help, but I don't want to take him away from his duties every morning. Nor am I sure an opponent is necessary for every practice. I wanted your advice on it as well, since you're my first teacher of self defense."

Ilena was looking at Justinian. "And your opinion on your capabilities at this time?" Ilena asked him. Mizi didn't know much about Justinian's level of understanding, but she knew he'd been practicing the same castle self defense form she was learning since he'd come to the castle several years before.

Justinian walked over to the sitting area to be polite and bowed to the two princesses. He took a deep breath. "Petroi and Thayne said I should decide if I could. I've been considering it. I do need to practice having restraint. Learning it at the greater levels first would be good. I'm sure I'd be so afraid of hurting Mistress Mizi that I'd have a *lot* of restraint. She's not someone I want to hurt nor am I afraid of her in that way."

"And if one of her clumsy attacks gets through to hurt you?" Ilena asked, her eyes narrowing just a little.

Justinian considered that. "I'd probably hold her hand or pause the fight until she knew she was in control again. I think that might take practice for my head to be calm about since it might put me into automatic teaching mode, but I don't think I'd become angry and retaliate." He took another deep breath and said, "If you're willing to let me try, I'd like the opportunity to practice and help Mistress Mizi."

Ilena's golden eyes wandered into thought again. "I think..., we'll want someone there from our Ministry to watch you the first few times at least, just to make sure so we don't get into trouble." Her eyes wandered back to Mizi's. "Take Delia to the practices with you. Maybe she can bring Ryan to practice with you as well so you have another person to spar against that's learning a different style. Not very many people who come against you will know the style you're learning, so that sort of practice is good for you as well." Ryan was another novice at learning hand–to–hand combat and so might need that sort of practice as well, Mizi understood.

Mizi rather liked that idea since it would be more time to work with her senior in the Medical department in ways other than on the hospital and intern testing. "I wouldn't mind sparing with Ryan, but we meet rather early in the morning which would be hard for him. I'll talk to Delia about it and ask her to come." That wasn't hard since Delia was her hairdresser. Mizi turned to Justinian. "Is there a particular day or days that work for you to come?" Justinian considered it and answered her with three options. "I'll suggest those days to my instructors and let you know." Justinian bowed and took himself back to his chair on the wall near his bedroom door, next to Reynold's desk.

Mizi had a thought. "When's the next Court of Ministers meeting? How much time would I have to prepare?"

Ilena chuckled a little. "Today, this afternoon."

"Oh, right," Mizi remembered now that had been on Rei's schedule.

"So in a week, or a week after that," Ilena answered for the more reasonable timing for being prepared.

"Okay. I'll set the goal to be ready for next week. Ah..., but how much before the meeting should the proposal be in the hands of the ministers?"

"I like to receive them three days in advance if at all possible, so I can fit reading them into my schedule. Two days is okay if it's a short and concise report. Lots of detail and I'd rather have it at least a week in advance. I think yours isn't going to have that much detail this time. If you want to give an updated detailed report before actually beginning construction, or a review after construction is over and you're looking for more funding, particularly from the Region, then that one should be given one or even two weeks before your presentation."

Mizi thought the timing in those cases made sense. "Thank you," she said. "And have you been resting enough and getting enough time out–of–doors?" She made the usual medical checkup last for this meeting. Mizi was the medic for the royals and Ore and Ilena's mistress so took this part just as seriously as she did any task given to her to do.

"Yes, Mistress Mizi," Ilena answered humbly. "Enough people here need to run as well on a regular basis that we've been taking time out each day to relax with physical exercise before each lunch. The Twins grew up in Kouzanshi so we're enjoying the snow and how it's different here than up in the heights of the mountains. It's wet enough here to pack very well into snowballs." She grinned and Mizi glared at her slightly until she ducked her head a little. "We don't fight to injury, just enough to get our blood flowing and warm up. Then we run to keep in shape until the horses are done racing us and demand we ride for at least a little bit."

Mizi sat up in surprise at that thought. "How are the Tarc horses doing in the snow here?"

Ilena laughed. "They quite like it actually. Except when it gets hard to find the grass under snow that's melted and frozen into ice. Then they show up at the gate and complain to the guards. The guards have finally stopped calling for us and just ask Rio to send to the stables that they need hay and grain delivered again." She tipped her head and added, "I think the horses might be learning to follow the stablehands back to the stables. They've come less frequently of late to bother the guards and Rio."

Mizi smiled. The short, sturdy Tarc horses were rather intelligent. She wouldn't be surprised if they were following the food back to its source. "Well, that's good, then. And how are you and Ore getting along now that he's more frequently back in the Rose office?"

Ilena sighed slightly. "We miss hearing him, Petroi, and Thayne on a regular daily basis from upstairs. Evenings are more close since we all need the time together, but Ore and I are still taking our couples time to be just us." She smiled. "It sometimes means we stay up later than we should since we want to talk to everyone we're missing, but it's been okay. I've made us take an afternoon off once per week since two weeks ago for that reason, too, so we can spend the time together just resting with each other. That's been helping our state of mind and our ability to work with more usefulness the rest of the time." Winters in Suiran rather required dutiful, conscientious vacation times.

Mizi sighed and relaxed. "That's good then. I've also been trying to remember to take some time each week to just be with my household. I think it's helping some." She'd complained to Ilena and Ore that she wasn't feeling very close to her staff and guards and they'd pointed out she wasn't taking much time to just get to know them and become friends with them.

"That's good," Ilena leaned back in her chair and relaxed a little as well. "And are you and Rei taking the time to relax together?"

Mizi wrinkled her nose. "I've been glad we set that into the schedule earlier. The rides together are brisk now that it's winter, but they help immensely. We're both so focused on things that are important that we need that and our morning practices to remember we exist to each other." She agreed with Ilena's grimace. "If I forget to slow down sometimes he'll stop me, but most of the time he's using me to keep going, so I'm having to remember it for us."

"That's a good thing to practice," Ilena encouraged her.

"Yes," Mizi agreed and rose to her feet. "Please continue to take care of yourself, Ilena," she requested.

"I will," Ilena promised. "And you as well. You're doing very well."

"Thank you." Mizi accepted Ilena's bow of the head and left the Lower office, relieved to once again be helped forward in her goals. It really did help her to have these meetings with Ilena.

Having Ore in the office more helped her, too, since she'd been missing him and now could visit with him a little there each day, too. She did think that the next time she and Rei went riding, she might try to see if he'd play in the snow with her. That sounded like a very good way to relax. He'd already suggested they take a sleigh ride as their next fun activity other than practicing horseback riding. Snuggling together under blankets sounded delightful to her, too.

-o-o-o-

Ryan sighed at the work in front of him. It was good that Mizi's push to get things done was helping him keep on track. It didn't help all that much that she kept being distracted by the financial things Ilena was having her work on. He needed her to help him with the advertising of the positions they needed to fill in the Department of Medicine. While it was probably a simple thing generally, he was really struggling with writing up the advertisement. He wished he'd kept one from Ichijou. His mentor Parmenia's description had been too vague and another round of letters would take too long.

Tap, tap. Ryan looked up to see Delia at the doorway smiling at him, her hand dropping from having knocked on the doorframe to get his attention. She was beautifully put together as always, being the First Princess' hairdresser. Her black hair was up in pretty curls pinned with delicate decorated hairpins, as if she was trying to bring some of the summer life into her winter day. "You seem a bit lost at the moment," she said. "Are you ready for today's practice?"

Ryan's eyebrows went up in surprise, then he slumped. "Yet again I'm distracted. It's a bit different this time, though." He frowned at the page in front of him.

"You're sitting up to the table this time," Delia teased as she walked over to see what he was doing.

"Well, that's true," Ryan smiled. "It's not helping me think better, though."

"Oh?" She was kind to let him talk about it.

"I'm trying to write up the advertisement for the intern openings here in the Medical department. While I helped with Ichijou's last one before I came here, that was about four years ago. Besides our needs aren't exactly their needs."

Delia read over it. "What's different?"

Ryan told her, needing to give his long–winded answer, hoping it would help him narrow it down to the single page he needed it to be. A half–page would be better.

"Well, what about...?" Delia thought it through and gave him a summary of one part of it. Ryan wrote it down.

They kept up that pattern until it was at least one page's worth. Then Ryan worked hard to edit it down to the half–page he wanted. When it was finally completed, he smiled at her shyly. "Thank you. I'm sorry to use up our practice time with that."

"Oh, it's okay," Delia waved a hand. "I know it's hard to focus when distracted, and I'd rather you were focused for the practice."

"Is it okay, to go ahead with it now that I've already kept you?" Ryan asked, concerned.

"Sure," she smiled at him. "I'm sure that a break for a physical work–out would help you come back to it fresh to make sure it's what you really wanted to say."

Ryan hopped off his stool. "You're right. Thank you for the help." She didn't say anything as she handed him his cloak then led him out of the department wing. They walked to the most open greenhouse where they'd taken up practicing while it was winter cold outside. The exercise did help him quite a lot.

When they were done and Ryan was resting, Delia commented, "You seem to have better stamina now than before. You only had to pause to rest once in the middle."

"I think so, too," he agreed. "It's nice to not feel so worn out just with sitting to my table, too."

"Justinian contacted me yesterday. He'll be helping Mistress Mizi with practices so she has a partner, but he won't be able to do it every day that she practices. We were wondering if you'd be willing to be a sparing partner for her, too, so that you both get the practice of sparing with others. It's a different style, though."

Ryan hesitated. It sounded rather large, actually. "Well, do you really think I'm ready?"

"We could give it a try. Even once a week would help you both to understand how to approach others. Most people you're going to have to protect yourself from won't be using the same style." Delia tried to be encouraging.

Ryan considered it. "Is it at the same time?"

"No. She practices in the early morning, so I'd come get you after helping her get ready for the day."

Ryan relaxed a little. "Well, if you're willing to come get me. I have almost as much trouble knowing when to wake up as when to do anything else." He smiled at his joke.

Delia kindly smiled back. "Okay. I'll let you know which day after we finish setting up the practice schedule." Ryan gave a nod. He already felt awkward about facing off against Mizi. She wouldn't be someone he'd ever fight. But, maybe if it was just two novices trying to help each other get stronger that would be fine. And maybe on those days they could come back to the department together. Likely his work brain would have woken up by the end of the practice and he'd already have comments or questions for her.

-o-o-o-

Airn Roland, Second Prince of Altherly, drew in a breath. Truly the dreary cold winters of northern Ryokudo weighed one's shoulders down. "I think it's time to be with people who are actually interesting," he stated to his aide Lord Erlic Yetherly and his guard Sir Ian Ulmer, "or I'm going to sleep without waking up in this boring garrison from now until the sun shines again." He'd been caught in it on his slow traversal of North road from Kouzanshi to Nijou by the snow storm that had lasted over a week already.

He'd actually been a bit reluctant to leave Kouzanshi. Practicing at the betting lists there had been exciting and a much preferred way to live life than in boring political studies. It had been the response letter from his royal Father that had pushed him to leave Kouzanshi. King Roland had been more open in that letter than he'd been before Airn had run away from the castle. *"Gael has become more determined to move from negotiations to actual war. You can return and learn how to supervise at a field infirmary, or you may go to Nijou and learn what the royals of Ryokudo can teach you. Perchance there will be a throne and home to return to if King Ryokudo will aid us."*

Airn had held that letter in his hand for some time, too stunned to process it at first. There had been some concern about Gael before he'd left, but he hadn't been paying too much attention to it since his sixteenth birthday had been practically ignored. The funny feeling in the pit of his stomach had made him squirm inside. He hadn't wanted to admit that war brewing would have made his father and brother be very abbreviated about birthdays. It made his running away seem very petty now. He'd wondered as he held that letter if he could face the young royals in Nijou. Based on the one time he'd talked to them, he was quite sure that pettiness didn't impress them.

He sighed at himself again. He hadn't impressed them regardless, other than to come out on top of the "regulars" at the fighting list. They'd implied that was expected of someone of his station, however. He scowled and rose to his feet. He led his men to the garrison commander's office and the aide he'd been assigned as his contact with that office. "Please teach me how to survive this winter weather if I want to travel in it. I need to be moving on to my destination." He was more than half–way to Nijou and wanted to be where he wouldn't have to worry about snow anymore.

He got blinked at like he was crazy, but the aide did eventually rise to his feet, go and put on his winter gear, and walk with Airn to stand on the garrison wall that faced towards Nijou. The aide pointed up towards the pale grey sky with the falling lightly swirling snowflakes around them. "This is snow that will fall for a long time, just like it has been. You know because the sky is light. When it becomes dark and the flakes fall thickly enough you think it's suddenly become night, three feet of snow will be on the ground in less than an hour and your horse will lose the road in that same amount of time. You'll have about four hours to death and we won't find you."

Airn swallowed. "If I run when it starts, can I reach the next village or garrison?"

"Usually, but going that way the clouds catch you unawares because they're coming up behind you. If you look up before the snow gets heavy and you see the darker clouds behind you, you'll have just enough time to start the run. Don't lose the roadway, though, and do stop at the first sign of people you see, even if it's a common house. Anyone will give you hospitality for that reason, but they'll also expect some form of service for it, or payment." That sounded reasonable, and kind. "If you're only a half–hour away from where you've just left, turn around and go back. That's much closer and safer. *Never* travel at night." Airn gave him a nod that he'd heard and understood.

The aide pointed to Airn's feet next. "You're fortunate you come from the west. You've got the best boots and coats for the weather." He'd bought them in Kouzanshi not having brought winter clothing from home. He'd wondered that the boots in the store had been at minimum knee high and on average thigh high. Since then the depth of snow that fell in this area had shown him why. "Your horse needs the same. You can't run your horse constantly when it's this cold, or the sweat freezes and then they do, too. Alternate the run with a walk to keep them at a temperature they can live at. Getting off and walking if you have to run too hard helps some, and keeps your own legs from freezing. They'll go numb and you won't know you're a cripple for life until you get off at your destination and discover you can't walk anymore.

"Most who have to move in weather like this will start with a slow warm–up trot, then run for about an hour. After a cool-down trot they'll get off and walk for about a half–hour, then repeat that cycle. Water yourself and the horse before beginning the repeat. You'll both be dehydrated in that amount of time, making you both mind–sick. That's another death trap when forgotten. But don't eat snow or eat ice, only drink water you've been carrying on your person to keep it thawed. Putting frozen water into you freezes the inside just as surely as it does the outside." He slightly glowered at Airn until he indicated he'd understood and would remember.

The aide turned to study the sky to the west. "There's no predicting if this is a snow that will end in blue sky for a day or so, or if the heavy snow is coming behind it. Sometimes a message comes and the messenger can tell us what he saw following him here, but that news will only be good for about half of the daytime at best." His eyes returned to blink at Airn and study him soberly. "There are a few old folks that have learned how to predict it based on what their joints tell them. I've yet to see any of them be wrong, regardless of if it's myth or not. If one of them speaks up at the inn before you leave it again, don't ignore their warning. Being bored someplace you don't like is better than being frozen."

Airn tried not to be impatient and gave him a curt nod. The aide turned away to head back inside, shaking his head. "Why they told you to move only in the snowy season, I'm sure I don't understand," he muttered to himself.

Airn knew slightly why, having heard their own words. He wasn't sure protecting himself from the vague possibility of other nations being threats was worse than moving through the winter snows, so he wasn't sure why they'd wanted that either. He was just as suspicious about if the four who'd claimed to be the young royals of the nation really were. He wanted to see them in their claimed environment of the castle to have it proven to him, and he was still going to ask lords of the castle if it was true.

Airn took himself to the stables next to ask questions of the bored person there about how to keep water for himself and his horse melted while out on the road in winter weather. And to learn how to put the winter blankets and shoes on the horses. He learned then that the garrisons were required to keep the roads plowed to the best of their ability, explaining one reason why they all had large draft horses in the garrison herds, not just the battle–trained ones.

After pondering on it for a bit, he asked if he could earn a portion of the cost for winter horse gear by going out with the plow group until the next clear day. He'd go as far on that day as this garrison plow went, then continue on his way. That seemed to be a safer start to the next leg of his trip, and gave him something to do daily that would be practice.

-o-o-o-

Amber walked up to Marcus, trying very hard to not be nervous. It was hard to find the balance between what she'd known before being brought into the Ministry of Intelligence offices and what they actually wanted out of staff instead of Agents.

It was made worse because Ilena hadn't kept it secret that she'd brought Amber in so Marcus could see if she'd make a reasonable wife for him.

"Marcus," she said, trying to be herself without being too much like the young ladies of the court, "could we go into town for a lunch or dinner away from the office? I really need to get out of the castle for a while. The snows and walls are making me claustrophobic." She brushed her curly brown hair out of her face with one hand, but couldn't help clenching at her skirt with the other. It was a reaction both to approaching him directly and because of bringing up the topic of her winter claustrophobia.

Marcus blinked his grey–blue eyes at her as he looked up from his writing work. He and Henry had a little of that to do every day, like all of the Ministry of Intelligence staff did, for all they did more listening and memorizing. "Sure, I guess. We should be able to get out but won't the trip to Falcon's Hollow be sufficient?"

Amber shivered. "Well, maybe, but we'll just be going there, then shut up again, then come back. I need to breathe." The monthly requirements to Ore's county were a nice break in the schedule, sometimes, but it was still winter. The manor home was smaller than the castle, if larger than their wing in the Royal Aide's building.

Marcus gave an understanding nod. "Maybe we can do lunch today. I'll ask Mistress Ilena."

A relieved Amber thanked him, then continued on to add a couple of logs to the fireplace. She'd taken to doing that to get some movement to her days and because her corner of the room went coldest first. No one had minded, nor complained about the heat, so she'd kept doing it. It had kind of been her test to see if she'd be treated like Justinian was if she just started to do something. She'd been a little surprised that she had been. Everyone had given her pleased looks for stepping in to do something that needed to be done without asking, and since then had just let her do it.

It had been surprising to her that going from the active days of being a maid of the castle — sweeping, dusting, washing, and such like — to the inactivity of being one of the staff of the Ministry of Intelligence was having such a negative impact on her mental health. She could barely sit still on any day now. She often wished she could still have a broom in her hands to at the very least sweep the room and the upper corners just for something to do.

Amber had been relieved when Rio had allowed that they could spar together for exercise and practice. That had seemed a good step for them and their partnership generally, too, since they were supposed to be spending time learning how to be partners. It helped that she didn't hate Rio enough to want to kill her anymore. But the sparring only happened for a short time in the mornings, while Ore and Ilena got ready for their day after Rio set out their clothes and drew their bath. By mid–day Amber was needing more activity again, and by mid–afternoon she was wanting to scream lately.

Ilena gave the four of them the lunch off, saying she'd eat with Rei and Ore. That meant they had to walk her to the Rose office, but that was on the way towards town, so that was okay. Somehow Amber couldn't be surprised Marcus had assumed that all four of them would go, for all she'd sort of hoped it might could be just the two of them. That was probably too much to expect just yet.

-0-0-0-

Rio held her cloak closely around her, her nose wrinkling up at the snowflakes that fell on it and her cheekbones and melted coldly on them. "Really," she muttered. "How do any of you wish to go out into this just to get out of the house?"

Amber's eyes came around to hers in almost a panic. Rio drew in a breath and held up her hand. "Sorry," she said contritely. "I know my life was very different." Amber gave an emphatic nod. Rio hadn't ever been allowed to leave one small room. The outside world was more than she could stand most of the time. "I wasn't ever cold, wet, or exhausted just by walking everywhere." She teased herself to say it.

Amber shivered. "And until I was working for Mistress Ilena, I was always in motion and all over the castle all the time. I've *never* had to sit still in one small room all the time in my whole life!"

Henry snorted at both of them. "And we were never shut in unless it was winter with the bullies who beat up on us the whole time because a pairing is always believed to be rich. ...Which is the opposite of the truth every time."

Marcus nodded in agreement. "Sitting still is very hard in the wintertime when one's used to activity. Is it being so hard, Amber?" he asked sympathetically.

She nodded emphatically again. "I'm about to go insane. Do you think I could have a broom in the corner to use when it's the worst?"

Rio laughed at her. "No, that would distract Mistress Ilena far too much. If you used it in the main hallway, though."

Amber actually seriously considered that. "That might give me enough exercise to be able to settle down again. I don't know why I hadn't thought of that."

Rio looked at her a little more soberly. "Because you got caught in the small one–room trap. I'd rather not think of anything beyond that. I'm surprised you don't."

Amber took a breath and seemed to settle a little. "Yeah. I wonder why not? I keep dreaming of the castle as a whole, but I've cleaned enough halls as an excuse to be inside in the winter...." She drifted off for a bit, then said, ruefully, "Because they were the worst as people tracked in the wet snow and just as often the mud in the early and late times when the ground was still freezing or was just thawing." She shuddered. "And after spring thaw is awful. I think I'll go back to being happy I can lord it over the other maids that I don't have to deal with that mess this next spring."

At that they all teased her mercilessly, but she enjoyed strenuously defending herself, it seemed to Rio. The non–painful arguments to get the stress out of their systems had been something she'd noticed Ilena was making them practice during their whole–family weekly breaks. They were to keep them short and not get into real angry arguments, but it was better than using physical violence. Once the verbal stress was out they could work out physically without hurting each other.

Rio was relieved when they finally reached the place Marcus and Henry were walking them to. As she removed her hood from her head, she was surprised to find a young person standing in front of her. The earnest face looking up into hers had large dark eyes that seemed to be judging her. She blinked back at them. "Welcome, I guess," the person said.

Rio raised an eyebrow, then lifted a corner of her lips. In the local whisper of Mother's Family, she scolded slightly, *Just because I'm not Mother, I'm not very welcome?* She was quite sure Henry and Marcus had been recognized immediately upon entering this place. Everyone knew them and that they followed Ilena.

The youngster jumped to attention, then bowed. "I'm very sorry, First Daughter." It had been a test to see if her voice was actually heard here in town and would be recognized. It had worked well.

Rio reached out her hand to rub the head bowed before her briefly, making herself do it since she knew touch was important, even though she herself found it difficult. "Can we please have the warm table? I'll take closest to the fire so the rest can at least breathe."

"O–of course!" The youth hopped to obey, leading them to an empty table near the fireplace. The room wasn't very busy but still held people talking and eating. The youth judged them all one more time once they were seated. "Why're you here together?" His eyes looked at Amber most suspiciously.

Somewhat humbly for her, Amber said, "I needed to get out of the office. Since Mother's put me with First Daughter, she had to come or she wouldn't have. She's kind to. Marcus and Henry were willing to come with us to keep us company."

The dark eyes went a bit wide and looked at the four of them again. He wrinkled his nose and said, "You're going to start getting teased for going out on dates. What do you want?" He listed off what foods and drinks were available that day. They placed their orders and were rather relieved when he left to go get them.

"The oblivious uninhibited young," Marcus said dryly. "And it would be worse if it was just one of us with one of you." Henry and Rio both shivered. "The problems with being known by everyone in a small town. The rumors go wild with just one thing that anyone thinks is suspicious. I wonder if that's why Mistress Ilena makes us all go out together? It's a lot harder to create rumors that way."

Nijoushi was the largest city in Suiran, it being the second seat of the Toukas and Nijou the castle of the Regent. Marcus was referring to the numbers of people in the city who were in Ilena's daywalker spy network, called the Family. The Family members liked to gossip just as much as they passed on information. Ilena made them differentiate the two clearly, however. It would be very bad to have gossip believed as truth.

Marcus put his chin in his hand, his elbow up on the table. "I wonder if we could create our own rumors the way we wanted to? We could send out the two of you on your own and you could gossip about us. We could start gossiping about you two, and then we could play games with their minds that confuse them terribly about who's interested in who. Then we'd send you two out with Petroi and Thayne and break their hearts because then they'd believe you're really in love with the Older Brothers. We'd get a lot of sympathy and free drinks, then." He grinned as the others roundly scolded him. Not one of them could keep the red blushes off their faces or necks.

Rio shivered inside. She'd never be able to go out to a place like this with just Amber, Petroi, and Thayne. It scared her so much to even think of it, for all she knew they were her protectors. To have to sit under the older brothers' scrutiny with only the small weak Amber at her side was more than she could bear. She wanted to reach out to hold Henry's little finger to chase away that fear, but because of the topic she didn't dare. He'd reject it anyway after that terrible tease.

"Marcus!" She had to scold a little more to get the fear out of her. "Please don't say such terrible things. You know I'd never survive having to have Petroi's cold glare directed my way for that long. I'd be a fainting wreck by the time we made it to a place like this and have to be carried back, then nursed by Mistress Ilena for days until I believed I was worth being kept alive again."

She was blinked at by all three others. "Is that really how you see him, Rio?" Henry asked quietly. Rio pulled her head into her shoulders and nodded at him.

"Hmm," Marcus mused, "but no one else does, except maybe Mistress Ilena. Everyone else loves him because he's so gentle and mild. He really does care for others, you know."

Rio looked down at her intertwined fingers a bit miserably. "I know," she said softly. "I just can't. I've had to work hard to get to where I don't get frightened every time he enters the room. I can do that now, but I still can't look him in the eyes. When I do, I still see what I expect to see, even if I know it's not truth." She sighed. "I'm working on that because I do want to see the kind I feel from him when he does talk to me, but even that's pretty rare." It wasn't often they had time to interact since they had such different duties. It was an old fear from her childhood, so was hard to erase because of that, too.

Henry was studying Rio. "I think we might need to make that opportunity happen more at the family days off, then. I'll let him know he needs to work on that properly. You should be able to at least be with him." She looked up at him, desperately wishing to tell him not to, knowing she shouldn't and couldn't. He pursed his lips, then said quietly, "Rio, if he's the only one near you, the only one who can protect you and only if you're close, you need to be able to stay in his protection until you're both safe again. For all of us."

Marcus had a frown furrow on his forehead. "Actually, we need to do that for Justinian and Reynold, too. I think they got far during the Tarc stuff, but I'm not sure they've settled properly yet either." He looked away, then said, "I'll take it to Mistress Ilena. Maybe she can think of a game we can play next time that would help everyone with that." His frown changed slightly but Rio couldn't tell why. She sighed. All three of them had been children abused by the Doll House, a nightwalker House that Ilena and Sasou had taken down. It was a shame Petroi looked so much like the Head of that House, the Dollmaker. They weren't anything alike.

A game might be good. Ilena was good at making lessons fun through that method. Still, Rio was just as happy that Amber turned the topic. She was glad Amber was good at that. It had been learned as a court game thing, which none of their household had much patience for, but it helped in even their more honest conversations.

-o-o-o-

Ilena sat up straight in some excitement. That wasn't an expected thing when she was being read to from a dry proposal. Her staff recognized it, though. She'd heard something to lead her to a treasure she wanted. When Reynold asked Justinian about it, Justinian shook his head, not knowing. Marcus walked over to let them know, since they wouldn't see it often. "Oh!" Justinian whispered. "Yes," he changed his mind to Reynold. "She looked at me like that right after I came the first few times I said things she liked." Reynold nodded thoughtfully and wrote a note about it on his papers on his desk. Since Justinian's title in the House of the Queen of Night was "Queen's Treasure", he'd get that connection very quickly.

Marcus smiled at them both and returned to his place. He was standing this afternoon. Compared to how much he and Henry had run as nightwalker kids in Kouzanshi, he was getting so lazy here in Castle Nijou, doing all the sitting and standing still. He and Henry helped Ilena as her Assistants in the Surian Ministry of Intelligence and were her personal guards, so he *was* working. He'd finally decided to spend more time up on his feet at least, and often worked out a bit in corners very briefly unless Ilena and the others were very engaged in their work. Then he could do more physical activity. It wasn't uncommon. Winters had been like this even in Kouzanshi.

They waited patiently for Ilena's secretary Leah to finish reading out loud the proposal for the repair of the Nijoushi south wall. When she was done, Ilena asked a few questions to make sure she'd gotten everything understood right and placed in order, then sat and reviewed what she wanted to say. Marcus shadowboxed while Ilena did that, but stood quietly respectful again when she started dictating her summary report to Prince Rei, followed by her recommendations.

Ilena turned to Marcus and Henry (who'd been sitting while working). Marcus figured he'd be picked to run the message to Rei since he was the most unable to sit still. "Henry, Marcus, you'll go into town after dropping off the summary. I want you to watch the process they say they'll use to repair the wall and bring back your opinions of it. I want you to see past examples of what they've done and see if it's really durable. We can use this a lot of places. It will cut their construction time by three-fourths and their costs to a mere fraction of what they should have asked us for.

"We leave in four days for this month's requirement to Falcon's Hollow. I want a meeting with them to see it with my own eyes and to have one of their men who researched the methods to go with us to the County. We've a need there it might be just the right answer to." Henry rose to his feet and bowed with Marcus. Marcus was just as happy to be given the larger research job, not just the paige job today.

"Is that always the next step?" Reynold asked them quietly as they dressed for the winter day.

"Yes," Henry answered as his scarf was finally wound around his neck, his hat having been put on first. "We're her researchers to see if the treasure is really a treasure."

Justinian suddenly was up out of his seat and holding onto Henry's arm, looking up into his eyes earnestly, the only thing that could be seen that wasn't covered up. "I really *am* a treasure, then. *You're* the one that opened the door to the carriage and...," he turned to look into Marcus' eyes. "You were the driver?"

Marcus smiled at the Second Prince's young manservant. "Yes. You were the package we were delivering through our message and delivery service business. The woman who bought you was one of Mistress Ilena's Agents."

Justinian teared up and threw his arms around both of them. "Thank you," he said around the tears in the back of his throat. They gave him kind pats on his back until he let them go and wiped his eyes.

"That was fun," Marcus said to Henry as they left out the glass doors to go over the roofs since Marcus very much needed the exercise and just walking on the ground wasn't going to do it.

Henry glanced at him. "Not often the package says, 'thanks', nope." He was laughing.

Marcus laughed back. "Nope. But he really has been a greater treasure than we would've guessed back then."

"True," Henry agreed as they jumped from the castle wall to the first building on the pathway to the Rose office.

"It was really something to watch him turn into the hunter last month," Marcus mused. "I caught that clue when he shied away from the pick-up person, then wouldn't let the traitor guard even think of moving. He told me he'd killed the pick-up, but that he didn't think it would be terrible since he smelled so bad." He glanced at Henry significantly as they ran down the roof of the second building on their path. "I could just barely make out the scent he was talking about under the usual unwashed man smells we're used to. Like Mistress Ilena, the Treasure said that he 'reeked'. I couldn't not test it."

"Well," Henry shrugged after the landing on the fourth roof, "she wanted that hunt as bad as he seemed to, so it was a good catch."

Marcus agreed. They turned for the roof of the crosswalk and took it as silently as possible and as quickly as possible once they were sure there weren't any observers. "What've you been thinking of for the business now that she wants us to expand into the Tarc horse messengering service with employees, of all things?" He wasn't surprised at Henry's roll of the eyes. While they were partners, and thus partners in that business, Henry wasn't much of one to bring others into anything they did. Ilena's long term goals there were rather important, though. "Would you want us to stay as owners of it, or give that over to someone else?" That's what Marcus really wanted to know.

Henry was quiet for the next drop to ground and climb up to a roof that the jump was too far for. "I've been thinking about that," Henry said. "I've been trying to from the business side, anyway. We aren't businessmen — at least I'm not. I think you could handle the hiring and training, and I could easily bring in the work and advertise, but can you deal with that level of responsibility on top of the ones we already have here?"

Marcus pondered on that for the next run and jump. He paused there on the royal office building roof until they'd been acknowledged by the roof guards. He still didn't move. "It's why I asked. I was thinking you wouldn't want to manage it. We could ask Mistress Ilena to do it but she has even less time than we do. I keep thinking there has to be some other way to run it than the normal way. I keep seeing what we did: run messages in Kouzanshi with the other nightwalker boys. They were competition, but none of us could've run all the messages all the time. It took all of us — especially when the lords all came for the conference. Not to mention that's who we're most likely to hire because that's what they know how to do, and do well if we pick right."

Henry looked at Marcus with wide eyes. "Actually..., we might be able to work something like that out. Not only do they know how to do the running, they know how to do it responsibly and solo or partner like we do. Could they be hired to be their own boss? Like we were all hired in town? They're just running exclusively for us. ...Or as part of their own business?"

Marcus frowned and shifted a bit. "Well, ..." He glanced at the guard watching them, then said, "Let's finish this run and talk about it on the way into town." They'd always prided themselves on being the fastest runners without delays to their deliveries and here they were doing just that.

Henry agreed and they dropped down to the new secondary balcony of the Rose office and entered as quickly as possible to keep the cold out of the office but then didn't move. "Master Rei, summary from Mistress Ilena. May we enter?"

They got called up to the front of the office with a finger, but Rei didn't look up from his work until the fiercely waggling pen finally paused. They waited by the door until he did look up, politely unwrapping their scarves so he could properly identify them. He blinked at them when they did finally walk up. "Thanks."

"No problem," Henry answered. "We'd rather you really knew it was us than die. And if you know we work by that pattern, you know whom to not trust."

Rei leaned back in his chair and gave them a small smile. "True enough."

"It's the summary and recommendations for the south wall renovations," Marcus said as he handed the report folder over. "Mistress Ilena was excited by it so we're being sent into town to talk to them about it next. She says they think they can cut the costs significantly. We're to confirm that."

Rei gave the report a suspicious look as he took it from Marcus and set it as the third report in a short stack. "And I assume she'll confirm it herself if it looks promising?"

"Yes," Marcus reassured him. "In four days on their way to Falcon's Hollow."

Rei's eyebrow went up. "And she was going to tell me that was on the schedule when?"

Marcus felt his face fall. They both bowed. "We're sorry, Master Rei," Henry said. "We'll let her know she's forgotten, but it's our fault for not remembering for her."

Marcus paused, then asked quietly, "Master Ore didn't tell you?" Rei shook his head. "We'll confirm that as well." That would've been Petroi and Thayne's to remember to remind Ore about. He'd been working in the Rose office regularly so they'd assumed he'd told Rei.

They were excused and immediately returned to the back door to let themselves back out into the cold. It didn't take long before they were out the Crane gate. They didn't go out that way by roof or wall since everyone walking on the busy street between the castle and Nijoushi would see them drop from the wall. They did use the roofs inside the castle until they were close, then they walked out like normal people. Marcus wasn't sure they'd ever be considered normal people, for all he did consider himself one. Just one that had been tossed out of his home as a child and made to live on the streets or die.

"I like the idea, Henry," he said as they walked the streets to the far side of Nijoushi where Jamison's business was located. "I think Mistress Ilena wouldn't want her horses going to someone she couldn't trust, though. The training and the horses cost a lot and to her are more significant than just hiring an apprentice then letting them go to be journeymen."

"True," Henry mused. His eyes were watching the people on the streets. Marcus did the same. They were finally dressed warmly this winter, but their eyes saw those like them: young, barely dressed warm enough to not freeze, running to keep warm and earn just enough to eat and earn a sleeping spot in a hidden safe house. They were very sympathetic. "But, if they're already of her House? We weren't the only runners for the House. And we'd want people from all across the Region and maybe even down into the southern parts of Ryokudo if the messages are going to go all over the nation."

"Well, they'd already have some allegiance to her, then. But there might not be enough that are willing to leave their home cities." That was hard. Not many people really wanted to wander and explore. "It'd be good to be able to hire all the good ones who want to, regardless."

"Would they be willing to join to the House?" Henry mused, then just as fast shook his head. "Most of those we'd want would be old enough to be wanting their own businesses by then. Some of the best for wandering are the freelancers, too. They might put Master Ore at their Head, but not Mistress Ilena." They pondered on that for the rest of the walk. Ore had been a freelancer nightwalker for most of his youth where Ilena was the Head of the House of the Queen of Night. Freelancers were independent and not prone to obeying Heads of Houses.

They tabled the discussion as they reached their destination and focused on their task of the day. In the end, they were rather impressed with the research that had gone into creating the new man–made rock slurry that turned into a material as hard as rock and stood on its own, even at the tall amounts of three–story buildings. They were told that for those heights it was poured over iron bars that supported it. For the height of the city wall, they were planning on making the foot of the wall just a little broader than the top so that the wall had a stronger foundation if they were going to build it new. If they could just repair the current wall, they'd pour the slurry into and over the cracks and only rebuild the weakest parts. The Twins asked a lot of questions until they felt they had enough answers for Ilena who'd know what to do with the answers and then what further questions to ask.

Getting back home to the castle was nice, since it was warm and cozy with a fire in the fireplace. When they gave the summary report to Ilena, she was even more excited by the new "liquid rock". Next on her list would be to go and see the work herself. That would be another opportunity to get out of the castle and be active.

Marcus was quite relieved to have had this day's run. He could rest sitting down after that, and nearly fell asleep. The dinner cart arriving woke him up, and a light hand on his head as quiet footsteps passed him by. He smiled, thinking it was Justinian, but when he turned to look at the back of the person who'd passed him by, it was Amber who'd done it. He stared after her, quite stunned and unsure how to take that. It took a bit to realize it was because he wasn't sure if it was a reward, comfort, or just a "hello". He'd have to ask her when there weren't quite so many people around.

-o-o-o-

Petroi had pulled Thayne back so they fell behind just enough to not interrupt. "Tonight, I need to drink," he'd informed Thayne. He'd been reminded by the younger four's trip out of the castle at lunch that he also should take care of himself so he could take care of his responsibilities rightly. Thayne had given him a nod that he'd heard and understood. They'd been following Ore so it wasn't the time for long conversations nor to fall too far behind. He'd just wanted to say it while he'd thought of it and they had a moment. They'd both remember better.

That evening, when Ore was safely settled in the Lower office for dinner with his wife and the rest of the household, Petroi and Thayne were excused so they could have their vacation. Petroi went to the wardrobe in their room off the Upper office of Intelligence and pulled out clothing for the both of them, handing Thayne his then carrying his own to his bed. Thayne raised an eyebrow at what had ended up in his hand. Petroi gave him a bland look. "We haven't been able to visit my favorite places until now because of Mistress Ilena's requirement to disturb the underworld. You should already know, since you introduced Master Ore to me for the first time at one."

Thayne slowly had a look of comprehension come over his face. It hadn't been a formal introduction and had been a while ago now at the Black Cat Inn, one of the Family establishments Ilena sponsored. As Thayne began to change he said, "Well, I guess I can't complain if we get to skip the seedy inedible food and I don't have to spend three months of pay on as small a meal as I can get in order to not have to pay a full year's worth. A home–cooked family meal will be a relieving change."

Petroi chuckled. "Yes." He ran his hand down the front of his new jacket. It would be nice to finally be able to be in one and feel presentable at the same time.

He looked up to catch Thayne watching him. "And yet, the vanity of the man really shouts he should be dragging me to one of those expensive ones," Thayne teased him. His new shirt was a new look for him, too. He shrugged on his new jacket, closer to the style the young lords of the castle preferred because he didn't care and had just grabbed something close enough to his size and sort of matched his blond–streaked brown hair. It hid his grey–blue eyes to have that much brown and gold. A grey–blue jacket would've been better. Petroi thought he'd order one for him before they went out again since he was the one who picked them out of the wardrobe for Thayne anyway.

Petroi considered that momentarily as he considered his clothing again. It was nicely tailored and, like Ore's preferences, an older adult style than the young men of the castle enjoyed. That was about the age difference between him and Thayne, too: nearly ten years. The jacket and pants were a medium silver–grey to complement his long black hair, but not so dark as to make him feel like he was in the Royal Guard's black uniform. He'd gone with a pale gold shirt that brought out the gold of his eyes. "I had a lot of business dealings to do outside of the Messenger responsibilities, and a Princess to represent." He'd been doing those jobs since Ilena was four years old, in Selicia.

Thayne was still studying him. Becoming a little softer he said, "And you appreciated the freedom to not have to wear a uniform all the time." Petroi looked up at him in some surprise. "Is that a problem to be back to it again?"

Petroi shook his head. "No, but to relax it is good to take it off for a while."

Thayne's slow smile came on his face. "Well, I've got the same answer to that, and I suspect it's even more so for Mizi's guards. Sam and Leon have had to wear uniforms since they enlisted. Brian and Kirk never had to wear them until they started following her. You at least got the practice early on then got to have a long vacation from it."

Petroi moved to collect their winter gear, tossing Thayne's cloak at him then pulling his hat, scarf, and gloves out. "It was good to wear one again, yes," he said in soft pride. It had meant his mistress had finally reached her proper place — something to be proud of for her sake. And relieving for his.

As they left the building out through the central room patio door (they never left out through their own window because they didn't want the world to know which one it was), Petroi turned his own almost–teasing look on Thayne. "Does it bother you? To be wearing a uniform every day now?"

Thayne waited to answer until they'd landed on the ground from the balcony and they'd turned for the Cat gate. "Nah. It's warm and easy to just throw on." He shrugged a shoulder. The guards outside the Cat gate unlocked and opened it for them.

"And the commoner who had to live too long as a nightwalker just cares that he is clothed at all," Petroi teased dryly as the gate clanked closed behind them and a key jangled to lock it again.

Thayne threw a punch at him and they mock–spared briefly as they moved down the road towards town. Thayne ended it first with a bit of a frown. "Were you noble in Selicia, Petroi?" he asked, made curious by Petroi's wording of the comment.

Petroi sighed as he looked at the stars over the city ahead. It was good there wasn't snow and clouds this night. It had cleared up finally during the afternoon. That made it easier to breathe. His mind went to the things he could no longer prevent himself from thinking about: the reason he'd needed this vacation night.

His next step took him close enough to Thayne he could lean his shoulder against Thayne's sturdy shoulder. "Yes," he whispered softly, saying one of the secrets he told no one. Thayne knew a lot of them now, actually. "It was the young noble boys that were brought into the barracks, to teach them how to serve the royals. After that training was when their fathers brought them into the departments and ministries to begin to teach them."

He paused, then added, "That was for the ones chosen to follow in their footsteps. More than one son for a father and the rest...." He drifted off. His home country, northwest of Ryokudo, across a high cold mountain range, was a place he'd not been in person now for over thirteen years. The coup had left both himself and Ilena without a home to return to. Suiran had been home now for both of them for that long.

"You were a younger son, then?" Thayne asked insightfully.

"No, and not always were oldest sons chosen," Petroi answered. His heart tightened for the totality of the burden he was carrying; although, that particular far–past time didn't hurt much anymore on its own. "I was the oldest. ...But too soon, before I was ready, I was an orphan. Because I was in the barracks, I was the only one left alive when the manor burned." Thayne's warm arm came around his shoulders. "Father had gone to visit the others. I have never been able to erase the suspicion they were assassinated all together because of the jealousies and chaos of the court." His memories of his family were what made him enjoy his visits to Mother's inns and restaurants. He'd very much loved his younger siblings.

The arm around his shoulders tightened briefly. "Thus why you like kids and learned compassion," Thayne deduced. After a bit he added, "And why you make a great herdsman."

Petroi spurted a little laugh. "Well, yes. Having two younger brothers and three sisters was good practice."

"So many!" Thayne was surprised. Petroi nodded confirmation. The look of compassion on Thayne's face was followed by him stopping their walk to hold Petroi in both arms in a hug. Thayne didn't say anything but it was kind that he recognized it would have been hard for Petroi to have lost so many beloved people all at once. "I'm sorry to bring it up," Thayne said after a bit.

"No. It is okay," Petroi forgave that. He moved and Thayne let him go so they could continue the walk to the north side of Nijoushi. Petroi did sigh, though. "Generally, that is tonight's reason for drinking."

"Okay," Thane answered, amenable to meeting Petroi's need to grieve a bit and remember the past.

After a bit of silence, Petroi said, "I did so well in the testing by the Third Prince and Princess because I was at the point in my grieving of being angry. They didn't tell us why we were competing that day. I was using it as a way to release the emotions that had built up to become too large for someone so young as me." Dryly he admitted, "I wasn't able to hit the older children quite so hard after that day. I had to become humble very quickly in my new sword lessons and work very hard to reach that same level of capacity they had seen that day."

Thayne had to laugh at that, but Petroi agreed. It had been a hard thing to have done to himself, if good for him in the long run. He went soft as he remembered that day. "I had worked out enough of the anger by the time the little Princess came onto the list that I could face her with the desire I had to face my siblings again, for all I was terrified to have her there. To have her not let go of my hand all night was the rest of the healing I needed that day. Like I didn't want to let any of my family go, she didn't want to let me go. It was something we shared. Something to give me the bravery to do what I had been ordered to do."

He remembered another thought he'd had in that past. "I wondered later if they had decided on me without the final bout being fought because I didn't have the family connections anymore to put me into a court position, but I had the proper nobility."

They walked into the northern part of Nijoushi. The traffic there was down to a dull roar from daytime activity. People hurried home to dinner on winter nights to warm back up again. Nearly as much ash was falling from the sky now as if it was still lightly snowing. That many fireplaces all warming up homes did that. Only the lack of clouds, save the small ones over those homes, said it wasn't snow. It smelled nice, though, to have the woodsmoke smell in the air. Petroi was able to relax a little more. That was one of the small joys he'd had here in this city for the twelve years he'd lived in it.

Thayne had had time to come up with his tease another three cross–streets into the city. "Well, I suppose it was a factor they appreciated once they learned it, but I'm quite sure it really was just that no one ever tells that little Princess 'no'. ...Except you once you overcame your own terror of her." The grey–blue eyes sparkled. "And I assume you learned how to do that out of self–defense or you'd have been beheaded many times over. I don't envy you that at all."

Petroi chuckled. "Well, that is true. But learning to say no wasn't really for that. I could do it when I learned it was the only way to protect her from her unwise decisions."

"Ooohh," Thayne nodded knowingly. "So *she* didn't kill you off before you could teach her how to be careful with others. I wondered how she'd learned even a little of that. She still keeps trying to do that. Are you sure you did your job right?"

Petroi slumped, playing along. Morosely he said, "Just because she learned to accept my 'no' didn't mean she ever saw anyone else as someone to care about. If she still won't answer to your 'no', you must not be real to her yet."

Thayne shoved him, then sighed and admitted, "Professor Shiotsu had to teach it to her, that I was more than an object. That was a harsh lesson for both of us." Shiotsu was the Head of the Medical Department at Kouzanshi university.

"Oh?" Petroi's eyebrow went up. Thayne didn't usually bring up what past he shared with Ilena.

Thayne went more sober than Petroi expected, his eyes looking into Petroi's. "At her worst point in her medical research she nearly killed me and injured him greatly. I missed the Kouzanshi university Lord's Conference when it happened because I was still unconscious." Petroi's eyes were wide in shock and dismay. Softly Thayne said, "She was much better after that, trying to take care of the people who took care of her, but it's always been hard for her to pause long enough to really consider it."

He looked at the people going past them, then added softly, "I rarely bring out the serious 'no' because I know that it will bring that time back up for her. I will never get a disobedient Ilena if I get serious. She still expects me to give her an actual physical beating as return payment. She flinches every time. I don't like to see it, so I don't do it."

Petroi stared at Thayne for a while, then silently had to admit that even in that they were equal partners. He turned them for the restaurant he wanted to eat and drink in that night. "It took that for me also," he said softly. "She was too small to do damage herself, nor had she learned it yet, but she cried in the infirmary when they made her watch as my injuries were treated. She was locked into the family suite while I healed there, and they made her help. That assassin was of a caliber I couldn't win against. The guards had to come to her cries for help, begging them to protect me before I died before her eyes."

He held the door open and let Thayne in first, both of them giving the check for safety of the interior and exterior as they did. "If she had listened to my warning, it wouldn't have happened. We were in the wrong place at the wrong time and got caught in the middle of things."

Thayne nodded in understanding as he pulled his scarf from around his face to let it dangle down his front. "She learned the lesson well, then. It's good you're still here."

"You also," Petroi agreed as he gave his sign to the waitress and pulled off his hat. That much was all it took to get crowded by youths and teens wanting to get hugs. He was quite happy to give them. That was what he needed most tonight, other than the drink and crying a bit. Thayne made Petroi introduce the youths to him so he could rub heads and laugh with them, too. Petroi liked that about Thayne, that he also loved the Children of Mother and was content to find joy with them.

4-5 Ante-Cold Solstice: Regional MoI Activities

Flandras, recent graduate of Kouzanshi university, walked aimlessly around the Nijou castle grounds. He'd been called up by Regent Rei and his professor Second Princess Ilena at the time of his examination. That had been surprising all around, but a great relief. To go from agonizing for five months on an issue he couldn't resolve until Ilena had helped him, to a graduate all within a half-hour had been more than he could recover from until a few days after it had all happened.

Writing the research paper had helped him recover and get over some of his depression at the not–so–nice things that had been involved in all of that. He'd almost chosen to not come a time or two, even. However, he'd not had anything better, and working for the First Prince of the nation wasn't a thing to refuse, for all he'd wondered how a mere mathematical statistical strategist could help two of the greatest strategy minds of their era.

That had been cleared up when they'd met with him his second day at the castle. He'd walked on proverbial air that day, after that meeting. He still believed he'd been born for this time. The Toukas were at a critical juncture. It was one of the reasons he was wandering the grounds now. He needed to tell them what his mind had uncovered but they'd not told him how to contact them, only told him they'd contact him.

Flandras sighed and hunched his shoulders up around his ears. He was at least warm enough in the winter cold here. Kouzanshi was colder so his winter coat, hat, pants, boots, and gloves were plenty sufficient. He was also used to a lot more snow falling than the light snow today. He could see two buildings into the distance or perhaps two and a half from his position. In Kouzanshi that was an excellent, nearly sunny winter's day. He blinked snow off his eyelashes and brushed off the frost his sigh had created on his upper cheeks so he could see again. A person was coming his way and he wanted to be careful.

The person glanced at him as they got into better sight of each other and that person paused. "Ah..., is it Flandras?" the person asked, as bundled up as he was so hard to make out. The voice was familiar, though. Flandras frowned, trying to place it. A hand was raised in greeting. "It's Marcus. Rio told me she'd run into you on your first day."

Flandras relaxed a little. "Yes. Hello, Marcus. How are you?" he asked politely.

Marcus shrugged casually. "Cold, busy, but well enough." Marcus looked around at their surroundings. "Are you lost?" he asked kindly.

Flandras looked around as well. "Not really, save in my head, I suppose." He rubbed his head, not wanting to say too much. This might be Marcus, but he was so bundled up Flandras wasn't sure. "You wouldn't happen to know where Princess Ilena's office is? She was my major professor and I was hoping to say hello to her sometime and let her know I've arrived." He hurried to add, "Not that I want to disturb her if she's busy, but I don't know how to tell that, either." It was hard to interject himself into other people's lives, but he really did want to talk to her. And Rei, but if he could get to at least Ilena he should be able to ask her about that, too.

"Actually, I do," Marcus answered. He turned and invited Flandras to go with him. "She's like most Ministers: very busy so very interruptable, as long as it's not for too long."

"Of course," Flandras hurried to say. "I'd appreciate it." He paid attention to their passage. He already knew which building Rio had said the Ministry of Intelligence was in. He was relieved when they neared the building he remembered.

Marcus introduced him to the guards on the outside doors to the building, saying Flandras was a friend. The building seemed to be similar to the one Flandras was housed in: multiple stories and two sides. The guards standing on the outside, and thus getting very much snowed on even though they were under a canopy overhang, seemed like those guarding most of the buildings on the castle grounds. They nodded and let the two of them pass.

It was inside that things were different. In Flandras' building, the main door let people into a lobby where the meal cart was brought. A set of stairs went up from the lobby to the second floor. On both floors there were long hallways to either side. One side was females and one males. Here, the lobby was open, but the halls to either side were closed off with doors and there were no stairs up. On either set of doors were two more guards each.

Marcus pulled down his scarf and removed his hat and gloves, giving Flandras a smile as he did so. "You'll need your identification here this first time," he explained. Flandras quickly removed his hat, scarf, and one glove so he could get to it.

Marcus led Flandras to the left–hand door. There, both guards inspected the badge, then looked at Marcus. "He's a friend of mine from Kouzanshi, but he's also a graduated student of Mistress Ilena's. He's asked to come visit her briefly. He can probably come visit generally, but I'll let Mistress Ilena say for sure." The guards gave nods and one opened the door to let them in.

Flandras shoved his hat and glove into one pocket. He'd left his scarf draped around his neck, but he pulled off his second glove now and then had his hands free to put his identification away. Marcus stopped him with a glance at him and a shake of his head. Flandras paused and looked around the newest space. There was a rather wide atrium area with stairs at the far end. To his right on both the first and second floor were five doors about as close together as in his wing. To his left were three doors on each floor and at two of them on the first floor were one guard per door. He was a bit surprised to see that. Security was rather tight here. Ah, but then, Ilena was the Second Princess and Minister of Intelligence. Rei must care quite a bit about keeping her safe. He approved from that standpoint.

He showed his badge to the guard at the central door and the second guard watched to see that one nod that the identification was legitimate. "Announce him, please," Marcus asked politely. "He's here to see Mistress Ilena."

The guard knocked once on the door, then opened it and said to the room at large, "Mister Flandras to see Princess Ilena."

Looking past both men, Flandras could see that this next room was also open, all the way back to windows and glass doors. The fireplace was crackling nicely to the right. Ilena had lifted her head from working at a desk central to the room, but about that far back. It looked like she wasn't unhappy to have him come. That was good. He took a deep breath and scanned the rest of the room as Marcus led him into it.

Henry was there, standing near Ilena. Rio had looked up at him from a rocking chair near the fireplace and was smiling a small smile to see him. The other girl... Amber he remembered from his first time in the castle, was there also. It was a rather full room for all it looked big at first. He noticed since there were three other men in the room closer to the door, one at a desk. They gave him nods and went back to working, he supposed.

He suddenly wasn't so sure. This was a lot of people to have around with what he wanted to say. It was too late now, he supposed, and sighed at himself.

"I ran into him out in the snow," Marcus was saying to Ilena. "He asked if he could come say hello, and I said he could." Marcus was a bit casual to his royal mistress, but she didn't complain.

"Welcome, Flandras," Ilena said with a smile. He paused again. She was the different she'd been in that first meeting. The Ilena he'd known at Kouzanshi had been flippant almost. Casual, almost flighty, save when she stayed toe-to-toe with him in the statistics and strategy. Then it had been more of a challenge enjoyed together. That he'd fallen in love with, like he loved the math and strategy from the beginning. He shifted, uncomfortable again, but as he glanced around the room her husband Ore wasn't in the room so he tried to shove that to the side again.

Today, like that other meeting, she was firmly and strongly in control, if more relaxed today than at that meeting. Very princess-like, actually. He could only slump and say to himself that it couldn't be surprising. Not only was she actually a princess, she was a Touka strategy genius. She knew how to play the parts to get what she wanted. That was becoming obvious. He wasn't sure he liked that, but he wasn't sure she wasn't being genuine. That he'd have to watch her for a while longer to know.

"It's good to see you again," Flandras said. His hands had clutched the ends of his scarf for something to hold on to since he was so out of his element here in this moment. Last minute he remembered to bow.

Ilena chuckled slightly at him. "It's okay Flandras. I'm as casual — usually — as you knew me to be in Kouzanshi. Particularly when just sitting in my office. I don't mind the interruption at the moment." She considered him for a moment more, then rose from her chair at the desk. "Give your coat to Marcus to put away and sit with me a while." She waved at the sitting area between her desk and the main door. There was a long low table there with couches on either side and chairs at either end.

She sat in the chair closest to her desk while Flandras nervously handed his coat over to Marcus, who only smiled at him and took both coats back to the main door to hang them on pegs there. Flandras had waffled on whether to keep his scarf in order to continue to have something to hold on to. He was surprised that Marcus had left it in his hands before he could get it stuffed into a sleeve. He looked at it, then shrugged and put it in his lap to hold as he sat on the couch close enough to Ilena to be polite.

"How has adjusting to the castle been for you?" Ilena asked.

Flandras drew in a breath, remembering that conversations should begin with pleasantries. It was hard to unlearn the researcher's constant drive to focus on their research, particularly when he'd been assigned to do just that from the beginning, having only one day to get used to the castle. "Given I'm working just as hard here as there, it's not much different until I come out of the office. Then I'm learning new things all the time."

Ilena gave a nod of understanding. "And you're doing okay with your room-mate?" she asked.

"Yes," Flandras reassured her. "He's been kind to help me learn the new way of living and has been helping me to remember to eat." He smiled. She smiled back, her eyes lighting up in a twinkle. That was new, too. He swallowed and looked away for a bit, drawing a breath. "It helps that I can learn spacial maps the same way I know statistical math."

"Ah, that's how you do it," Ilena mused. Flandras gave a nod. "And does that translate the other direction, then? You see the strategy as a map, ordered by the math?"

"Yes," Flandras said softly.

"We Toukas see it as boards," she offered. "Like chess boards, but very expanded. Sasou has them at multiple levels, even. Master Rei's is compact in comparison. Mine's expansive but only one level." She smiled. "I can't explain how that holds all the data, though, since the amount of data is rather large for holding on one space, but it works well enough for my brain." She got a musing look on her face. "Actually, I wonder. Ore called me the weaver when I said it out loud, what I do. I set warp threads, seeing them extending into the distant past and future, then weave the weft threads in as I set people and things in place, creating a pattern. So perhaps it's a mixture of boards and patterns." She pondered on that for a moment.

Flandras watched her, just observing. She was researching herself in that moment, he realized. A new data point had been added to that "paper" she was working on. He looked down and smiled, running a hand across his scarf without paying much attention to it. She was giving him an interesting look when he looked back up at her. He continued to smile at her. "You never stop researching, do you?" he asked.

"Not really," she agreed.

"Did they really make you a professor of strategy?" he asked her. He'd wondered at all the suddenness four and a half months ago.

"Yes, but only because that was what they desperately needed to graduate you. They'd have made me a general professor if such a thing exists," she answered. "I think Ore and Master Rei would've told them to make me a professor of research." She winked at Flandras and he had to smile again.

"I think that's becoming obvious," he agreed. "But were they really so desperate, to do that all for me?"

Ilena went very sober, surprising him somewhat. "Yes, they were, actually. This Dean is very serious about meeting his responsibilities to each student. You're that important to me, too, so I wasn't going to complain at all."

Flandras looked into her openly serious face for a while, then sighed and looked down at his scarf again. "Can I be allowed to come visit whenever I need questions answered?" he asked, really needing to be able to.

Ilena considered that. "Given we have history at Kouzanshi to claim, you probably can."

"And Prince Rei?" He really needed to be able to have access to the Prince as well.

Ilena shrugged a shoulder. "I can pass on your request," she offered.

Flandras frowned. He wasn't comfortable with that arrangement. He blinked at his instructor of strategy. "How do you handle the variable that won't settle?"

Ilena smiled as if to herself. "Never fully trust it. Leave it open and set into place things to block it if it should become betrayal. If it doesn't, then those things don't have to happen. If it does, you've already protected yourself as best possible." She blinked back at him. "Sasou's excellent at that."

Flandras considered the King's history, then nodded. "He's had to stay alive a long time on his own power."

"Indeed," Ilena affirmed.

"Is that still the answer even if it's you?" he asked.

"Always," she agreed quietly. "Setting any variable into a constant will skew the final result if it was a false constant."

Flandras relaxed a little. Ilena understood and wouldn't reject him if he kept her in his internal space as a potential traitor. While he knew he had to rely on someone or several people because no one could get through life distrusting everyone, he always had to have some level of uncertainty in that same space. Perhaps that was why he'd been struggling with her since she'd come back to help him understand the piece he'd been missing. She'd become someone completely different than he'd expected, than he'd placed her in his space.

It was his fault. He'd plopped her down in a space and thought she was just that, when she was so much more. He could have seen it back then. To have her be both airheaded and be able to follow his math mind was so contradictory that looking back on it he really should have. He'd been so focused on his research, though, and so desperate to have someone to talk to about it that understood.

It was an excellent example of the things he saw in the numbers all the time: the blind spots looked back on by historians that were so obvious after the fact. The very thing he wanted so desperately to not have happen to him or his math. He'd keep her in that place of distrust, having pulled her out of the hole he'd put her in, but he'd also remember it as his own lesson and humbly accept his guilt in the matter rather than place it all on her. He was quite sure that as Minister of Intelligence it was rather necessary that she be able to hide everything that she was. He'd learn it little by little until he could hopefully place her rightly, at least as best possible.

"You should keep that level of healthy distrust regardless," Ilena said soberly.

She blinked at him but didn't avert her gaze as he took his turn to study her. "Why did you keep me from attending the National Security Meeting?"

Ilena's expression went a little sad. He wasn't going to trust anything save what rang true to his numbers. "I couldn't get you here in time for the meeting, as much as both Rei and I wanted you to be."

Flandras shook his head at her. "Writing a dissertation can take place anywhere. You've known it, that you were going to have that meeting from before you were brought to this castle. You've wanted me here since you found me in the library. The Prince or King would've found out about me eventually, but was not bringing me here in a timely fashion because you wanted to cover the base that you'd found me without letting me work most effectively?"

Ilena shook her head. He was surprised that it was somewhat vigorously. "The landslide was a surprise to me. I had no idea I was going to be here as soon as I was. Things had to move at the pace set by that for the first three months. That pacing was set by both Ore and Rei. Did I know we'd have the meeting at some point? Yes. The scheduling of it was based on Sasou's timing: when he could be here for it."

Flandras frowned at her but she raised a hand at him. "It couldn't be the first time he came because *he* wasn't ready to let Rei know about Gael and Brulac. He was still testing Rei at that time. His pace is slower, one step at a time, wanting to know if the person being tested can stand steady before going to the next thing. Since I was at Rei's side, it was also obvious that adding that to the Tarc issue was more than he could handle. I worked hard to build up his strength, as did Sasou, so that by the time we *did* have the meeting he had the strength for it.

"I'm his teacher of strategy also: the strategy of kings, subterfuge, and spies. He's had little training in it at all yet. Sasou has me teaching that now that I'm by his side." She turned to look into the distance.

Flandras pushed on it. "What is it?" She was seeing a piece he needed to see.

Ilena looked back at him, sober. "I hate that royalty isn't allowed to trust other royalty, can't be true family, has to always do as you said at the beginning. Every royal — king, queen, prince, princess, even noble blood relations to them — will never settle. They can never be fully trusted, ever. Even Ore could decide at some point to kill me.

"The reciprocal is also a truth. A royal never trusts anyone. We can love and hold dear to our hearts our family, but family is never trusted, just like no other person is unless they're tested most harshly and survive the testing. No amount of testing will let one royal trust another royal. Ever." She blinked at him. "I hate it."

Flandras slumped and gave a small nod. That was indeed the piece he'd needed to hear. That critical variable entered his equations and settled them. He'd be able to come talk to her, he'd be able to track down a way to talk to Rei by himself, but he'd never hear everything he wanted or needed to hear in joint meetings. Only what they'd be willing to say in front of the other.

He rose to his feet and bowed. "Thank you for letting me visit and for answering my questions." Ilena gave him a nod. It was a cold walk back to his small office after that. It was sobering to him to learn how cold and lonely a place a throne was.

-o-o-o-

Carl looked up at the person who'd stopped at the table in the seedy bar. "Imagine running into you two here," it was said dryly. It took he and Liam both about fifteen seconds to recognize Corporal David Tellius. He was dressed in civilian clothing and looked about as commonly rough as they did. "Is this really where you hang out on your days let loose of the leash?"

"You're here," Liam pointed out and returned to his dubious meal.

Carl set down his mug from taking a swig in order to recover from his surprise. "Not to mention you've got the same sort of reputation." Liam raised an eyebrow but kept eating. He was practicing the "eat and run" habits of nightwalkers and ne'er–do–wells. It wasn't hard but it also wasn't habit yet.

David welcomed himself to their table and waved at the waitress for a plate and drink. Places like this didn't have more than one of each on any given night. He'd barely dug into his plate of food when another voice interrupted them. "Quite the crowd. I'm not sure I should interrupt."

Carl's eyes lifted sharply and focused on the speaker. "Yes, you should. Sit down. He's payin' tonight and I'm sure you've not had nearly enough to eat." The words were a scold, but more so that the person wouldn't run away. More than two to meet at a table and it made anyone on the shady side of life nervous, particularly in public places like this one.

The person was so wrapped up against the chill as to be nearly unidentifiable, but the scarf was pulled down from over their mouth and the food shoveled in even faster than it was for David and Liam. Liam took notes, but didn't change his personal speed. He was already nearly done eating. "Since when'm I payin'?" he asked gruffly. "I might pay fer meetin' a potential contact, but I am't payin' fer '*im*!" he pointed at David.

"An' 'ere I was about to thank ye, too." David frowned at Liam in mock dismay.

"*Pft.* Yer' earnin' enuf to pay fer yerself," Liam didn't let it go. He was liking finally having a paycheck at all. To have to waste it at places like this wasn't on his wish list; although, they'd be expensing it all to the Ministry regardless. It still rubbed him wrong. He'd rather spend any money on himself at nice places or on nicer things. That was new, too, to be able to have things to call his own, after only having the King's hidden woodcutter's cabin to even remotely claim before.

He sighed and set his utensil down, then leaned back in his chair and picked up his mug. He let the other two more newly come eat more as he lazily looked around the room. The newest to arrive asked around his eating without slowing down, "Why'd you want to meet up with me?" A glance did arrive on Liam as he looked back at the person. It was fast enough he wasn't sure if it was a suspicious look or not.

"The MoI's changed hands," Liam answered, making everyone at the table nervous suddenly. He kept going, "That means no one knows anythin' anymore. With the newest MoI a nightwalker Head the whole works's thrown into confusion." He frowned. "This one," he pointed with his head at David, "lost 'is main employer to the same MoI before she was put into place. It's confusin' ever'one. She keeps swingin' e'ery–witch–way."

Liam waved his free hand, then took a swig of his mug nearly wishing for just plain water. "The one you know," he pointed with his thumb at Carl, " 'ad to go lookin' fer new clients and assistants b'cause she then went and cleaned out the whole of the south of town and half 'is contacts, just to take it over 'n call it all hers." Carl shook his head in sorrowful agreement with Liam's shake of the head. "So he was lookin' fer new contacts and I was lookin' fer the same since the market's open."

Liam sighed to himself. He was copying the words of his family that he'd learned as a child and wasn't particularly thrilled. That was probably the hardest part of this job. He'd hoped the kings had let him leave it behind him since they'd worked so hard to. The princess had decided otherwise. He let his dismay show on his face since it matched the comments.

"I'm lookin' to know which way she's gonna fall in the end, or if she ne'er does so I know how cautious to be and just what she'll jump at and won't. Not to mention I've got work tha's come my way I'd like to get paid fer." He leaned forward on the table to rest an arm on it, putting down his mug because he really didn't want to drink what was in it anymore. He paused to get another glance thrown his way. It didn't look like he'd scared off the person, yet. Not that they should be scared off. They already knew what they were to be doing next.

Lowering his voice to an even quieter volume than normal, he said, "They say some of her own House is in the castle garrison's prison." His eyes went to David who gave a slight nod of confirmation, making the contact's eyes widen a bit and even the eating pause just momentarily. "I want to know if they're still loyal to her, or if they hate her for lettin' the soldiers keep them arrested fer the long–haul after they went and were loyal to her in Tarc. If'n she c'n keep them loyal in that sitchiation, then I'll know how quiet to walk 'ere."

Liam tapped his finger on the table. "I need someone not native to the city. Too many won't cross her now that she's moved against the Houses and set up the governance she wanted to see." He glanced at David again. "He's already inside and was left alone when she cleaned out the garrison. He can get you in and out again."

The contact thought about that for a bit, then asked, "And you're not willing to pay him for that effort?"

Liam smiled a little. "Oh, he'll get paid, but by my employer fer the job. I'm jus' not payin' out o' *my* pocket for 'is meal tonight. I gotta pay yer meal out o' pocket so you'll sit still long enough to hear my request."

The contact took longer to think, about to the time they were done eating their meal. The eyes came up to measure him. "And why're you breaking into the market now that she thinks the city's clean? Who are you to think you've got anything new that can be done in this city she's closing down to any of this sort of work at all?"

Liam looked around the room casually again, without turning his head much. A few eyes had been looking at him already. Most in the room and this part of the city wondered who he was and why he was hanging around Carl and now David on just enough of a regular basis to be noticeable. He dropped his volume down even more as he shrugged and said, "Just protectin' myself by not bein' present when things were noisy." He blinked at the person, then said, "I'm the last person standin' from the House of Daed."

All three of the people at the table stared at him in shock. He finally waved his hand and said, "Not an assassin. I know better'n that with that one. Just in the information business. Safer that way if I want to keep standin'." They all relaxed slightly, but still gave him disbelieving looks until his calm face made them believe it to some level.

"Well," Carl admitted, "information's about all she'll tolerate, unless it's honest nightwalker work." He grimaced. "That doesn't mean *she* won't use assassins herself, and she'll let the Regent as well if he asks, but tha's about it. So do stay out of that business if you value your neck. ...Which it seems you already do." He gave a significant look at Liam who nodded quite positive of that.

"What's the pay and when?" the contact asked.

Liam told them and added, "Now, if y'll agree to it, David here'll let you in t'night, then you give 'im the report. Then he'll help you escape back out into the wild."

The eyes turned to David. "And what makes it safe for me to go in with you? You could just leave me locked in there with them."

David understood. "I'm the one in charge of interrogations of prisoners, of all types. It's not all that uncommon for me to take bully-types in with me to get the more resistant types to open up properly." At the contact's blink he added casually, "Or as swaps to get people out."

The eyes went wide again. "*Pft.* Who'd go *in* to stay?"

David shrugged. "Someone someone else wanted to punish and didn't know they was headed for that punishment until they woke up already in? That's the usual way. Sometimes I can get them back out later since they aren't a known face, but that's harder so costs more."

The eyes narrowed at David. "So..., you'd take me in as the former?"

David waved a hand in negation. "Naw. That's not the job this time. He wants someone they'll talk to that isn't me. They already won't talk to me in that way since to them I'm the enemy. If I take you in as a temporary for a few hours while I try to figure out how to book you they'll talk, I figure. It's the other soldiers that'll think you're the bully to make someone talk." He gave a mean grin. "After all, that's who I usually come into town for this time of night, when I come into town for dinner." He frowned at Liam again for not being willing to pay for that dinner.

"Yer gettin' paid enough from the castle and from my pay to pay fer that yerself," Liam scowled back at him, still not giving in.

The contact gave in and agreed to do the job. Liam passed over the payment to him wrapped so as to not look like coin and gave David his as well. David promptly put his payment for the meal on the table and rose. Liam reached for his mug and held it. "I'll met you at the other place," he said to David, who gave a nod as he wrapped up in his scarf and coat.

As they walked for the door, a man at a table on the way reached out and held David back a little, a worried look on his face. "Be careful. You may have escaped the washing of the garrison, but I hear tell that the next on the list is the staff. Watch yerself."

David gave a grateful nod. "Thanks for the head's up. I will, now that you've said." A small coin slipped from his hand to the other man's as he pulled a glove out to put on. The two were out the door shortly thereafter.

Liam sighed a bit. The warning wasn't wrong. Ilena was focusing on the staff next, if she could spend even one–eighth of her brain on it. Right now it was a little less than that. It was good she had lots of spies in the staff to be working on it for her. There'd be plenty of data when she was ready for it. He slumped as he wondered if she'd be keeping the two of them busy on that project once she felt they needed more to do. He sort of hoped not and that she'd give it to Marcus and Henry instead. Or Mitchel.

-o-o-o-

Carl and Liam walked away from the Lower office of Intelligence the next morning after the Regional security meeting through still–falling snow. "Well, that was a surprise," Liam said as he drew a deep breath as if it was a sunny spring day. "I really didn't think she'd let me go of the office until spring thaw."

"Well, she and Lord Mitchel did have a point that you need to focus on what I need to teach you," Carl said. "Now that they're ready to let everyone go, we'll be getting busy, too."

"True," Liam answered in his quiet voice. They were headed for Queen Kata's wing and Carl's office there. He'd been left there because the Lower office didn't have enough room, nor did the Upper office. Mitchel's office was still there as well, but he'd gone off for his own next task rather than come with them. By the time they got to Carl's office, there should be a desk for Liam in it as well, making it a bit cramped. They wouldn't be there much anyway. Their nightwalker work was in the city and the little bit of census work they still had to do was going to be mostly out in the field as well.

They'd been partnered by Ilena at the beginning of the Ministry two months before the end of the last year, but Liam was one of Ilena's strongest restraints and supporters within the Immediate Family of her networks. It being winter when the claustrophobia of being shut in and snowed on for the whole season did things to everyone in the Region, Liam really did think he'd have been kept in the Intelligence office until this first year of Ilena's castle imprisonment was over.

When he'd protested, she'd shaken her head. "I'm used to it from birth: castles or manors and not getting to leave them much. We're using it as the excuse for Master Rei to keep Brulac and their spies in the castle believing I'm unstable and he can't control me, but I'll be fine. No one knows that's what you are, and if they do, they'll think the same. Ore's sufficient and so is everyone else."

Liam had noticed it. She'd not been using him any more than normal, and even less because she hadn't had so much time to focus on training him to his position anymore within the Immediate Family. Likely she was postponing his test until after the current more real threats were handled. He sighed a bit at that. He was under no delusion she'd forget to test him at some point. He might, though, so he hoped he'd been trained enough to just react properly when it came.

He wondered if he was even needed at all, then changed his mind. When she was quietly in the mews she was easy. When she was let loose to hunt in the outdoors was when she got dangerous. The last month had proven that in Nijoushi. Being the Naluk' in Tarc had as well. He'd been trained during the times she'd been dangerous. She'd call him back when she could fly free again. He felt his shoulders relax and had to dryly chuckle at himself. He didn't want to be not needed by her.

Liam continued his musings as they walked in their comfortable long silence they enjoyed and that threw off anyone thinking to trail them and learn anything. Carl didn't take his next turn until they were in his office, taking off their winter gear and trying to not be too claustrophobic at the space shrinkage the second desk had caused. "You were more surprising," Carl complained at Liam, giving him a bit of a glare. "What're you thinking, admitting last night you might be a Daed? That's more risky than anything you've done to date. You sure you wanted to do that?"

Liam raised an eyebrow at him. "Truth's always easier to remember than lies, and it's a strong answer to his question the whole city's been asking since I showed up."

Carl came full–stop and grabbed Liam's arm to pull him around so they were face–to–face. His glare was rather strong. Liam just held on to his cloak and looked back mildly. "That's too far!"

"Is it?" Liam wasn't sure why Carl thought it was.

"No one's going to believe it, and if they decide to, they won't talk to you at all! The King's the most feared of all. If any hint of a smell he's involved gets added to the conversation, they clam up and leave the city to not be seen by his operatives again."

"Why'd Sasou be involved with that name? His father did it," Liam stayed calm, but was getting a bit angry underneath.

Carl dropped his hold on Liam as if he'd suddenly realized he was holding a hot coal. He woke up from being frozen with a sharply drawn breath. "And you'll say his name casually?" he whispered. "You don't get to go out again until you've learned it properly."

Liam pursed his lips, then deliberately carried his cloak over to hang it up while he got himself under control again. When he turned around he looked at Carl in the eyes. "I told you already I don't ever want to kill anyone. That's why: because the previous King said I couldn't do it. I couldn't stay alive and not be my family. I love Mistress Ilena and am loyal to her because she said I could and proved it to me. He put me in solitude for twenty years and more. She pulled me out of it and claimed me hers."

He glared at Carl. "Sasou kept me there because he couldn't be bothered to worry about what to do with me. He already knew from my first testing she'd have me in the end. He's half the man she is. If the city's afraid of *him* then he's on purpose being the distraction so they don't understand what *she* is." He let the full scowl out. "And if *you're* afraid the same way they are, I think it's *you* that needs the lesson. I know to keep quiet about Sasou, and it's good to learn to keep that toned down, but...," he bit his tongue and moved to his desk to sit back against the top of it. He folded his arms and chose to scowl at the floor until he'd gotten back under control again.

Carl moved to his desk and sat down rather heavily in his chair to assimilate Liam's rant. When Liam had calmed down enough, he looked up at Carl. He was a bit surprised Carl was somewhat pale. Carl eventually looked back at Liam. Quietly he said, "I really don't want that lesson. It's been hard enough to work for her with the few brushes I've already had against that darkness. I stay away from House Heads for a reason."

Liam blinked at him. "How can you do your job if you're that cautious and afraid?"

Carl looked like he was going to be offended, then his face turned bitter. "*Because* I am. I won't ever be Minister or any top person in the intelligence field because I won't go that deep. I'm at the level of information gathering because that level doesn't have to. I can manage people and information so I sit where I do and let those willing to walk the darkness get what I need and bring it back to me. I live to pass the information on up because I know how to stay alive with that caution and fear."

Liam looked at the join of the ceiling and wall as he took that in. "I can see that. However, I'm going to naturally not be so afraid. The only thing I fear is Ore, and a very angry Sasou. I'm not allowed to be afraid of Ilena. She's trained me to act out of love for her so I have a motivation to ignore any fear that might come up."

Carl choked a bit. "Then you'd best be ready to act as your family."

Liam wrinkled his nose. "Yes, I had that open up to my mind in that moment. I was acting like them and really didn't like it. I'm working on figuring out how to balance that." It looked like having Carl as a supporting balance might not be the way, but if they could work even something out, that would be good. The start to that would be to work on his own balance, as Carl had said at the beginning. Liam sighed. "All right, I'll take the gentle lessons when we're out so I can learn how to not drop so deeply into the darkness. Having only worked with the Immediate Family until now I haven't had that side at all."

Now Carl snorted a cynical laugh. "No, I'd imagine not." He paused, then frowned a bit. "Is that why she scolded me last year for trying to fit her and the household into even some level of 'normal'?" He immediately rolled his eyes. "Of course it is. I want there to be a level of normal so I can relax and feel safe. And when they hand that to me, then she scolds me for believing it too strongly and relaxing." He groaned and put his hand over his eyes. "How do you even manage it? All of you?"

Liam smiled softly, understanding his quandary. "How do you manage to stay alive at all on the street, wanting to believe even the underworld can be safe?"

Carl dropped his hand and looked soberly at Liam. He considered that question for a long time. "I know it's not, but the nightwalkers aren't all dark. Enough of them are there for reasons they didn't choose that there's an understanding and a strata. They recognize I'm closer to the light and don't want to drop into the full darkness, like many of them. Each level of nightwalker calls to those who fit into it. Like the others, I run from those who're darker and choose to interact with those of my level. We know even that's not completely safe, but people need people regardless, so contact is brief, tentative, appreciated, and needed."

Carl considered Liam then said, "Let that one mention of Daed be a rumor only. That name runs as deeply in the fear of the underworld as Sasou's name does. We'll work today on a different background you can remember. If you need to work that deeply on occasion, it will be without me and you can bring the name out then. No one will be surprised that you keep it quiet except for those times and hide behind a different story."

Liam gave a nod of agreement. He asked a different but related question, "Why isn't Ore as feared as he should be?"

Carl raised an eyebrow. "Because he's a known friendly. He gets the job done but relaxes with everyone when he's not on a job. He's not afraid and he doesn't make anyone afraid. ...Well, except when it comes to Princess Mizi and Prince Rei. He's been firm that he doesn't hesitate to kill anyone who thinks to touch them. But people see that as part of his job so it doesn't affect them in dark ways."

Liam shook his head. He pondered on that, then asked, "I've been out of commission so long. What does the name of House Shicchi do?"

Carl paused to consider that. "It was an old House, failing and falling. It's no surprise to anyone it's gone now."

Liam pursed his lips. "And the name of House Thunder Fist?"

Carl shifted uneasily. "My level stayed away from that one. Those who love beating and torturing others — the bullies — enjoyed either working for him or boasting they could best him while at the same time granting him the respect of silence or distance if his men were around."

"So caution and some respect for the darkness?" Liam asked. Carl nodded.

Liam sighed. "Well, he's hidden it very well, then."

Carl's brow furrowed. "Who's hidden what?"

Liam shook his head as he rose to his feet so he could go sit in his own chair to relax a little while they got to work. "Maybe I should study him while working on this issue," he mused to himself. Ore had been able to hide himself excellently. Liam thought he'd rather hide similarly to that than how Carl was. Maybe it hadn't been the best time to transfer him out of the office. Well, then, but Ore was back in the Rose office more now, so he wasn't there to observe anyway. He'd review what he'd already observed and what the nightwalkers said about him when they were out in the field.

-o-o-o-

Mitchel walked into the hallway of the block of cells Ilena's people were in. There was one new person in them, but he knew who that was. He still stopped, frowned, and turned back for the door. "Who put the new one in?" he asked the door guard.

"Corporal Tellius," the guard answered.

Mitchel frowned more. "Well, tell him to come get him out and put him somewhere else until he's talked to me. That doesn't happen unless I approve it." He glanced back into the hallway of cells. "As a matter of fact, come get him out now so I'm not wasting my time. March him down there. If Tellius wants to bring him back up, he can do it when I've left again."

He was getting slightly dark looks but he glared at the soldiers on the door until one of them complained. "I don't care what the General does, I just care that Minister Ilena's not gone completely insane, and her people don't get out of hand. I've only got a few more days of being able to do that before they're let loose again." He scowled even more at the soldier until he did as he'd been ordered.

When the door was closed behind Mitchel again, he walked half-way down the hallway and spoke as quietly as he ever needed to in this place. "Oliver'll be back, on the complaint that he's one of you and I didn't know." He was getting a lot of interest generally.

When he was mostly done with this day's instructions and practice, the key rattled in the doorway and it opened. He glared at the interruption, it being Oliver and David. The other guards stayed to support David. David somewhat impatiently and rather perfunctorily said, "According to the records of both the city and castle, he's one of hers, so belongs in here. Is there a reason that's a problem?"

Mitchel scowled and asked for Oliver's name. He was given a false name and answered David, "I'll ask her about him. If he's lying, I might get to finally have some fun for once." Oliver properly paled just a little. Mitchel waved at the cells, his scowl not leaving his face. "I guess it's fine until then. Just add him in. I'm not quite done."

As Mitchel walked away from the guards outside the hall when things were finally in place, he mused to himself. "I wonder who to play with when they're gone? Such a shame the place has been cleaned out. Maybe I should randomly pick hallways for a while and see who got left behind."

6 Ante-Cold Solstice: The Anti-Touka Faction

Flandras was pacing, five steps from the entrance wall to the farther end of his office, then five steps back. The three wide steps from side wall to side wall hadn't been enough very early on. The five wasn't quite enough now, and only one circuit of the room altogether made him sigh explosively and reach for his warm winter gear. Impatiently he shoved his arms through the sleeves of his heavy cloak and did up the clasps. He'd already wondered why they didn't make and sell this sort of cloak here in the eastern part of the nation. Cloaks without sleeves or clasps were so easy to blow open by the bitter biting wind.

He jerked his heavy gloves and hat out of his deep pockets, losing one glove to the floor for his impatience and irritation. The hat went on first, then he was scooping up his lost glove and turning for his door. At the last moment, just before his hand touched the latch he was suddenly wide-eyed and turning for his desk. Dropping the gloves on the corner of the desk, he grabbed the papers scattered there from either side and shoved them together into a messy stack. He tapped them together, but didn't bother to make them any neater than they needed to be to shove them into the drawer of the desk. He had to wrestle the key on the chain around his neck out from behind the cloak, but this part was so important his heart was beating even more rapidly in his chest. He'd nearly forgotten to protect himself and the royals of the nation. That would be so very, very bad.

Once the drawer was locked, Flandras shoved the key back under his cloak and shirt, then was snatching up his gloves. He really couldn't afford such inattention here in this place. Being a researcher at the university it hadn't mattered so he'd not learned the pattern of protection. If today's mild fear could remind him, that would be very good. The door latch was turned and he was flinging open the door to find himself looking into a face. That was even worse and his heart stopped completely.

"Ah, I'm sorry," the person also dressed for the outdoors said and stepped to the farther side of the hallway. "I was just passing by. I didn't mean to startle you."

"Ah..., no, I'm sorry to suddenly come barging out," he managed to stutter out.

He got a small smile of forgiveness. The person waved their hand behind them a little. "I work about four doors down. None of us meet often. But you're new?"

"Yes," Flandras closed the door behind him. "I'd nearly decided I was the only one working on this floor."

That earned him a little chuckle. "Yes, that's common here, particularly in the winter. Because you've come at the start of that season it will be spring or summer before you start seeing more, unless like the rest of us you like to stay in your office after the cold leaves enough to let us out of our not-prisons." They rolled their eyes.

Flandras sighed and got them started walking for the stairs again, his body still needing the pacing. "Well, but I do need it today regardless of the weather. Five steps isn't enough to get anything out of my system and fresh air is rather required at the moment." His words came out rather firm.

"Quite understandable," the other said with dry agreement. It seemed this one's need to get the winter difficulties out included needing to talk to anyone other than themselves as the conversation continued until they were out into the cold. At least there was sunshine today and the walkways were finally clear. Snow–laden bare branches of bushes were all that decorated the garden area outside of the building his office was in.

Since Flandras had already used the excuse of needing to be outside walking as his reason to leave his work, he had to walk around the garden outside the building with the person he'd nearly run into until they'd found a reason to excuse themselves and he'd excused himself from their presence with a need to continue to pace to think about his work. He'd made sure to let that person do most of the talking and keep his own words from saying anything about himself he shouldn't.

Once he felt alone enough, he took himself directly to the Royal office building. He took the stairs up two at a time and went straight to the Lotus office. He kept his hat and scarf on until he was on the second floor but had the scarf unwrapped and hanging around his shoulders and down his front and the hat off by the time he reached the door. He paused just long enough to look the guards on Rei's door in the eye before opening it and entering. He wasn't going to intrude on the Rose office, but he knew the guards knew who he was and he wasn't going to wait for permission any longer.

It was a bit chilly so he kept his cloak on, shoving the hat back into his pocket. He glanced at the small fireplace in the fore–corner. It was cold logs waiting to be lit. Mizi must not be planning on arriving until late or wasn't going to be in on this day. He didn't light them. He didn't expect to be there long enough for it to matter. Instead he went back to pacing. That and his cloak would keep him warm enough.

His pacing was able to be slower now that he was in this room and his body was getting worn out from all the outdoor pacing he'd been doing. He took deeper breaths and tried to get calmed down generally, using the time to get his thoughts into order. He found it odd that this office had neither window nor door to the balcony. It was very much like his own office, actually, if larger in both directions. He paced it to calculate it. It was seven paces (nearly) deep and five wide. That was a nicer size. He'd rather be in this office, actually. Then he'd have ready access to the prince. He sighed. His brain had already done the calculations that it would be safer for them all, too. He added that to the list of things to talk about today.

The door opened. Flandras spun around then relaxed as Rei entered, leaving Mina on the door outside. His last thought blurted out. "Can I have this office instead? So it's normal for me to come here and talk to you? It's more dangerous for me to have to pretend to not be your aide, and not be able to contact you at all when the things I need to tell you are usually critical." It had turned into a real scold by the time he was done. The look of surprise on Rei's face brought Flandras back to his sense of his place.

"Ah, sorry," he paused and rubbed his head. He looked away. "The calculations have me tense. I've already calculated that if I'm assassinated on my way here with a critical piece of information the entire nation will fall. That was last week and I haven't been able to settle well since."

"Ah, well, that would be unsettling," Rei agreed. He blinked, then asked, "Will this be a long meeting?"

"That depends on what's long for you," Flandras answered. "Not likely, but I'd like enough time to tell you what I have to tell you and get some questions answered so I can move forward."

Rei relaxed into a listening stance, also likely not wanting to sit again. Flandras watched him for a moment. Rei was young enough he should need motion still, but he held himself completely relaxed with a stillness to him that spoke to far more internal stillness than just enforced restraint for the season or his rank. Flandras focused just a little more, but even Rei's breathing was relaxed and normal, not shortened like he needed to be told to take a deeper breath to be alive.

Flandras moved his attention to Rei's eyes. They were calm, his facial expression undemanding. However the longer Flandras looked into Rei's eyes, the more the brilliant blue filled up his vision and demanded unwavering loyalty and attention. Flandras' lip lifted up on one side. "Indeed. One of the best strategists of the Toukas. Even Ilena doesn't see everything. That was what I was wondering and needed to see for myself."

He smiled at Rei's slight mocking look that barely changed his face, almost only his eyes. Flandras broke off the eye contact and began a slow pace two steps towards the prince, which was all it took for that body to tense up and say that was as close as he was allowed. Then he turned for the wall closer to him to let the body relax, paced back the two and turned, then paced to the other side wall and back again to his original place. "How is it you also learned court testing?" Rei asked him, having watched that much.

Flandras turned and looked him in the eyes again, raising one of his own eyebrows. "And you haven't done your history research of me yet on your own? Or is such a question the natural way you throw people off from knowing how deeply you do know?" Rei blinked at him and didn't answer.

Flandras looked up to the corner of the room and casually said, "I spoke privately ...well as privately as can be given the circumstances of her office... with Ilena. She gave me the final variables I needed for the equations." He looked at Rei from the corner of his eye. "That no royal trusts anyone, not even any other royal." Rei seemed to agree with it, but again it was more in the eyes than anywhere else. The rest of him was just listening. "If that's really the case, then all of you are going to tear this nation apart when the lords finally act in a few years, or when you act against them in that same time."

Rei blinked and Flandras turned to look at him straight on and sober. "Ilena in particular isn't trustworthy at all by all my calculations and what information I've been given so far. I've got real data to collect next but I wouldn't be at all surprised to learn she was both helping you and King Sasou and working with the other hand with the anti-Touka faction in the lords against both of you. Why do you trust her? What have you put into place to prevent her from acting against that trust?"

Rei paused, then asked his own question. "Why is that your focus instead of Altherly and Gael?"

Flandras shook his head and answered, "Because they're all tied together. If the inside of the nation isn't stable it falls apart when external movements are made. I need this equation figured out so I can decide if it's even worth it to stay here in the castle. The answer to the question I just asked will let me decide if I continue to support the Toukas or don't."

"Ah." Rei looked down for a moment then took his turn to walk, moving forward until he was at the desk in the room. He pulled open the drawer and pulled out pen and paper. He motioned to Flandras and began writing. Flandras moved closer but waited until Rei was done writing. The page was handed to him.

"I can't talk to you openly in this office. One on the first floor I could if there weren't spies from every Ministry watching everything I do in this building. I'll consider what can be done. I also don't want to have you die with unspoken necessary data on your lips.

"Sasou has his own protections he's put in place against Ilena, knowing her from a very young age. I have Ore. Ore loves her, but is fully loyal and faithful to me. He watches her, keeps her restrained, and will punish her for me if it becomes necessary. He also knows more than she thinks he does and hides it even better than I. I know everything he knows." Flandras' eyebrows rose at that one. That was rather significant to the whole of the very detailed equation that had been coming out of these discussions he was having with the royals individually.

He put the paper on the desk and reached for the pen. Rei handed it over. Flandras pointed to that paragraph's last sentence and asked, *"From before she came to the castle? Or after?"*

Rei pointed to "before". Flandras drew in a breath and added that greater weight to the constant pinning Ilena's variable down. He continued reading. *"You need to add one more constant, but not to the written equations. Only keep it in your head. It's what I'm keeping the most hidden to be what wins us all of our battles. If you let anyone know I won't let you live."*

Flandras read that and paused. He blinked as the scene of his battlefield equations shifted in his mind one more time for him to see what it could be. *"Does it hold the whole of it pinned down into secure stability?"* he asked on the page.

"Yes," Rei answered quietly.

Flandras closed his eyes. Based on his conversation with Ilena he'd already added individual constants to hold the spinning variables of the royals down. Having the greater weight of someone completely loyal to a different royal as one of Ilena's constants helped. He similarly set constants owned by other royals next to each of the other royal variables. Then he tested to see if he needed any other constants. He could see that one constant that would be consistent between them all would cement the equation into being one of solidarity in the end instead of fracture.

He wrote, *"It's not necessary to know it specifically. Just knowing it truly exists and is present is sufficient to the equation."*

Rei shook his head and took the pen back. *"You are part of the equation also."*

Flandras blinked, then slumped a little. Right. If he went traitor, then the whole would also come falling down. He watched in some trepidation as Rei wrote on the page what that constant was. The words held his mind for some time. It was a very strong constant, if it stayed true for each piece. He'd have to test it for each one of them to confirm it for himself, but he nodded in understanding.

Flandras was done with that much. He bowed to Rei, but Rei didn't excuse him. Instead he stood thinking, perhaps making his own calculations. Finally he wrote, *"Are the war and the anti-Touka faction answers really tied together?"*

Flandras hesitated. "They could be if you decided you wanted them to be," he answered.

Rei pondered that answer then asked, "Has Ilena explained her variable?"

"She helped me understand that the Touka spin is controlled by a constant," Flandras answered. Rei nodded thoughtfully.

Rei looked at him with a testing look a little longer that then went to a more closed look. Flandras' brain instinctively recalculated. *"Would it help you to know Ilena has hidden guards watching over you? Or do you really need open access to me?"*

Flandras shivered inside for all he was still in his heavy coat and winter gear. His eyes widened of their own accord. *"That doesn't really help me, no. At the moment, she'll kill me faster than you will."*

Rei gave a firm nod of decision. *"From now on I'll expect you in the Rose office every day. Gather up your papers on your way in tomorrow morning, but don't tell anyone of the change. I'll let the door guards know on my way in in the morning."*

Flandras slumped in relief that Rei understood how to protect a critical value, even if a small one. He bowed and held it for a bit, swallowing the lump in the back of his throat. The pen scratched on the paper while he recovered. When he rose it said, *"You'll be very much out of your element and we'll be very distracting for a while, but until we've got the final resolution I want you where I can see you. We can move you into the Rosebud office after that. We'll let it out that I'm training you until then."*

"Thank you," Flandras mouthed without voicing the words. Rei gave him a nod and walked toward the door. In passing he placed a hand on Flandras' near shoulder to him and held it briefly.

As Flandras began to relax, Rei whispered, "Did Ilena give you physical support when you saw her?"

Flandras was puzzled by the question. "No?" he whispered back.

"Mmm," was all of Rei's response, then he was in motion for the door again. Flandras turned to watch him. He moved for the door himself as Rei passed Mina, saying quietly, "I think it's time to give Ore more time back in the Ministry on a regular basis. The balance isn't right yet."

Without thinking about it, Flandras followed Mina and Rei into the Rose office, but he stopped near the door to watch Rei. Rei paused by Ore's desk. "If Ilena's being too much the Researcher and Minister, how much more time do you need to be over there to calm that down?"

Ore looked up from his work in surprise. "Ahh, I don't know?"

Rei looked over his shoulder at Flandras, who blinked at them because Ore had looked also. "He's like that and she didn't do her usual to take care of it." His eyes looked back into Ore's which were still very wide in surprise. "I'll take to thinking she's going traitor already if that keeps up."

Ore went a little pale and shook his head. "I'll find out tonight and fix it," he promised, his eyes going back to Flandras. Ore frowned. "She should have if it's that obvious."

"That's what I thought," Rei said dryly and moved to continue to what looked like his desk. "Send him back with Mina to make my point more clear." Ore paled more and Flandras' eyes darted to Mina. Her court neutral had gone very cool. Flandras immediately added her to the equation. Then out of curiosity he looked at Andrew. Andrew was paying attention to the exchange. Like Rei he looked like he was only listening, but the eyes turned from a judging look at Flandras to a baleful look at Ore, which were only normal, to look into Mina's eyes. Flandras shivered yet again. Those two weren't to be crossed at all. When they showed up, Rei was angry.

Flandras took just one moment to scan the rest of the room. Everyone else was working hard, trying to not be interrupted, but he could tell that he needed to be in this room observing. Everyone in it was here for a similar underlying purpose to Rei, not just because he needed aides to help him with the work.

"Come with me for a moment, please." Flandras jumped to be addressed and had to turn his attention back to his more immediate surroundings. Ore was looking at him with some compassion. Flandras followed him back out to be taken back to the Lotus office. There he was completely surprised to have warm arms wrapped around his head and shoulders. "It's okay. You'll be protected sufficiently here. We don't let anyone die that we've claimed."

"That depends on who the 'we' is," Flandras muttered into the shoulder he was being held against.

"Weelll, I guess that's true," Ore conceded. "If it's Ilena I'll let you and Master know. Sometimes it's hard to tell when it's that and when it's as Master said and she was just too much the colder of her selves at the moment you talked to her. We're still learning her winter, closed–in self and I'm needed here for training for another week or so yet, if not more. I'm sorry you didn't get what you needed when you saw her."

"And this is just odd," Flandras said, since he already had a mixed opinion of the Consort.

Ore laughed. "Well, to most normal Ryokudans, yes. But you got adopted by the Second Princess, so for you it's what the inside of you needs."

"Not really?" Flandras denied it.

Ore let him go, studied him, then nodded and reached out a hand to rub the top of Flandras' head. He kept at it until Flandras finally sighed at him. The hand didn't go away for another few rubs after that. Flandras was surprised to find himself tearing up when it did. The arms were around him again, gently, and his tears came then. "You can let the ones go for when you were little, too," Ore said kindly. "You'll be able to work again, then, with much more ease. That's my role, is to be the gentle Father for those who need it."

Flandras' experience with him already said that wasn't what he was, but even that thought brought more tears. The lonely parts of him all wanted out at the same time as all the frightened and worried ones. There wasn't much he could do until it passed.

Walking back to his office with Mina was a struggle in recovering from letting out emotions like those all at once. He was glad she was silent for the walk, not demanding conversation nor asking any questions. She gave him a small kind smile at his office door. "I'd recommend just sitting still for a bit and finishing the recovery, or even taking a nap. Naps help one not have to think and the system to recover without the brain being involved."

"Ah..., this is normal enough even you can say it?" he had to ask.

Mina snorted. "Not that I'd ever let anyone touch me, but Father's rather hard to not accept at least once." Her eyes drifted away. "Mother, too, actually," she frowned. "Which is why it's rather hard for any of us to accept she wasn't for you. If that isn't fixed let us know. I'll need to take her out and work her hard as her punishment for completely missing it."

Flandras finally understood. He blushed. "Ah, no. Actually, Prince Ore already accused us of wanting to be intimate. That wouldn't be proper."

Mina blinked at him. "Oh. No, that would be a problem if he's already stepped in as the jealous Consort. He wasn't there when you visited?" Flandras shook his head. "Okay. I'll tell him. He'll know better how to handle that. You might get a visit from both of them, then. He's okay with it when he can be there to have that part calmed down." She gave him a sharp look. "At least I assume he didn't beat up on you ...instead of be Father for you?"

Flandras shook his head. "No."

"Well, that's good. We have to watch those two rather carefully. Wild as they come," she shook her head and raised a hand in farewell. "Rest. It will help." She closed the door and left him alone.

Flandras sank down at his desk, then did lie his head down on it and close his eyes. He wondered if all of this last little bit was what Rei had meant by, "*You'll be very much out of your element....*" He was asleep fairly quickly.

-o-o-o-

For some time after Flandras had been to visit and left again, the efforts in the Rose office had been the usual quiet industrious ones. The only sounds then were the scratching of pens on paper, the soft sounds of sheets of paper being turned, and the occasional sounds of people shifting, taking deep breaths between folders, soft coughs, and the like. With eight people in the room minimum on a regular basis now, those sounds were more frequent than when it had just been Rei, Andrew, and Mina in Ichijou.

A double knock came on the office door. Mina finished her sentence, then rose to go open it. On the other side was a paige with a message in hand. Rei's eye was on them since she'd put hand to handle. He sat up and quietly set his pen down as he recognized the paige. He was one of Ilena's. The message from Sasou might finally be here.

Taking a deep breath, Rei took the folder from Mina. He'd noted as as soon as it had been handed to Mina that it wasn't tied in the gold ribbon it should have been. All private missives in the nation were bound so that it was obvious that they'd been tampered with. That Sasou hadn't bound this one made it obvious to him that Sasou didn't want this one to be obviously anything at all. He wondered if he'd even let his closest aide review it. Michael Barrett usually read everything they wrote to each other, like Rei had Andrew read most of them as well if they contained things that would affect their relationships as siblings and royal peers.

It's normal. Ask Ilena what that means for the nation, if you're still unsure. As already discussed, the timing's difficult; however, because the lords of Suiran are complaining, and you asked, I'll see if I can get the Court to agree to a nationwide census.

Rei frowned at the letter. He wasn't sure even he completely understood what Sasou meant by this letter. It was obvious Sasou had thought he might not, given he'd been told to go back to Ilena again. He leaned back in his chair against the bright blue cushion and looked over at his third knight. "Ore, remember I wanted to teach you how to decipher cryptic messages?"

The black–haired head lifted from his work at his desk to blink golden eyes at Rei. "Yes, Master?"

"I've received another one for you to practice on." Rei stared at him directly in the eye. Ore knew who this had come from.

"*Oooh.* Like last time. Court speech like I'm supposed to be learning," Ore confirmed.

"Right. So learn it faster." Rei ignored the roll of Ore's eyes and held it out for Ore to collect. Ore arrived beside Rei's desk, opened the folder, then read it. When he was done reading it, Rei took it back and set the folder in his pile of work to take to his bedroom that night. "Think about it for a while. We'll discuss it later to see if you've figured this one out better than the last one." He pulled out his next folder to address.

"Yes, Master." Ore bowed a brief bow and returned to his seat.

There was the quiet scratching of pens on paper or papers being turned until there was a knock at the door and it opened to let in Mizi. Sam and Brian were already in the office, having been sent there by her that morning, now that she was refusing to have more than two guards with her at once. Kirk, Leon, and her secretary Tanner followed her into the room. Rei put down his pen and smiled at his wife. "Is it lunch time, then?"

"I'm a bit early today, having arrived before the lunch cart, but yes," she smiled back at him.

"Hello, Mistress!" Ore greeted her cheerily.

"Hello, Ore," she answered back kindly. "Ilena seemed to be in good spirits today," she said. "We had a good if brief visit."

"That's good," Ore relaxed back in his chair. "I'm sorry she's often very busy. If she was able to help you smile this morning, then it's indeed a good day."

Rei smiled to himself as he addressed them both. "Well, then, maybe this would be a good day to vacation a bit. Shall we all have an evening off and we'll go with Ore and his guards to the Lower office for dinner tonight to tease their office?"

Mizi's face lit up as Ore gave a nod. "I think that would be good for us, if you could tease us. It might mean you're relaxed enough," Ore teased Rei right back immediately. Then he just as immediately frowned. "Except sometimes your teases are that we think we're going to relax and then you give us more work instead."

Rei actually laughed at that one. It was so true. Even tonight it would be. Mina's look of approval agreed that was usually what Rei did to the pair to tease them, and was what they needed when they got too relaxed. "Well, we'll see. I won't promise anything," Rei teased Ore further, getting a small groan in response.

Mizi put her hand on Ore's shoulder to console him. "Even if he does ask one or the other of you for more, it will be good to come and just visit for a while." Her eyes took in everyone in the room, in particular her own people. She was still practicing telling when they needed time off. "I think an evening's vacation would be good for everyone. They are rather important this time of year, after all."

Several people in the room shuddered, and a few others hunched their shoulders up to their ears, but the stalwarts firmly held themselves. One evening vacation per week minimum was necessary in the Suiran winters. They'd take it even if just to go to bed earlier than normal, or to sit in a chair in front of a fireplace. At Andrew and Mina's raised eyebrows, Rei waved a hand at them. "You don't have to walk us over there. I've seen all your faces enough every day all day. We'll go with Ore, Petroi, and Thayne. That's sufficient."

Both of the couple gave him curt nods and glares–without–glaring at Ore and his guards. Ore held up his hand in promise to watch over the royal couple well. The promise nods from Petroi and Thayne were what made Rei's childhood guards relax, though, as he expected. He sighed at them internally. At least the four had a good understanding with each other, unlike Mizi's that were still trying to fit in at some level.

That reminded him. He leaned back in his chair and put his fingertips together in front of him. "However, we do need to have a relaxing time all together, too. I think the next vacation time after this needs to be at least a half–day of both households together. A competition or something to work out all the sitting inside we have to do all day every day."

People in the room sat up and paid attention, since most in the room were competitive. Probably only Aiden, Brianna, and Mizi weren't, although Mizi was learning to hold her own. "Petroi, Andrew, work something out, but include input from the others in both households. We shouldn't be making Aiden, Brianna, Grandfather, and Leah bored, left out, nor competitors." Both men bowed to Rei, neither one needing more work, but both of them needing the practice in talking to the members of the households and in working out what sorts of things they could do together. It would be hard to be all in the same building together once the new Regent's residence was built if they hadn't had free time to get to know each other before then.

Ore raised his hand. "While we might want to do something different, the last time we went as a household and Ministry, we walked to town for a group shopping trip and had a snowball fight on the way in. Then we let everyone have the evening off so we didn't have to see each other's faces any more than that. That sort of combination seemed to work well enough."

"Something like that, but I don't have the capacity to go into town," Rei answered. "The hills north of the castle, or the garrison, or one of the indoor locations we can turn into whatever we want would be best for me."

"We'll see to it, Rei," Andrew answered. Petroi promised it as well. Satisfied, Rei returned to the folder on his desk, wanting to get it completed before the lunch cart arrived.

-o-o-o-

At the end of the workday for the Rose office, Rei rose from the chair at his desk and picked up his evening stack of work. It was about four folders which was one more than he wanted but that one was rather important. That was the silent signal for everyone else to put down their pens and prepare to leave as well. There was a lot of muffling up in heavy cloaks, scarves, hats, and gloves. The gas lights were snuffed out and the fireplace logs separated for the night. They all left the office together and separated at the usual place Ore would leave the rest of them. Mizi and Rei turned off with them. The rest of their household continued on to the Old Regent's building.

"So, is it going to be happy teasing or work teasing, Master?" Ore asked on the way. He'd already told Ilena, in their ministry's coded whisper, that it was a vacation evening and Rei and Mizi were coming to dinner when Rei had said it before lunch. Mina had sternly reminded Ore that he was to see to Flandras as well, so Ore had told Ilena to invite him, too.

"Work, mostly," Rei answered.

Ore sighed a long–suffering sigh and slumped dramatically. "I rather thought so." Mizi giggled.

"It is good for you both," Petroi said without a shred of mercy.

"Indeed," Rei agreed. Thayne snorted a laugh as Ore went even more dramatically dejected, but he did pat Ore's back in some sympathy.

Leah, Rio, and Amber were at the food carts filling plates when they arrived at the door to the Lower office. They were greeted cheerily and the cold larger group flowed through the door to remove their warm outer gear and hang them up on the pegs just inside the door. The fire in the fireplace was crackling just as cheerily and was made to warm them up nicely. Rei made sure to hang on to his folders, not losing track of them during that time.

"Welcome Master Rei, Mistress Mizi, and Ore!" Ilena called to them as they finally turned for the main area. Ilena was sitting on one of the couches at the low table, waiting for them. Rei took up Mizi's hand in his free hand and pulled her with him to sit on the opposing couch. He wasn't surprised when Justinian was given the third seat on that couch next to Mizi. Ilena's household had an instinctive knack of knowing who needed what kind of support.

Having Justinian located there put the historian Reynold in the end chair. Ore made Ilena scoot to the middle of the couch, sitting opposite Mizi, so he could sit opposite Rei. Rei was a little surprised Ilena waved at Petroi and made him sit next to her, which he did with some tentativity at first that gave way to relaxation the longer he was next to her. Usually it would've been Justinian or Liam next to Ilena, but Rei understood it after Petroi had relaxed. It was hard for the childhood guardian to be away from Ilena all day in the Rose office, even if Rei did need Ore with him.

Since Petroi was next to Ilena that left Thayne without a place to sit, unless he took the remaining single head chair, but Ore motioned to Grandfather to take it. Thayne immediately pulled an extra chair from the side of the room and carried it to set it between Ore and Grandfather for Leah to sit next to her husband. Then he went back and picked up another to set next to Petroi. Reynold shifted over to make room for him.

Before Thayne sat down, Rei caught his attention. "Bring another over next to me for Flandras," he mildly ordered. Thayne bobbed his head and disappeared into a bedroom for one more chair. Flandras sat in it very tentatively, obviously uncomfortable with his placement but Rei was making a hidden statement that he was sure wouldn't be lost on Ilena even if she should question why. "I think you need more table space, Ilena," Rei dryly teased her. "Where will the rest sit if we add the chairs for them around this one?"

There were chuckles in the room as the remaining ten people took up places in whatever chairs were available. Ilena's tawny eyes sparkled as they came around to meet his gaze. "That's why I've asked Mister Balar to make the new building's dining room a garrison–style eating room with the long tables and benches. We'll all just sit wherever and have table space then, unlike laps like we do now."

"That would work," Rei agreed as he considered that option. "Benches aren't as comfortable, not having backs, but for fitting everyone in, it'd be fine. If we want more formal, we can always inform the kitchen to put together a formal dinner for us in one of the formal dining rooms."

Everyone in the room shuddered except himself and Mizi. He smiled. It had been a good tease of the group. These didn't need nor want such formalities normally. "I wonder," Ilena mused, "if the kitchen doesn't wonder why we don't more often, generally?" She looked over at her ladies. "How many carts did they send this time?"

"Four instead of the usual two piled high," Leah answered dryly.

"Yeah, they catered to you coming to us tonight," Ilena grimaced at Rei. He grimaced right back, not needing it any more than they did. Although, he was grateful the castle kitchen fed him at all.

The conversation continued around the table for the meal part of it. When the plates had been collected up, this time by Henry, Marcus, and Justinian, and whatever hands were there to pass them back out into the hall, Rei leaned back and pulled Mizi to rest on him. His cue was very quickly understood by the intelligent Ilena. "Petroi, Thayne, go pour up after–dinner drinks. You know what they like by now?" She raised an eyebrow at them.

Thayne smiled. "Juice for Mistress Mizi, wine for Master Rei, port for the two of you. ...Unless you're wanting something less sweet?"

"Less sweet," Ore requested, "but more than wine."

"Of course," Thayne answered. "Flandras, what would you like?" Flandras hesitated, unsure for a bit, then asked politely for juice. Thane accepted that answer calmly and joined Petroi at the drink bar.

The remaining members of the household began to disappear to their own rooms, save Grandfather who was also brought a glass of wine. "Will you be needing me to stay?" Leah asked, looking between Ore and Rei.

Ore raised an eyebrow at Rei. "I don't think so," Rei answered, "but that isn't mine to say." His eyes scanned the remaining people in the room. "It might be better for it to be Petroi," he said slowly, "if it needs to be anyone else."

"Petroi can answer from his room if we need him to," Ilena excused him as well to begin preparing for bed. Rei agreed. Petroi and Thayne placed the final drinks on the table and bowed as Leah curtsied. They took themselves out and Rei reached for his small stack of folders. He flipped each one open until he'd found the one he wanted.

Ore blinked at him. "I always thought you took work to bed because you were lonely at night and it was hard to fall asleep."

"Well, yes, but that's where I answer the most secret messages as well, so no one can inadvertently see what I'm working on. You'll be doing the same from now on, but you can claim it's hard work for you," Rei answered.

Dryly Ore answered, "It will be, I'm quite sure."

"And Ilena can help you with that."

Ilena rolled her eyes and ended up looking at Grandfather. "If it's letters to write back, you'll be helping him practice that part." Grandfather agreed, but then he was Ore's secretary.

Ore obviously already knew what Rei wanted to talk about, given he was the one who'd kept Grandfather and by his drink choice. He only did the port when he was planning on really relaxing. There was one piece of business they needed to complete first, though. Rei looked at Ore and tipped his head slightly at Flandras.

Ore swallowed his mouthful of drink and set his glass down on the table. He turned to Ilena who gave him her attention. "Flandras came to Master today to ask questions, I assume, but he was so tense he followed Master into the Rose office without any thought after their conversation was over. I gave him the healing of Father, but it was very obvious you'd not given him the comfort of Mother when he came to visit you." Ore drew in a breath and went apologetic. "Mina explained it to me after she took Flandras back to his office. Thank you both for respecting my boundaries."

He glanced at Flandras, then said simply, "Ilena, Master has said that you need to help him properly. Will you be Mother for him tonight while I'm here with you, to help him not be so afraid?"

Ilena put her glass down on the table and sighed. "First he needs to understand. I'm already an untrustworthy variable in his equation. If he can't trust Mother, it won't help much."

Rei agreed. It was why Flandras was here tonight. It was a lesson he needed and Rei wanted to participate and watch Flandras' reaction. He turned to Flandras. Flandras blinked at him, then said, "It was rather difficult to deal with what Prince Ore did. I napped like Sir Durand suggested and that helped some, but I'm still very confused. Was that event what you meant by I'd be out of my element? Because I very much was ...am."

"Yes," Rei answered that question first. "Let me help you expand Ilena's variable. It's actually it's own equation almost as long as the Touka one you've put together. Ore's is as well in order to match her's as he needs to provide a constant for each of her variables."

"*Each* of her variables?" Flandras blurted out as his eyes turned to take in Ilena again. Then his eyes narrowed. "You don't just play court faces."

Ilena and Ore both shook their heads. "I *am* different faces," she answered. "My household calls it 'broken'. I've been through life experiences so difficult that each face has unique needs that need to be met. Ore and everyone else have been trying to help me heal, so things are better than they used to be, but we're not completely there yet." She blinked and seemed to sigh a little.

"So, the way I knew you at Kouzanshi university?" Flandras asked, his eyes still narrow.

Ore smiled. "I like that Ilena. That's a unique place for her, the library, and thus a unique face. When she talks to you as the Professor, that's one we see here on occasion when she feels the need to lecture, but the happy bouncy Ilena only happens there. I call that one the Kouzanshi Ilena. I'm always all of me, but that one I can be the usual relaxed me with, just like with 'Just Ilena'. That's the woman who's still the Ilena of all of them but whom she's most uncomfortable with: the Ilena that isn't playing any faces or being any faces, just being herself. That's also my favorite."

Flandras studied Ore for a bit. "Is it okay to pander to the divisions?"

"Pander?" Ore's eyebrow rose just a little and just the hint of derision came out in his tone. Rei thought his lessons on being a high lord had honed his capability to play the game a little too much, maybe.

Rei took back over before that became a fight. He shifted to catch Flandras' attention and frowned at him. "Don't play those games in this room. Learning by observation is fine, they don't mind that, but the court push only makes them angry, particularly Ore. Ilena will accept it and deflect it most of the time, sometimes she'll laugh at you, but as you've already said, she'll put a knife into you if she's the wrong face to do it to." He'd learned a lot about how Flandras tested the variables of his equations in the one private visit they'd had. Flandras backed down and apologized.

Rei asked Grandfather to fetch paper and pen. When they'd been handed to him and the inkwell placed on the table, Rei put the paper on top of the folder in his lap. He wrote the equation for Flandras, keeping Ore's constant the same letter but a different one for each of Ilena's variables. "While we call Ore names consistent with what we call Ilena, he is, as he said, the same for all of them.

"M is for Mother, when Ilena's comforting those whom she cares deeply for and when she's tender. P is for Princess, the young Ilena that felt a severe duty to her birthright, who holds with exactness to the duties and responsibilities of nobility. C is for Child, the young girl who watched her family murdered before her eyes that needs the comforting arms of those who care for her and won't leave her abandoned to her fears and loneliness.

"R is for the researcher and professor, the genius student who loves to learn and teach." Rei lifted his eyes to tease Mizi slightly. "Mizi loves the combination of Mother, the professor, and the princess. That's who helped her stand by my side." Mizi smiled back and nodded agreement.

As the pen was about to go on the paper again Flandras got in a question first. "They can be combined, they aren't just separate?"

"Correct," Rei answered. He'd already been making the equation an addition problem. He pondered just a little then said, "When they're all zero then what's left over is 'Just Ilena', as Ore said. Most of the time she only comes out for Ore. We've seen peeks of her here and there." He pouted at Ilena, but she only blinked back at him.

"It's the hardest one for her to reach," Ore explained, "because she almost always has one role or another to play. The rest don't all go to zero often."

Flandras blinked and Rei went back to the equation. "Q is for the Queen of Night, who is deadly, impatient, and will kill you quickly without remorse." His eyes rose to look into Flandras' soberly. "That's who you're afraid of, and rightly so, but she's rarely that here in the castle. That's who she became so that I'd have a nightwalker intelligence network, and because of Pakyo Shicchi and his nefarious workings. He also created the Steward."

An S went down as the next variable. "That's the hard–working servant who faces others and expects to be faced with practicality and little waste of time. Those two are who won't play the game. If she purses her lips at you instead of just answering to it, stop and let it alone." Flandras swallowed and nodded that he understood.

"You're not likely to ever see the Naluk'." The N went down on the paper. "That's who she is in Tarc. Also deadly but also caring and a noble like the Princess, not like Mother. And contrary to the Professor, if her wisdom is ignored she kills if allowed to." Rei actually wrote those equivalencies and non–equalities on the page below the N part of the summation equation:

$$IO = MO_m + PO_p + CO_c + RO_r + QO_q + SO_s + NO_n + IO$$

$$N = Q + P \neq R \in (P \neq M)$$

Rei blinked and looked at Flandras to add, "When she's being my sister, she's being Mother and the Princess, mostly Mother and a little the princess since I'm a prince and her brother." He frowned a little, then asked Ilena, "And is some of that 'Just Ilena'?"

"Yes," she admitted to him. "Mostly, actually." Rei was a bit stunned at that revelation.

Ore raised his hand. "When she's being my wife outside of being casual here at home she's the Steward, Just Ilena, and Partner. If we need to face the world with nobility she adds in the Princess as well."

"Oh? You have a Partner category, too? Is it a combination of the others?" Rei asked, not having heard of the Partner before.

Ore considered that, then shook his head. "I'd have to say it's a combination of the others in varying levels, like a little of the Queen, Princess, and Mother added to a lot of the Steward. I made her add Just Ilena because that's who I love best, and drop the level of Steward, too."

"That's convenient," Rei said very dryly. Ilena glared at him. He turned to Flandras instead of answering her. "That's a good example of how well she can use them and intertwine them as she does play the game to suit her needs, but when she's each of them without restraint she can't come out of them very well. Each of the people who ate with us tonight are varying levels of restraint on her various selves that she's placed on herself. She didn't have Ore as a restraint until spring of last year when we discovered her.

"You could add each of them to the equation as well, but it's not worth it because that's getting too far into the details. It's enough to know that she knows she needs the restraints to be whole and has them around her. Ore's not the only one, he's just *mine* added to her equation." He looked up blandly at Flandras. The strategist understood what he meant.

Rei considered all of the parts of Ilena he knew about, then went very sober. He'd forgotten one of the small yet most critical things. He didn't have to worry about it too much when they were calmly in the castle. "There's one last piece that will cause the most chaos in the equation and makes it slightly unstable." Flandras' eyes immediately jumped to look into Rei's eyes. Rei wondered if he'd been hoping to have that one shown to him and likely he did. Rei pursed his lips. "So far the instability shifts always in the direction I need it to go, but it's not guaranteed." He added one more variable for Ilena, the related constant for Ore, then one more variable.

$$IO = MO_m + PO_p + CO_c + RO_r + QO_q + SO_s + NO_n + IO + F(O_f + \sigma)$$

Pointing to the final term of the equation Rei explained, "This is the wildness of both of them. F is for the Falcon. The falcon is the part of Ilena that wants to be free to do as she will, rather than be under the requirements and restraints she must be. It's a very small variable, but it's rather critical to the whole because it can cause unexpected changes if forgotten or not taken into account.

"Ore — when he's calm — is her handler and the constant, but her wildness can pull on his wildness strongly enough the constant becomes zero. His variable can then go even higher than hers, in particular if she's threatened in any way. It can go high enough to overwhelm the whole of what you expected. We had an opportunity to see that early on. He's become much stronger since then, but it's not to be left out at all. That variable is what we call the Stallion. Expect it to be that surprisingly fierce and sudden, too."

Flandras looked back at Rei just as sober. He gave a nod. "I'm glad you've not left it out. I've already put it into place for all Toukas, but I needed to know Prince Ore also contains it, particularly if it can be that strong. Knowing when it's most likely to happen helps as well."

Rei raised an eyebrow. "For *all* Toukas?"

Flandras' lip lifted slightly. "There's a reason your family has always used the eagle, hawk, and falcon to represent the members of the royal family. You all carry that small chaos that changes things ever so slightly beyond what people expect." His eyes studied Rei like they had before when they'd met each other privately. "You're almost to Eagle as well; although, you'll not likely ever be called that, not being King."

Rei blinked at Flandras in slight surprise, but Ore was nodding wisely. "Having to work with Ilena as she is and being strengthened by her is likely doing it: finishing making Master into what he really can become." He turned a puzzled look to Ilena. "Is King Brother doing that on purpose, too?"

"Likely," Ilena answered. "He's been working very hard to make sure Master Rei can stand on his own."

Once Flandras had settled that equation, which Rei handed him the paper for, Rei tested him. "So, now that you know, do you want to still test them all to truly understand how to fit them into your calculations?" His eyebrow lifted slightly and he watched Flandras. The others sat with the court neutral to make him decide what he wanted.

Flandras looked down at the sheet of paper in his hand. Tentatively he said, "Well, not the Queen of Night, nor the Naluk'." He paused, then frowned. "Prince Ore said there's the unique Kouzanshi Ilena?"

Rei shook his head. "I don't add her because she is unique to that location. I believe she added that one in because she had a need to meet, so it isn't part of this consistent base equation caused by others."

Flandras gave a nod without looking up. He was perhaps as disappointed as Ore was that Ilena wouldn't play that part anywhere else. That and the Professor were all he'd known before. He drew in a breath. "It would be good to understand the Steward and Princess, I think. But would the Child or Mother affect national politics?"

Rei went soft. "The Child is who became the Queen of Night and Mother. Mother's essential to understand because that's who created my other intelligence network. Those people love the Princess Ilena and give her great loyalty, the same as the nightwalkers give their loyalty to the Queen of Night. Once you understand Mother, and mix that in with the fear that the Queen of Night engenders, then you understand why Ilena's necessary to Suiran and Ryokudo." He looked at Ore, although he was more seeing the past. "Is it really necessary for him to see the Child, or just to understand what happened?"

"Understanding the history is usually sufficient," Ore answered.

Mizi agreed with him. "We all have enough empathy to understand how difficult and heart–rending that event would've been."

Rei turned to Flandras again and waited for him to decide. He finally lifted his head and looked Ilena in the eyes. "Come to the next City Council meeting if you want to see the Steward," she invited him. "Come to the next three or four Court of Minister's meetings to see that in slight measure mixed with the Princess, which is the closest I get on a frequent basis. You'll want to know those to understand how I relate to the lords, which really isn't all that different from most Toukas of the past." Flandras' nose wrinkled at the reference but he indicated he'd go.

Ilena's face went soft and compassionate, Mother coming to the fore to teach him that aspect of Ilena. "Flandras," she said softly, "I'm grateful that you were willing to continue to press forward to meet your own dream and goal, even though you were bullied by those who'd been your friends and you were disowned by your father. Your mother sends her love and often asks if you're doing well. I was pleased to be able to tell her that you'd been called up by the Regent. She was glad to know of it."

Flandras was staring at Ilena, stunned. "How...? I've never told you anything."

Ilena gave a soft, sad smile. "No. You haven't. But I've been watching you a long time. It was one of my Children that suggested you try Kouzanshi university that night you were spending your last coin at the inn, wondering if you'd be able to eat again now that you didn't have a home to go to." Her tawny eyes were slightly glistening. "I have many Children who are my eyes and ears at inns. So many frightened and angry people will tell their stories to a kind smile and open ears. I listen for dreams that cry out for fulfillment. Your's was one that I couldn't let die.

"The innkeeper was willing to let you sleep in the attic room and do his books in payment for that and food until we could get a carriage out to pick you up and take you to Kouzanshi. The Dean was willing to listen to my messenger so knew to be expecting you." She looked down at her hands, then smiled back at Flandras briefly before turning to look at Rei. "Sasou was his sponsor who paid for his housing, food, and clothing." Rei and Flandras both had their jaws drop. "When I explained what I'd found and what I wanted to use him for, Sasou asked no questions, only sent the Dean the requisition and requirement to bill him silently. I believe it came out of his personal purse, too, but he hasn't told me."

Flandras closed his mouth and swallowed. He was trembling slightly. Ilena motioned and patted the empty couch seat next to her. Flandras hesitated. Rei reached out and pushed lightly on his closer shoulder, also encouraging him. Flandras glanced at Ore. Ore nodded he should go, his soft smile that of Father.

Flandras moved to sit next to Ilena, shoving the paper rather automatically into his jacket as he went. They waited until he was perched a bit on the edge of the seat of the couch, still uncomfortable. Ilena reached out and took his hands in hers, holding them over his knees. "Flandras," she said softly, "thank you, on behalf of the Toukas, for coming and being willing to help us. I'm sorry it made you so afraid to be alone in the office. I was testing you, to try to learn if you'd still be loyal to your father and take to him and the anti-Touka lords what knowledge we need to give you to overcome him and the other anti-Touka lords. It's a hard place to have you and for you to be in. Can you live in it? Can you live with betraying him? Or should we release you?" She kept the final questions as gentle as the rest.

Flandras had already had tears streaking down his cheeks at her first words of gratitude, the touch of Mother doing that to people generally as they felt the reality of being needed and cared for by a real human other than themselves. He froze somewhat at the admission and questions, though. He stared at her through his tears, then slumped. Drawing a deep breath, then taking the handkerchief Ore was handing over Ilena's lap in one hand, the other still captured in hers, he wiped his face and considered what he'd say.

When Flandras' eyes turned to Rei, Rei kept his expression kind. "Thank you for caring about what I needed, while still being obedient to Ilena," Rei said. "I look for that kind of heart to be close to me. I'd like to be able to continue to work with you for a very long time."

At that the man broke down into sobs that he hid behind the handkerchief. Ilena let go of his hand and wrapped her arms around his shoulders. "If you've won Master Rei, you've done very well," Ilena said. Her hand rubbed his head comfortingly. "I'm very proud of you." They let him cry until he was done. It took a while, so the rest of them sipped at their drinks until then. Mizi held Rei's hand tightly and smiled at him. He smiled back, happy to just sit and rest with them in this room.

When Flandras had recovered enough to leave Ilena's arms and talk to them again, he said, "Father was always angry that I'd rather admire Toukas than be angry at them with him. I could see why the past Toukas had done what they'd done. I could also understand why the first lords would be angry about being conquered. It's illogical to me for the lords to still be angry today when so many good things have been done in recent history." His brow furrowed in some frustration.

"I want to support good people trying to do good things." His eyes went to Ilena, Ore, Mizi, then Rei. "I think you're trying hard to do that, from what little I've seen and heard. If I could influence things in that direction, I'd like to, for all I will tell you all sides the equations show."

Rei sorrowfully understood what was behind that. "And that will test us as well."

Flandras' expression went wryly self–incriminating. "Well, yes," he admitted openly. "But even so, I do want to stay and use the gifts I was given in the best way I can. I spent the whole day after our first meeting completely amazed at how much my unique gift is so needed at this very moment in Ryokudo history. To be here that day was to walk on proverbial air." He slumped and gave an accusatory look to Ilena. "You could have said so earlier when I was here, that King Sasou already knew who I was. It would've been sufficient to make me not quite so afraid."

Ilena shook her head. "I didn't need you doubting him, too. He needs to stay at the position you'd already put him in your equations and mind. He really is there, for all only Rei and I can see it. While it won't have as great an effect on the balance of strength we have when you add in numbers to the Touka variables, it will still have one that no other people account for." She pet his head one more time as he pondered that part of the equation.

-o-o-o-

Rei motioned Flandras to return to the seat next to him. This clearing was much greater than the tears Flandras had cried for Father. Distance from Mother would help him recover a little better. Rei wasn't ready to send the man to bed, which he likely really wished he could be. "So, have you had any thoughts on deciphering this one, Ore?" Rei tapped the folder in his lap, changing the topic to work.

Ore's brow furrowed. "It came unmarked, but by Ilena's courier, so King Brother wants it even more secret than normal. But it seemed somewhat unassuming even so." Rei let him consider a little longer. "Even if it had been read by anyone else, it wouldn't have been thought to contain anything secret at all."

"Indeed," Rei answered dryly. "Leaving off the salutation and who it was addressed to points to the high level of secrecy as well. I suspect that he didn't even let Lord Barrett read it. That's something that almost never happens." Eyebrows rose on the opposite couch. "If he'd tied it in his gold ribbon and not shared it, that would have given away the secrecy of it and it would have been translated the way he didn't want it to be in his own office." He narrowed his eyes at Ore, "That is: correctly."

He turned to Ilena and handed the folder to her. "It's actually you who I've brought this to. It's his message to you, not me."

"Oh!" Ore sat upright a bit. "Is that why he expressly mentioned her name in it?"

"Yes," Rei answered. "She has the answer to give me more directly, so he's written it so the clues tell her what to say. I've my guesses as to what the last half of the letter means, but the first half is hers to tell us."

The letter being short, he made sure his eyes were on Ilena, waiting for her eyes to come back up from the page. She repeated it out loud, but quietly, to make sure she'd read it correctly, since it was in letters that didn't sit still for her. Ore and Rei both nodded to let her know she had. Rei firmly didn't let her go, though. She needed to answer for him what she knew that he only could guess at.

She sighed as she closed the folder and handed it back. Mizi took it for Rei. He indicated she should also read it. She did then put it with his other three folders. She was confused as well as to what it might mean other than what it said on the surface. Rei needed her to have these lessons as well so if necessary he and Sasou could write similarly to her. That wouldn't likely happen soon, but it would almost surely be necessary at some point in their lives as royals of Ryokudo.

Rei wasn't surprised when Ilena first turned to Ore, including Mizi somewhat. She was always very good at helping him teach the finer points of being royalty. It was her first responsibility for Mizi and Ore, as a matter of fact, after keeping them protected. "The first part comes to me because the secret letters like this are based in a person's shared experiences with the letter–writer. He's referencing our shared childhood, from my first visit to Ryokudo. I told him then that the Selician court was falling apart, with open dissensions and assassinations nearly daily. When I'd complained to my Grandfather and Uncles, and eventually even the lords for this unruly court behavior, I was told that it was normal, the way the court worked, with smooth court words to justify what they were doing." Her expression went sad.

Rei's heart fell. "What we're living now is similar, just hidden rather than open," he said quietly. Ilena gave a nod of agreement. "In other words, the hidden sedition has been going on for at least as long as Mother ruled, and perhaps longer?" he asked.

"Yes," Ilena confirmed. "Likely longer. Even our shared Grandfather moved against the lords, not just the nightwalkers." She sighed and looked away. "Actually, in doing the history research on the Old Regent's building and thus more in depth on the nation, like Flandras said it's likely been a problem since Touka entered the area and took over all the small clans and nations that made up Ryokudo at that time.

"No people like to have to bow the head to invaders just because they're stronger and take over by force of arms. The First Peace King is called that because he didn't take any more land, stopped fighting, and tried to smooth things over just enough to get the lords of the lands to work with him and Touka generally. He left the lords, particularly in Suiran, as lords who already knew how to rule, save for the Kouzan head line and House Shicchi since that had been the Waldstaat king's line."

Ilena shrugged. "That didn't mean that the lords all fell in line, happy to become friends with Touka. I suspect at some level that resentment is passed down from that time in many holdings. It might be passed down in the commoners as well, but that's likely a lesser influence since most of what the Throne has done is to help the people of Ryokudo. But there's been no love lost between the Throne and the lords."

Mizi nodded. "My reading research around the edges is the whole history of Ryokudo, and we studied the Suiran history pretty extensively when I was working to become princess. I wondered that as we went on the progress. More than I liked of the lords were at best polite and many didn't want us there longer than we were there, if at all."

Rei gave a sad nod of agreement. "I did have to work harder than I wanted to have to; although, I did expect some level of that sort of testing since I'm both new and young. It's been the same here in this court. Most of the lesser court lords, from directors on down, can work with me fairly easily, but ministers and higher lords seem to enjoy standing in my way and arguing with me when it should be completely unnecessary."

He looked off into the distance, somewhat pensively. "I watched that happen with Sasou in Ichijou and hoped I'd be junior enough and just different enough in my approach that it wouldn't be so bad here." He looked back at Ilena, taking comfort in her compassionate look. "If it's already so entrenched in them, though, there's not much hope of just turning their opinions about me. It's the whole of the family name they're fighting against."

"Sadly, yes," Ilena agreed.

Rei slumped back into the couch and sipped at his wine. Mizi pressed his hand in hers and he pressed it back, glad he had her support, and the support of the two in front of him. Even Grandfather's and the whole of the Suiran Ministry of Intelligence's. It seemed a large thing to fight against history and things he couldn't affect now. He could only work from this point forward.

"Why does King Brother say he'll help because Master asked him for the census?" Ore asked.

"It means he's been waiting for me to decide what can be done, now that I've begun to see the whole scope of the problem," Rei answered back. "If it's lasted this long, and Mother couldn't move against the court, only holding it from exploding entirely when she was Regent, then they've been waiting for me to be here in this place. It's probably also why Sasou put me here so young." He gave Ilena a questioning look. "Was it desperation because things were getting so bad, or because he thought if I still seemed young and impressionable I'd be able to get them to turn better?"

Ilena shook her head. "Probably both. Between us we could clean them out of Nijou from a position of innocence, coming to it newly and knowing nothing of the history at the time. Even if we might have known the history, all of the royal family can claim it was the innocence of youth. If he'd waited until you were his current age, you'd be considered already 'tainted' by what Sasou learned young."

"Yes," Rei was dry. "I watched him learn the coldness towards the lords when he was still only fifteen and sixteen. I didn't understand it completely, but I watched how he acted towards them and how they responded from before then until I left Ichijou. It's actually why I spent more time with the soldiers than the lords. I didn't want to be seen siding with either side in Ichijou. I've always believed it important to be in as neutral a position there as possible." He shrugged. "It's very hard here to not act like him, though, when they're so entrenched in their unwillingness to move and help the country the way they should. I've been trying to make sure I feel my own way through instead of falling into his ways."

Rei let go of Mizi's hand to open the folder and look at the words again. "Ore, every phrase is important to review. Every one has meaning. We've covered the first two sentences, but you've only asked about one of the four phrases that are meaningful in the last sentence. I want to confirm the rest with Ilena and you can learn from them as we do."

He glanced at Grandfather. "I'm sorry to take up so much of your evening with this, but I do want you to know enough to be able to help him write up the response to it, if we decide it needs one. I'll be having him answer Sasou's letters, not just reading them and bringing the information to Ilena." Grandfather forgave him although it wasn't necessary for a servant to do so, just as it wasn't necessary for Rei to ask for the forgiveness. It was how Rei worked, though, and he was grateful he could and receive kindness in return. The obstinacy of the court wore on him many days.

Rei turned to the first phrase of the last sentence. "We've already talked, he and I, about how difficult it's going to be to fit in all of the things I want to accomplish this year, and what he wants to accomplish." His eyes lifted to Ilena's again as his finger tapped on his wine glass in slight frustration at all of the pieces of this very complex puzzle he was supposed to be putting together. "I don't think he's completely opposed to me requiring a census this year, but he still doesn't think that's the right thing to be doing this year, given how lukewarm the rest of the sentence is." Ilena gave that thought confirmation.

Rei continued to the next undiscussed phrase. "He mentions that he's willing because the lords of Suiran are complaining, but I never mentioned that in any letter or conversation I've had with him."

Ore raised an eyebrow and interrupted at that. "How would I know something like that, if I'm the one trying to decipher this?" he asked.

Rei shook his head. "You wouldn't, but you might be able to wonder it and ask me. You do that separately from reading the letter. Like when I requested to come have dinner only after Mizi arrived at the Rose office to keep the two things very separated from each other to prevent the others in the office from knowing they were related at all."

Ore considered that for a while, giving a musing nod after a bit. Rei continued on to Ilena, "Is that him saying that he'd like to use something like that as a pry bar between the lords of Ichijou and lower Ryokudo and those of Suiran? If he can create conflict between the lords that are against Touka?"

Ilena answered slowly, "I'd think so, yes. That would help him where he's been unable to affect them. Since you've said he's had to be adversarial generally against the lords, if working with them, then it's possible he hasn't found a way to get them to break up alliances with each other. He's not in a position where he can very easily. He'd have to find the inside cracks, like I used against Pakyo, and like we're hoping to use against Brulac. It's perhaps his way to tell you he can't?"

Rei took another sip of wine, considered that, then agreed. As his mind spun the words of the letter around and the answers, Ore hesitantly interrupted again. "Ah, is there any meaning in the last part?"

Rei shook his head. "It means what it says, but it's the part that lets me know he's lukewarm to the idea being the best choice for what to do to address the issue."

"Because he worded it like he didn't believe it would happen?" Ore asked. Both Ilena and Rei nodded agreement. "Oh. Okay. I think I can tell those kinds of things." They both glared at him slightly. He did that kind of thing all the time on his own, so he should be able to quite easily.

There was silence for a while as the others let Rei work things out in his head. Eventually Mizi shifted. "Ilena, this issue of the lords being antagonistic against the House of Touka, could this in part be why I'm struggling with Lady Brianna? And maybe with Brian and Kirk? Would they have been taught to dislike Touka from childhood?"

Rei squeezed Mizi's hand, knowing this part was very difficult for her. They needed to have allies in the lords, and use them where they had use, but to select one that wasn't already tainted with the resentment was so hard. She looked at him. "This is why Sasou didn't let even Lord Barrett read the letter and why Ilena tested Flandras. There's no way for us to know who's learned it from birth, and what information they'll pass on to the others. It's why we used Ilena's couriers, the only system we trust with sensitive information. It's why not even Andrew and Mina are here tonight."

Mizi's eyes had gone very wide. "Not even them?" she was aghast. "But they're so loyal to you."

"They are," Rei agreed, but with some sorrow in his heart, "but I've never been able to be sure with Mina in particular. Andrew's rather transparent, as you already know, but she stays a very closed book all the time. She does as she should, and the best do. The worst traitors also do the same so they can pass along the one or maybe two pieces of critical information at just the worst time. She's heir. She's very much on the high–risk list of being among the anti–Touka faction. I love her as a sister, but I can't ever forget that." Rei motioned to Flandras. "Even he knows he'll still be suspected of it by us, given Ilena knows who his father is. It goes into our equations, and his, because it has to for us to remain safe."

Mizi took a little while to process that, then turned her wide green eyes on Ilena. "And you recommended Lady Brianna to be my head nurse, when she could also be that and teach our children things contrary to supporting our own House?" Ilena's expression went a little sad, but she didn't say anything right away.

Rei blinked. "No, she was recommended first by Lord Aiden. Ilena agreed she'd checked Brianna's background." He narrowed his eyes. "But you did recommend Aiden."

Ilena nodded. "As one of three. You picked him."

Rei stared her down. "What are you teaching me?" He wasn't wrong. She was the same as Sasou.

Ilena folded her fingers together in her lap. "Why did you pick Aiden out of the five you were considering?"

"Because, of the neutral lords, he'd already been the most willing to work with me as a near–equal: to teach instead of obstinately block me." She let him consider his own words. "He has the patience to stand close enough to a Touka to try to get them turned for the lord's side, and at the least discover things the faction needs to know. He's lost his patience a time or two already, but it's not unexpected given how crazy our collection of persons is." He considered those moments. "But it's Lady Brianna who loses patience first." Mizi nodded agreement. "And who is more stern for the court niceties. I do agree that she's a very likely candidate for standing on that side, actually." He frowned at Ilena.

"Having lost her husband and being at loose ends, she was in a perfect position to be called up to head nurse. She returned to the castle earlier than I would've expected for grieving," Ilena said.

Mizi agreed. "I also thought six months not very long."

Ilena tipped her head. "I wanted to see why Aiden had recommended her. She certainly has all the proper skills and perfect background to catch my attention and be who the lords would like to see standing next to Mistress Mizi, particularly since the lords had learned by then she'd do everything in her own power to try to become the princess she believes she should be."

"It's been more than Brianna expected, though," Mizi said quietly, her eyes downcast. "She gets impatient so quickly now. She's very good at closing her mouth, but she wants to scold so badly sometimes. ...And I don't even know what the scold would be for most of the times."

"Nothing nice," Ore interjected dryly. Mizi had to agree with that.

"But, why?" Mizi asked Ilena again, imploring her. "Why would you put them there or give them that opportunity?"

Ilena answered her and Rei, "Because of what Rei's already told you. We can't know who unless we can know who." She blinked at them for her convoluted answer. Rei understood it.

"Like knowing who the spies in the castle are?" Mizi asked.

"Right," Ilena said. "I couldn't know if Aiden was in that list, but when he recommended Brianna, I was instantly suspicious he was. Watching her has pushed that closer to a confirmation. I think he still stands as neutral as possible, not letting much of anything out, like Mina doesn't if she's on that side. Lady Brianna truly didn't expect someone like you, but then the lords continue to underestimate you so likely didn't bother to take that into account when they brought her back here to the castle."

She smiled. "Lady Brianna was quite relieved to learn that I can stand in front of you. She's content to let you come here and have me do that when she can't anymore. But that's putting her in the Rose office more frequently, where she can be the more active one to let the lords know what Master Rei's doing there. That lets Aiden stay the neutral party, rather than a suspicious one."

Mizi looked at Rei with wide eyes again. "I'm sor–" Rei held up his hand.

"Mizi," he said gently, "as I said, I never forget it at any time." He waited until she settled, then turned back to Ilena. "However, already knowing that, what other thing are you trying to teach me?"

"How to see in the timing of kings," she answered him.

"What does that have to do with it?" he frowned, puzzled.

"We can't just go up and ask that faction of the lords what they're doing, what their plan is, or their timing. We have to have some of them close enough to watch, to ask questions to that might make them have slips of the tongue. Watching Brianna in the office, you've already begun to see for yourself and hear things." She turned to Mizi, "What are some of the major complaints from Brianna? When does she want to scold the most?"

"When I can't remember the simplest of court niceties," Mizi said sadly. "When I forget to *be* the princess and am just me. She tries, because she knows I need to relax in my own House, but that's the hardest for her. She also gets very frustrated when I'm trying to learn a thing the young lords learn but the ladies don't. She doesn't know how to do them so lets Lord Aiden do that teaching. He has quite a lot more patience for me than she does at those times."

Mizi considered a little longer, then added, "She complains, usually not in my hearing, when I've been thoughtless about taking care of her and the others."

"Hmm." Ilena considered that last one, as Rei added the first set to his board. "That's harder to know if it's because of a learned habit of complaining about royals in general or because she feels entitled to more respect and consideration. If it's the former, then yes, she grew up in a House already set against Touka. If it's the latter, it could just be a personality issue. You could test that a little more by actively doing something that could be a complaint against a royal but not about how you've treated her. That would be useful information, and be a final confirmation if it is the former."

"Would that be grounds for dismissal, that suspicion?" Mizi asked.

"Not really," Ilena answered as Rei shook his head. "However, as you've said before, the general incompatibility and discomfort of the both of you could be." She looked Mizi fully in the face. "I'm not going to ask you to keep her on just because Touka needs information on the anti-Touka faction. That's hard within one's own household, understandably. It would be sufficient at that point for Rei to say that he'll keep her in the Rose office. He'll already know what to look for and what disinformation to plant."

Ilena looked back at Rei. "You already understand that to keep them by your side is to have a way to do that?" Rei shrugged. That was already evident as well. "What's the other long–term reason to keep them there? It's your favorite reason, actually."

Rei blinked at her. "To continue to attempt to win them over to my side?"

"Yes." Ilena answered simply. "And in your case, that's essential, because you're the least Touka–like Touka in many generations. Even your father was more Touka than you are." Rei found that a rather stunning statement. "The House of Touka needs you to show that faction of lords that you really are different. The longer you keep them by your side, watching what *you* do, the softer they might become, learning that we *can* work with them, not just against them, if they'll let us. We very much need that for this nation at this time.

"I'm not sure it will be enough over the time of your life, since they'll want to know if you can teach it to your children, that balance, and have it be maintained. But, it will be something to sway even a few more away from that way of thinking. Each lord we win over, helps. Each of us gaining even a few means eventually they'll all give in and let us rule with their help instead of standing in the way of the full prosperity and peace of Ryokudo."

Rei slumped, finally understanding. "You've already won Lord Malkin." Ilena nodded. "And perhaps in working with Mina, I might have won Lord Durand."

"We'll hope," Ilena agreed.

Rei had already hoped that a lot over the years of coming to respect and appreciate Mina. He asked, "Was giving her the reward of Andrew enough to finish winning her over, or is it going to be only an opportunity for them to try to get to me even more?" He rather agonized over that issue, particularly when he'd let Andrew go with her to Nakaba when they'd worked for him on the war preparations against Tarc.

Ilena shrugged. "That won't be shown for another few years, I'd expect. Give it at least three, particularly once they have children." Rei could only accept that answer. He knew as well as she that people moved and changed slowly if at all.

Mizi's brow furrowed. She was looking at Ore and Ilena. "Did you give Ilena to Ore as a reward to keep him or as a reward to Ilena to keep her loyal?"

The three stared at her in shock. Ore finally snorted at her. "To ask us in person, surely you do still need to learn court politeness. That's rather rude to ask us directly, Mistress."

Ilena turned to look in shock at Ore. "That's far more direct than normal from you, Ore," she scolded. She sniffed and answered Mizi, "That means he's got ulterior motives and doesn't want you or me to know the answer to that one. It will cause us to have fights to know that about the other, Mistress Mizi. Ask it to Master Rei again when you're alone with him."

Mizi blushed as red as her hair. "Ah, I'm sorry. I didn't mean to."

Rei patted her where he could reach. "No, I won't answer that one with either of them here. They know the answers they need to know to that one. But yes, Ore was born in a House that was anti–Touka. By the time he left they were anti–peace altogether, and only given over to chaos.

"Yes, Ilena's a Touka and Toukas don't trust each other either, as much as we do love each other. That's just part of the same thing. We don't have the conflicts within the royal family some nations do, thankfully, but it's only healthy to remember that each one is also a lord. It's why I get frustrated with the constant testing from all of them but put up with it. They're still teaching me what I need to know to continue forward, so everything's okay. When they start letting the assassins get through or stop teaching me then I'll know to be worried." His eyes held hers until she understood.

Then he blandly looked back at both of the other two. Ilena only looked back mildly, letting him know she agreed with everything he'd said. Ore wouldn't quite look at him, still miffed at Mizi asking at all. "In Ore's mind, I may have needed to give my permission, but it was Ilena's father that gave them to each other, so your question is irrelevant." Ore was able to accept that answer, but Ilena gave Rei a slightly scolding look. He felt it was better to repair Ore's ire against Mizi than let Mizi remain that insightful just at that moment. As Ilena had said, that one was better answered in private, if at all.

Rei had one more issue that was still outstanding and he didn't like that it was. He reviewed the letter from Sasou and their discussion on it one more time. "Ilena, if Sasou would have a different answer for how to affect the lords would he already be moving on it?"

Ilena tipped her head in thought. "Not necessarily. He's been waiting for you to be in this place and to act as the Regent. He might tell it to you now, his idea, to see if you'll act on it, or he might wait to see if you'll change your mind and present something else. It also might be that he doesn't have an idea that would work and was expressing his depression over that fact in the letter. And maybe wondering how to use what you want to do. Was he asking you to expand what you're thinking of so he *can* use it in lower Ryokudo as well?"

Rei scowled at her. "Like I need to add one more level to the job I'm already carrying most of?"

Ilena sighed. "I can only guess, Master Rei. He hasn't told me either. Remember, he's already told you he'll tell you everything he can. But he didn't here. That would be my clue to say he doesn't know. He's run out of options he can see. And that he'd like to work *with* you on whatever the best answer you can come up with is. There are interconnections between the lower and upper lords, even though they started as three separate nations."

Ilena shifted and her brow furrowed a little. "Have your boards expanded to include the generations, yet, Master Rei? I would have thought the issue with Brulac would have given you the push for that to happen. But if you can't see in that way yet, you perhaps wouldn't see how important that interconnection is."

Rei's mouth dropped open. He closed it as he frowned and considered her point. "Go back even further. Remember the timing of kings. You can't go back just to when you learned the information," Ilena's voice ordered softly.

Rei began with the example she'd stated: the hand behind King Gastonne. To begin that, he began with Ilena and everything she brought with her, as she was the hinge point of that whole action. As that built up on the boards, he paid attention to the repeats of it. Learning about Pakyo Shicchi, about the disloyal court members, the corruption in the garrison, the precision she removed it with in all three locations. How he'd learned about the Lord of Tarc because there had been another hand involved behind Pakyo.

He'd worked hard to see that one, but she'd left enough clues there he could. Ore had asked him why Pakyo would give Ore up. Only having someone behind Pakyo could have done it: convince him to do what he wouldn't have normally done. It had been the same with the Lord of Tarc. Ilena had said it at the national security meeting. Her Seconds would never have been attacked by the Lord of Tarc.

They were a normal and natural part of life for him. Only someone who didn't want Ilena supported would do that. And thus it had only made complete sense for her to see that there was another hand behind the Lord of Tarc. She'd found Brulac.

His mother said that King Gastonne wanted her, like the Lord of Tarc had wanted Ilena and Pakyo had wanted Ore. Even just the reward of having Ryokudo to rule over would make King Gastonne move, regardless, since he wanted the Inner Sea access. But following all of that logic and history said that King Gastonne wasn't being given all of the information he needed to win his prize. Someone understood there was a person available to make him emperor of many countries. They hadn't told King Gastonne who that was. They were keeping that information to themselves and still only telling the king the old words he wanted to hear. Someone who'd want Ilena now from the time of the coup would be very, very old and not be given a young woman as a wife, even if they did want to be an emperor, but an heir would be young enough.

Rei watched as his internal boards expanded. He realized he'd always kept them small, had typically kept them relegated to the present and not-very distant future. He wondered why that was. History repeated itself. The past was what drove the present and predicted the future. He understood that for military battles, but for some reason hadn't applied it yet to the political arena. This whole evening had been based in it, though. The history of Suiran and Ryokudo's beginnings and how critical those decisions were, and how long–lasting the consequences. He drew in another breath and reconfigured his new boards from that long distant past. Then he added in the summary of the things he'd learned growing up in Ichijou, and then the more painful recent past as Regent.

Like he was to watch the lords and ladies for a long time to wait for them to show him in small movements where their loyalties really lay, he needed to understand the past of why they were that way. The interconnections between each of them, and between the southern and northern lords. The changes that his forebearers had already tried to make to help the lords understand how to work with House Touka. It was true that this was an insanely large number of generations for that irritation to have lasted. Why hadn't things of the past worked already? What was already in place that was supposed to be helping? How could they all work together to maybe get a greater shift in the thinking of the recalcitrant lords?

Rei just breathed for a little while. There was a lot more data to put on this new configuration of the boards he could see. Sasou had already begun to teach him the data he needed, long ago. Particularly of the lords here in Suiran. Now he was asking that Rei tie in that data to the lords of southern Ryokudo. Not to act there, but to work in tandem with Sasou, a combined effort.

Rei sighed. It was probably as bad as he'd thought, then, when he'd sent his question to Sasou that had prompted this letter in response. Perhaps here was an opportunity for that greater shift House Touka needed to see happen in the nation's higher lords. Perhaps that was what Sasou wanted to know about most. *Can we get the lords to move because we have this rare opportunity of war from outside to push them to see reason within the nation?*

He opened his eyes and nodded tiredly at Ilena. "Well, that did what you and he wanted. The boards have expanded sufficiently to reach the concept of kings and generations, for all I'm sure they're still young and small in comparison." He wrinkled his nose at her as she gave a small triumphant smile. He needed to rest his brain and let the current information settle so that he could add in his lessons from the last several years. Eventually his brain would sift through it all and point to one or more solutions. He rose to his feet.

Rei pulled Mizi up and picked up his folders. "I've got to let that rest a bit. I'll get back to you when I've been able to move it all into the future." Flandras was looking a bit disappointed, but that had been a very major stretch to his brain at the end of a long day after over a month of worry.

Ilena took Ore's hand and held it tightly as they rose with the younger royal couple. Flandras jumped to his feet. "We'll walk you all back home," Ilena said firmly. "I promise we won't talk about work, just let you rest." Ore agreed that they weren't going to just let Mizi and Rei walk themselves back to their building. All four of them would get into too much trouble with Andrew and Mina if they did.

When Flandras was seen to his building and Rei and Mizi were back in their own suite, Rei nearly too tired to undress for bed, Mizi caught up his hand. "Will you tell me now? About Ore and Ilena?" she asked quietly.

Rei was willing because it wasn't about anything on his boards. That needed to not be touched by his mind until tomorrow or the next day. They undressed while talking. "Ore was taught to be loyal to one lord. That was the Earl Shicchi until his brother broke the bond by coming to kill him for no reason. He chose no lord until he met me and tested me. He's loyal to me, and me alone. Even more than Andrew he's loyal without question. To give Ilena to him is to gift him what he's wanted for a very long time, so it's a reward, but he knows too much about her. It's a restraint on her which isn't so much a reward for him. He was offended because you insinuated that he wouldn't stay on his own without reward."

"Oh," Mizi's face fell. "I didn't mean to do that."

"No, you didn't, but because of what he knows about her it was a sore spot he didn't like having poked." He hugged her. "He'll be over it by tomorrow. She knows how to smooth such things over. He's her reward and bribe for good behavior, after all."

Mizi giggled a little at that. "Well, yes, that much is obvious." She lifted her head to kiss him. "Like I'm yours, I've guessed."

"Yes," he answered tiredly as he sank to the bed, undressed and ready to sleep. "They keep working me so hard I'm grateful they've gifted me you on a regular basis." He slipped under the covers with her and held her. "I'm glad you're here."

"Me, too." She kissed his forehead and held him as he fell asleep. Flandras would be the next person Rei talked to once all the data was settled. He wanted Flandras to do more of the heavy thinking for a while. His brain and stomach really did need the rest.

7 Ante-Cold Solstice: Liquid Stone

Ilena walked into the meeting room of the Falcon Studios merchant council within Balar's office building, her long black braid swinging behind her. She had Marcus and Henry with her, as usual, and had brought Liam and Carl along so that Carl could hear the outcome. She wanted him to be able to give the gossip to his contacts in the southern part of Nijoushi and to add comments as needed. As the head spy since the prior Regional Minister of Intelligence within that area he still knew more about the nightwalkers of that part of town than she did. She was pleased Liam was learning from him well enough since she wanted one of her own people involved there as well. The four stayed on the wall between the door and the seat that was hers at the large polished round table designed and built by the construction master himself.

When everyone was present, Balar spoke, pointing to the map that was on the table. "This is a close-up of the section of Nijoushi that Missus Ilena has suggested become the crafter's mall. Here's where the inn district ends," he pointed to a road in the corner nearest him. "This strip would be the crafter's mall," his finger pointed down a roadway, "and another three major city streets down is where her fighting lists are going in." That got people shifting uncomfortably. "I'm thinking of buying the last part of that strip for my warehouse if I keep it inside the wall. Regent Rei has asked that there be a buffer of space between where that would be and the wall itself, so there'd be enough room for the wagons to bring in my supplies, and it's not too far off one of the southern gates."

Ilena leaned forward and drew her finger in a circle around where the lists were being built. "These locations will be bought up by members of my House who know how to keep the lists hidden and protected." She drew with two fingers up two streets to the west and back down the two streets to the east of the crafter's mall road. "These could be bought up by your employees, by members of my Family who wish to have side businesses nearby such as restaurants, lesser craftspersons, and such, to be housing and businesses."

She looked around the table. "In Kouzanshi I've purchased all of the buildings around the lists to about three streets out from them. Now that Regent Rei has picked out his, I've opened up sales to the rest of my House. When they're full of people who I trust to keep the lists secret and safe, we'll open up the rest of that area to anyone who wants to help renovate that part of town. Here, I can begin right away to purchase the land and renovate the houses while the rest of the renovation of this part of town is going on."

She leaned back. "The Nijoushi nightwalkers are now settled in a similar way to how they're settled in Ichijoutsu. There's now a council of four Heads, with a neutral fifth, that each own a section of the city. Crafter's Row cuts right through the northwestern section of the Sage Seraph's district. If you stay here, you'll eventually have to negotiate with him. I own all of the south, including this area," she waved at the map, "and for now Crafter's Row. I'll fight for you for as long as you want me to and my nightwalkers want to keep it. If the cost becomes too high, though, we'll have to come back to this table and renegotiate." She paused to let them assimilate that much.

"One of the things that's been proposed generally for the city renovations is living districts. There'd be apartments built that would rent out at a cheaper rate than houses would, similar to the boarding houses, except with kitchens built in to each apartment. That would allow families that don't have enough income or time to own a whole home to still have a place to live. Grocery centers and other living goods stores would be built nearby, so that people can reach them more easily than going all the way to a far market district. I can see a few eating establishments going into those areas as well. Thus why I think your employees and my Family interested in such businesses can easily find places there. Less time walking around town means more time to be families or to rest.

"Mister Balar tells me you've talked already and have had time to consider the idea. Please tell me your concerns and the pros and cons as you see them." Ilena opened up the floor to them.

There was silence for a bit as everyone put their own concerns together with what she'd told them. "Will the nightwalkers really leave our businesses alone?" was asked as the understandable main concern.

Ilena paused, then said, "Not any more or less than they already do. However, we've cleaned up that district and the west side district the most, including the city guards," she scowled slightly, then returned to her negotiator's face. "Not only are we expecting a lot less crime generally, but we're expecting the guards to be serious about their duties to see to the protection of the businesses and citizens in those areas.

"Mister Balar will be keeping the nightwalkers as busy as he can this winter with the demolition of the decrepit buildings. I expect all of the construction companies to keep them busy from that time on in each district with the rebuilding or renovations. They're the only ones with time on their hands to work on those projects and a willingness to earn enough to eat. Not to mention the ones in the south are ready to pay for houses that aren't full of holes if they're getting enough pay from honest work to do it."

"While there might be reasons to expand to a new location for some," jewelsmith Calvin said, "in my case it doesn't make sense. We only cater to nobility and royalty. The nobles live in the north and east and royalty from outside Ryokudo only stay in the castle, which is right next door to Crafter's Row. I don't need more space to expand. I need merchandise being exported from the city, like we negotiated with Mister Marciel last month. That'll be sufficient for me."

Ilena gave a nod of understanding. She'd expected that one. "I do understand it won't be appealing to all of you, but many of you have already said in that same meeting that you're ready to expand even here in the city. The crafter's mall is a place where you'll be able to both expand in space and in clientele, since you won't have to rely on only residents of the city who already know where you are. Outside clients won't get lost if they just walk down the street to the crafter's mall and back up again. Plus most of those who come and stay on the west side have sufficient expendable coin for even the better crafters' products or they'd not have come in the first place."

Seraphina put her hand genteelly on the table in front of her and they let her talk. "I've been considering it, and I'd be interested in opening up a smaller shop than the workshop that's for display and sale of the nicer but more common clothing. I have several ladies that would be excellent at the sales and who prefer to specialize in such things. I'm not sure I'm ready to pay for a new building, however."

Ilena considered that, then said, "Could you offer them a loan? That once they've paid off the building costs it belongs to them? Perhaps they can put something towards that cost now. At said time, they could negotiate with you to continue to carry your name on the shop, or turn it into their own, with a fee coming to you if they choose the former."

Seraphina blinked, then said, "I could consider something like that as an option." With a glance around, it looked like others were suddenly thinking they could perhaps work out something similar. Ilena knew that the expansion was needed almost more because there were too many masters in each business. Those who had just enough dissimilarity to the head master craftsperson were the most likely to want to move out. This was a way for them to do it more gently and still have some level of income to the masters. The alliances didn't need to be torn apart. They just needed more space and more autonomy for the junior masters.

When all complaints and comments had been said by the people in attendance, Ilena said, "Take the idea back to your shops and discuss it there. Let them know housing, food, and expanded working space will all be available in close proximity. See if it's something that gets any interest. We can have the next meeting open to everyone who wants to come. I'd like for us to set a construction and renovation schedule in that meeting if you do want to open businesses there. We'll need to do that so Mister Balar can begin to schedule his employees. They can't all work on *all* of the buildings at once." She smiled and Balar was in agreement.

Seraphina shifted to rest her lightly clasped hands on the table. "Lady Ilena, there's one other topic we'd like to bring up to your attention, and request that if you can do anything, to please step in."

"I'll hear it," Ilena answered.

"You've been in your first city council meeting and we think you'll be in several more in the coming months. We're finding it difficult to get them to listen to us as business owners. It's a shared frustration with most business owners in the city. Their positions are appointed. Many of them have been in those offices for quite some time but still lack any knowledge of how to keep businesses happy here in the city. They seem to think odd civilian pet projects are more important, when our concerns are valid and not egregious."

Ilena blinked at her then looked around at the other masters. They were all in solidarity. "Well, I did think it odd that Master Rei had to have me there to propose the renovation plan to them for there to be any sort of resolution to the specific problem. He didn't say it before or after, but it did seem like in the meeting he was rather frustrated they hadn't yet come to him with their own proposal for the issue. Is it because they were waiting on him? Or because they're unwilling to offer options or financing possibilities?"

Looks went between the masters at the table. "It seems to be some combination, as far as that specific issue goes," leathercrafter Emerson said. "They do seem to like to complain, passing the complaints that come to them from the residents on up, but solutions are in short supply, suggestions or otherwise."

Ilena nodded slowly. "I'll watch them in the next several I'm to be in." She looked sharply at Seraphina. "Do any of you have solutions to your concerns to offer?"

Seraphina gave a sharp nod as others nodded as well. "It's in the appointments. It would be far better to have a better representation of all of the citizens of the city than just the lords or the more common citizens. It's hard to tell what drove the appointments, as well. The majority of them were set before we began our businesses here."

Rodney added, "I've thought that it would be better to have a vote for at least some of the positions. For instance, if all of the business owners in town, or on a smaller scale for each type of business, voted to have one or two of their own to be on the council, then there'd be better representation of the businesses. Even the common people aren't really properly represented; although, the council likes to *say* they're representing them. When nothing gets done on their concerns save the few that give the council the greatest publicity, then it's hardly fair to call it true representation."

Ilena waited but that seemed to sum up what everyone felt about the issue. "I'll consider what you've said and pay attention. Probably Master Rei can tell me what he's already seen from his place as well. Give me another two to three months to observe the city council. Likely he'll have me bring back for your consideration some further options he feels might help to solve the problem." She sighed. "Of course, getting the Court of Ministers to agree to such changes might be the greater problem, but he's been considering what to do about that rather difficult–to–budge group as well." She gave them a cynical half–smile. They were sober about that as well, but understood.

-o-o-o-

Ilena took Marcus, Henry, Carl, and Liam down to the southside of Nijoushi. That was her nightwalker territory to see to. She hadn't been back since she'd had her night meeting with all of the nightwalkers there. She also hadn't seen it in the daylight since her ministry had helped clean up the battle the previous month that had cleaned out the worst of the nightwalkers of the city. Today was a good opportunity to do at least a little bit of learning, ...and teaching. Carl and Liam both needed to learn how she really interacted with the nightwalkers.

Ilena started up on the roofs. She wanted to look at the city from above before she walked down on the streets. There was nightwalker traffic up on the roofs, as she expected to see, but it was rather light. Mostly it was messengers running messages from businesses in the south to customers or other businesses in the north. She had Henry stop one that looked like he was headed for more work, rather than in the middle of work. She wanted to know if the numbers of messengers was increased from before the clean–up of the nightwalkers in the city. She sat where she could hear the answers, but couldn't be seen. For all she had plenty of protection, Petroi and Ore had both been very firm that she wasn't to be seen if at all possible. They'd also changed out of their castle clothing into shabby nightwalker clothes to disguise who they were.

"Yeah, the business has picked up now that the area's clean enough to be safe for running. And the business is booming. We're a lot cheaper for getting communications sent around town than what they'd had to do back then. They like having nearly–instant answers back." The messenger was happy to be gregarious.

And are the messengers from our district, or coming down from the north side? Ilena asked Henry to ask. She was relieved when it was a popular way of living for the nightwalkers she was responsible for. Even better was the comment that they weren't afraid at all to cross House boundaries. Not just because of the city–wide truce, but because they were protected by being counted as her House. That meant they might be settling to some level of acceptance of that fact — which was what she was most hoping to learn today.

Because they already had a captive to interrogate that was willing to talk, Ilena asked after those nightwalkers that couldn't work as messengers because they were too old to move easily up and down the buildings. "Ah, most of them's working for the demolition and building, those wi' backs and strength, and even some who can only do the minimum." That was good. "That work filled up fast, though. There's still lots who aren't happy the coin's thin. Maybe... half?" That wasn't so good.

Ilena sighed to herself. She lay on her back on the roof she was on and pondered the options. So far they hadn't seen too many nightwalkers on the streets and in the alleys doing things that she should punish them for. For half not having things to do, a good percentage were probably those begging on the street corners. There still weren't enough people in the area with enough coin to share it in that way. Her finger tapped on her belly as she listened with half an ear to the rest of Henry's conversation with the runner.

When the runner was far enough away, Henry joined them and Ilena looked up into his brown eyes. "Thanks, Henry," she said quietly. He gave her a sober nod. "I think we'll go sit in a few of the safe houses. I want to begin to learn their voices and watch them to see what their greatest needs are." She sat up and wrapped an old ratty scarf around her face.

Henry looked a scary warning expression at Liam and Carl. "You'll go in first and let us know by code if she shouldn't be going in. We'll come in after her. She always sits in a place to hide and we watch her and only move in if they recognize her. It's not uncommon for them to threaten her, so that's not when to move. If anyone recognizes her, though, the whole room could become a war zone we don't want to see." Carl blinked and Liam looked a bit concerned, but they agreed.

"If they do recognize me, we'll gather up on the dais," Ilena continued the teaching so they could be a little more informed. "I'll let them complain at me there and answer to them. If we stay on the floor, that's when it gets dangerous." That they could understand and get behind better. She rose to her feet and adjusted her clothing to make it more unkempt and pulled her hat down low over her eyebrows. "We'll keep it short, too, since I'd like to get to at least three of them today, if possible."

Marcus made sure her black braid was tucked up well inside all of her other warm gear. He stepped back and inspected her. "You still make a great young man." He mock frowned at her. "Just when *are* you going to be a woman?" He dodged Ilena's mock attack. "Yeah, like that," he pointed out she'd only proved him right even more. They mock spared for a bit as Henry sent Carl and Liam ahead, then they were headed for the closest safe house.

They had an easy and short observation visit at the first safe house. The pathway to the second safe house was through some of the poorest streets of the south side. Ilena paused to drop down from the roofs and talk to several of the nightwalkers, most of whom were huddled up in alleys to be out of the cold wind of the day. She spoke kindly to them, asking when their last meal had been, what ailments they had, and if they spent their nights in the safe house or on the street.

She let them complain to her about how hard it was to earn any coin at all, finding out that in the main they'd been paid by other nightwalkers who'd had the corrupt coin in hand to pay with. That was a problem that made her frown. None of that coin would be available again, as far as she was concerned. Before she moved on, she gave each of them enough coin to pay for that night in the safe house, or a bite to eat if they'd rather.

The nightwalkers in the safe house were only slightly better off, since they had found ways to earn just enough coin for that and their one small meal of the day. Enough of those she talked to didn't get the meal, wanting the protection from the cold more. Or they alternated eating on the not so cold days and sleeping inside on the bitter worst days.

The trip to the third safe house wasn't much different. On top of the roofs after that one, looking towards the west from where they were in the center, Carl said quietly, "It gets better from here. It's here in the east and south that it's the hardest. Over there they're close enough to the visitors to town they can get coin and come back a little more easily."

"But there's businesses on the east side, too," Ilena frowned at him.

Carl shook his head. "Established ones with customers who don't come from outside the city. Messengers get sent between the nobility and the shops. It's rare that it's shoppers with coin to spend. Sometimes those who work there will drop a coin on their way home from work, but they all live centrally or north. They don't come down here."

"*Ah,*" Ilena sighed. She turned and looked back the way they'd come, getting an overview of the layout of houses and streets. "I think I'll be adding something new to Leah's plate. The four of you: find two or three places in the worst off areas, close by the safe houses maybe, that we can turn into places to hand out food. I'll bring it up in the city council meeting as another solution the Prince's representative has recommended for a problem they're refusing to resolve properly. That way any funding that we need can come from donations to the indigent and from the city itself. I can keep those costs low, and maybe others in the city will donate food, not just coin to run them. The city council can do the advertising to get the pats on the back and make the requests for donations." The castle kitchen didn't need to be sending so much edible, good food to the pigs. These people needed it more.

She turned northeast and headed for the next roof that direction. The castle–identifying items had been left at Balar's office so they could be disguised while doing the nightwalker research. It was time to go to her next appointment. They needed to change clothes again to at least look like upstanding citizens.

-o-o-o-

Done with that day's nightwalker research, Ilena sent Carl and Liam off to do their work in the city. She was headed for her meeting with the stone slurry researcher. Henry and Marcus took her to a building that was under construction just south of the south wall. There they asked around and were directed to the site manager. "We're here for an appointment," they told him.

He gave a nod and asked them to wait for just a moment then called to another person working with a material in a wheelbarrow. Ilena walked over to it, curious. "It looks like wet sand, almost," she said. It would have to be very fine–grain sand. It was grey in color, like the color of the mountain stone, but the man had been stirring it with a metal tool as if it were a thick soup. "What is it?" she asked him.

"A mixture of lime ash, fine rock sand from when the rock is cut out of the mountain, and water," he answered her. "It's taken a while to learn how fine the sand has to be and what the right mix is. I've found if there's too much lime when it dries it cracks too much, not enough and it won't hold together. Rather like egg in the cake mixture," he smiled at his analogy.

Ilena placed her hand over the wheelbarrow, close to the slurry. "It's as warm as it smells," she commented.

The man explained, "That's the water reacting with the lime. We already know it does that from making the soaps. I got the idea from helping my wife dump out the washbasin. My son didn't clean out the basin well enough one day and the next day it was a solid mass in the bottom where the stone dust and soap had dried out. I chipped it out and then sat and played with it until I got it figured out. She was happy when I quit monopolizing her washbasins." He laughed and Ilena smiled in response.

"They've been letting me play with it here," he waved his hand at the building around them. "I've had to scrap a few walls already, and it was easier to test on steps, but I think we've got it worked out." The stone researcher led them through the building explaining from the beginning of his experimentation through to where he was to that time. Ilena listened avidly and asked a few questions, but mostly just learned.

When they were done, having closely inspected the two two-story walls the man had put up a few weeks before, she took over, asking a ton of questions. When she was done with that Ilena rubbed her head. "I can see this needing more research. Take the time to build a few walls as high as we're wanting for the city's south wall. A few sections to tear back down if necessary, but I want you to start thin, not thick." The man blinked at her in surprise. "And I want to have someone who knows how to do this come with me to Falcon's Hollow. I've got another direction I want you to research."

"Oh?" he raised an eyebrow at her as she paused.

"I want to go down, but instead of open air I want to know how it handles the pressure of water. How well would it contain a large pond or small lake's worth of water?"

The man's eyes went very wide. "Whalll, I can't say as that's any easier to figure out than a tall wall." He looked around the construction site until his eyes found the person he was looking for. They walked over to him. "They'd like you to go research a new thing with the liquid stone. How it does being poured down into the ground to hold water."

The younger man's eyes lit up and he turned to Ilena, Marcus, and Henry. "That sounds like a fun project!"

Ilena turned to the grizzled researcher. "Can I take him from you for this other experiment, or do I need to wait until the wall research is done? I need the answers to both at about the same time, sadly."

The older man rubbed his chin with a frown, then said, "To take him for a day or two to see what yer needing isn't too bad, but I'm going to want to have his help on the wall, too." The younger man went pensively anxious, but didn't want to complain either. "Meybe he can work some on the lake research on the side at the times I don't need him so much." He shook his head. "We'd have to see. If there's not time for both...?"

Ilena sighed and considered it. "I guess in this case the wall's more important, but I'm going to lose a lot of land to runoff by spring thaw that I'd rather not.

Perhaps a temporary solution could be found for that if just enough research can get done around the edges for it?" That seemed to be a better possibility. "All right, then if I can steal him away right now, we're actually on our way there today. I'll have him back in a day or two." She looked pointedly at the man. "Get started on setting up the wall research. This place will wait for you to come back to it. If the client complains, let me know and I'll see if I can work out an arrangement with them."

The man pointed to the site manager. "He's gonna complain first."

Ilena gave a dry chuckle of understanding and waved at him. "Right." She headed over to the construction manager, the young assistant researcher trailing her with the Twins. "I'm stealing this one for two days –ish. I'll pay him for his time and he'll give you the company cut of it when he gets back. I want this project put on hold and the other researcher getting to the research for the south wall immediately."

"Ah!" the construction manager complained immediately. "We're already behind for the research he's done. He's finally just told us that's done and we can get the project finished."

Ilena gave him a stern look. "And if you don't already have all of your other hands trained to do the work now that he knows the proper ratios, then how do you intend to get the work done on the wall at all? He can't build it with his own two hands, nor the four if he includes this one." She pointed at the young man behind her with her thumb. "You can have one day for the researcher to teach all of your hands on this project exactly what they're supposed to do so *they* can finish it. Then he needs to be setting up his experimental site for building to the height of the wall. Jamison will have a much better price estimate for us once we know exactly how much material will have to be used in the building of the wall."

The manager was still a little pale. Ilena said as she turned away to leave the site, "Tell Jamison that I'll pay him a fee to let the process and recipe out of the company. Or he can have it stolen from him if he'd rather. This process is too important to let languish in only one company. Knowing what goes in it and the process to test it is sufficient for my researchers to figure it out as well. I'd just rather not have to waste that time all over again when war and siege may be on the horizon."

She was gone. The manager stood there frozen for some time before he jerked back into awareness. He ordered the researcher to begin teaching the rest of the construction hands on that project what they needed to know to have him gone from it after the next day, then took off at a trot for the company office. That last request and comment was above his pay grade and needed to be passed up.

-o-o-o-

"Is it really war preparations?" the young researcher asked Marcus and Henry quietly, rubbing his hat, making it wiggle so that he had to pull it over his ears again. All three of them were trotting after the fast–walking Ilena.

"Well..., yes," Marcus said quietly, putting a slightly sad expression on his face. "Gael's been threatening Altherly, who apparently has approached King Sasou for aid. That and Tarc were enough to make the royals wish to see we're protected here in Nijoushi properly before it becomes a problem."

"It's why the demolition and renovation's starting in the south," Henry added in a loud whisper. "If that sector goes up in smoke from the attacks we'll all go down.

Fixing the wall and maybe even putting it farther out to protect what's there now..., that's part of the preparations."

"Ah." The young man swallowed. "I see. ...And the lake or water stuff?"

Marcus shrugged. "Nah. That's a different project. As Mistress Ilena said, it's just to prevent the erosion of the land there. So that's time critical but not for the whole of the Region in the same way."

"Ah," the young man relaxed slightly at that. Then he shivered and nearly quit walking as his mouth dropped open. He gasped out quietly, "Did you say 'Mistress Ilena'? Is that the Second Princess?"

The Twins smiled at him. "Yes," they answered as he gave them better going-overs than he'd done on the construction site. Their uniforms, black wool castle cloaks, and swords told him the rest of the truth of the answer. So did the white sword sheath peaking out from under Ilena's black cloak when he looked back at her.

"And your name is?" Ilena asked him over her shoulder

"Russ, Your Highness," he answered respectfully. Then he muttered, "Oh." He'd just understood why the manager hadn't complained any more than that, and why the older researcher had told her to go talk to said manager instead of say he couldn't do what she wanted. One rarely told royalty they couldn't do things. At best the company owner might be able to complain and get some sort of allowance, but with war and siege on the horizon, likely not. He slumped a little, but went to some curiosity fairly quickly.

He was roughly the same age as the Twins and they were happy to engage him in further conversation, answering his questions about Ilena and what it was like to follow after her. They asked their own questions of him until they understood his background and why he was apprenticed to the researcher. By the time they were done, they could tell Ilena was quite satisfied and was likely going to really steal him away from Jamison's company if she could talk him into it. So they asked him why he was working for Jamison. It couldn't be too surprising it was because he was a nephew of the owner. That meant he had loyalty to the family company, so he'd be hard to pry out. They saw Ilena shrug one shoulder. She'd try but not so hard now.

At the end of an afternoon of walking the proposed lake bed at Falcon's Hollow in discussions with Foster, Russ, and the men who would lead the ice cutting business, they returned to the manor, sending Russ home to Nijoushi with payment for his time. The lack of information about the liquid stone's properties under water and the top half of the lake bed being very leaky peat were both pretty large concerns for getting the ice business up and going.

Ore led Ilena to the office for them to sit comfortably while waiting for dinner. "Do you think it will work in the end?" he asked for her current opinion.

Ilena shook her head. "I really don't know. I think there are a lot of ways to experiment with it, but we may be doing that way into the summer. We might have to shore up the part that's already been dug, hope for the best over the spring, and wait for the summer dry season to settle in before we can have enough experimentation completed to actually do the work. I'll keep myself occupied some over the next couple of days running the numbers to see if the cost of the experimentation and final construction costs makes it worth it at all."

She ordered the Twins, "When we get back, start looking for a researcher who'll research liquid stone for us. I expect Jamison to turn down the project. He won't want to share the recipe and he doesn't have enough people who know how to do it and also do the city wall. I'll negotiate with him for a little if he wants to make a proposal to see if something works out, but for us I think we really need a dedicated person not already committed to someone else."

"Yes, Mistress Ilena," they answered. She preferred having someone dedicated to her projects regardless.

7 Ante-Cold Solstice: Mizi's Household Review

Rei and Mizi's morning meeting was held after their early morning martial arts practices and breakfast, after they'd returned back to their suite to wash and get dressed for the day. Mizi had worried at first that she'd dislike having to cross the entire campus of the castle grounds twice in the morning. Since she'd gotten so busy with the hospital work it had been just as good she had the flexibility to stay in the suite for a while after they returned to it before leaving for her other morning activities, or even skip those altogether if she needed to. Some days had been so mentally stressful, she'd really needed that flexibility.

This morning her mind had been focused on a new concern, one that demanded immediate action. She sighed at herself. She just couldn't put things down once she'd thought of them. Most people pondered and scheduled things out into the future. If she didn't deal with them immediately, they became even worse stressors that weighed on her and prevented her from getting anything useful done. This was one of those. However, she was going to interrupt other people in order to get it resolved. The major portion of her thinking while walking across the campus and while practicing on the royal list had been focused on figuring out how to not annoy those same people with a "last minute" request of their time.

She let Rei go first, Andrew going over his schedule for the day. When Andrew was done, Mizi said, "Rei, I'll be at the Rose office for lunch today. The rest of the day I need to discuss with Tanner, but you don't need to be here for it. I can talk to you about it tonight."

Rei raised an eyebrow at her as he considered her. After a moment to think about that, he asked, "Last night gave you a new thing to worry about?"

Mizi hesitated, then said, "No, just a new thing to do that I need to get done right away, like I do when it's short and very distracting."

Rei smiled a knowing smile at her that Mina echoed. Andrew understood as well. They'd seen her this way often enough now. "All right," Rei agreed, but he looked to Tanner first. Tanner gave a small shake of his head to indicate there hadn't been anything major on the calendar he should know about that Mizi might be forgetting. There really wasn't since it was just the continuation of what she'd already been doing for the last three days to month. Mizi was glad Rei was willing to let it go with her promise to talk about it that evening. He rose to his feet, gave her a kiss and accepted his cloak from Mina.

When they were gone, Mizi turned to Tanner and observed him for a moment. "Tanner, you've been my secretary for over five months now. I've greatly appreciated your presence and assistance." At her pause to think of how to ask her next question, Tanner tipped his head in acknowledgement of her gratitude. "How do you think that's going?" she asked. "Are you content, overwhelmed, bored?" She smiled a little, knowing he was a little of all of them.

Tanner smiled back his small kind smile. He was about as tall as and thin like Ore, but was older than him by about ten years. He made her feel comfortable in the same kind ways Ore did. She'd always appreciated that. Knowing he was an assassin–grade guardian from Ilena helped that, too, but she didn't often actively think of that part.

"I'm content enough," he answered after thinking about what to answer with. "It's busier than just following you around in hiding, but it's rare you overwhelm me." He blinked, then said with a smile, "Save when you're running around on your feet all day. But that isn't really new either. I still had to do that before you brought me to your side." Mizi gave him a rueful grimace back. She'd been like that her whole life — either stuck to her desk for weeks on end or running all over to accomplish multiple tasks — so that wouldn't change at all. "I do like getting to help you with your good and noble pursuits, now. Having my hands help you with those projects isn't a thing to dislike at all."

Mizi had taught him how to help her with her experiments in the Medical department, then he'd helped her learn Ilena's whispered language. More recently he'd been helping her with the hospital proposal, particularly when she struggled with writing noble letters on her own. That was also new for him from the beginning of the hospital research, but he had a better grasp of what the lords might need to hear. She'd had him help with those also because as her secretary it would be his responsibility in the end to write them for her. He took those lessons seriously for that reason. He'd also become a third person to practice her hand–to–hand combat skills with and was an excellent and gentle teacher, in her opinion.

Mizi interlaced her fingers together in her lap as she looked at her hands. A lock of her golden–red hair slipped down over her shoulder. She'd been putting it up less now that she wasn't in the lab so much. She knew Rei liked to see it down so had sort of "neglected" putting it up more recently. Maria had taken to staying to brush it for Mizi on the mornings she was on duty. That had been nice, to have more of an excuse to visit with her first friend in the castle. "Tanner, our dinner conversation last night made me realize that I really need to step in and be proactive in understanding my own household and my comfort level in it." She looked back up at the one person she was quite sure she could trust in that group.

"Today, I need to interview all of the people I've invited to be in my household. Separate and in private. I'd like to give a half–hour for each person." His eyebrow went up but he waited for her. "I know that's hard, to have it be last–minute, but you've been with me long enough now. It's the same as when I asked you to stand with me, actually." She blinked at him and waited for him to remember that day. "Until I act on that thought and complete it, I won't be able to do anything else at all. Since that 'anything' happens to be the hospital presentation to the Court of Ministers, I can't delay it at all." His wide eyes said he understood that criticality quite well.

"What we've just talked about is our interview. I want to keep you, until your death or mine. I desperately need a secretary, particularly a man who can help me as I traverse the difficult path of communicating with other men. Even though you aren't a lord, you understand what I don't. You're willing to work just as hard as I do to learn the things you need to learn to catch up in the same places I do.

"As long as we're learning together, I think they'll think all the errors are mine, protecting you until you can step in as the knowledgeable secretary I obviously need. You'll take over writing those letters I can't stand to write, and I'll have enough knowledge to review them and know if they've said what I need them to say. That will be a comfortable level of oversight for me, and probably any secretary's preference as well." She knew Rei always reviewed Andrew's final letters, although they did it differently since Rei knew how to write them.

Mizi looked at Tanner soberly in the eyes. "Last night Rei and Ilena began to teach Ore and I how to read letters containing secrets sent between royals. I'll be teaching you what I learned. We'll need to know that skill as well so that if we need to communicate with Rei, Ilena, Ore, or each other we can do so without worry. You already know Ilena's going to phase out the whispered language. Writing will be the only way to exchange long–distance secrets after that's completed." Tanner looked as sorrowful as she felt about losing the spoken secret language. "Rei said she's allowed that maybe we royals may continue to use it, but the numbers of people who can pass it across far distances is likely to disappear so it won't be all that useful generally."

Tanner nodded his head. "Only when you're close enough to each other to hear it." He gave a small sad smile, "Which might be enough to keep you alive or at least in contact safely." Mizi agreed.

"Are you agreeable to the permanent assignment?" Mizi asked Tanner, wanting to get the main reason for talking to him this morning settled before moving on.

Tanner placed his hand over his heart and bowed. "I would be honored, Princess Mizi." He paused and swallowed, then said, "And it would give me great pleasure." He didn't move for a moment while she blinked and tried not to let the tear drip from her eye that had suddenly come up. When he rose, she realized he'd not moved because he'd also been fighting his own tears.

She smiled almost sadly at him, her heart rather full of gratitude. "Thank you, Tanner," she said softly. She had to pause to recover again slightly. "Please, stay by my side and protect me as well."

"Always," he answered just as quietly and they both had to look away to recover this time.

Mizi took a deep breath and said, "I don't want to inconvenience any more people than necessary today, particularly since there are a few I don't want to offend. I'll interview Ilena during our usual meeting. It won't be unexpected to her, generally. We'll see if she questions my total motive, but it doesn't matter since I'm doing it for my own peace of mind." She blinked as she reviewed in her mind the schedule she'd come up with. She'd need the walk to and from that for sure.

"I'll send one pair of the guards to the Rose office this morning and interview the other pair, letting them rest downstairs when it's not their turns. I'd like to meet with Delia and Maria also this morning, preferably first thing as they're already awake, but before they leave to do their own things. Either one can be next, followed by the other. I'll ask for Sam after that if there's time before we go to Ilena's. Brianna, Brian, and Kirk can go to the office this morning."

Mizi drew in a breath. "After we're back from Ilena's I'll speak to the nurses in turns. That should be enough warning this morning for them to be prepared for the unusual request." She slumped a little because she could with Tanner. "I really hate that they're so bored and useless at the moment, save for the few household activities. I'm hoping they can offer some suggestions of what they feel they could *do*." She pondered on that, then added, "And maybe I should ask Ilena what hers are doing and have her remind me why it was so important to have them come now when Rei won't let me give him any children for years to come." She pouted internally for a bit, then straightened back up and returned to her planning.

"Then we'll go to the Rose office for lunch and I'll talk to Ore before we start and Rei as usual while we eat." She paused because Tanner had moved. She looked at him in slight surprise until she realized he was trying hard to not laugh. "What?"

"You'll interview your own husband even though you're already married to him and he's lord of the household?" Tanner teased her rather severely.

Mizi exploded into a hot blush. "Well...," she couldn't quite recover. Sighing she said, "It was either include him, Ilena, and Ore, or forget three of the others. It wouldn't hurt to have a few less by the end, just for the sake of my memory. I almost forgot Leanna this morning when I was thinking about them, and barely remembered the nurses." She looked away and fought the embarrassment until Tanner had settled down again. He wasn't wrong. Her brain only worked at "full on" or "very partial" she'd learned. It was one of the other reasons to have a secretary, but she was still learning how to use Tanner in that way. Brianna and Aiden's lessons there had been helpful for both of them, too.

When Tanner was ready to listen again, Mizi continued. "I'll interview Brianna right after lunch in the Lotus office so she can stay in the Rose office. That won't interfere with her schedule overly much, nor interrupt her work since we'll be coming from the lunch break." She paused and bit her lip a little. "Then it's a little harder. That leaves Brian, Kirk, and Leon to be interviewed in the afternoon. I could bring them all here after I'm done with Brianna, so they already have the expectation of standing around doing nothing much, or I could stay there and interrupt their office work just long enough for the interviews. Because it's in the afternoon they could be prepared this morning before they leave."

She turned to look towards the main suite door. "It's not as private to have the interviews in the Lotus office for those three, but I'd like to have you send to Leanna that she arrive a little early for our usual meeting before the supplicants come this afternoon. That way I can not interrupt her schedule any more than required, and we'll be there for our requirement to hear the petitioners to the Regent." She looked back at Tanner. "I'm sure you can use the code and paiges, but I feel like it's going to be one of those days we're running around all day again. That many people has made it a full and busy day just for the interviews and one required task."

"Well, yes it is busy, but for you again," Tanner said gently. "Please sleep in tomorrow morning, or come back for a nap so your brain will be focused well enough."

Mizi wasn't sure how to take the scolding. Then she sighed a slow sigh out her nose. "Well, that's probably wise. Maybe a nap after the morning meeting and before going to see Ilena. Then I can come back to the report fresh and all this behind me." Tanner seemed satisfied with her decision.

Tanner took his turn to settle her suggested schedule into his memory, then said, "I'll let the household know this morning you'd like to meet with them all. I'd be happy to be your Voice to make the requests."

He hesitated, then said, "May I make that suggestion? That you do make me your Voice? I've observed them enough to think they'd take well to that when you're unsure of how they'll receive you directly. As you say, I've been learning all the things you've been learning, so it would be good practice for both of us as well." He looked at Mizi's expression of dismay and kindly added, "I think they'll eventually learn to hear your voice, and you'll get comfortable with how they respond to you. It just seems to me that perhaps this morning having that one less thing to worry you would help?"

Mizi considered all the requests involved in what Tanner had said, then relented. "You've learned to read me well, Tanner. It's true that I'd rather not this morning. If you do it I can observe and hear their answers, which would be enough. I still don't quite understand what the purpose and duties of a Voice are, but if we learn that together, too, then I think it would be logical to have you in the position as well." She wrinkled her nose at him. "Any formal lessons for that need to come *after* the hospital work has become a smaller thing in my life."

-o-o-o-

Below them a young guard's heart fell. He'd not heard the whole conversation, having been in the bath for the first part of it. He'd been hoping to earn that final position. He wanted to stand next to Mizi and be her Voice. To let all the world know what she did and would do to continue to make it better and push everyone forward in the good ways she wanted to so much.

He finished tying his boot, then impatiently brushed at the wetness blocking his vision. It was perhaps his own fault, for not letting her know openly what he wished to do for her. He worked hard to ignore the fear. She wasn't wrong to say that the numbers of the household were more than she truly needed. He didn't want to be one of those let go. Maybe he could help her understand these things of his heart during his interview time.

-o-o-o-

Maria trembled a little as she was let into the upper suite in the Old Regent's building by the guards on the door. She clasped her hands tightly in front of her skirt. She walked into these rooms half of the mornings and nights, each time grateful that she could, that she had something useful in the castle to do. This was different and felt so formal she was almost cold. Mizi had never spoken to the household through a Voice before, that she could remember.

Mizi welcomed Maria kindly and indicated she should sit in the chair near her. Maria shivered and shook her head. "Please, Mistress Mizi. I'm too nervous to sit." She was even having troubles drawing enough breath to stay conscious, she realized, so she focused on that for a bit.

Mizi had been taken aback by the refusal. She waited a bit, watching Maria, then sat back a little puzzled. "Why, Maria?"

Maria worked hard to not offend her. She'd sort of learned some wrong things in getting a little too relaxed with the Mizi that didn't understand nor fully live the formal of the castle. She wasn't quite sure how to approach the formal Mizi anymore. Since she didn't have any other answer to Mizi's question, she timidly gave that one.

"Oh." Mizi paused, then smiled a little. "Well, I wasn't intending on the interviews being severely formal, just a little more formal than the casual chats when we have the time to meet." She looked a little sad, Maria thought, actually. She tried to relax a little, but she still didn't sit down. "Maria," Mizi's voice was gentle, relieving her, "I greatly appreciate all your help to this time, since I asked you to come over five months ago."

Was it so long ago? Maria couldn't help but wonder.

"I also appreciate that you were the first one to be kind to me of the young ladies of the court," Mizi added. "Your patience with the wildness of Tarc impressed me, too. I don't think any of the others would have been willing to put up with that."

Maria shrugged a little. "We still had beds and a roof over our heads, and each other for company. I was glad to come home alive, since they're a scary people. It

80

helped to have the wives come visit. Then they were a little more like real people to me." She clamped her mouth shut tightly. That had been more words than she should have said, but when she was nervous it was harder to stop talking.

"Yes, it felt that way to me, too," Mizi agreed kindly. "It helped me that you never complained and that you helped encourage me." She paused, then said (again a little sadly), "I'm sorry that my busy brain can't find more time to fit you into my life, just to visit even. I'd hoped having you in the household would help that, and I do feel like I'd never come visit you at all right now because I'm so busy, but...," she gave a slightly helpless look to Maria.

Maria had to go sad as well. "I hope you don't mind I'm spending more time with you in the mornings."

"No," Mizi said. "I appreciate it, particularly since the brushing helps me calm down in the morning instead of letting me just jump up and run off before I even meet with Rei." She laughed a little at herself.

Maria let the concern that had been growing in her breast out on her face. It made it out into her hands that wrung themselves together, too. "Mistress Mizi, you really are moving at a very unhealthy pace. I know you aren't lazy or even languid like many of the young ladies, but surely you could walk instead of run every day?"

Mizi leaned back in her chair and blinked at Maria. "Well, I'm sure there are some who would think that." She glanced to the side. "Like Tanner and some of my guards, and Brianna for sure, particularly on the days she has to follow me around." Maria's head was nodding lots of agreement with her and them. She worked hard to get it to stop, blushing a little as Mizi smiled at her. Mizi sighed a little. "Well, until the current tasks are completed, I probably won't nor can I. But I will promise to be more aware of it. Tanner scolded me this morning as well, and gave me the opening to be kinder to myself. It helped to have the direct suggestion of something I could do."

Maria froze a little, then gave a small nod. "I can do that, I think. If I may?" she abruptly added, not knowing if she could.

"If you think of it in the brief times we see each other, yes you may," Mizi gave her permission. "I really do need the kind direct little helps." As Maria relaxed a little, Mizi watched her. It went on long enough, Maria trembled a little again. "Maria, are you content to work for me when I have so little time for you? I feel very bad about neglecting you so much. I do appreciate having your friendship, but —"

"Oh, no!" Maria couldn't hold it in at all. "I – I really like working for you." Her shivers were getting worse and she could feel tears were going to be next. She clenched her hands in her skirt to try and prevent them. "I – finally feel like there's a reason to wake up in the mornings, a reason to care that I exist. I – I know it's very little I do and can do, but," she couldn't hold back the tears, "I'm so very grateful that you asked me to come be with you."

She looked away, ashamed of the tears, but not able to do anything about them. "I think I'm a waste of your time since you don't hold teas that I could help with. And what little other things I know aren't helpful to you either, or maybe aren't, but...," she pulled the handkerchief out from behind her waistband and wiped at her chin then cheeks, then wiped her nose before that got embarrassing, too. "I'm glad that I can be in a place where the others are patient with me, too, and mostly kind. Strict I can live with, having had to do that for my whole life. But to not have to see the unkind faces, nor hear the awful words they say: I've been so much happier and content than ever before in my life." She broke down and sobbed into her handkerchief. "I'm sorry," she moaned around the sobs.

She heard the sound of leather being patted. "Maria, come sit, please," Mizi requested. Maria stumbled to the chair and sat until she could recover. Mizi's hand on her elbow helped. As the sobs subsided Mizi said, "I'm sorry to cause you distress. I'm not sending anyone away at this time, Maria. I just need to know for my own sanity what everyone thinks right now. Certainly we've all been through so many odd things together that by now anyone would know if they're okay with the oddness of our household or not."

Maria shook her head. "No. It's not odd. It's just being a royal, to have to do what has to be done. Nobles won't bend to do that, unless they're odd." She gave a teary smile to Mizi. "Most people wouldn't think a royal would have to do such things, but then if they didn't they'd be the first to complain it wasn't being done."

"True," Mizi said very dryly. "I think I watched Rei do more odd things in the first year and a half I knew him than even most commoners would do." Maria nodded her understanding. That didn't surprise her at all. He'd do them because they needed doing, for sure. Maria was surprised when Mizi added, "The least of which was helping to free an unknown foreign commoner from the bushes she was caught in and then defend her in front of another nation's prince. I thought he was quite brave to do that because it wasn't until the next day that I knew he was a prince of Ryokudo."

Maria gaped at Mizi. "That – that's very romantic, Mistress Mizi. Did you really meet that way?"

"Yes," Mizi smiled. "I was so nervous to learn he was the Second Prince, but he pretended like he didn't know I'd learned it and just kindly helped me back to Ichijoutsu and helped me find a place to stay. Then he took me to the castle and told the gate guards I was allowed to come inside anytime I wanted to."

Maria shivered. "Just – just on that alone? That's rather ...amazing."

"I thought so too," Mizi agreed. "I didn't go until I went for the intern testing. Then I had a reason to come and go that wasn't just 'because the Prince said I could'. That wasn't right, to abuse his kindness like that."

Maria sniffed as tears threatened again. She wrung her handkerchief a bit. "Mistress Mizi, you're the best noble I know. I don't know anyone who would have had that thought but you. Some would have been too afraid to go back, but most would have abused it even a little. But you had the nobility to refrain and the courage to find a way to enter honorably." She wiped the corner of her eye. "I love working for you both and seeing you both so in love." She covered her face again to catch the tears. "Please. Please let me stay. Although, I'll go if you really can't bear it."

"Maria," her ears caught the commanding tone Mizi rarely used, "look at me." It was said kindly even if ordered.

Maria obeyed. The green eyes commanded like the words had. "Maria, if you stay, I'd like to find something you can do besides just help me dress and brush my hair. That isn't enough to give anyone a true calling in life. I will need your help with the things the ladies of the castle know and can do. Eventually we'll do those things together. Right now there are other things I'm required to help with. Please write up a list of things you know how to do or would like to learn to do. I'll look at it when I can around the edges of everything else I'm doing. Maybe together we can come up with something that will let us work together more often. I'll at least be able to feel like I'm not just abusing your friendship if I can support you in meeting one or more of your dreams and goals."

Mizi ran her hand over her head distractedly. "And when we have time to talk about it, you can tell me what you do with your free time right now, since I don't even really know that."

Maria shook her head. "I'm still in some of the classes they teach young ladies, like Lady Brianna told you about. History, advanced comportment, and I still go to the dance classes," her nose wrinkled up. Mizi already knew she didn't really like that one, but since Mizi and Rei liked to dance she'd been trying. She turned away, a little embarrassed. "I did enjoy the one household accounting class they had us take, but most don't. They only learn it because it's required. Most lords have secretaries and stewards so the wives don't really need to know it."

Mizi had stiffened, worrying Maria a bit. "Maria, how well did you do in that class?"

"Well," she said. Embarrassed, she added, "I got the best scores in the class but didn't let on."

"Go take the next level class. You'll be the only young woman in the class I'm sure," Mizi said dryly. "I need help with the hospital accounting. It's my personal business and I need to make sure we're doing the books right, but I haven't got the time to take that class, too. Get high enough that the Ministry of Finance won't complain when they review the books. You've got at least one year, maybe a year and a half, until the construction is done. I can keep track of the financials up to that point. Then together we can stumble through the first year or two of actual training by the Ministry — if they'll do it and not complain." Her eyes were lit with that green fire of keen interest and a goal in sight.

Maria sighed to herself. "Well..., that would definitely keep me very busy for the rest of my life during the days." That slowed Mizi down so Maria could really think about it. Slowly she said, "It would be hard to be in the classes with the young men," she looked away, then smiled a little. "But to be able to match them at the same time as tell them you required it would be rather delicious payback and silence them quickly." She turned back to Mizi with the smile. "I'm willing to try. Is it okay if I let you know if it becomes too difficult?"

"Absolutely," Mizi answered immediately. "I want to know right away. And if it's just the studying, I'll help with that, because I want to learn it, too." She paused, then slumped just a little bit. "But I hope you can handle the first month or two on your own. Once the hospital is approved and construction begins, then I'll be a little more free ...except all the travel Rei wants to do this year." Her eyes drooped in a message.

Maria drew in a breath, then slumped herself. "Well, I'll let the instructor know I'll have to be missing classes at those times. But I think if I keep practicing I can be fit into the next class. And, if you require it, they'll have to assign me an independent instructor that teaches me on your schedule."

"Oh!" Mizi considered that, then gave a nod. "Get started with the class when it begins again. It will help you teach the young lords what we're like, too. Then you'll be both practiced enough to decide if you can do it and we'll be able to order other options when we're closer to the time to leave."

Maria liked that plan. Travel had made her pause, though. "Ah, I'm not really at a level of lady–in–waiting for Ichijou, which means for international courts either." It was hard to make that admission, but Mizi did need to be told directly, as she'd already said on multiple occasions not just today. "You should take Lady Brianna for sure to those. ...I could go as one in training, though."

Mizi's face fell a little, but she understood. She rose to her feet. Maria jumped up immediately. "Rei and I will talk about that and let everyone know before we go how we want to handle that. Thank you for coming to talk to me, Maria, and letting me know how you feel."

Maria curtsied deeply. "Thank you for being patient with me. I'm sorry to cry so much. I really have a long way to go."

Mizi paused before releasing her, and did so kindly. Maria escaped to her room to cry some more. She couldn't help the worry that she'd botched the interview terribly. Mizi was so kind it was very hard to tell just what she really thought, but she didn't lie when she said something. She couldn't go to Delia to compare notes since Delia had already left for her classes, most of which were teaching the other hopeful hairdressers how to do their jobs. Delia had gone first and Maria had fretted that whole time.

When Maria had recovered she washed her face then took herself out to the young ladies' educational building to pass along her newest orders. It would be different to have to go to the young lord's building for her new class once it started, but she was a bit excited to be able to try to do something she'd done well in. Then her heart fell. She hoped she wasn't made to do terribly with highly difficult material just so she had to admit she couldn't do as well. The pressure from the teacher was going to be awful if he agreed with the prevailing opinion of the Financial ministry. It was taught by a member of that important group, after all. She sighed, but could only try.

-o-o-o-

Mizi walked into the Rose office from the Lotus office after her session with the day's claimants to the Regent. She sighed to herself as she set her notes down on her desk. She'd work on them the next evening. The Lotus office was only open two days a week unless there were enough claimants she needed a third day to keep up with the numbers.

"Ready for dinner?" Rei asked kindly.

Mizi smiled at him, sure it was a tired one. "Yes," she said. "Can it be just the two of us in the suite tonight? I'm sure I need the quiet after having such a busy day today."

"Alright," he agreed. He took half a minute to look back at the folder in front of him and sign the document, then close the folder and put it on his outgoing pile. He rose to his feet and people began doing the same, chairs scraping on the floor.

Mizi looked at the full room. Flandras was new to the room today. Sam was quietly getting him to come out of his focus on his work. That made Mizi smile inside. It would take a while to train the tireless researcher out of Flandras. She knew how that worked. He, Ore, Petroi, and Thayne were all under Ilena's management, as far as Mizi was concerned, save for her being Ore's mistress.

Tanner was by the door, waiting with her cloak. He'd been with her and Leanna in the Lotus office. The rest of all of their household and Aiden made the room very full. Aiden was the only one she hadn't interviewed, but he was Rei's to worry about. Then she internally shook her head at herself as Andrew put his hand on her head comfortingly. She'd gone and forgotten the two who never left Rei's side. How she could forget two of her first friends in Ryokudo she had no idea. Truly it must be because she was very tired by now.

"Thank you, Andrew," she said quietly as he smiled at her. "You and Mina can rest tonight from watching over us, too. I'm sure I'll be sleeping half–way through the meal and he'll have to have Rutherford and Tanner carry me to bed." Rei gave her a wide–eyed look as Mina shook her head with a silent scold.

Mizi shook her head tiredly back. "Tanner already told me this morning. I'll nap in the morning after we practice and before I go to Ilena's. ...And he won't complain if you forget I exist and leave me in bed instead." She was rather wry. She knew they'd do it, too, if they thought she'd been pushing too hard. She wouldn't complain this time, for all she'd feel some guilt regardless.

It was comforting to walk warmly next to Rei, holding his hand. Being surrounded by their guards and household was as well tonight. It really had helped to talk to them all, even if things weren't completely settled yet. Their voices as they teased and talked now that their minds were free from the work was a nice background to the evening as well. Mizi let her brain just rest as she took in the sounds and let others guide her feet.

"Goodnight everyone," she said as Rei led her to the stairs. They wished her respectful evening farewells as well, but she was more focused on the comfortable chair in the sitting room that was waiting for her. Rei tucked her hand up into his elbow to help her get that far.

Tanner took her cloak and helped her out of her warm accessories. She was just as glad to not worry about them and move to sitting down. "Is that why royals and nobles need that done for them? Because they get home so tired even that detail is too much to think of?" she asked.

Rei spurted a laugh as Tanner chuckled quietly. "Not usually, no," Rei said, "but it can happen for that reason. Certainly when their heads are full generally it helps, too." He settled down in the chair next to her. His brilliant blue eyes studied her. "Are you going to fall asleep before you can tell me what you've done today to become so weary?" He said it lightly, but she could tell he'd be quite disappointed if she didn't talk to him first.

Mizi drew in a deep breath. "If I can change my request, just a little, please?" She waited to get his nod he'd hear the change request. "Can Tanner and maybe Rutherford join us? If Tanner eats with us he can remind me of the order so my mind can remember instead of just be tired. I'd also like to hear if he has any opinions or comments." She looked into Rei's eyes. "I want to know if he caught any of the small signs I wouldn't know to see."

"Those sound like good reasons," Rei agreed, nodding at the person or people behind Mizi. She sat back and closed her eyes to put her thoughts together and almost fell asleep. His hand taking hers brought her back.

His eyes teased her and she sighed and took the plate that was arriving from Rutherford. It would be better to just start talking. "After last night's conversation I realized that I'd been doing it again: sitting back and waiting for others to do things for me that I should be doing for myself." She looked firmly into Rei's eyes. "Maybe there are things I can't do that you and Ilena need to do, but only I can ask my questions and hear and see the answers I need to hear and see. I've spent the day interviewing everyone in the household and learning from the interviews using the court methods I've been taught."

An expression of great approval came on Rei's face. He nodded as he took a bite of his dinner and waited for her to continue. She took a few bites first or she might not get dinner in her at all for all the talking and exhaustion. That gave her time to remember back so far as the early morning again.

"I'm grateful that Tanner's willing to continue with me. We're working together very well." She gave a nod to him and he bowed his head back. "He's the only one I trust implicitly. If he's a traitor and murders me, then I think that would be fine. No one in the world is trustworthy at all then and it's not worth it to worry that hard. I'd just lie down and rest from all the labors of life. ...Like I feel would be so wonderful tonight." She sighed sadly at her food, ignoring the scolding looks of the men with her. "At least I don't have the tight stomach and severe worries anymore after today." She ate a few more bites as her thoughts moved to the next person.

After a few bites Rei said quietly, also looking at his plate, "Well, I can understand that, though." Mizi glanced up to see Rutherford blushing a light pink. Mizi gave him an understanding nod of gratitude. These two men both were like that.

"I interviewed Delia next," Mizi continued on after sipping at her drink. "As one of Ilena's Captains, I trust her as far as my security goes, but...." It was a little hard to swallow the next bite. "She still won't stay long enough for me to get to know her. It feels like she's a lady of the courts so much that she isn't really one of Ilena's. She understands what I need and when I need it, which is good for me, but the interview was ...perfunctory, I guess would be the way to say it." Mizi drew in a breath and paused, then picked at her food a bit. "She's busy with good things during her day, which helped me not worry so much."

Her eyes went to Rei's again. "That was one of the worries to settle, was if people were completely bored, since I can't be happy with that arrangement. They don't have to be as busy as I am, but like Ilena, I want to know they're working on goals that make them content and happy with life." Rei understood.

"I spoke with Maria next." Mizi set her plate on the low table in front of her and drank some of her juice to clear her palate. She sat back in her chair and folded her hands in her lap. "That interview was the complete opposite, quite surprising me." She blinked at Rei's glance. "Poor Maria thought I was going to fire her on the spot," she went softly sad. "She was very emotional, and grateful. I'm sure there are some who could use that sort of dramatics to hide duplicity and use emotionality to guilt a person into doing what they want." She looked at Tanner to get confirmation of the next statement. "I don't think Maria was. I know how hard it was for her to deal with the other young ladies before I became princess, before she knew I was going to. I believe she was being honestly concerned and grateful."

Tanner tipped his head sideways a bit as he considered it. Slowly he said, "I did watch her when you talked to her before you called her up, so I think that would be true. Certainly the spies who watched her then and now haven't seen anything to say she's anything other than what she appears. A young lady who doesn't fit in so doesn't have much to say to anyone, who tries hard to fulfill her duties. We don't know what goes on in her father's quarters, though, so we don't know if or how much information she'd pass on to him. She didn't know anything before you called her up. Mistress Ilena would like to have that one test before we settle on a decision."

Mizi considered that. "I can see wanting to confirm that much more." She turned to Rei. "There was one thing that came out of the interview that she can potentially do for me that would give her more to do than just the brief morning and evening tasks. She's going to see if she has an aptitude for accounting. If she does and wants to do it, I'll have her do the books for the hospital. I'll learn it by helping her study the material from the classes, but I haven't the time to add that to my schedule as a fixed study."

She paused, then said, "If not, then I might release her, but I've promised that if she brings me a list of what she can do and wants to do, we'll review it together to see if something comes out of it." With a sigh, she concluded, "I'd like to keep her on. I'm grateful to have a friend, but I just can't see being selfish for small reasons. One maid really is enough."

"You'd keep Delia instead?" Rei asked tentatively.

Mizi bit her lip, then shook her head. "I can't decide yet. We'll get to some of that at the end." Rei set his plate down and leaned back to let her continue. "I spoke to Sam next." She sighed again and this time slumped a little. "That was going right back to talking to Delia again. He claims to be content enough, did his best to settle any worries I might have, and was kind. But again, he was solicitous rather than honest. When the lords are that way, I feel like they're trying to help, aren't particularly against having me as Princess, but they're not going to let me know how they really feel or think about me being in my position. I'm the most uncomfortable with those people, which isn't really what I would wish for."

She shifted to get a little more comfortable and see Rei better. "That was enough to see the beginnings of patterns. I started categorizing them as I interviewed them after that. One of the nurses is like Maria, but because the nurses and I don't know each other as well she didn't become as emotional as Maria. She was open and expressive enough in the interview I felt comfortable with the level of honesty. They all have work they're doing outside the castle since I said they may to keep busy." Again she glanced at Tanner. He indicated he hadn't seen or heard anything of note.

"They let me know that Lady Brianna's been properly seeing to her position with them, too. She's asked them all to continue to study the newest research, experiment to confirm the validity of the research, and to keep their skills sharpened and up to date for when we should have children. One said that she'll come talk to them weekly to learn what they've been learning so she doesn't fall behind either. I'm relieved by that, actually." Rei nodded. "The other two nurses were calm and answered like Sam, although they weren't quite so stiff as Delia feels to me, but I've put them into the same category as them all the same." Rei seemed to have something to say but when Mizi paused he didn't interrupt.

"Ilena's doing well and is as busy as me so can wait to move into the new building as long as I can," Mizi wrinkled up her nose. "We also both agree more time spent getting to know everyone is necessary, too. That is, between the households. I'm grateful Ore's doing well." She blushed a bit. "He did scold me for calling him out to the tree and the bench. He refused to sit with me and stood like most of the rest did while I sat. I'd not thought about the propriety of it, I'm sorry," she said humbly to Rei. He gave her a slightly scolding look, but then relented, knowing they never would have anyway. "It was that I really needed to be at the tree more than he did by then," she chuckled wryly at herself. "At halfway through the day I already didn't want to be inside, for all it was cold." Rei smiled back at her, understanding that, too.

"Ah, and Ilena suggested that she and I change the pattern of our meetings to the off day from when you have the Regional security meetings. Then there isn't the gap for me, nor the continuation of being interrupted for her. If I go first thing on the days you don't go, she and I can move on to work rather quickly and it's a daily pattern for her." Mizi went very dry, "I told her I'd think about it after tomorrow morning when I had a brain again." The men chuckled at her.

Mizi reached out her hand for Rei's. When he took her hand, she looked at him soberly. "Thank you so much, Rei, for supporting me in so many things, even this. I was glad to have the opportunity to rest at lunch with you, even though it's awkward for us to have a meal at a desk instead of a table."

Rei smiled at her. "Well, they do all fill up the tables now, and then some. It was okay to have just the two of us for once, and this is nice, too." His thumb ran over her fingers, making them tingle. Mizi blushed a little.

She looked away and hunted for the next person, then felt her face fall as she remembered. "Lady Brianna's interview was the one I really wasn't looking forward to, but the one I needed do to the most." She frowned a little. "I did test her like Ilena asked me to. She answered my questions, but she gave me the most lord–like answers, and too many felt on the edge of honest, rather than fully honest." She looked at Tanner slightly helplessly. "Because of you asking me not to be alone with any of them, I asked Tanner to stay for all of them. I don't know how much that affected what they said, but I'm hoping not too much." Her stomach did clench a bit again now.

Tanner and Rutherford were done eating now, and Rutherford was collecting up the plates. Tanner waited until Rutherford was out of the sitting area before he spoke in his careful way. "Mistress Mizi, they pay attention to my presence, knowing I'm there, but like they treat any servant, I'm part of the furniture. What they say wouldn't be any different if I wasn't there. If they thought I was a spy and they needed to tell you something, they'd write it to you, or ask to speak to you without anyone else present." That helped Mizi.

Tanner continued, "I think that Lady Brianna's still as unsure as you are. You've asked her to give it greater thought over the next two weeks. As you both do that, perhaps one or the other of you will find the resolution."

Mizi had heard Tanner and agreed. She turned to Rei. "We're both uncomfort-able with each other now that we've had this much time to learn about each other. If there weren't underlying reasons for her to stay, I think we would've agreed to have her go today. We did agree that allowing her time at her home to rest and recover would be beneficial. If you'll let me go to Kouzanshi soon, that would be a good time to let her have that vacation. ...We could let Maria spend that time with her father as well, so Ilena's people can maybe see if something is said then that shouldn't be."

Mizi turned her attention to her hand in her lap. She rubbed it over her skirt. "I think that would help everyone, actually, to be able to have time away from each other. No one other than Lady Brianna was so much in need of it at the moment, but I think we might be getting close to it for some of the others."

She sighed. "Brian was as cold as Delia and as evasive as Lady Brianna. He's not usually, but then he's also been having a hard time since we got back with how slow I am to learn the habits of nobility. I've noticed he's been teasing the others more meanly, too. He also needs to be somewhere the rest aren't, but when I asked if he'd want to vacation at home again he said that's not really restful for him."

Blandly she looked at Rei and said, "He wants to be working in the Rose office and competing against Andrew there and in the list more. Walking behind a princess isn't what he really wants, even if being in your household is what he wants. That's what I think he's learned, based on what I saw in our conversation."

Rei thought about that, then said, "You'd let him go."

Mizi shrugged. "He and Kirk get along and he has the skills to defend royalty, and the nobility to walk behind them."

Rei sighed at her. "And that was as coldly noble as you've said he was."

Mizi couldn't help but give the comment and herself a cynical half–smile. She let it pass, though. "Kirk enjoys having Brian as a partner, and Mina to practice with. Those two things make it easier for him to follow me. However, he has his own reasons to stay as well that make him kinder and softer. I think he makes a good guard for me and he wishes to stay. If there were no Brian, I don't know if it would be enough, though.

"He answers more honestly. I suppose there are some that hide behind that sort of face, too, so I still can't tell for sure as far as loyalty goes." She looked away into the distance and realized she was fading even more, but she was almost done. "So..., I pushed him, saying he could go to Julie and I could have you write a writ to Ichijou if he wanted."

She smiled a little tearily at Rei. "I wouldn't have except I was done with the count being weighted higher than I wanted to those too much like the lords. I need more with me that *are* honest with me. I've learned enough from watching the lords of the castle and Ilena. His response that he really does want to stay watching over me was very honest, that first glimpse that was covered up by the hiding of the face with the respectful bow as he humbly begged me to not let him go, but he'd be obedient if it was my answer."

Mizi shook her head. "If that was a play, I'm afraid I don't know how to be hard to it." Whispering she said, "I don't want to let him go, now." Rei glanced at Tanner. Mizi was almost too tired now to be relieved that Tanner gave a tiny nod. She couldn't even interpret if it was a nod of agreement with her that Kirk was probably not the spy, or of agreement that she wouldn't be able to let him go.

She closed her eyes. "It was almost unnecessary, in the end. Leon's desperate to not be sent away, as desperate or worse than Maria. He refused to cry and let the others know, but the expression on his face said it regardless, as did his willingness to be openly honest with me." She glared a little at Rei. "I understand that such emotional pleas can be used against us women, particularly if they know how to twist the words to twist the emotions of a woman, but I'm not that type. Even if they do know I'm common and need honesty." She frowned as she tried to say it when her tired brain didn't want to formulate the idea for her.

She waved at Tanner. "His honesty, and Rutherford's, the tenderness with which they treat us, yet the firm hand of necessity. Leon's too young to have learned the firmness yet, which Kirk does know. Yet the tenderness he treats me with is the same. At the same time as I'm feeling deeply grateful for the relationship I have with Tanner, he's feeling the same. That's what I feel with Leon." She looked at Tanner. "I know you offered it, but I think I'd like to see if I can give Leon what he's asked for. If I change what I said, would that offend you?"

Tanner hesitated, then said, "Of course that's yours to decide, and perhaps all three of us should learn it at the same time so you can make that decision with knowledge. I have plenty to do if you wish for Sir Leon to do it."

Mizi gave him a grateful nod for his advice and willingness, and turned back to Rei. "Leon has asked to be my Voice. I've admitted I have no idea if I need one, nor what to do with one, nor why one is used. That's a lesson I need to have after I'm not so focused on the hospital. I can't make a decision on that now. Tanner had also offered this morning and acted it so I could not worry this morning. I think that made Leon panic a bit." She smiled softly. "He was determined to tell me today all his thoughts and wishes. I should've perhaps talked to him long before today. He's been uncertain how to approach me, I think. Maybe he'll have more courage now."

Mizi sighed. There was just one more. "Leanna's still as stand–offish as ever: kind, works hard, but isn't interested in coming to be part of the household. Teas at best outside of work, I think. But it isn't too unexpected. Because that's all the interaction we have it's hard to imagine she's a spy. Because I picked her early on before she knew I was to be your princess, and she hasn't changed at all since then in her personality, it's hard to believe she's part of the anti-Touka faction." She grimaced at Rei, "Even if her father was. I believe I've already won her to Touka. ...Her husband will be another matter. I can't get her to talk much about him, but she's ever so practical that it's not likely she says anything sensitive to him regardless."

Tanner smiled. "Well, that would be true. If anything, she's more likely to sway him to her way of seeing things, in the end."

Mizi nodded her agreement, then slumped back into her chair. "If you have anything you'd like to say, I'd love to hear it Rei," she said, "but please be short. I really will fall asleep very soon now."

Rei smiled gently at her. "I do want to talk about the patterns briefly. Hearing the rest helps me and it looks like it's helped you, which is good." Mizi nodded and tried hard to pay attention. "It isn't surprising to me that one of the patterns you see is nobility. That *is* how the nobles are, how they interact with each other, and even more with royalty. With calm politeness, without pressing their emotions on others. They don't require anything of anyone above them, although they'll make requests when allowed to, or if they feel it important to do so.

"Likely Maria and Leon both were embarrassed by their emotionality. Leon found it difficult to tell you what he wanted before now because it wasn't his place to. You asked in this interview, so he was finally allowed to answer it." He paused, then tightened his hold on her hand to catch her attention.

"Mizi, I wouldn't be surprised if the others were just as uncomfortable. They know you well enough now to know that you'll do such things out of a lack of knowledge; however, you should know. Most of the time if a superior calls in a subordinate for an interview, it's for a scolding. Praise is handed out quietly and in brief moments, save when royalty grants awards of arms and titles. Questions for information are asked in passing and only in private when personal information is being requested, or secret information is being passed on."

Mizi sat upright. "Oh! No wonder Maria was so distressed," she sighed at herself for not understanding again and causing problems. She'd have to apologize the next day when she had a brain again.

Rei nodded. "That wouldn't surprise me, that she'd be emotional if she was concerned she was going to be scolded."

"She said she wasn't sure what to do with a formal me," Mizi said.

"Because formality and scoldings go together, but they're still trying to understand you, and you them," Rei said quietly. Mizi gave a slightly miserable nod of understanding. "If the others were kindly, patient with listening to you and answering your questions, then that really is the best you could hope for and expect. Lady Brianna's insecurity coming through may also have been because of the nature of a formal interview, but she's had others with you before where the others haven't. It could also show just how weary she's becoming with how difficult it is. A long vacation at her home would likely be very good for her, I agree.

"Watch Delia and Leanna. Their level of interacting with you is a very good level for you to learn from. They'll help you to understand the interactions and relationships between royals and their noble subordinates." He smiled kindly at her. "Perhaps they're more like Ilena and are choosing to teach you what you need to know. Even if not, let them teach it to you. Then Lady Brianna and Brian will be able to relax better around you."

"Relax," Mizi moaned. "I suppose I do want them to, but that's a lot of change for me to make to get there, to be okay with that level of stiffness as if it were relaxing." She sighed.

Rei smiled again. "And thus why Ilena and Ore refuse to be stiff, even to teach you. Because they're determined to make even me find that level of relaxing that I never knew before them. Ore had to work very hard, but I was young enough when he began to want to get there. I still only do it with them, you, and these two," he tipped his heads at their men.

"And Andrew and Mina!" Mizi scolded.

"And them, when we're drinking," he agreed.

As she groaned and scolded more, he laughed quietly at her and pulled her up to her feet. He rose with her and led her by the hand towards their bedroom. "It's time to get you to the bed before I do have to have them carry you." He excused the two men to their beds, shaking his head at Rutherford's raised eyebrow. He could clean up after them in the morning. Mizi needed the sleep and Rei his wife.

As they undressed he added one more thing, "Mizi, have you researched for yourself just who each of them are? What family they come from? Where they live? What details surround their backgrounds?" Mizi froze and looked at him with wide eyes. He was looking at her soberly. "I always have Mina research everyone that comes into my life, the same as Sasou does before he lets them stay near me. Or him for that matter. Knowing who they are, even back a few generations, fills in a lot of holes. Often they either won't say it or you won't think to ask for it. No one has time to sit and have long conversations; however, a report read as part of the day is simple enough."

Mizi finished undressing and climbed in the bed as she said, "No, I haven't thought of it, but it's yet again a thing I've passively been letting others do. Since Ilena already has the reports on each of them, I'll ask her for them later, but...," she gave Rei a knowing almost unhappy look. "I'll go to the library and do my own research as well since I need to see it with my own eyes, like I needed to see and hear it for myself today. *Then* I'll have others just send me reports. For the household it's too important for me to delegate."

Rei sighed a little at her, but didn't protest. He did know it and why.

-o-o-o-

Following Ilena's household's habit of keeping everyone's winter cloaks and accessories easily to hand, a wardrobe had been added to the open lobby of the Old Regent's building. "I think Mistress Mizi actually met her limit today, surprisingly," Brian said quietly to keep his words from lofting up into the open space.

Kirk turned to watch the backs of their royals followed by Tanner enter the upper wing. All three still had their cloaks on. "Well, perhaps, since even Master Rei didn't pause. I'm not sure he believes she'll stay awake for dinner either." Leon watched those backs until the upper door closed behind them, a furrow of worry on his brow. He was concerned for Mizi's state of being as well.

"She does seem to get the most tired from having to be social," Lady Brianna commented in her calm voice. "Who didn't she talk to today?"

Everyone looked around at each other. Andrew's eyes were calculating and Mina's as judging as ever. "Not us," Mina answered, "but we're Rei's."

Lady Brianna gave a thoughtful set of nods and turned for the sitting area. "What was the reason for the interviews, if we may ask?" Andrew asked. He lay Mina's cloak over his arm with his own and took up his wife's right hand to walk them over to the sitting area. He placed their cloaks over the back of the chair next to the one Mina took.

It was Leon's turn to hang up his winter gear, but he took Maria's cloak from her shoulders first and hung it up before taking his off. "Thank you," she whispered to him as she added her scarf and gloves. Leon only gave her a nod, also wanting to listen to what was going on. Sam stoked the heating stove as Brian and Kirk picked up plates from the dinner cart and began to put food on them for Sam and Brianna. Maria headed for the cart as well to begin to fix Mina's plate. It had been rare the two ate with the rest of them, but they'd been doing it more frequently of late. Rei and Mizi had been as well, when they weren't eating with Ilena's household.

"Is it normal for Mizi to push herself so suddenly like that?" Brianna asked, having settled into a comfortable chair near the stove. She'd picked up the blanket that had been draped over it and now wrapped it over her lap. It had become her chair generally and the blanket hers as well. Maria and Delia had brought out lap blankets as well, particularly since they sat a little farther from the warming stove. Serving the plates helped keep them warm, though.

Kirk and Brian were headed for the folding tables Sam was already setting out. That had been the compromise to also having a large table in the room; although, it could have been put on the other side of the lobby. No one wanted to be that cold in the winter, so they'd decided to settle for individual small folding tables that could be brought to the chairs as needed. Leon was sure that as soon as it was warm enough the dining setting would show up. Someone would order it eventually. He fully expected servers to also show up at that point. It was odd to most of the nobles in the room to be serving themselves from a food cart.

It was just one of the many things of that sort Rei and Mizi didn't think about. Leon suspected it was mostly because it was the noble's wife's job to think of such things and Rei was still letting Mizi be trained by the rest of them. He suspected *that* was because Rei had never had a royal or noble woman in his life, given his mother's absence from it. Kata had only ever been at the castle once in the five years he'd been a guard there, which had been for Sasou's wedding to Aryanna.

"Where's Delia?" Maria asked, looking around. She'd come in just after those coming from the Rose office had, coming from her classes for the day and knowing it had been an evening Mizi would be late in the Lotus office.

The door opened just then to let in the last swirl of snow as the final four people of the household entered, the nurses coming from town entering with Delia. Leon made a hasty retreat from being near the doorway and that blast of cold. The food cart was still warm so making up Andrew's plate of dinner wasn't a bad way to keep his hands warm. The soldiers up on the upper level did keep the fire going so they could stay warmer, but the heat all rose up there so the lower level got colder than the rest liked over time. The soldiers got too hot when they came in to eat, but it didn't last long, usually.

When the new arrivals were settling around the sitting area or near the cart to dish their meal, Brianna asked her first question again. All four said Mizi had also interviewed them in the morning. The main prevailing feeling in the room was one of confusion. When they were finally all sitting down with plates in front of them, they looked to Andrew and Mina.

Mina nodded. "It's rather typical for Mizi," she said. "Sometimes she'll learn something new she hadn't considered and then she can't let it go. Her mind works at it, even preventing her from sleeping. She must act on it as immediately as possible in order to set it aside and return to her work again."

Andrew shook his head. "When she first came to Ichijou, she wouldn't act on them. She'd be distracted for weeks on end until Ore would make her admit what the concern was so the rest of us could set it at ease. Typically they were minor to us, but almost always they're related to her relationships with the people around her, I've noticed."

"Well," Brianna mused, "that would make sense given how difficult social interactions are for her generally." The others nodded understanding.

"Because we understand this from her past, we'd really appreciate knowing what the general need was. We also weren't at the dinner last night, but she said it was from that time," Andrew asked again gently.

Delia shrugged slightly. "I was first, after Mistress Mizi and Tanner came down and told us all that she wanted to interview us today. She just wanted to know how I felt about serving her now that we've all been together for five months. And she wanted to know what I was working on generally with my day hours. I'm rather busy but she seemed to be fine with what's in my schedule. It wasn't much more than that."

Leon knew it hadn't been. In fact, Mizi had worried that Delia had recently added to her schedule two mornings in the list with them. One to help coach Ryan and one to be Mizi's training opponent. Maria and she had shifted their schedules so that those were slightly simpler mornings for Delia. Maria had also picked up one more day of the week to serve in the suite so Delia had one extra morning of sleeping in to make up for the two extra–early mornings. That interview had gone well enough, he'd thought. It had helped him calm down as far as understanding what was going to happen in them, too. He even now worried about the comment from Mizi that she might ask some of them to leave, but the interviews themselves hadn't pointed to any of that yet.

Maria shifted, uncomfortable. "I was next, but I had no idea what to expect." She set down her utensil and clasped her hands tightly together. "I'm glad to know that this can happen, but I wish I'd understood it before. I was so worried she was going to scold or ask me to leave." She shivered and closed her eyes briefly. Leon had sat next to her on purpose. He lightly put his hand on her arm. She looked at him quickly, then swallowed and took in a deep breath. "She tried to relieve my worries and only thanked me and asked me what I might like to do with my time."

Her face fell as she looked at her hands. "Actually, she's asked me to add lessons and pick up a project for her. I'm not sure I can do it, but I'll try. I think it's going to be very difficult in the end, but she's willing to help me with it if I need it, and was willing to accept my suggestion for an alternate way of taking the lessons. We'll see how it goes."

She looked a bit despairingly over at Brianna. "I also was finally able to tell her I wouldn't be anything other than a junior maid in training at Ichijou, and that she should take you with her for sure. I'm not sure the message really got through to her, but she heard it."

Brianna sighed, but approved. "Thank you for trying your best. We'll keep trying over the next little while."

"What's this?" Andrew asked, his sharp eyes looking between the two ladies.

Brianna folded her fingers together and placed her hands in her lap. "Mizi still isn't anywhere near ready to go to Ichijou and be accepted as a Princess there. Because she can't train her own maids properly, even they'll be frowned upon. If I go with them, then at least the court can see there's *someone* in the household that's trying to train them all." She was firm, but the tiredness leaked out.

Leon said quietly, "I've been thinking about that." He received probably more attention than he wanted, but this was important. "I believe that Master Rei doesn't know how much training she needs, nor in what, because he never had the example himself to see just what his wife should be doing. Queen Kata was never in his life in Ichijou, being too busy with court responsibilities early in his life. Then she was here while he was there for the later part of his life and training. He never had an example in his life of what a noble or royal wife does and is. He doesn't know what's missing, so he can't teach it. I really do think we're going to have to do it, and in the way Mistress Mizi can learn it. She'll work hard and learn it quickly. Lady Brianna, if you write it up and present it to her — the things she must learn before she goes — I believe she could be ready in time."

Brianna actually rolled her eyes at Leon. "I'd rather let Ilena do it," she sighed at him.

Even Mina shook her head at Brianna. "You know she never had the example either," Mina said. "Even I can't teach it to Mizi at the level she needs. I can see she needs help, and I'm willing to help where I can, but I also never had a mother to teach me, only my father to tell me what to do that he required my help with."

Brianna slumped, but nodded her head. "I'll see to it, then. At least to getting the list compiled. Maybe once she's seen it, between us we can divide up the work. I really don't think I can do it all by myself this time."

"Nor should you have to," Sam lightly put his hand on her arm. "All of us can help where it works to do so." Brianna gave a grateful nod.

When Maria didn't say anything more, Sam cleared his throat. "I was next, I believe," he said. "Again, it was similar. Gratitude for the work done so far, followed by questions about my schedule and how I felt about how things were now that we've come this far. I did my best to reassure her. I think she wasn't completely satisfied, but it was hard to tell if that's because she's still struggling with understanding how to relate to nobles generally, or if she was hoping to hear something more. There wasn't more I could give." He looked slightly sad.

Mina's eyes had gone sharp now. "Are you all trying to teach her how to relate to nobles, then, too?"

"Well, yes," Sam admitted. "She's not comfortable with it still, but thus the need for more practice. She'll get worse responses in Ichijou, I'm quite sure."

"True," Andrew said, "but be careful how far you go with that without telling her that's what you're doing." The others were a little confused. Leon privately agreed with him, though. "If she knows you're training her, she'll have patience with it instead of take it to heart. Remember that to her, treating her like that is to treat her coldly." He frowned. "If she felt it necessary to talk to all of you, then you've already perhaps walked that line too far without telling her openly.

"As Leon said, being told it's lessons she needs to learn for Ichijou will make her work hard. Being told silently that you all still disapprove of her will only make her angry, eventually." Andrew shook his head. "And also beware how far you push her to *become* that. For her to show up at Ichijou and be someone completely different than what they're expecting will make them wonder if they or the royals were being blinded by a play at the beginning." His eyelids closed slightly, "Not to mention it will make King Sasou angry. He quite likes the innocent commoner who talks back to his face when he needs it, and who won't take pressure from the nobles that he has to fight with all the time."

Leon noted there were eyes that glanced at other eyes. He noted it, but stayed quiet for now. He also had been feeling uncomfortable for a while now with the silent pressure on her. That was why he'd finally spoken up. They were going about it the wrong way, and he was rather sure they knew it from her last set of lessons. They'd needed the scold, in his book.

The nurses took their turns to agree that their interviews had been the same as the first three had been. When they were done, Brian turned to Sam and drolly asked, "And did she interview Mistress Ilena the same as she interviewed Master Ore and Master Rei? Truly, did she need to interview *everyone* in the household?"

Sam allowed as how it had seemed like that. Leon blushed for Mizi's sake, but he couldn't defend her. The reason for it had been the same reason for why she might let some of them go. "It's relieving she remembered you nurses were part of the household," Kirk said dryly, echoing Mizi's own frustration, but in an unkind tease, nearly as unkind as Brian's questions.

"An ordered mind sometimes needs an ordered progression to get from beginning to end," Sam calmly scolded them both and they subsided. They looked at Brianna.

Brianna waved a languid hand. "It was the same for me. I did have to admit to her that I've been feeling overwhelmed and unsure, and she admitted the same to me. We'll continue on for now, however, as the original request was for three months after returning from Tarc. She's allowed that I might have a long vacation at my home if she's allowed to go to Kouzanshi for recruitment. I'm sure that might help me be able to think about the issue with a clearer head, if it can happen at all." She sighed. "I just don't know who to suggest as an alternate as the need for someone in this position is so great at this moment in time." Others nodded heads in sad agreement. Leon didn't disagree, since he'd been the one to suggest the lessons, he just wondered if there was someone else that could do it. Since he didn't have a suggestion right at the moment either, he stayed quiet.

Brianna looked at Brian. Brian sat forward and put his elbows on his knees, clasping his fingers in front of him. "I was the one who couldn't stand to come back here for hours just for interviewing," he admitted to Rei's pair. The rest of them knew he had been. "It didn't seem to me that whatever she needed to talk to us about would be that terrible, because it never seems to be with her. My interview was the same, and I handled it about like Sir Sam did his." *Except more coldly,* Leon felt.

Kirk nodded. "Also for me. She did ask if I wanted to be transferred to Ichijou, but I reassured her here was sufficient for me."

"Were you offended by the suggestion?" Brian asked. "I would've been."

Kirk shrugged, uncomfortable with being asked. "Not really. I know she asks with concern, not with the noble's hidden intent to see it happens one way or the other eventually."

"Do you think she was trying to see who of us to ask to leave?" Maria's hands were wringing her blanket in her lap now, her knuckles rather white. "Some days I feel...." She didn't finish it.

Brian snorted as Kirk shrugged. "It didn't seem like it to me," Kirk said.

"And yet, there are more of us than she can keep in her mind," Brian said. "It wouldn't surprise me if that was one outcome." Leon lightly put his hand on Maria's arm again as she tensed up. Brian turned to him. "And did she talk to you last because you're the least, and first to go if she does clean up a little?"

Leon held his tongue fiercely for a few seconds before he answered, "No."

"But to even ask to be her Voice. Really?" Brian asked scathingly.

"Brian!" Maria scolded, not able to hold it in. Leon appreciated it, but he tensed his hold on her to make her withhold. She pulled back her next words and he stepped in.

"Brian, Mistress Mizi asked us what we each wanted to do. That's what I've wanted this whole time. I'm willing to wait until she understands why she might want one. If she chooses not to have one, then we can talk again about what she might want me to do for her. It's enough. I'm quite sure by the time she reached me she needed a friendly smile, with the three of you being so cold to her just before that." He glared at all three, and included Sam. Really, they were all too much like his older brothers and even his father on occasion. Smiling worked so much better at getting people to do what you needed them to do.

"But it's such a large jump, from lowly soldier to Voice," Brian said with the court neutral voice.

Leon forced his scowl off his face, but it was difficult. He was somewhat relieved when Mina stepped in with the court cool response. "Leon's not wrong. Mizi does leave something positive for the end of something unpleasant she has to do. It's her personal reward to herself." Mina gave the cool not–quite–glare she was so good at giving. She got one back from Brianna and slightly apologetic looks from Sam and Kirk. Brian stayed cool and disapproving. Leon didn't get any apologies, but he was ignored for now which was nearly as good so he let it go and refused to say anymore about his interview. Most of the rest knew it had been the same as the others, since they'd heard it from the Rose office, like he'd heard the ones before him.

Andrew and Mina considered everything they'd been told, then thanked the members of the household for letting them know. "Lady Brianna, if you suggest a lesson plan to her, be sure it's after the presentation to the Court of Ministers," Andrew said as the summary. "Be sure you let her know that you've been trying to give her lesson opportunities to practice facing lords and ladies. Include it in the list if you feel it that important." Brianna bowed her head.

"When you discuss who can do what to help her, please let her know that I'll be continuing to help with those lessons," Brian said coolly. Brianna tipped her head.

As Andrew and Mina rose to their feet to return their dishes to the cart, Mina paused and looked directly into Brian's eyes. "It's true that most of the time she has things to say that are trivial, questions that show she has much to learn, but beware. She's most direct when angry and scolds immediately and publicly, not caring who might hear it. She's very aware that it needs to be heard in the moment by the person who needs to be scolded. If your lordship is so important to you, please don't step into her ire at the wrong time or you'll be quite embarrassed." She turned coldly away and took Andrew's plate from him to move to the cart.

Andrew looked into Brian's eyes and let him read that it was a truth. "But you should already know that," Maria said quietly. Leon was shocked she had the courage to interrupt. "She's already shown that at all of the teas. She has no fear when she's angry." Andrew gave a confirming nod, then turned and joined Mina at the foot of the stairs. The rest were quiet until they'd closed the door behind them.

Brian turned and looked Sam in the eyes. Quietly he asked, "Even in Ichijou she was like that?"

Sam confirmed it. "Even there. Perhaps even more so there. It was rare, but even Ore was scolded until he settled to understanding what she wanted. Master Rei was scolded most and he never forgot any one of them."

Brian blew out a breath, then rose to his feet as well to pick up his and Brianna's plates. He silently took them to the cart, then collected the two folding tables to put them away. "Will you stay up, Lady Brianna," he asked solicitously.

"No, I don't think so," she answered tiredly. Brian helped her up, then took Sam's table to the wall as Brianna folded her blanket to drape it over her chair again.

Leon lightly took Maria's elbow in his hand again and held her back from rising to her feet. Instead he rose and took both sets of their dishes to the cart, and then collected their tables to set them against the wall with the others. By the time he got back to Maria's chair most of the household were in their lower wing or were moving that direction. Leon sat down next to Maria again and waited silently with her until the lower room was empty, save the guards above.

"Maria, thank you," he said quietly while looking into her eyes. "Please, you don't have to defend me. I'm grateful you care, but I don't want to have the mud they're throwing at me thrown at you, too. I can understand that it was difficult for you to face Mistress Mizi this morning. To be called in without warning, when we're all still trying to learn her and our places is difficult. I think if you can remember what Kirk said, it may help you. She's almost never hiding things behind what she says and does. I believe she was trying to respect our privacy, for all it was perhaps unnecessary."

Maria's face crumpled a little. "You really don't think she'll ask some of us to go, do you?"

Leon let his scowl out. "It wouldn't hurt to have a few go." Maria put her hand over lips that curled up, understanding who he meant. "But, I think it's a difficult thing for her to make a decision like that. She cares overly much, some might think, but it's also hard to decide generally. I'm not sure she asked questions today that would help her answer to it so I can't be sure this was that sort of interview." He really hoped it wasn't anyway.

He pondered on what Andrew had said, then concluded, "I think I'd have to agree with Lord Andrew. He and Lady Mina have the experience to understand Mistress Mizi. If she were getting concerned because so many were feeling so cold to her, she'd wonder if she was doing something wrong and want to understand that. For all she might not understand how to be a lady, nor how to relate to lords and ladies in that way, she does have a good sense for how people are feeling about her. To talk to us one on one would let her know for sure how that was going. She was near to crying out of desperation by the time she talked to me. I'm not wrong that she very much needed a smiling face by then." He sighed a bit.

Maria's face went soft and she patted Leon's arm. "I'm glad you can be that for her," she said softly. "Some mornings she can't even leave the suite unless we give that to her to encourage her for the day. I'm glad she has a project she's focused on. Those help her move forward each day."

Leon agreed with Maria. He felt it was why of all of them Maria wouldn't be the one sent away. Her smile was rare but made anyone who saw it willing to face the day, even grey cold winter ones. He smiled at her now and was relieved to have her smile back. If she was feeling better now, then he could also. He'd nearly not been able to withhold himself this long from talking to her, but he didn't want her to know he'd heard her interview. She'd be very dismayed to know it.

He helped her rise to her feet, then added a few logs to the warming stove to keep the guards warm a little longer while she folded her blanket and lay it over the arm of her chair. He held his elbow out to her and escorted her to the door and to the door of her room, wishing her a quiet goodnight. She smiled for him one more time before closing the door.

He went to his room, the central one in the hallway on the men's side. The suite above him was quiet, but he wasn't surprised. They'd talked long enough that even if Mizi had stayed awake to give her report, they'd be sleeping now. He drew in a long breath and worked to set aside the worry of the day so he could sleep. Tomorrow was another day and Mizi would be busy with her report again. He'd listen to hear if they woke her up or let her sleep in. He rather hoped they'd let her sleep. He'd be able to fall back to sleep as well, since Andrew would wake up Sam to tell him before they walked out. Mizi really did need to slow down even a little bit. Maybe after the Court of Ministers.

8-11 Ante-Cold Solstice: Delegation of Princes

"Mizi, are you still doing history research for the nation and region?" Rei asked her the next morning.

"Ah, well, to some degree, as I said. It's the reading I do when I need to unwind or have a bit of time on my hands." Mizi blinked her green eyes at him, having paused in pulling on her leggings. He let her finish that and get her comfortable casual dress on over her head before continuing. She was still doing research and report writing with Ryan in preparation for the Medical department intern tests in addition to her report writing for the hospital presentation, so wasn't dressing up in the court dresses generally. Rei thought she was quite beautiful in the dresses, but he also enjoyed getting to see the slightly more relaxed her that he'd fallen in love with at the beginning.

"I'd like to have you do some research for me in that area," he asked her as he took up her hand to lead her to their breakfast table.

"Okay," she immediately agreed.

Rei leaned over to whisper in her ear before opening the door between their bedroom and the sitting room. "Find out which Suiran lords have already been replaced and when, and which ones are still of Houses from the founding of the Region."

Mizi blinked, then gave a nod. While it might not decrease Rei's workload much since he wasn't sure he could wave his hand and give all lords not from the founding a pass, it would help him greatly to know who was most likely set against them the most strongly. "Should I add anything of note?" she whisper–asked back. "Like if it was rewards from royalty, or simple appointments?"

"Yes, please," he answered. That would help, too. If the House had been allied with Touka before, perhaps they'd be more inclined to side with Touka now. That didn't always bear out, but again, clues like those helped him sort things so he knew what to focus the most on. "It doesn't need to come soon, as I know you're focused on other important things, but if you could make that your history study for a bit, I'd appreciate it."

"Of course, Rei." She gave his hand a squeeze and he opened the door, the smells of breakfast already put on plates coming to their noses and making his stomach growl just a little.

As they were finishing eating, Andrew and Mina arrived for the first–thing–in–the–morning meeting. Andrew went first with Rei's schedule. It was one of the usual mostly–quiet office work days. When Mizi had finished telling him what her schedule for the day would be (also a simple and usual list), Rei leaned back in his chair to look at both of his aides. "Andrew, I'm going to stay here for another hour or so this morning. If you want to stay and wait for me, make yourself comfortable. Mina, I've got some research to send you to do before going to the office. We'll meet you there." He handed her a folder.

His requests weren't too unusual to these of his aides, for all he'd not had to do it since they'd been doing research on Pakyo Shicchi. They bowed and Mizi gave him a kiss before accepting her warm winter accessories and cloak from Tanner. Andrew settled into one of the chairs closer to the main door as Mina, Mizi, and Tanner left the room. Rei moved to his desk there in the sitting room and pulled out a pen and paper and started writing.

"Is it a letter?" Andrew asked. He usually helped with those.

"No. A mini–report," Rei answered. Andrew settled into a more relaxed state, knowing Rei could handle those on his own.

Rei's writing hand was actually tired by the time he was done writing. He set the pen down in the drawer, then massaged his hand. A blank folder from the side drawer had the papers slipped into it and he was nearly ready to go. "I'll be right back," he said to Andrew and took the folder into his bedroom to collect the other folders he'd brought to the suite. He paused to hand Rutherford one of the papers from the folder. His manservant took it, slipped it into his jacket, and returned silently to his cleaning up of the bedroom. He'd just finished with cleaning up the bath room.

Once there were four folders in his hand, Rei returned to the outer sitting room. Andrew was standing, holding Rei's cloak. Rei walked over to him to accept the weight of it around his shoulders. Out of habit from taking care of Rei, Andrew was settling the warm winter hat on his head, making sure it covered his ears. Rei sighed at him, but let him do that and settle the scarf around his neck. "It's not too tight?" Andrew asked at Rei's expression.

"No, it's fine," Rei answered. "I'm just not ten anymore."

Andrew blushed slightly and defended himself. "Well, you do have your hands full."

Rei just sighed and accepted the gloves. He didn't let Andrew have the folders, though, holding them under his arm instead while he put the gloves on. Andrew got his winter gear on and they were out the door. It was a cold and windy winter day, with snow being swirled around. "I can only tell it's day because the flakes are grey instead of black," Rei quipped.

"Indeed." Andrew was walking very close to Rei. He always was a little nervous outdoors in this kind of weather. It was harder to see potential attackers because visibility was so poor.

Rei grasped Andrew's elbow and steered him in a different direction than they usually walked. "What is it?" Andrew asked him quietly.

"I've got someone to stop by and see on the way," Rei answered only loud enough for Andrew to hear him. "And I'd like to go by a different way generally today." Andrew understood and they went into their more stealthy mode of traveling by foot in castles. He still didn't go very far from Rei's side, but they became two co-workers, muffled against the cold, just walking together for company in the miserable weather no one wished to have to be out in.

The stop at the office Rei headed for first was brief and only to pass a folder over. It was a request for more research, again a simple unassuming thing to be researched that shouldn't take the person too long to complete. Rei had Andrew distract the office head with a question. It wasn't uncommon for Andrew to visit places for Rei but he didn't want to be seen there himself. As soon as the folder was with the person he wanted it to be with and had received a surprised nod, he left the room and waited for Andrew in the hallway, hiding in the recess of a doorway that wasn't used because bookshelves had been placed in front of it in the office behind the door.

When they arrived at the Rose office, Rei went first to his desk, letting Andrew remove his winter gear first. He picked up three folders off a stack, adding them to the stack in his hands. He shuffled them and set the whole of them on his desk, then removed his winter gear. He handed the pieces to Mina, who was standing waiting to receive them by then.

Once he was free of the winter accessories, Rei picked up the stack again and walked to the far end of the Rose office to place two of the folders on Flandras' desk. "Here are two more you can learn from," he said casually. He'd been giving a few folders to Flandras each day since he'd come. He didn't want the statistician to be completely bored while in the office. Training him to be useful while he was there and then later in the Rosebud office was better than wasting his time.

He dropped one off on Brian's desk, another on Brianna's, and the fifth on Aiden's desk. "Kirk," he said and carried the final folder on to his own desk. He was sitting by the time Kirk had arrived in front of his desk. "Take this to General Garen and stay until he tells you to return. I don't know if he's already gotten things written down or if he can get it written down quickly. We have messages to run to some of the garrisons and I can't send Ore two places at once." He handed the folder over. Kirk took it, bowed, and headed for the cloak pegs to dress for the weather.

-o-o-o-

Garen looked at the contents of the folder with a very puzzled expression. "Are you sure this is the folder I was supposed to get?" he asked Kirk.

"It was the one Master Rei handed to me. It was one of a small stack, though, so I suppose it could have been confused with another one if they'd gotten out of order?" Kirk wasn't sure.

"What did he say when he sent you?" Garen asked.

Kirk told him what little he knew. "That you might or might not be ready to send a message back. That you both had messages to run to some of the garrisons, and that Lord Ore couldn't be sent two places at once. I'm afraid that was all."

Garen sighed. "Well, it wouldn't do to send you back and waste the trip. He might still send you again with the proper folder, but I'll try to guess as best I can so you don't have to." He gave an understanding grimace and Kirk smiled back in gratitude.

Kirk had taken off his gloves and hat after handing the folder over to General Garen. He didn't remove his cloak though until the general waved at an empty chair over by the doorway to the office. It wouldn't do to get too warm inside. Then one only froze when they returned to the outdoors. Kirk had been reminded of the warm gear of home when Flandras had come to the Rose office for the first time. Northwestern boots were so distinctive and so very warm. His were almost worn out so not quite so warm anymore. They were still his favorites, though. He'd been regretting not buying a new set while they'd been in Kouzanshi. It hadn't been cold enough then to remind him he was needing them. He didn't have an easy way to get a pair he would like shipped to him, now that Julie was in the islands of the Inner Sea.

He spent the next little while thinking about her as a pleasant diversion from being rather bored. He'd been perhaps a little *too* excited to learn that he could have her as his wife if she was willing. While she'd wanted to have the time to come to terms with the somewhat shocking news that she was the child of completely different parents than they'd grown up believing, she'd actually had more time to consider it than he had since she'd been the one suspicious it was so. He supposed his proposal was more shocking to her than that news had been.

Still, she'd had as hard a time leaving him the last night on the road south of Kouzanshi as he'd had saying goodbye to her again, knowing it would be many months, maybe more than a year, before they saw each other again. He rested yet again in her promise that she'd come to Nijou after her veterinary training for the messenger birds. He was very much looking forward to her arrival and was hoping the new Regent's building would be finished by then so that she might be willing to say yes and stay with him.

For all thinking of Julie was pleasant, he could only do that for so long. Sitting was rather hard when he only had thinking to do. He'd ask Garen to call him back in and go out to practice in the list, but he wasn't sure he'd see the stick in his hands given today's weather, and that kind of relaxing hadn't been in his orders.

Rei was a very focused Regent. Play time was play time, and it was only as often as necessary. The rest of the time was work time or taking care of the body time (that is, sleeping or eating). For a nineteen year old that sort of intensity was rather impressive. It was even more impressive that he was actually being productive the whole time it was work time. The six folders being passed around the room weren't empty, nor did they hold things Rei hadn't touched. If he was handing them out, he'd decided certain things needed to be done by staff, not him, and he'd summarized what that work was for them so they could focus on getting it done expeditiously.

Kirk took in a deep breath and sighed just a little. He was older by five and a half years and some days he felt very much behind Rei in capacity and office work skills. Not to mention focus. He'd been surreptitiously watching Ore when he was in the office and taking notes. Ore couldn't sit still very long either, but somehow managed to not be scolded. It had been relieving that Kirk had been watched but not scolded the few times he'd experimented with doing what Ore did to sit still (including not sitting still but instead getting up to stoke the fire or something similar). He wondered if he was going to become Rei's next Messenger because he'd been displaying those similar traits. He wasn't going to complain if it meant he got to be released from the office to run messages regularly enough he could get the need to be active out of his system.

It also helped that Mizi was getting better at telling when he needed to not be sent to the Rose office. On those days standing in the medical wing was better than sitting still, hunched over a desk, only moving fingers to write. Of course she kept him busy as well when there was experimenting to do but that was more fun than work for him.

With her writing up things more than researching right now, he'd been trying to quietly work out in the corners of the office she worked in, trying to not disturb her or the other medics. When she was working in the Old Regent's suite there was plenty of time to work out in the open area of the outer lobby. She was willing to let them stay out there where they wouldn't bother her focused working, but they scolded her when she told them *all* to go to the Rose office. That wouldn't do.

One of the things that had helped all of them was having her talk to them a little more frankly after the first time she'd made them all work too hard too long without rest. (That had been before this most recent interviewing time.) Brian had been plain that he'd be just as happy working at a desk in the Rose office where it was quiet. Kirk had been the opposite, explaining that he really did need more activity and truly enjoyed helping her with the research. That had split them up most days, but not all of them.

Sam was good either place and Leon was still mostly confused in the Rose office. Sometimes Mizi made Leon work in the Rose office anyway to get the practice in. Those were the days it seemed she wanted to have longer days of quiet. Often on those days she'd apologize to Brian and make him go with her and Sam. Today she'd taken both soldier guards with her but Leon stood on the wall better than either of Brian or Kirk, having had more practice.

Kirk frowned a bit as he thought on the youngest of the guards. Brian had been rather harsh the night before. It wasn't a bad thing for Leon to have the aspiration to be Mizi's Voice, if she cared to have one. It wasn't even surprising, given how much Leon looked at her with stars in his eyes. Kirk wondered if that's why Brian was so harsh with Leon. Brian was the opposite, wishing Mizi would learn nobility faster. His immediate letting Brianna know he'd not be letting up on how to relate to him and other nobles said it plainly. However, Leon also wasn't wrong in that. Mizi did need a kinder hand with her lessons. If Brian continued on as he was, he was likely to push her wrongly. Kirk wasn't surprised Mina had warned him of it severely.

Today, with Ilena and Ore at Falcon's Hollow, the four guards had walked Mizi to the medical building first thing. Brian had commented to Kirk on their walk to the Rose office how he truly felt sorry for Tanner. Mizi still didn't really see him very well, still more often than not forgot him. Kirk had reminded Brian that Tanner had said he preferred it that way in that household conversation they'd had. Also, Kirk had seen that while in her medical office Mizi was doing better and remembering to give Tanner something to do before losing herself in her work. Since a lot of her work was writing things up, she was giving a small part of that to Tanner every day she was there.

She more often lost sight of Tanner when they were in the Rose office. Kirk thought that was because there were too many people in the room for Mizi to remember more than a few of them at a time. She was so focused that most people not directly related to what she was focused on weren't there to her. Which *should* be the case when most of everyone around her were personal aides and staff. It was Tanner that kept an eye on everyone around her so she could be safe, and that was as it should be as well.

"Sir Leander," Garen called and waved him over to his desk. Kirk rose to his feet, holding onto his winter gear, and walked back over. "Have you traveled much in the eastern and southern parts of Suiran?"

"No," Kirk answered honestly. "The progress was my first time."

Garen rose to his feet and led Kirk over to a wide map cabinet. He opened the top drawer and pulled out the map on the top, then set it on the top of the cabinet. "Here's the castle," Garen oriented him. Kirk did know how to read maps, so he gave a nod of understanding. "This marker is for the garrisons." It was a triangle and they were placed mostly along the roadways, farther apart than the little villages and inns travelers would stop at overnight as they rode wagons from far place to far place. In the east part of the Region, though, there were several garrisons that were along the borders that weren't near populated places. Those were the ones Kirk had missed, going with Mizi up Castle Road.

Garen drew his finger along the North Road from castle Nijou to the west. "You know this part well, then?" Kirk nodded again. "Regent Rei will be sending Lord Ore that way and hope to keep it long enough to get the need to run out of his system, but short enough Ilena doesn't become difficult." Kirk understood that balance might be hard. "That's still a lot of garrisons not reached." Garen waved a hand from the east part of the Region and around at all the rest of the garrisons. "A single Messenger by horseback, moving fast enough, can get it done in about two weeks in the summer, maybe less. But you do need to know where you're going, and if it's you, you'll be going in weather like today. It'll be easy to get lost out by the border."

Kirk wrinkled his nose. "Well, add another half-week, then, to the winter travel time so I can take those parts slow enough to not pass by it when I think the gate's just another three trees standing together."

Garen chuckled. "True enough. I've got a soldier I can send with you for at least the eastern part. They can bring the message back up Castle Road while you continue on to the easier garrisons along Suiran Road and up the intermediate roads." He paused, then said, "Or, Regent Rei has said that he could send Brian that way, since his family lives that way. Then we'd send you down Castle Road then west. That would cut out some of the time you were gone." Kirk could see that, too.

Garen put the map back into the cabinet. On the way back to his desk he said, "Study the Rose office's copy of that map and let him or me know what you think you can handle. I'm sure Princess Mizi would rather not lose you to the winter snows and wind, so we'd rather not be too rash about it." He picked up the folder. "Give this back to Prince Rei. I've done my best to guess what he wants."

As Kirk put on his cloak, hat, and gloves again, Garen asked, "Do you know why they're still keeping four guards for Princess Mizi? I could use my two back again."

Kirk paused. "Brian and I have teased that it's because all four of us would have to fight it out, with the best two left standing getting to stay. ...Which makes Leon depressed and then argue back." He smiled a little. "And with Sam sent by the King no one can move him but the King." He sighed and went a little more serious. "But we're actually wondering it, too: how many of us they'll keep in the end, particularly once both households are moved into the new Regent's building. Lord Ore and Lady Ilena are her first guardians and she surely doesn't need six."

"Is mixing the four of you up her test to see who works well enough with whom, to see who she'd like to keep?" Garen asked.

Kirk shook his head and picked the folder up from the desktop where he'd put it to put on his gloves. "I don't know. It could be." He winked a solemn wink. "If that's the case, Brian loses. He'd rather be in the Rose office being lazy."

Garen snorted. Even he knew neither royal was that nor did they let their staff be. Kirk took himself out of the office and back into the bitter swirling wind. If he wasn't careful he'd be lost just trying to get back to the Rose office. Then he'd not be sent out as a Messenger at all since that was a lot easier of a distance than to the eastern mountains.

-o-o-o-

Flandras kept his head down when he was in the Rose office. Everyone save the oldest two in this office and Rei's first two aides had been at his graduation testing, so knew what he did and had met him, even if only cursorily. Rei hadn't bothered to introduce him much at all. Although, after the first opening comments from Rei to Ore about him, everyone had assumed Flandras was part of Ore and Ilena's group. That meant no one talked to him directly save Ore and his guards when they paused to greet everyone when they came. That was a bit lonely, since he felt somewhat ostracized, but at the same time it was somewhat relieving since he didn't have to come up with small talk that hid what his real assignments were.

Not that anyone talked about their assignments, unless it was a question critical to getting the work completed or moving forward expeditiously. He'd already been trained at this point to add his questions to his summary of the documents he was being given if they weren't of the critical kind. Even important ones were to be written down since asking Rei to change his thoughts from one thing to another was what he liked least. Once he'd picked up a folder, that was where his thoughts focused, so that was when he could answer the questions easily. Flandras found that a pleasant way to work, actually. Because Rei needed it for his own sanity, it was gifted to everyone. If Rei had already been working on the same topic, the folders came to them with comments from him, sometimes necessitating research before the final summary could be written up.

Flandras had been working on one that morning when Rei had come in and given him the two new folders. He'd ignored them in favor of finishing the one he was already working on. (That had been another lesson Flandras had learned by observing the workings of the office. If you were sent out of the room you went immediately, but if new work was handed to you, you finished what you were working on already first.) The second folder (the first of the new ones – one always did them in the order they'd been put down on the desk) had been somewhat simple to complete, being done by lunch time.

Flandras was ever so glad they didn't have to walk through the frigid winter weather to find food in the middle of the day. Excused now from the lunch table to return to work, he sat to his desk and opened up the final folder. (He was never given more than two in a day at this point in his time there.) As his eyes read the words written on the paper, they got very wide. He almost didn't catch his reactions in time. That was one of the harder things to remember. He wasn't alone in his lab or personal office anymore. He was with others who'd read all of his expressions and tensions. He allowed himself to take in a deep breath, then let it out and lost himself in the words on the page.

You'll calculate every option I have. My answer from Ilena is so large that I haven't the time to walk through every permutation of every option available to me. I need to know which ones end with the most optimal results for both critical issues. When you're ready you'll give me a report of coded summary options and percentages of success, casualties, generational consequences, and long-term affects on all castes. My personal preferences are weighted to kindness, temperance, patience, and education. This time I'd like to add in greatest effect that results most rapidly in prosperous and peaceful living for all, even if those other preferences have to take a lesser weight.

Flandras closed the folder and pulled his folded notes out of his jacket. They were getting a bit worn as the stack was somewhat thick and it had been a while that he'd been carrying them back and forth. He made sure his ink well was full, pulled a new sheet of paper over, and began to copy from his notes. He made changes based on Rei's desires and weight preferences, then calculated. He followed that process for option after option already spinning around in his head since he'd seen the full scope of the problems until his shoulder was touched and he blearily came out of the page in front of him.

Rei's brilliant blue eyes were looking into his kindly. "It's time to be done for the day." Flandras blinked in a bit of shock. "Can you stop and come back to it or do you need to get to a better stopping point?"

Flandras looked back at his page, realizing his mind had become more hazy than it should be. He shook his head. He'd gathered all the papers up, and was about to shove them into his coat again when a folder was handed to him. As he put the papers in it, he saw it was the same one Rei had given him the order in. That made sense. He shouldn't just leave that one sitting around either. Once it was put together, he held on to it tightly. It seemed Rei approved. "I'll work on it a bit more tonight," Flandras told him. At the scolding look he got in response, he added, "Just enough to get to the end of that thought."

"Do sleep tonight, Flandras," Rei scolded dryly anyway. "You've got plenty of time to work on it. Practice that, too. I don't require sleepless nights. There's always lots of hard work here in this place. Resting the mind is crucial to not making mistakes."

Flandras took in a deep breath, rose to his feet, and bowed. "I'll remember," he promised. He held on to the folder tightly, only letting Rei hold it briefly while he dressed in his winter gear. He held on to it while eating a cooled meal at the food cart in his dormitory entrance hall. He held on to it when he got into bed for the night, not bothering to finish the calculation. His mind was already too tired to continue as it was, and he was already afraid of being the one that caused the one fatal, foreseeable miscalculation. He woke up a few times in the middle of the night to snatch at the folder for dreaming it had been stolen from him or fallen from his arms into very bad locations. Each time it was as it should be he relaxed back into sleep, holding it tightly to himself again.

-o-o-o-

There was a great bustling around the courtyard of the Soldier's gate. Prison carriages and wagons were being loaded up. It was time for the final clearing out of the prison, the last of those sentenced to pay their due to society.

Nobles in wrinkled clothing but also in cloaks were led out by soldiers. Their wrists were manacled together and their feet were bare. Those who'd been higher lords were grumbling at their lady wives or sons and heirs about the cold snow and ground. The most prideful walked in silence, heads held up just as proudly as they'd always walked. They were let into the carriages four at a time and made to sit on the same bench together. Chains were run through their manacles and locked to sturdy rings set into the side walls of the carriages. It took two prison carriages to hold them all.

The common prisoners were brought out in light cloaks and were allowed their boots. That was because they were locked in the same manner into the open prison wagons. While they might be getting execution as their sentence (or so the shovels in the supply wagon suggested), they weren't going to have to have their toes frozen off first. It was assumed the nobles had been given the sentence of bare feet so they couldn't run off when the caravan of carriages and soldier guards on horseback had to make their stops on their way east to the prison manor they'd be staying at for the rest of their natural lives. The carriages would warm up fast enough with that many people in them.

The whole of the caravan eventually was ready to go. Garen confirmed the instructions with the head of the guard detail, then ordered them off. The horses strained on the yokes and the carriages and wagons got moving forward. The complaining creaks and grumble of wheels against the road were preferable to the complaints of the lords. With a sigh out that puffed as a cloud in front of him, he shook his head and turned for his office. He knew there were still a few spies around watching that display, but none would see the true sentence carried out except those in the caravan.

It wasn't his to worry about any more. Now it was in the hands of the Suiran Ministry of Intelligence. He was glad to have his part in it all done. He had a lot of other things to be thinking about right now. Having the garrison prison cleaned out to minimal prisoners was a relieving weight removed from his responsibilities.

-o-o-o-

Sasou was going through his mail in the Office of the King in Ichijou, as he did every morning. He had four folders he was holding in his hand, undecided if he wanted to read them first or save them for last. Looking at the remaining stack of folders in front of him, he decided to open these first. The rest would be work he'd have to focus on and would get lost in. If he read these first he'd maybe have a good attitude while facing that work. Besides, he was supposed to gift himself good things on his birthday, wasn't he? Skipping out on work hadn't been one of those things, so this would be sufficient.

Happy Birthday Brother,

I'm pulling my hair out but will spare you that in this letter. Mizi and I have sent you a gift that should be presented by Aryana at your birthday dinner ...just so the rest of the court knows I still remember you with respect.

This letter is my personal gift to you: Yes, I'm still alive and doing all the work you don't want to do up here, and things seem to finally be stabilizing in the main. (Other than the outstanding issues you're already aware of.)

Sasou was nicely surprised that Rei actually continued on to chat about random things going on his life. He was relieved Rei was keeping out most of the things that were worrying him, so as to not add darkness to this gift he wanted to give his older brother. The chatty length of the letter let him relax and appreciate he had a capable younger brother who cared about him. It was already one of his most favorite presents of the day.

Sasou set the page down when he reached the end and untied the folder with a red cord next. He was keen to see what his "corespondent" had to say. Mizi was the only one who'd openly said that she'd be happy to be that for him. Well, maybe Ilena's request back when he was nine counted.

Sasou,

Happy Birthday. I've been working hard on the idea of building a hospital outside of Nijoushi and running it as a business, following in Ilena's footsteps as best I can. In the process of doing that I've been having lessons in writing letters to lords more full of fluff than substance. I hope you'll be okay with me using this opportunity to write a letter of the sort I much prefer to write. I would think if you only ever receive correspondence of that kind, you'll appreciate it more than most.

Sasou couldn't hold back the snort of laughter. Mizi was ever so right. He did enjoy getting her letters when she sent them. It was the same when she faced him and talked to him with open honesty and directness. He much preferred being approached that way over the foggy words that the lords and ladies used. It was refreshing, even if he might feel like he'd been sucking on a lemon slice. (Mizi's letters weren't ever that bad.) Sour notes or true meat to chew on was much better than the aftertaste of ash. She'd even relaxed enough, or been trained in letter writing enough now, that she'd not used an honorific in the salutation. That was nice as well, that she could approach him with the right level of casualness at the right times now.

He continued to read her letter. It contained quite a bit more about her hospital–turned–business idea, which meant she was likely very focused on that at the moment. He knew how it had likely come about, but she kindly left that out of her letter, like Rei had left those things out of his.

Sasou picked up the letter from his mother next. It was as usual short, just a desire to greet him on his birthday. It also included a scolding tease of a pat on the back for finally getting his wife pregnant and doing his duty to the nation. He sighed at her for that, but was pleased she'd taken the time to let him know she cared.

Sasou then picked up the final folder and briefly wondered why there wasn't a fifth this year; although, having Mizi's be an additional one was nice. He untied the gold, green, and black ribbon and slipped the page out of the folder.

Sasou, (I feel like I should add "you bastard" except I don't have a reason to.)

Happy Birthday. Ore says the same. Grandfather says, "Be happy you got that much. I'm just as glad to not have to write it for him." And he also sends birthday wishes. He's just grumbling and relieved because Shicchis are worse letter–writers than you.

Ah. That would be why there wasn't a fifth letter. And likely there wouldn't ever be one. It was okay for it to come with Ilena's letter, then.

Sasou paused then, blinking at his sudden thought. *Wait. If Ilena can't write, then who's writing this one?* He had to calculate that, then laugh. Poor Leah. She was a good woman to write it exactly as Ilena dictated it. Then he wondered if some of the additional swirls to the letter — like the parenthetical part of the salutation — was Leah herself. ...Or maybe it was Ore. It was the sort of thing the thief–turned–lord would say. Sasou could only shake his head at the whole of the ministry. Really, he could probably consider the letter to be from all of the crazy bunch, then, if he wanted to.

He continued to shake his head at much of the letter. It was as meandering as a mealtime conversation in the office there. He wondered if it had been written at a lunch and everyone had added to it. He put himself into that setting as he read it and did in the end feel like he'd been there with them. He had to immediately take up his eagle feather pen and blank paper to write back to Ilena and that crazy office just how he'd reacted to it. And to scold just a bit since he wanted his turn to do so. But, he was grateful. It was another way to help him relax and feel loved.

108

When that letter was done, he continued to write responses in the reverse order he'd read them in. A short reply to his mother. A slightly longer one to Mizi to thank her for working hard on the hospital ...for all the reasons she was doing it for. Then it was Rei's. He paused and tapped his pen for a bit. That was a harder one. Finally, he put the pen to the paper.

Little Brother,
Thank you.

Sasou glanced up as he cleaned up that much correspondence from his desk and caught his aide relaxed back in his chair, looking at him. Michael's eyes sparkled, "It's good to see you smile." Sasou gave him a nod.

He didn't offer the letters to Michael and his aide didn't ask to read them. These were important to Sasou's soul as a man but weren't critical to the nation staying whole between the royals. It was instead the proof that the nation's pillars were working well together, a relief to them all. Sasou held on to those feelings tightly for the rest of that day. He very much needed the positive distraction from his own worries.

-o-o-o-

Osterly to Princess Mizi: Prince Airn has left as of this morning. He's expected to arrive at the castle mid–afternoon today. Mizi sat upright in shock. She'd been listening to the slightly more frequent reports that Airn was traveling the road even through the snow, but she really hadn't expected to hear that this morning. She looked around the table in the office of the Regent's suite. Her notes for the next day's presentation to the Court of Ministers were more scattered than she usually liked notes to be, echoing her internal stress about the event. Her nose wrinkled up.

Rei had said that he was going to tell the Ministers that Sasou had agreed to support Altherly against Gael, in the hopes that would help them see the wisdom of having a new medical facility built. He'd also warned her that it might make them not quite so willing to approve funds for it as they'd want to wait to see what the war assistance would cost the Region. Mizi could only understand. She was a bit resigned to that already, since she wasn't sure funding was going to come from public funds anyway.

She considered the state of her table, the state of her mind, and what she was. Then she called for a paige to be sent to the suite. It wasn't her typical but it needed to be today. Paiges were usually sent to pick up people, knew how to take them to their rooms, and she just didn't have the time to do it herself today. Her orders to the paige included that he stop by the Châtelaine's office to have rooms requisitioned for the prince and his two aides. That office knew what kind of room a young visiting prince should be given and where. She was quite glad to let those in the castle who were there to help the royals help her today, and it was good practice for her, she was quite sure.

As a last minute order to the paige before she let him go, she added, "He's here for lessons. He can have his first one tomorrow at the meeting of the Ministers. See he's brought for it and he stands in the back. Whomever is assigned to bring him should stay with him to answer his initial questions. Any that can't be answered he can ask to us again when we've got the time to sit down with him. See he's taken to the library after that. We'll send for him when I know what his schedule will be."

The paige bowed as she excused him and she turned back to her piles in relief. Mizi's last comment before her head bent to the work was, "Tanner, please remind me the day after tomorrow. Thank you." She barely registered his quiet answer as she was very soon lost in the work again.

-o-o-o-

Prince Airn couldn't be surprised to be placed into the care of a paige when he was let into castle Nijou by the guards. "Princess Mizi apologizes for not coming to welcome you directly," the paige said respectfully once Airn was in the castle grounds proper. "She has a presentation tomorrow at the Court of Ministers she's preparing for." That did make him pause. She wasn't much older than him, and she was going to face that august body? He could understand why she'd be focused on that. He himself had stood in such meetings, wishing to be anywhere else. "She'll meet with you when she can after that," the paige finished.

They were being led through the beginnings of snowfall again. Airn was glad they'd been able to ride under cloudy skies without so much snow during this day. The road had been clear enough to make the travel uneventful. The building they were led to was fairly close to the gate they'd been let in through. It was rather grand in a solidly imposing manner, yet was also graced with sculpted details that made it not merely utilitarian. He made sure to count that they were led to the third door on the left of the main open entry atrium.

That door opened onto a short hallway which had one door on the left and two on the right. "Your men may have the rooms here on the right," the paige waved a hand at the doors, then turned to the door on the left. He pulled out a key to unlock the door, then handed it with a small bow to Airn. "This is your apartment." Two more keys came out to be handed to Erlic Yetherly, the senior of the two with Airn. "If guards ask who you are, just let them know. The garrison has been informed of your arrival. A paige will arrive tomorrow two hours after the breakfast cart is delivered to take you to the Court of Ministers for your first lesson." The paige bowed, then asked, "Do you have any further questions for me at this time?"

Ian Ulmer waved at the hallway door they'd entered through and asked, "Which key unlocks that door?"

"Any of the three," the paige answered. That satisfied Airn's guard. They could lock up and be safe enough. The paige hesitated, then added, "Because you're here under the protection of the Regent, you're under the protection of his Minister of Intelligence. She'll personally murder anyone who even thinks to do anything to harm your persons. Her people will be your housekeepers. She's asked me to let you know so you can *all* sleep soundly at night." Airn was impressed with the scolding glare the paige gave Ian. It was rare for someone so young to scold his men and get away with it. The paige then sighed and added, "She's the most paranoid person in the castle. You can let her worry about that." He gave a rather direct look to Ian. "No one in the castle wants her eyes on them, so please, do relax at least a little."

"Ah!" Airn jumped in to use this opportunity. "I've heard that she's a well–known nightwalker? ...The Queen of Night?"

The paige nodded rather morosely. "She is."

"Truly?" Airn mused in slight surprise. "Well, perhaps I'll have the opportunity to meet her sometime while I'm here." He waved a hand of dismissal at the paige. "We'll be looking for our escort tomorrow." Not like he was wanting lessons right away. He'd kind of thought they'd not let him vacation any further upon arrival at the castle, though.

The next mid–morning Airn did get to see with his own eyes that, indeed, the red–haired young woman was the First Princess of Ryokudo and that the same pale–haired young man who'd sat before him to a meal and given him his requirement for staying in Suiran was sitting on the Regent's throne. His eyes searched the Ministers until he found two black–haired younger members of the court before that throne. The same woman who'd recognized him in the lists of Kouzanshi had a medallion of ministry around her shoulders and the man who was next to her was the same one who'd been by her side there as well.

Airn sighed, then tried to pay attention to the court. Certainly seeing how it differed from the ones he'd been in at home was something to learn, but he didn't expect it to be all that different. The Regent had a herald, the same as Airn's father did, so that the royal didn't have to do all the talking and have a sore throat by the end. Airn asked the paige who it was. He was told it was Count Andrew Marciel, the Regent's personal guardian and aide.

Surprisingly to him, Airn's attention was caught very early by the proceedings themselves. Andrew opened the meeting, then said, "Regent Suiran wishes to inform the Ministers that King Ryokudo has informed him that Gael has broken off all peaceful relations with Altherly, and is preparing its armies and navies for war. The missive from the King informs the Regent that he is to begin preparing companies to support Altherly according to the treaty of support the King has signed with King Altherly." There was disturbed stirring in the ministers and their supports that matched the disturbed stirring in Airn's heart. He hadn't been prepared to have his other concern confirmed so quickly.

"Regent Suiran will order the landed and court lords of the western quarter of Suiran to begin to prepare men to be part of the companies that will enter Altherly, and the remainder of the lords to begin to prepare their men to defend Suiran if Gael should overtake Altherly and arrive at Ryokudo's border." There were some open protests. Rei indicated to Andrew that he should let the ministers give their concerns. Airn wasn't surprised that the ministers would rather have it the other way 'round, so that there would be more men on the border itself.

There was quite a lot of push from the ministers for the Tarc to be used as well, Airn assumed to protect more of the people of Ryokudo. When that topic got pushed hard enough, Ore moved to stand forward and answer. Airn leaned over to the paige and asked him why and learned that Ore and Ilena were Interim Grand Duke and Grand Duchess of Tarc, they and Rei having overcome that nation while Airn had been playing in Kouzanshi.

He stood in rather a lot of shock at that news while he listened to Ore explain that the Tarc had even smaller numbers per lord than the lords of Suiran, particularly since they'd gone in and won that nation. He might be able to bring as many to the battle as any single earl would, but not much more. Certainly if they had more years to allow the young to grow into swords they might have more. The ministers were disgruntled, but it seemed they couldn't argue it any further.

Rei proposed an alternative course of sending a portion of the men from the Suiran internal holdings to Altherly, leaving sufficient at the western border to defend there, and then a sufficient number from the eastern portion of the Region would be called up and trained so they could be used to help defend Ryokudo as necessary. That option was received more favorably and the ministers happily argued the border lines of which lords would have to pay the earliest price.

Erlic chuckled to himself at that point. Airn raised an eyebrow at his teacher of all things courtly. Erlic leaned over and whispered to Airn, "The Regent understands courts well. The first offer was the opening for the court to complain. This offer was the one he wanted accepted. He knows how to let the court entertain itself while giving him what he wants. Do watch him well." Airn gave a nod that he'd heard and could see how it had been done.

When that topic had been addressed sufficiently, Airn was slightly surprised when the next topic was about a census of Suiran. The ministers between him and throne frowned in some concern. One of the ministers asked, "If we spend the money now to pay for a census, then have men die in Altherly, won't we have wasted our time and money? Shouldn't we wait until the warring is over, then gain a rational and real count?"

Andrew stayed quiet. Rei considered the question, then answered, "You're not wrong; however, the imbalance of funding has become quite a problem for the Region. Can you continue to maintain the current balances in your Ministries, waiting on any further possible funding of essential projects until after the King has declared our borders sufficiently safe again? Are you willing to consider which of your own projects could be shifted to less funding until we can call for the census again?"

As the ministers considered his questions, Erlic nodded sagely. "Yes, he does understand his court very well. Likely he saw these issues early on when he was placed in that seat. He'd still be doing the census, most likely, just so these would stop whining about not getting enough funding for their favorite useless projects. We'll see if they can give him a satisfactory and useful answer. That will let us know if they're worth anything at all." Airn gave him a slightly scolding look. The excessive pride of Altherly wouldn't hide from these royals that Roland had the same problems in their own courts, should Touka come and visit during peace times there.

Airn was impressed that Rei didn't let the ministers stray too far off the topic of his questions to them. Rei rerouted them from the beginnings of accusations. He pointed out needs on both sides of the issue when ministers strayed to favorite off–topic whines. And, in the end, when the ministers were finally made uncomfortable enough with the topic without coming to any sort of full resolution, Rei called for the issue to be tabled so that everyone could consider it outside of the meeting.

The meeting was opened up to issues the ministers wanted to bring before the Regent. Airn and his men weren't surprised when most funding issues were blocked early by subtle reminders of the first two issues. "Those are the reoccurring ones that they've been asking for funding for too long already, aren't they?" Airn whisper–asked Erlic.

"Most likely," Erlic answered dryly back.

The paige with them nodded his agreement. However, when the Regent got a sterner look on his face after one minister spoke up about desperately needing further staffing, the paige whispered to them, "That Minister and the next two who'll likely speak, the Regent's been punishing on purpose because they've been completely against any of his policies and refuse to listen to his direction."

At that, Airn paid close attention to how Rei spoke and responded to those ministers. Airn was a bit surprised that in the exchange with that minister, Rei negotiated a slightly softer stance with the minister when the minster seemed to give some slight concessions. The next minister wasn't quite so willing yet to work with the Regent and Rei remained impassive and unrelenting. The third minister Rei worked very hard with to get him to admit he might be willing to meet Rei in even some slight way. Still, Rei had to be disappointed in the end, only getting icy responses at all.

Airn was a bit surprised when Erlic turned to the paige and asked, "Will the Regent remove them eventually if they won't work with him?"

The paige considered it, then said, "You might want to ask him that yourself, but based on how he's been moving since arriving, I wouldn't be surprised if he did. He's just put in one of those to replace a corrupt Minister that was removed, about a half–year ago now. It's been hard for him that someone completely competent has been a larger thorn in his side than he'd hoped. Some of us have wondered why the Minister hasn't been more grateful to be given the position and trust. It wouldn't be that hard to work with Regent Rei. He's very reasonable for a Touka," the last was said rather dryly.

Ilena went last of the ministers. She'd barely opened her mouth to give an accounting for her ministry, as the other ministers had before moving into their specific issues they wanted to bring before the Regent, when she was being attacked, surprising Airn at first. "And you've said nothing about Gael moving on Altherly this whole time? Do you have no intelligence on that nation? Only on our own to interfere in the doings of we who are trying to get the work of the Region done?" Airn blinked. It had been words from the icy minister.

Ilena held her ground and answered calmly, "And who am I to speak out before the King has allowed me to speak? He told me directly that until he'd finalized what his decision was going to be regarding the request from King Roland I was to let no one but Regent Rei know what I was learning from Altherly and Gael. Until Regent Rei was allowed to open his mouth today, wasn't my mouth also sealed?" She stared the minister down. He didn't back down at all, but he did let that answer to his accusation.

"*Ah,*" Erlic sighed in understanding. "They can't accept he's put *her* into a high position. ...And that the King supports it." Airn worked that out, then agreed that the king would've had to if she was already Interim Grand Duchess of Tarc. That would be a position assigned by the King, not the Regent.

Ilena was allowed to continue her report to the Court of Ministers and Regent after that, but a few times one or the other of the two who hadn't relented this day added other barbs and pointed questions. Ilena calmly responded to all of them, or ignored them if they had no purpose. The paige taught them, "The first Minister would have joined in with them until today. He's reached his breaking point this last week and won't fight the Regent on that point any longer. He needs to be released to getting the job of his Ministry done, not be part of the petty fighting. That will be relieving for all of his staff, that he's finally opened his eyes to that part. Regent Rei allowed as how he understood that it didn't change the Minister's perspective nor his disapproval, but he was grateful the battle wouldn't be fought in this room any longer."

Ah, that's what that was, Airn thought, now understanding the messages under the words and slight concessions that had been spoken earlier.

When Ilena's report was completed, Andrew moved the meeting to the next portion of it: a request for a report on the renovation of Nijoushi. Airn watched with slightly widened eyes as Ilena walked to the front of the room. She stood facing the court from just before the throne dais. "According to the approval of the Regent and this body, deconstruction of the old decrepit buildings has begun. The day following the last meeting of this body, the bid and proposal for updating the south wall was received." She looked down to reference some papers she was holding. "The bid was for one third the cost that was expected." That got a lot of interest from the room.

"There has been a new product discovered that can be used to build the wall with, or to reinforce it. It's a 'liquid stone' that hardens as it dries until it's as strong as stone, but not quite as hard as granite. Because it can be made on–site, the costs to cut and transport stone are removed from the bid, making up the majority of the cost decrease. Slightly less persons are needed for the setting of the material. What stone is used must be ground into a fine powder before being added to the liquid slurry. At the scale of the height of the wall, they will also need to add in steel reinforcement. Thus materials cost is higher generally.

"It's expected to take the same amount of time to build or repair the wall as if cut stone was used; however, there's some hope that it can be reduced as some of that time is early experimental time. Nothing that tall has been built with this material yet." She looked back up at the court from reading from the notes in her hand. "Having gone to inspect this new 'liquid stone' myself with other masters of the craft, I'm quite impressed. Once the early experimental phase for height is completed, it's my belief that they can have the wall completed rather quickly.

"They've sent one question that needs answering before the final acceptance is sent to them. They've said that they can potentially pour the liquid stone around the existing wall, reinforcing it with the liquid entering the weak places and strengthening them. This would complete the work even more quickly and cost less than building a whole new wall. However, that leaves all of the businesses outside the wall still outside the wall and at risk. Given that we now understand that there's even some slight risk of war reaching Nijou and Nijoushi, that might have some bearing on the decision: lesser protections, or speed of completion."

Immediately there was a question. "How much does reinforcing the existing wall cost in comparison to rebuilding?" The guests in the room were surprised it was from the less icy Minister that had made concessions with Rei. He definitely had less fight in the question than the other two had had.

"He's the Minister of Finance, Minister Hulmer," the paige whispered to them.

That's complex, was all Airn could think of to that point.

The numbers were given, then the summary of them, "That's one–fifth the costs in materials, but a similar number of workers, and one–fourth of the time."

One of the more calm ministers in the room stepped forward frowning. The paige named him Minister Rotius, the Minister of Interior. "Those businesses are rather critical to the funding of the city and the Region as a whole. It's good that we've had prosperity long enough to expand outside the wall, particularly with good trades. It wouldn't be good to not protect those assets. If they have to rebuild their businesses and restock their materials, that could be a long wait for the city to be renewed again, with even the renovation having to wait."

"And if the new wall is destroyed even in some slight way, it would be better to wait to rebuild at all. With the sad state of the current wall, reinforcing it now would be better. Then potentially building the new one after any warring is over might be more prudent," another minister pointed out.

"Then that's a total of more than one would hope to spend at all, particularly if war never reaches this far east," Hulmer countered back dryly.

The arguments for the two options, and a few for doing nothing just yet, bounced back and forth. Airn was a little surprised when Rei called for a vote and a sufficient majority voted for the current wall to be reinforced. "It's less expensive, will still protect the city, and the outer wall may never have to be built, saving that cost," Erlic summarized for Airn. "It's possible he didn't postpone this one because he wants a faster resolution and only cares that enough of the court wants one as well. He likely heard enough to make his own decision as well. The earlier one, he didn't hear enough to make a decision and none of the ministers were willing to consider the answer he does want to have them make. Choosing when to have a vote or not is as much a part of the dance as what people are willing to do or not."

The following argument was how that project would be funded. That the ministers were a little more cautious on, but Airn learned yet again from that how a royal should come to the table with answers already in hand to offer. Rei offered several ideas, as did Ilena, some of them similar but stated at different times in the argument. "Minister Ilena is acting as his ally," Airn learned from Erlic. "They discussed this before coming so she could know what points to bring back to the table for him, so it's not always only coming from him. It's extremely difficult to fight alone when none of the others are willing to consider what the royal considers reasonable. While they don't like hearing it from her either, it's at least a different voice."

"So..., having an ally in the court can be rather critical," Airn said. He could understand how tiring it would be to fight alone all the time. He often felt like that when arguing with his father and brother, when they both turned the same arguments on him. He sighed, not surprised that was one of the relationships between those two. However, that was royal allied with royal, like here. Likely it would be far better to have an ally among the lords or ministers if possible. Their words were considered differently. He wondered if it was possible Rei didn't have one yet because he was still too newly come to the Regency. He asked and received some level of confirmation of that reasoning.

When that argument was resolved, Ilena turned to Rei and gave a summary and stated that a contract to that effect would be written up and passed around for the proper signatures. She was excused and Andrew called for Mizi to make her presentation to the court. "Mmm," Erlic mused as Mizi walked up to the front to where Ilena had stood. "She also doesn't get a good reception here." Airn hadn't felt it, so he looked around again. It was true that the court hadn't particularly *relaxed* to have Mizi called forward. He wasn't sure it was any worse than before, though.

Mizi took a breath and spoke to the court nearly as directly as Ilena had, as an equal rather than as a humble weak woman would. Airn supposed he wasn't very surprised given his first interaction with the four; however, it would be as unusual in his home court so he perhaps would've been if she'd appeared there first. As

Mizi introduced the idea of a hospital for wounded and ill persons to the Court of Ministers there was perhaps a slight relaxing of the members thereof. When that became more obvious, Airn looked a question at the paige.

The paige moved forward to ask one of the lesser staff members standing at the rear of the room, then returned to Airn's side. "Before, she sat in the throne as the Regent's representative. They ignored her then. When she'd interrupt them and scold them for not properly considering the Regent's views and needs, they fought. This is different. Plus she's a trained medic, so this is something she has knowledge on."

Erlic looked around the room, reevaluating the ministers again. "I think they'd find this a more suitable use for this Princess, then?"

The paige blinked at them blandly. "Likely," he agreed.

And get her out of their hair, Airn thought slightly bitterly. It was how he felt when his father and brother gave him things to do that took him away from their home: like he was annoying and a waste of their time and attention.

He wasn't too surprised when the final resolution to the request was that the minsters approved of the idea, but wanted more research, definitive names and places, and time to come up with possible funding options they were willing to "gift" the First Princess. Likely it was to punish her for her earlier "hubris" they were still annoyed with. Airn sighed, but was rather impressed with Mizi regardless. She'd used a lot of courage to talk to them when they'd started on adversarial ground and had received as positive an answer as she could have. She'd also been very rational and firmly grounded in facts and useful information. She hadn't faced the ministers with vague ideas and fluffy thoughts.

When the court was adjourned, Airn turned and walked out first with his men and the paige. "That was very educational," he teased Erlic. "I learned that I'm not the only royal that's unwanted." Erlic clucked his tongue at Airn with irritation but Airn ignored him. He turned to the paige. "What's next?"

"The library," the paige said neurally, not getting into that fight.

"Why?" Airn asked.

"Because all young men being educated at the castle start there," the paige answered. He spoke directly to Erlic. "You'll continue his education from where you left off, using our library to do it, until the royals of Suiran can fit visiting with him into their schedules. They'll all give him assignments to add to the list you've already got. They'll be able to find him if he's there or in the garrison, if he wants to have them talk to him. It will likely be in between other required activities, so somewhat random as they walk from one place to the other, at least for now as they try to get caught up from the Interim Investiture."

"When did that take place?" Airn asked.

"At the beginning of last month," the paige answered.

Airn blinked. "And how long did it take them to overcome Tarc?"

"One week."

Airn froze and stared at the page. "You're lying."

"Nope," the paige answered back, almost daring Airn.

Airn turned to Erlic. "I think we'll study a little bit about who the Tarc are first." He wanted to know just how easy a job that had been, to have only taken one week. The paige took them to that part of the library and left them there, pointing to one of the history books to read first. Airn pulled it out and skimmed the beginning. By the third chapter he was walking for the first chair he could find. Half–way through it and he had to flip back to the beginning again to look at the early dates and compare them to the dates in the middle. He flipped to the back of the book, skimmed that chapter, hunting for dates.

When he was done, he looked at Ian. "Go find the most recent book you can on the relations between Suiran and Tarc." He held the book in his hands, staring at it. "That is one of the harshest people this nation had to face in its history. How could they have won in only one week?" He was still not believing it at all. "I need to hear that story. Did Tarc become so weak since then?" He eagerly snatched up the book Ian brought to him, but even it didn't tell him very much. "There's nothing after this?" he asked. Ian shook his head. Airn sat and mused while Erlic finished skimming the first book, then flipped through pages in the second one.

When Erlic was finished, he handed the two books to Ian. "History of Ryokudo is next. General summary, please." Airn was nodding. He'd need to know that, too, to understand the current generation and why they'd been able to best their worst enemies. He missed Erlic's secret smile. It wasn't a fight to get him to study when he was suddenly keenly interested in the current realities and in getting his personal curiosity satisfied.

"Mistress Mizi, you asked me to remind you today that Prince Airn is in the castle and you need to visit with him," Tanner said quietly in their meeting the morning after the Court of Ministers.

Rei raised an eyebrow as Mizi sighed. "Thank you, Tanner, for the reminder."

"And Lady Brianna has requested some of your time." Mizi sat quietly as Tanner went on to tell her the rest of the things on her list she'd set aside for too long already. Included in it was Ryan's concern about the intern testing preparations she'd been ignoring out of self–preservation.

Rei held up his hand to stall Andrew from telling them about Rei's day. "You haven't been able to divide your focus between tasks," he scolded her gently. "Either delegate, refuse, or learn to divide your attention. That was Ilena's first lesson to me. As royals we can only focus on what we should focus on. What are you doing with those tasks already that fits the requirements I've just given you?"

Mizi drew in a deep breath. That was very direct for Rei, but she'd earned it those five days ago. He'd been more direct in his teaching since that morning they'd let her sleep in instead of go to the list. "I've had the paiges settle Airn into the castle and instructed his aides to continue his education where they'd left off until we can go see him. I'll stop by to welcome him properly, but I don't plan on spending any more time on that than I have to for now.

"I'd like for you to come up with something to give him to do that you think is important for him to learn about. Stop by the library when you've thought of it to welcome him yourself. Once he has his assignments from you, me, Ilena, and Ore if he wants to give one, that should be enough to keep him busy for some time. We can visit him when we have time, or if he sends a paige to ask for us to come. If you want a more formal introduction of him to the court, I need to know."

Rei thought about that, then indicated that he'd follow through on his part, said he'd think about if he wanted a formal introduction, and allowed that was a sufficient level of interaction and commitment of time from Mizi.

Mizi considered the other tasks. "I can probably fit talking to Brianna into my schedule sometime in the near future, but I'd like to talk to Ryan first to see just what he needs from me next. Delia's been filling in here and there for me she said when I talked to her before. I'll apologize and listen to what his list is, then consider it with a more rational understanding of my capabilities to let him know what I really can give to the intern testing and teaching."

Rei held up his hand. "You need to know what my schedule for you is going to be as well before you commit to any further time for him. I'm sorry that's been in flux, so you haven't known it. I'll bring that to you this evening. Listen to what he says, but don't promise him anything today."

"Okay," she answered humbly.

"Specifically, I'm thinking I'll allow you to go to Kouzanshi ...in five days. You'll be gone long enough in this weather you shouldn't commit to much of anything that's long–term."

"*Oh*," Mizi sighed. She bowed to him while seated. "Thank you very much." She swallowed at the unexpected emotions that came over her. She was grateful he was going to allow her to accomplish the next important task to the hospital moving forward. It would also help Ryan, though, so it was good to know she could say it when she talked to him. It would be hard because Rei would worry the whole time she was gone.

Knowing that addition to her schedule helped her tell Rei about the remaining things on her schedule, most of which could be delegated or could be removed from her list for now. Once she'd done that, she could turn to Tanner. "We'll go talk to Ryan today. I need to know his list as early as possible, and let him know about the trip to Kouzanshi. He and I'll need time to come up with what I need to say to the researchers."

She worried her fingers in her skirt, then said, "I think I need to know that and Rei's schedule for me before I can commit to a time for Brianna, but I'd like for it to be before I go. It wouldn't be kind to make her wait until I get back. Plus I want to send her on vacation during that time, so we can talk about when she'd like to go then." Tanner nodded as he added those two things to her schedule for the day.

After a bit more thinking, Mizi said, "I'm not ready to face Airn just yet. I still don't know what I'd have him do and I'd like to say both that and my greeting to him in the same meeting. I should make my request in his behalf to Ilena today when we meet this morning." She turned to Rei, "I told her three days ago that we'd meet on the off schedule like she suggested, so this morning is her and my meeting time, next. I'll go to the medical department after that. If there's time today, I'll work on what I might suggest to Airn. If not, I'll do that tomorrow, but I'll for sure meet with him before I go." Rei gave an accepting nod.

Mizi indicated she was done. Rei looked to Andrew. Rei's schedule was the usual Rose office work with one meeting during the day. Then Andrew raised an eyebrow at him. "And I suppose that finalizing the year's schedule is now on today's list?"

"Yes," Rei answered. Andrew made a note in the folder in his hands, then closed it.

Rei rose to his feet, pulling Mizi up by the hand. He kissed her and said, "Thank you, Mizi. Please keep trying. Taking care of you is important, too."

"Yes, Rei," she answered quietly. She already knew that he was like that. She'd just forgotten it in the stress of the end of last year and the beginning of this one. She drew in a deep breath and let it out slowly and quietly as the cloaks were brought to them so they could go out and do those things important to this day. She was grateful he reached out and took her hand in his and held it tightly as they left the royal suite. She pressed his hand back. While she knew he was teaching her more directly because he cared, it was hard to not feel like it was somewhat severe scolding. Having the warm connection of his hand helped her not feel that quite so much.

When they reached the door to the outer lobby area of the building, Rei gave her a kiss as Andrew opened it. The rest of their household was waiting below the upper landing for them to come and tell them what the day held. When they reached the main floor, Mizi motioned to Tanner. While he might not end up her Voice, having him let them all know what she wanted helped her so much, she'd learned from that one day. She let his quiet voice soothe her. She wasn't surprised he'd learned who to have go with them as guards by now. Sam and Leon would be quiet supports. She might take Kirk the next day, but it would depend on what Ryan said today.

When Tanner was done passing out the assignments, Mizi stepped forward slightly and addressed Brianna specifically. "Lady Brianna, Tanner has passed on your request. Please give me a day or two to understand what the schedule needs to be next, but I'll call for you as soon as I can." Brianna gave her a curtsy of acceptance. Mizi turned to Rei and gave him a small smile. "I hope I recover soon," she said quietly. "Maybe today will be restful enough, to just sit with Ryan."

Rei put his hand on top of her head gently. "I'll hope so, too." His expression and tone were kind. She was so glad she was his wife, to be able to be so close to his support every day now.

-o-o-o-

Minister Eadsley, Minister of Public Works, looked up at the quiet clearing of a throat in his office. He blinked at the man standing in the door. "And you are?" he asked, not sure he needed yet another interruption. His office was finally settling into a level of mild chaos from the grand chaos caused by having his most useful assistant taken from him.

"Vicount Mortenson, to serve in your Ministry, by request of the Regent." Eadsley sat upright in some shock and looked at Mortenson a little closer. He wasn't very reassured, actually. The man looked like he'd spent most of his life living in the luxury of his title, likely passed down from father to son for many generations. If the Prince still wanted to punish Eadsley he looked like the sort of "help" that would do just that. The only juxtaposition was his voice that sounded like he'd had a throat injury in the past.

Eadsley sighed, but said, "Well, I suppose any helping hands at this point are useful." He called out the door for his most pressed division head and waited for him to arrive. Mortenson stepped just inside the door to be out of the way of said arrival. "Please train him to do whatever he's capable of helping you with," Eadsley waved a hand at Mortenson, then returned to his work. That was all the time he could spare and cared to as well.

"Please come with me," his division head said quietly and the two men were gone from his office. Eadsley allowed a small scowl out, but let it go for now. Mortenson would let them know within the week if he was useful or not and by a week later Eadsley could legitimately let him go if he wasn't.

When his division head stopped by briefly to report that two weeks later, Eadsley was rather surprised to learn that Mortenson was not only capable of at least helping reasonably, but that the head was pleased with how organized he was. Eadsley relaxed just a little bit, but wondered what concession Rei wanted from him.

-o-o-o-

"Hello, Ryan," Mizi said cheerfully as she entered the front staff research room of the Department of Medicine. Ryan looked up from the tall work table with a smile on his face. "The meeting was as fearful as I'd thought it would be, but I managed to survive."

Ryan chuckled with her. "It does look like you might have taken a little damage," he sympathized. He handed her a tea cup that had been sitting on the table near him. "I thought I'd have this for you, just in case, anyway."

"Thank you, Ryan," she said, humbly grateful. She sat down in the tall chair across the table from him and sipped at it. "I think I've forgotten it this whole time, when that's the use of it from the beginning." She sighed, enjoying the flavors of the tea the two of them had created together to help Ilena and thus just about any woman who needed to relax and rest. "Tanner, remind me of the tea."

Tanner bowed. "I'll just make it for you, or have Maria make a pot of it for the mornings you work in the suite office."

"Yes, please," Mizi said, relieved to have one more small action that would help her. Wryly she said to Ryan, "I over did. Rei's watching my schedule more carefully to make sure I don't do that again and that I learn a better pacing. I had almost all of my household scold me in the week before the presentation, but I couldn't relax until that was done." She slumped onto her elbow and rested her chin in her hand. "So I get to relax here with you today." She smiled as Ryan's face lit up.

"That said," she put her arm back down and went a little more serious, "I need to hear from you where you are and what the schedule is. We can discuss what you think I need to participate in, then I'll take that back to Rei." She smiled at his slightly worried look. "But, he let me know this morning that he'll let me go to Kouzanshi in five days. That may interrupt what you need me to do, but maybe it will be alright?" she asked him.

Ryan had frozen at that news. It took him a while to blink back to awareness. "I think that would be good, but let's talk about the schedule and see. I'd like your help with some things that we might be able to fit in after you get back, but it would be a postponement from what I'd originally thought of."

Mizi nodded. "Generally for the next five days I'll be here every other day at this time and the other day I'll be here an hour earlier. Ilena and I changed our schedule to give us a better flow each day." She smiled. "Today was a day for Ore to be at the Intelligence office, so he came down kindly to greet me. He even stayed for some of the meeting to make sure I was doing okay. I think I worried everyone."

Ryan looked at her with his sober expression, then said, "Even me."

Mizi sighed. "I'm sorry," she said. "It's very hard to see that I could go a little slower when it takes so much effort to begin and I know we're going to be gone from the castle so much this year. Rei will have that calendar finalized by tonight. That will help all of us, I think." Ryan agreed with several silent sober nods.

"Do you think we can get the initial list of possible testing questions written before you leave for Kouzanshi?" Ryan asked. "I was thinking that if they left Kouzanshi shortly after you did, we'd need to be prepared with them rather early."

Mizi considered that, then answered slowly, "It might help to get me into the thinking of what I want to say in Kouzanshi, but...," she frowned. "Maybe. How far have you already gotten?"

Ryan reached for a set of pages near him on the table. "I've got the outline of what topics we should cover and a beginning to the questions."

"Oh, that might not be too bad, then. You can finish if we can't get to all of them?" she asked, unsure.

Ryan sifted through the pages and pulled out a smaller stack. "These are the topics I was hoping you could work on." He handed them over.

Mizi took them and was soon lost in reviewing the notes. It was nice to read Ryan's neat handwriting for once instead of her own. She remembered to sip at the tea, and ask Tanner for writing tools before she got too lost into the work of the day. It was nice to be back for a bit in the environment she was most comfortable in.

Tanner interrupted them at lunch time, then reminded them they needed to have their calendar planned before that evening. They switched to that task until it was completed. "Thank you, Tanner," Mizi said quietly as she handed him the calendar summary for them to reference that evening. She turned back to the table and her testing questions. "Please continue to interrupt me with alternate necessary activities until I learn to do it myself."

He bowed to her and put the page into a folder and that into his jacket. Then he quietly left them alone again to their work. She was grateful that she didn't have to do any of the other things today. Tomorrow would be soon enough to think of the rest of the activities on her list. Or tonight even.

-o-o-o-

"Mistress Ilena, Master Ore, please come into the city to have dinner with us tonight," Petroi invited them.

"Oh? For a specific reason?" Ore asked.

"For me to relax," Petroi answered.

Ore's eyebrows went up in surprise. "It won't feel like more work?" he asked.

Petroi shook his head. "Not if it is just the four of us. But the two of you can call it an almost–date if you wish," he teased a little.

Ore's smile twinkled in his eyes as well as graced his face. "That's fine with me," Ilena answered from the floor below since Petroi had asked it while they were in the Upper office. Ore agreed as well.

"You'll allow them to go without the full guards?" Henry asked in surprise from below.

It was true that Petroi was the one who required the full six most of the time. "We will be on the north end," he explained. He could just make out Henry grumbling under his breath. It wasn't part of Ilena's nightwalker territory so wasn't the safest area for them to be in without full guards, but it was second best because it was part of her Family territory.

"Then put the Family in the area on alert," Marcus suggested, also from below. "That way they'll be watching the streets for you at least, and know to be on call if things don't go the way you want them to."

Since that was wisdom, Petroi sent that notification out immediately. That calmed the Twins down. "Sleep early tonight," he told them. "You two also are needing rest." He got back silence so they at least acknowledged he wasn't wrong.

Petroi called Justinian upstairs to Petroi and Thayne's bedroom an hour before he wanted to be leaving the castle for dinner. "Tonight, please make my hair presentable." He abruptly handed the suddenly in shock Justinian his brush. He was already somewhat pleased Justinian had been able to knock on his door rather soon after being called. The practices at the household weekly vacation times together did seem to be helping the three most skittish.

He could see Justinian begin to tremble. Petroi judged that and decided it was suppressed excitement, not fear. "A–are you sure?" Justinian asked, but his eyes were already taking in the clothing Petroi had chosen for that evening. It was similar to what he'd worn into town with just Thayne when they'd gone to the north end before, but slightly more formal in tone, with the shirt more simple and understated.

"Yes. I have always represented the Princess to the businesses in the north of Nijoushi. Now that I am here, I can properly do so. It would be good to have them begin to see that even I am in my proper place now." Justinian agreed almost more because he wanted to brush Petroi's hair, which had been the first interaction Justinian had ever initiated with Petroi. Petroi reined him in with a stern look. "You only have a half an hour to complete it, and it must be refined, not fancy."

Justinian gave several nods of promise to keep the look matching the clothing and Petroi's goals, but it looked by the trembling of even his hands now it might be very difficult for him to have that much restraint. Petroi led Justinian into the bedroom, going to the desk and pulling out the chair. He turned it so that when he sat in the chair he could watch what Justinian did in the mirror, so he could help with that restraint. It was good that for having such a marvelous distraction Justinian didn't even pay any attention to the fact that they were the only people in the room. Petroi was quite sure Justinian would have been too nervous to do anything at all if he'd let Justinian have the time to think before announcing the request. Petroi was hoping this test would mean he could have this final piece to his city ensemble regularly.

Justinian drew in a great breath to calm himself down enough, then there was a pause. Petroi looked into his eyes by way of the mirror. "Um...." Justinian blinked at him. "While I have been thinking of what to do since Mistress Ilena said we'd need to be able to make all of you presentable at Ichijou, I've not learned anything in the castle for long hair except for the ladies. I'm quite sure you don't want that." Petroi glared at him and he swallowed. "Can I have a few extra minutes to try some of the basic things I need to test? Just because I can see something in my head doesn't mean your hair will let me do it."

That Petroi could allow for. He'd rather thought he'd have to. Men of Ryokudo didn't have their hair this long. He kept it this way because it had been his way to make his statement of who he served when he couldn't say it any other way. He'd not been able to grow it to the nearly–floor–length Ilena's was currently, but having it grown to the small of his back was to have it at the length Ilena's had been when he'd had to cut it to disguise her at the time of the coup in Selicia, and was sufficient.

He stiffened when Justinian went to the desk and picked up scissors. The murderous look he was sure was on his face made Justinian freeze in the way Petroi had expected him to on first arrival. Justinian shook his head rapidly. "Just to trim the ends. In order for any proper look to hold, the ends can't be ragged. I promise: only what little is necessary."

Petroi held the murderous intent to remind him of that promise until Justinian put down the scissors again on the desk. He trusted Justinian with scissors and his hair much less than with the brush, for all Justinian had cried to cut the little bits out from underneath to hold Ore's markers and be his braids in Tarc. Petroi turned his head to confirm Justinian's work while he was at the desk. It was shorter than he would have liked, but he had to admit having it be no longer ragged was nice.

Because he'd moved Justinian brushed it out again, then with great focus he was lost to the hairdressing for a while. Petroi watched his face. He could tell when Justinian was unhappy that a certain thing he tried didn't stay in, likely for the weight of the hairs. He could also tell when Justinian was pleased when specific things did work. After about ten minutes of that experimentation, Justinian took another deep breath and gave a nod of his head to himself. "Rio will you please bring me a handful of hair pins and the small hairclip from the desk in my room?"

he asked just loudly enough to be heard by Rio in the office down below. Rio had the third best ears after Ilena and Petroi himself.

Justinian's eyes rose to look into Petroi's in the mirror. "I picked up the hairclip the last time I was in town from the haberdasher's that's carrying such things now from Ichijou. Because I was quite sure you didn't want very curly and wasn't sure curls would stay in besides after watching Rio work hard on Mistress Ilena's hair, the best way to get any kind of look other than straight down or ponytail is to have it ornamented slightly. Will that be okay?"

Petroi blinked and thought about that. "We will see," he decided. He wasn't completely opposed, but he still was going to keep Justinian restrained today.

He wasn't surprised when Rio handed the items over to Thayne at the entrance door to the Upper office rather than come into the bedroom off said office herself, nor was he surprised when Thayne stayed to watch. Petroi narrowed his eyes at Thayne through the mirror. "Go get dressed now if you are going to shirk on the end of your work to be entertained instead." Thayne meekly did as ordered. He knew when Petroi was peeved enough that the requirement was that and not a suggestion.

Knowing very well what the lords and young lords of the castle liked for hairstyles, which was still curled for all it wasn't like the ladies, Petroi wasn't surprised that the hairpins were for keeping pseudocurls in his hair. Justinian put up half the hair, on one side, then stepped back to survey how the effect was. With a frown, he shook his head and pulled all the hairpins out, very gently. He focused on the hair and the pictures in his mind, then gently brushed all of the front hairs out of Petroi's face to the back of his head and gathered up the small handful into one hand. With a few twists to hold them into a miniature ponytail, he picked up the hairclip.

Once the hairclip was in where Justinian wanted it, to hold the first set of hairs in place, then he tried again with the curling and hair pins. He had to still try the curling two more times before he found a way to combine the two in a way that pleased him. He looked up into Petroi's eyes in the mirror. "That's harder, to have to experiment, instead of just put something in I already know, but I think that might be sufficient for today?" he asked.

Petroi inspected what he could see of the handiwork. "I think it might be. Will my hat and scarf undo it all?"

Justinian's expression went to a bit of dismay, then to some resignation. "Well, this is why the ladies wear the larger cloak hoods rather than the snug winter hats," he said. "Loose keeps in some warmth but doesn't destroy the hairdo. You wouldn't have to have the hood so loose as they wear them, but the walk into the city won't be pleasant if you do as the young lords and refuse a hat at all."

He looked off into his mind again. "I think as the hats from the haberdasher are becoming more popular, the curly look will begin to transition to more straight looks, or at least calmer curls." He frowned at the work he'd done. "I'm not sure how they're combining hairclips and hats, though. If you put a more formal hat on, the hairclip wouldn't even show."

Petroi couldn't know, nor Justinian until they arrived in Ichijou. "Maybe you and the other staff could be sent ahead by a few days, so you would have time for training there before we arrive."

"Not a bad idea," Thayne agreed. So did Ilena from below. She was directly below them now, also getting dressed by Rio for their night out.

"I'll help you get dressed for the weather," Justinian promised Petroi. "That way you can be in town and have it be nice. Messing it up on the way back won't matter so much. You can leave the pins and clip on your desk for later or call me and I'll come help take them out." That last made him nervous so Petroi held out his hand for his brush to distract him, since Justinian would otherwise forget he was holding it and take it with him. Thayne got up from sitting on the side of his bed to watch and got them all moving to the door, which also helped Justinian leave the room before he could think of his worries any more than that.

They picked up their winter weather gear on the way out of the upper suite door. They wouldn't put them on until they were in the common room of the main floor suite and Ore and Ilena were ready to go. To keep Justinian company, the two older young men walked down the stairs with him inside this time. "Thank you, Justinian," Petroi said on the way.

Justinian glanced at him, then flushed as he looked away again. "You're welcome," came the soft response. "You'd look good in a hat," he added.

Petroi narrowed his eyes at Justinian and shook his head. Ore had purchased a hat and they looked too much alike to the eyes of the Ryokudan. He didn't need to be mistaken for his master when the man was far too jealous already. If that confusion ever came up in Ichijou, it would be either his firing or his head on a pike. He wasn't interested in either happening ever. That was why he still kept his hair long. Ore wasn't ever likely to grow his out. He didn't have that kind of patience.

"I do miss the Tarc braids, though," Petroi said a bit wistfully as they entered the Lower office common room.

"You what?" Thayne asked in surprise.

Petroi nodded. "They keep the worst of the hairs out of my face while letting me not have a headache from the ponytail."

Justinian was nodding in agreement. "That's why I thought of that way of doing it for you tonight. To have the same effect. ...Not to have the braids, though." He was going to drool if his mind went any further in that direction so Petroi handed him his winter gear to juggle as his distraction. Still, Justinian's mind wandered that path a bit. "I should get out the braid board and make sure I still remember how to do them, though. I don't want to forget...." He was lost in his mind, his mouth closing to words. Petroi left him alone.

Thayne gave Petroi a smile and whispered, "Going to regret that for a few days, aren't you?"

Petroi shrugged. "Maybe, but he will be down here and I won't be." Thane had to give him that.

Petroi then had to endure Ore's jealous inspection. Petroi focused on Ilena's pleased reaction instead, staying calm for the both of them. "Justinian got me a hairclip as well," Ore said. Petroi rather froze inside at that. "I don't have any idea how that would work in my hair, though. It works well enough on yours."

Justinian woke back up. "That's why I've been wondering how to put the two together. Maybe they don't." He was still mostly not present. Petroi decided that if they didn't mix hairclips and hats, then on days Justinian put the hairclip into Ore's hair, he'd wear the simple ponytail those days.

-o-o-o-

Rei sighed and rose from his chair to pace from his desk to the fireplace where he could warm up and pace back before he got too hot. He paced that path only enough to warm up, not wanting to distract everyone else too much on that side of the room. Then he paced the path across the front of his desk, between it and Andrew and Mina's desks. That was his cue to them they needed to get ready to hear the words he needed to say to work out the final thoughts in his head. He'd been thinking through his plans and what he was willing to sacrifice.

When they put their pens down and looked up at him, he stopped pacing and leaned back on his desk. With a little frown wrinkle on his forehead, Rei said, "While I really don't like the thought of sending Mizi out on such a long trip while we're still in the winter blizzard weather, I think she needs to continue to move forward on her goal while the ministers are still amenable to it. I know Ryan's already postponed the intern training and testing longer than he should have for her sake so she could focus on reaching the level she needed to be at to become my princess. He shouldn't go unrewarded for his patience."

Rei paused, his frown still on. He looked around the room a bit aimlessly, absently noting again that Ore and his guards weren't in the room. Rei had asked Ore to stay in his office in the Ministry today to confirm Ilena was still handling the winter claustrophobia well. Rei needed to know if it would be safe enough to send Ore with Mizi like he was thinking of doing. "While Ilena's been having her good days, I think it's been good to have Ore in here on a regular basis to prevent them from fighting. Some mornings at the security meeting they're already at each other, barely past breakfast. He even severely scolded Mizi the other night for a slip of her tongue."

Andrew and Mina both raised eyebrows at him. After considering that for a moment, Andrew asked in some surprise, "She called his loyalty into question?"

Rei nodded unhappily. "Inadvertently, but yes. I smoothed it over as best I could and corrected her once we were back in the suite. ...I think it would be good to send Ore with her to Kouzanshi to let them have the time to both settle back into the relaxed state they should be with each other. That's best done while doing something that's a familiar pattern.

"When I broached the possibility with Ilena before, she said she should keep Petroi and Thayne here with her. After that night, I'm in agreement with her. So, I'll send Marcus and Henry with Ore if I send him with Mizi."

He looked out the tall windows, the golden curtains framing them only pulled enough to let in light and the least cold possible. They'd be closing them soon as the sun was already setting and then it would just be cold air seeping in. "Garen's got enough information ready on the war games and conference that I can send Ore with the message to the garrisons along the way. I'm going to see if Kirk can be my other Messenger now that Ore's not so available."

He turned to look at Kirk who was now paying attention. He seemed rather eager to be sent, but Rei had been paying attention. Kirk was ready to get out of the castle and run, like Ore was. He'd been studious at the map table whenever he needed to get up from his chair. "Can you handle the eastern garrisons?"

Brian's head came up at that. Kirk gave a nod. "I think so."

Rei's attention went to Brian next. "Do you know where they are sufficient to not get lost in the weather, or should I send Kirk east with a garrison messenger?"

Brian hesitated. "I know where the back roads are for most of the northeast part of the region, but I haven't been to the garrisons on a regular basis. If it was a heavy snowstorm I might miss them, particularly the two farther south along the mountains. The one at the southeast end I've never been to."

Rei considered it, then said, "Do you need vacation time outside of the castle? I could send you with them. You could stop at your family's home, stay there a few days, and return while Kirk and the garrison messenger continue on. I'd like Kirk to go to all of the eastern ones so he learns how to find them. If he's going to be my Messenger, he'll need to be familiar with them all."

Brian sat back in his chair to consider that. "I wouldn't need very long, but getting out of the castle walls for a bit would be good for me." He wrinkled up his nose. "Having to sit inside the tighter walls of the family home having my sister pester me in person wouldn't be so nice, though. Garrisons are better than that. It is between the Northeastern garrison and the next one down, so we could stop overnight there. I'd probably return again the next day when they've left. That would be enough if I could have one more night at the village or here in town to pretend I was on a longer trip." He gave a wry smile.

"Okay," Rei agreed. "Kirk, I'll let General Garen know tomorrow morning I want a garrison messenger to go with you for the eastern section. You've already been to the Castle Road garrison to know where it is so he can come up that way with the message. I don't want Mizi away from the castle longer than she needs to be, so you'll handle the central garrisons as well as the southern ones."

"Yes, Rei," Kirk answered, sounding relieved rather than put out about the longer passage. That was sufficient. "Ah, will you send Leon and Sam with Mistress Mizi then?"

Rei shook his head. "She rides double with Ore on those trips. It will be more than they've had before to have Marcus and Henry with them." The heads of those two had come up and they were looking at him in some dismay. (Mizi had Tanner with her in the Lotus office.)

He gave the pair a dry look. "I'd rather hold on to you here and be able to send you out as the rescue if they get into trouble on the way back. Garen wants to have you more for a bit if you need to be getting more physical exercise than you are." They found that surprising. "I'll ask him in the morning when he'd like to be seeing you and let you know."

"Ah," Leon was in particular rather distressed. He paused, not quite sure how to say his concern. "I'd rather not be dismissed and returned to the garrison," he finally got out.

Rei stared at him for a bit, making him very uncomfortable. "Well, that's Mizi's to decide," he finally answered. Leon turtled his head a bit, but knew that he'd have to take that as his answer. The sympathetic look Kirk threw Leon's way was interesting, as was the fact Brian didn't.

Rei stood back up on his feet and motioned at the guard on the patio door to close the curtains against the chill that was reaching for him. He reached for the folders on his desk he'd be taking with him to his room for the evening. "Ah, and Flandras," he looked over his shoulder at the head that had risen to look up at him in some shock, since any interruption for the man was shocking to him, "be at the Ministry of Intelligence first thing in the morning."

"Ah..., yes, Rei," Flandras answered. He continued to watch as Rei headed for the cloaks on the pegs by the door, taking a little bit for it to register that the work day was done. There was the general shuffle of papers and scraping of chairs as people rose from their work to prepare to leave the office.

-o-o-o-

Ore, Ilena, Petroi, and Thayne were seated at a round table in one of Ilena's Family restaurants in the northern business district of Nijoushi. As the food had filled their bellies, they'd been able to begin to relax together. The wine was also helping Petroi and Thayne relax. They'd keep that minimal tonight because of the higher alert they needed to be at for having the royal couple out of the castle and them the only guards with them.

The door to the restaurant opened and four men walked into the room, like many had over the course of that evening. However, this time it was a little different. They scanned the room, then began to head into the room without waiting to be seated to a table. As they took off their outerwear another man in the room, already seated, rose to his feet and barred their way. Quietly he refused them from continuing on.

Petroi's head tipped towards the confrontation so that Ilena turned from her listening to Ore and looked. She sighed. *Let him come.* It would be better than having the confrontation turn into something worse. The four men continued on to her table. "Brendan," she acknowledged the Sage Seraph when he arrived by the table. It wasn't usual for one House Head to walk into a place acknowledged to be owned by another, particularly when the other House Head was present in it. However, they were technically in territory claimed by the House of the Sage Seraph. This confrontation was already coming, unresolved in the first council of the Big Four.

"Princess Ilena," Brendan bowed to her a bow of a high lord to their liege. She wasn't surprised. "I'd like to speak with you for a bit." Given that he was the wealthiest of the nightwalker Heads living in the city proper, he was dressed for the room and nearly as well as Petroi. He'd made sure his Lieutenant and two guards were nicely clothed as well, that or they also had enough wealth from claiming the whole of the business district now that the city nightwalkers had been restructured.

Ilena looked over to Petroi. "You'll need to apologize to Lord Petroi first, then." Brendan's eyebrow went up in surprise. "It's his vacation evening and you're here to talk work."

Brendan inspected Petroi. "I'm sorry, but yes, it is work."

Petroi studied him coolly long enough to get his displeasure across then relented slightly. "Well, I suppose it can't be helped. And I would far rather it was resolved so I can continue to frequent my preferred eateries ...undisturbed." He made sure both Heads got the point they needed to resolve it so he could.

Brendan drew in a breath, then gave Petroi a slight bow. "Thank you, Lord Petroi." He was finding it awkward to hold to expected politeness. It spoke to his focus being on the nightwalker side of things, for all he'd chosen the timing for the confrontation. However, Petroi was a high court lord — being an Earl — so the politeness was required to him, not just to Ilena.

Ilena motioned to the table between Petroi and Thayne. "You and your Lieutenant may sit with us, but the guards will need to find another table. There isn't room." There was a brief time of shifting of chairs and removal of cloaks before the newest "guests" to the table were settled enough for the conversation to begin in earnest.

"It's the businesses I'd like to discuss," Brendan began.

Ilena leaned on her elbows, her interlaced fingers under her chin. "I can understand that," she answered. "Flynn suggested you learn from me and you said you'd be willing. Now would be a good time, before any more of your street folk freeze." Without waiting for Brendan to do more than open his mouth, she launched into the lesson she'd taught the Gold Lion. Flynn had pointed out to her that each Head really did bear the responsibility to see to the street people of their districts.

The street nightwalkers were those who lacked hope, so much so they wouldn't even attempt to go inside the safe houses to stay warm and protected from the winter weather. Not all of them could be encouraged to give life another attempt nor be tempted to desire hope again. Some weren't fit for any sort of human company at all, having given up even their own humanity. Those Ilena took care of, but she'd had to agree that having the House Heads help her by not stepping on what was rightfully theirs to do was only wise.

When the lesson was over, and it looked like Brendan had at least absorbed enough to follow through once he'd mused on it all for a while, she said, "Taking care of the least is my gift, those who won't move in nor find hope. That's what I do. You won't be able to move some of those street nightwalkers out of your district no matter how much you'd wish to. How shall we deal with those who are mine to take care of?"

Brendan had to blink again to reconfigure that she'd been the first to challenge him. He furrowed his brow. "What do you do for them that they return anything to you?"

Ilena leaned back in her chair to consider the question and the asker of it. "And if I told you that would you also take up that responsibility?" Brendan blinked at her, then pursed his lips. She shook her head at him. "You can't just let them die, Brendan. You already know they're wishing they could, but when the body refuses then something must be done.

"I open houses for them that they can hide in, that they can find some warmer corner away from the wind than in an alley. When the worst of the weather comes, crusts and crumbs appear for them, gifted by members of my daywalker Family who know what it is to come from dark circumstances and have thus learned compassion, even towards those who are dangerous. If they seek to give anything back, I accept it and don't refuse it, as it's a sign they might someday bloom again, but I don't force it. Yes, that makes them a net loss from the business perspective, but the small gratitude, the single tear, even the look of awareness full of poison from usually dead eyes that lets me know they've been touched by something outside of themselves is sufficient payment."

Brendan had sat back in some astonishment at her words. "And you send *daywalkers* in to deal with them?"

Ilena smiled a small smile. "Well, that depends. Most of the time it's better to send in the street nightwalkers who've been given the hope to move forward in life again. That gives them something positive to do to help them in that forward movement, and they already know how hard it is for those who won't to open up at all, having come from the next–closest thing themselves, but yes. Sometimes it is better for a daywalker to go and have compassion on them. Those find it easier to accept the compassion of those who've never had to live their life. It takes patience to find the right person to connect with them. It's just that the daywalkers have just a little more to offer and give than the nightwalkers. Of course you could have those of your nightwalkers who are willing to be compassionate go out and beg that additional small meal to take to them. It doesn't *have* to be from the hand of a daywalker."

Brendan studied Ilena for a while. This time she let him without interrupting him. "Do you do it to gain some loyalty from them?" he almost accused.

"Most of them don't know it's my hand directing it, no," Ilena answered. "I do go and talk to the few here and there if those who are my hands ask me to, but it's rare. On the rarer occasion I've had a need that my networks say such a one is best to meet. Those I do gain the loyalty of first or it'd be dangerous to ask them to do what I need to have done."

Brendan leaned forward casually with his elbow on the table and his chin in hand. "So..., tell me more about the daywalker network."

Ilena let him take it to the point he'd arrived wanting to discuss now that he had the background she'd wanted him to have so they could. "They were in the same sort of situation as the nightwalkers, only locked into prisons of their lords' making. I've released them so they also can walk with hope again into lives full of what they want them to contain." She'd surprised him again.

She waved her hand at the establishment around them. "Unlike the nightwalkers who can't see how to move out of the safe houses and into their own houses, these have dreams they want to reach. I help them reach them. Some were nightwalkers but most never were. Nightwalkers find attaining this sort of goal very uncomfortable."

"That's the freelancers," Brendan said with a glance at Ore. Ore gave off an air of agreement as Ilena gave a small nod.

"I don't have to do much for or with the freelancers," Ilena said. "They're already working for their goals. That's why they're his. In Tokumade every servant was afraid they'd be the next to die to Thunder Fist. I carefully and slowly helped them to escape, then helped them begin to live the life they'd always wanted to if they could get out from that place. I take the daywalker child that's thrown out by a parent who won't care. I help them arrive at a place they can live in without fear while learning to work hard for their own future."

She went sad for a bit. "We can't catch all of those before they're in the nightwalker world, losing hope already, but we do try when we see it. It helps that there's now the orphanages, but they also don't cover every case." There were plenty of young still entering the House safe houses on a regular basis so they all knew it was true.

"So..., what do they give you back in return?" Brendan asked, fishing for what he could take a portion of for himself.

"Gratitude, love, loyalty, and information if I should ask for it," Ilena answered. "That should be obvious, however, given my position."

"Not like any of them would give that to me," he grumbled at her. She only shrugged.

After thinking about it for a while longer, Brendan's brow furrowed. "So, how do you get paid for anything?"

"Mostly I don't," she answered. "Not in that way. It's why I own shares in the businesses I've created. I get paid that way, just like any business person. It's why you're the wealthiest. You've also learned that's the right way to earn income."

He waved his hand again. "And do you own shares in places like this?"

Ilena looked around the open room of the restaurant. "Not once they've paid off the loan for the purchase of the building. And that small percent goes to pay for the next location I purchase for the next dream I want to help fulfill."

Brendan narrowed his eyes at her. Shrewdly he asked, "Is that why you protected Crafter's Row but didn't bother with the rest? Those *are* your businesses you don't want to pay my fees for, but these aren't, so they'll have to pay them for you?"

"What a crude way to put that, Brendan," she scolded him. "Have you even attempted to negotiate with them yet?"

Brendan's eyes went a little wide at that question, and the scold. "Well, no. I needed to talk to you first to even understand how you see it."

"Well, shall I call the owner out then, to talk to you? He's already been standing there watching us quite nervously for a while, wanting to know what I think I'm going to do with *his* business and you sitting there." Ilena raised her hand and motioned. A middle–aged man came almost immediately. Ilena rose from her chair and offered it to him, then stood behind him as he sat almost as immediately as he'd come from the back. Brendan stared at him for not even blinking an eye at having a princess act like that.

"He's only just reached the point of his education to understand," Ilena said in quiet explanation to the man.

The man gave a sharp nod, then clasped his fingers in front of him on the table. "I'll hear it, then," he said shortly.

Brendan took a moment more, then said dryly, "I take it you've all been waiting for me to show up, then?" He didn't get much more than a scowl for wasting the man's time when he had work to do. Brendan put forth what his typical "business" proposition was.

When he was done, the owner of the restaurant was scowling even more. "I don't need protection. I don't answer to threats, and I don't need anything you've got to offer. I realize you're new to this strip, but I'm surprised you didn't learn it in your strip already." Brendan sat up stiffly in surprise and looked at Ilena.

"Tell me, Brendan, what arrangement do you have with...," she mused, then named three places in the area of the north that he'd been Head over for longer than the full north. Her gaze that landed on him judged him.

He blinked back at her, then slumped. "Oh. *That's* what they're like."

The man across from him rose to his feet. "And don't forget it," he pursed his lips at him. "I suppose you can go talk to them all to learn who we are, if you want, out of all the many here in town, but the answer won't be any different from a single one of us."

Brendan gave a tired nod of his head and waved the man off who was already leaving him behind to get back to work. Ilena sat back down. Brendan sighed. "I take it they're all like that because of where they came from?"

Ilena gave a wise nod. "They'll never be afraid of any man again and will stand up for their principles and rights to a man, woman, and child. Even if they didn't come from Tokumade. The thing they gain isn't hope when they leave their past behind. It's courage."

"*Ah,*" Brendan sighed quietly. He rested for a bit, then rose to his feet. He bowed a more respectful bow to Ilena. "It's very different to work with a Princess, indeed." He bowed briefly to Petroi. "Thank you for the time," he said. His cloak was around him and his other warm clothing in hand and he and his three were out the door soon after.

"I think...," Ore mused, as they watched them leave, "...that he's going to go find the Gold Lion to drink his misery away in company. Or perhaps the Black Ram if he's desperate enough." The others at the table laughed quietly.

Ilena shrugged. "It always works best to have the owners teach them what's allowed and not allowed. It's their rules after all, not mine." She gave Ore a small bright smile.

He leaned over and gave her a kiss. "I did always wonder how you worked at this level. It's harder to see than at the nightwalker level." She just gave him a secret smile. "I think I approve," he whispered in her ear.

"Oh, that's good then," she answered and called the waitress over. "Refills please," she requested.

-o-o-o-

Petroi and Thayne raised hands to interrupt the waitress. "Tea for us please," they requested. They'd had their one. While there was truce, the Sage Seraph hadn't promised them safe passage home if he was actually irritated, so they wanted to be sharp enough on the walk home.

Most patrons had cleared out of the room by this point, it now being late enough in the winter evening. Petroi looked around the room to confirm by just how much as they waited for the drinks. Once those were on the table, he sat back and put his hands in his lap and looked at Ilena. She swallowed her sip, set her cup down, and went to a "listening politely" pose. Petroi's eyes went to Ore as well and he also prepared himself. He could only hear in his head, *You're very obedient aren't you?* It almost made him sad. They both played parts so well it couldn't be told if they were being honest or not; although, in his case he was sure they wanted to be kindly polite at a minimum.

He studied them for a moment more, then said, "Thayne, muss up Master Ore's hair until he cries uncle and really relaxes." He reached over and grabbed Ilena's braid and held it — and thus her in place — while he tickled her until she did cry uncle. When that was all out of their systems, including his, he sighed at them. "See? Work did undo it all in the end."

Ilena sighed back at him. "And as you said, it needed doing. I'll be sure to have him pay you back."

"Thank you," Petroi said. That meant if the Sage Seraph or any of his people forgot to leave him alone when he was eating out to relax, he got to exact his own payment and be forgiven for it. However, now that they'd been able to relax again he could get to his actual reason for calling the couple out. "When I brought Thayne out before, he pointed out to me that I was still having troubles for not being open with you, and for not asking for help from Mother and Father as I ought to. So, can you now be relaxed enough for that?" He raised eyebrows at them, but they were very quickly into those personas to his relief.

"Grief has been a problem for me when the winter darkness becomes too much," Petroi admitted to them. "This time, because Thayne has helped me begin to heal it, it truly does need to be healed so I can let it go and move forward." Ilena immediately reached out her hand to him and he took it to hold it tightly. Ore's look was sympathetic.

Petroi spoke to Ore. "You don't know, but Second was a woman, not a man. It was, I believe, Mistress Ilena's only male–female pairing before Lady Leah's brief pairing with Liam." Ilena gave a small nod. Ore's eyebrow was up, but he was also already beginning to guess. Petroi took a deep breath. "We were husband and wife." Ore was immediately up out of his chair and walking around to take the now–empty chair to Petroi's other side. The warm arms of Father were barely around Petroi before his tears were falling. "She gave her life to save mine, knowing what importance I held for Mistress Ilena." The hand holding his firmly trembled slightly. The pain in Petroi's heart was still sharp, but it truly did help to be held in the arms of Father.

This time he didn't sob as he had when he'd admitted it to Thayne when they were first getting to know each other. That level of pain and self–recrimination had been released then. This was the regular sorrow that came when the loneliness of winter depression sat on his shoulders heavily. "Master Ore, while I do love Mistress Ilena and want to see she's protected, it isn't what you need to be jealous for. ...Truly," he whispered because that's all that would come out around the lump in his throat, "I am jealous that my own wife can't be here with me to smile with us and also participate and to be my comfort at night."

"*Ah,*" Ore sighed and slumped. "That I can understand," he said in sympathetic misery. A chair scraped as Thayne rose to move to Ore's seat. Ilena moved and Petroi knew Thayne had taken her other hand. Even she still grieved.

"She was one of the few who loved to smile with me, and would tease me like Thayne does you," Ilena told Ore. "She was strong of heart and of stout loyalty. It was her that came to me and told me she'd come to love Petroi and wished to support him in that way. I allowed it, then regretted it when her loss became both of our severe losses and grief. It was the same for the Messenger of Kouzanshi. He was my most capable and loyal from Tokumade, one who held on to the positive in life even in that place. I knew I wanted whomever I put at his side to learn all of his traits, particularly that one. Thayne has learned it well, and I've been glad." Ore sighed sadly for all their sakes, but he only let them grieve, giving them his kind presence that understood.

When Petroi had let that grief go enough, he rose from Ore's shoulder and embrace to pull out a handkerchief to wipe his face. He quickly caught Ore's hand, though, before he could move away too far. "From both of you, I need one more healing from my childhood, that even Mistress Ilena doesn't know. Thayne reminded me of it on our walk into town last time, then scolded me later that evening when I said it was healed." He gave a wry smile. "I will listen to his wise advice now that we have come this far." Thayne was giving him a, "*you'd better*" scolding look that made Ore stay put also.

Petroi looked down at the table in front of him, only seeing the past for now, not wanting to see their faces until the story was told. He explained the deaths of his family and when that had been in relation to being brought to serve Ilena. How hard it had been to know as a young child that he'd have no future after that save to remain a soldier of the barracks, a life he really didn't want to have to live because he wasn't really a man who could only live to kill.

There wasn't much more to the story or the grief, but when they both threw their arms around him and held him, and then both said how proud they were of him and how glad they were that he was and had been part of their lives, he could only cry once again. The results of the experiment to understand the healing of Mother and Father was obvious this time. He'd needed the arms and love of his parents for a very long time, like Ore had taught Ilena she also did. It truly did help him to receive that final comfort he'd never been able to receive from his own parents because they'd died so far away from him and so suddenly.

When that was cried from his system, Petroi was wishing he could down another glass of wine to finish chasing the emotions away, for all the help and comfort was appreciated. He did sigh and drink some of his tea regardless in order to replace some of the water that had left him through his eyes. He motioned Ore could return to his place and he and Thayne rearranged again. Thayne moved to sit next to Petroi bringing his cup along as well. The warm presence next to him and unspoken approval and relief was sufficient.

When Petroi had recovered enough, he looked at the royal pair again. Ore and Ilena were holding hands, so that Ore could help Ilena finish releasing her grief. "There is one other thing you need to know, although only for considering into the future. It is a pain of mine, but only temporary, since it is also a joy and pride." This secret he hadn't told Thayne yet. They'd gotten worried until the final phrase and Petroi was glad he could relieve them of any further worry on that part.

"Second and I had a son," he said simply. "Because we hid we were married to protect us both, we hid his presence even more. He doesn't know he is my son, but I have watched him closely and trained him as best I can. He grew up in the border between nightwalker and daywalker. Second placed him in a Family foster home and would visit him regularly. He spent much of his youth running the streets since he would follow her to the safe house. He watched me there and followed me on more than one occasion.

"When he had learned just enough from me, I had him taught by the teacher now teaching Miss Contina how to speak Selician. I have sent him there to the castle barracks with a letter of recommendation. If he learns his lessons there, and how to win the trust of the Selicians and how to be a young lord, then I will let him challenge me when he returns to see if he could stand in my place later."

All three others at the table were staring at him in shock. "When winters come since I have sent him, I miss him, too, and wish I could see him. It is only an addition to the other sorrows and as I said, temporary. The Family there give me regular updates and he is doing well, working hard to best me, so they say," he smiled. "I don't know whether to admit who I am to him when he comes again, but it will definitely be after the challenge so he isn't weakened by the knowing. I would like it to still remain a secret regardless, I think, to most of the world." He blinked at them. "Like Mitchel wishes his secret still were one."

They looked away, knowing that was still a sore point for Mitchel. It wasn't unreasonable for Petroi to wish it for the same reason. He might not be so much a target anymore, but it could still be dangerous. He really didn't want his son to die when he was all the family Petroi had now, and he was the only treasured remnants of Petroi's wife in his life other than memories.

Ilena finally blew out a breath. "Petroi," she complained at him a little, "wasn't this supposed to be a vacation night? And here you've said such heavy things." She pouted at him. He only raised an eyebrow at her. She slumped. "Well, I hope you've healed even some. If it comes on you again, let us know. Sometimes an additional hug is necessary even if you don't say anything, just to chase away the gloom when it comes on. It's why Marcus and Henry both will come up to me and just hug me until they can let go. Marcus in particular lost his father roughly and his mother just before, as you heard before." She rolled her eyes at Thayne. "I still don't know why Thayne won't come get his hugs."

Thayne smiled at her. "Because my Mother sits right there," he tipped his head at her. "What you did when Ma died was what I needed to release the grief right then and after with Da'. I've been grateful I haven't needed to carry it with me, other than the soft moments of memory. It's been harder to carry the death of the Messenger, but being with Petroi has been helping with that, and tonight was good."

Ore put his chin in his hand and almost glared at Ilena. "And since when does Henry get healing hugs from anyone?"

She looked away and both of the older guards scolded her also. She sighed at them all. "Okay, he doesn't. But he's a nightwalker. Remember, they have to be forced, most of them. He's too angry to let it out on his own, and even more private about it than Petroi." She gave Ore a speculative look. "I think he'll come get it from you when Rio's had enough time to work on him and teach him that life can be soft for him too, and that he's okay when it is."

"That's like..., seven to ten years from now, if not twenty?" Thayne said dryly.

"Well, yes," Ilena admitted. Then she smiled. "When it happens, then I'll know that Rio finally has learned to care for anyone other than herself. That doesn't happen naturally until then anyway, after they aren't tired all the time from chasing after their own young children."

Thayne leaned on his elbow now and gave Ilena the scolding look. "How is it that you can observe and know all these things, and still not see your own supports with compassion?"

Ilena's eyes went wide at the accusation. Then her face fell. "Thayne, would that I could force anyone to open their eyes to see what I see so they'd have the compassion I have." They blinked a little to see tears enter her eyes. "I have to be blind, particularly to those closest to me, or I would only ever be unkind. I expect all of you to tell me what you need when you're ready for it because you already know I'll give it as soon as you ask. To give it at any other time is to damage your trust in me, and for you to come to believe I don't trust you." She looked down. "I also learned that one the hard way, early at Tokumade."

Ore lifted her hand to kiss the backs of her fingers. Her smile for him was teary. "I've been trying to find the balance here of not just being only blind," she said, "but also train all of you to speak before it becomes so hard." That was true. She had been scolding them to open their mouths better.

Petroi considered her, then said, "When you see it, come tell us and we will talk to them and remind them to come talk to you. Thayne's reminders and scolds to me were helpful. Sometimes it takes that, too." Thane agreed with him.

Ore's eyes narrowed. "And if it's one of these two, come tell me and *I'll* scold them." They looked at him in mock horror but had to relent. For all they didn't like to be pushed either, he wasn't wrong that they were perhaps the worst for keeping their mouths closed and not acknowledging their own stress was getting too high. The lessons of this winter were good for all of them.

Ilena looked at them both, then she pursed her lips and with some irritation turned to Ore and said, "Petroi's jealousy will kill Thayne. Scold him to fix it." Petroi sat frozen while Thayne sat in shock. "It will also bleed into the whole of the Immediate Family and we'll have to remove him altogether." Petroi's head was already shaking itself in denial.

Thayne turned to look at him with wide eyes, then he pursed his lips as well and turned to Ore. "He can't bear to face and forgive that he wasn't allowed to stand at Mistress Ilena's back those many years. The Twins and I are very careful to never talk of those times save the few times he needs to understand me better. I don't need that killing intent brought up when we're trying to learn to be partners who work together."

Petroi couldn't face them any longer. "Surely it isn't that bad," he complained at them.

"Well, actually, it is." Petroi whipped his head around to stare at Ore for saying those words. Ore looked at him directly in the eyes with the challenge that held him. He waited, holding his breath, as Ore judged him.*

When Petroi had submitted to the authority of his master just sufficiently enough, Ore ordered, "When you can say *I* have also felt that bitter cold wind and humbly admit that *my forgiveness* was the right answer, then you may act on that jealousy, ...but only to voice it so we can help you. You will restrain yourself with your partner and the Twins to prevent that from doing the damage it will do to all of us." The pupils of Ore's eyes narrowed slightly, which was rather dangerous when pointed at Petroi. "If you don't, I'll give you triple the damage you do to them and you'll be on probation for a week. One additional week for each slip, until you are removed and replaced."

Petroi swallowed slightly. This was the Ore that would be obeyed or death would be the swift answer: the Queen's Knight, the Suiran Nightwalker King, the Second Prince of Ryokudo. He drew in a soft breath, then rose to his feet. He backed up a wide step so he'd still be seen by Ore and went down on one knee and bent over it, putting a fist on the floor in the humblest bow of a servant to their liege. "It isn't a thing I ever wish to act on," he said humbly. "If Thayne will warn me of when it comes, I will remember this moment."

"Then I'll no longer keep my mouth closed," Thayne said, almost as menacing as Ore in his cool answer. Petroi nodded his head without looking up. It didn't help him that Ilena's warning against having such things forced held so much truth in that moment. However, he couldn't say they were wrong to force the issue now if it would bring so much trouble to the Immediate Family. He'd spend the next week or so meditating on the issue to scrub it from his soul.

---

*Ore recognized this the very moment he understood what Petroi was to Ilena up on the mountain before the fight against Pakyo. If Petroi still hasn't been able to see it for himself and face it, then Ore is going to step in firmly now that others have asked him to.

13 Ante-Cold Solstice: First Full Household Activity

Mizi stared at the page in front of her, feeling rather miserable and as if she was suddenly back at the time before the Court of Ministers again. Rei had set down the year's schedule on the desk in their sitting room, then put his hand on it and shaken his head at her. "This is work. Now is dinner time, where we don't work, according to your requirement."

Mizi had drawn in a breath, then motioned to Tanner. Tanner had added the desired schedule from Ryan. They'd spoken about both after that dinner. Somehow they'd been able to work out what might be an acceptable schedule to Ryan but she still had yet to talk to him about it. Instead of going straight there this morning, she'd decided to give Brianna time for her requested meeting first thing so Brianna could go to the Rose office after their meeting.

To Mizi's dismay, the page she was looking at impacted that schedule greatly, and had as critical a time limit on it. She remembered Ilena's cool face as she'd taught Mizi how to properly face a lady or lord as a royal, the page in front of her reminding her sharply of that lesson. She drew in a quiet slow breath, then looked at Brianna with no expression on her face save the court slightly interested yet mostly impassive one, desperately hiding behind that mask in the moment. "Thank you for taking the time to write this up and for letting me know what you've observed. Your concern is kind."

Mizi tried not to let her swallowing be obvious. "Rei has just been going over the year's calendar with me, so I now have a better idea of when we need to have this learned by. Let me review the list with him, and the timing. There are perhaps more things here than will fit into my schedule between now and then. I'd like to make sure what we work on is what he feels is most critical. If there's additional time, we can work on more than that." She almost excused Brianna right then, but then remembered she had one more point of business with her.

"I'll get back to you as soon as we've decided, so you can also know your schedule. He's already allowed that you may go to your home for vacation time while I'm in Kouzanshi. I leave in four days, first thing in the morning. You may leave anytime after we've talked about this and stay for as long as you need. He expects I'll be gone about three weeks if weather's bad the whole time. We'll hope it's for not much more than two weeks, as there are many things to be working on." Her heart fell. This new list was most of that "many". She worked hard to not let it show on her face.

Brianna was as surprised about the updated schedule as Mizi had been to read this page in front of her. She sat a bit stiffly, then bowed her head. "Yes, Mistress Mizi. I'll let the manor know right away to be preparing for my arrival. Thank you for seeing me this morning."

"You're welcome, Brianna." Mizi excused her and sat stiffly until she heard the hallway door close. Then she moved the page in front of her over on the desk and rested her head on the desk. She closed her eyes. She would've never thought her prior education to nobility under Ilena was so limited. She reviewed the new list in her mind, then had to admit that it really did contain mostly things Ilena found irrelevant in her own life. Some were things Ilena didn't know either. Mizi had been able to tell some of those things, but she'd missed so many. She wanted to cry, she so badly wanted to be done with the nobility lessons.

A soft knock came at the door and Tanner went to see who it was. A brief moment later a warm hand was on her back. "Mistress Mizi," Leon's kind voice was almost as quiet as his footsteps had been. "It's okay. You can do this too."

Mizi sat up and looked at him in surprise. He paused, then said, "If you'll excuse me?" She nodded in her shock. He pulled a chair around and sat down next to her. "May I see the list? Everyone added to it, but I don't know what the final outcome was."

"Everyone?" she asked, her mouth very dry as she pushed it closer to him. He gave her a sad smile back but didn't really answer the question. He reviewed the list, then reached for the pen and ink waiting at the side of the desk.

In short order, Leon had marked most of the lines with numbers, from one to three. He smiled softly at Mizi as he slid the list back over to her. "They only see I'm young, like you are. They rarely remember that I also was at Ichijou. Many of their expectations aren't the same as the main castle's. It's one of the things that causes minor conflicts between the lords of the two castles. Those things specific to here I've left unnumbered. You can think about doing those later if you care to learn them."

Mizi glanced at the page and was relieved to see it was more than two things on the list. She didn't think about it too hard beyond that at the moment. She looked back at Leon, still wanting to hear more reassurances, needing to feel not quite so inept. "I've ordered the rest in importance from one being most important to three being lesser. Only you and Master Rei can choose which ones you'll learn and have the time to, but if you have at least that much, I think it might help?"

Leon smiled again as Mizi nodded almost automatically. "I have a mother who raised five daughters. I'm not a lady to teach them to you, but I do know what's expected of a high noble house and in Ichijou. Please come to me if you're not sure. I'm happy to observe and let you know what I see. Maybe that also can help you."

Tears entered Mizi's eyes as she said, "Thank you so much, Leon. I'm very grateful you've followed me and encouraged me from the beginning."

Leon rose to his feet and bowed. "Truly it has been my only wish to do so since you arrived at Ichijou. Your smile that made Prince Rei smile in return caught me. Your willingness to work hard to walk by his side, when he so desperately needed someone to care for him in that cold and lonely place made it become a determination, Mistress Mizi.

"He'd come to the barracks looking for any place to distract himself from that loneliness. His kindness and concern for the people of this nation found outlet there that made all of us appreciate he was our Prince. He's only made us more and more proud." Leon's smile was genuine as was the glint of tears in his own eyes. "I don't know how many others could see how much your presence was so needed by him. In just your first visit, when he told us you could come and go as you pleased, that was enough for me to understand what you could do for him if you would. You have my gratitude as well." He bowed to her again.

"Well, then I'll be able to continue forward working to stay by his side," Mizi said, encouraged by his gratitude. "Please do help me. I'll be counting on you in this. Although I'll work at a better pace this time, if I can," she sighed at the list.

"Even progress is enough, Mistress Mizi," Leon encouraged her. "They watched you before. The distance you've already come is more than enough to surprise them. There are just a few more things that will be important. Those are the number one items. Please, if you can, do at least those to a level they can recognize you're working on them."

She drew in a large breath of courage and nodded. "I can probably do that much at least." Leon bowed again. Mizi rose to her feet, leaving the list on the desk. She'd review it with Rei and they'd discuss it in the evening meeting. She motioned to Tanner, who brought over her cloak as Leon moved his chair back. They'd go to the medical department next, but Mizi planned on considering what to say to Airn as they walked that distance. She wanted to meet with him at or just after lunch this day to also have that done and not hanging over her. Rei had at least approved of that habit. Getting things out of the way when they needed doing was better than having them dragging as weights waiting to be done.

-o-o-o-

Rei walked into the Lower office of the Ministry of Intelligence all business as usual. As he shed his scarf and cloak, Andrew barely grabbing them before they fell on the floor, he said, "Ilena, Flandras has been working on the calculations for me. He's close to ready to submit his numbers, but I noticed he's struggling with some details." He was settling in his place at the head of the seats around the table. He'd sent Mina on to do her research for him that he'd assigned her that morning.

Ilena glanced at Rei, then turned to look at the desk behind and farther down the room from her. "Reynold, he needs your detailed eye to teach him what he needs to know. He's yours for the rest of this time until his questions are answered or you know what data to research for him."

Both men froze then turned to stare at each other. Flandras took a deep breath and headed over to Reynold's desk. "It's details about the lords," he admitted.

"The anti–Touka faction's the main topic," Rei said mildly and looked up at Garen. The other two flinched again.

Justinian jumped up and offered his chair to Flandras. "Come sit here. I may be able to help, too, if there's research to be done." Flandras sat and they were quickly into quiet discussion.

"Garen, when do you want Sam and Leon for the initial visit? They're primed, but you should want them most when Ore and Mizi are on their way."

"Today or tomorrow would be fine. Then they'll be ready by then," Garen answered.

"Fine," Rei said. "Ilena do you have to do the one week prior security check for Mizi and Ore to go to Kouzanshi?"

"Nope." She was just as short as he was being. He paused to stare at her, letting his brilliant blue eyes do their job of commanding for him. She scowled at him. "I've got a whole Family's worth of agents who do just fine at it without us having to do it, too, particularly when you and she are in a hurry, they've been just fine this whole time until now without it — because of *my* people not yours — and none of us can spare any more than that at the moment."

"Good," he answered. "Mizi says she can be ready to go in three days, leaving the next morning, on the seventeenth." He blinked at Ilena's sudden relaxing. She still stayed just a little cool to match his brevity today. However, Ore had stiffened somewhat. Rei ignored that for now. "You'll still have Marcus and Henry go with him?" Those two guards stiffened, but the other two didn't, telling him just how much they both knew Petroi needed to stay with Ilena.

Ilena gave a sharp nod. She turned to Henry. "Can you two be ready for recruiting on the trip?"

"Yes," Henry answered. Ilena was satisfied with that and turned her attention back to Rei but Henry wasn't done. "It's that they'll need to know how to run a city for you since you're currently very focused on the renovations. We'll need to add that training into the schedule."

Ilena's eyebrow went up. "Remind me when we go through the Ministry schedule at our meeting later." She got a positive response and gave Rei her attention again. "Have you decided on if they go with a carriage or not?" she asked him.

"Not," he answered, turning his attention to Ore. "You'll go as you usually go: together on one horse. I want her gone the least amount of time possible as I'll be worrying the whole time about all of you. Do what needs to be done, including the messages to each garrison, but don't take any more time than you have to. If you run into troubles, use the network to let us know. I'll send Sam and Leon with a garrison sleigh if you need rescue because of the weather."

"You won't send even them?" Ore asked in surprise. Rei shook his head. "What about Tanner?"

Rei shook his head again. "She doesn't need him for that part, for all he's helpful. The fewer people who go the better. I'm only having Ilena send Marcus and Henry because of her ulterior motive and because I *will* get into too much trouble if it's just the two of you now that you're married to people other than each other."

"Ah," Ore shut up, understanding that very well. Chaperones from now on in cases like this protected everyone.

Rei let them know what he was thinking for having Kirk go as his Messenger, wanting he and Brian to leave at the same time as Ore and Mizi. Garen agreed to have his final message to the garrison commanders ready by then, as well as assign a garrison messenger to help Kirk learn the paths to the eastern garrisons.

"It's perhaps made just a little more difficult because Brian does want to go with Kirk at the beginning. I'd like to make sure Kirk knows something that Brian won't or shouldn't; that can test if they've started working together, but I think they haven't." He clasped his fingers together in front of him. "I also want to make sure we've pulled out the parts that shouldn't be written but need to be told to the commanders." He glanced at Mitchel. "You're sure the commanders of the eastern garrisons are all loyal?"

"Yes," Mitchel was firm. "Like Ilena kills traitors, your mother made sure that all of those garrisons stayed clean. They all know the criticality of their placement." He motioned to Carl. "If you want fast confirmation, we can send Carl to his other place of work directly after this meeting. He'll know from the discussion today what to listen for and can come back with the answer before Kirk gets back."

"Good." Rei sat back up and scanned everyone in the room. "You'll tell no one outside this room what was said in it at this meeting or the data will be skewed." He got obedient agreement and turned the time over to the other's summaries.

-o-o-o-

Garen looked at the two soldiers in front of him. Older and wiser, Sam was holding judgment as he should. He wore the white uniform and cloak of the military men, having received his commission and position from King Sasou. Leon, always the eager younger one, was very unsure so was holding himself stiffly so he didn't let the worry out. He should technically also be wearing the white uniform, but he'd practically begged to wear the black one when he'd been knighted by Rei. The compromise was that he still wore the white cloak with his military commission badge on it. He hadn't been removed from that office, after all. He'd just had "guard to the First Princess" added on. They were reporting at Garen's office as ordered to by Rei.

Garen rose from his desk and reached for his military–issue white cloak that was slightly nicer than most since he was a general. "It's time for your test, Leon," he said quietly. Leon's heart was suddenly beating twice as fast as it had been. Ilena had already passed him to Agent in her network a few weeks ago. It was hard to believe that he'd be sent away by Mizi having that as part of his resume now, but he still worried greatly. The teasing of the young lords in their group didn't help him, nor that none of the others could reassure him. Only the interviews not leading to action yet helped at all some days.

They walked out to the list field and selected wooden practice swords. Leon took his stance and then did his best against Garen. Somehow he was glad it was the General. That was much easier than against Ore in hand-to-hand when that was a more recent skill he'd learned. At least they both knew how to test, not just beat up on the person they were testing. A few things made Leon reach hard, but he knew that the peculiar way each person fought meant that he had to reach in the immediate moment like this. He'd actually been practicing in the lists of both castles every extra moment he had, just to reach this goal of following Princess Mizi. He'd known early that if she was going to reach this place, and he wanted to as well, he really did have to be good enough to defend her in any situation. Thus he took this testing very seriously. He didn't want to be taken away from it now that he had it.

Garen called a halt to the physical sword test. Surprisingly he then began a verbal test as if retesting Leon to the position of Agent in the Ministry of Intelligence again, except Leon recognized some of the questions as being from his final military testing before he'd been given his commission. He answered every question promptly and firmly. At the end Garen paused, then asked, "What does Princess Mizi need most from her guards?"

Leon blinked, then answered with all seriousness, "Protection from the threats she can't and doesn't see. Protection from the lords who mean her ill will. Someone to make her smile and remember the world doesn't hate her."

"And are you committed to doing all that for her and everything she asks of you, and that you're ordered to do by Prince Rei and Princess Ilena?"

"Yes, Sir, save if Princess Ilena orders something that would harm Princess Mizi."

Garen considered that answer, then gave an accepting nod. He waved Sam to come closer so they could all talk without being loud and overheard, and so they could be a little warmer. "As far as anyone in the castle is to know, you've been reassigned to me temporarily while Princess Mizi is in Kouzanshi. Your orders are to arrive here early in the morning of the seventeenth, as soon as you can after Prince Ore and Princess Mizi have left the castle grounds."

He blinked at them and said even more quietly, "You'll be following after them as travelers on the road. Hopefully nothing will happen but a quiet ride to

Kouzanshi and back. Prince Rei wants to know if they're followed or attacked. If they're followed, try to get descriptions and even names if you can without exposing yourselves. If any of them call for help on the network you'll rush up to help them, so make sure you're not too far back, but don't be close enough to make it obvious."

He handed his wooden sword to Leon. "You'll both arrive here again tomorrow at the same time you did today. Go to Corporal David this time. He'll give you the schedule of places and times for their stops and take you to a private room to review the map. Plan how you'll follow them and how you'll stay not–suspicious to others on the road, and as not–recognized as possible. The next day, bring any casual clothing packed in a bag to be left here. We'll see it gets on the horses and they're ready for you the following morning. We'll have different outer gear for you to wrap up in once you get here that morning. You'll walk back out of my office wing as the new people you'll be for the rest of that trip."

Garen addressed Sam. "If you need to stop in at any garrison, you may let them know who you are and that your orders come from me, but keep Leon's name secret. He's just your aide for the trip." Sam nodded.

Leon asked to make sure he understood, "So we keep to the pattern each day we already have, but at the same time as today each day we come here to set the new pattern?"

"Yes," Garen affirmed. "The final day before they and you leave, you can let it loose in the office in the afternoon that you've been assigned to me all day every day until they get back, and I've asked for you to be in the garrison even at night. Tell Regent Rei and get his permission. That will be enough to let them all know what they need to know."

They saluted and he excused them for that day. On the walk back to the Rose office, Sam said softly, "I suspect we'll be more on call on the trip back."

"Why?" Leon asked.

"Four days isn't long enough to even be told they'll be headed out on North Road, but in that time plus the time we take to get there and do what she needs to do, they'll have plenty of time to plan something."

"Ah." Leon understood now why Rei had said in the office he'd rather keep them back and send them as retrievers by sleigh if trouble happened. He could use that excuse and so could they if trouble came at the time it was most likely to.

-o-o-o-

Ilena sat at her desk with her fingers steepled in front of her. She looked over her Ministry members. "Before Carl gets to leave, we'll have our meeting." She turned her focus on Carl. "It won't be a bother to take Liam this trip, would it?"

Carl shook his head. "I think we've reached the point where they understand we've got a partnership going here in Nijoushi. If that carried over to there, particularly if he goes looking for similar people to pay there as here, it wouldn't be surprising."

"All right. You understand what to do from the previous meeting." It was a mere confirmation. Ilena asked Liam, "Do you need anything from me or Ore before you go?"

"No," Liam answered, "just a promise you'll both be good for those left with you," he looked at the rest of the household, "and that you'll be kind to them while keeping them in line. I think they've been doing rather well, given the circumstances.

Remember that Mistress Ilena always does better with praise when she gets rough." They all sighed at him.

"You'll miss it to leave now," Ore said, "but it's household vacation day this afternoon. I think that will help generally, too." Carl was quite relieved to hear he'd be missing that event. Liam seemed to find it perhaps sufficient.

"You're both excused, then," Ilena said to them. They bowed and headed for Liam's room so he could pack.

"Henry," Ilena turned it over to him next.

Henry said, "We need to fit in time for Petroi and Thayne to run in Nijoushi with us so we can take them to the places we're going at the moment for the city renovation project. Right now that's a lot of time at the south wall and in the southwest part of the city spying on the liquid rock researchers to figure out their formulation and methodology, since they won't come out of that company and that company won't share. We'll introduce you to the researcher who's agreed to work on it for Mistress Ilena. She asks us questions and we go find out the answers and take them back to her. She's fairly close to coming up with a similar product."

"She?" Petroi raised an eyebrow slightly at Henry.

Henry and Marcus nodded. "She's another marginalized intelligent female that loves getting her hands dirty. She's quite keen to one–up the men who invented it. No one but Mistress Ilena is paying attention to her right now, since we found her for the project. ...Which you also need to know how to do because she needs assistants. The building takes at least two and four is better, but she doesn't have the income to pay them."

"It will come from the County funds and my pocket," Ilena interjected. "But we can't get her the additional hands until she absolutely needs them, so yes, they need to know how and when to pull them in."

Henry added, "The 'how' includes grooming them to accept the work and then that their boss will be a woman. We've found two potentials and were about to start talking to them. We can show you what we do with one of them and then let you see if you can do it with the second one. If you start to lose him we'll step in and help so we don't. She needs male strength to lift and move the forms and final product — it is still stone. You can try to find the third one on your own once we've explained it. Another woman might be fine for that so it's a little more open in the possibility field."

"I've specifically asked her to research how it would be different underwater than just in the air," Ilena added. "That would make it just different enough she might be considered a separate researcher who happened upon it at nearly the same time to prevent Jamison from becoming too angry. Petroi already knows how to make it look unrelated to me at the start, so that part should be simple for them." Petroi agreed with that statement.

Ore considered the timing. "This afternoon we'll all have to be here and Eldest most of all since he and Mister Andrew have put the family activity together. Tomorrow we need to prepare the river for the travel now that we know it, so they can be doing the security checks at the right time. Master will likely want me in the office for a good portion of the last day as he adds to what I'm supposed to say in little bits and pieces all day, like he usually does. But I suspect we could excuse them from the office to run?"

Ilena considered her schedule. "Falcon Studios will be having a meeting that morning I need to be at. They could come after that. I've got to meet with Mister Balar after, so we could let you know when the meeting's done and I can meet with him until you get there. Then we'd have most of the day for the teaching and practicing."

"You'll stay in town?"

"If you're going to be in the office all day, yes," she answered Ore. Since it would help her to be distracted, he didn't complain.

-o-o-o-

"The weather's been weird recently," Carl complained to Liam. They were dressed in common brown cloaks, heavy pants, worn boots, and thick jackets that had seen better days. It was the layers underneath that were slightly better at keeping them warm. Their winter hats, gloves, and scarves were similar: getting a bit threadbare but still warm enough to be sufficient. "You think it's going to be a day of snowfall and when you finally get outside it's calm. You dress up as warm as possible, hoping to not have your eyelashes freeze your eyes closed, and then wish you'd worn your spring gear." He scowled slightly.

Liam chuckled. "True, but after three weeks straight of snowfall, it's nice to have the calm. Given we're about to travel, that's even better."

"I suppose," Carl sighed. He held up a gloved hand. "I'm for sure going to splurge on new gloves if it's a profitable trip." He wiggled the fingers that had the tips worn off enough to have holes in them.

"I'd appreciate the same," Liam agreed. He pointed to the place in his knitted hat where the threads were worn enough to have been torn loose from themselves, as if the ends were trying to be his hair for him.

Nijoushi was busy this mid-morning since it was good weather. It wasn't sunny by any means, but the grey clouds were the lightest in color they'd been in a long time and no snow was falling. "It's a bit difficult, though," Liam frowned now. "The public carriage will have already left and I'm getting too old to walk for a full day." While they could have used horses, particularly Liam, their personas wouldn't have had them. Liam's Tarc horse would have stood out the most.

"Oh, there's ways," Carl said casually.

Liam got to learn that day how Carl already had a job set up with a merchant that let them hire on to help get a load of goods to the border. Liam didn't see money change hands, but a packet of letters went into Carl's jacket in an inner pocket when Liam was supposedly not looking. Liam wasn't trusted yet so he pretended to not notice.

They helped load the wagon, then were on the road after a quick lunch. Carl was the driver, knowing where to go. Once they were out of the city and on the road, Liam asked, "Going to have some light reading at night, then?" Carl's lips curled up but he didn't say anything. "And how far are we going with the supplies?" Liam asked a while later.

"Just the border checkstation. There are people who work between the villages we'll pass them on to and get our information from." He sighed. "It'd be good to have more time there. For you to really get trusted we'd need to stay at least three weeks to a month, but they'll want the information faster."

Liam mulled over that. Carl wasn't wrong. "And if I stayed and you left?"

Carl considered that for a while. "Maybe, if your mistress can spare you that long." He gave a sidelong look to see what Liam thought about that.

Liam shrugged. "I won't be very useful for the foaling, so I could stay. We could also use the code and both stay if it's necessary. They didn't give us a return time. They only want the information."

Carl shook his head. "They know about the code and will hear it when it arrives."

Liam shook his head back. "There's ways."

Carl gave him a suffering look for returning his words back to him. "You'd at least best get approval for staying away that long, since she didn't bother to ask nor tell before we left."

That was wisdom, so Liam did. They got the approval to stay as long as it took for Liam to be accepted and to find work to bring back with him. *But don't cross the border yet.*

Liam chuckled. "What?" Carl asked.

"She already knows where you go and what you do there."

Carl sighed, defeated once again. "I don't like to cross the border anyway," he complained. "It takes too much effort unless I wanted to add the persona of a merchant doing business in Brulac. That's even more effort." He wrinkled up his nose. "It's not a fun place to be one of those, or anything for that matter. I'm just as happy to be a Ryokudan."

Liam leaned back against the wagon driver's seat back and looked at the white scenery they were passing. The pines were dark green under their white blankets. The deciduous trees were grey ghosts. He was just as happy to be Ryokudan, too, but the way Carl had said it made him wonder just what was going on in Brulac generally. So far the words of Kata's spies hadn't been very complementary at all. The spies Ilena was sending in as lords had reached their manor two days before, according to Mitchel. He wondered if any lord of Ryokudo would really flee into Brulac, traitor or not. Probably not, if they had a clue of what it was like there. ...Which they probably didn't.

-o-o-o-

The two royal households gathered after lunch on the day appointed by the Regent for them to spend vacation time together. Petroi and Andrew led them to the royal list in the garrison. There they made everyone who had live steel on them leave it on a table set up near the watering station, save for the four royals who were allowed to keep theirs. Four garrison guards watched over that table to make sure the cherished weapons stayed on the table. Four guards were already guarding the entrance to the list as well.

Chairs had been set up at the edge of the list near the outdoor fireplace that warmed the enclosed space just sufficiently for those who were on the list to not freeze. Those who weren't fighters in their group and the four royals were invited to sit. "You'll be the examiners," Andrew explained.

Petroi turned to the fighters of the two households and motioned to the other table set up closer to the list zone. "Please select a marking weapon equivalent to what you would use." Lightweight sticks had been wrapped in soot–filled gauze or chalk–filled gauze. "Black for Mistress Ilena's household, white for Master Rei's."

145

"What are the balls for?" Kirk was looking between the black marking tools that had many small tied balls of soot included, where there were very few chalk–filled ones on the white side.

"To simulate thrown weapons," Petroi answered. Eyebrows raised, but hands collected those things they understood well enough: sticks long or short or a handful of the marking balls. Andrew had spent that same time scolding the royals that they were to properly keep themselves out of range of any weapon, even the mock battle ones prepared for today.

Petroi called for Delia and Maria to join the fighting group of Rei and Mizi's household, then began the rules for this "game". "Please hit each other lightly. Thin sticks still hurt and will break all the more easily, for all we have padded them to not hit nor break quite so badly. When the judges determine a hit is a killing blow, you must retire from the field, or at a minimum refrain from further attacks. A blow to an extremity should be considered sufficiently damaging that limb is out of play. The goal is to protect the Regent and his wife." He put his hands on Delia and Maria's heads. "That is, for the first round, where their household will be the defenders. We will go twice. The first time as a practice warm–up battle, the second as a more serious learning battle.

"Then we will trade places and we will protect Rio as Mistress Ilena and Justinian as Master Ore while those who protect the Regent and his wife will attack. Again it will be a practice warm–up battle followed by the learning battle." Wide eyes were staring at Petroi and glancing at Andrew and the royals. Petroi drew in a deeper breath. "During the practice battle, Andrew and I will stay out as coaches. If we need to continue to do so for the learning battle we will, but we would rather set up the strategy and be included so the full strength of the households can be understood."

He allowed everyone to settle to the idea of this first event of the vacation. "Why?" Leon finally asked in a bit of confusion. "We won't actually have to fight against each other, will we?" That was said with a little more suspicion.

Mina dryly answered, "We'll hope not."

Petroi shook his head. "Our worst battle was one like this. We had even more than this number set against us. They were also mixed: excellent sword masters and skilled nightwalkers. We lost beloved companions who were strong and just as skilled and some of us nearly died as well. It would be good for both sides to understand just what that means, given the uniqueness of this generation of royals that wish to stand at each other's sides. You will all need to keep them alive, even in such extreme cases."

He turned to soberly face the four royals. "You will not participate both because we don't need you accidentally harmed, and because we don't need you accidentally harming us. You will, however, watch closely to see how what you would think to do would affect the battles, how you would need to defend yourselves, and what attacking would do to those who are your defenders. Sometimes holding still is the best answer."

He turned back to the participants. "If either of the substitute royals are marked the battle is over. That includes if they are marked by weapons of the defending side. The goal is to prevent them from being harmed, but if all the defenders are down then the battle also ends, for they have been captured at that point." He turned to the two royal stand–ins. "You will do what the defenders say to keep yourselves protected, but not actually attack anyone. Do defend yourselves." They gave him nods.

Mina raised her hand. Petroi let her speak. "Our most frightening battle was against lords and soldiers, and it was me all alone to protect Rei until Ore could get Andrew freed up so they could come help." She waved at the open list. "This is as open as my fight was and I hated it. When Ore gave us an opening so we could run to the wall to defend I felt much better. A wall's as good as a partner when one's all alone. Such a practice would also be good."

Petroi nodded. "This practice will be better as you will have multiple partners to help you defend, but yes. In our fight we were surrounded and kept in the middle of the room. Thus why an open space for today. They are the most dangerous."

The participants moved to the middle of the list, Delia and Maria standing in the middle with Tanner standing with them, a handful of chalk balls in his hand. Mina, Brian, Kirk, Leon, and Sam took up positions around them, facing outwardly with their chalked "swords". Thayne, Henry, and Marcus considered that formation then formed up into a triangle with Thayne in front and Marcus and Henry to either side and behind him. Thayne faced Brian first specifically. That surprised Rei's household guards because they knew Thayne's swordsmanship wasn't up to the skill level of Brian's. Given Thayne was the only one with a mock sword in that group, they weren't sure why he'd picked Brian to be his opponent.

Just before the command to begin was given, Mizi opened her mouth and shifted, but Petroi shook his head at her and she subsided with a frown furrow on her brow. She watched the combatants intently, like the others were. "Lay on," Andrew called out.

Thayne moved forward to engage Brian, stepping slightly into Mina's left-handed range as well, fully catching her attention. As soon as Brian and Mina were committed to engaging Thayne but before the others could move, Marcus and Henry ran to either side and threw one soot ball each, then a second each. The third was out of their hands before a thrown chalk ball hit Henry in the shoulder. "Hold!" Andrew called out. Soot and chalk had to settle a bit in the area around the three active swordspersons before the results could be seen.

There were sighs all around. "The Regent is injured and the First Princess dead," Petroi tallied the results. "Tanner is injured, Leon is dead, Sam has lost his sword arm. Thayne has lost his off–arm, Brian is dead in three days from now of a belly wound and thus would be on the ground at this point, and Henry has lost his dominant arm. Marcus is still alive and whole as is Mina." The combatants look around to see what had "killed" the royals. Maria had soot on her head and Delia on her shoulder. Tanner's throwing arm also had soot on it.

"Oh, good job getting a hit on Henry at all, Tanner!" Ilena praised him, since he'd have had to throw his ball with his off–hand.

"What have you learned?" Petroi asked the defenders.

"That it's *very* hard to defend against small thrown things!" Leon answered immediately.

"Indeed," Petroi answered drolly.

Mizi raised her hand and this time Petroi let her speak. "The very first thing I learned when put into any sort of battle situation was to crouch down and make myself as small a target as I could. All the time I'd do that first, now. I don't want my head taken off with a back–swing and I don't want to be in the line of sight of any attackers. So if Maria's going to do what I'd do, it would be to do that.

"I plan on only using my knife if I have no standing defenders and I want to defend them or myself. And even then I'd use it more from a crouched position if I can. I also practice running since I agree that a wall or corner to defend against — or not being there at all — is much better than in the open."

Petroi turned to look at Rei. He stared back until he finally sighed. "It's not what I practice, but I guess with the evidence I can't disagree that being small at the beginning is better than not." His eyes went to Delia. "I assume you weren't hit in the head because you knew it was coming and turned?"

Delia nodded. "Yes. If you couldn't tell, you would've been dead," she agreed. "Henry threw it, not Marcus, so I almost didn't move in time. Henry threw his first one at Tanner, not me, knowing that Tanner would be as bad against them as the two of them were against us."

"So, why did you face me first?" Brian asked Thayne. "And you even opened yourself up to Mina and let yourself get wounded, knowing full well what you were doing. Why?" They all wanted to know.

"I was the distraction," Thayne said. "Any wounds I could get in on the hardest pairing would slow the two of you down." He waved at the rest. "I could've picked an easier pairing, but the two of you would have moved to engage the two who could take down the targets but who aren't the best swordspersons. When there's a serious goal to reach, sacrifices are considered acceptable, so an off–arm wasn't a thing to care about." Kirk and Brian both shuddered. They'd find it hard to sacrifice in that way.

Ore asked, "Are you sure you don't want us to help? Three against that many looked rather small for what might typically be sent."

Petroi gave him a bland look. "Perhaps when they have had enough practice to need high level opponents; however, we all know you never miss and Mistress Ilena kills with only a look and a tap on the shoulder. It is sufficient to place you with our minds only. Andrew and Mina would be dead first, with Brian and Master Rei falling shortly thereafter, with the rest of us barely taking the first breath from the call to begin. Then you would beat up on Kirk together for fun while Sam and Leon tried to hit shadows of where you had been when their eyes actually saw you, or where they guessed you might be in the moment." The others laughed, trying to hide it to be even a little polite, but it was so very true.

"Oh, good!" Mizi said, a laugh in her voice. "I'd be able to knife them in the kidneys while they were distracted then!"

Everyone laughed as Ore and Ilena looked offended, then went hang–dog sad until Mizi rubbed their heads and promised she wouldn't really kill them, as long as they didn't try to kill everyone else. Ore sighed and said, "And thus why they can't practice here either. We wouldn't see it coming."

That practice took a couple of hours. Petroi and Andrew kept the spectators busy being commentators, giving advice as they saw the battling from the outside. A few times Grandfather made suggestions on alternate battle practicing they could do as related to moves that were tried by one side or the other. During the break between which of the two households was defending and which was attacking, Brianna asked why the noncombatants were present also, not because she necessarily needed to know but because she felt that perhaps that lesson should be taught while the other was being taught.

Andrew answered the question. "Because all of both households need to understand the criticality of their roles. Even all of you who don't study fighting methods will be called on to protect the royal families when present with them. You nurses already understand collecting up the child you're assigned to protect, to flee with them if it looks like we'll be overcome." He waved his hand at the center of the list activities. "You also should consider how you'd defend them if such a situation were to occur and we the guards were falling. While you might not pick up a fallen sword, there are things you could do and would need to do."

He pursed his lips, then said, "In the battle Mina talked about, we were in a place that had both loyal and traitorous soldiers. How could we trust any of them, not knowing which was which? It made the battle that much more difficult for not knowing, not being able to call on any of them. The household must be fully trustworthy to always support the royals because that's their last line of defense. In our case, a retreat to a safe place until others could sort out the traitors from those who were loyal was required."

Ilena nodded. "In our case, I also sent out others to weed out the traitors who'd given us away to our enemies. We didn't move again until that was completed."

"Even so, calling for soldiers if we've been taken by surprise is an acceptable thing for you to do," Andrew instructed the noncombatants. "We'd hope you'd never have to, but even standing before blades to be that slight time advantage would be your duty and obligation. Being the distraction, the vaguely seen person that they send a few after to be a few less actually following the royals: such things are what you can be considering."

When the battle rehearsals were over, Petroi and Andrew led the households inside to a small fire–warmed ballroom that had been set up with tables for them to have an intimate dinner at. The Chef and Châtelaine had apparently been very relieved to be told to set it up for the royals this evening. They'd decorated almost too much in their exuberance and the tables were filled with delicious foods by the servers as they settled into their chairs. Rei, Mizi, Ilena, and Ore rather automatically took the central chairs in their typical order. They were pleased when Andrew and Petroi frowned at the rest of the household members until they mixed themselves up at the tables.

They didn't hurry through dinner, taking the time to get to know their neighbors at the table better and to recover from their exertions of the afternoon. As the final set of plates were being removed from the tables by the servers, the Nijou Royal Chamber Orchestra was entering the room and setting up on the opposite side of the ballroom. It looked like they were also happy to dust off their instruments and have their skills and practices be appreciated by the royals tonight. Mizi and Rei were quite content to get to dance together in a comfortable environment. Ore and Ilena lit up the same as the younger couple did.

Not everyone in Ilena's household knew the ballroom dances, but Marcus, Henry, and Thayne surprised Rei's household by showing them they did, and quite well, too. They took it upon themselves to teach the nurses who didn't. After a quiet discussion, they talked the chamber orchestra into playing some of the common dances and those pairings taught Rei, Mizi, and those of their household who'd learn those dances. Ilena and Ore had the most fun that night since they knew them all: a surprise and delight to Ilena who didn't know Ore knew the common dances. Ore was surprised to learn Leah and Grandfather didn't know the common dances so they spent some time teaching them those dances, too.

Brian and Kirk had begged off of dancing the common dances, but they watched them all the same. Leon led Maria out to dance them and both of them blushed to stumble through them, but they had fun regardless. Brianna danced the noble dances with both Sam and Aiden, who'd been dragged along this time by Rei's frown at him when he'd tried to escape at lunch time. Petroi also had her dance with him a few times, wanting to get to know her a little better and let her know him as well since he was the most familiar of Ilena's guards with the noble game but she'd not had the opportunity to learn that yet. Marcus danced a majority of his dances with Amber, making her blush prettily and him too at times, particularly when he had to pause and teach her a dance she didn't know.

By the end of the night, all four royals were content that the goal of the vacation had been met. Not everyone had enjoyed all of the activities, but everyone was relaxed and nicely worn out having done good things together they could share. Ilena sighed and took Ore's hand. She smiled at Rei, then raised an eyebrow at Mizi. Mizi gave a contented nod. "Thank you, Master Rei," Ilena said to her brother. "You're such a good husband. And getting to be a better young man every day."

Mizi squeezed his hand. "Yes, Rei, thank you. I think it's helped quite a lot. It would be good to do this again in a month and regularly."

Rei agreed. "I'll get it put on the schedule as best we can fit it in."

"We should include at least a quarterly ball we include others of the court into, then," Ilena said dryly. "They'll get too jealous, otherwise, not to mention their pants in a twist to not have us allowing them access to us at all if we're going to have fun."

Rei paused and rubbed his head. "Well, actually, that would be a good way to include another reward for those lords doing what I want them to be doing."

Ilena and Ore both spurted laughs. "Well, that's a truth," Ore agreed. "And a better reason to be on our feet that much than just walking around after a dinner." Rei and Mizi both agreed with that. Ore then mused, "But, I wonder if they'd really be okay with the common dances?" Ilena laughed aloud at that. Rei threatened Ore. Ore waved a hand of defense. "Okay, we'll leave those out on those quarterly events," he gave in. "It can be our little family secret."

"Yeah, like the dinners Mistress Mizi, Ore, Petroi, and Justinian make for us!" Ilena agreed. "Although having dinners like this is nice so they can rest, too."

Mizi smiled. "It's nice to make the dinners together, even so. Even that's comradeship with family."

Ilena looked around the room. "Hey, any of you in Master Rei's household know how to cook? Our family chefs are looking for more to join in with them the next time we fix our favorites."

She was looked at with wide eyes, then Kirk blushed in his ears and raised his hand. "I'd sit in the kitchen with Julie at her foster parents' home. She cooked and I'd help for something to do, but I don't actually know any recipes."

Tanner raised his hand. "I know simple dishes since I helped cook the dinners before mother returned home from her work. I'm not sure anyone really wants to eat them, and I am very much enjoying that I *don't* have to cook as an adult."

Mizi smiled at her guards. "Well, then next time I'll take the two of you. Kirk can be sou chef and Tanner can sit, keep us company, and help with the emergencies. When Julie gets here, she can join us, too."

"Next time can we have the time in between to go back and change so we can dress for the dancing?" was requested. Many of the group agreed, among both the men and the women.

The four royals looked at each other until Mizi answered, "Sure. It is fun to get to dress up properly. Even the common dances are more fun when dressed up. I do know that from watching them."

"All right, then," Andrew bowed to them. "We'll be sure to add that into the schedule. But no escaping in between."

Ilena laughed and Mina snorted. "Now you've made it sound like we're all prisoners to herd around and make do this," Ilena scolded Andrew. He blushed and apologized.

Mina was scowling slightly and opened her mouth, but Ilena gave her a high look. "Shall I come make *sure* you're dressed properly and honoring your husband in doing his duty to his liege?" Ilena threatened.

Mina went pale and paused, then shook her head, not saying anything. Ilena had had her revenge and would be paid every time this was done by the household, particularly since *she'd* be made to pay it every time by Ore as well. Mina was rather dejected for a while after that. The reminder that Ilena played best by having the most patience was a bit harsh for someone who hated to dress up, particularly for balls. Ore and Rei both shook their heads ruefully at Ilena. She ignored them, as usual.

"And there it is," Brianna pointed out to the others. "The royal game played by those who hate it most."

Ilena leaned forward on her elbows, interlacing her fingers at her chin. "Yes, Amber did come back and tell us that story. Reynold," Ilena pointed at him and he tried to hide by turtling his head a bit at the far end of the table, "was keenly interested and added to her understanding." Ilena's amber eyes turned to sparkle slightly at Ore. "Ore in particular was quite tickled that she figured out how he fit into it. I quite love to watch him for that very reason. He can tease all of us and sit back and enjoy the consternation it evokes. Mistress Mizi's just scary." Ilena was laughing silently at her. Mizi just rolled her eyes but then gave a nod of agreement.

Rei looked at all of them, then leaned on his elbow. "I think I missed something important?" Ore and Amber, with commentary from Ilena and snide side comments from Ilena's guards, had fun getting to regale Rei with the theory of how the royals played the court game, but only in the royal hierarchy. When they were done, he slumped just a little. "Oh. That. Yes, Ore's always been Sasou's bane. I deal with it by ignoring everyone else when they play it. I haven't got the energy to care enough to participate."

"Oh, I don't know, Master," Ore disagreed. "You've gotten very good at throwing them at me lately. You just like to draw out the suspense."

Rei looked at him sidelong, then shrugged. "Maybe it's that, and maybe it's that I finally can find the words to tease you with lately. ...Or are they the same thing?"

Ore rubbed his knuckles into Rei's head. "I wouldn't know *...Little Brother.*"

Rei pushed Ore off. "Of course you would. You're the one teaching it to me." Petroi and Andrew broke them up at that point. Ilena was laughing too hard to survive much longer.

-o-o-o-

Rei paused in his walk to his bedroom as he passed the desk in the sitting room of the suite. He was relaxed and ready to sleep after having had the afternoon to observe the two households together. Getting to dance with Mizi again had been good as well. He looked at the paper on the desk, thinking it might be a note from Rutherford. It took a moment for the words to register. He got colder and colder the farther down the page he skimmed. "What is this?" he asked before the coldness would come out too strongly in his voice.

Mizi's voice was as coolly neutral as he'd ever heard. "I met with Brianna this morning. That was what she brought to me. Attached was her expectation that it all needed to be learned before we arrive in Ichijou."

Rei had to ball his hand into a fist to prevent it from crumpling up the paper. He took the time to breathe two calming breaths. He turned to look Mizi in the eyes. She looked back as fearlessly as ever, but seemed to be neutrally calm. He waited.

"Leon came after I excused Brianna. He encouraged me by pointing out which things wouldn't be well received in Ichijou and then by ordering them by importance to that court. He was kind to offer to help, saying it would be sufficient to show them that I'm working on learning the most important things."

She drew in a breath. "I left it at that point, knowing we'd need to review it together and decide what there was time for. Again, in this, I'll not learn anything you think I don't need to know, and will focus on what you do consider necessary." Rei relaxed slightly. Mizi pursed her lips and Rei waited to hear what had angered her out of it. "While Brianna brought it to me as the person who'd be in charge of teaching it to me, Leon said it had been added to by everyone."

Rei's fist clenched. He said very quietly, "Then in the morning we'll see if we can guess who suggested what, shall we?" Mizi blinked in slight surprise but nodded she'd work with him. "Tonight I'll enjoy my wife," he held out his hand to her. She took his hand and he took them into the bedroom.

As Rei kissed Mizi and felt her red tresses in his hands, he was able to calm down enough to think rationally again. As he moved into softly loving her, he felt again the sorrow in his heart for her sake that had already been motivating his lessons to help her not work herself to death. He realized then that much of his anger was that they'd moved without understanding he was in charge of her training now, having taken that up with her last lack of understanding of her limits. That pointed out that he himself wasn't communicating well with them so they could understand. He let that go with a promise to himself to figure out the answer to that problem later.

He focused on appreciating the finer parts of having a wife for a while. When they were both satisfied and his body was able to relax sufficiently, his mind was capable of returning to ferreting out the sources of his anger. He needed to do that much before falling asleep so his mind could work on the solutions while he slept. He lay on his back, holding Mizi with one arm as she lay nestled by his side, her head on his shoulder. It was warm in their bed, covered with three layers of blankets and soft sheets. His eyes were closed as he let the anger show him where it had come from.

He couldn't be surprised that a good portion of it was what had been irking him for the majority of the time he'd been Regent already. He really didn't want to have to fight the lords and their blind "requirements" any more. To have even those of their household "turn traitor" and add to that list with an actual list against his wife had made that irritation explode into anger against all lords generally. He drew in a deep breath and let it out in a long breath, forcing that anger to go out with it. He already knew and had practice in letting that one go to be replaced with duty and a choice for patience.

He was just as ready as Mizi was, actually, to have their household properly cleaned of potential traitors and only full of people they could trust and relax around — as much as he could relax. He'd been able to move more confidently towards that goal since she'd told him the summary results of her interviewing each of them. Going over the list in the morning to see if they could tell who had suggested what would be somewhat guesswork but would be a good test of if he understood the members of the household rightly now.

The anti–Touka faction moved deliberately, slowly, and were a terrible road–block to everything good the royals wanted to get done in the nation. Sasou had been giving Rei lessons in that specifically for the last four years. While it wasn't open rebellion, nor violent war, it was still a rebellion that needed quelling. Rei went back and reviewed everything that had happened since he'd arrived in the Regent's seat, using his expanded boards to see it. The expanded boards did help him do that much better than he'd been able to before.

If Sasou hadn't instated Rei when he had, if Rei had been even a year and a half younger, if Ilena hadn't been made to appear when she had, if Tarc hadn't been tamed expeditiously.... So many ifs together. Because Rei had been placed when he had been, almost too early, still too innocently young to really know what he was doing, Suiran had been interrupted from adding to the national rebellion in any meaningful way. His and Ilena's actions the previous year had upset the balance just enough with uncertainty it was holding for now.

It wasn't really even a matter of Touka falling. It was the preservation of their nation as a whole. If Touka fell in the internal rebellion, Ryokudo would assuredly be invaded by Brulac regardless as it became completely take–able. The chaos of the lords who thought they knew best but who had no idea of what that would do to them would prevent them from being able to fend Brulac off.

From the years of studying the lords, he knew the lords weren't a unified group. There wasn't any one lord that they'd all put into the place of king if Touka was removed from the throne. That lack of leadership would put the nation back into small warring groups. Such a situation would be simple for Brulac to enter and fill the vacuum of leadership.

However, that made Rei grasp hold of one name. He held it in his imaginary fist tightly. His other internal hand reached for another person and held it as the opposing force. ...He had a question for Sasou that needed answering. It was one he could ask by Ilena's Family after Mizi's guards were gone from the castle.

He reviewed the boards one more time. One other slightly surprising and very worrisome thing came out of his thinking tonight. Sasou was most assuredly behind the surprising arrival of Ilena to Rei's view. If he let her, she'd kill Sasou for it, too, ...eventually. Rei shivered. That would have to be addressed openly so it didn't happen.

Mina and Andrew entered the office part of the Regent's suite the next morning, as they did every morning for the royal couple's meeting. They both noticed the paper sitting on the desk, a surprising thing to have there because the couple kept their living quarters so neat as to be nearly sterile, and Rei never left papers out anywhere. They stepped up to the desk and scanned the page.

Mina's breathing nearly stopped in her throat. She could feel Andrew stiffen beside her. *This list....* She knew what it was, but to actually see it made her feel a chill she hadn't felt for a very long time. "Andrew," she whispered. "This is far beyond what was discussed, ...isn't it?"

Andrew answered with a sigh. "It won't go unanswered by Rei. I'll stay close by him until he knows what he wants to do." He was rather sad, it sounded like.

"You knew?" Rei's voice was next, surprising them. He had come out of the bedroom holding Mizi's hand.

Andrew paused then answered, "It came up first with a concern related to things a noble and royal lady needs to know that Ilena and Mina couldn't teach but Lady Brianna should be able to. Those things, it seemed, could be useful to suggest. However, when they took it too far into trying to teach her how to face nobility how *they* wished her to, we warned them off, telling them that both of you would be angered if they went that far."

"Mmm," Rei answered. "Then I *might* still let you two handle it ...this time." He closed the door to the bedroom. Andrew and Mina both sighed very quiet sighs. Mina's chills hadn't been wrong. She knew these two now very well, and they were both very angry.

Still, there was silence on the issue while the young royals ate their quick breakfast and listened while Andrew and Tanner went through their schedules of the day. When that was done, however, Rei ordered, "Mina, please go down and hold the household here for now. I'll send Andrew down with my message in a bit."

Mina rose to her feet, bowed, and took herself and her winter gear out of the office immediately. She noted as she arrived on the upper landing of the stairs that most of the household was awake and mostly done eating breakfast. Mina and Andrew had already eaten, usually being the first to do so. "Rei has asked that everyone remain here for now," she told the room generally as she reached the third step above the ground floor. That made those who usually left immediately after eating remain, most of them hesitantly returning to their seats to wait. She stopped and stood at the edge of the sitting area. She kept her attention generally on the room, but also somewhat on the door above, waiting for Andrew to come down.

There was always a bit of nervousness inside her when she was waiting for Andrew to appear. She knew he was always with Rei at those times, but having her own side cold made her seek for it to be warm again. As they'd told the household the day before, the time they'd been forced to be separated had been very difficult for all of them.

Brianna paused by Mina's side as she returned from putting her dishes on the cart. "I've noticed that you're often being sent on errands recently. Is that typical?"

"It is," Mina said. "I'm Rei's feet. Andrew is his hands." *And we're his second and third brains and sets of eyes,* she added to herself. Brianna bowed her head briefly in thanks and moved on to sit again in her chair by the warming stove.

When Andrew arrived by Mina's side, he was holding a folder. He wasn't letting anything out about what had been said in the suite. She kept her eyes on the household, knowing that her other job was being the eyes that should see the small clues to report back. Andrew pulled out a page from the folder and set it on top of it, then pulled out the special pen he used to take notes with as he walked with Rei. She shifted just enough to glance over and see it was the list the household had given Mizi.

He looked at the household members, then mildly said, "Rei has asked that I get a count of who wishes to have each line item worked on by Mizi from the list Lady Brianna gave her yesterday morning. A raise of hands is sufficient." He looked down at the page in front of him and read off the first line. Mina watched the people in the room for their reactions to each item. From the corner of her eye she watched as Andrew wrote down not a number but the first letter of the person's first name, save Lady Brianna's which would have been the same as for Brian's.

She noted that no one was particularly comfortable to have this being called out openly, but they were sufficiently obedient. She also noted that there were two who never rose their hands. The nurses also didn't, being mostly confused by the request and list. That is, until the final line was read. That received unanimous hands, even two of the nurses, but then she would have raised her hand as well for that one. Mizi really had overdone with the hospital. It was admirable, but unconsidered.

Andrew put his pen away, folded the page, and put it into an inner pocket. "Thank you," he said to the household. He drew in a breath, then said, "Rei apologizes for not speaking plainly enough. He'd already as of the day after Mizi's presentation begun teaching her to maintain a more sane schedule. Having another list of things to do land on her desk in the middle of that made him realize he'd forgotten to make that clear." As Mina was watching them she saw Brianna's face begin to pale.

"He therefore has asked me to make it more clear for him. Please remember to bring such things and questions about the same to me or Mina first for review. We're happy to let you know how they'll both react, and what they need. Because we've been somewhat disconnected, please answer a few questions for me. What was it Mizi asked for when she asked for your help?"

There was silence for a bit in the room until Brianna answered, "When she brought me the list of things she wished to learn, it was to understand how to face the ladies of the court."

Kirk raised his hand to chest height and added, "She's asked that we be more clearly open about things she lacks when facing her staff."

Andrew gave them nods, then waited. When no more answers were forthcoming, he asked, "What has Rei specifically asked for?"

That took them a bit longer, then Brian answered, "That we let Mistress Mizi know when we have a need she's not seeing, and that we show her how to interact with her staff appropriately. ...And that we remind her when she needs to rest. Both have asked for that."

"And have you been doing those things?" Andrew asked mildly, but he'd changed just subtly enough that Mina knew he was now upset with them.

"We've been trying to," Brianna answered for them humbly.

Andrew pursed his lips ever so slightly, then said to the group, "I'll state clearly what they're wishing for. Please from now on, teach as if Mizi is really a student, not someone who already understands. Use your kind words to remind her, but let her make her own decisions. She's promised to be more open with what she's willing to do or not do when you do that. That way you all can learn together.

"Please remember that you are staff, not lords and ladies in this situation. If you can't remove that mantle when in this building or in either of their presences, please consider resigning. They already treat with the lords and ladies the way they wish to." That got more than one face going pale and Brianna's hands clenched just ever so slightly. The lips pursed on the two who potentially hadn't participated in the compilation of the list.

Andrew continued, "Rei wouldn't have had to step in to teach Mizi a better balance of her time and efforts if you'd been answering to the requirement to see she rest when she should, which is why he took it over. Please try to be more aware of that from now on. It isn't uncommon for either of them and we still must watch for it regularly, warning them openly. When he's decided she's learned it well enough from him, he'll more openly let you know she should be ready for testing on it." Even Mina stiffened a little. That would be Rei testing them as much as Mizi. She hoped they all practiced it better with her from now on.

"Lady Brianna," Andrew called for her. She stopped breathing for a moment, then rose to her feet and approached Andrew. He handed her the folder in his hands. "Here are the things they're willing for her to learn. It will be after she arrives back from Kouzanshi, the two of them have confirmed her schedule, and the two of you have had time to meet." Brianna took the folder and curtsied. Andrew excused her and she returned to her chair, looking like she might faint along the way. She likely only remained upright because her spine was ramrod stiff.

Andrew turned to the nurses and excused them to begin their workday. They quietly headed for the cloak wardrobe. "Mizi will come after we've reported to them. She'll be going to the Department of Medicine to continue her work there today. She's asked that Kirk and Leon go with her. The remainder of you are to go to the Rose office."

Andrew turned to Mina to excuse the rest of the household and give her quiet orders. "You're to come up and receive further instructions after they've settled a bit. He wants for you to be able to answer any questions once I'm gone in."

Mina gave him a sharp nod, then put her hand lightly on his arm to hold him in place. Leon had gone over to Brianna. Mina listened closely to hear him apologize to her. She glanced up into Andrew's eyes. He was angry. She gave a nod. "Leon," she called to him as Andrew turned to stand slightly behind her right shoulder now.

Leon turned to face them. "Yes?" he asked.

"Why would you apologize to Brianna?" Mina asked him.

Leon drew in a deep breath and straightened his back and shoulders. "Because I was the one who suggested the list be written, not understanding." He bowed to them and apologized again but to them this time.

"Why would you do that?" Mina asked neutrally.

Leon pondered his answer before giving it to them. "Because I remembered that Mistress Mizi had said she needed more direct instructions than they were trying to teach her with. Because she'd used lists before, I thought having it written would help her be able to understand what they saw lacking and be able to choose from it what she'd wish to work on."

"And how were they trying to teach her before that?" Mina asked.

"By presenting the face they wished to have her answer to." Leon wasn't pleased by that method. Nor were Mina and Andrew since that was exactly what they'd been asked from before by both royals to *not* do.

She was a bit surprised when Andrew asked Leon, "Why did you visit with Mizi right after Lady Brianna presented the list to her?" Several people were surprised that he'd done that, including Brianna herself.

Leon hesitated, then answer a bit sadly, "I didn't know what was on the list, but I was worried. It was dismaying to walk in and see Mistress Mizi so despairing over the list. I encouraged her the best I could. I don't think anyone intended it to be something she'd have to face all at once or even fully, but be something she could choose from and work on as she saw fit. Particularly since the last item was included to hopefully remind her. I'm not sure she saw it that way, though." He was sad by the end of his answer. There were a couple of others who didn't see it the way he did. Either they wanted all of it, eventually, or it was something else.

"Thank you," Andrew said to Leon, since he'd been honest and answered their questions. He turned and walked back up the stairs to return to the suite above.

Mina stayed where she was. Eyes returned to her from watching Andrew. She relaxed slightly on purpose. "If there's anything I can answer to I will," she let them know. No one looked at her right then, so she ignored them, knowing it would take some time and none of them might. There wasn't any pressure to talk to her, but the lesson they'd just given them taught them how the two of them worked so they'd know for the future. Andrew scolded. Mina listened and taught neutrally.

-o-o-o-

Rei held Mizi snugly in his arms, her soft warmth comforting. He was leaning against the wall next to the door to the atrium of their building. He was holding her leaning against him so her head was resting on his chest. He thought he might have grown again. She seemed closer to his solar plexus today than usual. Or maybe it was their angle against the wall. "You can hear well enough?" he asked very quietly. She nodded and turned her head just enough to uncover the other ear and look up into his eyes.

Her green gaze was as brave and trusting as ever, for all she was worried and still a little upset. He thought this would be a reason to have two chairs in this hallway, set against the wall to either side of the door, but he didn't need to sit all the time and then he wouldn't have the excuse to hold her. It was a bit odd to see the arms of his that held her and feel how broad his chest had become. He'd been such a scrawny young thing until about a year ago. Having his father's broad chest suddenly show itself on his own person was surprising and a bit... well it pointed out he could also be vain. He worked hard to suppress the blush at the thought.

He bent down and kissed Mizi on the lips to distract her so she wouldn't notice the blush. Andrew started talking to the household then, so they could both be properly distracted by that. Like he'd been teaching Mizi the finer points of how royals gained information, he'd openly taught her this one before they'd come to this location. One reason to have a Voice was so that the royal could hear things they wouldn't otherwise. And so the Voice could see the reactions that would be hidden if the royal was present.

She'd already learned on her own that it let them see without distraction when they were present. He was rather proud she'd done that one on her own. She usually did learn things like that rather well, which was why he only stepped in when she needed him to. Being able to use opportunities like this when they arose was good, too. He kissed her more as Andrew walked down the list. The room below was silent other than that, so it wasn't going to help either one of them: to hear it yet again. Going through it in detail the once this morning had been more than either one of them could stomach.

When Andrew began talking again after the list was completed, Rei whispered very quietly directly in Mizi's ear how each thing was a couched scold. He was continuing the education Ilena had already been teaching her in the court setting, but this was for small group settings and was how the lords did it for their households. She didn't need to know so she could repeat it. She needed to learn it because he was quite certain they were doing it to her. She needed to become upset with them when they did and do her own scolding. She'd get that connection on her own once she internalized the lesson.

Rei watched Mizi's face as the household answered the question about what Mizi had asked for them to do. She wasn't too happy with the answer Brianna gave, but she didn't say it was wrong. She did agree that Kirk had remembered rightly, but it was what she was most upset about. That they hadn't done as she'd asked and been open with her before then in more gentle ways.

Rei let her know that Brian had worded his answer to what Rei had asked them to do in a way to protect them. It hadn't been exactly right, but because Rei had asked them in the lord's way, there was the leeway for them to claim to have been confused and misunderstood. Which they would've said if he'd been present.

The first statement from Andrew was from Mizi. She nodded when he was done. He'd said what she wanted him to say. The second statement was from Rei and was his clear warning they weren't to walk that path any longer. He'd no longer have any patience with the attitude of lords and ladies in his own house. He was willing to let them go amicably if they couldn't live with it. That had always been his way. For all they'd been doing well enough in the Rose office, sometimes it took this long or longer for the people he tried out to become staff to settle or choose to leave.

He closed his eyes as he listened to the final biting scold. Andrew softened it as best he could, but it was necessary. It had been their responsibility, given to them obviously, and they'd not fulfilled it again so he'd had to take it back. He held her more tightly, not explaining this one to her. They'd already talked about it before they'd left the room. She squeezed him back, her promise again to watch herself better into the future. He sighed a slow breath out his nose. He did know how hard it was to watch that one. Andrew wasn't wrong that even he still needed the regular reminders.

When Andrew began passing out the assignments for the day, Mizi looked up into Rei's face again, a question on her face. He shook his head at her and didn't move. "The questions and answers to them at the end are the most important," he breathed into her ear. She nodded and settled again. Rei was pleased when Mina picked up on something important at the beginning. He also wanted to understand Leon better. He listened closely to Leon's answers. Not being able to see Leon's face meant he'd continue to reserve judgement, but that much went into his calculations.

Shortly after that Andrew opened the door and stepped through it, then closed it behind him. He pulled the list out of his jacket, unfolded it and handed it to Rei. Rei only let go of Mizi with one hand to take it since there still might be things to hear. He scanned down the list of initials on each item, then showed it to Mizi. She scanned down it and then nodded miserably. Almost all of them were from Brian and Brianna. That wasn't surprising at all. Many were from Sam, also not surprising. The only one with everyone's letter wasn't a surprise at all and Mizi slumped her head back onto Rei's chest with that one.

Rei whispered to her, "Because they all watched it, understood it, and yet let it happen, they all must pay that price." She nodded her understanding. What was surprising to him was that Delia's name was on two of them but that Leon and Maria had refused to participate. Rei handed the paper back to Andrew and pointed to their initials, asking the silent question.

Andrew leaned in close and whispered, in a tease for him, "Mizi sympathizers." Rei snorted softly at him and Mizi giggled very softly. Andrew smiled gently at both of them, glad he could lift their spirits even a little. Rei sighed and tried to relax even a little for his aide and best friend. Andrew always worried the most for him at times like this.

They waited as the household either left or settled. Rei stood up on his feet when they heard Mina's footsteps on the stairs. He took Mizi's hand but didn't begin to move until Mina was through the door and it was closed behind her. "Sometimes they'll ask the final question at the last minute," he explained to Mizi in a whisper again. She indicated she understood and they all walked together to Andrew's door. Mina looked at Rei with a raised eyebrow, but he waited until they were inside her and Andrew's room. Quietly he explained, "She kept Leon."

When Andrew and Mina only nodded, Mizi asked, "Why does that matter?"

"Which rooms are everyone in downstairs?" he asked her soberly.

Her brow furrowed. "I guess I don't know," she answered him. He left it at that. She'd go learn it now and learn her next lesson in the process.

Mina asked for the list and pen. She made one note at the bottom, "*Sam - Sasou's tester?*" Since she and Andrew both were Rei's he wasn't surprised she was wondering it.

Rei rubbed his head. He could see it, but it wasn't clear. He closed his eyes. "Likely he was testing Mizi at Ichijou," he answered softly. "I don't know if he'd change loyalties now that he's not where Sasou can watch him. Certainly having that ratio of looking like a supporter might put him there, but," he frowned, not willing to settle that one yet. If he was still loyal to Sasou, part of Sam's job would be to test everyone in the household like Sasou tested anyone who came near Rei. In order for that to be effective, Sam would have to be trusted by the household members enough for them to show him their true loyalties.

He turned to Mizi. "That gets resolved by removing those he's appearing to sympathize with, then seeing if he goes back to being merely supportive of you." Mizi pondered on that resolution, then allowed as how she could see that. "As long as he's testing everyone we might not see it, though. When we've agreed with what he's seeing, he'll settle. If he's turned, then he won't."

Quietly, Andrew then Mina let Rei and Mizi know what they'd observed. It was their usual detailed report, but it was only Mizi's second time to hear it. When they were done and Rei had added the details to his board, he sighed.

When he, Andrew, and Mina finally left the royal suite to head for the Rose office, the others who were waiting to go to the Rose office were gathered again in the sitting area, dressed to brave the weather. Before Rei left the stairs, he let his eyes review those gathered there, keeping his expression the court cool that expressed just the slightest hint of disapproval. "It's good that we'll all be separated for a bit to our various tasks in and out of the castle in a few days. Perhaps that will help everyone by the time we come together again." He continued on down the stairs followed by Andrew and Mina who had paused with him.

As he passed Brianna, she curtsied deeply and humbly. Sam, standing next to Brianna, also bowed humbly the same, neither rising until he and his two aides had passed them. Brian, standing behind the other two also bowed, but stiffly. Rei thought that even if he wasn't released by Mizi, he might be leaving on his own rather soon, if he was allowed to by whomever was giving him his orders. Rei's words had changed their vacation time into probation time. They now understood that he'd be testing them himself when they returned, not just leaving it up to Mizi to decide.

-o-o-o-

Mizi was happy to hunt for the guest in the castle this morning. She'd decided to do that next in order to finish calming down from the first–thing–in–the–morning scolding. She'd received some of her own, not just the household, but Rei had been gentle enough, she supposed. He'd been much more clear than he usually was, perhaps trying to correct his own errors in the whole thing. It was just hard to have the whole debacle interrupt her so horribly.

She sighed to herself and looked up at the sky. She wished it wasn't a grey day today. A little sun would help her so much. She was very much looking forward to her trip to Kouzanshi now. Getting out of the castle walls would help, too.

A light touch came on her elbow halting her forward motion slightly. She turned to see Leon looking at her, his expression hidden behind his scarf and hat. "Mistress Mizi, I'm sorry, but I've orders to appear at the garrison in just over a half–hour, for the duration of one hour. It's been added to my schedule as of yesterday morning. I can see you safely to the Medical department but then should go. I have things to prepare ahead of time." He bowed deeply. "I'm very sorry."

She looked at where they were and realized she'd just turned for the library rather than continue on to see Ilena. She paused, then asked, "For one hour?" He indicated she'd heard it right. "Well, I can go at or after lunch, then," she said, setting that expectation into her schedule so she'd remember it. "For how long is the requirement?"

Leon hesitated, then said, "General Garen has said it will be that schedule until you leave for Kouzanshi. I'm sorry to not have said it before now. I thought he would have received your permission before giving the order."

Mizi wondered a little at that herself. It wasn't normal for anyone to interfere in the affairs of her household like that. "Please find out who did give him the approval when you go today, then," she requested. She'd like to know since, like Rei had asked her to not say yes to anyone but him, she really didn't want her guards to say it to anyone other than her. She didn't think they would have either.

Kirk bowed a bit. "I believe I remember Master Rei telling Sir Sam and Leon to go talk to General Garen yesterday. I can't say if he was the one to give permission for the longer schedule."

Mizi was a little puzzled that Rei wouldn't have told her, but he was as distracted as she'd been with the hospital, so it wasn't out of the realm of possibility he'd forgotten to tell her. "Well, do still ask General Garen, Leon."

"Yes, Mistress Mizi," he said humbly.

Mizi frowned a bit more, then remembered. *Mizi to General Garen.* She waited for the message to be passed, walking them back to the path that would take them to the Royal Aide's building. When she heard his response back she said, *Who is it that gave you permission to have Leon every day?*

After a bit she heard, *I'm sorry if you weren't told, Princess Mizi. It was Prince Rei that decided it. Shall I wave it for today?*

Mizi frowned, then said, *No, but I'll not have a second guard while he's gone. Please send someone to stand in his place at the Medical department until he can be released back to me. Have them meet us at the Lower Office of Intelligence.* That would allow them all to be obedient to Rei. Garen agreed to that requirement which settled her a little. She was wishing very much for some vacation time now. Or at least some quiet time by herself in a safe place. Sadly that wouldn't be the Medical department today since that place held more work for her.

When Mizi was finally settled in her office with her notes and the questions she was working on for Ryan in front of her, she really wasn't able to focus. Ryan had appreciated receiving the official schedule for the year. He was focused on fitting what he needed Mizi to do into that schedule now. She'd asked the substitute guard to stand on the door Leon usually did, but hadn't asked Kirk or Tanner for anything yet.

Instead, she stared out the window, that being all her brain could do this morning. Kirk settled into a more casual stance, resting against her desk. "At my home, when the fire wasn't warm enough to reach me anymore, and there wasn't any sun to relieve the grey, I'd go hide with Julie at her foster parent's home. That's when I got to watch her in the kitchen, and at her other indoor chores," he said.

Mizi turned her head to look at him, not really able to lift the sober tiredness she felt. He looked up into his memories. "I never really understood how she could get the spinning wheel to work. She tried to teach me, but I was quite miserable at getting the pattern of the speed of the turning and the tension of the wool I was holding. She quite laughed herself to gasping and I had to stop so she could breathe again." He smiled at Mizi. "Did you ever have to do that? Learn to spin?"

Mizi shook her head. "No. Because I helped in the inn, I mostly did washing, sweeping, dishes, and eventually some cooking." She paused to think about that, then said, "I was never fond of cleaning the bath rooms. I would whine and complain about that until they promised they'd help with it so we could all wish together that we weren't running an inn." She smiled.

Kirk laughed a sound that helped brighten her day just a little. "I can imagine. I'm sure I haven't been in any inn that's had the customers care so much about the bath rooms, save when they aren't clean because they themselves won't care enough. Then they can certainly complain enough." Mizi nodded her agreement. That had often been the case.

"I've heard Yamanzar is a warm place. Did you ever have to worry about so many cloudy days in a row? Or snow?" Kirk asked.

Mizi shook her head. "We get almost no rain, particularly in the main part of the country. It's mostly desert sands and rock there. The coasts get moisture that rises from the Inner Sea, so there are some trees there. No snow, though." She shivered a little, "The sands hold the heat of the day for a little while, but then the temperatures drop rather quickly. It can get as cold as Kouzanshi in winter at night."

Kirk shivered in sympathetic reaction as well. "Brr. So take my heavy cloak with me even if people look at me strange."

Mizi smiled a small smile at him. "Yes. And the blankets are heavier. More like the Tarc blankets because we also don't have sheep, but even heavier."

"Even heavier than the Tarc blankets?" Kirk found that hard to believe. Mizi nodded firmly. Kirk sighed. "Well, maybe we can all *not* sleep outside in Yamanzar then, or huddle even closer than we would have in Tarc."

Mizi had to give a little giggle at that. "Yes. *Not* sleeping outside would be my preference, as would be staying by the coast. It doesn't get that cold at night. The moisture in the air seems to be what also holds in the heat longer."

Kirk narrowed his eyes at her. "And..., does that mean it's harder to breathe, too?"

"Well...," Mizi averted her eyes for a bit to tease him, then answered, "yes, it is. About like it is in Ichijoutsu, if a bit warmer so harder to breathe."

Kirk did give a longsuffering sigh to that. "Well, if Mistress Mizi could live there and survive, it can't be that bad a place. I mean, you've survived the cold and snow quite admirably for several years now. To be able to live in both places, you're very strong."

Mizi looked into his blue eyes and only saw kindness. "Thank you, Kirk," she said quietly.

He blushed a little and looked away, then said a little sadly, "I'm sorry I didn't help you more in the ways you needed. I'll remember to say things when they need to be said..., to you and to others." He looked back into her eyes as he said the last.

Mizi looked back then gave him a nod. "I'll hold you to it," she said softly.

He looked away again briefly, then rose to his feet. "How many more questions does Ryan want to inflict on you before he tortures the potential interns with them? Or is it you that he's hoping will be the torturer so he doesn't have to be hard on them?" He was looking over the papers on the desk to draw her attention to them.

Mizi waved her hand over them. "I think he said he wanted them to be able to sit agonizing over their papers from sunup to sundown for four days and then walk away hopeless of ever working for any castle in Ryokudo."

Kirk gaped at her, then broke out into a full hearty laugh. She smiled at him. "Oh! You mean he just let you loose without any boundaries at all, and you've not figured out where to stop?" he teased back just as firmly. "Well, we can't have that. Let's start with: just how *long* do they actually need to be sitting at the table. *Then* maybe you can stop writing questions and start getting rid of the completely unnecessary ones. Then you can be done by lunch and hand it all back to him and rest for the rest of the day? Hmm?" he raised an arch eyebrow at her.

Mizi covered a laugh with her hand. "I'm sure it's not *that* bad," she pretended to defend herself. He shook his head at her as if she were hopeless and she slumped and "gave in". "Well, certainly defining a time first might be of help," she agreed. It was easier to face the work after that. She was grateful for his strengthening, and then for his firm requirement she stop for lunch later, and then his reminder she'd wanted to do something after lunch so she didn't forget that, too.

Leon was back by then, so they had a quiet meal together with Ryan. Kirk sat next to Ryan with Leon across from him and next to Mizi. Mizi was just beginning to feel like Leon was a bit stiff and uncomfortable when Kirk moved before she did. "Leon," he said to get his attention. Leon blinked at him. "I'm sorry I've kept my mouth closed this long. I've promised Mistress Mizi I won't anymore. I'll keep Brian in line from now on. He doesn't need to be so prickly all the time. Even I've been uncomfortable with his unkind teasing of you and the others. I've just not known how to scold him while still being the partner he needs."

Kirk paused, then said, "I've been watching Mina, Andrew, and Ore, since Mina teases Ore like that and Ore likes to tease generally. I think I can try some of the things they do; although, I'll have to learn how Brian will take them."

Leon looked at Kirk with some surprise, then a bit bitterly said, "I'd appreciate it, since I don't appreciate the belittling at all ...of me or of Mistress Mizi."

"Me?" she asked, then waved her hand. "Never mind. I don't want to know." They silently agreed with her and let it go without an answer.

Ryan gave them all a sharp–eyed look, then said offhandedly into his bowl. "Trying to have a new family group isn't easy. I couldn't even begin to fit in until Mizi and then Ore came."

Kirk ruffled Ryan's hair. "That's because they were the first ones to let you have the space to fit in." Ryan almost–glared at Kirk, but Kirk only smiled back. "And Ore's the only one who helps you practice relaxing." Kirk put his chin in his hand, resting his elbow on the table casually, and blinked at Ryan. "So I think I'll step into that slot, too. You also get to be a younger brother."

Ryan gaped at Kirk while Mizi laughed. "He does need more of that kind of older brother," she agreed. She was relieved when Leon relaxed a bit more.

It was enough she could turn to him and lightly place her hand over his hand where it was resting on the table. "Leon," she said gently, "thank you for thinking of me and trying to be helpful. Just remember in the future that there may be things in the background you can't see. Taking things to Andrew and Mina first will be best for everyone. Or even Ilena if you can't get them to have any time for you." She wrinkled up her nose. "Even I have a hard time pinning down any of the three of them, and it already sounds like Rei needs that scolding again if he's forgotten to ask me first to have you. I don't like to give up either of you two." She frowned at the Rei she was going to talk to.

It took Leon and to some degree Kirk some time to unfreeze. Kirk was first, a bit of panic on his face, "Has he told you that he's chosen to test me as a second Messenger? I'll be gone at least twice as long as you'll be, leaving at the same time. I'm to take the messages to the garrisons Ore won't be going to, returning by way of Kouzanshi and North road."

Mizi's mouth dropped open and she blinked, then almost had to dash a tear away. With a scowl, she said, "He most definitely needs a scolding to leave me out of this many plans of his!" An evening return scolding would surprise him, but now he very much was due one. All three young men at the table looked away from her face, not wanting that scolding or any part of it directed at them.

"Well," Kirk finally said, "I do hope you'll forgive him for his own distracted winter brain eventually. I'm sorry to tell you so suddenly and late." Mizi snorted a soft breath at him, but did relent somewhat eventually.

-o-o-o-

After lunch, Mizi took Kirk and Leon with her to go talk to Airn. Leon asked Ilena's Family network on the air where they could find him. She was relieved he was in the library. Curious, Mizi asked the network what Airn's usual daily schedule was since he'd come to the castle. They informed her that the first half of his mornings were spent exploring the castle and talking to those who had time to answer his questions. He then went to the garrison and practiced on the list. He stayed there for lunch, then went to the library for the afternoons to work on his studies. He'd discovered where the young lords had dinner and typically ate with them since then. Before then he'd eaten a few times with the servants, also asking them questions.

Mizi smiled to herself. Airn had at least been following Rei's instructions to not only be with one class or type of people. She wasn't surprised he'd gravitated to those he could understand best and not feel completely out of place, though. When they'd entered the library, Kirk bowed slightly to her and asked, "Will we be here for longer than a few minutes?"

"Yes, I'd expect at least a half an hour," she said.

Kirk stepped behind her and said, "Then let me take and carry your cloak. It's not healthy to wear it the whole time." She let him take it off and took off the rest of her winter gear to hand that over, too. Leon had also shed his in that time, then held Mizi's things while Kirk followed suite.

When Kirk would've taken Leon's burden back, Leon shook his head. "At least one of us must be able to get to his sword. I'll put these where we can watch them when we get there so both of our hands are free." Kirk agreed. Mizi smiled to watch them fuss over her, even though that was their job and why she appreciated having them with her. Leon looked at her in time to catch the smile and blushed. She just turned and led them into the library to let him recover. Behind her Kirk shoved Leon and Leon growled back, but Mizi knew it was to help Leon.

Mizi found Airn's aide first, sitting at a table with cloaks on chairs and books, papers, pens, and ink pots strewn on the table. "Sir Erlic, welcome to Nijou," she said quietly for the sake of all the studying students in the room.

His head came up from reading the book in his hands. He rose and bowed to her. "Thank you, Princess Mizi. It's been a joy to have a willing student finally." His eyes twinkled at her.

"I'm sure it is," she smiled back at him. "What's been his choice of studies here at the beginning?"

"Actually, you four young royals and what you've done in the short amount of time you've been active in the politics of the nation," he said a little dryly. Then he teased, "Thus necessitating quite a lot of history studies of the nations outside Altherly, a topic I couldn't interest him in at all before now."

Mizi was delighted and let her eyes sparkle back. "That's a very good start, then. Were his studies of Altherly's history sufficient before he left? I'm afraid our library will be woefully inadequate for that study."

"It was sufficient so that when he returns he'll only need to review the significant details to fit them into his new understanding of why such things are necessary," Erlic was pleased to report.

"Wonderful. If I may, I'll test him a bit on that. We've just learned some new things from our teachers, Rei and I, that he should probably also learn for the sake of his own nation." She mused on what else she might have him study on his own.

"Ah, if I may ask, who are your teachers?" Erlic asked, curious.

"Ilena and Sasou," Mizi said. Erlic blinked then bowed his head in thanks for the answer. Mizi shrugged a little. "When the royals are the most intelligent people in the nation, and the older ones wish to see the younger ones able to rule wisely, it's best to let them do it if they have the time." She frowned at Erlic. "The lords can have too much of an influence to sway the royals away from what's best for the people as a whole if they have greedy designs."

Erlic blinked at her, then bowed. "And will you be able to remember that, Prince Airn?"

Airn stepped two more steps to come past Mizi and bow as an equal to her. "Princess Mizi. It's a pleasure to greet you again."

Mizi curtsied to him, also as an equal. "My pleasure as well. Welcome to Nijou. I'm terribly sorry to have had to make you wait to be greeted."

"Not at all," Airn forgave it quickly. "It's been warm and far less boring than being snowbound in a garrison." He smiled a court smile that Mizi returned. "I could certainly wait until you were no longer in the middle of preparing for and then presenting to the body of Ministers. Your hope for sponsoring a new hospital is admirable, and the meeting generally was educational." He paused, then said a little hesitantly, "It's still hard to believe that Gael has actually refused peace since I've left."

Mizi sighed a little sadly for his sake. "I'm certain that is quite difficult to believe. One never wishes to have such terrible times come to their own home. However both our spies and the King's witness is that it's so. You were sent by your father, using quiet and perhaps desperate means, to our courts so that we could see to your safety. King Sasou confirmed it to us five weeks ago." She waited politely for him to come to some level of sorrowful acceptance of the news. "We'll do our best to help as we can in Altherly. We do want to help you to become what you were born to become. We'll hope to keep you distracted with important things until you can be called back home.

"I hear you have many questions. Are there any I can answer for you today? I've not got a lot of time, but I can answer what I do have time for." She turned for one of the chairs not currently full or occupied by books. Leon pulled it out for her so she could sit. Airn sat as well once she was seated. Mizi saw Airn's guard then and welcomed Ian to Nijou as well. He bowed, but remained standing, like Leon and Kirk were. Mizi would rather have the three sit, but already knew from her lessons they wouldn't. She was relieved when Erlic did sit down again. Then she could focus on Airn.

"I must admit," Airn began to answer her question, "my first curiosity to quench was if the four of you who'd surprised me for that brief meeting were really the royals of Ryokudo. It seemed such a fanciful thing after there'd been time to sleep on it." Mizi smiled. Airn shook his head. "Everyone in the castle I talked to confirmed it, and it was obvious in the Court of Ministers, to see all four of you there. It's still very hard to imagine it, though. I'm very much used to having my father and oldest brother in those positions. You're all much younger than they are, like me."

"I suppose that would be true," she answered. "Even in Ichijou you'll find that to be true. The oldest people there are the ministers. King Sasou isn't much older than Ore and Andrew. It comes from them losing their father when Rei was only three. Queen Kata ruled until Sasou was able to sit the throne in Ichijou. She held the Regent's throne after that until Rei could be sent. We're all relieved he was capable enough to take it when he did." She put her piercing look on and stared at him in the eyes. "Because we understand that even youth may need to rule, and do it as wisely as possible, is why we want to see you strengthened as much as we can. If things go badly, you may also be in our position unexpectedly, having to sit a throne before you believe you're ready."

Airn slumped slightly and looked away pensively. "Yes, I've had those thoughts at night since the court lesson." He looked back. "Would it really be possible?"

"With enough support from your teachers and your countrymen, yes," Mizi replied firmly. "However, that was the one thought I had that I wanted to make sure you understood. You must know if Altherly's lords support your family in their place. If they desire to have anyone of your family on the throne, they'll recall you happily. If they don't, they won't welcome you back kindly if your father and brother should fall, but the nation stay sovereign against Gael. They'll want to put their own king on the throne. If you don't know, you need to learn it, then decide how much you'll want to fight to return to that throne. If they don't put someone on it who'll support the people and peace for the country, it might be that you should fight with your people to regain the throne. It would be wise to be prepared for either circumstance." Erlic nodded wisely in agreement.

Mizi let Airn think that through for a while. His brow was furrowed with concern. He finally looked between Mizi and Erlic. "How would I find out? That's not going to be in the library here, and I don't think it wise to return home just yet, since Father hasn't recalled me." Erlic let Airn know he was thinking rightly, but didn't say anything yet. Airn's eyes went to Mizi.

She let him think about it for a bit longer, then softly said, "If you trust Sir Erlic to truly be on the side of your father and family, you can start with asking him what he knows. Sir Ian likely also can answer you to some degree. That would help you begin to know who to be asking deeper questions about." Airn glanced at Erlic just a little uncomfortably but Erlic was still sitting passively, letting Airn learn this lesson.

"Once you have some names, you can take them to Ilena. While her spies in Altherly are few, she can get the information you request. She'll make you pay wages eventually if you ask for so much that her office must devote hours to research instead of occasional moments here and there. It certainly wouldn't be wrong to ask for a summary report of what her Ministry knows about the lords, though. You'll only be letting her know you're working on your lessons to ask for that." She stopped and waited, seeing if that helped him think of other options.

Airn considered that with a frown, then finally looked into her eyes again. His expression was guarded now. "Is it possible to trust Ryokudo?"

Mizi shrugged slightly. "If King Sasou or Rei were interested in expansion, they'd already be preparing to march into Selicia. They now have the last remaining royal of the previous regime in hand, and a vendetta against the current king. Before Selicia strengthens itself from getting rid of the spies that kept them unbalanced would be the best time to enter. They're not and they won't. It's enough to keep ourselves continuing forward in peace and prosperity as much as possible. I believe King Sasou has agreed to help your father only because Gael also threatens Ryokudo's peace."

Mizi shifted in her chair to lean back a little, resting her back. She lightly clasped her hands in her lap. "No one knows the far future, and the near future can only be guessed at and hoped for." She lifted her eyes to look directly into Airn's eyes. "We haven't put you into prison, nor killed you, nor demanded a ransom. We're trying to teach you what you need to know to be the prince you can and should be in Altherly. If you can use that much to trust us for now, that's perhaps the best you can hope for."

Airn slumped just a little, then gave a nod that he'd understood. "If I wanted to correspond with my father, could letters be sent?"

"Since Ilena did before, I'd think so," Mizi said. "Her courier service is very secure, and she tries to have it be fast service as well. You could have a paige take any letter to her office and she'd send it for you, I'd think. Or you could have it sent to the courier office of the castle."

"Thank you," Airn said. He sat in thought a little longer, then changed the topic. "Why have King Sasou and Prince Rei allowed for a known nightwalker Head to become a royal? Isn't that putting themselves into a difficult position?"

Mizi tipped her head to the side as she thought about that. It was true that there were going to be, if not already were, lords who wouldn't be able to stomach that. "I don't know," she answered finally. "It isn't at all unusual in Ryokudo for the royals to know exactly what's going on in the nightwalker world and to affect it rather severely as needed. You're right that it's not typically a spoken thing, nor put in the faces of those who'd rather not think of those kinds of people. However, Rei has officially stated that Ilena's been his Head of Intelligence since they were both much younger.

"She'd been kept in hiding inside the worst Head's House while working to undermine it for King Sasou's sake. While there she built up her spy networks. To the royals of Ryokudo she isn't a nightwalker Head. She's the Suiran Minister of Intelligence and has been working to get there for many years." She blinked at Airn. "That's used as a check against the lords who think they can get away with their own evil deeds in the dark behind the royals' backs. We've yet to see how the lords in Ichijou will take it, though. They might face it differently than the Suiran court has."

"How do the people see it?" Erlic asked.

Mizi smiled slightly. "Those who know her love her, both the nightwalkers and those who live lawfully. Those who don't know her apparently love me, and she protects me, so between us we keep the whole of Suiran happy enough." She shrugged, "That's a generalization, of course. I'm sure there are people you could talk to that don't like either of us." She tried not to think of all the young ladies and young lords of the court that scorned her and Ilena. They hadn't been asked about.

Airn frowned suddenly. "Two questions come from that. Why have you only said for you and Princess Ilena, not for Princes Rei and Ore? And," he turned to

Erlic, "can I, or should I also have my own person who can gather intelligence for me?"

Erlic bowed his head to Mizi, asking her to answer first. Mizi pondered it wondering herself for a moment, then she said, "Of course they know or don't know, love or don't love Rei and Ore. But I think a people's loyalty can be told much more easily by how they feel about the princesses. A king or prince is going to have those who set themselves against them regardless. If an argument comes up in the court, if a new law is set into place someone doesn't want to have to obey: emotional ties that might have been in the past are replaced by irritations of the present or future. Princesses don't have to have that distance from the hearts of the people, nor are they going to set policy and law, unless like Queen Mother Kata they have to sit the throne."

"Ah," Airn sat back and nodded. "That makes sense." He turned to Erlic.

Erlic blinked back at him. "Do you want to have them?"

Airn's brow wrinkled. "I think I should."

"Why would you?" Erlic asked. Mizi watched as Erlic treated Airn the same way Ilena treated Mizi and Rei. She wasn't too surprised to see it again in this setting.

Airn looked away into his thoughts, then said, "If I have someone who can get the information I need to have, whom I trust, then I won't be surprised or as uncertain as I feel now." He scowled a little, "And I would've known why Father wasn't available to talk to me. He could've at least told me *that* much." He scowled at Erlic in lieu of his father. "Why didn't he?"

Erlic sighed a little. "Because you weren't mature enough to tell, based on your behavior in the castle. I did disagree with him, that it would have been better to have tested you by letting you know. I believe he was feeling too distracted by it all to drag you into it as well."

"And he didn't delegate it to Owen why?" Airn wasn't satisfied sufficiently by that answer.

Erlic shook his head. "I don't know," he answered softly.

Airn blew out an irritated breath of air, but that was all in the past and the answers in the minds of people he couldn't go ask. He turned back to Mizi. "I think you've given me a lot of things to think about. I don't want to keep you longer than you have time for. Thank you for coming to visit with me."

Mizi rose to her feet. "I'll be leaving on travel shortly and won't be back for several weeks. When I return, I'll come find you again."

Airn rose to his feet and bowed to her as she curtsied. "I'll look forward to it. Safe travels."

"Thank you," Mizi smiled and left to head for the outdoors again.

"How old is he?" Kirk asked as he helped her into her cloak at the door.

"I think sixteen," she answered.

"Ah, yes, he does still need to do some growing up, then," Kirk commented. "If they didn't tell him, they had reasons. That's not something to keep quiet about to family."

"Yes," Mizi agreed quietly. "It does make me wonder what life is like in their castle, though. Perhaps they've generally coddled him too much until now."

"That could be," Kirk mused.

"At sixteen, Rei was already running several regions of the country and all of the northern garrison business," Mizi said somewhat dismissively of Airn and proudly of Rei.

Kirk chuckled a little. "It wasn't possible to coddle him. There already weren't enough people to do the work." Leon was in complete agreement.

Mizi, however, pondered on that then said, "No, that's not it. King Sasou and Queen Kata already knew what they wanted him to do, probably from either his birth or at least the death of his father. They didn't waste time nor let him waste it either. They did let him run from the castle when he needed to, but the more serious he became the more work they let him have to learn from. It's the approach of the generation before that sets the importance of learning the skills on the next generation. If strengthening responsibilities are withheld they aren't prepared, and it's the king's own fault."

She sighed and slumped just slightly. "Thus why too many of the kings around us are failing in their own duties to their families. He's not wrong to be upset they didn't tell him, nor give him more trust from the beginning. I hope he can fix that for himself, now." Kirk lightly put his hand on her shoulder until she could let that go and move on to her next responsibility for the day.

-o-o-o-

Rei blinked and drew in a silent long breath. Mizi's hands were on her hips and her scowl was rather fierce. She'd not scolded him this badly in some time. He was trying to calm his heart enough he could listen to the important words — which was all of them since she usually didn't say more than was necessary.

"I realize that you're trying to help, but to not include me in the planning to the point of forgetting to tell me who you were going to do what with in our evening meetings is going too far." She drew in a breath to halt the words flowing out of her mouth, her lips pursing at the end of that. "Keeping your mouth closed on *everything* to *everyone* when you have secrets to hold on to isn't the right way to live. Set the secrets down in the office that *really* are secrets and remember to talk to me about what needs to be talked about." She followed her requirement with the scowl again.

Rei breathed carefully again and considered her words. She wasn't wrong to be upset that he'd planned to use her people completely without her consent. He'd only told her he'd figure out how to test them, then not said anything since then to her. "I'm sorry to not properly communicate with you," he said humbly. She relaxed slightly but still waited on him.

He considered the other part of her requirement, then slumped inside just a little. "And I'll try better to remember to leave work in the office and enjoy coming home to you in the evening to rest." It was true that he'd been so focused on all the problems troubling him that even their evening meetings had been brief and nearly non–existent. His lips had been too tightly sealed generally.

"Thank you," Mizi said, still a little stiff with her anger, but it was better.

Staying humble, Rei explained, "I've been watching Kirk in the office. He's like Ore. He needs activity. I need a Messenger who isn't Ore. It's a lot harder to send another prince out in that role and Ilena's keeping him very busy regardless. I'd like to test Kirk, to see if he could do it. He seems to be interested in it as well.

Would it be okay if I sent him on the routes you and Ore won't be going on this time?"

Mizi drew in a breath to switch from scolding to considering the request. "It will be hard for me to have him gone even longer than I'll be gone, but for this time I can see why it was a practical time for it." She frowned and admitted, "He's one I'd rather not have gone from my side for very long generally."

Rei nodded. Softly he said, "I do know that. However most of the time when I send them out for that it's not for this long. The winter weather is what makes it so long this time." He pondered on it, then said, "I can try to keep most of my need for him to the other times of the year and use garrison messengers when I can in the winter. You know why that's not enough this time." He looked into her eyes until she indicated she did understand. Since he'd still used Ore as his Messenger before Ilena had come, Mizi did already know how long it took on average.

Rei reached out his hand for hers. She lifted her hand and he only took her fingertips in his, then led her to the desk. There he pulled out a piece of paper and the ink and pen. He wrote, "*I'm sending Sam and Leon after you, but don't want the rest of the staff to know that's what they're doing. Their requirement at the garrison until you go is to distract those watching them from understanding my true actions. They're to be your and Ore's backup if you're ambushed. It's more likely to happen on the way back than the way out, but I don't want them far from you.*"

He looked up into Mizi's eyes. She'd been reading as he'd been writing so there was only a small delay before her green eyes were looking searchingly into his blue ones. She relaxed and nodded her acceptance of his reason for Leon's schedule change. Likely learning it was Sam's as well was new, but for that reason she wasn't going to get mad again.

"I've allowed Brian to go with Kirk for the first few days, so he can have vacation time away from the castle. He'll only be gone maybe five days, then help in the Rose office." As she nodded, he turned to the paper again. "*The evidence is most strongly against him as being the mole. I'm using it as an opportunity to let him contact any of the people he's an informant to. Ilena's people will be tracking him and what he says to whom while he's out.*"

Mizi slumped and sighed but wasn't very surprised. He wasn't surprised she wasn't. She'd already been struggling with Brian and his unwillingness to let her be her own self in her own home. Rei paused, then wrote, "*I haven't decided whether to keep him on and feed him information or not. Please consider it and let me know if you have a preference when you return from Kouzanshi.*" She gave him a nod. She seemed happier with that way of going about it than him just deciding, but he knew now she would prefer that. Making the decision together would perhaps help both of them.

He considered her for a little while, then wrote, "*Do you want to make the decision on whether Brianna stays or not?*"

Mizi's countenance fell into sorrow again, like it did every time she thought about Brianna now. She reached for the pen and he handed it over. "*If I did release her, would you keep her on in the Rose office? She's very good there, it seems to me, and it gives her something to do.*"

Rei hesitated then took the pen back. "*Possibly. There are reasons to keep her on and reasons to let her go.*" He tapped his finger on the pen, then wrote, "*I may begin to put pressure on Aiden to propose to her. That way he can't continue to hide behind her and I can choose to let her go with gratitude for her help during the time we needed it most. I'd like to keep her protected from the other lords who want her for her dowry. She's actually in a rather critical position for me as far as that goes. I need to keep her close just for that reason.*" He'd done enough research now to understand just how critical that part was. He suspected the anti-Touka faction lords were putting more pressure on her than they should be by threatening her for her financial and landed position.

At Mizi's wide eyes, he sighed in frustration and shook his head. "*It's only the germ of a thought for now. A need in the future that's on the board. I need to protect her to some level, but I don't have enough information yet to do it right.*" He appreciated her sympathetic pat on his arm.

Mizi took the pen again. "*So for now keeping her in the household protects her until you know?*" Rei nodded. "I think I told you that I've given Brianna the next weeks off to visit her home while I'm gone," she looked at him with a raised eyebrow.

"Yes," he confirmed for her.

"Maybe that will help enough for us both to know what to do," she said. Rei pulled her into a one–armed hug and kissed her on the side of her head. It was hard for all of them, this learning to become a household. Eventually it would calm down into its patterns.

-o-o-o-

The first City Council meeting of the year with the Regent was rather full of guests. Ilena was there with those of her staff who needed to be there. Balar and Jamison were also there. Representatives from the other construction companies of the city were as well. Ilena was called forward to speak first.

"Regent Rei asked last month that city renovation feasibility studies be requested from the construction companies of Nijoushi. Those studies have been requested, with a submission due date of the end of this month to the Office of the Regent and each member of the city council for review and comment. The Office of the Regent will get their comments to the studies returned to the construction companies and the council members as soon as possible thereafter."

Ilena drew in a breath and moved to the day's specific topic. "As regards the south side of the city in general, it's been determined that the sad state of repairs of the buildings in that area are a hazard to the livelihood of those who live there, and to the city as a whole should a fire break out in that district. Such a fire could set that whole quarter of the city to blazing and much of the rest of the city as a result. Thus a contractor has been hired to remove those buildings that are unoccupied and too decrepit to truly be housing for man or business alike.

"In the personal review of that district by the Regent's representative, it was also dismaying to learn that the south wall and the areas directly around it are in a similar state of disrepair. Any flame on either side of the wall would just as likely jump it and continue on. Any war coming to this area and siege to the city would find that part of the wall very vulnerable. All the enemy would have to do is set the buildings on the outside of the wall to burning and the wall would crumble and allow the fire to continue on into the city.

"Thus, a proposal for reconstruction of that wall has been requested, both one for simple repairs and one for adding a new wall that continues the west and east sides but which is placed far enough south to protect those businesses that were added outside the wall after the city became peaceful and prosperous enough to necessitate building outside of it. The Regent's office was pleased to learn of a new 'liquid stone' that could be used to merely repair the old southern wall so that it can stand firm again. The Court of Ministers has voted that option be the one considered as the most cost effective but useful option."

Ilena waved towards Jamison. "Mister Jamison will present that proposal to us today."

Jamison moved to stand in front of the council to the front side of the throne dais. He summarized the costs for each proposal, then made his recommendation for adding the new wall and removing the old wall. One of the council members proposed possibly making repairs of the most damaged parts of the wall and keep it as a fall-back defense in the event of a breach of the new southernmost wall. Jamison was able to give them an estimate of adding that to the proposal.

There was some debate on the issue for a while, not only on which proposal of the project they'd select, but on who was responsible for paying for the project. For those council members who didn't want their favored projects' pots dipped into, they argued that it was the throne's responsibility to see to the protection of the citizens. Ilena reminded the council that the ministers had only approved sufficient to repair the wall.

Rei further argued through Ilena, "In requesting this proposal, the Regent is seeing to the protection of the citizens, being very concerned about it since the wall is the main line of defense should war come. However, the costs can't be borne by the throne alone, nor is it considered a fair thing to have the whole of the Region pay for it. It's suggested that a city tax be levied to help pay for a loan if additional work is done. In this way the payment for the work to be completed can happen over a longer period of time that wouldn't be as grievous to the citizens as a shorter–term required payment from the city, particularly as we wish at this same time to begin renovations to the city as a whole."

That led to an intense round of arguments. The council really wanted to have the new wall built farther south. There were a few merchants present who stood up to protest the new wall as their businesses required more direct access to suppliers. Being inside the wall would be an inconvenience.

The council members that wanted them protected pointed out that the businesses outside the wall could move back inside the wall for protection with the room that would be made available to them from the desconstruction of the old buildings. When that wasn't sufficient to sway them, Ilena asked the businessmen if it would be sufficient to make the roads in that area more broad so that wagons of goods could more easily bring the products into and out of the city, and requiring the gates in the south to be similarly wider than in other parts of the city wall. After some consideration, it was tentatively agreed that might be sufficient.

That settled most voices, so the vote was called for. The council agreed to the loan option, and the simple repair to the wall that the regional ministers were willing to help fund, but left it open for requesting an expansion of the wall to the south after they saw what the renovation in that district did. If there wasn't enough room in the end to allow the businesses to move back inside the wall, they'd bring that option back up again. After the vote was finalized, Ilena excused Jamison and called up Balar to have him give a summary of the deconstruction plan.

The following questions from the city council ended up with them requesting that Balar be the one responsible to find the owners of each building to inform them of the intent to destroy or reconstruct, with a lead time of at least two or three months if they were occupied so that people could find alternate housing. There was debate over where the people who lived in buildings that really did need removal or reconstruction would go. In the end it was recommended that a set of apartments be built first to be temporary housing. The council also decided that the city would sponsor lower–interest loans for those persons who would have to pay for their homes or businesses to be renovated or rebuilt.

The council pushed for a stipend to be paid to the homeowner if they had to move since the throne and city were requiring them to move. The Regent and his staff argued that it would be like the city or throne was purchasing the home and land from them. That wasn't so pleasant a thought, since the council did like the city being owned by the citizens. It was enough to table that request. The rest of the business of the council before the throne was abbreviated due to time and the prevailing atmosphere of too much money already having been spent for that day.

Ilena sighed as she walked out of the meeting. "That was a normal meeting, yes?" she asked Rei. He wrinkled his nose at her and nodded. That meant she'd learned just who were the most reluctant to let anything useful happen, now that she had practice in seeing it. She set her Nijoushi spies to learning as much about those council members and their family history as possible. She had Leah add their names to the slowly growing list of potential nobles and families set against Touka generally. "Maybe we could find and groom younger members of those families who are more interested in seeing proper change happen than in holding on to ancient grudges," she moped to Rei before they parted.

Rei glanced at her, then answered quietly, "I wish we could. Even a few would be better than where we are now." Ilena agreed wholeheartedly. He gave her an almost mean glare. "I would think between your office's research and Mizi's, you'd already have that list to hand to me in a few days?" Ilena froze then gave him a dark look, but she agreed. Having those persons in the castle for direct training by Touka sooner than later was better.

-o-o-o-

Ilena watched the Falcon Studios council members and their many assistants walk out of the conference room in Balar's office building. She really did enjoy working with them all. She was also grateful that they were willing to put up with her as she tried to help them and herself and all of Suiran (and Ryokudo on the side). The meetings were always a good lesson for her on what worked at a negotiating table and what didn't, whether she understood each person's motivations yet or not, and on how people changed little by little as the world around them changed. It had been another good meeting for all of that.

Balar turned to her when they were the last two in the room (plus her guards). "What's your preferred solution on the old wall?" Ilena asked him.

Balar sighed and sat back down in his chair. "I'd have complained more if it weren't for your suggestion to make the streets wider down there. Having the products arrive expeditiously is sometimes critical. It's one of the reasons I wanted to put the warehouse down there to begin with. I'm just as happy to be inside the wall regardless."

"Thank you for being willing to keep your warehouse as the anchor," Ilena said humbly.

Balar grimaced at her, but nodded a curt "you're welcome". "Not like it's an anchor so much as a protecting wall itself." He glared at her, "But if your drunk nightwalkers come make a mess of it, I'll move it again."

Ilena blinked at him, then said, "That would be why I'll be putting the buffer between them." She leaned over to pull the map where they could both see it better and picked up the wax pencil resting on top of it. She'd brought the map this time. It was already marked up with notes of where the Studio heads and assistants wanted their new buildings.

"Here's the section I'm buying up to keep the lists protected." She drew a rough rectangle that Balar knew contained the lists. She drew ovals around the streets to either side of the main Crafter's Mall strip. "These sections, roughly, I'll be buying and building living districts for the Studio employees in the northern two-thirds, and Family in the southern third." She drew a light line at that third level. "I'll get this map back to you on our way back to the castle from Falcon's Hollow after the foaling. I want to specify exactly what goes where as far as apartments, grocery stores, and restaurants, etc., so you can give me estimates for each building. Once I have that I can go sell them to the people I have in mind."

She sat back and folded her hands in her lap. "I do expect that the apartments will fill with other city-folk, not just mine, but it will be enough. There'll be a few houses mixed in here and there, and I'd think the rest of the streets beyond those will be mostly houses, but that can be part of the revitalization proposal I'll put out when Rei's approved it. I'm thinking that maybe the main street of Crafter's Mall should also be wider to accommodate the higher foot and wagon traffic we'd like to see there, not to mention parking of those wagons while allowing other wagons to pass. So maybe a minimum of five wagon width's for that street. Then at least three on the other side for deliveries. That will be another buffer since any thieving nightwalkers will be more visible to city guards walking those streets." Balar nodded thoughtfully.

"We should choose carefully what the actual anchor at the far end of that section should be. It could be just that the road narrows to the three wagon width's of normal market ways and we continue the businesses on down." Without drawing on the map, she pointed to a place off center in the middle of the first rectangle she'd drawn. "The lists are actually here, so that the main market traffic isn't directed straight to them, but they're still easily accessible." She pointed along a short section of the next road south from that rectangle. "If you put your warehouse somewhere on this road, on the north side, then begin the wider roads and the rest of the updated warehousing south of that, you'll be joined rather quickly by companies moving out of facilities that need to be demolished."

Balar rubbed his chin. "So..., focus on that section while I'm waiting for your final notes to this one and make them the main part of the revitalization proposal beginning?"

"Yes," Ilena said. "If there's already people willing to buy in an area, and people willing to move in, it becomes a place that work can start." She looked him in the eye. "And you can pass this concept on to the other construction companies. If any of them can find buyers in any sections other than this one by the time their feasibility studies are to the castle, it's that much faster we can get final approval and get the revitalization started. If they think they can find the money within their own companies to buy up sections of land to build on, and then sell after the new buildings are in, that's something to get the push going."

"Can I make them pay to tear down things in those areas, then?" he half–jokingly asked.

"Of course," Ilena answered immediately. "And if they'll only pay their own to tear down, that's fine, too. There's a lot of that to be doing at the moment." Balar understood.

Balar rubbed his head. "You know, it's going to take a whole team of people to do the research to find out who owns what building down there, contact them, and make sure the communication's happening right."

"And you should keep track of what properties trade hands in the mean–time, too. I'm not the only one who's going to buy up properties while they're cheap," she agreed. "Find three or four realtors that work that district and have them team up. They'll love the additional income the sales will bring in since they've been starving, too. They'll not only know or find out who owns the properties for you, they'll be more than happy to bring in new residents to bring the property values up. Delegate it to them and they'll hire the more they need to keep track of the details."

"That's a useful idea," Balar was pleased with the suggestion. He made another note on the sheet of paper he'd already been putting notes on. This one to put up notices on the boards all over the south side to have all realtors of the area meet him in his office for a group meeting. It would be easier to tell them all at once what was coming up and get them on board. If they knew ahead of time what properties were wanted, they'd focus on those first as well.

"Henry," Ilena waved him over. Henry looked over Balar's shoulder, then took the pen and added the names of three people to the sheet of paper.

"These are the realtors that are selling the properties she's looking to buy." Henry pointed to one. "This is the one who sold the properties where we're putting the lists." He looked into Balar's eyes and handed the pen back. "Just so you know." He returned to the wall.

Balar made small notes next to those names and returned to focus on Ilena again. After inspecting her for a bit he said, "I hope that we can keep the rumors of war coming to Nijoushi as just that: rumors." Ilena couldn't say. Balar slumped a little. "Well, I hope you'll sleep in while you're down there and let some of this go for even a little bit. Rest is good, too."

Ilena slumped a little, but gave a nod. "Ore's good about making me let my brain rest, for all it's hard to get it to shut up sometimes when it gets this full."

"That's good," Balar was firmly in agreement that it was a necessity. He'd already needed it himself more than once. This was such a big project and it was only one of the big projects on *her* plate since she was helping hold up Rei. She was good at delegating and reminding others to delegate, though, so he hoped she wasn't going to collapse before it was done. "Where is he, by the way?" he asked, referencing Ore.

Ilena rose to her feet and smiled at Balar. "Master Rei called him back into the Rose office to help there again. He really hates being chained to that desk, except he's where he can see his master and tease him when it gets bad for the both of them." She bundled up for the cold snowy day in ratty nightwalker clothing as she talked. "I'm glad winters here are nicer than in Kouzanshi. My last winter there with him, Pakyo firmly declared he'd never go in winter again." She laughed as Balar smiled. "So he sent me instead." They both shook their heads. "The Kouzanshi 'Pakyo' already knew how to live those winters with patience: indoors with a fireplace and runners to do the outdoor work. I had it easy then."

She gave Balar a hug and headed out the door with the disguised Twins. They were met by two thugs who stepped up to block her way. She blinked at them. "Ready to run a bit?" She was looking forward to watching Henry and Marcus train Petroi and Thayne. Running the roofs would be good exercise, and watching how they talked people into doing things for her would be fun. Plus she could get some of her own work done, too.

Ilena wanted to make sure the soup kitchen project she'd put Leah in charge of was working smoothly. The castle kitchen and city restaurants had plenty of leftovers they'd been encouraged to send to feed those nightwalkers of the south side who were starving otherwise. Leah was in charge of organizing the Family for these sorts of projects generally. It made her happy to have something useful to do that wasn't just rewriting reports. Particularly because she only had to organize it and then order people to do things, all things she could do without leaving the warmth of the Lower office. Ilena was happy to be the person who checked on the progress in person on occasion. She also wanted to sit and listen to another two or three of the safe houses to get to know the people in them. They could join in one of the lines for their own lunch and listen in the safe house while eating. That would do both things at once.

17 Ante-Cold Solstice: First Day on the Road to Kouzanshi

On the day Mizi and Ore were to leave for Kouzanshi, Ore turned from fetching his cloak from the common room of their suite to see Ilena walk out of their room heavily covered head to foot in thick warm clothing. He knew she was wearing the usual clothing underneath, since she'd put them on that morning. She had a round hat with a flat top all made of fur on her head with flaps that covered her cheeks and ears. It had strings hanging from the flaps so it could be tied under the chin.

Over the brown uniform of the Suiran Ministry of Intelligence was a thick quilted coat with fancy embroidery on the shoulders. It looked like the fur was on the inside as fur peeked out from the collar, cuff, and hem of the coat. She had heavy gloves on her hands and a scarf around her neck, although the collar of the coat was high. On her legs was another layer of leather leggings over her pants and on her feet were sturdy boots that looked large enough to have three or four layers of socks under them. He tipped his head sideways as he looked at her. "Can you really move in all that?"

Ilena smiled at him. "This is the standard winter gear of Tarc. Even though they don't get snow as deep as here, the winter wind is very harsh and cold. I can move, and I'll be very warm and protected while we're outside. I'll really wear it for the foaling, though. The ride will be short in comparison, but I may as well wear it there as try to pack it."

Ore knew better at that point than to bring up the possibility of a carriage taking her to Falcon's Hollow for the foaling. His wife loved to ride horseback almost more than she loved him, and just slightly more than she loved competing in the knife fighting ring. "But do you have warm clothes for Third and Fourth Sons?"

There was a tap at the outer door to the courtyard of the Lower office of the Ministry and they braced themselves. It opened and the frigid air of the northern mountains of Suiran swirled in the room with the just–mentioned pair. "We're good, Father. No worries. If Mistress Seraphina makes one set, she makes them all." Marcus reassured Ore. It was true that both men were dressed similarly to Ilena, coming in from having gone to fetch and ready their horses for the trip to Kouzanshi.

"Hoh? Where's mine then?" Ore asked, raising an eyebrow.

"In the wardrobe," Ilena waved her hand at the door that led into their bedroom. "You can wear it now if you want."

Ore looked at the three already wearing it askance, then opted not to. He'd grown up in these cold environs, most of it with only a thin blanket and hat over his threadbare clothing. He was already almost too warm indoors with his thick castle–issue cloak and warm winter clothing. He wasn't complaining, though. He hated the cold for the same reason from his youth. He just also liked to have the flexibility to defend his mistress and it looked like that would be hard in the thick leather winter gear.

Ore was very much looking forward to being close to his mistress again. Since being assigned to the Ministry of Intelligence as Ilena's Assistant he'd not had much time to be with Mizi, at least in comparison to what he'd been used to before when he'd followed the First Princess as her first knight. He was looking forward to being able to spend this coming two to three weeks with her again.

"The horses are ready," Henry let them know. "If you're ready?"

Ore stepped up to his wife and hugged her. He laughed. "It doesn't feel like you. You're twice as large as usual, and all stiff."

She gave him a kiss. "It's me. I'll keep Master Rei happy and you keep Mistress Mizi happy, so you can stay happy for me."

Ore's eyes lit up. "I think that'll be an easy assignment. Except, of course," he leaned in again, "missing you will be hard." He wouldn't walk out the door until he'd given her a long enough kiss he thought it might hold him until dinner or thereabouts. Their intimate morning should keep him for at least two days, though. He was thinking the coming weeks would be hard. Even being able to be with Mizi again it would be lonely at night. He'd never been fond of lonely nights.

The four with Petroi and Thayne, who'd be staying with Ilena this time, left the room out the same door Marcus and Henry had come in from. They mounted their horses outside the Cat gate to head around to the Soldier's gate where they were meeting Mizi, Rei, and their guards. Ore was riding Fenrier this time, so Mizi could ride with him as ordered by Rei, so he made Ilena ride with him for the short ride to the garrison gate.

-o-o-o-

It was a dark and bitterly cold early morning for both royal households. There was one relief, however. The snows had stopped the day before and the sky had cleared overnight. All of those headed out for their travels would have blue skies this day. They hoped it meant an auspicious time for travel generally. The steam from the noses and mouths of person and steed alike made what few local clouds there were. They disappeared very quickly as the dry air sucked the moisture away, save what froze to fur and muffler.

While he still had Ore to help him with Ilena, Rei pulled the two of them aside to speak with them privately. Rei looked at Ilena and soberly asked her, "Ilena, will you let Sasou be? We both need you to be able to face him in Ichijou having forgiven him."

Ilena drew in a breath. She blinked at him. "You've seen very deeply this time, Master Rei," she said quietly. He waited on her answer. She ran her hand over the top of her hat, looking down at the ground as she decided what she could and couldn't do. Finally she looked up at him with tears in her eyes.

Rei reached out and put his hand on her shoulder. "Ilena," he said softly, "he does still love you, but his duty is his requirement. Let it go. It was the only way to get you freed from House Shicchi in time."

She turned her face from him a bit angrily, but that was to be expected. "There were other ways than such treachery that nearly cost me my life."

"Maybe in implementation," Rei had to agree, "but it had to be the Earl's plan and decision or he'd not have ever let you go. Even your plan included him making that decision."

Ilena held on to it just a little longer, then finally she slumped, her long breath of resignation out making a great fog in the dawn air. Ore and Rei sandwiched her in gentle hugs. It had been a harsh thing to be nearly assassinated and injured so severely for the sake of keeping the nation whole. "He did wait as long as he could before he had to take your freedom from you," Rei pointed out.

Ilena growled, but not with any serious bite to it. Ore kissed her on the tip of her nose, the only skin uncovered on her face. "And I was very glad to have you again sooner than later, and living instead of dead in the end." She nodded to that. She was able to relent shortly after that.

Rei still made her answer him once they'd released her, his blue eyes boring into her amber ones. She drew in a breath and stood straighter, then she bowed her head to him. "I'll accept that it was necessary and not retaliate against him for it."

"Thank you," Rei said. While it wasn't a promise to not assassinate Sasou, he'd accept that answer as sufficient for now. It was perhaps wise to allow her the loop hole. They wouldn't know the far future for a long time to come.

Rei moved them back to the waiting horses and riding companions. He hugged and kissed Mizi one more time as Ore turned to say his farewell to Ilena. Rei then helped boost Mizi up onto the back of Fenrier, who was excited to get to go out on a long trip. His winter blanket, displaying Ore's coat of arms of a sleeping cat, covered him enough to keep him warm and the run would warm him up the rest of the way.

Mizi's extra warm clothing, in two and almost three layers if one included the cloak over the heavy coat and lined pants, made her look twice as big as she actually was. Her red hair was completely covered by the thick hat with ear flaps tied under her chin. Rei held her gloved hand while waiting for Ore, his own also so gloved they could barely tell they were holding hands at all save by looking.

Ore finished kissing and hugging Ilena and mounted Fenrier, sitting in the saddle in front of Mizi as they usually rode. He was as equally as bundled as Mizi and it was equally as hard for Ilena to let his booted foot go as it was for Rei to let go of Mizi's hand. Winter travel happened, but carried risks that made it hard for loved ones to be comfortable with it. When Ore teased them enough, Ilena let him go and took Rei's other hand. That made it easier for him to let Mizi go. Ilena had already said her goodbyes to Marcus and Henry so with final waves the four were off down the road. They didn't wait long to move up to a gallop and were soon out of sight.

Rei waved at Sam and Leon, giving them permission to leave for the garrison, then turned to Brian, Kirk, and the military messenger. "Please also take care in the weather. With today being nice, perhaps it will stay nice long enough for you to learn the routes to the eastern garrisons. The landmarks are different in driving snow." He smiled at his tease that the military messenger echoed. The three bowed from their saddles and they, too, were soon out of sight. Rei leaned over to Ilena and asked quietly, "Would you be able to hear Sam and Leon's horses from here so we can know they're on the road, too?"

Ilena squeezed his hand and walked them slowly to a place where she'd be able to. The clear air would make it easier to hear. Andrew, Mina, Petroi, and Thayne followed along after them, the only other ones to have come out into the weather. The pinks of the beginning of sunrise lit the area around them enough to see that the snows had left another eight to nine inches on the ground. It wasn't an even layer because of all the swirling winds that had accompanied the clouds, so they could only estimate. The winds today only lightly swirled the looser top snow around their boots and the walkways in eddies. Ilena kept them to the pathways where the snow wasn't quite as deep.

"You also might not want to hold hands for too long here," Petroi scolded gently.

"Oh, right," Ilena let Rei's hand go and they both sighed a little. There wasn't anyone other than the few required castle guards to see them holding hands, but as the sun came up they'd be seen better and others would begin to come out to go to their workplaces. "You'd think they'd all have figured it out by now, but I guess we don't really come out enough for them to learn it."

"Not really, no," Rei agreed. "It might be even harder once we're all in the new building together. Then they might really wonder if we two couples have decided to all share one bedroom. The rumors just before the wedding announcement were rather concerning." He shuddered.

"Weelll...," Ilena pondered on that. "I suppose there is that risk. I'll make sure my rumor people make those who think it feel quite embarrassed for even suggesting it. The maids will be able to confirm it anyway, since they'll know whose rooms they're cleaning."

"True," Rei relaxed a bit and pulled his cloak around him just a little more. The wind was picking up as the sun finally poked up over the horizon and sparkled red and gold sparks off the snow. That reminded him of his wife so he looked up at the sky. It had reached the color of his brother's and his eyes. That made him smile. "The Sun has risen to meet the All, and her bond sister, the Naluk' walks with him."

Ilena giggled. "And the Marluk' has left his Seconds to watch over them." She looked teasingly over her shoulder at her guards.

"Indeed," Petroi answered dryly.

"If we didn't stay, who would make sure you behaved?" Thayne teased.

"And the Naluk' has sent her Seconds with the Sun and Marluk', with the All watching over them, ...I guess to see that they behave?" Ilena added. She slumped. "Not like any of us need that. We're all behaving rather well right now, I think." She leaned her shoulder against Rei's shoulder, still needing human contact, and his in particular. "It's hard to have to show them we aren't. I'd far rather just relax."

Rei snorted. "So would I."

"So you've delegated?" Ilena asked.

"Yes," Rei sighed the word. "I think it's helping Flandras to be able to talk to Reynold. He's very anxious about all the details since present numbers are so different from past numbers. He's very focused and I have to pull him out of his work every evening to tell him to go to bed. But I'm hopeful that he'll be done about the same time the rest of my helpers are. Then I can synthesize it in one large go and rest relatively soon after that myself."

Ilena patted him on the back. "I'll hope so. I'm ready any time you need to walk through the final few until you're happy with what you want to do. Like you and Flandras, I see a large number of options, but he's not had the practice with the practicals enough to understand quite so well how to reach what you'll be trying to reach. Are you trying to reach just the one plan?"

"No. I'll pick what I think is best, but I'd like to bring the three best to the table." He gave a teasing glance to Ilena. "I want to have my turn to teach you two." Ilena snorted at him. "Besides, neither of you will be content if I don't let you argue with me."

Ilena laughed with him. She tilted her head, then her eyes followed movement on the other side of the tall outer castle wall they were walking past.

Rei stayed silent so he could also hear the hooves of the two horses headed out to follow Ore and Mizi. As they continued on past them, he turned their feet towards the Royal Aide's building. "I may as well have breakfast at your place since we'll all be meeting there first thing anyway," he said.

"You're welcome to come," Ilena said kindly. It would help them both to have each other for company that morning.

-o-o-o-

Amber sat up in her bed, rather suddenly actually. She looked towards the window. The heavy curtain was pulled over it to keep out the cold but she could tell that the sun wasn't up yet, or was perhaps just coming over the horizon. It was her usual time to wake up, then, perhaps. She shivered and wrapped her arms around herself. Perhaps Rio would also be awake then. "Rio?" she asked in a normal to perhaps slightly louder tone of voice. "Can you come here?" She was hesitant to ask for it, given that in the past Rio had usually entered her room to scold her, save once, but she really did need some help this morning.

She eventually heard footsteps on the passage between their rooms and a single knock on the door. Amber shivered, then slipped out of bed and went to unlock the door. She was grateful that Rio had been respecting that boundary since they'd finally been able to not fight all the time. Rio's eyes widened to see Amber shivering so. She stepped into the room and took Amber in a very gentle hug. Amber had decided the hugs were so gentle because Rio herself had a hard time giving them.

"What is it?" Rio was already dressed for the day.

"Did – did you help them dress this morning?" Amber asked.

"Yes," Rio answered. "That made it a very early morning."

"I'll let you nap later, if you need it," Amber said.

Rio stiffened slightly, Amber hoped in surprise not rebuke. "That's thoughtful of you. Thank you. It might be better to let me sleep earlier at night, actually. Mistress Ilena's going to need me to sleep with her at night to get through the nightmares, so my sleep will be interrupted for a while," she was rather dry.

Amber blinked but shivered a little more fiercely in sympathy for a moment. "Nightmares?"

Rio nodded. "Mistress Ilena has a nightmare every night. Master Ore's been with her to keep them very brief and comfort her. With him gone, there's only me to help with that; although, the worst ones only Leah can comfort. Thank goodness they're very rare now."

Amber considered that for a bit, then gave a nod. "Okay. I'll ask Justinian to help me with cleanup after dinner so you can go to bed earlier." She drew in a deep breath and asked, "Will – will the Twins be okay out on the frozen road for so long?"

Rio consider the question, then answered softly, "Yeah. They've been messengers out on the road so much now not much holds them down. They know where all the hiding places, odd woodcutter's huts, and kind farmer's places are all over Suiran. It's probably for that reason over any others that they're the best to send with Mistress Mizi and Master Ore. They'll keep all of them safe should a winter squall come through."

Amber slumped in Rio's hold. "Well, I'll hold on to that, then."

Rio released her a little to look her in the eyes, a puzzled expression on her face. "Winter travel worries you that much?"

Amber couldn't meet her eyes. "My... mother died to one. She was only going to the village to check on one of the women who gave birth and it caught her on the way back."

"Ah," Rio said sadly, her arms coming more warmly around Amber again. "And you'd not like to lose Marcus before you even have him." Amber could only nod miserably. "Well," Rio rubbed Amber's head soothingly, "as I said they'll watch out for each other and should be just fine. If anything they'll have a grand time getting to talk to all their acquaintances on the way. It will be perhaps more vacation for them than anything, really. When they get back and tell us all their stories, we can be very jealous all we want and whine at them for it to get out the worries, too, without letting them know that's what we really were the whole time." She gave the surprised Amber a grin.

"Well," Amber had to admit, "I suppose you'd worry about Henry, too."

Rio blinked a bit in surprise as she took that thought in. "Well, I suppose I do use him for stability when I'm uncertain so I'll have a few moments of shock he's not around, but that doesn't happen too often here, and I've lived without him a lot. This is a first to be with them nearly all the time." She let Amber go and led her towards the bathroom. "You go get the water started and I'll pick out the clothes, if you'll let me. What color do you want to accent with today?"

Amber had to admit that she did need to get her day moving forward before Ilena and Rei arrived for the day's breakfast and security meeting. "How about green for the reminder of spring and for hope."

"Great choice!" Rio said cheerfully to help Amber and let her go. Amber forced herself to not think hard about who was missing as of that morning, nor of her mother, and headed for the bath room where she quickly cleaned herself off. When she returned to her room, Rio was sitting on the settee with the curtain pulled just enough for her to be lit by the early morning sun. It was also likely because she'd been thoughtful and closed the door to the room. Amber already knew that was difficult for Rio. Being by the window she could feel like she could still escape. Amber's clothes, including the green shawl Lady Seraphina had made for her, and matching green stockings and belt were laid out on the bed.

"Thank you for staying to keep me company," she said humbly to Rio. That part hadn't been necessary, but had been kind.

"They're not back yet," Rio shrugged, "nor is the cart here yet, but I think it will be soon."

Amber got dressed, thinking about Rio and Henry. She'd been doing that almost every time she thought of Marcus, actually. As her head came through the bodice neck, she hesitantly asked, "Rio, those two really are so close that sometimes I wonder if Marcus *could* ever get married. What will Henry do, to not be able to be in the same room with him? They already can't do anything else without the other one." So far everything they'd ever done had been all four of them together. Amber had experimented with asking Marcus if they could go out without specifying and it really had been all four of them. He didn't even think of it being just the two of them. Well..., she still might be under "training", but that's what the training said, was that it might never be just the two of them.

Her bodice settled over her shirt and skirt, she put the belt on while Rio thought of her answer. Rio finally snorted. "Well, I guess you aren't wrong. I can see them both shivering in the middle of the night, wanting rather desperately to ask you if you'd mind if Henry came and slept on the settee like Master Ore did on Mistress Ilena's every night before they were allowed to be together." Amber glared at Rio who smirked sympathetically back.

Amber pulled on her first boot, not sure she could ask what she really wanted to. Finally she took a deep breath and asked it a bit timidly. "Rio, would *you* keep him company at night, if he needed it?" She glanced worriedly at Rio from the corner of her eye as she tied the final knot on her boot. She was sitting on the foot of her bed, where the clothing had been.

Rio drew in a sharp breath as she shook her head. "I do trust both of them more than most, even at night because they've proven they can comfort Mistress Ilena properly, but...." She looked away and bit her lip. "I don't know. I think he'd have to have a really good reason." She sighed. "Even Mistress Ilena will need to learn how to sleep alone eventually. We all have to do hard things we don't want to. ...I probably wouldn't unless ordered to."

She watched as Amber tied the second boot on. "That's the only reason I ever learned to help Mistress Ilena through the night. They showed me how, then ordered me to keep her at Tokumade so she wouldn't leave it to go to Petroi's side after his life–threatening injury from the Doll House battle. She had to send them back out again so there was only me and Miss Leah to do it, and I was the one in the room all the time anyway."

Amber was sympathetic. "That must have been very hard, then." Rio nodded and rose to her feet. She waved at the door. Amber walked to it and opened it, then Rio could follow her out through it. The smells of the freshly cooked and warm food reached their noses as they walked for the stairs to head down for the cart and the waiting plates they were to fill next.

"Rio," Amber asked as they picked up the first set of plates, "do you think Henry likes you?" She glanced up to see the old smirk on Rio's face. She shook her head at Rio. "Yes, I do like to gossip about the pairings in the castle, but I can't help but wonder it. He's very good at helping you relax and yet not restrain you so you're afraid. It's so different from what I've seen. It's more like Master Ore's gentleness with Mistress Ilena, sometimes."

Rio's eyes went a little large until she blinked and returned to putting the last bit of food on the plate she was holding. Her brow furrowed as she thought about the question and the first plate went back on the lower shelf of the cart so she could pick out another empty plate to fill next. Amber let her think about it as she finished dishing the plate in her hand and did the same.

"Why would you think of it that way?" Rio finally asked. "He's very good with people and knows what they need generally. That's one of the things he learned to survive on the streets and was honed by Mistress Ilena in what she ordered him to do."

Amber drew herself up and looked Rio in the eyes. "Because I could do that: have our partnership be based on helping Henry and Marcus."

Rio was shocked. Finally she said, "I'd have to think about that for a while. It's not something I've considered at all." She frowned. "I'm not sure I want to, though." She paused, then gasped in surprise and quickly looked back at Amber.

"Not that I don't care about them, or about your and Marcus' relationship." She bit her lip, then said, "I'm just... not sure I can turn that way when Mistress Ilena's already a large handful by herself, even the smaller part I have to carry." She was pretty uncomfortable.

Amber finally shrugged and returned to their work. "Well, think about it I guess. I'll keep thinking of other possibilities. Have you thought of any yet?"

Rio stayed uncomfortable, but Amber wasn't surprised. She rather thought Rio hadn't been thinking at all about what their joint goal could be. She did seem to ignore things she didn't want to think about. It was her selfishness, like Amber had hers. Finally Rio said in a small, quiet voice, "I'll work harder on it." Amber gave her the *"you'd best be"* nod and pursed lips, but let it go at that. They didn't need to fight over something this important.

-o-o-o-

"Mistress," Ore said over his shoulder after they'd been on the road long enough to get past Nijoushi and onto the stretch of the North Road towards Osterly and eventually Kouzanshi, "are you warm enough?"

"Yes, Ore, thank you," she answered. "It usually helps that you're my shield from the wind and my muffler is very warm."

"Oh, good," he answered, relieved. "Please let me know if you get cold, particularly in your legs. We'll want to get off and walk a bit to make sure the legs stay warm enough. Riding in this much cold is different. We'll let the horses walk more often so their sweat doesn't freeze to them and cause damage, too."

"Okay," she answered.

For all he'd said it in an asking way, Ore would make sure they walked whenever their horses needed it regardless. Having your friend and method of transportation suddenly incapable was bad in this kind of weather. One didn't want to be walking away from a dead horse into a sudden snow squall while still twenty miles from the closest inn or home. He'd made sure to check Fenrier's shoes before they left the castle for that same reason. He'd asked Ilena why the Tarc horses went without shoes and it was mostly because they didn't do so much walking and labor as the Ryokudo horses did (and because of the lack of metal there). So he'd made Marcus and Henry check the feet of their horses. That had led to an interesting discussion about the differences between the two breeds of horses' hooves generally, although Rei had made them keep it short.

Because today was finally a clear day after nearly a week of snow, there were plenty of other travelers out on the road, trying to get where they needed to go next before the snows started up again. Business was done based on weather in the winter, more than time. However, they'd been some of the first of the day's brave to leave that morning, so they were for the most part being the first to break the new snow on the road.

They eventually came upon a patrol coming from Osterly garrison driving four draft horses pulling a wide road plow behind them. The plow paused so they could go around it without being buried by the snow that was being pushed off the road. "Is the Nijoushi garrison doing the same from the city, or do they go all the way?" Mizi asked Ore as they got going again at a slightly faster pace now that they were on more clear ground.

"They'll meet up in not too much longer, I'd think," Ore answered. "We left before even they were on the road. We might have made just as much time if we'd waited."

"Why didn't we wait, then?" Mizi asked.

"Fewer people to know who'd left when," Marcus answered dryly.

"Ah," Mizi understood.

"Not to mention Master Ore needs the run," Henry said just as dryly from the other side.

"Master's always early when he wants something to be done with," Ore gave his answer.

"True," Mizi said. She paused, then asked, "I'm not sure how he's feeling about the hospital in general, since Ilena said I shouldn't talk to him about it in detail until after the Court of Ministers had heard it. We've only been able to talk about it in brief in our meetings. Do you know, Ore?"

"I think he thinks it's a fine idea, Mistress," he tried to reassure her. "He has so many things in his head that it's often hard for things to come out of his one mouth. If he had five or more to say things, his thoughts might be able to come out better for having the more places to escape from." Mizi laughed at the imagery. "He understands why it could be needed, so I'm sure he's grateful you're working on it."

"That's good," Mizi sighed and looked off towards the forests. The part of the road they were on was high enough to look over them and see how the foothills of the mountains rolled. It was a beautiful scene, particularly with the brilliant sun in the blue sky overhead. It made for painful seeing with the sunlight shining off of the white snow, but they were all protecting their eyes by having their hats low over their eyes and their mufflers high over their cheekbones. Even Fenrier had similar eye protection today, with the eyeholes of his hood being slits instead of full open circles. The Tarc horses seemed to be doing fine by just closing their eyes partially and their thick eyelashes providing the rest of the shading they needed.

By the time their stomachs were rumbling in hunger, Osterly was in view. Ore took them directly to the Osterly garrison for their somewhat late lunch. They ran into the garrison surgeon, Bonner, who'd worked on Ilena when they'd first found her. He was leaving the garrison cafeteria as they entered it. They greeted him then were a little surprised when he also greeted Marcus and Henry.

Before Bonner could leave her, Mizi called to him. "Ah, Doctor Bonner, you have a lot of field experience in setting broken bones." Her hand went to her heart to curl a little there. "Would you be willing to teach what you know at the hospital once it's built? I'm headed to Kouzanshi to bring back staff to be trained for it, but I'm sure someone with actual experience would be very helpful to have access to."

Bonner looked at her in a little surprise, then bowed to her. "Princess, that would need to be answered to by the Captain. I'm certainly willing, but my time and duties are determined by him."

"Thank you," Mizi answered him then turned to Ore. "Please see that you bring it up to Captain Grey when you speak with him, that I'll be needing Doctor Bonner and calling for him when we're ready for him."

Ore bowed with his hand over his heart. "Yes, Mistress," he answered soberly. He gave a sober wink to Bonner when Mizi had turned away, satisfied with that answer. Bonner was mystified, but this wasn't the time or place to say more than that.

As they slid into seats across from each other with full plates in hand, Mizi asked Marcus and Henry, "Did you two spend time in Osterly?"

"Yes," Marcus said airily. "We've been messengers generally all up and down North Road. Some of our messages were for soldiers from family members so we'd get permission to eat before having to leave again." Henry nodded, already digging in to his food. Marcus dived in as soon as the words were out of his mouth.

"Will it be like the other times you've had messages to pass along, Ore?" Mizi asked after her first few bites of her lunch.

"Yes, I think so," Ore answered. "It's a brief message to pass along, since Garen put together the written orders." Henry had possession of the message bag Ore had pulled the specific folder for the Osterly garrison commander from. Ore turned a stern look on the Twins. "You'll stay here and keep Mistress company while I run up and talk to the commander, so I can find all of you when I'm done."

"Yes, Master Ore," they sat up and saluted, then returned to eating again. He snorted at them, making Mizi giggle a little.

"At least you'll have company to tease," Ore told Mizi. She smiled at him. She always had company when he left her as she always took the opportunity to talk to any soldier who passed by her, and they loved coming to talk to her. At least this time, her first as Princess of Ryokudo, she'd have guards instead of sitting alone without him. That had been the hardest part of his orders when their trips had included him having to be Rei's Messenger at the same time before.

Ore finished eating before Mizi, but that was on purpose. That was their pattern so she still had something to do for part of the time he was gone. He excused himself from her presence and reached for his dishes. Marcus frowned at him with a little shake of his head, so Ore picked up his folder instead and headed for the commanding officer's office.

"Captain Grey," Ore said upon knocking on said person's door.

The captain rose to his feet and bowed. "Prince Ore. Welcome." He moved to leave his desk but Ore waved him back to his seat and closed the door behind himself. As he sat in one of the two chairs across the desk from Grey the captain said, "You'll still be so informal, even as to not change your patterns in your travels with Princess Mizi?"

Ore lowered his eyelids at the couched scold. "We've been sent away from the castle because I can't stand to be practicing nobility any more, nor can she. We can pretend on this trip Mistress needs to go on that we've not changed stations. Master's ordered it besides, so we get back fast enough his worries about winter travel can be lessened even somewhat."

"And you'll still call them that even now?" The tease was dry. Ore shrugged. He'd rather and hadn't settled on any other names to call them yet. The habit was sufficient for him. "Is it so great a need to travel in the depths of winter?" Curiosity was better than teasing.

"The year will be very busy," Ore answered. "Her business is with medics in Kouzanshi, to call them to Nijou for training there. She's asked me to let you know she'll be calling on Doctor Bonner to come and train at the hospital once it's ready for such things." Grey raised an eyebrow but Ore didn't answer to it just yet. He handed the folder in his hands over to the captain. "Master's business is this."

"And he'll still keep you as a Messenger?" the captain mused in quiet surprise. Ore glared at him, but Grey ignored it, opening the folder to read through it. "War games is it?" he continued to muse quietly as he read. "A reunion conference would be a fun diversion," he added a moment later. When he was done, sharp eyes rose to look into Ore's. "And the secret message is...?"

"The reason the Assistant Minister of Intelligence and a royal is the Messenger," Ore scolded him back just a little. "It isn't just war games. War comes. King Brother's agreed to help Altherly against Gael. There's a possibility Brulac will invade while our back is turned to it. The goal is to make sure they don't, but the garrisons on this side need to be watching for it." Grey had sat up sharply with wide dismayed eyes. "The conference and war games are the peaceful excuse for beginning to get everyone ready. The hospital is the same: an excuse for a medic Princess to have something to do that the court approves of while preparing a place for the wounded fighters to be treated."

Grey slumped and sighed. He rubbed his forehead, then pondered the combined messages until he nodded. "I'll see to it here. Will any of the men be called up from this area to help Altherly?"

Ore shook his head. "The Court of Ministers decided that before we left." He told Grey the boundaries of which holdings were going to lose men sooner than later.

Grey added that to the things in his head, then asked, "Anything else?" Ore shook his head. Grey leaned over his desk and clasped his fingers together. "It was so surprising to learn at everyone's last trip through here that Earl Pakyo's steward had been the missing Princess and that the Touka brothers had decided to acknowledge her as a Princess of Ryokudo." Ore nodded agreement. That bit of news had surprised him as well. Grey's eyes pinned Ore sharply, though. "It was even *more* surprising to hear most recently that *you're* the missing heir to these lands. Does that bother you, to not have them?"

Ore blinked in surprise, then shook his head. "I learned early that the position was cursed. I'm far more relieved to have the curse of the Shicchi's off the people of this land. Master's worked hard to find someone capable and kinder, and I'll hope that person repays his trust with loyalty. I'm content with the holding that's come to me with my current titles." He smiled a fond smile. "Ilena let me bring the householders in myself so I can know them. They've all got the courage to face me with smiles so I can smile at them. Ilena holds me so the darkness doesn't come. It's good where we are."

Grey studied him soberly for a bit, then relented. "That's good then. Let me know if it becomes too hard to beat back the beast and I'll come do it for you."

Ore's eyes went wide, then he slumped a little. "All of Ilena's guards do it quite well, thank you anyway. She's put both of her Messengers behind me just for that reason." Grey let out a spurt of a chuckle. "Well..., I asked for the first one since he can tease me out of it before it gets that far. The other one...." Ore shuddered. "He's one of those quiet, kind persons that'll suddenly strike with the blade so you're dead before you even know it."

Grey laughed quietly. "Well, it sounds like they're good for you, then." Ore readily agreed. He reviewed the beginning of their conversation and decided Grey had been testing him, not teasing or scolding. He sighed. He'd forgotten how much effort and work this garrison had put into dealing with his older brother for so many years. Grey would for sure want to make sure this prince wouldn't stray on those paths.

Ore considered him, then asked, "Are you married?" Grey blinked at Ore at the sudden surprising question. "Or, is there someone somewhat young here that learned how to face Pakyo reasonably well?"

The captain considered that question, then answered, "Yes, there are two."

"If you've the time now, I'd like to meet them," Ore rose to his feet. They couldn't stay too long, but it would be good to fit this in now.

Grey rose to his feet, not complaining. One didn't complain about lack of time to a prince of the realm; although, Ore wasn't given to abusing that privilege. From the perspective of the royal it felt more like expediency. A royal didn't have time to waste, nor did they care to waste the time of others who were getting needed and useful things done. He mused on that as they walked out of the offices and down the hallway. "Are you already thinking of the future?" Grey asked quietly, fishing for Ore's reason for the sudden request.

Ore looked at him out of the corner of his eye. "As ordered as my brother's wedding. I have yet to understand why the Toukas *want* to have the beast still roaming around. Having someone who knows how to temper it early would be good, no?" Grey shook his head in resigned agreement with Ore.

Ore met with the two young soldiers, asking them questions about how they'd dealt with Pakyo. (He wasn't interested in acting like him to test them. He had no desire to put into their heads that he was his brother.) Then he took them to the practice list and sparred with them briefly, wooden sword to wooden sword. While he wasn't the best at that, he knew what it was like to spar against Andrew and Mina.

When he was done, he turned to Grey. "Transfer them to the Nijou garrison where they can get more lessons in until I need them. I'll let Andrew know they need special training. Mina would be happy to help, too, with both sets of lessons." He rolled his eyes. "You can let them know what I want them for after I'm gone." He turned back to the two soldiers. "Thank you. I'll stop by to talk to you every now and again to make sure what you're learning is what I need. I may not call for you for a few years, but please be working hard." The three soldiers bowed to him and he left, headed back to Mizi. They needed to be on the road. It would already be dark by the time they made it to their next stop.

-o-o-o-

It didn't take long from when Ore left the table before soldiers were stopping at the table where Mizi, Marcus, and Henry were still sitting. Marcus had taken his and Ore's dishes to the kitchen and returned to sit next to Mizi. Mizi was happy to talk to the soldiers who stopped by. She wanted to know how they were doing. She was glad that the Twins knew how to help relax those who were a little uncertain that they could talk to her now that she was actually a princess.

Marcus and Henry were telling a story when Mizi noticed one of the younger soldiers off to the side, watching them. Mizi motioned him over. "How are you today, Private Vince? Is your mother well?"

Vince bowed a little stiffly. "I'm well, as is mother. Thank you for asking." The private hesitated, then asked, "May I ask why you're traveling today?"

Mizi nodded her head. "I'm going to open a hospital just east of Nijou. Head Medic Ryan has sent requests for apprentices and interns to apply to the Nijou Department of Medicine over the next month. I'm going to Kouzanshi to request a few researchers I met there come for that time so they can learn what the castle expects. I'd really like for them to help me run the hospital." She smiled. "It seemed a good excuse to escape the castle walls at the same time: to go and personally ask them to come."

Mizi kept her answer to that. She'd been learning so much about reading the court faces that the small non–verbal cues she was picking up from the young private said that he was reserving himself for more reasons than merely shyness or nervousness about her being raised up to a princess now. It made her sad and slump inside a little. She didn't really want to but she wondered if he was merely unhappy with her being so relaxed with the soldiers, or if he was perhaps a child of one of the noble houses that were unhappy with Touka. The latter might mean he was fishing for information that could be used to send assassins against her eventually on this trip.

She let the sigh out and looked at him gently with that sorrow. "I've been relieved to have found a project the lords of the castle can approve of me doing. It's been very hard to be accepted by them." When she received the slight approval rather than the sympathy, her heart hardened just a little. She tried hard to not let that out in her interaction with him.

"I'm sure that would be of great benefit to the area and Region," Private Vince said politely. "Perhaps I'll let my sister know of the call for apprentices. She's been working with a medic to learn the skill."

"I'll watch for her, if she should decide to come," Mizi answered back just as politely. She let him escape thereafter. *Mizi to Rei. Add the House of Vince to the list of those potentially against.*

Marcus and Henry threw her glances. *Are you sure?* Marcus asked her quietly. Mizi gave him a single sorrowful nod. They gave her sympathetic looks.

At a break in the conversation going on around them where he could, Henry took his and Mizi's dishes to the kitchen and said while on the way, *Third Son to North Road Children. A son of the House of Vince has been told Mistress is on her way to Kouzanshi. Watch to see if communications are passed along and report negative actions on our way back.* Mizi could only approve. It would be good to see if it bore out and be protected if it did in ways none of them wanted it to. She did raise her eyebrow at the title he'd given her. Ilena's household didn't usually abbreviate to Ore's way of calling her. Marcus smiled his teasing smile at her. She rolled her eyes back at him.

As she distracted herself with paying attention to the fun conversation that Henry and Marcus were leading the others in, she noticed that a few times the soldiers were referencing prior times the Twins had been in Osterly. When one of those comments was made again, she broke in. "You know Henry and Marcus from before?" she asked the person who'd made the reference. She noticed the slight tension in the Twins as more than that person enthusiastically filled her in on how often the Twins were there. It sounded like it was nearly as often as Mizi and Ore had been there, perhaps for over a longer period of time. She leaned forward on her elbow. "What's your favorite story of theirs?" she asked generally. She got to see them blush as her question was answered with great dramatics and laughter.

It was fun to focus on such things, but it didn't completely prevent her mind from remembering Rei's statement to her that he never, ever forgot in anything he did that he was a target. That anything he said could be used against him. That any important information that he let slip in public could be used to remove him from his place. She was glad that her castle training had helped her see what she'd needed to see so that she hadn't said more than she should have. It left her core sober.

Even that helped her to understand Rei a little more. He liked to relax like this, but he never, ever lost his sober core. The only place that ever happened was if they were having an intimate party with just his close friends. Even then, he likely never lost the sorrow and care. She'd seen it in his face when he'd admitted he couldn't even fully trust Andrew and Mina, his closest friends and aides.

That thought was one too many. Mizi dropped her hand down between herself and Marcus and took his pinky in her pinky and ring finger, to hold it tightly. He didn't let on, but shortly he was closing down the conversation, with Henry helping him smoothly. The three of them rose to their feet, Mizi letting Marcus's fingers go so no one would see. "May we go and talk to the stablehands, Mistress Mizi?" Marcus asked politely. "So we can do the job Mistress Ilena's asked us to do?" Mizi agreed mutely with a nod. Marcus let Ore know in the code that he'd find them in the stables.

They settled Mizi nearby the fireplace in the stable so she'd be warm enough. The doors to the stable were kept closed to keep as much heat inside as possible. As the Twins once again turned to conversations with the stablehands, Mizi looked around for the head of the stables specifically. When he'd come to her, since one of the stablehands had gone to fetch him for her in the end, she said, "It seems to me that the open fires in stables would be very dangerous with all the straw and hay in them." She waved at the fireplace. "There's a new heating invention that we've recently been blessed to have installed in our building. It's a heating stove that keeps the open flame contained behind doors. The metal of the stove warms up and releases a rather large amount of heat for far less fuel consumption than a fireplace. I think they'd be far safer to use in the stables."

She looked into his eyes. "I understand that's an unplanned–for expense to suggest it, but in only a few years the decrease in cost of fuel will pay for it." She told him the name of the company it could be purchased from, having learned it from Ilena while waiting for him to be fetched. "Please put in a requisition for the heating stoves for this garrison's stables. One per building might be enough for now. After the initial experiment if you need more stoves you could ask for more. I'll let Rei know I've recommended it and why so that if the expenditure makes it all the way to the castle for approval they'll have at least that word to maybe help you." She looked around at the people and horses. "We won't be able to protect the people of the Region if you all lose your way to see they're helped quickly."

The head of the stables thanked her, then stayed and politely kept her company until Ore arrived. "I'm sorry I'm late, Mistress," Ore bowed to her formally, hand to his heart.

"It's okay, Ore," she smiled at him, for all it was still a sad one in the main. "I've had plenty of company and good companions." Marcus and Henry were disengaging from their conversation and sending men to get their horses saddled. Ore talked briefly with the head of the stables, then they were mounting and getting on the road again. Once they were far enough from others, Mizi's shivers had to be answered to. She wrapped her arms around Ore's middle and rested her head on his back. She let the slow tears drip from her eyes into her muffler.

"What is it, Mistress?" he asked quietly. She could only shake her head, not able to get words out around the sorrow in her heart and throat.

Marcus answered him for her, explaining about the encounter with Private Vince. "*Ah,*" Ore sighed and placed his hand on her arm to comfort her. "Yes. It is hard to be met now with such obviousness." He let her cry a little more, then said very dryly, "At least your first time wasn't to be drugged and wooed into a bed you didn't want to be in."

Mizi froze and blinked, then had to chuckle. "No. I suppose I'm grateful for that. I'm sure I'd have no idea how to respond to such a thing."

Ore nodded knowingly. "I didn't either, actually. Justinian saved me. I was very grateful for him that evening."

Mizi agreed. "I'm grateful Marcus was there," she said and looked over at him. He rode closer to them and reached up from his shorter Tarc horse to wipe the freezing tears from her eyelashes with his gloved hand. Before it could get very far away, she caught the hand in hers and held on tightly. "I'm so grateful there are kind people in the world," she whispered. Ore patted her arm as Marcus nodded at her. They let her fall asleep and nap, keeping her on the horse. Unexpectedly it was harder on her than she'd thought, to be social and have fun as a royal. Likely because "having fun" now had a new, not so happy definition.

-o-o-o-

When Mizi was sleeping, Marcus handed her hand back to Ore so he could tuck it in under his hand with her other arm to keep her on Fenrier with him. Ore frowned. They weren't going to get to run much this leg of the trip, even if she were awake. They were headed into the north mountains on the hardest, if shortest, leg of their trip, as far as terrain went. "Neither of you've been up to this one yet, have you?" he asked Henry and Marcus. They hadn't since the new Northern Pass garrison had been built after they'd been called into the castle.

He sighed and whisper–sang back to the castle. *Father to Mother. We were delayed too long to get to the Northern Pass garrison at a reasonable hour. Is there a small empty manor we can stop at for the night in Tokumade lands? If not we'll have to stop there tonight.* It would be at the new Earl's new manor home, but he still didn't want to if he didn't have to. An empty building would be better from his perspective. ...Until he remembered the "chaperoned" status they were supposed to be holding to as well. Then he wanted to run away, too. He amended his question, *Father to Mother. That is, one that doesn't hold lords and ladies? Common folk who can be our witnesses to good behavior would be just fine. As long as there's an empty room for Mistress.*

About eight minutes later the answer came back. *Mother to Father. There's the waystation between old Tokumade lane and the passage to the Northern Pass garrison. They have enough rooms. Just let them know you're headed for them.*

Father to Mother. Perfect. Thank you. I love you. He'd forgotten about the waystations her Family had used to help him pick up the final set of witnesses against Pakyo. They were part of the messenger service the Twins were setting up.

Until now they'd been used by her Family to transport people being moved by Ilena from bad circumstances to better ones. He sent the request to the waystation, which really was a family who supported Ilena in a home larger than most that also stabled extra horses, letting them know they should arrive in about three hours.

The road had already been cleared by the garrison earlier that morning and the sky had stayed blue all day so far. If Mizi stayed asleep, they'd just canter the whole way. The Tarc horses could do it regardless and Fenrier would rather move fast than care about the cold. Ore reached around both sides to pull Mizi's cloak up around her and him until he could just hold on to the edges of it to keep her and her legs enclosed between his back and her cloak. That should keep the space between them warm enough and help hold her on. "Is her hood up tightly enough?" he asked Henry. When Henry was satisfied that Mizi's hat and the cloak hood would stay put, he gave Ore a nod. Ore urged Fenrier up to a canter and held him there. The gallop they both wanted to go would be too much in the cold.

Ore was pleased that Mizi's regular practice riding on her own helped her body ride at the canter better than she had before she'd started learning. That had been the most uncomfortable pace for her when they'd been traveling together before. Since it was uncomfortable for the horses too, for too long, he averaged their speed at the canter but let them rest at a trot when the horses needed it.

"Will you keep all of the waystations?" Ore asked the Twins. "Or will you narrow it down to just the ones needed by the messenger service?" He'd not used all of them that time he'd learned about them. Just the ones they'd thought he'd reach on his pathway. He thought he'd missed this one they were headed for, remembering his last one had been near Osterly and the one before that beyond the one they were headed for. Of course, he'd been going on over thirty–six hours of not–sleeping by then, so he wasn't sure he was remembering right.

"Won't know until we've had people run it a few times," Henry answered. "Sometimes the drops down the central roads make the runs go to the half–way points instead of the full running points between the main cities. Then we'd need them all if speed's of the essence. We're still trying to decide if that's important."

Ore raised an eyebrow and glanced at him. Henry shrugged. "General messages it won't matter if they show up in three days or a week and a half. How many emergency messages are there really, even now? Most of them go by the messenger birds that are faster than horse regardless. Speed's good and fun but to ask the families to continue to hold open spaces when we aren't using them so much anymore...." He shrugged again. "As I said, it will take experimentation. Certainly during times such as we're expecting we'll want to keep the option open, but that will hopefully be over in four or five years. That's not the generations she wants us to be setting up this business for."

"True," Ore had to give him that.

"Not to mention the Tarc horses have a different distance and stamina ratio," Marcus said. "We'll begin to learn that on this trip, but even that will need experi-mentation."

"Did you get any interest in Osterly?" Ore asked them.

"Some," Marcus answered. "Most of them like the regular military pay. They are more adventuresome than most city nightwalkers would be, so we might be able to wiggle those few out. The math will have to be done once we have an idea of the numbers of persons interested, to see if we can pay them enough to make it worth it to them." He shivered a bit, still somewhat traumatized by the difficulties he'd had trying to learn the math for the Duchy books.

"Will you advertise generally, eventually?" Ore asked as his next question.

"Probably," Henry answered. "We'd like to get just a few to be the equivalent of business partners here at the beginning for the experimenting. Then we'll see from there."

Ore let there be a pause, then asked another question. "So, when you two came out of Kouzanshi it wasn't just to gain information. You were running the messenger business?"

They both gave him long looks before Henry answered. "Yes. Running the messages paid for the travel. Later, when the work of gaining information and witnesses against the Doll House got going in earnest, we moved up from horses to a carriage and took more people packages than letters, some days."

"Ooh, like Justinian thanked you for?" Ore asked, referencing a conversation from earlier that month.

"Yes. We picked him up, dropped him off at the castle, picked Reynold up from there, and dropped him off at the closest house to Tarc, where they took him by horseback. We were needed back here so didn't go that far."

"Why didn't Reynold say anything then, when Justinian thanked you?" Ore asked, curious.

"None of them knew it was us. A different person escorted them into the carriage. We were just the driver and guard. No one looks at them, or cares," Marcus shrugged. He smiled at Ore. "Justinian's just intuitive like that." Ore silently agreed.

"Where's the carriage now?" he asked, not having seen one used by them. Not that they'd needed it.

"We sold it after that operation," Henry answered. "Mistress Ilena had the waystation wagons built during that time and before, so they continued to be in use for her other purposes. They couldn't be taken into the cities like a simple carriage could be, and not remarked on." Ore nodded his understanding. The high–sided farm wagons with false bottoms would stand out in any city.

Henry got in the next question before Ore could ask another one. "Are you really okay with being the Assistant Minister, when you've been Rei's Intelligence head since he took you?"

Ore stayed silent while he pondered on his answer to that question. "It's fine," he finally said. "For all those titles are lesser or greater, to the Family and House we're equal. That's sufficient. I can hide behind the lesser title enough to get done what needs to be done. Master approved it when I was told what she wanted me for." He wasn't surprised they'd want to know.

"Is it being stifling to have so many lessons on a thing you already know?" Henry continued.

Ore shrugged. "One can always learn something from anyone. Everyone in the office listens to those lessons so it helps all of us to one degree or another. And it isn't wrong for the Uncles to want to be sure we've understood what they've learned." The Twins understood that perspective.

"Why do you even now continue to hide that you've known us and Thayne from before Mistress Ilena was found by you and Mistress Mizi?" Marcus asked.

Ore's eyes turned darkly on Marcus and he swallowed a bit. Ore's tone was equally as cold as he ordered, "Because Ilena never needs to know about that time. What she learned on her own is enough."

Marcus bobbed a bow at him. "You should know, though," he warned, "Mistress Mizi is already learning on her own that we've crossed paths at the garrisons. That many soldiers can't keep quiet and don't know to. She'll begin asking questions in another garrison or two."

Ore gave a nod that he'd heard. "I'll think of how to say it to her," he said, closing the conversation and making it clear they were to continue to keep quiet about their brief shared past.

-o-o-o-

"Welcome to Nijou," Garen saluted Sirius because he wanted to, then held out his hand.

Sirius clasped his hand with a small smile. "Good to see you again, Garen. You've gone up in the ranks nicely. Welcome."

Garen shrugged. "Getting tapped by both the First Prince and the Second Princess all unexpectedly will do that."

Sirius gave a genuine smile to that. "Yes, well I did have the opportunity to witness that in Tarc. Quite the Touka team, those two."

Garen chuckled in agreement as he led Sirius away from the bustle of the courtyard around the Soldier's gate. Sirius had brought with him his staff of about five total adjuncts, secretaries, and aides. Those tagged along behind the two generals. An entire squadron of soldiers had come with him, too, but they were here to be reassigned by orders of Sasou. The quartermaster was taking charge of them to get them into rooms.

Garen walked Sirius to the office he'd been assigned and let them into it, then handed the full set of keys available for the room over. There were enough desks in the room for them all and they filed to their usual locations. Most garrisons, particularly castle garrisons, had the same sorts of rooms in them so they had their learned places. Once they had their office things settled, Garen waved a hand at the staff. "Can we let them have the rest of the afternoon and evening off to go learn their rooms and get comfortable again with the place? Or would you rather put them right to work and come with me?"

Sirius snorted at him. "You mean you want to put me to work right away. I'd rather you let *me* have a vacation day. I've been on the go since I got here the last time. None of the Toukas let me rest. For them, the ride to and from places is sufficient."

Garen laughed and waved a hand. "True enough and I'm sorry, but I need to talk to you today. Then you can have your vacation, even for three days except for the security meetings, while you try to process it all and decide what you want to add to my thinking." That made him think of something. He looked the staff over again. "Do you know who of these Ilena trusts? The meetings are in her office and always top secret. You can't bring them all and she kills anyone who betrays her trust." He said it very soberly and got more than one pair of eyes looking at him in shock.

Sirius looked between his frozen staff and Garen. "She didn't there," he said quietly.

Garen shook his head. "If anything secret was said, it was in her code, I'm quite sure. They have to speak the code too much everywhere else. If they didn't talk openly in their office, they'd forget how to speak to normal people at all."

"She's really as bad as the nightwalkers claimed?" one of the corporals asked.

"Yes," Garen answered simply, not knowing what they'd claimed. It hardly mattered. "She'd rather not be, but she has no qualms at all to act on her paranoia." He paused, then added with a shrug, "Ore's actually worse, but it rarely comes out. They're the Nightwalker King and Queen of Suiran because of it."

Sirius nodded slowly, "And Grand Duke and Duchess."

"Indeed," Garen answered dryly. "I hear the Tarc are just as bad." He got back agreement from everyone in the room. They'd seen it.

"Well," Garen waved a hand and let the atmosphere lighten up again, "pick wisely, but for now they don't get to hear what we need to talk about."

Sirius excused his staff to go find the quartermaster, saying they'd meet back up for dinner if he wasn't called to that by Rei. He needed to know where he'd be sleeping as well and they could find that out for him. When his staff were out the door, he turned a bit of a scowl on Garen. "Did you really need to do that, scare them all so severely?"

"Did I?" Garen asked mildly, moving to sit on the corner of one of the desks. He wasn't ready to sit in a chair yet. "Get comfortable," he waved at the room. Sirius took the closest chair and swung it around to face Garen and sat. Garen clasped his fingers together and put his thoughts into some sort of order. Everything had built up enough it was hard to not be able to say it all all at once.

Sirius frowned at Garen. "They saw what those two do in real life, there, when they've got knives in their hands and are serious. It's not a comforting feeling at all."

"No, and it shouldn't be," Garen answered. "I've not seen them serious, but I've watched them practice on the list and I never want to be what they're seeing. I have had her mad at me in the middle of an acting session and that was bad enough, since she wasn't really acting at that moment. The entirety of the south side of town and some of the west was in an uproar when they cleaned out the unsavory nightwalkers shortly after they got back. I walked the burial grave once I got my desk cleaned up enough I could go see for myself what they'd done."

Garen looked away for a bit, remembering that walk. The group grave long and deep, being dug even more long as he walked it. "Most of the killing wounds were small, normal nightwalker attacks. There were a few I had to ask the people bringing them in on the wagons. They said the dead with no wounds were Ilena by hand, which she prefers apparently, the eyes and jugular wounds were Ore. Every driver could point to their kills if they were in the wagon."

Sirius blinked. "Ilena's kills in Tarc were neck and face kills by blade, the longest wounds. Everyone elses' kills were the small ones, yes."

Garen considered that, then nodded slowly. "I can see that. That's how they practice on the list: live steel, long knife for her, hand knife for him."

"Why? Why are they practicing on the list, and why not in the private list?" Sirius asked curiously as he leaned back a little in the chair.

"I asked them to, and Rei approved it," Garen answered with no emotion. "The soldiers didn't know Ilena, only the rumors. Ore'd already gotten them to relax around him, so they don't mind him being there practicing. To them, he's just doing his duty, like them. Her on the other hand...." Garen slumped a little. Quietly he said, "If you don't mind, I'd like to off–load and I think you need to know since you'll be leading a lot of the work for the Brulac–Gael initiative."

Sirius leaned his elbow on the desk next to him. "Yes, we'll have a lot to talk about there. Sasou gave me an earful about those two as well, that they aren't to know he or I know."

"Well since I sent half of it to him, you may already know most of it then." Garen still needed to say some of it. "It hasn't been easy to be the spy getting into their network. ...Her network. She trusts no one for all she knows she needs to act like she does to have any work get done that needs doing." His eyes looked into the distance, his mind on his memories. "It surprised me she was so willing to go along with training me and the men I assigned to learn how to be in her network. Then it surprised me she was willing to train us to learn her secret language. It wasn't until later that I understood that she already knew that Sasou or Rei would want to have someone they trusted on the inside. It doesn't matter to her which one I'm working for. She nearly lumps them together into one, save she trusts Sasou less than Rei, who's still very much in the dark in her eyes."

Garen turned his attention back on Sirius. "He's not. I'm reporting to him also: the same stuff. The things he asks me to be paying attention to say that he also knows more than he's letting on to her about — or anyone, for that matter." He paused, then added, "It's been fascinating to learn from Ilena how the Toukas think. She's been letting me research how she manipulates and manages so many people at once. I'll notice something and go to write it down and she'll make me take it out or rewrite it, congratulating me for seeing it rightly, then preventing me from letting anyone know. I don't bother sending those to King Sasou, or to Rei. They already know those things." He shook his head and it turned into a shake of his whole body. "The lords of this nation don't stand a chance," he whispered.

Sirius' eyes came to look at him sharply. Garen shook his head. "They already know there's a faction of the lords set against them. If it came down to it, the Royals would lead the people in an uprising against the lords and replace them all to a man by common men with better loyalty and management skills. And they'd win in the coup without calling up a single soldier to fight for them, and without the nightwalkers, too, most likely."

Sirius sat in a bit of shock at that news. "Not even?"

"Nope," Garen believed it to his core. "It would be harder with just the commoners, but they'd still win in the end. The soldiers love the brothers enough to obey, in the main. The northern nightwalkers will follow Ilena and Ore without question, and *all* of the nightwalkers will obey King Sasou, including those two. They just can't use those two castes and keep the loyalty of the commoners, and they already know it."

He looked away into what he'd learned. "Even so, the coming war will solidify their hold on the commoners to finish solidifying their positions while they're still only in their twenties." His look went back to Sirius. "*I* won't be standing in the way of that. If any soldiers do, it's your head and mine that will roll, given Sasou's placed you in the position of knowing their secrets now." Sirius finally went a little pale. "And it'll be Ore or Ilena's hand that'll do it."

Sirius considered that for a while, then said quietly, "Thus why your warning to even the staff to walk carefully around them."

"Yes," Garen answered quietly. "I only take my one aide who's already in their network with me to those meetings. They send everyone but him out of my office when they want to talk privately here. Select carefully. If you don't know who they trust in your staff, take none or ask them beforehand who they'll let come with you. They already know what they want to know about them all. They'll tell you if you ask, let you sweat swinging if you don't, wondering if you picked right or if they now believe you to be completely untrustworthy. They know your men better than you do in that regard. Since I didn't know anyone in the garrison command staff office before coming, I just went with who they gave me. It was the safest thing to do."

Garen let Sirius consider that for a while then changed the topic. "We'll get to what King Sasou wants you and me to do about Brulac in a minute. I want to talk about my pet project first and pick your brain there. That will let you have another hour or so of vacation before you tell me what King Sasou wants me to know about the war." He gave a small smile to Sirius at the tease.

He was glad he at least had that one reward he could focus on instead of the royals and their doings. It was vacation for him to think about the military reunion and war games. Honestly, the war itself was as well. Spying on and researching intense Toukas was an intense workout mentally and emotionally. It helped everyone else that they stayed quietly in their offices most of the time. They were content to do so to keep the rest of the country from really knowing and understanding them. Garen wasn't sure he liked that part of his job, but he was stuck with it now. He took a deep breath to try to let that go and turned his thoughts to what he preferred to think about these days.

Sirius held up a hand, his expression sober. "Before you leave that topic, let me ask a question." Garen tried to not let his face fall as he gave a nod he'd hear it. "Would the Princess kill the King, if given the opportunity to?"

Garen blinked then thought about that. "She's not likely to, no. I don't think it's in her plans. *Could* she, if she thought it necessary or became angry enough? Yes. *Would* she? I don't believe so. She's not interested in being hunted down and killed or stuck in a prison somewhere. Would she send an assassin? Not likely for the same reason, although — again — she could."

"She could run to Tarc once the deed was done," Sirius said quietly.

Garen paused again and had to think about that one harder, but again he shook his head. "You'd be thinking after they were strong enough to defend her. That won't be for a very long time, from what they've been thinking and saying in the meetings. I wasn't there, though. I don't know what our forces' chances of winning are given what level of healing they'd have gone through."

Sirius gave a thoughtful nod, but didn't let Garen know what he thought of the Tarcs' strength. That was fine by him. He didn't want to think that hard about the intrigue between the Toukas. It was hard enough to have had the realizations he'd already had about the intrigue between the lords and the Toukas. He moved the topic on to the military reunion and war games they'd be having. Sirius would need to plan the one in the northeast corner as Garen couldn't leave his post in the garrison. Sirius would teach Garen how to have them at all while he was here. He was looking forward to it.

Mizi felt as if her hands were bound by ropes and as if she were enclosed in a sack. She felt a rocking as if a rocking on a boat out to sea. It was as if she were kidnapped again, waking up to a place to make her afraid.

"Mistress. Mistress!" Ore's voice called to her. She struggled and gasped, trying to free her hands from the bonds, to return to wherever Ore was. Her hands were released, but a person grasped her around her middle and pulled her over. She began to fight in earnest. She was placed on the ground and released. The cloth over her head and face was brushed back and cold air was suddenly entering her lungs. Cold enough to make her cough, her fighting having to pause so she could.

"Mistress, it's okay. I'm here." Ore's kind but worried voice said more closely in her ear. His warmth was by her side as she lay on the ground, trying to not breathe through her mouth to have the cold burn her lungs.

Mizi tried to pry her eyes open, but it was dark. "Ore? Where are we?" she managed to get out.

"We're at our sleeping place for the night. What is it?" he asked her. "I'm sorry we woke you up poorly."

"I'm not kidnapped?" she asked him.

"No," he said in kind sympathy. "We had you wrapped up to be warm while we rode Fenrier. You were sleeping very soundly."

"*Ah,*" Mizi sighed, trying to place where they were and why. She supposed riding a horse might feel like being at sea, and a sleeping, dreaming mind would make the terrible connections she'd had. "It's so cold," she complained sleepily.

"Well, I'd pull up your muffler, but I think you'd have fought even more, for thinking we were trying to silence you," he answered dryly.

"Probably," she agreed.

"Well, if you think you can stand, we'll get you inside for a warm meal and a more comfortable bed," Ore said with the calm practicality he used when she needed to be moving forward. A hand slipped into hers and pulled.

She pushed against the ground with the other one and got up to stand rather unsteadily. "I think I'm still at sea, though," she said. "My legs don't want to work."

"That's from riding without stopping to move them for the last three hours," Ore said and tucked her hand into his arm to get her moving slow enough her legs could get used to the movement again.

"Three hours!" she was somewhat aghast. "I really slept that long?"

"Yes," Ore laughed silently at her. "I think the stress of planning the hospital and having to present to the Court of Ministers made you miss a lot of sleep?"

Mizi slumped. "You'd be right," she admitted, finally beginning to remember why she and Ore were out and traveling.

A rectangle ahead of them opened up to spill out light and warmth. A young man let them in and closed the door behind them. Mizi looked over her shoulder to see Henry and Marcus following them with the bags for the four of them in their hands and the message bag over Marcus' shoulder. The young man seemed to have left the house after they'd entered. "I'm sorry," she said to them, but they shook their heads at her. One of them had to be the one who'd taken her down from Fenrier so Ore could get off.

"It's good to know you have the right instincts," Marcus smiled at her. "You don't need to change that, nor apologize for it. We'll try to remember it right for next time, though. It's not good to frighten you."

"Yes," Ore agreed. "Next time they'll let you choke on the cold air first, then finish waking you up."

"Ore!" she scolded, earning her a teasing grin from him. He was being serious while teasing her at the same time, as usual, to set her at ease and get her out of her head and her worries. She squeezed his arm and let him go to look around the open room. A fireplace had a happily crackling fire in it, logs having been added recently, likely on their arrival. There were a goodly number of comfortable chairs and a couch in the room, as well as a few side tables. Beyond that room was a door into the farther parts of the house. It looked like the dining room was next and maybe the kitchen a little farther down the hallway.

"It's one of Ilena's protective waystations she uses to get people to safer locations than they're coming from," Ore explained as he pulled his gloves off, then his scarf.

A woman came bustling into the fire–warmed room. "Welcome." She introduced herself and her family, then turned to Mizi. "We have this room and one above you could sleep in," Irene offered. "Or," she glanced at Ore and also offered, "the men could sleep upstairs and Mistress Mizi in the room with my daughter, Abigail. There's an extra bed there, and four in the guest room."

Mizi immediately said, "I'd be happy to share with your daughter tonight. It's been a while since I've been able to have a fun sleep–over; although, I'll likely do more sleeping that chatting and laughing, given how tired I am from the day." She smiled a happy smile to let them all know she was quite okay with that arrangement.

"Ah, Mistress doesn't want to be alone tonight and is kind to make sure I'm not either," Ore smiled at her, getting to the point she'd been hiding with the ease he did. She often wished she could tweak his ear for doing that to her. He turned to Irene. "That will be fine if she says so."

"As long as you don't then spend all night down here awake watching the door," Henry dryly scolded Ore.

Mizi giggled, knowing Ore would do it, too, if they let him. It was nice they could tweak Ore for her. "Yes, do sleep Ore," she mock–scolded him, too. "If you fall asleep in the saddle tomorrow, I won't get my nap for having to hold you up." Ore gave a heavy sigh and slump of his shoulders in mock submission.

Irene smiled tolerantly and politically turned the topic. "I've food waiting for you. If you'll follow me to the rooms to put your things away, we can get warmth into you so you can sleep well." She did show them the next room was where they'd be eating, then they were going up a set of stairs. The room over the front sitting area was as large as it, with another fire going nicely in it. The men picked their beds and dropped their bags and winter gear on them. Mizi followed Irene down a hallway like the one on the first floor to a back room where Abigail was finishing putting a third warm quilt on the second bed in the room. Mizi thanked her for being willing to share the room and bed with her, then put her winter gear over the arm and back of the chair at the foot of that bed.

Ore appeared with Mizi's bag and put it on the foot of the bed, his eyes scanning the room. He'd want to know how to help her if he needed to, but she was just as happy that this could be a safe place and he'd not have to. She was a little surprised when the matron paused and glared a bit at Ore. "You'd be the overprotective husband or boyfriend, but please remember that in this house if you walk into this room we'll not hesitate to attack even you. We also protect our daughter."

Ore drew back a little in shock. He shook his head. "I'm sorry. It's very much habit now. She's been stolen out from under our eyes a few too many times for my liking."

"Like, once," Mizi rolled her eyes at him. "And that a long time ago now."

He scowled at her slightly, "And how many more times was it tried that you don't even know about?"

She humbly relented. "Probably more than that once is more than I care to know about." It didn't help that her waking had been an open reminder of that once. And that his scold tried to bring up the memories of similar situations from before he'd been her guard.

Ore was mollified but still took a while to not be quite so stiff. He bowed to Irene. "I'll not enter unless it's absolutely essential. Master would so super scold me that I'd barely feel your beating for my ears being torn off my head." That seemed to calm Irene down enough they could head back downstairs to the dining room. Mizi and Marcus turned the conversation to lighter things so Ore could calm down and the air between them all relax again.

"What time would you like to leave in the morning?" Lewis, the man of the house asked. He'd come in with his son, Lorence, to join them in the dining room to report their horses had been seen to. They'd been given warm drinks, but not food, so Mizi could tell it was late enough the family had already eaten their dinner.

Ore tapped a finger on the table, his lips pursed. "Adding in the new Northern Pass garrison really makes this part difficult. If we make it a short visit, it's still a ten hour day by winter's travel. We can't make it much faster at the first part because of the mountain passage. We could run the last half of it if it were slightly warmer and stays clear. That would shave off enough hours to arrive by dinner time." He sighed and his eyes measured Mizi. "We could stay up there, but that wastes time. Half a day in a place that's still not really even finished with construction and where we could be trapped if it snows until the soldiers clear the passage."

He slumped a little and looked at Lewis. "Master wants to know if he should plan on closing that garrison in the winter when the snows come, once they've fully completed the construction on it. I'm to confirm it this trip. If the snows block the full passage enough, it doesn't have to be a prison for them over winter. It's just that we're newly come from all of the conflicts with Pakyo and Tarc, so there's some level of concern about the passage we didn't know about from Tarc into Suiran, for all it's a difficult one." That was understandable. As was the practicality of closing it down if it was impassible in the winter time.

"The old mare says it will stay clear through tomorrow, at least," Lorence commented to his father.

Lewis gave a slow nod. "You could go up there and come back here," he said. He tipped his head towards Mizi. "She could stay here and relax if she's not needed for the visit. That might ease your mind a bit as far as the difficulty of the passage goes."

Ore was uncomfortable with not having eyes on Mizi, she could tell. He looked at Marcus and Henry. They were nearly as uncomfortable. Finally they sighed.

"We'll split up, but we'll both be imagining the sudden winter squall that separates all of us for a month of fear and worry. It's just as hard for us to do that as for the two pairs of you, you know," Henry said. Ore's eyebrows had gone up.

Mizi was a bit surprised as well. "You don't have to," she said, then glared slightly at the Ore who wanted to protest. "It'd only be for the one day, not for any nights, and no one but the Family knows where we are. I'd rather you had both of them if that squall did suddenly show up so that you could all get back here safely."

Ore considered it, then quietly said, "I think we need to take this to the other half and get their thoughts on it, particularly Master's since it's his order." Mizi could understand that wisdom. "I'd like to be on the road before dawn. The early part we don't need much light but we'll need all we can get once we're up on the mountain's shoulder and until we're back down from it. The rocky ground doesn't give much purchase. I'm not sure having snow on top of it's helpful. At least it's still patchy rather than full rock like above the garrison is."

After dinner they sat on chairs and beds in the guest bedroom, Mizi included, with a window open towards the east. *Father to Mother and Master. The waystation family has been kind and offered to keep Mistress for the day while we visit the Northern Pass garrison. We need your advice and thoughts on who should stay with her and who should go with me. She says I should take the Twins with me, but as you well know I'm not comfortable leaving her without eyes I know on her, for all I'm grateful to them for the offer. Mistress isn't worried.*

The Twins don't want to be separated for the same reasons Master's worried since before we left, but will do as ordered. We'll take her with us if you wish it, although the passage is worrisome. Their mare says it will stay clear through tomorrow, so making it a single day–trip should be simple enough if we stay here again tomorrow night, putting us back onto the usual travel schedule thereafter.

Mizi ran through that in her head again while they waited for it to be passed along. Saying it all at once helped on the other end, but made the communication take longer for the larger saying at every person along the line. "Sending the messages this way does seem rather cumbersome and awkward," she finally said. "It's kind of them all to be willing to help in this way, but I can see why it would be hard to keep the verbal lines like this going."

The other three nodded. "A letter is much simpler and if only one or two messengers carry it, much less taxing as to the numbers of helpers needed," Henry said. He looked away. "Mistress Ilena's been able to continuously add new members to the Family and House until now, but she won't be able to so very well anymore. The lines actually do have an attrition rate as people move, get new responsibilities, and such like. We'll be having to cut down regardless, as the number of available persons to help shrinks. And rather sooner than perhaps we'd like is when it should happen, to show some gratitude and give them some relief."

Mizi sighed and put her chin on her arms, as she'd moved to be sitting back against the wall of the bed second–closest to the window, her knees up in front of her. "That's certainly true. It was quite invaluable while Ore was in Tarc and we were in the Northeast garrison, and I'd expect it to be that in the coming conflict. And I'm sure it's quite helpful for the passing of information expeditiously to the Ministry, but it is quite a great amount of volume for them to carry in that way." She frowned a little. "Will all of it then come by written means?"

"Most will," Marcus said quietly as they were now waiting to hear back an answer. "If it's critical and very secret, it's likely to still come by way of personal messenger who speaks it in our ears. Mistress Ilena will only ever trust that form of communication for the most critical things. The person who witnessed it has to tell her directly or she won't believe it." Mizi understood that, while also understanding it was quite paranoid of Ilena.

Nijou to Father. Making it a day–trip up to the garrison is fine. Father can't go alone. Master is trying to decide the rest, finding it perhaps as difficult as you all are.

"That's Master Rei, Mistress Ilena, Mistress Ilena," Marcus muttered more to himself. Mizi agreed with that assessment, though. Somehow the patterns of speech of the person came through.

She sighed and moved closer to the window, near Ore. *Mistress to Master.* That was rather awkward, but she understood that they still wanted the code names to be used rather than the actual names when it was the long–distance code. *Really, I'll be fine. The family is kind and I'd really like the opportunity to relax for a day while not having to overly worry about Father. I can talk to you at our usual time in the morning to help us both. I'm sure Mother has picked her waystation families with care for the protection of her Children. Even the matron of the home had no troubles scolding Father with fire in her eyes tonight.* Ore turned red, but Mizi felt he deserved it.

They waited again until they heard, *Nijou to Father and Mistress. It's fine. The Twins going with Father will help Mother and them, not to mention they need to know where that garrison is and how to get there. I'm likely to make them take over Father's Messenger duties after this anyway.* The Twins rolled their eyes, but it wasn't a surprising thing to hear from Rei. He'd use Kirk and them, plus the Twins' business, as they'd already been talking about.

Father to Mother and Master. We hear and will follow through. Sleep well tonight. We love you.

Mizi nodded her head, glad he'd put it that way. She patted Ore on the head. "You sleep well tonight as well, so I don't worry about Fenrier slipping on snowy rocks and throwing you. Your eyes will need to be sharp." She went to Marcus and did the same. "Thank you for today, Marcus. Sleep well also for the same reason. I need you to come back whole, too." She went to Henry and bowed slightly. "Same for you, too, sir." She scolded slightly sternly.

Henry smiled for her. "I'll see to it we all come back, the same as we all will. Given a fair day it should be a simple one for all of us, really."

"Exactly," Mizi said firmly. "The worries only hold us down and interfere. I for one will be glad to have no one around who cares *what* I am ...other than a Child of the Family." She sighed to herself. That would be the best present of the day. She waited long enough to hear the goodnights and loving wishes from the castle, then took herself out and down the hallway to the bedroom she was sharing.

"I'm sorry to take so long to come back," she said to Abigail. "I hope it hasn't disturbed you too much."

"Oh, no," Abigail said. "It's better for everyone to understand so the worries can be settled." She smiled at Mizi and Mizi was grateful for it. Mizi dug through her bag and pulled out her warm nightgown to begin to get dressed for the night.

"Is it true that Prince Ore is also your boyfriend from a long time before?" Abigail asked.

Mizi smiled. "That is a very old and very wrong rumor. He's only ever been my guardian. He does love me, for which I'm grateful, but it's more like the love of an older brother for a younger sister," she looked at the young teenage girl as her head came though the neckhole of her nightgown, "like you and your brother. He'd be first through that door to take a man down if he snuck in, I think?" The girl had to agree.

Mizi tucked her clothing into her bag and moved it to the chair, then pulled back the blankets and top sheet from her bed. "Oh, that's going to be very warm. Thank you for making it for me," she said, although she sadly had to run her hands over the sheets and pillow and under the pillow to confirm it was safe. She hid her knife under the edge of the pillow as well. They weren't precautions she wanted to take, but had to for the sake of staying safe and for the practice of the same. She had people who relied on her to see she did now, particularly since in this place she'd said she'd stay safe for them.

Abigail had snuggled down in her bed further as she'd also commented on how warm it would be that night. Mizi wasn't surprised the next question was another common one. "Were you really born common?"

"Yes," Mizi said as she lay down and pulled the covers over her. They were heavy but would warm up very quickly. Once she was settled, she explained, "It's been a very big change and adjustment. Not all for the nicer, either. It's hard to make the lords happy with me, some of them. But I'm very glad to be married to the man I love the most. Are you hoping to marry for love?"

"Oh, yes!" she was answered. "I don't know who yet, as all of the boys in this area aren't worth it, but I do hope to someday."

Mizi smiled. "It was like that for me, too, in Yamanzar. It was so surprising to learn the young lad I'd run into by complete chance was the Second Prince of Ryokudo. He was the second person I talked to when I entered the country. He was very kind, even to helping me get to Ichijoutsu since I'd gotten a bit lost. It was hard to not like him right away. That feeling only grew stronger with every passing day and visit we had, until I was very much in love with him. I couldn't believe for a long time that it could be something I could dream for, though. Princes don't often get to marry for love. We've both been very blessed we were allowed to and were helped by others to get there. When I remember that, it's easier to face the difficult lords and the more stressful times."

"It's not just a perfect romance?" she was asked with some surprise.

"Oh, no. The romance is perhaps as perfect as it could be. It's that life for us is like life for everyone: hard most of the time, taking a lot of work and patience. When you come home you get to relax. It's that way for us. Once we're in our own suite together, we can relax together, and that's very nice."

"How old were you when you met him?" was the next question. That was much better than where conversations turned next when Mizi was talking to young ladies of the court.

"I was thirteen, nearing fourteen," she said.

"Oh! I'm fourteen!" Abigail was very surprised. "Were you traveling with your family?"

"No. My mother died when I was very young and my father put me in foster care with my aunt and uncle. They died when I was eleven and I ran an herb shop from then until I was thirteen. I'd left Yamanzar on my own, so was alone until Prince Rei found me."

"That's so sad!" Abigail was quite sympathetic. "I wouldn't be able to do that," she shivered in her bed at the thought. "I love to help my family and am so glad to have them. I don't know what I'd do if I didn't have them."

"No, that's understandable," Mizi agreed. "It was hard at first. I'd helped my aunt and uncle with their inn until they passed away, so I knew just enough about managing money so I could live. I sold the inn, because that was more work than any one person can do on their own, and bought a small herb shop because I love working with plants and their medicinal properties.

"The grannies of the neighborhood helped me learn it since they wanted to have a close enough place for their own ailments to be treated. There was another shopkeeper on the block that helped me get suppliers for the basic herbs, and I learned how to go hunt for the easier ones in the woods to save my own money. I loved learning how to do all that and helping other people. It was being told by the government official that I had to close it all down by order of their First Prince that made me leave. I thought I could work as a medic here in Ryokudo.

"After I met Prince Rei, I learned that the Department of Medicine in Ichijou was testing for interns. I studied very hard and passed the test. That meant I could be in the castle and learn what I wanted to learn. It helped to be closer to the one person who'd been kind to me, too."

"When did you meet Prince Ore?" was asked with the bated breath of a person excited to hear more of the story.

Mizi smiled to herself. She was enjoying telling it, since it brought back happy memories, even though it had been hard work, most days. "I wasn't wanted in Ichijou by the lords, like here in Nijou now, because Prince Rei would come talk to me: a commoner from another country. One of them hired Ore to chase me out of the castle. Instead, Ore saw whatever it was that Rei, Andrew, and Mina saw in me that gave me their approval, and he eventually refused to try any more. I was working hard against him, since I was very determined to stay where I was. Rei asked him to protect me instead and he agreed. It came as a surprise to me that Rei would think I'd need protecting, and made me begin to wonder if he was also coming to fall in love with me, as embarrassing as that thought was." She smiled to herself at the memory of that realization.

Abigail giggled in agreement. "That would be so romantic, to be assigned a personal guard by the Prince himself."

"Umhm," Mizi agreed. "Of course we both then had to gain the approval of the older brother, just like your family has had to gain it from my 'older brother'," she chuckled. "King Sasou's scary when he's protecting Rei. We had to work very hard to get his approval, but in the end Ilena managed to help us get there. She's been very supportive and kind. She's the older sister."

There was silence for a bit from the other bed, then quietly came, "My older sister was like that.... She was to be married to someone but got an unexpected injury that she couldn't recover from. We've all been sad since then that we couldn't help her recover."

"I'm sorry to hear that," Mizi said gently. "That is hard." She let the silence go for a bit, realizing that this bed was probably that sister's bed. "Well, I know it's not much, but if you'd let me be the older sister again for a day, tomorrow, I'd be happy to help you around the house."

There was a sniffle from the other bed and a muffled, "Umhm."

Mizi got up out of her now warm bed and walked over to lie down with Abigail and hold her while she cried for a while. She should be the older sister now, not just tomorrow, since she'd brought the grief up. Eventually she was thanked and pushed lightly back out of the bed. "Go warm up again. It's only going to get colder."

Mizi realized then that the back bedrooms didn't have fireplaces. Likely they were only warmed from the heat of the kitchen fire below during the day. Mizi patted Abigail on the head and obediently went back to her own bed. "Good night," she said kindly and received the same. She lay there thinking for a while longer, falling asleep without really knowing she did. She was looking forward to the next day already.

18-19 Ante-Cold Solstice: A Relaxing Stop

Mizi woke up to the quiet sounds of Abigail preparing for her day. Birds were already chirping outside the window and, as she peeked her eyes open, early morning sun was already coming in through the window. Mizi sighed to herself and sat up with pursed lips. "It looks like they let us sleep in," she commented, not pleased to have been left without goodbyes being said, for all she was sure Ore had firmly wanted her to get enough rest. He really didn't like goodbyes and much preferred to be on his way so he could get back so he could worry less.

Abigail agreed with a shy nod. Mizi got out of bed and went to her bag to pull out clothes Maria had packed for Kouzanshi. She wouldn't need the heavier traveling clothing today. She carefully picked one of the few outfits that she could get dirty if necessary since she expected to help in the kitchen. "They'll have food waiting for us in the kitchen, when you're ready to come down," Abigail said as she paused at the door to let herself out.

"Okay," Mizi said cheerfully. "I'll be down shortly. Then I should talk to my husband for a bit. He'll be eating his own breakfast right about now, so I have that long." That would be in the garrison cafeteria this morning so he had the distraction and in keeping with their patterns. It would be easier to talk to him once he reached the Rose office.

"Okay," Abigail said, then left, shutting the door behind her so Mizi could get dressed. Mizi dressed quickly, making the bed neatly and making sure her bag and clothing were also neatly packed. She paused, then closed up the bag tightly and put her knife belt around her waist. She'd been reminded that clothing needed to be protected as well. She might be able to tell if things in her bag were rearranged if she closed it now, but if she just left it open, she'd never know. With a sigh at this new state of things once again, she left the room, closing the door behind her as she went, just out of force of habit.

"Good morning Irene," Mizi said to Abigail's mother as she walked into the kitchen. "Thank you for the comfortable bed last night and for the food. Did Ore and the Twins get out okay this morning?" Her lips pursed just a little again as Irene handed her a plate, readied for her when Abigail had come down, no doubt.

"Yes they did, Mistress Mizi," Irene answered. "Master Ore was quite certain you'd be unhappy with not being woken up but was just as firm that you were to be allowed to rest. He says you can call and scold him, but you should do it fairly soon since we don't have people to pass on messages once they're up on the shoulder of the mountain."

"Oh!" Mizi paused in surprise, then shook her head as she set her plate down at the small kitchen table and sat. "I would think not. But I don't...," she paused, then said, "I'll scold him briefly before I talk to Rei, then, which I need to do directly after eating. Once I've done that requirement, then I'd like to help around the house, if I may." She smiled briefly at Irene, then tucked into her breakfast. She did actually need to scold Ore and hear from him to know he was okay. She sighed at him once again. He really did know her too well by now. She looked up at Abigail and wrinkled her nose up. "Do you scold your older brother as well?"

Abigail giggled. "Well, yes. Particularly when he teases too much."

Mizi nodded a knowing nod of agreement. "He likes to use the nicknames for us all the time. Maybe I should start calling him that instead of by his name."

Abigail and Irene both laughed at that. "Irene, Ore said this is one of Mother's protecting places. Can you tell me a little more about that?" Mizi wanted to know and wanted to get the food into her rather quickly so she wasn't interrupting Rei too late in his morning.

She listened as Irene explained what the waystations were and in brief how Ilena used them. When the explanation was done, Mizi was mostly done with the food as well. She shook her head. "What Ilena's done already in her lifetime amazes me. It's been done because she had a need that also met others' needs, but all together it's rather astounding." Soberly she looked into Irene's eyes. "Thank you so much to you and your family for being willing to stand ready to be one of those who aids those in need. Abigail said last night that you lost your oldest daughter unexpectedly. I'm very sorry for your loss." Irene gave a wordless nod.

Mizi rose to her feet to take her dishes to the kitchen sink, refusing to let Irene take them. She wanted to wash them herself. "Does running this waystation make you members of the Family, or allies?" she asked.

There was a pause that made her look over her shoulder. Irene was giving her a studying look. "In our case, allies with limited knowledge. We know the long–distance code so we can know when we're needed. ...Do you not know how to see?"

Mizi blinked, then turned back to her dishes to consider that question. "Well..., no, I guess not. I'm considered a Child by them as far as the Family network goes. I had to learn the long–distance code on my own. I wanted to be able to hear Ore's reports while waiting at the Northeast garrison since I wanted to know he was okay." She rinsed her plate and picked up her fork to wash it.

She paused before rinsing it. "Now that we're in the castle again, I can under-stand why they didn't really want me to know it. I've been learning quite a lot about the darker side of my home that I was quite blissfully unaware of before then." She rinsed the fork and picked up the drying cloth to dry it. "It's actually nice to be here this morning and not have any reports passing by my ears at all. I'm sure it will be just as noisy as normal by afternoon, however."

She turned to look for where the fork should be put. Irene had moved to be closer to her and reached out her hand for the fork. Her smile was kind. "It is hard when it's the bad news that's passed along most often. But you do hear the positives as they come, I hope?"

Mizi paused, then gave a nod and picked up her plate to dry it. "I do like hearing the brief stories of who's had a baby, or gotten engaged. And I've noticed a few will send along funny stories as well."

"Yes," Irene gave a firm nod. "No one likes to hear only bad news, and Mother does like to know that her Children are happy now. Focus on those when you can and let the rest go as best you can." Mizi gave a nod and a final wipe to the plate and handed it over, learning where utensils and plates went so she could put them away at the next meal. She hung the cloth back where she'd picked it up from to let it dry. "But if you don't know how to see, then how did you guess that we were an allied house?"

Mizi answered, "By feel. Rei chose ally and his translator explained why that was the right answer for him. You have that feel this morning, but I think to stand up so quickly to Ore last night made me think it. Children might tease, but they don't ...bark, if you'll excuse me for saying it that way," she was blushing, but that was the only term she could use that fit how it had felt. "Or, I suppose I could use Ore's term and say 'super scold', except it wasn't quite that either."

Irene was blushing a little herself. "I'm sure I didn't need to be so firm, but I was suddenly quite irritated with what I'd seen."

Mizi chuckled. "Yes. I've had my own hackles raised more than once by that look of judgment he gives to every room I walk into that he's not allowed to stay in to watch over me with his own eyes. It's really that he's jealous of that requirement, not jealous for me. Nor is he complaining about the accommodations. He's complaining that his master won't let him be the true guard dog he wants to be." Mizi bared her teeth and growled, curling her fingers in front of her, then barked. "He'd sometimes rather be that than a man, when it comes to my safety."

She laughed with the ladies of the house, then relented. "Well, but I'm very grateful for it, in the end. He isn't wrong that he's protected me many times, most of them so well I don't know when they happen. The first assassination attempt I knew about against me at the castle surprised me. Ilena made them let it happen to begin to teach me what it would mean to really be a royal, although they still protected me very well." She shook her head. "Well, I'm going to be late talking to Rei if I don't go now. I'll be back shortly," she promised and headed for the stairs.

Mizi did scold Ore first so he could feel loved and remembered and so she could feel better, too. She'd remembered that he'd said back in Osterly that he felt loved when he was scolded by Rei. She'd really not believed it then, but today she thought maybe he'd not been lying and she could finally understand why. Then she talked happily with Rei for a bit, doing her best to cheer him up and give him enough of her attention to hold him for the day, grateful that they could still do this. She thanked the people along the line as well before closing the conversation. She was sure they'd rather be passing along cheerful messages of care and concern when they could, now that she did have to ignore all the negative messages that came in.

-o-o-o-

"Well, that's very convenient!" Leon said as his ears perked up and he and Sam listened to Mizi and Rei's morning conversation. The evening conversation between Ilena and Ore had been rather normal to them, since they'd done that when in Tarc. The Ministry business was still being done all the time in the afternoon, too, so they almost felt like they were still home, to some degree.

"Well, they did do that when Mistress Mizi was at the castle and Master Rei at the Northwest garrison before," Sam said.

"True, but we couldn't hear it then," Leon said. "It helps to know what the plan for the day is and that they're about to go right at the moment we want to know. I hope we can use that every day. That would make the traveling so much simpler."

"True," Sam agreed congenially. They were already on the road, having left Osterly as soon as there was daylight in the sky. "It helped quite a bit to learn they'd stay put at the waystation today, too. Now we'll for sure be ahead of them."

Leon agreed enthusiastically. He wasn't too thrilled to be traveling in this season. It was his first time to do the winter snow travel and he was a bit nervous about the trip. Sam had reassured him he'd done it for several years as a younger soldier, so that had helped or Leon would've also asked for a guide from the garrison. He'd only done the one trip on North road during the progress and that hadn't been in the winter. He shivered in his warm clothes, hoping the trip wouldn't put them at risk and that Mizi and Ore wouldn't be attacked. It was going to be enough for him to learn how to travel in the winter in Suiran.

He sighed at himself for his lack of courage, but there were too many horror stories and rumors told down in the southern part of the nation about winter storms in the north. They were usually told when people said they were moving north. His brothers and sisters had done that to him when he'd stopped by his home on his way north to Nijou from Ichijou. His father hadn't been too happy he'd taken a perceived step down in status, but he'd earnestly explained to his father his real goal: to stand behind the one he fervently believed would become the First Princess of the nation. That was definitely many steps up from being a gate guard at Ichijou. He might be worried about the winter weather, but he was also oh, so proud, to have reached the goal he'd been working for; that he'd been right from the beginning.

He hoped that would be enough for his father to agree to his next goal. As the fourth son of a noble lord, he had more leeway than most, though, so he didn't think it should be *too* hard. The greater difficulty would be if he had competition. That was the hardest part about this sort of goal. It would be out of his hands almost all together. He sighed to himself and tried to not worry about it again. Instead he tried to enjoy the fact that it wasn't cloudy, snowy, and grey. It was actually nice for once. He didn't have to worry today.

-o-o-o-

Mizi paused before leaving the guest bedroom, having gone upstairs again to that room to talk to Rei since it faced the castle and was out of the way of the family. The middle of that room was just open enough. She practiced her martial–art dance there, just enough to get the full form done twice. She couldn't do the rest of the practice, but opportunities to do it at all were going to be infrequent as long as they were on the road. Then she headed back downstairs.

"So, what can I do to help? I've heard there isn't much to do inside in winters, but don't have much knowledge of it since Yamanzar is a hot desert country and a medic is *always* busy." She smiled and looked around. Indeed, it looked like they'd already done what little cleaning to the house it needed. Then her eyes were caught by a corner of the kitchen. "Bring me your herbs. I'll work with them and see what I can do to help with that."

"That would be a help," Irene agreed. She was at a spindle and Abigail was holding carding blocks. A basket of wool was in front of them. They left their tools and walked over to that corner and pulled down the trays and tied bundles of dried herbs likely collected over the growing seasons.

"Do you have packets or cloths I can put them in?" Mizi asked. Irene put down her part of the burden and headed for a linen closet. A packet of what looked similar to handkerchiefs was placed on the table. Mizi was satisfied and pulled the herbs over. She was soon lost in the identification of them, sorting them into piles of things she could combine into useful mixes and things she should just keep separated. One thing she set to the side.

When she was ready, she pulled the cloths to her and began breaking up the stems into shorter lengths that she laid out on the cloths. Those things to be kept individual should be kept wrapped so they could be kept efficacious longer. "Ah," she interrupted the quiet conversation of the other two. "Paper and pen, please? I don't want to write on the cloths but I don't want you to be confused. And would you want me to pin the papers to the outside or put them inside the packets?"

Irene sent Abigail for pins and went to the front receiving room for paper and pen. While they did that, Mizi relaxed a bit, then realized she'd become very lost in her work, like she did when she was in her office in the Medical offices. That was sad in this place. When they'd returned, she smiled at them. "Thank you. I'm sorry to get so lost in the work instead of being pleasant company. I'm afraid I fell rather quickly into my habits, having my hands busy with what they already know."

"That's all right," Irene smiled. "We were just having Abigail's daily lesson. I'm glad we weren't disturbing you."

"Oh, no," Mizi said, slightly dismayed they'd be worried about that. "I'm more worried I'd be disturbing your day. I'm grateful you're willing to let me be here."

"Your professional help with the herbs is more than we can repay," Irene said respectfully.

Mizi paused in some surprise. Then she ruefully shook her head at herself. "I certainly wouldn't make you pay for something to keep my hands busy, and I do love to work with herbs generally anyway. I'll also try to be more aware so I'm not just a part of the table and chair." She laughed at herself a little self–consciously. They all returned to their work and Mizi tried harder this time to pay attention to what the other two were doing while also doing her work. She really did want to know what mothers in Ryokudo did to teach their daughters. This was a rare opportunity to learn a little of that.

When it looked like Abigail had sat at the wool as long as she could stand, Mizi called her over to the table and took a turn to teach her what she'd done to store the individual herbs, naming them and what their base use was. Then she called Irene over, and showed her the one herb she'd set aside. "This is a look–alike herb." She showed them the details of what was similar to the real herb, then what wasn't. "In this case, this one has some benefits, but not enough for us to use professionally. If you want to use it, you'll need to use three times as much, but not steep it as long, since it has some not so nice effects if it's too strong." She looked to Irene, letting her decide.

Irene was obviously disappointed it wasn't what she'd thought it was. "Well..., for this winter, I'll still use it, but I'd like to get some of the right herb. What should I look for again?"

Mizi paused, then said, "I'll write it down. Even I'd need that reminder. I'll write down the formulation for this one, too."

"Thank you," Irene was grateful. Then she turned to Abigail. "And thus why you need to learn to read, even as a woman." Abigail slumped, but Mizi firmly agreed. She turned to writing and Abigail dutifully watched her form the letters.

"Did you have to learn new letters, too, when you came to Ryokudo?" Abigail asked Mizi somewhat suddenly.

Mizi paused, then smiled ruefully. "Well, yes, actually." She wrote the name of the plant in her native language, which was much curlier and more like Ilena's secret written language, actually. "That's what I'd write for this plant there."

Abigail's eyes were very wide. "And you still passed the testing? Don't they make you write for it?"

Mizi nodded. "I had to work *very* hard to learn how to read and write very quickly in Ryokudan. Since I really only had to know the technical terms for the herbs and medical methodologies for the test I didn't have to learn everything all at once, but learning those things helped me with the rest."

"How long?" Abigail asked, almost as a challenge.

Mizi sighed. "About three months, a little less by the time I learned of the request for interns."

"So fast!" Abigail was shocked. Even Irene was impressed.

Mizi shook her head. "It was most of a year before I had the rest learned. I'm grateful that for at least most of the countries around the Inner Sea we all speak the same trade language and use the same numbering system. Having to learn how to understand the spoken language and I'd have missed the intern request altogether since it took me three years to really be able to hear and speak royal Ryokudan." That had been a requirement because she was in the castle itself where it was spoken almost exclusively by anyone outside of the Department of Medicine, and thus mostly there as well. The others had been patient with her to help her learn it.

"No wonder you said it was mostly work," Abigail sighed and put her chin down on her arms on the table. "It makes my eyes cross some days, to try to read."

"Yes," Mizi sympathized, "but it's well worth it." She finished writing up her instructions and gave half of the herb to Abigail to cut. She showed Abigail how long to cut the stems, then chatted with her while they got that one completed. She showed her how to wrap them up so that the cloth became a soft envelope that held the herb in so it wouldn't spill. She handed the paper to Abigail and she pinned it onto the cloth and added it to the completed packets.

Mizi stretched and looked at Irene. "Do you mind if we pause here for lunch? The rest I'll make into mixtures and label them with what they do and proper measurements and timing." She waved at the remaining herbs waiting in their piles. Irene blinked a bit in surprise, then rose and headed for the ice chest.

"Abigail," Mizi drew her attention to the waiting herbs, "will you help me with them, too? We have to take the leaves off of most of them, or cut the stems down very small, so that we can measure and make the correct ratios of the herbs. We can't just dump them all together at whatever number was harvested. Some herbs are very potent and others aren't at all, like the look–alike. We don't want to cause harm by having too much of the first kind, and if we don't add enough of the latter kind it wasn't worth bothering to add it at all, except we usually need its properties.

"Sometimes we need the secondary properties of herbs. The main property might be nice, but not part of the reason for the mixture; however, the secondary property of the herb buffers, or makes safer or easier for the body to use the main properties of the herbs we need. Much of the experimentation at Kouzanshi university in the Medical Department has to do with discovering those kinds of properties." Mizi waved her hand a the individual herbs. "Most people know about the main properties. Some researchers find new herbs and experiment with what they do, but most of us are experimenting with mixtures to find new or more potent ways to help those we know about do their job better, or with more effects added in."

Mizi smiled. "I like to experiment with tea mixtures. Ore's very brave and will try things that taste very bad, or that have bad reactions. His stomach is now very much iron, but I do try to not poison him. Ryan likes to study mixtures that do more than one thing. His favorite one is one that helps broken bones not hurt while they're healing. He added a pain–relieving herb to boneknit, then had to find the right buffering herbs to make them work together in concert at the right amounts."

She paused, then said quietly, "Ilena's was similar, but she also added in one that healed bruising and muscles, and another that made people sleepy, which we usually try to not add in, but she needed it for Tokumade. It took her a long time because it had so many different effects she wanted and finding just the right set of herbs that would work together was hard. It's particularly hard to get the seeping timing right for teas. To make what would have been a poultice into a tea was the hardest for her, I think."

"She used it both ways," Irene said quietly as she began to set food on the table. "She'd hand over the cup at the end of the seeping time, having only the brief time between the punishment given and when she had to lock them in. They'd drink it before entering the coffin, then place the remaining herbs as a poultice on the wounds once they were inside. They still cried themselves to sleep, but it was a relief to be able to, knowing the tea, the poultice, and the sleep would all help them heal."

Mizi studied Irene. That was enough to say she'd been there during that time. Which made Mizi wonder why Irene wasn't a Child. Then she knew. "You wanted to help her there," Mizi stated. Irene gave a curt nod. Mizi paused, then said, "I'm glad you weren't broken by living there. You're very strong."

Irene looked into Mizi's eyes, then she turned to retrieve plates and a knife to cut the salted meat with. Mizi studied her further. "You watched her go through her own punishment. Her coming out of it alive impressed you that much?"

Irene spun around to stare at Mizi with wide eyes. Mizi only looked at her with the court face that said nothing other than she was observing, perhaps judging what she was seeing. Irene drew in a deep breath, choosing to be careful in what she answered with, rather than just reacting. That showed some level of understanding and restraint. "I was young enough that I'd already forgotten she'd been put in that punishment by the time she was released from it. The person of skin and bone, that couldn't even stand, that looked like she should be dead, was a sight I'll never forget. I asked my mother who it was and had to have it retold to me all over again. I was in shock for a long time.

"I watched her recover. I watched her stand with strength even after that, and I wanted to be like that. I wanted to be able to face difficulties with courage. It took me a long time to learn that courage was fears faced regardless of how much that fear wanted to make me run away and cry in a corner. When I learned that hidden part of how courage worked, then I truly understood how much it helped her when we'd be obedient to her so that she didn't have to be so afraid.

"She never once faced Earl Shicchi with fear on her. Only when one of us would catch his eye did she have fear on her face. Only when she was the one between us and him was she able to find relief. The punishments she took were...," Irene stopped and shivered. "It didn't take long before everyone understood that if she gave an order it was to be followed with exactness so that we — and even more she — didn't have to." Irene pursed her lips, then turned away for the final things to put on the table, but the sorrow on her face was enough for Mizi to understand.

"Thank you for understanding, and for protecting her as best you could," Mizi said softly. "We're very grateful for all of you doing that. We love her very much, too." Irene arrived with the final things and began preparing the plates for the three of them, her face showing some level of gratitude. "I love seeing her smile now, knowing how precious it is. Even I obey her guidance, knowing it's only to help me grow. I do like getting to scold her, though." Mizi smiled at the glance she received. "Like Ore, she likes knowing we care so she likes to get into trouble so we can."

Tears escaped Irene's eyes although she refused to look at Mizi. "Gentle scolds are so much better," she agreed, letting Mizi know she'd been listening to her conversations and likely had been worried about that, or testing her to see what she'd say as a scold.

"Indeed," Mizi sighed in agreement. "Still. I do turn the tables on her and praise her more often than scold. She really does so much better with that. She just never learned it herself, not ever having it since she had to run from Selicia, ...save from Leah. I had to learn to keep it brief and light, though, because the first time I tried it she cried very hard."

Irene's laugh spurted although the tears kept falling. "I'm sure she needed it."

Mizi nodded several times in agreement. She took the plate she was handed with a soft, "Thank you."

Lunch ended with Irene putting away the food and Mizi kindly making Abigail wash the dishes while Mizi dried them and put them away. "Do your men work outside of the house during the day in the winter, on clear days?" Mizi asked before they were done with the work.

"Usually," Irene answered, "but today they have other work. I sent lunch with them." Mizi was curious. Irene smiled. "Today they're watching the backs of those who left without you. None of us were comfortable with there being no voices in between. They're only two, so they'll only be able to run emergency messages, but that will be enough."

Mizi blinked back sudden tears of her own. "Really," she said softly, "it is so very nice that there are kind people in the world." Irene patted her hand in passing as she returned to her spinning. Mizi turned herself and Abigail to the herbs on the cleared table. It was nice to pass the time in productive work and company rather than in worry.

-o-o-o-

Ore was quite relieved that the day stayed nice, the horses didn't stumble, the conversation with the commander of the garrison was brief if pleasant, and his review of the passage sufficient he could pass on the order for them all to leave and spend the rest of the winter at Osterly. They wouldn't have to return until the pass was done being a river during the melting season. They'd have to send up soldiers to review when that started and when it was enough of a trickle that enemies could creep down from Tarc. Once they'd learned and reported on that side of winter, then the schedule of winter's hiatus could be set in full.

The return to the waystation was uneventful as well, and they arrived in time for dinner. Ore was a little surprised to be greeted with a hug from Mizi, but the waystation family greeted each other the same. "I've finally learned what to call you!" Mizi's face was bright with a tease.

Ore got very wary. "I think you've relaxed her *too* much," he complained at the ladies of the house. "Mistress teases so very rarely." He closed his eyes and braced himself.

Mizi's peck on his cheek was followed by, "Welcome back, Big Brother!"

Ore's eyes flew wide and his mouth fell open. He stood there stymied for a while, then he ruefully said, "If you'll say it too often, I really will start saying the other names waiting for you and Master."

Mizi paused and looked at him with her calm judgemental look. "Well, then perhaps I'll let Rei know to start as well, if he will."

Ore put his head in his hand as Marcus and Henry chortled. "And now I want to tickle you as if you really were my Little Sister, but that won't do just now, I think." He glared at Mizi but she only gave him a smile.

"I think you've won greatly against him today," Henry said, looking between the two of them. "That's a rather large victory, actually." Ore decided to trounce Henry instead as his alternative. Henry took it with a sigh at the end. "The Older Brother always has to get it out one way or the other," he explained to Mizi. She didn't look like she liked that alternative. Ore would be okay if it made her not do it quite so much. He still wasn't ready for it.

"Still," Ore relented slightly, "it's good to see you happy, Mistress. Our work went well and the day stayed nice. Even if it snows now we'll be able to be in Kouzanshi with time for you to do your work there."

"That's good," Mizi answered, then she smiled at him. "I've offered to cook dinner tonight. Will you be my sou chef?" The men of the house gave the ladies of the house wide eyes at that statement, but Irene only smiled patiently at them.

Ore shrugged. "Okay. But you'll make me want to make one of mine."

Mizi blinked at him, then said, "I'm not sure they'd have the spices. Can you make one of the ones you learned that the rest of us can eat?" She considered it, then named one of the more simple ones Ore had in his repertoire that didn't include the Selician spices.

"That's fine, if that's what Mistress would like to eat." Ore didn't *have* to make his favorite all the time.

"You'll really cook?" Lorence asked, quite surprised.

"Of course," Ore answered. "It's what we two siblings do to spend time together and to help the rest relax," he teased a bit.

Mizi agreed seriously. "We've done it since Rei put us together and he needed a night to seriously relax. Even Mina and Andrew were begging us to figure out what to do to help him." She wrinkled her nose at Ore. "Ore wanted to knock him out or make him drink enough to have to sleep all through the next day, but Andrew wanted to lock Ore up in the prison for even suggesting it." Ore rubbed the back of his head and didn't look at anyone. "I suggested a small dinner party and offered to cook. Ore took up the challenge and we cooked enough for thirty that night, since I was used to cooking for an inn full of people and he just followed my lead. It took a few more times before we found what the right quantities were, so now we can cook for the fewer."

She paused, then sighed and slumped. "Except now we're calibrated for Ilena and a few others, too, so," she looked around and counted, "well, I think we can not overdo if we stick to one dish each."

"I'll enjoy getting to watch you two for the first time," Marcus said with a smile. "I'm jealous that Petroi and Thayne get to help you since Petroi knows how to cook, too." He winked at Lorence. "We had to miss out the last time because of that. You know: the youngest brothers don't get to do what the oldest ones do unless they're out of the way."

"Well, it's making me hungry already," Lewis said heartily as he clapped his son on the shoulder. "Shall we go get washed up and set the table, so they can put the food on it all the faster?" The rest liked that idea, although Lorence wrinkled his nose.

Once they all had washed hands and Ore and Mizi had aprons on, Irene set the rest to chores, or made them sit to the table out of the way. Then she asked what ingredients they'd need. After they'd negotiated based on what was available in the house, Ore and Mizi set the extra hands at the table to cutting so they could get the pans and stirring utensils negotiated and set out on the fire to warm up.

Ore felt himself relaxing into the kitchen work. It was what he needed, except Henry tapped him on the head in passing when he got a little too relaxed. "Hey, Older Brother, not quite so much teasing or we'll have to step in."

"Right," Ore answered. He pondered on what he needed and said, "I need a work–out after dinner, I guess."

"Obviously," Henry said dryly since he'd already had to take it once that evening. "What can we do that doesn't leave the two of us in their beds for three more days while Mistress Mizi heals us back up? Be thinking of that while your hands work. We really *aren't* the Older Brothers, and you know it."

"Yeah," Marcus pouted sadly and dramatically. "We really are thin sticks that snap easily. There's a reason we dance from a distance."

Ore gave them a nasty grin. "Target practice?" They complained at him loudly until Mizi scolded all three of them.

True to the four of them, they dragged the teens into the fun of the kitchen as well as kept the parents entertained until the food was ready. Then everyone was busy carrying it out to the dining room to set the parts of it on the table. Ore and Mizi removed the borrowed aprons and everyone sat. Irene looked at them all sitting around her table and said, "Truly, we appreciate that you decided to stop here. Thank you for the visit, and for the cooking tonight."

"Our pleasure," Mizi said with soft kindness. "Thank you for all you've done for us during this time as well."

"Please, eat," Lewis said and passed Mizi's dish to his wife for her to begin the meal.

The conversation was lively and full of laughter and smiles that night. Ore smiled to see Mizi's shoulders fully relaxed again. This visit had been what she needed, which helped him, for all he did need to get out the physical components of his own stresses. His back and shoulders needed to swing a sword around, actually, for all he kept rejecting the idea. He really hated practicing with the sword. But his mind kept remembering the slow practice on the horses with the swords before they went into Tarc. And the sword dance of Selicia as well, for all that felt a bit too gentle for what he needed this night. The stretch and weight of a sword in his hand would work out his back muscles so they could relent and relax tonight.

When dinner was over and they were all crowded in the kitchen, or going back and forth between, cleaning up, Ore got Henry and Marcus' attention. "You two haven't done much sword work on the back of the horse."

"Ah," they looked at him with wide eyes. "Actually, none at all."

He nodded. That would do. They swallowed a bit. "We'll do the practices Petroi, Thayne, and I did on the way to Kouzanshi last time. They work best for those of us who don't really like to hold swords. We can warm up and end with the sword dance." They slumped and relented. Those were all things they could do and would be gentle enough on them. Plus give them that one more thing they'd had to miss out on so far because the older brothers weren't there to "be in the way".

He paused before leaving the house to ask Lewis, "Have you got an extra sword I could borrow for this practice? Or something roughly the same weight and length as a short sword?"

Lewis disappeared briefly and reappeared with a sufficient sword a little longer than Ore used normally. He waited until he was outside of the house to pull his own short sword. He tested them in each hand, then put the longer one in his right hand and his short sword in his left. He carefully didn't swing it around wildly. This part was new for him. That decision made, he put his short sword back in its sheath and held the borrowed sword point up in front of him. Marcus and Henry fell in behind him, their swords held the same. "The usual," he told them, then began.

The male attacking part of the dance was done first, slowly, followed by the speed round. It was as good a meditation now as Ore's martial art was when he worked out that way. After a pause to breathe, they began the female defensive part of the dance, the opposing one to the one they'd just finished. That warmed Ore up nicely and he was ready to move in more strengthening ways. He whistled for the Tarc horses, who came out of the stable since they'd told Lewis their stalls shouldn't be closed up. There was a snorting from the woods and Ore wasn't at all surprised. He did sigh, though. "Okay, Kesheb. Come on. You haven't done this with me before now either, so we may as well learn it all together tonight."

His own Tarc horse came out of the woods, having followed after them this whole time. Ore frowned at him. "But you really have to go back after this. We're going to be gone so far and long that you'll become lost in any snowstorm and I won't be able to find you. This isn't the time of year for you to learn this passage. Next time we go to Kouzanshi with Ilena maybe, since she won't ride double with me." Kesheb looked away from him but he stared the horse down until it submitted, lowering his head to the ground.

Ore sighed at him, and held out his hand to touch Kesheb's forehead. He mounted the horse bareback since he didn't have the right saddle for him. The other two finished saddling theirs, mounted, then sat at the ready. Ore taught them what he'd been taught by Petroi, only this time he held both swords, one in each hand, making the left mirror the right as best he could. That was a much better balance than only holding one sword. It made his back ache in funny ways to only have the one. The slow sword dance of the horse, the weights on his back and arms, and the warmth of his blood flowing were just what he needed.

"I think we should skip the final sword dance," Henry said, eyeing Ore when he called a halt to the practice. "You're already sleeping."

"I haven't talked to Ilena yet," he frowned at Henry.

"All the more reason to," Henry said firmly. "Go give the sword back and go up and talk to her while we wipe the horses down and settle them for the night. That will be the rest of the relaxing you need: to talk to your wife."

Henry wasn't wrong. Ore slipped off Kesheb, told him to go with Marcus and Henry, then went into the house. He left the sword on the dining room table, since he couldn't find Lewis in the outer part of the house and didn't want to disturb him if he'd already gone to bed. The climb up the stairs was what told him just how tired he was. He had to pause briefly two–thirds of the way up, then remember to keep going before he slept right there.

Opening the window helped him get the cooler air again to wake up a little. He called to his wife and was glad to hear her respond. He'd already let her and Rei know they'd made it back to the waystation safely when they'd arrived so they didn't have to keep worrying. Now he just told her about the fun they'd had at dinner and what he'd done to finish relaxing.

Mistress is so very relaxed after today, too, he said happily and sleepily. *It was good to come here and let her stay. She even teased me severely, very much a rarity for her. She's threatened to start calling me by a nickname now, but I've told her not to. I'm not ready for that level of casualness. It's still hard to accept what I've become; although, I think it's slowly becoming better.* He sighed, not really wanting to think about that today after relaxing so much, but it was true. He'd not fought it so hard today, the positive side of that place.

I'm so glad you've both been able to relax, Ore, Ilena said. *My thanks to Lewis and Irene for helping you both so. I'll wait to hear the nickname from her in secret so you don't have to hear it until you're ready. Or at least until they decide you're ready.* Ore rolled his eyes at all three of them as Marcus patted him on the head, having come in during the wait for the response to come back. She took her turn to tell him about her day.

For all he loved his wife greatly, and did need these nightly visits with her, sadly Henry wasn't wrong. Ore was asleep before her part of the conversation was done. Henry sent on Ore's love to her and told her of the achievement, also as rare for him as it had been for Mizi. They could only chuckle at the both of them and tuck Ore's blankets up around him. "A good day," Marcus sighed happily as he settled into bed.

"Mm," Henry agreed. He always took first watch when they were away from home. He'd have some good warmth inside to carry him through it until it was Marcus' turn. The physical exercise with the sword had done him good as well. He agreed with Ore. That slow way of moving made a lot more sense for learning sword work.

-o-o-o-

For most of the rest of the trip to Kouzanshi from this point on, they'd reach the garrisons at dinner time and stay overnight before going on to the next one. Ore spent some of the time on that first leg from the waystation thinking about what he might say to Mizi if she started asking difficult–to–answer questions, but he really did prefer answering such things in the moment. He was well used to distracting her now, but she'd been practicing in Nijou so it might be another level of difficulty to learn to match this time.

Ore sighed. He really wanted to do the full run on this day. It was still clear enough. He just wasn't sure he wanted to arrive at the garrison early in the day. Then he'd just pace a lot while waiting around, wanting to be on the road again already. They'd be having a late lunch at the inn on the way. Perhaps a run to that far so they didn't have grumbling bellies would be good, and they could be a little leisurely at the inn. "I need the run," he let them all know. "It's warm enough now. The inn will be warm, too."

The Twins waved at him as Mizi patted Ore's head, telling him to stop giving them excuses. "It's okay," Mizi said. "You can run. I'll hold on tightly." The Twins gave him the nod they'd be fine and watch her. Ore blew out a deep breath, then leaned over Fenrier's neck. Mizi's arms tightened around Ore's middle and they were running. It was always a fierce pride to Ore that when they ran they could cut down an eight to ten hour travel time to only two to three hours.

He watched the coats of their horses so that at the first sign of sweating a little too much he slowed them down to recover. He kept up that rotation, the walking only adding to the time they needed to get the stomachs to be ready for the lunch that was next. It also allowed for Mizi to have the resting from the run. She might be practicing such a thing for short distances, but for the long runs it was new and tiring since he hadn't done full runs with her ever before. He missed Ilena a little with that thought, but it helped that Mizi was willing this time. It also helped that Mizi was bright–eyed and exuberant at the end of the first run. "It's like you can leave all the worries and stresses behind, running faster than they can catch up to you," she said, agreeing with why he liked to run.

At the stable inn they made extra sure to wipe down the horses. Ore was particularly concerned about how the hair of the shaggy Tarc horses would have held in the sweat closer to their bodies so that they'd become sick before they could know. He pulled up in some alarm and ran out of the stable. He gave the whistle for his horse to come, then somehow wasn't surprised when Kesheb did show up. He scolded the horse softly as it shivered upon arrival. He immediately took Kesheb into the stable and rubbed him down vigorously. "You didn't walk when you should have, did you? It's really not safe in Suiran winters to be on your own. Please take better care of yourself. And I'm sorry I forgot you'd not leave on your own for all I scolded you last night."

While he dried and warmed Kesheb back up, Ore frowned in thought. Mizi came and crouched down next to him while he was rubbing a leg. "He's as stubborn as you, isn't he?" she asked, though kindly.

"Yes," Ore sighed at his Tarc horse. "He wants me to ride him so badly, and is so jealous of Fenrier, I can't keep him away. He's also learned it from me riding Usuri for so long and making him learn by watching. I'm just glad Ilena had enough time to train him how to run without hurting himself before now, or he'd still be practicing that bad habit this time. Breathing in this much cold air while fighting the body will make any horse sick." He was quite unhappy. "In the end, it means he's really still too young to be wise or he would've gone back when I ordered it last night."

He paused in his rubbing and Mizi rose to her feet and patted Ore on the head. "Well, he'll learn sometime." Ore rose to stand and move to the opposite side of Kesheb. "I think he got cold enough this time to learn why we walk?" she asked, appraising the horse.

"Hopefully," Ore replied, back to the rubbing.

"Maybe we should just take him with us?" Mizi asked. Ore wasn't sure.

"He'd learn the passage that way, and not get lost in the future," Henry said, arriving from having finished with his horse.

"I'd pay to leave him here, locked in until we get back, but I don't want to pay for the repair of a broken stable door," Ore complained at his horse. "It would punish him for having followed us in the first place. But...," he frowned again.

"It's not kind," Mizi finished for him. Ore just gave an unhappy nod. That wasn't how to deal with the familial horses of Tarc.

Now that Kesheb had followed them this far, he couldn't be abandoned. Not only were horses generally herd animals, needing their own kind for their mental and physical health, the Tarc horses had been bred and trained over generations to be family to their clans. He sighed and called to Ilena, *Father to the Naluk'. If a Tarc horse is halter led behind another horse, is it a punishment to them, or a training? Kesheb's followed me and won't return.* He didn't want to push Kesheb into further depression, and anger was going to be next if he didn't handle this right.

-o-o-o-

Ilena's head rose from her work at her desk and her mouth dropped open in shock. Justinian and Reynold were looking at her with eyes just as wide as hers. After a moment she said, "Well, I guess he would since he's a free stallion. Usuri's the head stallion and would stay with the herd, which is enough protection." She closed her mouth and leaned back in her chair, rubbing the top of her head. "Hmm...." Her eyes went to Justinian again. "Go run upstairs and ask Novare. I don't know the answer to that one, but I'll pass the answer back to Ore."

Instead of going upstairs inside, Justinian ran to the patio, keeping the door open the least amount of time possible. With a lot of concentration and strenuous effort because it took three tries, he jumped up to catch the upper balcony floor, then pulled himself up the railing until he was over it and properly on the balcony. Ilena watched that with just as much bemusement as the question from Ore had brought her. "He's asked us to help him learn it," Thayne said dryly. Ilena chuckled quietly. Any strengths the young man wanted to learn by his own efforts were fine by her.

They heard his feet patter across the floor above them towards the inner door, a pause, then his feet running back to the balcony door again, then his voice from the railing as he called to Novare and asked the question. "Went and got a cloak *after* the fact," Petroi said, just as dryly amused.

"I wonder whose?" Thane mused in a tease. Petroi only shrugged at him. It didn't really matter. They didn't bother to point out that it would've taken just as long for him to grab his cloak hanging on the peg by the inner door and run upstairs on the inside.

Ilena lightly tapped her finger on the arm of her chair while waiting for the answer from Novare, who'd have to have a translator at Falcon's Hollow ask him and relay the answer. She wasn't too surprised by the answer that came, since it was as natural as any of the things the Tarc did with their horses, but she hadn't wanted to guess wrongly. She motioned for her cloak and it got grabbed up by Reynold and tossed to Thayne who'd moved three long paces closer to the door but Reynold had been closer. Thayne tossed it to Petroi, who'd caught Ilena's hand so she couldn't do more than rise from her chair before the cloak got to her. He gave her a scolding look and put the cloak around her shoulders. "Don't take too long."

She rolled her eyes at him, but gave a nod she'd be quick. She was out the door and up next to Justinian rather quickly. She patted him on the head. "Thank you. You can go back in now, or do you want to stay?"

Justinian shifted from one foot to the other a few times, so she pulled him in front of her and held him inside her cloak to keep them both warmer, both of them facing towards the west. *Naluk' and Treasure to Father.* Justinian blushed to be included. *Tied behind the saddle and made to come behind another horse*

219

is a punishment. Halter tied to the pommel and the halter kept short is training. Lock him into a stall until you're ready to head out again. That will be a sufficient solitude punishment, as long as the other horses are around him to let him know you haven't left him behind. Then give him the training distance to let him know that you're unhappy he followed you, but you're going to give him what he wants. You'll need to watch that Fenrier doesn't punish him, too, for being made to have him that close.

Once you think he understands and is learning his lessons well enough, you can have Mistress ride him close by Fenrier's side. He'll be humbled enough by then for her to ride. If he's not, you know what to do to be sure he gets there. He does need to learn that Fenrier is of higher ranking in your eyes. You can test he's learned it by having Mistress ride Fenrier and you ride Kesheb. If Kesheb stays humble and lets Fenrier lead for a day or two, then he'll have perhaps learned something for at least a little while. She chuckled quietly.

Justinian turned his head and then brushed back the hood of his cloak to look at her. She looked down at him. "Kesheb is still too high–strung to let it last longer than this trip. He'll continue to fight for dominance against Fenrier for a while. Ore will have to work hard to find the balance between the two of them. They're too alike."

"Ah," Justinian nodded and turned back to the west again. "Like Petroi and Thayne."

Ilena stiffened and turned him around again. "What?" He didn't repeat it, just looked solemnly into her eyes. She finally relented and sighed. "Yes, and if you see that come up, feel free to attack them or separate them. Ore super–scolded Petroi before he left and Petroi promised to accept any words of warning from Thayne. He'll take them from you, now, too. Like Ore and the stallions, while I can work with them both, I can't scold because that only adds fire to the flame." She looked at him sadly, wishing it wasn't so, but they were both Messengers for a reason, and it was what made them too much alike.

Justinian had stiffened this time. "*Attack?*" he mouthed, completely surprised she'd allow him to release the King's Assassin.

Ilena leaned down and whispered in his ear so only he'd hear, "Once, to make the proper impression. They'll survive it because you care and they're that good. And only for that reason." She rose to look into his eyes again.

Justinian considered the requirement and his ability to follow through, then gave her a sober nod. She smiled a small smile at him and patted him on the head, then turned him around to hold him again since he was beginning to shiver again with the cold. *Father to the Naluk' and Treasure. Thank you. I think that will work best as well at this late a time. When I get back, please teach me how to make him stay behind.*

Justinian and Ilena sighed at the same time. "He never will," Justinian said morosely.

"Probably not," Ilena agreed, "but we can hold him here as family who say no because there are good reasons why. I'd rather have him here where I can send him after Ore if troubles happen on the road. It's okay for him to learn the passage this time for that reason." Justinian nodded wisely. Ilena sent back her agreement, love, and ended the calling. "And have you really jumped down yet?" she accused Justinian.

He looked up at her and with a twinkling smile answered, "That's easier. I just use the dance to land."

"Good enough," she answered, and let him go first. He ran inside, put the cloak where it belonged, then ran back out and jumped down. He immediately paused, one hand still on the ground as he looked to his left to see the person standing there, waiting for them at the lower patio door.

"And shall I let him practice now?" Ilena asked very dangerously.

There was a slow intake of breath, then quietly Petroi answered, "No, Missus Ilena."

She still waited until Justinian had risen before she was over the railing and standing with him between her and Petroi. She looked her first guardian in the eyes. "Petroi, I do love you and need you greatly. I'm sorry for what circumstances have done. Please, do your best to overcome that jealousy." She waited for him to turn his head away from her, the pain unable to be hidden. "What can I do?" she asked him.

"It pains me to have the accusation when I wish to be kind," he answered her almost sullenly.

She motioned to Justinian. Kindly and softly she said. "He's the one who said it. If he's seen it to say it, then it's needful to face it." The impassive look Petroi gave to Justinian told Ilena what she needed to know. "Justinian, do you see what he needs? Shall we both teach it to him?"

"But... it's sad," Justinian complained.

"Necessary. We go to Falcon's Hollow next," she didn't disagree with him, but she couldn't afford to feel that just yet.

Petroi looked at them, confused. "The anger wants out, Petroi," Ilena said to him. "It's that anger that will make you act against what you want to do. Anger must be let out with physical action." She let him consider that concept just long enough for him to admit to himself that perhaps might be the case, then she motioned at him to come at the two of them. "Fight to prove to yourself you're really in the place you want to be in."

She and Justinian were already at highest alert. She'd already made sure Petroi had reason to be angry with the both of them, just enough to bring it to the surface. He moved very quickly. She moved faster so he couldn't take Justinian down, giving the small young man just enough space to move out of the way, then take his turn to attack. Together they watched and worked hard to allow Petroi enough fighting time and effort to get the stress of the anger out of his muscles, facing him seriously without causing him serious injury in return.

They spared until Petroi stopped and held up his hand. Ilena didn't wait for him. She immediately began to tease him on a completely different topic that wasn't hurtful until he was scowling, then scolding her. She let him continue to scold her, pushing him if he needed it, until he suddenly stopped and stared at her with a surprised look on his face. "What was that?" he asked her.

Ilena relaxed a little and smiled. "Anger gotten out of the muscles then needs to be released through shouting or scolding, which is better. It isn't necessary for it to be related even. Just the act of scolding gets the rest of it out of the system." Petroi looked at her with a sad but more relaxed expression this time. "I'll still let you scold for that time, though, if you need the words heard," she offered humbly.

Petroi sighed and then did softly tell her the words that he needed her to hear. Ilena gently shoved Justinian back inside before he got started since the young man was getting very much too cold after a heavy workout and no cloak. Ilena humbly listened to this scold. She really did very much want for Petroi to heal and knew that much of this pain had been held in for a very long time.

When she'd apologized again and promised again to not ever hide from him again, he sighed and relaxed. She still wasn't done, though. She called Thayne out. Thayne came wearing his cloak and carrying Petroi's, that he placed around his partner's shoulders, since he also was now chilling from his workout and then standing still in the cold. "Petroi," she instructed firmly, "what was just done needs to be done again, only this time it needs to be final and for all of the rest of the past you're jealous for. Then you must let it go as soon as it comes up in your breast, every time.

"Look at Thayne. Tell him what you need to let that past and that jealousy go. Yes, I used him as a guard in Kouzanshi. Yes, I also used Marcus and Henry for that and information gathering. I need them here like I need you here. All four of you are that important to me and my work. Only you remember the princess and the princess can't let you go. But they must also remain and help you without you taking out your jealousy on them." She pursed her lips and tried to patiently let him face this part as well. She knew he wanted time to recover but he'd not do it. He'd not be able to open up again unless she started all over again.

When it looked like Petroi didn't have words and was going to be resistant to attacking, Ilena turned to Thayne. "You begin. You already have words that need to be heard, and he *does* really need to hear them, Thayne."

Thayne blinked at her, then pursed his lips and began scolding Petroi for not being able to let the anger for the past go enough that they could really become the partners they needed to be. Ilena slowly eased back towards the door into the suite, then entered and motioned to Justinian. This time he did snatch up his cloak before trotting out the door. He stood just outside it. Ilena moved far enough back to not be visually present, and observed. They'd be able to open up better and release this tension between them if she wasn't present, as she'd already explained to Justinian earlier. Even if they saw him, it wouldn't interrupt that flow. Seeing her would. She still wanted a referee in case they got too serious with each other.

The confrontation between Thayne and Petroi was shorter than it had been for Petroi and Ilena. When Justinian shook his head she opened her mouth, but before she could give Justinian the order, the words that poked Petroi's most sensitive spot were out of Justinian's mouth. She smiled sadly. He'd been able to protect her and step in where she'd asked him to because she couldn't. Truly he was a treasure to them all, for all that got him into trouble because the very angry Petroi had been woken up. This time Petroi fought Justinian and Thayne until they were sitting on him and he had tears streaming down from his eyes.

Once Thayne had recovered enough to speak, he said, "I see you've finally had enough of a beating for the tears to come, just like Mistress Ilena taught."

Petroi's face twisted. "I never did want it," he said.

Justinian patted him on the head. "No, but you really, really needed it. Now you can heal and we can hug you without being dead before we know it. You need hugs more." He leaned down and gave Petroi the hug he needed as Thayne got off of Petroi and let him sit up to receive it. Thayne still needed to finish scolding gently until Petroi could apologize honestly. Then Petroi could say the final words of pain to Thayne he needed to say and Thayne could hold his shoulder in understanding.

Ilena sat down hard in her chair and let out a long quiet sigh. Now they could all move forward again. She closed her eyes and hummed a song of healing peace for all of them.

-o-o-o-

Ore followed Ilena's advice, but he made sure Kesheb was wrapped up in a warm horse blanket and in a stall near the stable fireplace. He also made sure he fed and watered Kesheb. He wasn't sure the horse had found much to eat at all on the way. There was some yellow-green scrub grass in short supply under the snow but that wasn't much food. The Twins had fed and watered Kesheb the evening before, after their practice, but then had told him to go back home. Obviously Kesheb hadn't done that. Ore made it clear to Kesheb he was not just disappointed, but very sorrowful. Kesheb hung his head, but then he'd been doing that since he'd been shivering. Once the sweat had been wiped off of his back and Ore was rubbing his front and final leg, he'd snuffled Ore's hair in apology.

Ore sighed now and reached out to put his hand on Kesheb's forehead. He was worried that the horse had already made himself ill, but he wasn't fevered as of yet. He turned to the stableboy and tossed an extra coin at him. "Come get me immediately if he shows any signs of illness. He's a young idiot, but he doesn't deserve being ignored while having to live his consequences. I'll see if the innkeeper will let me buy the blanket."

The stableboy nodded. "He keeps them around for this and similar reasons." He named the price for it and told him to pay the innkeeper, then added the price for the felted horse "boots" often used when the snow was deeper. Ore thanked him and told him to pull out a set of boots to have ready. It was going to be expensive having a fourth horse with them they didn't really need, but he couldn't let his second favorite horse suffer. He made Kesheb sit down in the stall to rest, then collected up Mizi, Henry, and Marcus, who were waiting by the fire for him since they weren't in a hurry.

"I'm sorry, Mistress," Ore said as they walked to the inn. "It might slow us down if he does become ill, but we'll hope that was sufficient for him to warm up and be ready to go."

She gave him a slightly worried glance, but gave a forgiving nod. It wasn't like they could do anything else at this point. It was just that they were on time right now. They were prepared for snow delays but being able to move quickly while they had clear skies was important.

Ore tried to relax again while they ate. It helped that the Child of this inn came and served them and teased them all, plus entertained them with some funny local stories in between serving others at the inn. Getting warm food into themselves was good, too. When Mizi started giving the three men looks, Ore leaned on his elbow and looked her in the eye. "It's fun to have the Family around. Did you know that *every* inn and village restaurant on North road has one of her Children in it?" Mizi's eyes went wide. "I didn't know it until she sent me to go fetch the witnesses against Pakyo."

Mizi went thoughtful, then said, "Irene asked me if I'd been taught to 'see'. I told her I hadn't, but I properly recognized her as an ally because she has the same air to her Rei does. Could you see them back then?"

Ore shook his head. "I didn't learn that until I had the second set of witnesses at Falcon's Hollow. You remember she gave me the rose and herb? That was to let them all know they could begin to teach me the things I needed to know." He pointed at the Twins. "I met them before that at the Black Cat Inn. It was pretty obvious regardless that they were her Family because they were so grey that night from not knowing if Ilena was still living and okay."

Mizi paused, then cautiously asked, "Is it okay if I learn it? How to see the Children at places we go?"

Ore blinked at her, then leaned back. "I think so. Then if you needed help you'd know who to trust. That was what I needed it for the most. We ran into a spot of trouble and I had to just accept their word, which was hard for me to do. I made them teach me after that. Look at each inn we stop at and pick them out before they come up to talk. They get so excited I'm around they can't help it." He grinned at their server who'd come up again to see if they needed anything.

"Well, you've always been a popular guy," the man grinned back at Ore.

"When no one knew me?" Ore asked, unimpressed. Then he turned suddenly to the Twins, interrupting the answer to the question. "By the way, I've been wondering.... Thayne told me Ilena let the Family know who I was when we left Kouzanshi after Mistress had earned her diploma, but I know we've been watched over a lot longer than that." He frowned at the server and complained, "And then they say things like that. ...Is that from when I was up here in the early years, or is it something else? I really don't like that people knew who I was that far back when it was so important that I stay in hiding."

The Twins glanced at each other. The server shook his head. Ore glared at the two who didn't want to answer him. "I know he's not supposed to answer. That's a high level question only those authorized to answer will answer. Since you're the ones here, you can answer it."

Marcus actually waited for Henry to decide for once, instead of just giving in. Ore let him have the time to figure out what he could say. Henry waited for the server to remove all the empty dishes save the mugs, then leaned on his elbow, and rested his chin in his hand. "Mistress Ilena had everyone watching *all* of the 'Ores', particularly as Pakyo turned to hunting specific ones." Ore nodded, remembering being told that. "You know that everyone likes to have their fun, too." Ore paused, then slumped inside and gave a nod that he did know that.

"The betting pool heated up quite a lot when there were only three left. There were a lot of excited people when you were the last one, you disappeared, and she stopped caring up here, only ordering the ones in the south to keep an eye on you there once she found you again. If the one who could stay hidden the longest and stay alive after being the only one injured enough to die was the one she was *really* hunting for, then why wouldn't the Family be super happy for her and excited to see you with eyes that finally see them?"

Ore groaned at Henry's very wicked teasing grin and put his hand over his eyes as his cheeks and ears flamed red. Mizi tried not to laugh, but she couldn't quite hold back. "I think it's good they've liked you for a long time," she tried to console him, "and even more that they were willing to watch over you for Ilena. That meant I could have you beside me in Ichijou and since then." Ore peeked out at her and her kind smile. "I'm sure learning there was a full betting pool doesn't make you feel any better than knowing Andrew and Mina enjoy betting on Rei and me do us, but at least it's over now, right?" Her eyes teased him with their green sparkle.

Ore put his head down on folded arms on the table. "Even Mistress," he groaned. "Mister Andrew and Miss Mina don't even compare to an entire *Family pool*. ...And no, they haven't stopped like those two have since you scolded them. There are three going right now just for her and I alone, with five more for the guards since they want to see more weddings and babies."

Mizi sat in shock for a moment, then patted Ore on the back. Then she paused. He peeked at her to see her glaring at the Twins. "Wait. Tell them they aren't allowed to include Rei and me."

"Oh, it's very much too late for that," Henry said calmly back at her. "How do you tell several thousand people they can't?" Mizi's face flamed as well. "For you two, if anyone *not* of the Family hears about it in passing, they want in and won't relent until they are. You're the most popular paring in Ryokudo for generations."

Mizi slumped and joined Ore on the table. He pat her back in return sympathy. "Ilena ignores it and doesn't care, as usual. I try not to think about it," he offered what advice he could. "The guards are a mix of loving to play with it and ignoring it." Mizi nodded her head, but still took a little while to recover.

The paige had been respectful to Maria. "Vicount Reed requests you have lunch with him today." Maria couldn't say no. She wondered what her father wanted with her. While he did call for her on occasion to talk to her, she was staying with him right now in his quarters in the castle while Mizi was away, as her vacation. (She didn't have a landed location to go visit.) He could have just told her at breakfast that he was coming back to their quarters for lunch. Particularly because when she'd asked if it was to be at a different location the paige had denied it. Perhaps her father had wanted to make sure she didn't leave to go to one of the young ladies' luncheons. Not that she would have. She hated them as much as Mizi did.

"Welcome, Father," she curtsied to him as he entered the open living space at the entrance of their suite in one of the middle lords' buildings.

"Maria," he gave a kind response, for all he sounded busy as if still trailing his work back with him. Likely their visit would be surrounded by that sense of business until he went back again since he was interrupting his work day. She'd already set out plates for their meal, the food having arrived before him. Surprisingly, he gave her a kiss on the cheek as he passed her on the way to the dining table. "Thank you for staying to talk to me."

"Oh, it was no trouble, Father," she said with a bit of a blush as she followed him to the table and sat down across from him. "I had no pressing activities today. The vacation has been rather peaceful, actually." She only had three morning classes now as she waited for the accounting one to begin. That meant she could mostly stay warm and comfortable, if a bit bored. She'd gone to the library a few days before, after her classes, to pick up some accounting texts to begin her studies early. She figured even if it got boring after a bit, or hard to understand, she could still spend some time on it each day and not be completely bored.

Reed looked at her a bit sharply at the word "vacation" but she'd found she needed to remind him of it on a regular basis in order for him to not be quite so confused as to why she was in his suite again. His mind was often lost in the clouds of his work in the Ministry of Scribes. Like her, he'd always loved to read when there was time and he greatly enjoyed writing as well It was a good place for him to work.

Because he was focused, he didn't waste much time on pleasantries. "Maria, tell me a little about each of the young lords in Regent Rei's household, perhaps starting with young Leon Tenisson."

Maria blinked as her breath was taken away a bit. Still, she considered Leon, then said, "He's been very kind to me of late, particularly two weeks ago when Mistress Mizi interviewed all of us. She was so sudden with it we were worried about why she'd done it." She frowned slightly at the food on her spoon and tried to repress her shiver. "The experienced aides told us later that she's like that when she's had a sudden concern cross her mind. She must see to it at once so she can return to her duties without worrying over it." Her father nodded his understanding. Maria figured most busy people were like that, actually. She gave her father a suspicious look but he wasn't looking at her. He was focused on his eating at that moment. "We're still not sure what had concerned her but it seemed to help her to have a review of each of us."

"Was it a timing issue?" her father asked.

Maria had to figure out what he might mean by that. "Well, it was just over five months since we'd been called up, barely two months since we'd returned from Tarc. Perhaps she suddenly realized that had been long enough to see if we were comfortably settling into the household. Brian and Kirk said that she's been trying to work on learning how to care for her staff, but even they thought it odd timing for that." She had to shrug. "Sometimes Princess Mizi's mind is rather unfathomable."

"So I hear," Reed said dryly.

Maria shifted uncomfortably and decided to change the subject back to what he wanted to know about. "Well, so Sir Leon is kind, very energetic and enthusiastic, if somewhat sensitive." She blushed just a little as she focused on her food. She'd really enjoyed getting to dance with him at the family activity ball. It was easy with that activity to understand why Rei and Mizi enjoyed it so much. "He works very hard during practices on the list, or so says Sir Sam. He's very dedicated to serving and protecting Princess Mizi.

"The other young lords have been teasing him since then, so he isn't quite as happy and sometimes will come to me when he's had enough of them." She wrinkled up her nose, not happy with them either. They didn't need to be unkind just because Mizi had done something strange.

"What are they teasing him about?" Reed asked.

Maria felt a little uncomfortable, but answered, "That he'll be the first of the guards released when she finally settles to who she really wants in the household because he's not as practiced a fighter as the rest, and is the youngest." She frowned deep enough to almost have it be a scowl, but that wouldn't be proper so she didn't go that far. "I think they're wrong. He's her favorite of all four of them. He knows how to help her relax and smile. She's told me herself how much she appreciates that and his kind devotion since she was at Ichijou."

She looked up to see her father watching her with a rather piercing look. She clenched her utensil a little tighter, not quite sure what he was looking for. "Anything else?" he asked her.

Maria fished, then shook her head, letting her hair fall in front of her face some as she reached for her glass to have a drink, hoping to recover. Her heart was beating a little more rapidly than normal. "Tell me about the others," her father said almost casually as he went back to eating.

Maria blinked, then said, "Kirk's the youngest of three sons of a landed baron on the western border south of Kouzanshi. We were introduced to the woman he wants to marry when we were on the progress. She's a researcher like Mistress Mizi is. She was welcomed kindly by her and Princess Ilena, for all she was rather uncomfortable once she learned they were the royals. He can be nice if he wants to be, but often goes along with Brian since they're partners. — Sir Sam is Leon's partner which is odd since Sir Sam is so old, but they both came from Ichijou. — Kirk likes to fight left–handed like Sir Mina so they practice together a lot." She put her utensil to her lips as she thought some more, then shook her head. "I don't know very much about him other than that."

She took another bite of food and wrinkled up her nose. "I don't like Sir Brian. He's cold and teases meanly, even Mistress Mizi in ways she can't understand it's happening. *I* think he'll be the first let go, not Leon. He's the best fighter out of all four of them, though, so he's a good protector. I think that's what makes it harder for her to decide." She paused there as she ate.

"What about Sir Dane Malkin?" Reed asked.

Maria looked up at her father in surprise. "Well..., I don't know. He's part of Master Rei's staff, training under Sir Mina. He and his brother Sir Tairn are at their father's manor over this winter. Master Rei has to trade when he has Sir Mina and Sir Andrew with when he has Sir Tairn and Sir Dane." She pursed her lips as she tried to remember Dane from when she'd been called up and before they'd left for the progress. That hadn't been for very long and she wasn't one of those in the Rose office.

"I don't know him well. He seemed competent and nice enough. Sir Tairn is more strict than he is, but I think oldest sons are that way?" She wasn't sure but it did seem like it to her. Her oldest brother was as strict and focused as their father was, which left a little room for being kind and loving to family if things were going well in the household.

"Will Sir Tairn be staying at the castle?" Reed asked at her pausing again.

"No," Maria returned from her introspection. "He's helping to train Sir Dane until his father's ready to have him take over Nakaba. Sir Dane will be staying since he's Sir Mina's replacement when she's called to Yosai." She paused, suddenly confused. "But Sir Tairn is Sir Andrew's replacement.... I wonder how that will work out?" She sighed and slumped a little. "I think Master Rei's going to struggle for a while. Maybe they're testing to see who can be moved from following Mistress Mizi to who can help Master Rei?" She shook her head. She didn't know when they didn't talk about things like that in the brief times she was in the suite.

"And is there anyone eligible in Prince Ore or Princess Ilena's household?" It was asked a bit coolly as if Reed didn't want to even be asking it.

Maria immediately shook her head though, to relieve him of any worries there. "No. Rio told me most emphatically that none of the unmarrieds there are eligible or interested. That is, Princess Ilena already has made matches for them, or they've told her they don't want a wife on top of their other responsibilities. I think it's a shame since they're nice enough, but no."

Reed relaxed and pondered as he finished his meal and downed the last of his drink. Maria took the time to also finish without having to answer any more questions. That had been rather a lot. As Reed was leaving, he paused and asked, "And are there any eligible young ladies?" He waited for the answer with a raised eyebrow.

Maria knew he was looking for a wife for her oldest brother who'd be coming home from Kishi Knight's school very soon. "Not really, no. Delia has confided in me she doesn't want a husband, but it's Princess Ilena that would decide for her if she cared. I suppose the nurses might be, but they're getting old. Rio's definitely not interested and Amber's been brought in for Sir Marcus to decide if they could work out okay. It's a bit sad that I'm the only one that cares to dream about such things among both households."

Reed gave a musing nod and let himself out of the suite. Maria's eyes widened slowly as the last of her words made it up into her brain. Then the import of all of the lunch interview added itself to that thought. She sat down rather heavily and suddenly in her chair again, her legs not able to hold herself up. A hot flush rose up to her head from her heart and her hands clenched and shivered. *Surely he's not gotten letters!?* It seemed so sudden and soon. Was she really so old as to be considered eligible? Wasn't that just pleasant dreams, not reality, to care what the young men looked like and saw when they looked at her?

Her hands went over her face as she tried in vain to get her heart to calm down. Her whole being shivered rather violently. *Who? Who had sent letters?*

-o-o-o-

The Regional security meeting before Mizi and Ore had left the castle had been focused on deciding what rumors they, Marcus, Henry, and Kirk would spread in the garrisons and villages along the way. They'd also hammered out the final messages from Garen and Rei to the garrison commanders. In the end there'd been one secret folder that Kirk had been told to carry on his person and let no one see but the garrison commanders. Then there had been a sack of folders tied to his saddle, one folder for each garrison to be left with the commanders containing their specific orders for the upcoming conference. War game orders had been summary since Garen was still working on the specifics for it.

The Regional security meeting the morning the pair left the castle was summary with a bit more focus on castle and city issues, since those topics had been set aside in favor of the other issues for a few meetings. Garen excitedly passed on the news that Sirius would be arriving that afternoon, the clear day helping him and and the company he was coming with make the final distance with good speed. Rei had lost himself in his work at the Rose office after that meeting, it being his usual way to distract himself from not having Mizi in the castle. It was more difficult at night, not having her in the bed with him, but he'd expected that so just did his best to ignore his emotions and sleep anyway. They'd already agreed to use Ilena's network again to talk in the mornings, like they had before.

The next Regional security meeting after that, two days later, was the last one before Ilena would be gone to Falcon's Hollow for the foaling. She was looking forward to training at least two of the household there in how to be Tarc youth. Rei could only smile at her when she got that excitement in her eyes. The Naluk' lived even in Suiran, for all she didn't come out often.

Rei wasn't surprised when Ilena suggested at that meeting that they might want to lengthen the time between security meetings for a while. With her and Ore out of the castle, they were going to be either non–existent for a while, or long distance over the network. There were still some sensitive things Rei didn't want said over the network, but they shouldn't stop having the meetings altogether. At the end of that discussion, they decided that Rei and Garen would continue to meet with Mitchel at the Lower office. Mitchel and the Ministry staff knew as much as Ilena and Ore and had just as many answers, since they collated and summarized it for the Minister and her Assistant. If there were questions only the two could answer that weren't too sensitive, they could ask the question on the network and get an answer back still during the meeting time.

In the end, Rei found it a bit regrettable that Mizi and her guards had learned about the secret code, and then had learned how to listen to it. Ilena could only agree, when he complained slightly to her about it at the end of the dinner they had together in her suite the night before she left for Falcon's Hollow. "But, in the end, it must be phased out anyway," she told him. "We can use it as a sibling and spouse secret, but this really is too many people to know everything that needs to be known. Thus why I'm sending Marcus and Henry recruiting for horse messengers.

It's a business that can pay for itself, but it will be the way messages are run in the future."

"It takes so long, though," he almost whined.

She could only pat his shoulder sympathetically. They were sitting next to each other on the couch so their sides weren't quite so cold. "The only thing faster and more secure is to be able to read minds over any distance, and that's not possible."

Rei blew out a breath, then leaned his head on her shoulder. "I'm glad you're here," he said, closing his eyes. "I can just let you worry about it. I'd still like to have it in place in case of emergencies, though."

"You're not wrong, that it would be highly useful for that," Ilena agreed. "Even the flag method the Brulac use was for that very purpose from the beginning. Any way people try to make information secret can be decoded eventually. I won't stop thinking of what can be done, and we'll wait to phase out the network until after we're back to stability again with our neighbors and hopefully within as well."

Rei agreed with that level, relieved to know it wasn't going to be sudden. He still needed to be able to talk to his wife across long distances, to know she was safe and okay. He frowned a bit, wondering how to use that when he put together his plan. "I think it's my turn to borrow a couch," he said, feeling his body relaxing even more.

Ilena chuckled. "And I've always said yes to anyone who asked me for it." She turned to hold him more comfortably against her, wrapping her arms around him. "I love you, Rei," she whispered. "Thank you for being my brother."

"*Umhm,*" he murmured sleepily. "By the way, I really need more letters read before they're sent out. I'll give your office that list later. Learning where sent letters go to was very helpful. Even more helpful was knowing they were about marriage proposals and not traitorous actions."

Ilena chuckled slightly. "And thus where I get a lot of information and why we write ours in code. It really is one of the least secure methods, for all the most reliable." Rei had to agree. When Ilena let him go to lay him down on the couch, already asleep, they covered him with two blankets and gave the other couch and two more blankets to Andrew.

Ilena took Mina's hand and dragged her into her bedroom. "Let's have a sleep–over since Master Rei decided it," Ilena demanded. Mina rolled her eyes, but didn't really want to leave her husband there to go sleep in her own bed alone, so agreed in the end.

Petroi complained at them a little from above in his room for making yet another opportunity for the castle to think Rei and Ilena were having an affair while Mizi and Ore were away. Ilena just ordered him to see the rumor mill had the story straight. He punished her the next morning by having the rumor mill pass around that Rei had stayed to keep her in her room so she wouldn't run away to follow after Ore and Mizi. Of course, then people believed that was what she'd done anyway because she left that morning for Falcon's Hollow, to be gone for two weeks.

Since that helped the story Rei wanted the mole to believe about the relation–ships between the royals, he ignored it and did his work. It didn't surprise him that both Aiden and Brianna believed it. When they finally confronted him about it he did tell them he'd given her permission to go to Falcon's Hollow for the foaling while Ore was gone, for something to do to keep her busy. Saying it that way also kept the story the way he wanted it.

-o-o-o-

Two mornings later Rei picked up the rather thick folder that had shown up on his desk at mail delivery. He opened it and his eyes went wide. "This is several days early, unexpectedly." He was used to proposals showing up last–minute as the people working on them were always waiting on data to arrive to add to them, often last–minute as well. He flipped open the one underneath it and wasn't at all surprised. "Mina, Balar and Jamison have both sent their studies earlier than expected."

Mina looked up from her work in surprise, then shrugged. "They've both had Ilena show up in person to talk to them. They're also the two largest companies. Maybe they have good people they delegated it to."

Ah. That Rei could understand. He picked up both folders. "See these are delivered to Falcon's Hollow expeditiously." Mina rose to her feet and collected the folders from Rei. She walked to the door and called for one of the paiges and handed the folders over. After giving the paige instructions, Mina returned to her desk and her work. Rei had already selected the next folder from the stack and moved on.

-o-o-o-

Mistress Ilena, the first two of the feasibility reports have come.

Ilena paused in her work in the foaling cave in slight surprise at Leah's words. *Alright. Go ahead and read the first one to me. I'm mildly busy but that should be taken care of now. Postponing anything in that regard is worse than not.*

Agreed. Leah's voice was as mildly wry as Ilena was feeling about it.

Ilena continued to pay attention to the foal and mare as they worked hard for the foal to finish being born. She didn't mind when Leah paused to rest her voice. The report was quite long, as expected. She ran through the details to that point, settling them into her memory where she could retrieve them when she was ready to summarize for Rei. The summaries were as much for herself, though, so she could also forget the unnecessary things. The report would still exist for her to go back and review if the details became necessary.

For all Ilena could memorize everything, and rather unconsciously did, she'd been working lately on selective memorizing. Things like the feasibility reports wouldn't be needed past this beginning research phase into the revitalization, other than for reference if problems cropped up with the construction companies them- selves. It wasn't necessary for her to clutter up her mind with such things when she was going to have at least another forty years of data to also remember past these twenty–five she'd already lived.

Ilena had cleaned up and was ready to rest by the time Leah returned to reading the report. She listened while pouring up a hot cup of tea sweetened with honey and warming her hands on the now–hot mug. She sat on the feeding shelf to rest, leaning her head back against the wall. She closed her eyes and melted into the sound of her nurse's voice. It had always been a sound to calm her and let her know that the world would be alright even if it was hard in the moment.

She was startled back into awareness as the horsemen brought another panting mare into the cave. *Pause,* she requested to Leah. The voice stopped by the time the men had the mare lying on the floor of the cave and Ilena was beside them. When their brief conversation was over, Ilena realized that she wasn't sure if she'd slept through some of the report or not. She ran through the summary in her head, then repeated that back to Leah. *Let me know if I lost the thread somewhere,* she requested.

Leah didn't answer for a bit, then said, *You've left out the last two sections I read to you.*

Ilena sighed at herself in a little frustration. *I did fall asleep, then. I'm sorry. Please go back and start there again.* This time when she was done with the mare and foal, she had Leah pause for longer, actually taking a nap until the next mare was brought. That helped tremendously.

It was hard that Ore wasn't with her, for all she was studiously trying to not think about that. She was working hard to practice being without him without it affecting her other than normal loneliness, keeping herself busy during the day working hard enough to sleep more soundly at night. It helped that they'd shared the bedroom so much now that his presence was there with her regardless. She still didn't sleep well without him, but Rio had been kind enough to help with being a roommate again when Ilena called for her in the middle of the night on the hardest nights. Eventually even Rio would hopefully be married and not available, so Ilena knew she needed to break that pattern, too, so she'd not asked her to be there every night.

Already, though, Ilena had called to Ore in the middle of the night from the manor roof, grateful to her very bored nightshift Family. She and Ore had chatted not only with each other, but with them as well on those nights that had been hard for both of them. That had helped all of them, she felt. She'd slept better those nights after the chats. She appreciated she could now, but was working hard to learn the strength for even that to be gone.

When the next mare was brought in, it was two and Novare came with them. "Justinian sent me to help you," he said to Ilena. "He says you're needing company." The herdsman from Tarc was happy to have her present so he could talk in his native language. Currently the only people who knew how to speak it were more often at the castle than here at the county. He was teaching it to Thom and Edward since Ilena wanted them learn it as part of their lessons on Tarc.

Ilena smiled at him. "Well, yes, in a way. I'm listening to voices on the wind, so I'm not lonely, but I do keep falling asleep, so having another person here is probably good for me," she eyed the two mares, "particularly with two this time. Do you think we'll be getting more from now on?" she asked as she settled next to the mare Novare wasn't with.

"Perhaps," he said, eyeing the mare he was with and calming her gently.

Ilena considered that, then called back to the house, *Leah, read one more time until I tell you to stop. Send Thom and Edward out to the birthing cave. We're to the point they should be here helping.* It was going to be hard to get the reports worked into the schedule, but they couldn't languish. She'd barely be back in time for them to be presented to the city council. Rei needed the time to review and put together his words for that meeting. She was so glad for people who could and would step in to help her. She sent a "thank you" to Justinian for sending Novare before getting lost in the foaling and report reading again.

-O-O-O-

"Andrew," Rei said as he, Andrew, and Mina walked to the Rose office. It had been one week since Mizi and Ore had left the castle. His two closest aides and friends had refused to let him sleep in, making him still get up for his practices even though it only made him miss having his wife more, to not have her nearby doing her practices as well. That plus dinners with only the aides or the few of the household not out of the castle now that Ilena was gone, too, was going to make him really sleep in from depression soon. He'd rather nip that in the bud early.

"Yes, Rei?" Andrew asked kindly.

"Schedule a dinner with Prince Airn for tonight or tomorrow night. I'd prefer intimate with he and I at a table and you two and his two guards at another. You four may as well eat at the same time." He rubbed his head, then added, "If it goes well enough and I can stand to sit with him for that long, we'll have a few more while the rest are gone and maybe have them at one of the larger tables so you can sit with us. I'm sure he eats with them like I do with you, and I'd like to hear what his aide has to say as well. It looked like there was some teaching going on in the Court of Ministers. I'd like to be sure he's learning useful things." He rolled his eyes at Andrew who gave him a knowing look back.

The three of them had had many such training moments when Rei had been at the same age Airn was at now. Because Rei now had the experience of sitting on the throne of the Regent, he had a much better sense of what was important than he'd had during the training lessons. It was likely Airn would listen to that voice of experience. Rei would have if it had been available.

Andrew was calling for a paige immediately. Since they did roam outside even during snowfall, one showed up eventually. Andrew gave him the order to find Prince Airn and invite him to dinner with Rei that evening. Rei wasn't surprised Andrew hadn't let him have one more dinner to get more depressed. He was a little surprised Andrew added an order to the paige to then go to the chatelâine to set up the intimate dinner.

"Won't having it be formal so suddenly be a bit stressful?" Rei scowled at Andrew once the paige had trotted off.

Andrew gave him the bland look he did so well. "If this one's more formal in the seating, it should be more formal in the presentation. Not to mention if you're finally going to acknowledge he's in the castle, the rest of the court should understand you do really know how to host a Prince of another country, other than at your wedding. Your presentation is almost as bad as Ilena's and that's not good when you're trying to set your place now."

Rei slumped inside a little. He gave a small nod, telling Andrew he'd understood the scold. Presentation to the court was actually important, particularly since he'd made such a forceful opening statement with the scolding High Court. Just because he preferred to relax didn't mean he should let formalities slide. He drew in a deep breath and sighed it out, making his own small cloud in front of him. He'd complain about the cold, just for something to complain about, but everyone in Suiran knew there was no sense in making that complaint. Suiran was cold in the winter.

He'd invite others of the court to join them at the dinner, but there wasn't anyone else to invite just yet. Plus, because this dinner was more an exploratory meeting, it wasn't really the right timing to include others of the court. Once he'd had this one, and maybe one more, he could entertain them both by having a more formal one with members of the court. It would be a waste of effort as far as parlay and negotiation went, but having a crowd around would help Rei. He entertained himself for the rest of the walk to the Rose office coming up with a list of potential invitees to said possible dinner. It might be mostly the young lords of the castle, actually, as a first. The dinner that had included them before had opened his eyes a bit to the fact he might need to be knowing who they were better. Over time they'd become his directors and ministers, after all.

-0-0-0-

Airn tugged at his jacket, frowning. "If you wanted to be able to be dressed in your favorite clothing, perhaps you should have thought to bring at least one formal outfit with you when you ran away?" Erlic scolded Airn.

Airn scowled at him. "And you could have brought one for me with you if you knew that far back I was going to end up here. Given Father told you to be sure I did, I'd think you'd have thought that far ahead?" He was a bit surprised that closed Erlic's mouth rather satisfactorily. Usually the scolds from Erlic couldn't be countered so Airn only ended up feeling rather miserable. As Ilena had seen quite quickly in Kouzanshi. He turned away to blush at the memory without Ian or Erlic seeing it. He'd definitely needed her comfort and understanding, but it was quite embarrassing that it had been so, and so public.

Airn tried to leave the jacket alone. He'd bent his pride enough to take the offer of the chatelâine's office to have proper attire sent to him, and had selected this outfit from the four that had been brought for him to review. It wasn't what he was used to, though, and he'd rather be representing his father and nation in his own clothes. It felt like he was a beggar. "Can you at least send to the castle and ask that they send a few things?" he grouched at Erlic. "I know they're generally more focused on the important things of staying sovereign, but this won't be the only time or place I need to represent Altherly. It may be even more important in Ichijou, if they're really going to send me there as well." Ilena had hinted they might.

"Certainly, Your Highness," Erlic answered neutrally.

Airn turned to look at him in surprise. Erlic only answered that way when Airn had done something right. He was rather shocked that such a request that could be considered vanity hadn't been an incorrect one. But then, his intentions hadn't been based on vanity, other than his personal preference for his own clothes.

"If you'll list which things those would be, I'll see a message is sent to your manservant. Shall I ask for him to come as well?" Erlic continued.

Airn paused and considered that seriously, a thought–frown furrowing his brow. "If it's safe for him to come, yes, I think so. I don't really want to drag him out of the castle and country, but...," Airn went pensive, not wanting to really face that he might not have a home to go back to. "Well, again, while I don't think it's quite so important here, it may be at Ichijou." He got another indication of approval from Erlic and sighed internally at his aide. "We can write that letter first thing tomorrow morning," Airn said. "Ian, my coat, please." It was time to go meet with Rei.

They were led by a paige that carried a lit lantern by its handle. It was a cylindrical tin box with slit holes poked into it to prevent the wind from blowing out the candle inside. Airn noticed that the usual lanterns lit on the outsides of the buildings they passed were also covered with similar lantern shades. It made the night rather dark, actually. It was only enough light to be able to tell where the entrances to the buildings were and mark the passageways. "Is it so windy for all of winter?" he asked the paige.

"Yes," the paige answered. "We know when spring's coming because the winds die down to about half and start to tease us with the smell of warmth and wet earth instead of cold ice and snow." The paige shuddered with the cold just a little. "Of course, it's teasing because it still stays cold for about another month. It's just that the winds change from west and north-west winds to more southerly winds, bringing the scents of the spring that's coming to the lands south of the forest and bog. When the south winds become the most prevalent and the west wind stops fighting with it, then we know we can start to shed the heavy warm clothing."

The paige glanced at Airn with a teasing look. "Then we switch to the rain boots, waterproofed cloaks, and carry shovels to dig ourselves out of the mud as the rains move in and start to melt the ice at the foot of the mountains. That comes down quickly as sheets of water to make us think we live on the sea instead of the land. Some have said we should at that point change out the sleigh runners to boats and oars." He chuckled as Airn shook his head. He just might want to be at Ichijou instead of in Suiran. The weather in this Region was quite abysmal.

Rei welcomed Airn to the small formal dining room that had been set up and decorated for them. Airn was rather surprised that it was. Ivy curled around the few pillars in the room and was set out in the center of the two tables and had small white flowers tucked into it. Airn was relieved Rei welcomed him as an equal to this table. "Thank you for taking time out of your schedule to invite me. The greenery is a pleasant change of view."

"That it is," Rei agreed with a smile. "Our gardeners insist on having as many greenhouses as the Department of Medicine. I think it's so they can be both warm and encouraged through the winter."

Airn smiled back. "I can understand that. It's been difficult to adjust to the quantity of snow and depth of the cold weather. I've been wondering if it's the mountains?"

"It is," Rei agreed, escorting Airn to the more highly decorated table set with two place settings. "I've asked for a second table to be set up for your men and my aides." He gave a bit of a grimace as he sat down. "I'm without any family to eat with and I'm sure the three of you eat together as frequently as my aides and I did only a few years ago. They may as well eat when we do as stand around and starve when it's just the two of us."

"Thank you," Airn said for them as he took the second chair at the table. Andrew was seating Erlic and Ian at the other table. When they were sitting, he held the third chair for Mina, then sat himself. Servers came to the tables and poured drinks.

Rei picked up his glass, swirled the liquid in it, then sniffed it. He held it as Airn picked up his glass and brought it to his nose. Airn blinked in surprise. "It's ...a grape juice?"

Rei slowly smiled. "My wife can't hold any alcohol at all, and you're only sixteen. If you'd like wine, we can ask for that after we have food in us. I've been practicing, but still would rather keep my wits about me more than relax to wine. Light juices have become the staple at the head table...," his eyes narrowed in a dry look, "when we don't have members of the court at it, anyway."

Airn snorted a laugh. "I'll accept that as a complement, then. But, Princess Mizi isn't here?"

Rei sighed as the glass left his lips to return to the table. "While it's hard to have her gone, because the hospital needs to be set up here at the beginning of the year, she's in Kouzanshi to win the heads for it herself."

Airn did remember that the ministers had wanted her to have the persons actually in hand before they'd be any more willing to help her and that she'd said she'd be gone from the castle for a while. A little hesitantly he asked, "She's willing to bend to the minister's wishes so far as to travel herself in the winter weather?"

Rei looked away. The servers were setting the first course of the meal on the table in front of them now. Rei waited until they were done and had moved back to the wall again. "While it answers to them, she'd already asked to go before they requested it. I'm sorry it pulls her away from hostessing you." Rei picked up his fork to pierce the fresh salad on his plate. He looked back up and gave Airn a dry, somewhat lonely–looking expression. "Since I'll be having quiet dinners while she's gone, I thought I could fill in for her on occasion until she returns."

"Thank you," Airn said quietly, turning to his plate of salad as well. Again, it was fresh greens and vegetables as if it weren't winter at all. While the meals they'd been served until this time hadn't been lacking, certainly the castle chefs had worked hard for this meal. It was possible that the greenhouses only grew enough of the fresh greens for the occasional formal meals. Perhaps he could get a tour of them as a warm diversion and lesson in the next day or so. Then he grimaced a little. He also wouldn't be surprised if the court lords demanded more of this sort of meal than the Regent. Most of the food that appeared for him was also the warm foods that staved off some of the chill of the air, so that much was also appreciated.

"I saw you at the Court of Ministers," Rei said, moving the conversation on. "Will you tell me what you learned?"

Airn wrinkled his nose, then sighed. "Quite a lot, actually. Princess Mizi is very formidable, for all the lords don't like her very much. I was very impressed with her preparation and logic." He paused, then added, "Actually, I was impressed with all of you coming to the meeting so prepared to face them." He glanced up at Rei. "How long did it take you to learn how to do that?"

Rei smiled a small smile of reminiscence as he considered the answer to the question. "My brother taught me that while I was still quite young. He said he learned it from our father and that it was what held the nation together after Father's death. Because Sasou had to face the court from the young age of thirteen, he had to be very armed with facts and blocks to their arguments or they'd have wrested the throne from him and Mother, although she was rather iron–fisted generally. Worse than Ilena, back then." He grimaced. Airn raised an eyebrow but let him continue.

"Since it's what Sasou trained me to early and first, I've always done lots of research before I act, making sure I've already blocked them before I even walk into the room. I'd say that it didn't really sink in as to just how important it was for me to be able to do it until I came here. I was quite glad that it was habit by then, though. The Suiran court wasn't thrilled to have an eighteen year old placed over them, even if I am a man now." Rei sat back in his chair, his salad finished. "I waited until I was nineteen to force them to listen to me, though. Most have been relieved to have me finally say what I'm willing to accept or not accept. Only the few remaining stubborn heads won't back down."

Airn nodded. "Yes, we did see that, too. And it seems to be centered around your desire to have intelligent women standing with them?"

"It is," Rei agreed. "At least that's their openly stated reason." His eyes took on a testing look to them that Airn recognized from the looks his brother and father gave him.

Airn straightened to look Rei in the eye and consider that point. The salad plates were taken up and he waited until the next course was set before them before answering. Some of that was testing how much time Rei would allow him to consider his answers. He was somewhat surprised at Rei's patience, but he'd already shown he'd rather not have the servers hear the full conversation they were having.

"The nobles always have ulterior hidden reasons to be truculent," Airn said softly. "While ours also expect the women to be hidden from their view in matters of state, I've already come across several well worthy of respect. I would've been surprised to hear one speak in our court of ministers, but because I'd already met your wife and Minister of Intelligence, it seemed natural in that meeting that they'd address it. Just as natural as the ire they both evoked in those 'stubborn heads' of your court." He gave Rei a sympathetic look.

He leaned back to rest from the eating and added, "It was interesting to have Sir Erlic point out that Princess Ilena is your ally in those meetings, helping you to press your own agenda forward. He said that the two of you had discussed even that before the meeting so she'd know what points you wanted her to support. It made me think of the times my older brother has supported my father the same." Rei glanced at him as he took another bite of his meal. "It made me think that it might be better to have a lord as an ally, as the other lords will react differently to a peer than to a royal." Airn returned to his meal as Rei gave a thoughtful nod.

"It's difficult to find such a one," Rei admitted. "If both royals have the same goals for the nation, that's a simpler ally to find. Most of the lords don't want to take a side, and when it's the side of a royal or a peer, it's much harder to pick a royal. They must defend their ministries, departments, or relationships on that level against their peers." He noted Airn's nod. Airn already knew that sort of thing went on. "However," Rei was looking at Airn again with that piercing look so he paused and paid attention, "it's also harder for the royal to select an ally from the lords."

Rei pursed his lips as Airn waited. "To have a fawning lord do everything the royal says is to have a lord that expects to receive favoritism, special consideration, and under–the–table deals that benefit him over the others. Such a thing is on the road to corruption of the land as a whole because it either corrupts the royal or openly allows corruption into the court. It's better to use the lords where and as they are to maneuver the whole of the court to where it needs to be." Airn was trying hard to not have his jaw drop rudely.

"Do you remember when we talked about the census in the meeting?" Rei asked. Airn did. "The first lords to speak up were the moderates, and those who I knew would bring up the financial concerns to continuing with the census. When the moderates speak first, there's an issue that truly needs addressing. The fawning lords and the cantankerous lords speak first when they have an ulterior motive but not a rational reason for being for or counter to the issue. Learning how to get the moderates to speak up is perhaps advanced lessons in that arena, but is rather critical to being able to move anyone in the group. You understand why I tabled that one?" Rei asked with a raised eyebrow.

Airn nodded. "To give them more time to think, because it was more of a reason to push other things later in the meeting, and because it wasn't as critical as some of the later issues that you did force an answer to."

"Mmm, yes and no," Rei answered. He let Airn eat a little before explaining further. "Those were certainly reasons, yes, but I also needed them to feel the discomfort of not being able to face themselves in the mirror I was holding up. Many of them have an unwillingness to help me help Suiran. It's their ulterior motive in being recalcitrant. Enough of them have chosen to be obstinate that it's become necessary for me to test just who's merely been trained to be that way and who might have traitorous reasons." Airn couldn't help himself from staring in shock this time.

Soberly Rei said, "I was using it as the opportunity to see who was in which position. Those who are willing to work with me were willing to listen to options and consider a proper resolution. Those who are being pressured from the outside by those counter to helping me were the most uncomfortable. Those who were angry and became icy the longer the debate continued are those to watch carefully.

"Such things are also necessary for a royal to learn. When you know who the enemies to peace and prosperity in your nation are you can begin to pen them in so they can't do severe long–lasting damage. Over time they can perhaps be replaced with better leaders, if you can find any." Rei was rather unhappy at the last statement. Airn wondered if he was having troubles finding reasonable people to work with in the court, or to be replacements at least.

"Everyone sees the world with the understanding of their upbringing and education, their experiences," Rei said earnestly. "For a royal, it's particularly important to see not through eyes of selfishness, but of open humility, a willingness to be taught. The eye a proper royal looks through is through the experiences and eyes of the people of the land, the common man and woman." Airn blinked. "If they can't provide for the land and all the people in it, then there isn't prosperity. Where there's no prosperity, peace falters.

"When you find a noble who sees with those eyes, hold on to him tightly and listen to his words with sober reflection, even if it's a scold to you. Those lords who see through the eyes of the common see through the eyes of true royalty, thus they support both sides: the whole of the nation. Most of the lords who fight against Touka in our generation have been blinded by the upbringing of their fathers and their fathers' fathers who were angry so many generations ago that Touka came and conquered, making this land a nation instead of city–states. They can't let that distant past go and see the good that's been done for their own people in our time."

Rei shook his head. "I won't say that my family's been pristine over those generations, but it should be that *everyone* has an open humble view, one that can allow for changes in people, even royals. Ilena has the greatest gift of our generation in relating to the common man, and she's beloved in Suiran because of it. My brother's won many of the same sorts of hearts in lower Ryokudo, if perhaps not as high a percentage. Those lords who've seen it and have been willing to bend are just as beloved by their people and by us.

"It saddens us that so many of the court are insular and don't want to go outside of the castle walls to see it. They only want to hold on to their petty ancient grievances or blind selfishness that take away from the full prosperity of our nation. Even their own. If they'd let them go, they'd have the more they wish to have to help the nation with. Instead, they put the iron balls on their own feet and then whine to have to drag them around." Rei sighed as he pushed his empty plate away from him to rest his folded arms on the table in front of him. "Thus, my current royal duty is to teach them that's what they're doing and to attempt to help them reach the understanding they need to reach to let those iron balls go, even if they don't give up their prejudices."

The sharp eyes looked at Airn again and he swallowed a little. That was a rather large task for someone as young as Rei. He already knew how hard it was to fight that kind of weight, just from watching Altherly's court. "We can't change their minds, except very slowly. However, we *can* teach them truths through logical reasoning. Then if they'll turn against reason we can use that as the proof to remove and replace them. Truths and facts must be presented for that to happen, and to prove to even them in some small degree, that because *they're* irrational, they're incompetent and unfit to fill their position." Airn realized that Rei was answering Erlic's question to the paige.

"So you'll replace them when you find someone suitable and capable of doing the work, who sees the people and wishes for the prosperity of the nation, but only after you've taught them and proven to them that they're the problem they're complaining about?" Airn asked.

"Yes," Rei answered soberly. "And it really is the hardest to do the very first of those things. There are lots of people who have wisdom, or skills. But to find one who can actually lead and knows how to make firm decisions, and who cares enough to care about the whole Region or nation, rather than their own needs or their family's needs, is quite a rare thing to find at all. That's why it's better at the beginning to see if they'll change themselves once they understand the full facts and truths they're currently blind to. They're in their positions because they've been trained to do it, and do it well. They're already capable. They just need to be a little less blind and the nation and region could prosper even more than it does now, blessing everyone."

Rei let Airn ponder on that lesson while they ate their dessert. Airn was grateful, just like he was grateful it was a warm cake with a lightly sweet sauce on it instead of a cold dessert to remind him of the cold outdoors. The lesson had actually been rather heavy, for all it wasn't out of the ordinary from what his lessons with his father and brother had been. It was all said differently enough, though, that Airn comprehended its full importance. He wanted to say that his station and situation were different, but they weren't. Not really. He as Second Prince would also be given a position of similar importance to what Rei had been given. He also could be a royal ally in the courts when he was finally ready to step into those shoes.

"I think I'd like to continue to watch you in the Court of Ministers," he finally requested as the meal neared its end. "I think learning how to see as you see by watching it there would be best."

Rei gave an accepting nod. "I'll suggest you come to the monthly meeting with the City Council as well. The lords at that level have the same problems. Ilena and I will be facing them similarly as well." Airn agreed and thanked Rei for the lesson and evening. "Learn how to research and send your aides out to research. Discuss with them how you'd address common issues that have come up in your own court. Learn outside of the real thing how to face them with confidence when you get back." Airn accepted the assignment, grateful that Rei was optimistic. He needed that encouragement.

The weather kindly held for Ore and Mizi for the three and a half days following their stay at the waystation, beginning to snow again when they were half–way between the last North Road garrison and Kouzanshi. They were grateful it was a normal snow rather than a squall, for all it was heavier than the light snows they'd had at Nijou before they'd left. Ore's explanation to Mizi about every inn having a Child of Mother in it held, as did the Twins' explanation they were a messenger business from long before, so Ore didn't have to field difficult questions from Mizi. Both relieved him greatly.

They arrived in Kouzanshi hungry, having bypassed eating lunch in favor of getting through the snow into Kouzanshi as quickly as possible. The Tarc horses were now familiar with stables enough that they stabled them in the larger, busier garrison stable. That made them a little nervous, but even Kesheb had had enough experiences now on the road to stay humble about it. He'd learned well, for all Ore had had to keep Fenrier calmed down the first day Kesheb had been on the halter lead by his side. Once the two horses had established dominance sufficiently the trip had been smoother, if not perfect. Kesheb hadn't wanted to be trained to that position longer than that first day and a half. Ore had made him do it anyway all the way to Kouzanshi. He'd see if the two horses would behave on the way home, then let him free of the halter lead.

Eating dinner in the full and noisy garrison cafeteria was another slightly stressful time for Ore since Mizi got even more clues. These he could pass off when he reminded her he'd had to work there while she'd been in the city for her two–year study at the university. He'd never talked to her about what he'd done then, so she politely didn't pry this time either. He sighed a sigh of relief at that, then turned the topic. "Mistress, I do still need to go up to the Northwest Pass garrison. Do you want me to help you talk to the professors tomorrow or the next day?"

Mizi paused in her eating as she considered it. "I think tomorrow. I can talk to Shiotsu in the morning and have him spread the word for a group meeting to be the next day. Then we can go talk to those individual people I really want to have come. Would that be okay?"

"Sure," Ore answered. He turned to the Twins. "Then you can be free tomorrow to do the business Ilena wants you to do in town, and walk with Mistress the next day. I'll have the Family and garrison guards watch over me for all of you while I run that errand." They gave him nods of acceptance.

"Oh!" Mizi said, sitting upright. "If you're going to be in town," she looked sharply at Marcus and Henry, "will you please pick up some of the local winter boots for Kirk? He mentioned his were worn but he'd forgotten during the progress to pick some up because he'd been so busy with Julie. While we were here I thought we could pick some up for him."

They gave her curious looks. "He's going to arrive up here anyway during his rounds, Mistress," Ore told her. "We'll not be going to the garrison south of here as it's close to his father's lands. Master thought he'd like to visit, and it's fastest to return to Nijou along North Road."

"Oh," Mizi said in a bit of disappointment. "Well..., but I'd like to pay for them."

Henry and Marcus looked at each other, then said, "If you'd like, we can take the payment to the shop and let them know, then let him know which shop to stop by when he's in town. That would be better so he can get ones that actually fit him instead of us having to guess his size and fashion preference. He's one who likes the fancier things."

"Well, I had noticed," Mizi agreed. She found it odd Kirk was a bit vain considering he was so relaxed all the time. "That would work for me, then." She fished into her belt and pulled out a small bag of coins and handed it over. "I set aside this much for them."

Henry took it and put it away safely in his jacket. "We'll see it's taken care of," he promised.

That evening Ore took Henry with him and left Marcus to watch over Mizi. It was easier to use the Family network from the top of the city wall where it encircled the garrison than to talk from their rooms, even if they had snow piling up on their shoulders and heads. Henry asked if he could go first and Ore let him. *Mistress to Sir Kirk Leander. When you reach Kouzanshi, please stop by,* Henry named a shop in town. *I've paid for new boots for you there. Please don't forget to pick them up. We didn't reach snow until half–way to town today, so you have that much more time of good weather. Take care.* He sent the end of sending code, to let Kirk know he didn't have to respond.

Ore took his turn to call to Ilena, also sending along the weather report to the castle. They wouldn't get the snows until the next day sometime. Likely Kirk had been able to make it to all the eastern mountain garrisons just fine. He'd just have snow in his face for most of the trip back west unless this was a shorter snowfall than the last one.

-o-o-o-

Kirk was lying in a comfortable bed with his hands behind his head, having been fed warm food, when he heard a message being delivered to him in Ilena's code from outside his door. He blinked in surprise but listened silently to it. When it was done he smiled softly. *If it's not too much trouble, send a thank you back,* he requested. He'd noticed that Mizi enjoyed gifting useful needed items to people she cared for. He'd not really expected her to buy him Kouzanshi boots, though, when he'd told Brian he was thinking of picking some up on this trip. Sometimes she heard things when they were talking quietly while watching over her at her work.

He was actually at an inn tonight, the distance between the Four-Corner garrison and the first one on South Suiran road being twice the distance a horse could go in the winter. There weren't as many garrisons internal to Suiran as there were on the borders. It had been very nice to have the good weather for all of the eastern garrisons. It was true that he'd not have found the three against the hills very well in driving snow. He'd asked his guide to point out the winter landmarks in the hopes that might help him next time.

Kirk frowned just a little. The second night of the trip they'd stopped at the Umber manor for the night. Baron Umber was as stiff as Minister Eadlsey and as old fashioned as Kirk's father. He supposed it was good that Brian got along with his father better than Kirk did with his own, but perhaps it had been good the princesses hadn't gone there for the progress. He'd raised an eyebrow at Brian, being surprised that their garrison guide had been invited to eat in the kitchen with the staff as if he was a lowly guard. Brian had whispered in the code that his father held to the older traditions, which explained that much.

Kirk had tried to let that be enough, on the outside, but he'd been rather uncomfortable because Brian's sister's maid had been present at the table. That only happened in such families if the daughter was considered wild and unmanageable and needed an extra hand on her. Kirk hadn't thought Gwenn much out of the ordinary for a young lady of a House. He could understand it from the perspective of them no longer having a Lady of the House to sit at the table to help teach her children how to be polite, but Brian had told him before that his mother had passed away recently. Surely the Baron's stern hand would be sufficient to keep anyone polite at that table without the help of a servant. He felt sorry for the daughter. Kirk could only imagine Gwenn must be stifled, or would be as she got older.

He'd not liked the maid generally, though. Her eyes were piercing and intelligent, rather than humble. When Baron Umber had asked Kirk politely for what reason the Regent was sending a personal messenger out into the weather for, the maid had listened with her ears, if not shown it in her face. Kirk hadn't said much in answer, only enough to be polite and include a slight scold that if the Regent had a reason anyone would go, and then to explain it was as much a training for him as a vacation to let him get his excessive energy out. Since that was a normal reason for anyone, and the weather was at that time nice, it had been accepted easily.

Because Kirk had had two garrisons to visit the next day, he'd excused himself to bed early so he could leave early the next morning. He'd been given a nice room on the second floor, but noticed that the garrison guard was given a small one on the main floor in the staff section. He'd paid attention to which one so he could wake the man up in the morning if necessary. Once they'd been on the road in the morning headed for the Northeast garrison for that stop, he'd asked the guard, "Did you learn anything, being kept with the servants? That surprised me."

The guard had given him an interesting look back, then said, "Well, it was informative, yes, but more than hear things, I was asked questions. I didn't need the advances, either," that was said very dryly.

Kirk had looked at him in shock and the man had nodded back. "Why would they have the guts to do that to a soldier of the castle garrison?"

He'd gotten a shake of the head back. "I have no idea. I set them in place quickly and also excused myself to bed early, wishing locking the door would be sufficient."

Kirk had agreed, glad they hadn't disturbed him. The House chatelâine would've had the key to let anyone in if they'd wanted it. "You'll be wanting to sleep in the saddle some today, then?" Kirk had smiled sympathetically at him. "I'd let you do it now, if you could. I *do* know this leg just fine."

Kirk frowned even deeper now. He was starting to wonder if he was the best partner for Brian. While they were young lords together of equal standing in the castle, Brian's past experiences were different enough from Kirk's that they might clash more often than he'd want. Kirk wanted to marry Julie because he loved her, but he was going against the traditions to marry common, now that they knew her heritage. Brian could very quickly become as impatient with that as he was about Mizi's common background. Julie at least had been raised noble to some level, so that might balance it out.

If Mizi was working on trying to decide who to keep because she didn't need four guards plus a secretary–assassin at her side, Kirk was coming to believe it wouldn't be surprising if Brian was released. That would be hard to make that decision, though, because Brian was a good enough guard to keep in that place. He was the best of all four of them, as a matter of fact, unless Kirk was fighting left–handed.

He shifted in the bed and stared out the window for a bit, enjoying the last bit of starlight he'd see for another long while. The snows would start on his way to the garrison the next day. He was hoping they'd be light since he was at the farthest distance from them he could get and still be in Suiran, but sometimes they were heavier and wetter because of passing over the boggy woods.

Finally he sighed. His instincts were telling him that he should stop practicing with Brian left–handed. That might be the only advantage he'd have against Brian if Brian turned against him or Mizi. Something in that House wasn't right, which meant something might not be right inside Brian, when it came to being in the position he was in: too close to a royal. It might not hurt to suggest it to Mina, too, the next time she worked with Kirk. It made Kirk's stomach tighten uncomfortably to think these thoughts about his partner. They needed to work together without reservation.

-o-o-o-

Shiotsu sighed as he set the paper in his hand down on the tall narrow worktable that was his in the Medical Department. He was sitting on his tall stool as he usually did, more leaning against it since his legs were as long as the stool was tall and then a little longer. He glanced down the wide table to the teapot. It was just starting to steam. He reached for it and poured up a cup of tea, then he replaced the pot over the small burner in its iron holder. He was lost in his head for a while before he remembered to pick the cup up and sip from it.

That drew him back with a little start of surprise. He held the cup in front of him and inspected it, then sniffed at it and took another sip. He sighed again as he set the cup down. It was Ilena's tea, the one he'd call her home to the department with whenever she'd been in Kouzanshi. He knew she was in Nijou, but he couldn't be surprised he'd picked it out all without thinking. He wanted to talk to her, to hear from her if what Mizi had told him was really true. To be able to comfort her while getting even more comfort in return just from having her soft smile in front of him.

He rose to his feet and took his tea cup with him to sit in the overstuffed chair that had been her bed for over half a year when she'd been there doing her research, years ago. He slumped back into the chair and sipped at the tea in silence until his wife and assistant Tiana came around the corner of the great herb cabinets and stopped short, her nose sniffing the air. She gave Shiotsu a slightly worried look. "Really?" she asked, wanting to know why that tea was what he'd chosen.

Shiotsu shook his head. "Completely lost in my head until I tasted it," he ruefully scolded himself. "I'd even get on the carriage and leave immediately now that I know where she is, except I'm needed here and there's no point to going, just for head rubs and purrs." He almost didn't catch the sudden tears. He looked down at the teacup, then hid behind it again.

Tiana walked over and put her hand on his shoulder. "Is it really so bad? What can I do?" she asked softly.

He could tell her part of it. "Gael's preparing to go to war with Altherly. King Sasou's agreed to send support and Lord Yosuko has agreed Kouzanshi will be where they'll bring the seriously wounded of Ryokado to for healing. We're to make sure we've got enough stock and find places to put the wounded for their tending." He looked away from Tiana, towards his table. "The royals are hurting and I don't want to face war any more than they do. It's too hard." He drew in a deep breath and sighed it out as Tiana wrapped her arms around his neck to hold him.

"You really are surprisingly a softy," she teased him quietly. "One of these days I'm going to have to spill it to the students when they get so mad at you for being so hard on them."

Shiotsu snorted at her. "And then pick up even more work they leave for anyone else to do?"

She sighed softly. "Well..., no."

"Then you'd have to be the harsh general," he pointed out.

She slumped, giving up. "Well, okay. I'd rather be that just to you."

Shiotsu chuckled. She did do well with that much firmness, and he knew he needed it when she did it. He wrapped one arm around her, mindful of the tea so it didn't spill on either of them. "Thank you, Tiana,' he said. Then very quietly he whispered in her ear, "The hospital is partially because they think we might be attacked from behind once we're fully committed to Altherly. We can't keep the best. We need to encourage them to go there."

Tiana stiffened with a sharp intake of breath, then she shivered. Shiotsu agreed. He held her just a little more tightly to strengthen her, too, then he let her go so he didn't lose the tea. He rested the cup on the arm of the chair and looked her in the eye. Her hand had taken his and he held it firmly to give them both the comfort they needed. Neither of them liked to have their peaceful patterns of life interrupted like this, for all it did happen.

"Mizi's threatened to send Ore after anyone not at the presentation. Please make sure you remind them early enough tomorrow so they have enough time to wrap up and get moving. Today she and Ore are going to personally talk to those she wants the most. If those come to you, remind them that being called up by royalty doesn't allow for refusal except in very extreme circumstances. If she can tell them why she wants them, they'll go without question." Tiana agreed. Even they'd go if she'd called them up for all they loved being over the department.

Tiana had been getting their current set of students started for the day while Mizi and Ore had talked to Shitosu. The paper on his table was the request for interns for the Nijou Department of Medicine for him to post on the wall of the department. He'd put it near the door so people would see it when they left, and he'd been asked to have it copied and put around the library. He'd have enough copies made to put it outside in the hall by the door and a few other strategic hallway locations.

He drew in a breath. "She's doing the university presentation because the notices won't get enough people in time. Prospective interns and medics need to begin the trip to Nijou within this week. I'm glad Ilena's people could tell us early enough for us to have everyone prepared at least for coming to the presentation." Knowing to have that venue announced and prepared a week ago had helped immensely. Sudden morning–of announcements were pointless in a place where researchers were so

244

caught up in their studies they wouldn't even lift their heads to see, breathe, or eat for days on end.

He sighed and slumped even further into the chair and ran a hand over his face, letting go of Tiana's hand to do it. Once Ore and Mizi were gone it would be quiet again save for preparing the hospital there in Kouzanshi. He closed his eyes. Tiana's hand came softly on his head, rubbing it a little. His internal cat ear flicked a thank you at her which came out as a small smile on his lips. "Just ten," he whispered. The cup was taken from his hand and he heard it land with a light thunk on his table. Tiana had her own research to do. Once she was settled at her table, Shiotsu was lost to a cat nap. Maybe he was getting old to need one after such small excitement in his morning, but he really wanted to escape for one brief moment.

-o-o-o-

Ore was relieved that Mizi managed to explain well enough why she needed the specific researchers to come to her hospital. She'd allowed as how they could bring their research with them and continue it there. That had won them best. They'd be able to practice on actual patients to see if their research was effective once the hospital was going. The training time had been a little harder. She'd had to allow that the one she wanted to be the head medic could come later, after it was built. He was already a well–known name with lots of experience so really didn't need the training at Nijou. It would be sufficient that he'd agreed to come do it.

They had lunch with Shiotsu and the other medical department staff and students Mizi knew, followed by a slow walk back to the garrison since Ore didn't want to shut her into such a boring place for a long time. Still, he had a job to do there so there was where they were going and would sleep at again that night. "Will you be okay if I require you to be in your room until I come get you again?" Ore looked at Mizi from the corner of his eye a bit sharply. He'd not normally be so demanding, but in this case he was rather firm.

Mizi studied him, then gave an accepting nod. "I can finalize my presentation while you talk to the commander." She then smiled a little, "And take a nap if you take too long. That might be a nice change of pace for once."

Ore stared at her in mock surprise. "Mistress would sleep in the middle of the day?" He put the back of his hand to her forehead. "Does that mean you might be sick? Don't become sick."

Mizi laughed at him and he smiled softly back. "Well..., it would be good if you'd rest," he allowed. "Mistress works hardest of all and needs the rest where she can get it." He put his hands behind his head. "Not like lazy Ore at all, who finds any corner or tree branch to hide and rest in until he's called back to work by one who manages to find him." Mizi gave him a scolding glare, then rolled her eyes at him. He heard in his mind the scold that she knew he worked hard as well. It was a common interaction between them.

He dropped his arms and slumped a little as he realized he hadn't actually been able to escape that way since he'd been made Assistant Minister, and maybe even before then. "Why did I want to become a Prince again?" he asked her.

Mizi patted his shoulder lightly. "Because you love Ilena and care about me and Rei. Those are very good reasons. If it had been because you wanted power and fame I wouldn't have approved at all."

Ore laughed at her this time. "And of course, what Mistress wants, she gets."

Mizi walked mock proudly for a few steps, then let it go and smiled at him again. "Well, I'm grateful you're willing to consider my wishes in the matter. It's good to have you at my side again for this trip, too."

Ore looked away in embarrassment. "Well, I'd rather be here than seeing you go off on your own." He frowned at her, "Particularly when we all need the time away and this is important work." She looked away this time, but gave him a nod of agreement.

He made sure she was safely in her room then ordered one of the two soldiers that had accompanied them in Henry and Marcus' place for the day to guard her door. He took the other one and headed for the garrison commander's office. He was finding it hard to remember even he needed the additional guarding. When his frustration with it would rise he'd remember his very first moment to be personally attacked for his new ranking and that would settle quickly. He didn't need any rumors going around at all, nor did he want any openings for others to sneak attack him in social ways.

General Joshua Monroe, Commander of the Kouzanshi garrison, welcomed Ore to his office. He wasn't very surprised Ore closed the door to the smaller office so those of his staff in the large outer office couldn't hear their conversation. (He left the guard out there as well.) Ore sank into a chair opposite Joshua, on the other side of his desk. That did surprise the commander. "It's going to take that long?" he asked. Sharp eyes studied Ore and Joshua leaned back. "Or is it you're finally worn down?"

"The latter, honestly," Ore admitted, "although, it will also take that long." He wrinkled up his nose in a grimace. He was usually very, very brief, and if he closed the door the meeting usually was only twice as long. They'd worked together now for three and a half years in brief passing meetings like those, but the commander had read Ore's reports so knew him well enough.

"It's hard to go from Head of Intelligence to Second Prince, I presume? And a surprise." Joshua was astute.

"Certainly a surprise," Ore agreed. "It's probably harder to have become the Grand Duke of Tarc. I really wasn't expecting that one at all." He shook his head. Joshua raised an eyebrow. "And in the end, it's all the hats that sit on my head at once now." He smiled the ironic wry smile of the nightwalker. "It's hard enough just to be my wife's husband. I prepared for that during those years here, studying the Queen of Night as ordered." He gave a small involuntary shiver that Joshua agreed with. "I still have to face Zade. I was quite happy to not do that last time we went through. I'm hoping he doesn't really know it's me yet." He raised an eyebrow of question.

Joshua tapped his steepled fingertips together as he considered the answer. "Lord Yosuko might not really know until he sees your face together with the knowledge. You might get one more cordial visit with him if you don't announce yourself to him, but someone's going to point it out eventually: that the person who was supposed to be hunting for and punishing the Queen of Night for him is actually now her husband." The sharp eyes came on Ore again. "Even Prince Rei asked us to keep quiet about it when he was here for the progress and inspection."

Ore wasn't surprised. "It would be better for me to not talk to him for the brief time we're here, then. I think we need to hold that surprise until it's really necessary for him to know. ...That might be in Ichijou," he mused. Joshua agreed with him. "Has he asked you if I have any last reports for him?" Ore asked.

Joshua answered dryly, "He wants *everything* you have on her to date that he can use as a weapon against her when he goes to Ichijou himself."

Ore slumped. "I was afraid of that. I've been struggling to determine how to narrow down everything I've learned since she showed up in our lives into something he can have." He reached into his jacket and pulled out a folder and slid it over the top of the desk. "Here's my final report to you. You can judiciously pick out what he's allowed to have and consider the rest as secret national security information he isn't allowed to have no matter how much he whines."

Joshua picked it up and skimmed the first few paragraphs, then flipped through pages. He closed it and put it down on the desk. "I'm going to assume it's already been edited to *actually* keep out the state secrets."

Ore indicated he was correct. "But you'll still find it very interesting reading. There were a lot of things I couldn't find out and we didn't know. Top of which was that she was the lost princess." The commander completely understood that hidden fact was one they'd never have known on their own. It was why becoming Second Prince had been so surprising a thing to happen to him. Ore smiled a bright smile. "I also finally learned what she does with the money she takes in from the lists and the taxes on the nightwalker Houses. That was a fun thing to learn, and not at all out of line with how she was already working."

"Oh?" Joshua asked, interested in hearing that answer that had escaped Ore's research for this long.

Ore shifted and went more serious. "Yes. She pays it into the war fund of the Region and nation ...just as directly as she pays for Kouzanshi to stay a nice city to live in." That surprised Joshua enough he sat staring at Ore for some time. Ore's sharp gaze stared him down until Joshua had thawed enough that Ore added, "And that *is* one of the state secrets not included in the report. I just thought you'd like to know."

Joshua finally rubbed his temple. "I did get some comments in reports that it seemed like there were suddenly fewer nightwalkers in town and just as suddenly they'd returned. She called for her House to go into Tarc?" Ore nodded silently. Joshua drew in a deep breath, trying to come to terms with the concept. "She paid for them all?" Ore nodded again. Not sure he wanted the answer, the commander asked tentatively, "How many?"

"Over two thousand across Suiran. Double that if you include her daywalker network."

That nearly made the commander faint as he went pale. "*Daywalker?* ...And *four* thousand she called to the field?" Ore nodded a third time. That was roughly equal to the number of soldiers in one of the cities of Suiran or more. "Would they follow her in a coup against the Regent?" he asked quietly.

Ore shook his head. "She won't take anyone on that isn't also loyal to Touka. But Master's put me by her side regardless, to make sure." He gazed at Joshua for a long moment then said quietly, "I do love her, and have since we were children, but I've promised Master that if she becomes a problem, I'll take care of it." The commander could only nod.

Ore shifted and changed the subject. "As to why I'm *actually* here, it's because Master's sent me with orders and information about the Nijou garrison and Kishi Knight's school spring exhibition. General Garen's quite excited we finally get to have war games in Suiran again and has been very busy coming up with things to teach everyone." General Monroe went very dry and neutral. "You get to come out and see us for a change!" Ore gave him his signature grin. The general stayed neutral then and through the whole of what Ore had to tell him.

-o-o-o-

Marcus was happy to be home. He and Henry were both able to relax in a way they couldn't in Nijou. They'd left the black–sheathed swords and black castle cloaks in their room at the garrison. They didn't need that much attention in the city, and they needed to be able to go into their usual nightwalker haunts. Royal guards would get sour looks and no information. They'd be recognized eventually under their winter clothing, but they didn't need the connection made quite so strongly in the Kouzanshi nightwalkers' minds. Henry had reminded Marcus that they should be cautious today since that's what they were now. They might get a different reception than even when they'd come for the progress: they didn't have Ilena with them this time.

Marcus, the one with the instinct to see without knowing he'd seen anything, was the first to grab Henry and pull him back. At the same time he grabbed and twisted the arm of the person who'd reached out. The crack of the bone was louder than the sound of the knife that hit the seven feet of snow on the ground. Marcus pulled the assassin close enough to scowl into his face and make him gasp in pain. "Just because she's not here doesn't mean we've gotten soft. Just because someone thinks they don't like her doesn't mean we aren't still in the top of the House for a reason." He shoved the man away in anger. "I'll let someone else in the House kill you. We're on orders and don't have the time to waste on the likes of you."

A passing person nabbed the back collar of the injured man and hauled him into the closest alley. They'd interrogate him first to find out just who'd had the audacity to hire him, and just why he'd been stupid enough to take the job.

Marcus stayed close by Henry's side as they strode quickly for their destination. "It's only going to get harder, isn't it," Marcus complained quietly to Henry.

Henry glanced at him and then the people on the street on the other side of him while Marcus watched the street on the other side of Henry and listened with his ears to the street behind them. Their eyes also kept track of the roofs around them. He wasn't happy to suddenly *not* be able to be relaxed at home. The streets were the usual busy of Kouzanshi, since the people didn't change their life habits just because of snow. They hurried from place to place when they had to be outside if the snow was particularly bad but that wasn't today. The only difference was that they were using their second–story windows as their doors. The shops all had doors that opened onto balconies on each floor so their customers could enter more comfortably than clambering through smaller windows.

"Probably," Henry answered him. "Over time, anyway. We've always been retested every time we've come back, but yeah, I do expect it to be more like that every time. Particularly when it's just us."

"Back to the old days," Marcus wrinkled up his nose. Every nightwalker had to earn their place and hold it. He was going to be done with that very soon ...like as soon as he chose to marry Amber. "How do the old nightwalkers that settle down manage to be free of it?"

"Hmm," Henry mused on that as they passed through an intersection to head for a particular alley where several good businesses backed up to each other and those nightwalkers who worked with horses held the delivery teams. One of the in–city stables was nearby there and was where they were headed. They wanted to start passing the word about the fast–horse messenger business, and those young men would be the best place to start. "Either they defend like that until they're forgotten, or they die, or they move to where no one knows their face."

Marcus sighed. "Not really what I want, when we're going to have to come with her every required time for the university and I'm going to want to bring Amber and then kids with."

Henry shrugged slightly. "True. Maybe we should talk to her about it." Her meaning Ilena, Marcus understood.

"Guess I will," Marcus answered. He was glad they'd been left alone at the beginning of their trip through the city. It was likely uncovering their faces in the boot shop to give Mizi's order for Kirk's boots and pay for them was what had given away who they were. The attacks had started after that place.

They spent the next little while talking to the horseboys and runners who had time to listen about the possibility of leaving Kouzanshi and working as fast–horse messengers. They weren't surprised to get only about one in every three or four to have interest but no willingness to commit just yet. It would take word getting out that it was a lucrative job. New things that weren't certain were harder for them to want, particularly if they didn't want to leave town. Spreading word of the business was still good at this point, though.

It was at the stable that they got a better reception. The older stable hands knew about their messenger business and already knew how to ride. There were two who were ready to move up and move on from the stable. They focused on talking to them in more depth, then told them the training would be at Nijoushi as soon as they could arrive there. Ilena had decided she could train them initially on the pack horses of the small herd of the Immediate Family since they were getting fat and lazy from not being used at all. When they were trained enough by her for the riding, Henry and Marcus would take over and make sure they understood how to run long–distance messages. Then they'd be taken to Falcon's Hollow to get the horse they'd keep as their partner until they were ready to retire.

Once they'd heard the arrangement for paying for the horse and lessons one man asked if they'd be able to obtain a second horse to carry more messages or to be the second horse if they needed to have more speed without killing the first horse. "That's actually a good idea," Henry agreed. "I think if you were doing well and had enough profits that could be arranged." He added dryly, "However, if you think you'll get a whole horse train, that won't happen. Two's probably the limit. The herd owner's a bit particular about that sort of thing. You'd have to be pretty convincing beyond that."

Marcus nodded. "Accuracy, followed by speed, are the things that will bring in the best profits. One horse of this kind is sufficient for speed and will bring in good profits. Two will be all you'll need to be serious businessmen."

When the two men were satisfied they understood what the business would be and how much autonomy they'd have, Henry and Marcus left them. Their final words were again encouragement for them to go sooner than later. "I'm glad the concept of letting them be their own individual business while using the tools of another company was received well," Marcus said. They'd done the same for Ilena when they'd started out. They'd not had horse nor tack. She'd purchased the same for them and they'd paid her back from the profits of their messenger business.

In this case they knew she didn't want to let the horses really be owned by the messengers, so it was a lease. If they wanted to not have to pay for the horse or horses, they'd have to return them and purchase their own Ryokudo horses. Of course, they could do that anyway from the outset. It was the Tarc horses' capabilities they were marketing to the men. That would be what the brave first people would be proving to themselves and those who might come after them into the business.

They talked the sales talk at three more stables finding that many again or fewer at each one. They could only hope that even two of those who'd been interested would come before the spring and summer traveling began. There'd be no training during that time, save by the householders of Falcon's Hollow, which might be enough but they and Ilena wanted to be the hands–on trainers for the very first few to see if the whole concept would really work.

By now it was getting towards dinner, the right time to go visit at the main safe house in town. They purchased food they could eat as they walked and had it eaten before they arrived. Damas, Mandor, and Zeph were waiting for them in the safe house, which was rather full as expected for this time of day. "That was far too many attacks on our persons this time," Marcus complained at them soberly. "What's going on? Have you let the House get soft?" He and Henry weren't soft at all when all three of them attacked the Twins at once.

It wasn't usual for the Twins to fight the challenge the Messenger would have had to, but Marcus' words had been the call for it to happen. Probably more *because* it had been him. If a more minor correction and test had been acceptable Henry would have challenged Zeph. It was one of the ways the nightwalkers of Suiran were like the Tarc. If the Left Hand of caution pointed out the need for correction it was usually a more severe punishment than if the fiery Right Hand did.

Mandor, the Lieutenant of the loyalty of the members to the House dropped out first, acceding that to have had that many people on the street be so disobedient to the representatives of the Head there were things that needed fixing in the House and the city. The whole of the city owed allegiance to the Queen of Night and so should have left the Twins alone.

Zeph, the Lieutenant of the loyalty of the members of the House to themselves put up a good fight, but eventually he yielded to Henry. Henry had to hold him down, watching for him to begin again if Marcus couldn't withstand against Damas. They were a little surprised when it was Damas, the Lieutenant of the House's loyalty to Ilena, who withstood them the longest. Marcus used one of the moves they'd learned practicing against Justinian to finally get Damas in a hold he couldn't get out of. That castle martial art was the only one not known in the practice lists of Kouzanshi.

"Why?" Marcus demanded angrily to know from Damas before he'd let him go.

Damas scowled at him. "Taking us from the city for even six weeks made individuals in the city decide they could relax. How can we know all of who that is until they move?" He very much wasn't happy either. "If you've cleaned a few more off the streets and helped us teach them all again where they stand, maybe they'll finally relearn their lessons."

Henry glared into Zeph's eyes but Zeph looked with his eyes over to Mandor. Mandor placed a hand down on the dais and bowed to the two of them. "Lord Yosuko has also increased his pressure on the Houses, hiring mercenary nightwalkers from outside the city. The first two to attack you were from inside the city, testing. The remainder were those."

At that both of the Twins scowled and let their captives go, standing ready to defend again, but the Lieutenants only moved back to their places on the dais. Henry pursed his lips then said, "It's not to leave this room." He got obedient nods from all three. "Lord Yosuko has also increased the pressure in the court of Ichijou. Now that the Queen of Night is also recognized by the Crown, he believes he can attack her on that side as well for his perceived slights." His face told of his complete distaste and disregard for that person. "The King knows and they're working on the final defense and potential removal of Lord Yosuko that was started when Mister Ore began to do Prince Rei's work in Kouzanshi."

Marcus gave a nod of confirmation. "It wouldn't be unexpected to have the pressure increase generally against the House on both sides. However, he's only made the Toukas angry at his continued unwillingness to become wise. Let the other Houses and businesses know quietly to send any further written complaints to the King's attention at Ichijou, frequently. Additional letters to other Ministries of concern and complaints to open their eyes to his lack of capability would be good as well. Increasing the pressure back on him in that way will lead to the city finally being able to work as it should, as they've all been wishing for it to be."

All three bowed to them, accepting that order with some relief. Henry turned to Damas. "It couldn't be helped. Regardless, it's a sufficient test of the other Houses as well. See that those that were most interested in raising their hands against the Queen of Night are leaned on and their Heads replaced if necessary. Such occasional testing is required, as you already well know." He shook his head, "Particularly now." He took in a breath and said, "King Sasou has agreed to aid Altherly against Gael. Wounded will be brought here for healing. It'll be hard enough to keep out those who sneak in with them. Clean up the city again before that begins.

"All job desks are to begin to advertise for men to go into Altherly with the Prince. Men are being sent, not just monetary and physical aids. The lords of Suiran are still as generally difficult as Lord Yosuko. The Queen of Night would like to see more men protecting Ryokudo and the Prince than they're expected to provide." The Lieutenants were scowling. Henry kept going. "However, only those who come from here to River road will go into Altherly. The others will be held back until more need to be sent, and we'll hope they don't need to be." Everyone agreed with that.

"When will they go?" Danel asked.

Marcus shook his head. "Have them listen for the call and watch for the men of the lords to arrive at the border. They should join in with them and say that they're the prince's men when asked what holding they come from. At the earliest it will be Autumn–Three before the Prince comes himself. There may be training for those who'll fight before then. That won't begin until after the end of Spring–Two. The garrison commanders are being called to a general war game and war conference to coincide with the Nijou garrison exhibition and review. Once they've returned from that, they'll know who's to run the training and how. '

"Won't Gael already be half–way through Altherly, then, by the time we go in to help?" Barakka asked.

Henry shrugged. "Maybe. They might also already be at our own border. Touka isn't concerned so that's not so likely." Since that meant all three of the young royals, the Lieutenants and the room generally settled somewhat. None of the nightwalkers liked hearing they could be embroiled in war by the end of the year. While they might join in on the looting and other such things, even nightwalkers preferred to not have their lives disrupted that much.

When Henry and Marcus had received confirmation that order would also be followed, they turned to the room at large. "This is for the information brokers, but also for anyone who has ears. Starting roughly at the beginning of the second week of next month, begin to listen for people who have a new thing to sell in regards to the war and our involvement in it, or who want to buy. The Regent's on the hunt and wants to know if the person sent this way is trustworthy or not." Faces that understood had eyes glint with the look of the hunt as well.

"Tell us on the wind right away. We'll hear all of it and determine it. Mark who asks for and pays for it. If it's landed lords' contacts, they want to know that also immediately, and which ones. It's time to clean them up as well, although that's going to take a few more years to settle." They all knew how slowly the crown had to work against landed lords who commanded men, in comparison to the rest of the corrupt they'd been able to clean out expeditiously.

With those orders given, the Twins could sit in their places on the dais and talk to the Lieutenants about more detailed things that didn't need to involve the whole House. Slowly the room emptied of the nightwalkers who worked in the night and the rest settled to sleeping. They didn't stay too late. They still needed to keep up with Mizi the next morning, and they needed to confirm Ore was okay and would stay put in his room and sleep for some of the night as well.

Ore stood stiff in disapproval in Zade Yosuko's office early the next morning. He'd stayed up to hear Marcus and Henry's report the night before and he was not pleased at all. He worked hard to put on a false humble front to Zade, at least one that said he still recognized he was the commoner and Zade the lord of the city. It would be the last time he did, though. "I've come to make my final report. Master has said he's reassigning me to other projects, but I can do this much."

Zade blinked at him in some surprise, then scowled slightly. "Is it because she's been recognized by them?"

"She's told them everything about herself they wanted to know," Ore agreed with him. "Learning the most secret secret did it: that she's the lost princess." At Zade's angry, impatient look, Ore shook his head at him. "It was irrefutable proof she couldn't have created herself. There's no doubt it's her." The memory of the tattoos on his wife's back and the feel of them on his fingers rose up in his mind. He missed her very much but this wasn't really the time; although, the memory was much more preferable to standing in front of this lump of a lord and having to listen to him.

Zade's lips pursed. He then drew himself up to stand as the imposing lord, which he did when he thought he was being crafty, and proceeded to interrogate Ore for all the traitorous details he wanted. Ore let him ask, answering the ones that wouldn't make *him* the traitor. Ore claimed he had no knowledge to answer any of the others, save one that would make Zade show his hand later.

When Zade was done with the interrogation, Ore asked his questions. "It was noisy on the streets yesterday and last night. Apparently you've been hiring mercenaries to take down the leaders of the House of the Queen of Night?" he raised an eyebrow at Zade.

Zade went slightly paler than his normal pale, then shook his head. "Why bother?" he said very grouchily.

"Because if the royals support her, then of course you'd have to resort to other means to get her out of your city." Ore said it rather practically. Then he shifted and went to confused. "Have you sent her a letter yet, asking her to please pull out and let you have your city, now that she doesn't have to be in hiding and now that you know where to send the letter to?"

Zade stared at him like he was crazy. Then he looked away and waved his hand. "Eventually."

"Eventually?" Ore was surprised by that answer. "Why wait?" He wasn't surprised when the answer was contrived and said nothing. It did make him supremely curious as to what was going through the man's head. Perhaps he'd finally understood how much of the city she was propping up for him. Ore wasn't sure that was likely, but he couldn't know if Zade wouldn't tell him. "Well, if that's all you have for me, that's all I have for you," Ore said respectfully. Zade considered it, then waved him off. Ore bowed. "I'm sure I'll see you here and there," he said and took himself out of the manor home.

Ore shivered to get the weight of that dark building off his shoulders as he stepped out into the morning again. Even the grey snowing clouds felt lighter than that house did. Maybe Zade was so incompetent because he kept himself buried under that heavy rock. His brain couldn't work right.

Ore had gotten the brief subtle clue he'd gone looking for. *Father to the House. Get the evidence we need to add to Lord Kouzanshi's conviction that he is the one hiring mercenaries against the Queen of Night. Father to the Family. Find at least two, three would be better, who'll trade true testimony against him in person for protection from the House.* If they worked together they might have what they finally needed. That plus an audit of the manor's paperwork. From early on he'd had Marcus and Henry put someone on becoming Zade's secretary's drinking buddy. He wouldn't ever go traitor to his lord, but they could distract him long enough to prevent the incriminating paperwork from being destroyed.

Ore drew in a deep breath as he brushed the snow off Fenrier's saddle and let it out as he swung up into the saddle. This morning he didn't have guards here in town since he'd not wanted them seen with him. He picked them up on his way back through the garrison, then left through that gate for the Northwest Pass garrison at the Ryokudo–Selicia border.

This time of year the Northwest Pass garrison, located at the highest pass the roads through the mountains went through, was snow–bound. People didn't travel between the two countries in the winter. Supplies were still sent up once a month though, so the guards and Ore knew the way quite well even with all the snow.

It had been winter four years before when the plague had shut down Kouzanshi in quarantine. He'd traveled from the Northwest Pass garrison to Kouzanshi quickly with Rei, Andrew, and Mina to learn why. Rei had been rather frantic then, with both Sasou and Mizi in that city. So frantic he'd sent Ore in to be with them and help them come back out again. When the city had been opened back up, Ore had gone back up to the Northwest Pass garrison to retrieve Rei, Andrew, and Mina back to Kouzanshi. He was glad that wasn't the reason this time.

The ride to and from the Northwest Pass garrison took far longer than the time it took Ore to give the commander of the garrison his orders. Not really to the liking of this commander was the additional order that a portion of his men would be joining in on the fighting in Altherly. With relations between Ryokudo and Selicia currently neutral to "doing better" the Regent thought they could spare about five hundred men to the Altherly–Gael war effort. Those soldiers wouldn't be called for just yet. This was the warning to be preparing, with the actual date to have the men on the road told to him at the conference and war games.

There was one other new order. "Tell the messengers to King Sandras that Ryokudo has joined on the side of Altherly to protect our own western border, and to be watchful of Gael coming from those roads. Ask them to confirm if the spies of Selicia agree that Gael is bent on major conquering. See if they want to ally with Ryokudo sufficient enough for talks to open if it looks like Gael will try to enter both nations if Altherly does fall. We'll do our best to keep the border points here protected, if they'll protect theirs from Gael."

Ore hesitated, then added quietly. "And ask them if they'll keep their Tarc border protected if Brulac decides this is the perfect opportunity to attack from our rear. It's simple enough to take a force through Tarc and the people there never know of it. If such a thing happens, we need to be informed immediately so we can go throw them back out. Tell them this is a request from the Grand Duke of Tarc. We will of course protect those borders as best we can, but the Great Fall is scaleable by those determined enough to enter by that way."

After his late lunch he and his guards were back on the road again. Ore rode in silence, his mind worrying over Tarc. The reports from there were still that the people were trying hard to understand the revised Laws as put into place by Rei. Generally the clans' daily lives seemed to be calmer and the people a little more content, if still occasionally confused. The most worrisome news was that it was still hard for them to police the whole of the Great Fall that separated the plains of Tarc from Brulac. He was going to discuss that one more time at the next Regional Security Meeting he went to once he was back at Nijou. They needed to send more men — either soldiers of Ryokudo or nightwalkers — to that border to see it had more eyes on it to keep it protected.

-o-o-o-

Maroz stonily looked out over the land far below the escarpment of the high plains of Tarc. The grimness he felt filled him with a soberness and anger that fed his heart's despair. It was his duty and his payment during these winter months, however. He ground his teeth again and turned for the tent of those who protected this empty part of Tarc. The strong biting cold wind from the northwest blew into his face, making him scrunch up his cheeks to protect his eyes. The warm embroidered hat would have blown off of his head if it weren't for the tasseled ties holding it on. The top of his head and his ears were grateful to his third wife for making it for him the previous winter. He didn't like the reminder that she'd been one of his wives who'd decided to die to Chaos and darkness. He was still grateful in this season.

He tried his best to not have the tent door open long. The front area was small, a place to keep that cold out as much as possible. When his cheeks felt warm enough, he lifted the hanging wall and entered the next area and pulled off his gloves so he could have fingers to untie his ear flaps and take off his hat. The fire in the middle of the room snapped cheerfully and what little smoke came from it went up and through the open hole at the top of the tent. He was glad to be able to return to the small warmth. It was another thing to be grateful for: warmth to survive the bitter cold of Tarc winters. He tried to let the small gratitudes lift the grimness his duty had left him with, even if only by that small amount.

"It's done then?" the head of the cloaked figures in the gathering room of the scout tent asked Maroz as he continued to pull off the outer layers of his winter clothing. The others didn't really need to be sitting around with their cloaks on. He'd decided they'd forgotten they existed as a separate element from them since they even slept in them. Surrounding this gathering room were other rooms where they kept the food supplies and had a privy room, but it was rare any of them left this room to sleep in one of the cooler sleeping rooms. He did, when he needed to relax away from the strangers.

Maroz gave a sharp nod. "And the plain below is clear. Will they even come to see the dead, to know we aren't letting them in?" That one thing confused him, that while they saw a few come to climb the escarpment every now and again, no one came to search the bottom of it and return with news of accomplishment or failure.

Wolter scoffed as he scratched at the scraggly beard that was growing on his face. That was another slightly odd thing about the strangers. They barely had the capacity to grow beards at all. Thin hairs that curled, sure, but it looked like they'd be old men before the beards filled out enough to even be close to matching the beards of young Tarc men. Others of the Children of Chaos and Change in the tent chuckled in scorn with their leader. "In that the Tarc are perhaps wiser?" Wolter grinned. "Sending a partner with them to make sure the job gets done if one fails would help them be wiser about getting it done, yes?" Maroz shook his head, still disbelieving the laxness of a nation that wanted to take over Tarc now that Ryokudo had weakened it.

The weakness of Tarc was the fault of those who'd not been willing to leave darkness behind. He'd been one of those until the day he'd received the punishment of an unwise clan head. His unmarked clan head braid brushed softly against his face as he bent to sit at his place around the small fire that kept them all living. He'd left his marker with Head Clan Head Ore. They'd allowed him to keep it if he wanted, but until his clan was his again he'd go without it. If they found him worthy at the next Marluk'nak', then he'd be willing to receive it again. He could tell he'd likely need at least two years. He sighed and accepted the warmed drink handed down to him from the man in charge of food this day.

He closed his eyes and reviewed his requirement one more time. The other men went back to the conversation they'd been having before he'd arrived. Most of the time he couldn't follow what they said when they spoke to each other — then they spoke in their own tongue anyway. Most of them had learned Tarcian by now, having nothing better to do in their lonely watch on the escarpment in the cold, giving him something to do himself.

Originally he'd been ordered to go with the Storm Clan after the Marluk'nak' of Chaos and Change to learn again how to lead a clan in strength. After talking to Zerak', that clan's head and one of the Seconds of the Head Clan Heads, and pondering on what he'd learned, he'd gone to Ore and humbly asked to be able to protect his clan's lands for at least a time before going to learn at the Storm Clan tents. Zerak' had admitted that there was worry about the Grouse Clan lands becoming a place spies would get through, and perhaps Brulac would even bring a full war party up the escarpment there to attack the rest of the clans without warning while they were weak. Protecting his clan was the first thing a clan head did, then it was protecting his herds and his land.

He'd been allowed to send his herdsman, two servants, two of his older children who'd been salvageable, the clan pigs and chickens, and the herd to the herd grazing grounds. To ask another clan to take care of the animals as well as the people was too much when the water and grass were still available to them. He'd had to take a moment to recover from his surprise at Ore telling him that a small group of his own men had already been assigned to watch the escarpment, but it was wisdom for the Head Clan Head to see to the protection of all of Tarc. It was already given it would be a lack of wisdom to not care and the Marluk' would never be accused of lacking wisdom, since She was his wife.

Maroz blew out a breath as he held the mug close to his lips to warm them before taking another sip of the drink. It only a held a little alcohol and was flavored enough to fortify and not be a completely boring drink. This life was very different from the days of noisy lounging in the council tent with his many bondsmen — most now very dead — and nightly sleeping with his many wives — most also now just as dead. They'd given themselves up to their pride and love of the darkness his father had taught them and that he'd continued himself. The bitterness in his mouth as it twisted wasn't helped by the drink. The two didn't meld well.

He smiled a more real smile as the noise of the men with him rose up enough to catch his attention. They were just as noisy as his men had been, and for the same reasons: boredom and a need to boast and position themselves. He'd been learning, though. "Bannet, Rory, you're late to your duties," he pointed out firmly but calmly. The two froze, then frowned at the others they'd been arguing with. Seeing as it really was their turn, and they'd been getting loud because they were the most bored, it was time for them to move.

He was pleased when they didn't argue, just rose to their feet, bundled up, and headed out together. Wolter gave Maroz a slightly praising glance as the winter wind chilled the tent again briefly. He pretended not to notice it as he sipped at his drink again. Zerak' had given him as much wisdom and advice as he could before Maroz had left him. One was to not ever challenge the head of the group, but to make sure he challenged all the rest of them as he began to understand them so that he was an equal to the head of the group. He couldn't challenge the head of the group because that was who was testing him. To challenge that one would be to say he wasn't willing to be obedient in learning his lessons.

Maroz asked Wolter, "Will the end of the winter's cold bring more or less of the spies that enter through from Suiran?"

Wolter was thoughtful as he blew on a refill of his mug, the steam rising up from it as the fire worked to rewarm the interior of the tent. They kept the fire small as the supplies from Ryokudo came regularly but in small bundles since all of the watch camps along the escarpment needed supplying. "It's harder for men to walk in the winter winds, but it's easier to increase patrols in Suiran and Tarc when the weather is warmer ... for the same reason." Maroz returned Wolter's ironic smile. "I think even Master Ore and Mistress Ilena are interested in knowing which it will be."

Wolter frowned a little. "I think if it increases, they'll have Clan Head Prota take them out closer to the border. They'll need to send the message then that the border is no longer crossable at all." He rolled his eyes. "Maybe *then* they'll bother sending someone out to see where all the spies have gone and give up." His tone said he didn't believe they would.

Maroz gave a wise nod. "Well, they'll at least find out where all of their spies were sent to die then." Wolter snorted agreement. Maroz had just sent the most recent spy told to "walk the clans" by the Fox Clan Head over the edge with his throat slit. The fall *might* not kill them and they didn't want mights and maybes to come back and haunt them. He'd taken on that task as his duty. For now, they'd let Brulak believe their spies were being allowed into the Tarc clan lands to learn things. He'd been wondering if spring would bring a change to that.

He set his hands to rest in his lap, holding on to the half–empty mug. "Well, when they decide that, I'll return to the Storm Clan for my lessons there. I'll need to start the herds on their rounds then and see if those watching over them survived well enough and if they think they'll be enough to see to them during the wandering season." He looked at the men in the room. "If you'll still be here into next winter, you'll see me again then."

Many shifted uncomfortably, but a few merely shrugged, including Wolter. Wolter's eyes saw what Maroz's did and he smiled slightly. "Well, likely some will wish to be rotated out for others. The open plain is harder for them to live in than where there are places to hide."

Maroz considered that then said, "Well, any who wish to stay in the end, I'd happily take into my clan as bondsmen. Maybe sometime in my learning year or years I can enter Suiran long enough to see these hidden places to understand why they'd rather hide than stand proudly on the grasses." That got the men into a rowdy conversation of descriptions of forests, mountains, villages, and cities (including the usual arguing) that kept them all busy and Maroz entertained.

-o-o-o-

Rei walked into the Regional Security meeting in the Lower office and froze briefly. His heart rate jumped up as a message began coming into the office. He deliberately but quietly removed his cloak and winter gear in order to calm back down at least a little while he listened. The news coming in from the border was news he'd been wanting badly.

He listened as Liam and Carl reported by way of the code, and in code, too, what information they'd gleaned from the checkpoint at the border. The report included rumors and information that were going into Brulac from Ryokudo and what news was coming out about Brulac itself. The former helped him as he'd hoped. The latter was actually a bit relieving. It sounded like the Brulac Minister of Intelligence was still doing very well at preparing the people to rise up against their King in insurrection. He raised his eyebrow at Mitchel when the report was finished and asked for confirmation.

Mitchel mused, "It does seem like it. The amount of comments from the common people as to their dissatisfaction is rather high, from the reports." He shook his head. "Sometimes that's the way to get the people ready to go to war generally, though. If their anger is already being pricked, then it can be turned against a neighboring nation rather easily. The reason we put them moving against Ryokudo out about two to three years is that the push in a direction for the dissatisfaction and anger hasn't happened yet. There's still an even push from both sides: against the King of Brulac, and against Ryokudo, with neither being fanned yet. We're listening closely there because once there's enough dissatisfaction, the flames can become the bonfire rather quickly."

Rei frowned. "Meaning, if we do enough here for the Minister of Intelligence there to notice it, we could have them in our borders this year rather easily." Mitchel let him know he'd understood. Rei could see that being the reason his brother wanted him to drag them in by the end of this year, or early next year. If the people were already at the point of inflammation they might be able to bleed it off so that they'd not approve a restart later. If they repelled it easily, with a high death rate on Brulac's part, it might even turn the people against the King of Brulac sufficiently that the Minister of Intelligence would have to take that opportunity to topple him, nicely distracting him for a long while — at least until he solidified his own reign. Rei could see the benefits of doing it that way.

He turned and looked over to Flandras, sitting in the third seat where Reynold and Justinian would be sitting, in his now–regular place for these meetings. Flandras sat up straighter, then gave a nod. If he had spectacles, he'd have pushed them up on his face, Rei was sure. "I'll make that firm, then," he said.

Rei paused, then said, "Run the calculation for the long–term consequence. Once their MoI has solidified his claim to the throne — if he doesn't sit it they'll be in chaos for even longer — what's the probability he'll hit us quickly versus let his successor take over and decide if he wants to take Ryokudo or not? And what are the consequences of each? Go out as long as you can go, at least to the end of the next generation or into the following if possible."

Flandras blinked at the final requirement, but gave him a nod and pulled out his folder of papers and charcoal stick, availing himself of Reynold's currently unused desk. Rei sighed at him internally for still using the poor–man methods when he was now in the castle, but left him alone to his work. Flandras could really only guess if the man would want to finish his own personal goal of owning all of the nations bordering the northern shores of the Inner Sea. It was the long–term consequences that the numbers would show with more clarity.

-o-o-o-

Mizi took in a deep breath, closing her eyes to ready herself. She let the breath out slowly and clasped her hands in front of her. She was dressed as the princess today, but not overly much so. It was a simple enough dress that Tiana hadn't had any troubles helping her get dressed in it. Fixing her hair had been more complex to consider, so she'd just brushed it down and clipped back the front hairs at the center back of her head. Her exterior was ready. Now it was time to become internally ready for her presentation to the university. Following the calming routine trained into her by Ilena that they'd practiced together helped her calm her mind.

When she was ready, she gave a short nod to let Marcus and Henry know she was ready. They walked into the lecture hall of the university from the professor's door and small office behind the main lecture floor. The room quieted save for the rustle as everyone rose to their feet to bow or curtsy. They held the respectful pose until she'd stepped up onto the platform where Shiotsu was already waiting for her. Marcus and Henry went to the usual guard positions at the front of the platform, dressed in their formal black uniforms, their swords at their sides. Their firm stances helped her relax into her own formal position as she sat in the chair that had been set on the stand for her. She'd not brought the crown, but she was wearing the pin of the First Princess. She'd thought that would be enough in this setting and had been small enough to pack in her one bag.

The lecture hall was somewhat similar to the Tarc Marluk'nak' and Ilena's lists in that the floor in front of her rose up to upper doorways so everyone in the room could see and hear her. Ore hadn't been too thrilled that she'd be at the bottom if something should be thrown at her, so the Twins had already been subjected to firm scolding to be watching for something like that to occur. Ore had included scolding her to be watching in case she needed to dodge to save herself.

She looked up at all of the students and staff that had come, grateful that they filled more than half of the room. Marcus had teased her before they'd entered, trying to get her to relax a little, that most of the people there had come just to see the red–haired First Princess. That might be true, but sometimes even the unexpected person who heard her, felt the importance of what she needed, and decided to go was the one most needed in a critical moment.

Shiotsu was being her Voice at the moment, introducing her and her cause. She'd told him to announce the internship testing at the castle beginning in two weeks. If they passed that initial testing they'd be trained then tested again at the end of the training. The internships were for working in the castle Department of Medicine under Ryan and for working at the new hospital under Mizi and the medic she was calling up to head it.

Shiotsu listed off the requirements for consideration that they were looking for. Certainly strong skills in medicine, but also surgery, nursing, midwifery, chemistry, and botany. Any who had skills they thought might also be useful were welcome to go, or to talk to Shiotsu to see if he thought they should go. Mizi hadn't wanted to keep it too limited since many of the students and researchers had specific things that they studied that could be helpful. She'd discussed those details with him the morning before.

She kept her hands clasped lightly in her lap and watched the faces in the room. They were respectful and listening closely. She had to work hard to ignore the ones that were obviously just there to look at her. This was the "standing on the wall next to Rei" she'd known she'd have to do. If the people wanted to see their princess she wouldn't cower away from that duty she had. She showed them the face she wanted them to see: mild kindness, as peaceful as she could get to today, soberness at the topic, and the calm strength Rei and Sasou exuded to her best ability. She made sure she continued to breathe full breaths as well. Passing out wasn't acceptable and was one of the things she'd laughed at Ilena for but had become very grateful for as an early lesson. Calm breaths kept her calmed.

When Shiotsu was done, he bowed to her and turned the time over to her. Mizi drew in a breath and spoke loudly enough to be heard but not shout. The shape of the room would carry her voice sufficiently. "Thank you for coming today to listen to our request," she said. "I've come myself to ask for help with the hospital because the need is sufficiently urgent. The winter snows are difficult to travel in and we're sorry the necessity is that you do so." Ilena had agreed with her that her example of traveling in them herself would encourage others to do the same.

Mizi waved her hand at Shiotsu and smiled a little. "We aren't asking that *everyone* leave the university and the needs that are here, but we do need those with research and leadership experience to come and help those who'll answer to the call from other places." She put her hand in her lap again and went back to sober. "There are many needs for you this year. One of them is here as well. Gael is threatening Altherly with war. King Sasou and Lord Yosuko have agreed that Kouzanshi will be a place that any severely wounded from that war can come to be treated, if it begins in earnest. If you wish to help with the hospital but feel your skills will be useful for that, then stay and come east once that war has been finished and peace has returned to our area."

A few mutters had begun at her statement of the war. The news of that was still being spread for all Ore had told the Kouzanshi garrison about it yesterday. "If you decide you'd like to help at any of the locations, please go to the Medical Department and let them know. While we want to allow for preferences, if we don't have enough requests for any one of the three, Head Shiotsu may ask you to reconsider." Shiotsu's shoulders slumped just a little at the load he was going to have to bear, but Mizi knew he'd lean heavily on Tiana, too. Hopefully they'd both delegate if they needed to. She'd encouraged that, too when she'd talked to them since that was one of the lessons they were all learning.

Mizi drew in another silent long breath. "The greatest numbers needed is at the hospital. If you're still a student learning your art, then stay, finish your studies, and come when you've received your diploma. We'll pair you up with those who've already learned what they need to learn so you can pick up the work easily. There will be a six month apprenticeship followed by a review that won't be anywhere nearly as hard as your diploma exam, for all it will likely be rigorous." There were smiles on faces in the crowd that she smiled back at.

"The construction for the hospital will begin as soon as the ground has thawed enough for the foundation to be dug. Until it's built, those who will be working there will work in Castle Nijou's Department of Medicine." She turned the time back to Shiotsu who answered a few questions but she'd told him she couldn't answer any beyond what she'd say.

When the meeting was over and she was in the little office again, seated in a chair there, she could only pluck at her skirt, the other hand curled over her heart. Marcus went down on one knee in front of her and took the restless hand in both of his. "Mistress Mizi," he said kindly as he looked earnestly into her eyes, "you did well. Breathe deeply two deep breaths."

Mizi did as Marcus said. When she could drop the hand over her heart to rest it in her lap he patted the hand he was holding. She dropped her head to rest on his shoulder. The sorrow she'd been holding in ever since she'd been in the National Security Meeting and had learned war was on the horizon filled her. Being busy with the hospital had kept it at bay, but now that she'd done her final plea, it had come to the fore too much for her to ignore any longer. The sum of sorrows since then was more than she could contain, suddenly.

Marcus and Henry were silent as she sobbed quietly, although Henry did hand over a handkerchief for her to hold to her face. Mizi was worn out when the sorrow and tears released her. Marcus patted her on the back soothingly as she wiped her nose and cheeks. She couldn't help that the tears continued to drip for a while. "Well," Marcus said gently, "I think that was very needed, yes?" She could only nod. "A nap is definitely next," he said kindly. "We'll get you back to the garrison by the hidden ways so you can't be waylaid or seen. We'll wake you when Master Ore returns, or let you sleep if we can't. A long deep sleep would be okay, too."

"Okay," she said quietly.

Henry bowed and slipped out of the hallway door, likely to fetch her things from the Medical Department where they'd left her traveling clothes. Mizi stayed quiet, recovering, until Henry brought the bag into the room with Tiana following him. "I've confirmed they're safe," he said, as he set the bag down next to her. "Put the pin back on to wear it back, though. If we have to drop the bag to defend you, that's the safer place for it." Mizi nodded. They each left out one of the two doors and stood guard while Tiana helped her get out of her dress.

"I think they make them so maids have to help just so the maids have something to do," Mizi said wryly to Tiana.

"It's okay," Tiana said with a smile. "I don't mind helping." When the dress was off, Tiana paused, then put her arms around Mizi. Into her ear, Tiana whispered, "It must be very hard, to have to face war might come." Mizi nodded her head, her heart squeezing again. Tiana sighed and squeezed her a little more tightly, then let her go to fetch Mizi's traveling clothes. "I hope it doesn't come," she said quietly. She handed over the clothes and folded the dress carefully.

"Me, too," Mizi agreed, pulling on the warm pants first. "It was so very hard to hear the news at the end of last year."

"And you've been holding it in all this time," Tiana said sympathetically as she traded the shoes that went with the dress for the winter boots. Mizi only sighed in answer and put on the shirt and jacket. Tiana looked up at her. "We'd come if you asked."

Mizi shook her head. "I do love you both and your skills are critical, but we need more trained students more than we need to take you from this place you're needed so much. Please recruit more actively for the department and bring on another assistant or two to help you with the greater numbers. In this thing, more hands to do the work means more people who can survive." She had to blink back more tears and draw in another deep breath. Putting on her boots helped her move forward.

Tiana's warm hand coming lightly on her head helped. Mizi's self–preservation instincts kicked in, though, and she rose to step away from her friend giving Tiana a sad smile. "Thank you so much for your help and comfort." She called the Twins back in and they came immediately, to her relief. They quickly put on their cloaks and winter gear. Henry picked up Mizi's bag and Mizi looked at Tiana one last time. "Please give my love and regards to Shiotsu, but we'll leave now."

Tiana curtsied as Henry opened the hallway door and checked the hall, then led their three–some into it. Mizi pulled her cloak hood up over her head as they walked down the hallway, glad Marcus stayed walking directly behind her so her back didn't prickle. Once they were out into the city, she took Marcus's hand and they moved very quickly through the side streets and alleys. "Can you go up?" Marcus asked her when they were in a quiet alley.

"That's very high, but I can try," she answered. "I'm supposed to be practicing when there's opportunity to." She really wouldn't mind not being where people's eyes could see her.

"It's the jumps, though, Scamp," Henry frowned at Marcus.

Marcus shook his head. "From here to where we're going I think she can do them."

Henry's frown didn't go away, but he finally agreed. "We'll die if you're wrong and Master's not here to be her spotter."

They helped her find the finger and toeholds. It worked her muscles in ways she hadn't since she'd been harvesting in the trees around her village in Yamanzar. She ignored the fall to the ground that was now three to four stories down like she was ignoring the tears still falling in her heart. The snows in Kouzanshi had only covered up the first one to one–and–a–half stories so the climb was tiring and demanded focus.

The first jump to cross a narrow alley was heart–pounding, but once she understood it she did okay. Henry always went first so if he needed to catch her hand he could. Marcus coached from the beginning side and followed after her. "You're doing much better for your first time than I did," he complemented her once she had a feel for it. "I was about half to three–fourths your height and he was about a quarter of his weight so I almost got dropped a lot." Mizi glanced at him and gave him a brief, wan smile, not wanting her voice to be heard while she was doing this. Not letting anyone know she could do this would save her one day, she was quite sure of it.

When they could see the walls of the garrison, they coached her in how to climb back down. She wasn't surprised to slip and fall the last half–story. They were very concerned, but she shook her head at them again. "It's I'm now too tired. The fingers wouldn't hold. Snow is soft enough," she whispered to them. They let her rest before getting her up on her feet again. She was glad she could just follow the hand holding hers to her room and bed.

Henry dropped her bag off in the room and took Mizi's cloak Marcus handed him. Marcus looked into Mizi's face soberly, then took her in one more hug. "Why can't I even trust my close friends anymore?" she asked him, the tears coming again. "She was only being kind, but that was too long to be alone with her and not worry she was going to do something." She sobbed once as he again patted her back, then ran a hand over her head to help her calm a little better. He walked her over to her bed, took her boots off of her, helped her lie down, then covered her with her blankets.

His warm hand ran over her head a few more times. "Sleep. That'll help you recover best. We'll watch over you." She nodded her head but didn't relax enough to really sleep until the door closed behind both sets of footsteps. A few warm tears continued to escape her eyes until she really was sleeping.

-o-o-o-

"I think I'd like to compare notes with Justinian," Marcus said wryly to Henry once they were sure Mizi was sleeping. "Was it this hard for Master Ore his first time to really realize what position they're in?"

Henry considered that, then said, "I wouldn't be surprised if it was, actually. Remember he needed to hear Mistress Ilena's scolding of the noble hussy and they both needed the last brief visit before Kouzanshi. He couldn't let her go for a long time, remember?"

Marcus did remember with that reminder. "Well, yes, that was rather similar in effect, wasn't it?" He slumped against the wall and crossed one foot over the other. "My own realizations were the same, for all we were a lot younger." Henry reached over and rubbed the top of Marcus' head briefly to comfort him again. Marcus looked up and sighed out his own worries. "I'm glad I can relate, though." He closed his eyes.

"Well, no you're not, but it's good you can comfort her the way she needs," Henry answered back. Marcus just kept his eyes closed and ears open, glad Ore had insisted on rooms with no windows for once, at least for him and Mizi. He and Henry had been obedient and not really understood why Ore had put the two of them to either side of the royal rooms since Ore knew they needed the windows and each other to sleep right. It probably wasn't helping Marcus that he'd not slept well the last two nights. He understood it today, though. Mizi wouldn't have been able to sleep with a window this afternoon unless one of them had been up on the roof, too. That was a cold watch in the winter.

"I also need the sleep," he admitted to Henry. "Can you take first watch and let me sleep for an hour?"

"Okay," Henry answered quietly. Marcus was immediately in the nightwalkers' light sleep that any unexpected sound or movement woke them up from. A light touch on his shoulder woke him up.

"My turn," Henry said. "I've gone as long as I can." That meant it probably wasn't even that hour, but Marcus woke up enough to actually have eyes on the hallway. When Henry was asleep enough, he quietly walked down to the hallway door and opened it a crack. The soldier guard on the door turned to look at him. "Send a paige in," he asked. When he got a nod, he returned to his post.

A young soldier was let into the hallway a little while later. Marcus met him farther down the hallway. "See the watch chief knows to send in four more to guard each door tonight inside the hallway, not just the two on the hallway. And see he knows we'll kill any traitors and demand even more guards to replace them. We're all triggered and need the sleep to become rational human beings again. I think he'll understand."

When the soldier had gone off, Henry cracked an eye open and glared from it at Marcus. Marcus shook his head and used the House nightwalker signs to indicate they'd leave as soon as Ore got back from his trip to the Northwest garrison. They'd be guarding empty rooms. They were all that paranoid now. Henry relaxed and agreed with Marcus' assessment.

Marcus slipped into Ore's room and packed for Ore, not that there was much to do. Ore traveled light. He carried Ore's bag into his own room, packed his bag, and carried them out into the hallway. There he crossed the hallway and entered the sitting room that had a corner window. He set the bags on the floor there in a hidden recess, then went back and stood on the door while Henry packed his bag. Henry returned to the hallway and slipped into Mizi's room to pick up her bag and added those two to the others.

While Henry was in the sitting room, he called in the sung code for someone they trusted to pick up the bags and get them to a safe place they could retrieve them from. Then he asked for a regular report on Ore's progress from the Northwest Pass garrison back to Kouzanshi. When he returned to the hallway Marcus traded him places again. "I'll be back quickly," he reassured Henry, then he was gone, into the sitting room to put his winter gear on again.

In short order he was out through the window of the room and up on the roof. He ran across the garrison roofs until he was at the outer wall. The skies over the mountains were medium grey and the snow that had fallen all day seemed to be heavier. He wasn't sure if it really was or if it was just his current pessimism.

Fourth Son to Father. The Sun has fallen and fears to rise again. Marcus shivered to say it that way, but he wanted Ore to understand the seriousness of what was going on. *The river that came from her eyes when her task was done was more than she could recover from. The more full understanding of her station has become a larger rock than she can carry. The nap she threatened has become her healing blanket, but it won't be enough. Your saplings aren't too far behind, honestly. May we meet you at the crossroad and sleep securely and soundly tonight outside the city?*

He walked back and forth across the top of the wall to keep as warm as he could and to prevent the snowfall from turning him into a snowman. Eventually he heard back, *Father to Fourth Son. You know the safe places If one could be found that has silent trustworthy servers who understand well enough how to be unseen, that would be good. I'm still nearly three hours out from the crossroad. Will she sleep long enough for me to come in and all of us leave together? That would be better.*

Marcus hesitated, then paced as he considered the answer. He wanted to leave right then and have the Family bring Ore to the safe house so he and Henry could sleep, too, but Ore wasn't wrong that Mizi should be allowed to nap as long as possible. He also considered how long it would take to get to the safe house if they couldn't leave until evening. Finally he answered back, *Fourth Son to Father. We'll wait for you. I'll have the place prepared to feed us a later dinner and have rooms made up.*

He sighed and sent out the message to the place he could trust this night. It wasn't even an hour's ride on a nice day. He hoped that would put them there only two hours after they left the city. The snow would have to hold at about where it was now, though. If it reached very low visibility, they should stay at the garrison. None of their horses knew where it was.

He returned over the roofs again to the wing their rooms were in. He confirmed that they had a trustworthy roof guard, sent by the Family, then dropped over and in through the window. Their bags had been taken. He confirmed they'd receive them back on the way out of town. He shook out his cloak and wet gear and left them to dry, laid out on the furniture. Then he was back in the hallway. He raised an eyebrow at Henry who shook his head. Mizi was still sleeping.

Marcus sighed and leaned back against the wall again. "Okay. You can really sleep this time," he said, since he'd been keeping Henry up.

He was a bit surprised to be getting a hug next. "It really will be okay," Henry said quietly. "There are a lot of things for her to learn, but she's strong enough. If she could cry for you, you don't have to worry quite so much. You know Mother always calls them cleansing tears to clean out the soot that fills up the house too much. The trip home will be sufficient for her to finish recovering." Since Henry never hugged anyone except Ilena to keep her still, Marcus had to recover from his surprise before he could relent and relax some of his tension and worry out. "That and your smile," Henry added as he released Marcus to smile at him. "We're all proud of you for being able to do that for her, by the way, even if the rest don't know about it yet. She's a harder nut to crack than Master Ore, almost."

Marcus rolled his eyes. "True," he agreed dryly.

"I'd always wondered who she'd cave to," Henry mused as he returned to his resting pose against the wall on the other side of the door. He gave Marcus a curious look. "Do you know why it was you?"

Marcus leaned his head against the wall, then said softly, "I think because I'm *not* anyone she has to please, nor am I stiff." He pondered a bit longer then looked sidelong at Henry. "Probably she'll do that for others of her own staff once she knows who she can really trust. She prefers the quiet kind types who can make her smile, and she already has some." He drew in a breath and let it out. "I guess it's okay to be the substitute for now, for all that's not easy either." He shrugged his shoulders up around his ears. "Why are they all so difficult?"

"Who? Women, or royals?" Henry teased him.

Marcus snorted at him. "Yes." He spent that guard shift pondering on Amber and if she really was going to be that difficult. He sort of guessed she might not be since she was a lot more accommodating than the women he knew who were difficult. Still, relationships meant hard work regardless. Thinking about the next steps in their relationship was a rather calming thing to think about today.

-o-o-o-

Marcus was on his second round of guard watch when the door at the end of the hallway opened and Ore walked in through it. Henry was instantly alert. They watched Ore's face and stride as he walked towards them. Marcus moved out into the hallway and met him far enough down from the bedroom door that they could talk quietly without disturbing Mizi. "She's still asleep, but could probably be woken up at this point," Marcus said quietly. He explained everything that had happened all while the amber eyes stared unblinkingly at him. Ore's worry for his mistress almost always got translated into slight aggressiveness. Marcus faced it the humble but unmoving way he faced Ilena when she got the same way.

"Why you?" Ore asked nearly the same thing Henry had asked.

Marcus gave Ore nearly the same answer, but added, "But, you should ask her yourself since I'm only making guesses. She's been needing it and asking for it in small ways since we got on the road, that reassurance that she's okay being who and what she is inside, and that she can be safe in this world she's trying to learn to live in." He drew in a breath and asked his own question he'd asked before. "Was it this bad for you when it was Justinian who helped you, the first time?"

Ore paused and frowned, going into thought. "I didn't have so much the pressure from everyone around me, since I already had the tutoring in being noble. I think that's worse for her." He went wry, "I also had as much training as you two as a youth in how everyone was going to kill me if I wasn't careful. She's newly come to that, as well. Her youth taught her to fight those who wanted to steal her away and sell her, not kill her."

Marcus shivered. "Yeah, that would be harder to have to get used to."

Ore frowned at Marcus, looking him up and down for a moment, then his arms were also around Marcus. "Why? Why does her fear make you afraid?" he asked.

Marcus swallowed against the tears that clogged up the back of his throat and gave in and held Ore back rather tightly. "Probably because it *was* that hard to be a child suddenly thrust into the uncertain world of the nightwalkers when all I'd known before that was the quiet life of a mother's love."

"Ah," Ore patted him on the head and held him until Marcus could shiver, sigh, and let his past go again. He moved away from Ore a little bit, letting him go and being let go. He just breathed a bit, then realized Ore was looking at him like he was still odd. He gave Ore back a puzzled look and his hand was being raised.

Marcus stared at their hands, his forefingers holding on tightly to Ore's two outer fingers. He blushed rather hard. "That's what she's been doing to me, too." He dropped Ore's fingers. "That's the need for protection from outside oneself." He sighed and drooped, waving his hand. "I really shouldn't be needing that anymore, having Henry and already being trained, but I guess it's part of the package of memories she woke up." He rubbed the back of his head, not quite able to meet Ore's eyes.

When he did glance at Ore, his tawny eyes were sparkling. "Really, you and Justinian the most remind me of that title of mine. I'm still not sure how to take being Father sometimes, but moments like this do make me smile." He grinned at Marcus as Marcus blushed again and groaned at him. Ore's hand ruffled his head as he relaxed and said, "Well, but if you can help her because you understand, then that's good." He moved past Marcus and headed for the doors to their rooms. He asked back over his shoulder, "So what do you want to do in your need to run away to a safe hole?"

Marcus blinked in surprise, then ruefully admitted to himself that's what he'd been doing this whole time. He sighed at himself and followed after Ore. "Wake up Mistress Mizi, have us use the excuse of going to check up on Kesheb to escape from the garrison with the horses, then not come back. The safe house is ready for us and they'll hand us our bags on our way out of the gate."

"Already?" Ore turned back with a surprised look on his face. Marcus didn't smile back. Ore slumped a little, then gave a nod. "I left Fenrier saddled." He paused outside the door with a bit of a look of consternation, then looked at Henry. "You or him? Which will scare her least since I shouldn't?"

Henry looked down the hallway at Marcus. "I'll go," Henry said. "You've only just gotten him down to slightly rational. She'll set him off again at this point." Ore gave an accepting nod and Henry tapped on the door. When there was no answer, Henry turned the handle and checked, then quietly entered, leaving the door open. He put a light hand on Mizi's shoulder until she roused. "It's time to go, Mistress Mizi," he said. "Master Ore's arrived."

Mizi turned to look out the doorway, then was up and out the door to also hold Ore tightly. "Yeah, I told you so," Marcus said dryly, quite sympathetic.

Ore had been taken somewhat by surprise but he gently held Mizi. "They said you'd received more of a scare than you were ready for," he said kindly.

"Scare?" Mizi's voice was a little muffled. She pondered on the use of that word, then said, "Well, I felt more sad, but I was surprised how difficult it was to trust Tiana when it was just us two in the room while they guarded it so I could change. That was hard as my worry something would happen before I was done only got worse." She sadly asked, "Why can't I even trust my friends anymore?"

Ore patted her on the back. "Because you've had that fear for several months now and not told anyone so they could help you." He pushed her back a little, holding her by both shoulders to look into her eyes. "Having our household as your example, and Master, you can only distrust. Having your household hold a traitor in it as well, and now there's no one to trust outside of the few you already did.

"You *can* trust. Very few people *actually* want to kill you. It's a level of awareness to have, not one of trust or distrust. Remember that Master trusts *everyone* first, then lets them show him who they are. Even the traitorous assassins he tries to win over before punishing them." Ore's face was soft. "That includes me, and it worked in my case, for all I'd already been won over before he asked me." Mizi looked into Ore's face, searching for the hope she was looking for.

"How do I get to that level around all the worry?" she asked him.

Ore pondered that, then said, "Time and experiences always help. Master's doing his best to free you of that worry as soon as he can. Maybe by the time we get back he'll know so you can be free of it. I don't like to see you this worried, either." He looked into her green eyes soberly. "Learning the skills to trust that you can keep yourself alive helps, too. Work hard when you're practicing those, focusing on the strength you're earning and why and that part will become more firm against the worry, too."

Mizi nodded. "Marcus had me practice going up and across the roofs today and I wanted to learn it regardless of whatever else I was feeling. It did help some."

Ore nodded. "Yes. Things like that and your daily martial arts practices." He sighed and let go of her shoulders. "And when it gets bad like it did today, you do what you did. You ask for the help to get through it. Even Master still does it when he's surprised by something too similar to events that were frightening in his past." He looked away for a moment, not expanding on that for now. When he looked back at Mizi he smiled for her. "Well, Marcus is quite sure that you need to escape the city today not tomorrow, and sleep in a safe hidden place tonight to be able to sleep at all, and so they can sleep as well." He raised an eyebrow at her and she blushed.

Still, she threw a grateful look to Marcus. "Yes, actually, that would help me a lot."

Ore put his hand to his chin. "Well, we'd have to leave from the stable, and then not get lost in the dusk we're going to be walking away from the city in. But he says the place isn't so far. It might be a late–ish dinner?" he asked her to confirm it one more time.

Mizi did take the time to consider it longer, but then shivered and shook her head. "I don't like the feeling of running away, but I won't sleep if we stay and the tears want to keep coming back. Saying we're trying to get back home to keep Rei from worrying too much would be okay?"

Ore smiled. "Very well. We're hurrying home to Master. That works. If you'll get your things, the bags are already ready for us."

Mizi's eyes went wide, then she was hurrying to obey. Marcus and Henry retrieved their things and they were all walking out of the hallway. Ore turned to the guards on the hallway door. "Pretend we're here until at least morning. Master's expecting an ambush of some kind on our way back. We'll get a head–start and hope they miss us in the passing." He was bowed to and they were on their way to the stable.

They talked publicly about Ore's worries about Kesheb on the way. They did check all of the horses, to be sure they'd been well taken care of. Ore then went to the stablehands and ordered the other horses to be saddled and readied to go out. "Because Mistress has become a bit claustrophobic again being shut up inside the city," he claimed. He tied up Kesheb to Fenrier's saddle horn again, confirming the training he'd done on the way to the city, and they were outside in the snows.

A wagon met them outside the city and garrison wall, at a far enough distance and down in a fold of the mountainside so they were hidden. Marcus made sure the bags were secure inside and outside, then tied them onto the back of his and Henry's experimental messenger saddles. When Marcus was at Henry's horse, Henry put his hand lightly on Marcus' head and gave him a knowing look. Marcus blinked back up at him, then gave him a soft nod.

They left Kouzanshi behind at as fast a canter as they could. The soft sheets and beds that night were so comfortable that Marcus was asleep very fast. He'd almost skipped dinner he was so tired. He was glad the snows had cooperated for them. Coming home to Kouzanshi had been more difficult than he'd expected. It would be okay to come back on only the rare occasion.

Brianna walked briskly into the large open lobby of the Old Regent's building, pulling off her gloves from the fingers. The trip to her home had been welcome, and not depressing for once. The quiet of her own space had helped her calm down and face her new life a little better as she'd had time to let what she wanted percolate into the spaces that had been too full for too long. As her hand reached up to push her cloak hood off her head, her eyes were caught by a surprising thing. One of the chairs in the sitting area off to the left was occupied. It had been mostly empty during the day since Mizi had turned her focus to the hospital.

As soon as her winter gear was hung in the wardrobe Brianna turned her feet to pass by the occupied chair. "Hello, Tanner," she said kindly. "It's unusual for you to have vacation time, and to spend it out in public areas." She smiled at him.

Tanner looked up at her and smiled a small smile back. "Well, out in the open was preferable today. Master Rei gave Rutherford a few days to go visit his sister so he could also get out of the building. It was kind of him, but with Mistress Mizi still gone it leaves the rooms a bit too quiet. Here I can sit and tease the guards and they can tease me if we get too bored."

Brianna frowned at him as she thought about that. "They didn't allow you leave to get out of the castle as well?"

Tanner blinked at her. He finally said, "Each of us get our turns. Now is Rutherford's. Yours is just ending. Sir Brian's was earlier." He said it with such dismissal she had to let it go.

Still.... Trying to be sympathetic, she said, "It's hard to see them forgetting you, Tanner. Do be sure to complain at them a little more when you have needs."

Tanner raised an eyebrow at her. "Isn't it what a servant's supposed to be, is forgotten but useful?"

Brianna snapped her mouth closed and drew in a breath through her nose. When she'd recovered, she curtsied to him slightly. "Thank you for the reminder," she said as humbly as she'd been raised to speak. He only blinked back at her as she turned to walk for the lower hallway door and her room. Only once she was through that door did her brow furrow slightly.

Both scoldings from Tanner had clashed with what she'd been in her home, but pointed so excellently to what her trouble was. Finding the balance between being a servant in the royal household and being used to running her own household was more complex than she was managing to meet, particularly with the royals being so young and thus like children in her mind.

She sighed a little sadly as she set her little travel bag down on the foot of her bed. Her maid would be along soon with the clothing bag. She looked around the single room she had in the building. She knew that in the new building it would be an apartment, but it would still feel small compared to her manor home. Was this really the place she wanted to be in, even if it was an escape from the traditional expectations the other lords and ladies placed on her? She'd been placed in such an *un*traditional household and place to serve that it had unsettled her too much. To be back home where things were hers and traditional had been calming. To have Tanner remind her of those traditions that were expected by Mizi and Rei had been so unexpected, given he was one of the household that was least traditional.

Brianna paused, then sat down in her chair in a bit of surprise. That wasn't true. While Tanner was from the most wild of the two households, she couldn't think of anything in it that was outside of traditional expectations, save Ilena acted like a man and was in the position of one. The rest of her House was actually run very traditionally. Brianna slumped and almost whimpered. It was only she that had been placed untraditionally in the Rose office, and thus had assumed even Rei's household was so. That's what the scold had reminded her. Mizi was actually trying to learn what the traditions were so she wouldn't misstep.

A shiver ran through Brianna's core at the final sum that stared at her with cold requirement. Rei, Mizi, Ore, and Ilena were *royals*. She still needed to learn to stand in her proper place in the hierarchy, as a servant of said royals. They'd ordered her to assist them in the ways they needed her to, but even that was proper and traditional. Her hand moved slowly up to her cheek to catch the wet tear before it could reach her chin, staying on her cheek as her mind and heart tried to find their footing again. She really didn't know what to do.

-o-o-o-

"Ore," Mizi said, her hands clenching more tightly on Fenrier's reins. Ore was testing Kesheb for this part of the journey back to Nijou, which had been difficult until recently when Kesheb had finally settled unhappily back into being the lesser of the two mounts, for all Ore was riding him. The snows were thick enough now that they were traveling at the standard careful winter travel rate from one village to the next and no farther, so Kesheb was getting lots of practice in the winter travel requirements, too.

"Yes, Mistress?" Ore answered her.

The return to Nijou was bringing back to Mizi's mind all of the uncomfortable things waiting for her there. "Can I talk to you about something I need to work out?"

"Certainly," he smiled at her although all she could see was the crinkle at the corners of his eyes. They were all bundled up again against the cold air. Mizi would be glad to be back and get to rest in the warmth of "home" again from that aspect.

She drew in a long breath. "I tested Lady Brianna like Ilena suggested I should, to see if I could tell if her complaints were habit from a trained past or from general irritation." She couldn't help slumping as she looked away from Ore for a moment and bit her lip under her muffler. She tried not to let tears out since they'd only freeze on her eyelashes. "Honestly, I'm not sure I can tell. It was hard to catch her at a time she didn't feel completely stressed out, in order to rule out the irritation." She looked down at her hands. "Because her stress level was so high generally, I gave her leave to go to her home for a while while we were on this trip. General rest and the few nights out haven't been enough for her."

Mizi sighed. "Maybe once I get back, if that helped, I can tell better, but...." She looked over at Ore feeling a bit miserable. "If she can't relax generally, or finds it too hard to be with us long–term..., then I think it would be best to thank her and kindly let her go. She's been a great help, and I don't want her to think I hate her...." She slumped even more. "And I don't like thinking that either one of us is going to feel like a failure." Ore's hand reached up to pat her knee at that. She was grateful he was kind to try to brush away the unnecessary thoughts and emotions, but likely they'd both have that one anyway regardless.

Mizi's eyes besought Ore. "If I let her go, will the others be upset with me? They've been working very hard to help her, too." She really didn't want to upset the whole of the household. She was already in internal chaos over it all herself.

Ore considered her question and the people of her household. "I think they can see how much stress she's under, like you can. A gentle letting go wouldn't harm any of them, particularly since they all know you're still in the early phases of learning what you need." His golden eyes came back to look into hers with the piercing look he used only when he was passing on serious words. "Those who do become angry or upset may be those who need to be reconsidered also."

For all she didn't want to have to do that either, Mizi could understand why he'd say it. Certainly it could be a clue to which of her household was the mole, assuming it wasn't Brianna herself. She gave a small nod of understanding and went back to musing, trying to get the sorrow and worry to settle. Fenrier shifted a side–step closer to Ore and Kesheb. Mizi rather automatically pulled him back with the reins firmly. "Very good, Mistress!" Ore complemented her.

Mizi woke back up to her surroundings with a start, then shyly smiled. "He's taught me well, how to control strong–willed horses, hasn't he?"

Ore laughed. "Yes. You can finally do for him what you've already done with me for years." His eyes caught her surprised ones as he gave her a very kind look. "You can do it, Mistress. You already have the strength and gentleness in great measure inside of you. You can't know what's inside of her until you get back. To worry over it too much now will only make you continue to falter. Trust yourself and her and the right thing will happen at the right time. Even she's considering it like you are. You can come to the right answer together. That isn't right now."

Mizi sighed, holding Fenrier in place as he tried to get too close to Kesheb again. "Okay." She paid closer attention to Fenrier for a moment, then said, "Perhaps we should return to a faster pace again. I think he needs to be distracted."

Ore laughed. "See? You even know how to do that for him. You'll be fine, I promise. ...And I agree with you. Take him up to a canter. He hates it, so it will distract both of you quite nicely."

Mizi groaned to herself, but obeyed. As part of training Kesheb, Fenrier had to be the horse that set the pace for the group. Ore wasn't wrong. She needed the distraction and lesson, too. She also wasn't too fond of cantering.

-o-o-o-

Three reports showed up on Rei's desk at unexpected times over the course of two days. When the final one arrived, he paused and set aside the other work he was doing. By rights there should be a fourth one with them but his wife wasn't available to do her research so it would have to be added later. He'd known that would be the case anyway. He set the three folders in front of him, blew out a breath and got to work reading.

When he was done, he took the time to sit back in his chair and compile them into a cohesive whole, putting them into the order that his mind demanded. He wrote down that organized pattern before he moved on to analyzing it. He only did that cursorily, to come up with the questions that came out of the data. That is: the mathematical results questions. When those were written down, he added one sentence to the end of the summary report. *"I'll meet you at Ilena's in the morning to discuss."*

He'd been having Flandras go to the Lower office of Intelligence every day at the same time every morning since the first time he'd told Flandras to meet him there. That made it so Flandras got the real–time information at the every–other–day meeting and had the help of Reynold on the other day. Right now that meant Flandras worked in the quiet on his own for that hour or so, since most of the ministry were at Falcon's Hollow or on the road. This was Rei's ulterior reason, though: so he could meet secretly with Flandras when they needed to talk.

He slipped his summary and all three reports into one of the folders, then rose to his feet and walked it over to Flandras. "This needs your attention immediately," he said. "Sorry to interrupt."

Flandras shook his head and took the folder, pushing aside the work in front of him. "Yes, Rei," he answered humbly. Rei sighed and ran his hand through his hair as he looked around the room aimlessly. "Andrew." He walked for the door to the office. He didn't want to get dressed for the cold, but he needed to stretch his legs and let the emotional impact of that information go. He could walk the halls of the building and that might be sufficient.

When the door closed behind him and he got going, he suddenly stopped and looked at the shorter person behind him. "Andrew's working on more important things than me today, and I'm better at scowling than he is," Mina said dryly. Rei sighed at the both of them, but let it be. She wasn't wrong and they did both know him that well. He'd be able to pace the halls without being bothered by the other people in the building. He was lost in his head shortly after.

-o-o-o-

Rei woke up rather excited and early the next morning. He was finally going to be able to move forward today. Not long strides but finally with useful knowledge. He pursed his lips as he headed for the bath room. "Rutherford," he called quietly.

His manservant showed up in the bath room shortly after Rei had already started lathering his wet hair. "Yes, Rei?" he asked in his quiet, kind voice.

"I'll be meeting with Flandras this morning at Ilena's." He threw a glance of meaning at Rutherford. Rutherford bowed his head in understanding then left the room to change what he was laying out on the bed for Rei to get dressed into. Rei quickly finished his washing and skipped the soaking.

On the bed were a castle staff uniform and standard issue black cloak. The uniform was new as he'd outgrown everything before his wedding, but the black cloak was an old favorite for clandestine work. It was long enough to hide his white sheath. Rei was dressed rather quickly. He collected up his folders of that night while he waited for Rutherford, who came out of his room in Rei's clothing and cloak. "Thank you, Rutherford," Rei said quietly.

Rutherford's eyes crinkled as he gave Rei a smile. "It's been a while. The clothing is very roomy now."

Rei spurted a little laugh. "Thus why you've tucked the pants into the boots and rolled up the sleeves?" Rutherford laughed silently with him as his eyes sparkled. They both pulled on hats, gloves, scarves, and pulled the cloak hoods over their heads. Rei opened the door for Rutherford and bowed him out. He was quite enjoying himself, actually, mostly because it had been since Ichijou that they'd played these roles. Rutherford gave the guards at the doors nods, although they only saw the hood move. Rei followed him down the hallway and opened the door at the end for him again.

272

They walked through the pre-dawn morning and snowfall to the office of Intelligence by a slightly circuitous route, including a few hidden hallways, but didn't waste a lot of time. Instead of letting the guards at the building see his face, Rei took Rutherford around to the back side of the Royal Aide's building and tapped on Grandfather's window.

When no one answered, he worked the latch until it opened. It was impossible to get to the opposite side of the wing unless he went over the roof or around the main castle wall altogether. While he did know how to get up on roofs, Rutherford didn't. Climbing in through the bay windows set relatively close to the ground was simple enough. Rei made sure to keep their sounds as quiet as possible as he closed and latched the window again. Rutherford was already unlocking the room door but he waited until Rei was with him again to open it. They made sure it was locked again before they left it.

Rei was relieved they'd arrived before the inside door guards had. They went across the broad hallway and Rei pulled a key out from under his shirt. He unlocked the door and they slipped in and relocked the door. They traded clothing, then Rutherford was headed out the door again to sit in his cloak in the hallway. Rei lit a few lamps then headed for the fireplace to get the fire started. The room was rather cold since this wasn't the typical morning to have a meeting in the Lower office, and no resident of that suite was present in the building.

Jefferson and Colin would eventually arrive upstairs to do their work there. Flandras had told Rei before that he'd been working in that office with them so that they didn't have to worry about two fires, and him the only one in the Lower office. Rei didn't want to disturb them this morning, though, so wanted to at least take the chill off the air. He pulled two of the chairs over to be in front of it so they could be close enough to the fire to keep it small. He sat in one and was lost in his musings until he heard Rutherford's voice in the hall.

That would be Hue and Sailte arriving for their guard duty. It was sad that while they did get vacation by having other guards assigned on occasion, they didn't get vacations when the household did. They were still expected to show up and protect the premises. His own on his suite and his office were the same. The royal guards were the only ones who had that requirement, but he was able to be relaxed in his own home because of it. It was also why they only got infrequent vacations. If the royals didn't recognize the faces of those guarding their own doors it made them very nervous, and if they didn't know who was going to be watching their residence while they were out of the castle that was even worse.

When things settled down out in the hallway again, Rei went back to his musings. The next sounds were of the breakfast cart being brought. He'd told Rutherford in his written instructions that he'd eat a very light breakfast on these sorts of mornings so they didn't take too much of what had been brought to others. There might be enough food for unexpected guests, but the food portioning in the castle was rather tightly handled for there to be minimal waste.

Shortly after the cart had been brought and left, Rutherford entered with a plate. When he handed it to Rei, Rei quietly said, "Come eat with me, please." Rutherford bowed and headed back out to bring his plate in. They sat in front of the fireplace where the log Rei had added when he'd heard the cart come snapped lightly. They ate unhurriedly since they still had another hour before Flandras showed up. When the food was gone, Rei handed his dishes to Rutherford. "You can go now," he said.

"Thank you. Have Hue send Jefferson and Collin in. Tell my two I'll meet them in the Rose Office."

Rutherford bowed to him, gave him a slightly concerned look, then exited the suite. Rei rose to go bring back the one small table Lena kept in the room. It had been made by one of her crafters and was a sales display piece more than a used item of furniture. He didn't want to move away from the fire to sit at the desk, for all it was almost warm enough that far away from the fireplace now. He added ink and pen to the table and a few blank pieces of paper from the desk.

Jefferson and Collin arrived through the door, somewhat surprised, while Rei was pacing, not really wanting to sit still during the time he was usually walking to this office. He'd missed his sword practice, too, which would also get him into trouble with his usual two guards and aides. That lack of morning exercise made it extra hard to sit still.

"I'll need you two to be my guards to the Rose office this morning," he said to the two. He knew they were trained well enough by Ilena. "When Flandras and I are finished I'll call you down so we can go." He paused, then added, "And it would make Rutherford, Andrew, and Mina all feel better if you stayed in this office. I don't want our conversation to disturb you any more than it has to, though. Having the usual guards on the outside really should be sufficient. Do you know what your ministry's preference would be? This won't be the only time this happens."

They considered it. Collin finally said, "I know Master Ore would scold you rather severely, to not have someone in the room with eyes on you that they trust." Rei nodded. It was the same for the others and the who wasn't surprising, either.

Jefferson offered, "Lords Petroi and Thayne are still receiving their reports at Falcon's Hollow for now, so our load isn't so heavy at the moment, particularly in the mornings. If one of us is down here and one upstairs to take the few reports that do come in, perhaps that would be sufficient?" He raised a tentative eyebrow at Collin.

Collin considered that then agreed. He offered to stay in the room and Jefferson bowed himself out to return to the Upper office. "I'm sorry to bore you, then," Rei said to Collin.

Collin shook his head and smiled. "I do have work I can do, particularly if you won't be needing the desk?" Rei gave him leave to go up and get his work, denying a need for the desk. He went back to pacing, not stopping when Collin arrived again; although, he did make sure he wasn't near that door until he saw it was Collin at it.

"Pacing won't bother you?" he asked when he was near the desk and Collin was settling.

"Master Ore's favorite activity in the office, and the Messengers aren't much different when they need to move while thinking," Collin rolled his eyes a little.

"I resemble that," Rei smiled and got a tolerant smile back.

They kept each other silent company until there was a single knock at the door and Flandras entered. Rei had been surprised to hear that "a few reports" in the morning was at least three at once, almost constantly following one another. He was glad most of them bypassed the area around his office, if this was only a few. The numbers he did have to hear while in the Rose office were already more than his brain had liked at the beginning.

Rei turned for his chair at the fireplace and waved Flandras over to the other one. Flandras arrived at the chair and hung his cloak over it. The folder he carried was beginning to be worn and a bit darkened. He never let go of it, unless it was on the table in front of him in the Rose office. "You could have brought the other papers in the folder they'd been in. You're about to lose the hinge for having so many papers in one folder. It helps to keep them ordered as to which one is important in the moment as well. One for the details and one or two for the topics at hand." He looked impassively into Flandras' eyes until he got an accepting blink.

"The ones that answer yesterday's questions first, please." Flandras opened the folder and counted out the top five sheets of paper and handed them over. Rei poured over them, rather automatically double checking the math as he went. When the data was in his head, he closed his eyes and fit the numbers into his own board. Having the expanded board that included past generations and the future ones coming up did help him immensely. "Can you calculate out further into the future?" he asked Flandras.

"I can, but the numbers get rather fuzzy too far out," Flandras answered.

Rei frowned as he glanced through the papers in his hand again. "Show me one of your calculations that go as far as you can into the future." He watched, unsurprised, as Flandras hunted towards the back of his stack, in the oldest calculations. He took the page he was handed. Flandras pointed out the beginning of the equation for him. Rei read through it and considered which numbers were most relevant in the equation and then in the answer.

Once he understood that much, he went back to the pages in front of him. He marked five of the possibilities. "Calculate these again out another sixty to one hundred years. Focus less on the current variables and more on the consequence of the choice. The variables are hard to pin down, I get that, but the consequences are more concrete," he looked up into Flandras' eyes.

Flandras was in his head now, seeing the equations. He blinked and looked at Rei again. "Okay, I can do that. Do you want percentage chances on the consequences or ...?"

"Yes," Rei answered. He rubbed his head, then asked for the next set of data he needed, from the more general first set he'd asked Flandras to put together that also contained the calculations for when to begin the fall of King Gastonne. It needed to coincide with Gael entering Altherly but exactly when was one of the calculations. While he wanted to only look at a subset, he wasn't sure he could. He didn't want to miss something he shouldn't. The summary should be enough, though.

Flandras pulled out more like twenty sheets of paper this time. Rei sighed to himself. "Collin, two empty folders, please." When Collin had handed them over, Rei put the first set of papers into one and left the other on the table. He was rather relieved when Flandras chose on his own to take the rest of his stuffed folder to Collin and ask for about three more folders to sort the rest of the pages into while he waited on Rei.

Rei marked the equations this time as he found them. There were too many pages to go back and find them later. When he was done, he was about done with doing math, too. He'd have to learn to not check the math as he went, and just trust Flandras. It was hard, though, and for probably the same reason Flandras was rather paranoid. Any mistakes such a major decision was based on would be rather devastating to either one of them.

Rei did let his brain rest for a bit before thinking of what was next. Moving from math to actual strategy wasn't really all that simple when he'd been that focused on the math. "It really is amazing to me that you don't need to ask me questions," Flandras said quietly.

Rei looked at him with wide eyes, then shook his head. "I didn't ever go to the university for the same reason Ilena hated it. My brother and mother didn't trust them to teach me what I needed to know at the age I was learning it. I learned this sort of math when I was about nine and already had a strategy board by then as well, although it was still small. It was mostly the castle and I was working hard to expand it by a year later." He sighed. "Still, it took Ilena's lesson for me to understand how limited it still was." He wrinkled up his nose. "I still don't know why Sasou's made Ilena teach me so much that he could have."

Flandras was silent for a bit, then said, "Maybe he wanted there to be an excuse for the two of you to have to get to know each other? I'm sure if you asked him it would be because he was too busy trying to stay alive."

Rei laughed. "Well, that's true. He relied heavily on the tutors he and Mother picked, for all he made sure he trained me personally in the things he found most important. I do know that he didn't teach me about having a spy network because Ilena had already told him she was going to do that part. But you'd think he'd have done the full boards, knowing I was already working on that." Rei rolled his eyes and sighed at his older brother. "Of course that's the way he tests. He waits to see what people do for themselves, then doesn't really make them stretch more than that. Ilena leads people along as far as they can go before she gives up. I've about decided it's a time thing more than a personality difference."

Flandras considered that, then said, "Well, yes, but...," he frowned. "Reynold says she knows quite a lot about motivating people. Maybe King Sasou's only learned what's necessary there rather than studied it as much as she has? She can see the clues that a person can still be pushed forward where he can't spare enough attention to it?"

Rei sat back and interlaced his fingers. "That might not be wrong." He closed his eyes and added that to his board, then gave a nod. "Which is why she also needs to review them. I can see this much," he waved his hand at the papers in front of them. "She can see if people can be motivated to accomplish it and even perhaps who. Sasou can see the full political board for the whole of all the nations of the Inner Sea, and for the lords of our own nation...." Rei stopped hard. *Then why did Sasou want him to pick the solution?*

He sighed. His instinctive reaction was to say it was because it was his final test for this part of his understanding. He wasn't sure that was all it was, though. Maybe it was also because the three of them needed to learn how their skills and talents worked together. Also, for the sake of peace in the nation they needed to be united in their decisions when they were of this level of importance.

Rei stayed quiet for a little while longer, finishing letting his brain rest and move over to his other requirement. He slipped the twenty pages into the remaining empty folder on the table. "I've marked the ones that I need you to add the information from the latest set to. Mizi will have specific Houses to add to them when we get that far. I'll let you know what to set those variables to when I get her report. We'll keep to these potentials for now, but I'll keep in mind the rest in case other things come up." He handed both folders over to Flandras, who now had five slightly thinner folders to carry around. It was still better than the one falling–apart folder that he was about to lose pages to the wind from.

Rei looked at that folder, then held out his hand for it. Flandras gave him a curious look but handed it over. Rei reached for a blank page and wrote on it, then slipped the page inside and handed it back. "Leave this on your desk today when you leave the office. I want to see who picks it up." Flandras drew in a breath, but gave him a nod.

Rei rose to his feet and separated the logs in the fireplace, then returned the table and chair. Flandras returned his chair to its place and put his cloak on. By then Collin had collected up his work and was headed for the upstairs to put his things away and get his own cloak. Rei took Flandras into the hallway to wait for Collin. He glared slightly at the guards in the hallway. "Do not, under any circumstances, let anyone know of these few visits we'll have here, even once they're back." Sailte and Hue both bowed.

When Jefferson walked out with Collin, Rei looked at them. "One of you needs to go over the roof so it looks like I'm one of the three of you walking out of the building." Both men sighed and Collin turned around and went back into the Upper office. When Jefferson had reached them, Rei had put on his winter accessories and pulled his cloak hood up over his head. "Pretend you're needing more exercise than pacing in the hallway can give you, so you're walking with Flandras for a bit," he ordered the other two quietly. They understood.

He'd get back to the Rose office just fine with Flandras, but then he'd have to endure the scolding from Andrew and Mina. They really didn't like being left out and unaware, but he wasn't ready to include them in this just yet. Andrew would figure it out eventually, then stop scolding. He'd only look at Rei with sad eyes until Rei was ready to be open. He hoped he could be some day.

"Prince Rei," he was interrupted before he'd barely turned for the outer hallway door. He turned back to Sailte and Hue. "May I ask, did you know you were making us royal guards when Mistress Ilena was brought to the castle at the beginning?" Hue asked.

Rei considered his answer then said, "I knew much of what she was, but not that, no. It was sufficient, though, and not much different. The Queen of Night needs special handling that the Princess is entitled to and the Minister of Intelligence required."

"Thank you," Hue bowed. "I've been wondering for a long time, but only you can answer to it. I appreciate your trust."

"Thank you for remaining trustworthy, both of you," Rei answered back quite seriously. Sailte bowed his gratitude as well. Rei and the two with him were out the door and shortly back out into the cold snowy day again. At least this time there was daylight to see by.

-o-o-o-

Andrew pursed his lips at the slight man that had entered Rei's quarters. He'd refused to budge from the room when he and Mina had found it empty upon arriving to pick Rei up for his morning sword practice. The guards had said that two men had left the room. Only Rei, Rutherford, and Tanner were supposed to be in it at all. Tanner was also missing, so it was unknown which two had left. With no windows that could be opened, one of them had to have not come in the day before. Andrew was quite sure they'd brought Rei to the room the night before, so it was more likely it was Tanner that had been ordered to either hide or take the night off and not come back.

Andrew had been fighting very hard to not be super angry. "Why?" Mina had asked quietly. "Why is it so hard this time?" It certainly wasn't the first time Rei had escaped without them, and usually Andrew chased him down. It also usually helped to know that Rei had taken at least the minimal required precautions, but this time it wasn't. Andrew had shaken his head and tried to chase that down: the cause of his anger. That was hard because he didn't want to. He just wanted to scold very severely.

When the door finally opened much later than Andrew wanted it to, he wasn't surprised to see it was Rutherford, not Rei. "And you left him?" Andrew growled at him.

"With two in the room with him, guards at every door, and instructions to tell you to meet him in the Rose office."

The last didn't help Andrew at all. "Why?! Why is he doing this now? Particularly when neither Ilena nor Ore are here to keep the assassins under their control?" That was part of his problem, suddenly. Scolding did usually help him understand why he was upset.

Rutherford raised an eyebrow at Andrew. "Where do you think Tanner's been this whole time?"

That answer stunned Andrew into silence for a moment and he had to relent just slightly. He didn't think Rei had ever learned to have hidden guards, but to use Tanner as one meant he'd learned the wisdom of it since the assassination attacks. "He's not interested in dying young," Rutherford continued, removing his cloak and then accessories, laying his cloak over his arm neatly, a learned and habitual motion. "He has important things to be doing before that can happen." He turned to put his things where they belonged, in the open wardrobe by the door. It had been placed there when the one on the main floor had been brought. Rutherford had refused to allow the royal winter gear out of his sight and reach. He and Tanner both kept their winter things there as well.

When those were put away, Rutherford turned and scowled a bit at Andrew. "I do think you need to learn to trust him — and me — a little more. You're the one that trained him and he's an adult man of responsibility now. His father's manservant trained me, and he was trained by their Grandfather's. While we keep very quiet about it, we really aren't to be tested." Andrew was surprised at the quiet but forceful sense of imminent threat that went with those words. He backed down and Rutherford began to turn for his room door. "You know him well enough to know he has good reasons for everything he does. It's time to let him be the man he is. Step back and watch instead of distrusting everything he does, or he should train someone new who can support him properly." There was nearly disdain in Rutherford's voice.

"Are you angry?" Andrew asked him quietly. "Have I mistreated you?"

Rutherford paused but didn't turn back to look at him. "You underestimate everyone you talk to, Andrew, and call it healthy distrust. It's a weakness you need to fix or one day you'll find that someone who's more than you can handle. That will be a sad day for the Prince." He was gone, into his room.

Andrew let that answer settle into his brain, then he turned to Mina. "And how am I supposed to fix that weakness?" he was still bristling.

278

Mina pursed her lips and took her time. "He said it. Step back and observe more, without making judgments. Actions speak loudest, but you can't hear them when you're jumping to conclusions while you're walking up to talk to them. That can get a knife in your gut before you can open your mouth to take the breath to speak."

Andrew raised an eyebrow at her. "You agree with him?"

Mina almost glared at him. "Actually, yes, I do, now that he's said it so succinctly. I haven't been able to place my general worry, but it was that. I've been trying to tease it out since Rei asked me to watch over the office while he tests everyone. He wasn't wrong to guess that some of them are more relaxed when you're both out of it. I suspect they still worry about me also, since I haven't heard much said openly during those hours, but...," she shrugged, "watching you when you walk into it has opened my eyes to that worry."

Andrew blinked, really not sure how to take that from his wife, for all she was often blunt. He finally bowed to her just a little stiffly. "Then I'll work at it," he promised. He wasn't quite ready to bend in humility given how angry he'd been just before then. He was suddenly struck with a thought and an eyebrow rose. "You think the mole will attack me and I'll miss it because of that?"

Mina looked away and bit her lip slightly, but gave a nod. "You are the closest and best. It would be you that would be taken out first." She looked back at him soberly. "Like during the households defense practice. If you'd been standing in the circle at the beginning it wouldn't have been Brian and me Thayne would've faced. It would've been you, and Brian he tempted. And the distance attacks would've had you as at least one of the early attacks. They can coordinate so would've attacked at that one instant Thayne had thrown a complex attack at you. The small blade would've killed you. You still don't look for them. The sword is all you use and all you see: the very problem Rutherford has pointed out."

Andrew stood with his feet planted a little wide to maintain his stance firmly enough he didn't fall down with the scolding he was receiving. It wasn't so much that his wife was scolding him, but that she wasn't wrong at all and so he was scolding himself. When he'd recovered enough, he more humbly promised her and himself — and Rei —- that he'd work more diligently at fixing that weakness.

When they arrived at the Rose office and then Rei did as well, Andrew only looked at Rei and observed him. His back was firm. His pace was sure. A worry sat on his shoulders, but he wasn't being a rebellious youth at all. When he turned to look Andrew in the eyes, Rei's expression was sober, perhaps a little sad, like it had been since he'd been given the difficult task of coming up with the best options to protect the nation from war. If that's what he was feeling, he was coming from trying to learn a little more to move a little closer to that goal. Andrew sighed to himself and wished once again he could take that burden from the young prince. Quietly he asked, "Did it help move you forward?"

Rei relaxed in the small ways Andrew knew how to read. "Yes," he answered quietly back.

"Then good," Andrew answered. He had to bite his tongue after that, remembering Rutherford's scold. He did need to practice letting Rei know he trusted him to be what he'd been working to be until now. He turned to his paperwork to let Rei get to work, and to let him know he wasn't going to scold, nor say any more than that. There was a pause, then Rei was turning for his desk to begin his day's work.

Fast–moving snow squall coming.

Ore's head came up sharply. That wasn't good news to Mizi's ear either. They were walking the horses at the moment and themselves to get their legs warmed back up again. It was already hard to see very far through the snowfall. "Mistress trade me horses," Ore said kindly, but she could tell he was very worried. She handed him Fenrier's lead and took Kesheb's. "Stay here for a moment until we're ahead of you. I'll go first to lead the way. Don't lose sight of Fenrier."

"Okay," Mizi halted Kesheb and held him still. He stayed for her, having had the practice now, although he shifted. She just stayed as calm as possible given the news.

"You two stay to either side of both of us," Ore ordered Marcus and Henry. They moved up to either side of Mizi, then waited. As Ore looked back, then halted Fenrier where he wanted him, he added, "Is there a waystation close enough ahead to stop at? We should send everyone back home but them so they don't get caught in the squall."

Mizi stiffened, a memory coming to her as Henry answered about the waystation. "No, Ore! We can't send them home just yet. Sam and Leon are with us but I don't know where. If they can't hear where we are, they'll panic and come looking for us when they might not need to." Ore stared at her wide–eyed in surprise.

Mizi shifted, then got on Kesheb knowing they should get moving sooner than later. *Mistress Mizi to the North Road line. Please find out where Sam and Leon are. They're traveling the road nearby us but in hiding.*

Ore, Marcus, and Henry mounted and they got moving as fast as they dared, which was a canter at this point still. It wasn't galloping weather even if a squall was coming. When they heard back several minutes later that the guards were in front of them Mizi said, *Everyone from Kouzanshi to us should go home. Everyone not on the North Road line also until the squall stops. When we pass you, please go home. I'm very sorry to keep any of you out in the squall if it catches up to us. Everyone between Sam and Leon and the next village, please also stay so we can know they've reached it safely. They'll want to know we've reached the waystation safely as well. Once that message passes between us, everyone in that stretch can go home.*

The closest voice to them answered, *Mistress Mizi, we have hunting blinds we stay in, in this weather. We'll be okay, but be obedient. The message of your safety will need to reach Nijou and Falcon's Hollow before the rest of us between that stretch go home. They'll know that much.*

Thank you for letting me know, she answered, relieved. They heard her message being passed on in both directions. Before they'd gone even ten more minutes, the word came that the squall was nearly upon them. They couldn't move any faster for all their stomachs tightened up with worry and wished to be able to. They secured their hoods, made sure they were wrapped up tightly, and then the winds and thick snow were upon them. Ore's regular calling to the Children on the road with them kept them where they needed to be as they lost complete sight of the road at all, and only the slightly darker grey of the forest to their right remained a landmark at all.

Mistress Mizi to Sam and Leon. Where are you?

Having that follow the news of the squall coming lifted Leon's spirits slightly from the knot of fear in his stomach. She knew they were there and cared. Since they didn't know *exactly* where they were, Sam only said *We're here, headed for the village.* They'd already been moving when the news of the coming squall had reached them. Sam had ordered Leon to fall back to come behind his horse and not lose sight of him.

They didn't hear anything for a while, then they heard orders passing by them. Since he was already watching Sam's shoulders because he was so worried, Leon saw him slump in relief. Leon agreed. He thought Sam would've turned around and gone to join them just because they wouldn't have known so would've sat and worried even more at the village inn. "How long do the squalls last?" he asked.

Sam shook his head. "Half a day to a week or slightly more. There's no knowing at the beginning. They'll likely report when it lessens at the far end again just because everyone likes to know those sorts of things as soon as possible."

Leon crunched his head into his shoulders. He really didn't want to have to live through a snow squall, but if they *did* live through it, he'd at least know how to do it again.

"If it takes us too long to get to the village, we'll need to trade places so I can rest my horse," Sam said. "If I stop, go around me and make sure I'm still awake and alive, then you'll be lead until we get there as your horse won't have had to work so hard until then."

Leon swallowed. "Okay," he answered. He hoped they were close enough. He swallowed again and hunched down when the word passed them that the squall was nearly upon them. He followed Sam's lead to make sure his hat, hood, and cloak were tightened down, then the wind slammed into his back, making the mane of his horse fly up. And then he could barely see the back of Sam's horse and the road, mountains, and forest were gone. He wasn't at all surprised Sam called to the Family along the road as they went to make sure they stayed on the road. A few times they almost got too close to the trees. He hoped there weren't any drop–offs like closer to Osterly. He couldn't remember any but he'd not been looking for them specifically on the way out.

Leon shivered and did his best to not think hard at all, just keep his horse's nose close enough to Sam's to feel the warmth so the horse would stay awake and not get lost. He was surprised at how fast the snow built up on his horse and he brushed it off, and then himself as a large chunk of snow fell off the top of his head and some from a shoulder. He reached behind himself but the wind was blowing most of the snow off the rump of the horse. It wasn't any happier to be out in the snow than he was. He kept them as clear of snow as he could when it would get thick and hoped they'd arrive safely and stay alive.

The word that the village was the next Child was very relieving. Somehow he was surprised that they had four children in just the village line, but since he couldn't even see the houses in it, save as shorter–than–tree shadows, he supposed they were just as needed. The final Child was the one in the inn. Somehow they managed to find the stable behind the inn, get their horses taken care of, and then find the inn again through the driving wind and snow. Before they went in Sam whisper–called, *Sam and Leon to Mistress Mizi. We're at the village inn and will listen to hear you've made it to the waystation safely.*

Leon sighed in relief as they sat down to a table near the fireplace. They weren't the only ones who'd been caught out in the squall, and there were three more that entered behind them, but that was it. As they all warmed up, the complaints to get out the worries, then the stories to pass the time helped Leon to finally relax himself. "It's my first snow squall," Leon said to Sam more quietly than the stories that were being told in the room to everyone by everyone. He shivered slightly. "Thank you for getting us here safely."

Sam gave him a kind, understanding look. "They're no fun, but it was a *lot* easier with the Family to help keep us on the road."

Leon got up to walk to the bath room but stopped at a window on the Kouzanshi side. *Leon to the North Road Family. Thank you.* His gratitude was all he could give them, but it was deeply heartfelt.

-o-o-o-

Ore reached out and brushed the heavy wet snow off of Fenrier's shoulders in front of him, then brushed it off his own shoulders. He'd switched with Mizi because he'd wanted her on the more sturdy horse of Tarc behind Fenrier. Kesheb wasn't complaining too hard at being behind the larger horse that broke the snow on the ground better. Marcus and Henry's horses weren't fairing quite so well since they were still to either side of both of them where they could see both Fenrier and Kesheb to not lose them. Visibility was very bad.

He called out to the Family on the road once more and felt the comfort of having them answer him. He and Fenrier knew the road well, but it helped to have others helping them. They'd been taking the route slowly since the snow squall had caught up to them to not have the horses tire too much, making sure they all stayed just warm enough.

There was motion to the side and behind Ore and he looked back. Henry was coming up to be beside him. "The garrison should be close as well. Shall we try to find it?"

Ore shook his head. "The waystation's closer. But if you know of a common home even closer than that, we could stop there."

Henry shook his head. "They're all set back too far from the road. The waystation's safer than getting lost in the trees."

Ore sighed. "It'll be fine then." He looked closely at Henry's horse and nearly called a rest stop right then, but their attention was caught by a sound on the wind. Ore used the code more loudly since the snow muffled sound, the opposite as it had been in Tarc. They were answered again and felt relief.

Twenty minutes later they were in the waystation courtyard, their weary mounts' heads hanging down, but relieved to be where there was a barn and hay. They led their horses into said barn, still more of a large dark shadow than an edifice in the snow. "I could sleep right here with them," Mizi sighed as she removed the military issue saddle from Kesheb.

"I know, right?" Ore said tiredly. "But that wouldn t be kind to our hosts." They were glad to have the help from the family father and son to get the heavy tack placed neatly and dried off while they fed and watered their horses. "Not much room, though," Ore said, looking through the full stalls.

Henry raised his hand. "Our two can be in the same stall if there's a birthing one. They don't need large."

Mizi looked at the three Tarc horses. "Or all three can stay out here. They don't have to be in the stall to appreciate the roof over their heads."

"That's true," Henry agreed. He negotiated that while Ore took Fenrier into the one obviously empty stall.

Mizi took that opportunity to go to the door and call to the Family line, letting them know they'd reached the waystation safely and they could all make their last reports and go home. Ore rubbed Fenrier's head and took off the sleeping cat regalia cover and blanket. He didn't need to be wet and cold. He hung them over the outer wall of the stall to dry, then took a quilted warming blanket from the son. "Thanks."

"You're welcome," the lad answered politely. "Do you all always take care of your own horses?"

Ore smiled at him. "Not this one. I send him to the stable at home and let those who're paid to do it pamper him. Those three, we just take the saddles and blankets off and let them loose. They know they're family and stay close. But when we're out, yes, we do, particularly in the winter since we want to know they'll be okay."

The lad gave a nod of approval and trotted off for blankets for the Tarc horses. Marcus stopped him and shook his head. "Their fur is thicker and needs to dry or they'll chill, in the reverse way. Once they're dry, then see that they get light blankets, not our winter ones, or they'll get too hot. Only if they're sick, or we're worried they're going to be, do they need the warming blankets. If you'll stay with them after dinner and watch them? If they start to shiver, even with the light blankets, then come get one of us and we'll check on them. This is their first Suiran winter so we're watching them more closely to see what they really need."

"Okay," the boy was willing. He pointed the direction of the house so they didn't get lost just going the wrong direction and they carried their bags there. The man of the house had already gone in.

They tried to not have the front door open too long, but a fire was blazing in the front receiving room's fireplace. That chased the chill back out rather quickly. "If you'll come with me?" the man of the house requested. They followed him upstairs. The space above the receiving room in this house had actually been divided into four small rooms with a hallway down the center.

Marcus rolled his eyes at Ore. Ore sighed. "All right. Mizi and Marcus in the outer two rooms, me and Henry here on the house side." It wasn't the normal way the castle would've wanted them to do it, but he'd already paid the price before for them trying it with the guards in front and the royals in the back. He really did need to have his ear on Mizi, which he couldn't do so easily if he was across the hallway. And if Marcus and Henry couldn't be in the same room, they at least also had to hear each other. They needed sleep so he wouldn't fight it this time. It still put Mizi in the most protected location they could, save for that being the front window location.

Marcus frowned at the same time as Ore did. "Okay, reverse that," Ore agreed before Marcus could complain. "I'll need the window for the fresh air. I forgot I need outside corner windows and would rather Mistress was inside." The inn had been a slightly different situation since they'd all been in "inside" rooms. Not having the corner hadn't been easy. He'd just tried not to think about it. He slumped. "I guess I'm very ready to be home."

Mizi patted him on the shoulder and headed for her door. She looked back at their host. "I'm sorry that we have no idea what time of day it is, but I think we need to at least nap first. Please tell your wife we're sorry to not eat her warm meal first. If she could keep it warm for us our stomachs will wake us back up before too long, I'm quite sure." She was kindly dry about that. They'd fought the snow enough they really hadn't eaten in quite some time. Ore was happy to have her make the decision, though.

Marcus followed her into her room to leave her bag there, then took his into the other room across from hers. Ore followed Henry and let him put Ore's bag in his room, then he followed that in and dropped his cloak and winter gear on top of it, sort of setting it out to dry. He was taking off his boots so as to not get the bedding dirty when their host knocked and entered, asking if he could take said sodden clothes to the fire to dry. Ore waved his hand and waited for him to be gone again, then fell onto the bed and drew up only one blanket over him. That would get him to wake back up later when Mizi called for him.

Food called him before Mizi did, the smell rising up from below. He sat up and decided to just pull on one more pair of socks instead of his boots. He fished in his bag for them, pulled them on, then walked to the door and listened. It was pretty quiet. He poked his head out and found the hallway empty and the smells stronger. He tapped on Henry's door, then Marcus', then Mizi's. "Mistress, dinner's ready and we should eat," he called to her only loud enough to get her attention. He didn't need to shout to the whole house, although warning them they were getting up wasn't bad. He waited until she said she was up and coming, then went back and made sure the Twins were getting up.

Their hostess was putting food on the table as they arrived in the dining room. "It smells too good to wait anymore," Ore smiled at her. "Thank you very much for letting us stay and escape the weather."

"You're very welcome, Father, Mistress Mizi," she curtsied to them once her burden was placed on the table. "My name is Heather. My husband is Rory and my son is Dyson."

"It's a pleasure to met you," Mizi said kindly. "Ore's quite right, that this smells so good. We're sorry for the necessary intrusion." Marcus seated her while Henry did the same for Ore. Ore let it happen since the Twins needed the practice. "Have you already eaten? I hope you'll join us if not," entreated Mizi.

"Rory's taking Dyson his meal and confirming your horses," Heather explained. "We'll sit with you once he returns." Mizi accepted that answer and Heather disappeared into the kitchen again to fetch the next thing to the table.

Ore leaned on his elbow at the table. "And how often have you two stopped by here before now?" he asked the Twins, wondering it and wanting small conversation.

"Some," Henry said with a shrug. "We don't often have to impose on the waystations since we more often have messages for people at the villages. We weren't ever the speed couriers either; although, we do well with that in town," he winked with a smile.

"Fastest in Kouzanshi when Mistress Ilena called us out of the city," Marcus agreed proudly. "So we still practice, but on the horses it's more fun to lounge and let them do the work." Ore chuckled as they laughed.

Heather paused, then set the plates around the table. When she reached Marcus, she searched his eyes. He looked back at her, his pleasant look on his face. "And you ran the carriage, which did come here," she said after she'd sat Henry's plate down and had her hands empty again.

"Well, yes, we did that, too, when it was needed," Marcus agreed with her, although he'd gone just a little wary.

Heather looked back at him again. "May I ask what happened to the young frightened lad that wouldn't leave his room to come eat?"

"Well, there were more than one of those...," Marcus hedged, then he sat upright. "No, you mean Justinian, don't you?" Everyone at the table smiled.

Heather looked at them curiously, just a little wary herself. "That sounds right, yes," she answered.

"He's doing very well," Ore answered her, a little proud himself. "He's my manservant and learning to combat his fears very well. He's one of the bright gems Ilena's quite proud of." Ore smiled. "He keeps surprising himself at what he can do now that he's free to be himself."

Henry nodded. "We won't be letting him go from the Immediate Family any time soon. Every time he surprises himself, he surprises us in good ways. He even tops Marcus some days at being able to get Mistress Ilena to relax and smile. He's relaxed quite a lot since she called him up for Master Ore out of the obscurity we'd hidden him in at the castle."

Heather relaxed. "Well, that's good to hear. I worried about him most of all those that came through here. He was such a small thing to be carrying around all those fears and worries."

Ore smiled kindly. "He still does carry them, but we're helping him to set them down when he's ready to let them go. And he's been a great support to many of us already. He learned to be strong, carrying those burdens. We hope to help him stay strong with the good things now." The rest from the castle nodded agreement.

"Justinian knows how to cook," Mizi said brightly. "So we've added him in to our cooking group. Even that's been a brighter sparkle to add to all of us. I've greatly appreciated his gentleness, too. If I need to see sunshine I can go find him and gently tease him. Even if it's dark grey winter outside, his smile is the best thing to think the sun came out briefly."

Henry chuckled. "See, Marcus. Even Mistress Mizi likes him better than you, by a slight margin." Marcus pretended to pout at him.

Mizi reached over and took his little fingers in hers. "Well, but Marcus is very needed, too, just like all of you," she gave a scolding look to Henry. She let go of Marcus when she'd realized she made him blush. "Thank you, Marcus, for being a comforting person in my life, too." She now blushed a little. "I'm sorry to impose so terribly before."

Marcus shook his head, but then said soberly, "I understand it very well, Mistress Mizi. What you felt that day was what I felt every day growing up in Kouzanshi. Those kinds of sorrows and fears are difficult when there's no relieving of them, and no way to release them. That you could do it then was good for you. I hope you'll continue to heal and not hold them in so much in the future." Mizi slumped a little, but agreed she'd take better care of herself in that way, too.

Rory entered the house then, by the sound of the door opening and closing behind him. Still, all four watched to see who came through the door to make sure. Heather returned to the kitchen one more time as Rory hung up his cloak. "The horses are doing well," he reported. "The small ones have dried out well enough and seem to be fine with the lighter blankets as you said. They've picked their favorite spot and are huddled up sleeping." He turned a smile on them. "They apparently made Dyson sit down in the middle of them. He was nearly sleeping on one of them when I arrived with the meal."

"Yes, they're bred to be family to their clans. They take that responsibility seriously, particularly for the children, taking it upon them to teach even the human children how to take care of themselves." Ore was rather pleased they'd included Dyson in their care, returning the care he was giving to them. "I do hope they didn't scold you for leaving him out there?"

Rory shook his head. "When one of them complained, Dyson scolded back, saying he'd been given the responsibility to watch over them. They asked me if that was true and settled when I spoke soothingly." He shook his head. "I don't think I've ever seen horses that could understand humans and their language so well."

Ore agreed. "I do like how they've been bred and raised by the Tarc. I understand why they're Ilena's favorites." He smiled, then remembered. "Justinian was taught by a Tarc mother horse how to ride and be comfortable with horses." He smiled up at Heather as she blinked at him, then sat in her place. "That was an early experience for him that began to teach him he could do things he'd never thought he could. It was good he had the opportunity for such a gentle teaching, and the right sort of horse to do it for him."

The food was passed around the table and they enjoyed filling their bellies with it. Ore, Mizi, Henry, and Marcus had fun taking turns telling simple light stories about their time in Tarc and about Justinian when they fit in. Like at the other waystation, they helped with clean–up, saying again many hands made light work and they'd rather keep busy. After, Mizi settled in the receiving room near the fire with Marcus and Henry. Ore went upstairs and put his boots on. "Mistress, I'll go out and talk to the horses for a bit," he said when he was back down in the receiving room. He picked up his cloak and put it on.

It wasn't until he looked back up at her that he realized she was studying him. He raised an eyebrow at her. "Don't freeze or stay out too long," she answered him. "Just because we've reminded you of home doesn't mean you don't need more rest. If you can't fall back to sleep, do your workout and then dance until you're tired enough again to sleep."

Ore took a moment to digest that, then closed his mouth and bowed to her. "Yes, Mistress," he said. He was a little surprised she'd seen the reason he was going out. He really didn't sit still very well generally, but it was true that it had been talking about Justinian that had done it. He shrugged to himself a little irritably as he walked out the door. He wasn't sure he wanted Mizi to be reading that deeply into him, even if he did need it on occasion.

Ore went to the stable and checked on Dyson, more than he did on the horses. Talking about Justinian had made him want to have someone young around to distract him from his old–age responsibilities. He had fun settling down warmly with the horses, making them complain at him because he made them shift, being bigger than the small lad. Kesheb moved over enough to put his head in Ore's lap. That helped, too, to be able to pet the big heavy head of a horse while he told stories to Dyson. Watching his eyes sparkle until they were starting to close in sleep was fun, too.

At that point Ore lifted him to his feet. "While we're grateful you've watched over them until now, to make sure they stay healthy, they don't need to be slept with when you need proper rest and warmth." He rose to his feet and walked Dyson back to the house and made sure he made it in.

The receiving room was empty so he said his quiet goodnights to Dyson, then pushed the minimum amount of furniture back out of his way and did an abbreviated– for–the–space workout. When he was done with that, he just lay on the floor for a moment, then realized he was going to fall asleep in that place. The bed would be warmer so he heaved himself up to his feet and walked himself up to the bedroom. He would've tried calling for Ilena to talk to her, but the snow hadn't let up at all. He hoped the people between them were warm in their own beds. Still, he stayed sitting up in bed, looking out the window until his eyelids were closing before he lay back and finally worked to sleep for real.

-o-o-o-

Rei watched in amazement as the afternoon messages were delivered to the Rose office. It wasn't just a stack. Three different people wanted to hand–deliver their messages. He immediately waved at Mina and hid back in his work on his desk. Mina rose to her feet to go to the door. "I'm sorry, the Regent hasn't the time to hear your additional requests and arguments today. We'll take the reports and review them. You may appear at this month's City Council meeting with the Regent and make your verbal additions at that time to both parties involved." She held out her hand for their reports and firmly didn't let them do any more than that. When there was finally one protest, she added, "If you didn't put it in writing in the report, that's your decision, isn't it? They're only feasibility studies. There'll be time for more heavy details later."

Mina closed the door firmly behind her and brought the reports to Rei, setting them down separately as their own stack. "Do we send them to Ilena right away?" she asked.

Rei frowned. "Ask her," he ordered. Mina did, going to the patio briefly to do it, then leaving the door open just slightly so they could hear the answer when it arrived.

Leah to Mina: The full foaling has begun. She won't be available for several days. I suggest keeping them at the castle until we return. She's completed the review of the two that arrived early.

Mina closed the patio door, walked past Rei's desk to pick the reports back up, and continued to the inner door. She listened for a bit, then opened the door and waved over a paige. "See these arrive safely at the Lower office of Intelligence for Ilena to see to when she gets back. Then go see who let those three onto castle grounds and send them for punishment. That is not to be repeated by anyone." She was quite firm. It was bad enough the lords in the castle could get away with standing outside the door; although, even that had been decreased rather dramatically when he'd assigned Mizi to take care of them.

His head popped up. "Mina, were they minor lords?"

She stopped then glared at the paige reaching for the folders. He took them, then swallowed. "I'll find out," he answered.

"And who they were specifically, please," Rei requested loud enough to be heard. The paige bowed and ran off. Mina closed the door and turned to look at Rei. "When we have the names, find out if their palms were greased, or if they have an interest or ownership in the companies. If the former, firmness will be required. If the latter, we can smooth it over in the City Council meeting. Your reasoning was sound and sufficient." Mina gave a nod so Rei went back to work, since he really *was* very busy and was desperately trying to not worry about his wife since he knew she was safe enough. It was just the delay and the heavy snow still falling outside his own windows that made him anxious.

-o-o-o-

Mizi and Ore couldn't leave the waystation for two days of heavy snows. Ore was pacing the receiving room impatiently before it let up. Mizi had to calm him. It really was that he wasn't able to talk to Ilena during that time, but she understood because she also wasn't able to talk to Rei in the mornings. As soon as they could tell through the windows that the sky was lightening and they could see the trees that surrounded the householder clearing, they prepared to leave. They were roughly half–way to the next village so there should be enough time to get there. They were grateful to their hosts, but didn't waste their time getting on the road again. The horses were unhappy but resigned. Even they knew that stable wasn't home.

Ore pushed them so Fenrier and Kesheb couldn't fight and had to work hard. He didn't have the patience to deal with them. He put Mizi on Kesheb again for this part of the run and told her to keep Kesheb firmly in hand. They were all worn out by the time they made it to the village inn but it was a good sleep. With an early morning they were on the road again, half an eye on the clouds behind them. Mizi talked briefly with Rei before they got going to let him know they were on the road again.

Ore called to Ilena that night from the next village and didn't get a response back from her. *Father, she's firmly focused on the foaling, I'm sorry. But, she is okay.* Leah's message was perhaps reassuring but didn't help Ore's impatience to be home. He had to stuff the jealousy down the next morning when Rei and Mizi were able to talk to each other again. He knew they both needed it as well. Four days was already too long for either couple.

The next night they stayed at the waystation they'd stayed at on the way out. The snows had gotten just heavy enough to slow them down so they couldn't reach Osterly. It wasn't a snow squall to keep them from riding at all, though. They enjoyed their visit with Lewis, Irene, Lorence, and Abigail that evening but were back on the road early so they could get to the castle before the next night if at all possible. Ore's answer from Falcon's Hollow had been unsatisfactory again and he was now getting upset. It wouldn't do to be poor company that much.

Rei met Mizi, Ore, Henry, and Marcus at the main entrance to the castle when they arrived late in the day. While they might have left from the Soldier's gate because of other reasons, Rei had ordered them to arrive at the proper gate for royalty so the lords would know Mizi had done her duty in Kouzanshi for her hospital project. He'd been listening to the reports of their coming so was present and watching for them to arrive, Andrew and Mina standing with him. Mizi had asked on their way in and been told that Sam and Leon had arrived shortly before they had, relieving her.

"That's surprising, to have you controlling Fenrier," Rei said into Mizi's hair as he held her tightly to him, glad to have her back safely.

Ore smiled. "They both did very well in their lessons," he agreed.

Rei raised his eyebrow at Ore. "And why Kesheb?"

Ore frowned at his horse. "He was too jealous and followed us too far. It was that or let him die to the cold and starvation. I wasn't ready for that. He's been learning his lessons as well. Next time if he won't stay put he'll have to fend for himself as his lessons. I think he did learn winters here aren't to be taken lightly." Both Kesheb and Mizi nodded in agreement, Kesheb ending his with a firm shake of his head.

The stablehands and porters had arrived by then. Their bags were removed and they ordered the horses to go with the stablehands. Since the snow was still falling thickly and home was very much wanted by the horses, too, they went willingly. The seven humans hurried into the castle, wanting warmth now, too. Rei held Mizi's hand in his elbow to have her close to him. Ore was a bit surprised when Rei led them to the Rose office directly. "No relaxing in warmth first?" he teased a bit.

Rei looked at him out of the corner of his eye. "It's warm enough, you can give your report there, and ...there's something there you need to deal with before you go on."

"Hoh?" Ore raised an eyebrow at him but wasn't enlightened any more than that. Instead Rei asked for Mizi's report immediately as they walked. Ore wasn't surprised Mizi left out her emotional responses to the stress, but when they were done talking about it, he did say, "Mistress has more to say when you're safely in your bedroom." Mizi's wide green eyes swung around to stare at him. He looked blandly back. "Consider it practice for letting people know what you need ...before it gets that bad again."

Mizi blinked her wide eyes at him, then slumped and shivered. "He's such a cold tyrant," she complained at Rei. "They both are. I don't have to miss Ilena when he's like that."

Rei had been looking at her in some concern, but at that he agreed. "Well, I'll hear it later, then," he didn't let her off the hook for following through on Ore's scold, so Ore relaxed again. Rei already knew Ore didn't do that unless there really was a need for it. Ore did tell him what it had been before they got to the Rose office since that wasn't something that should be said there, but should be part of his own report. Rei made Marcus and Henry say it as well, since they'd been at the university with Mizi at that time.

When they were done, Rei sighed at Mizi. "I'll assume Ore thinks there's more to it since he wants you to talk more later." He patted her hand. At Ore's glare, he added, "And yes, I do have things to say to you that might help as well." They were at the door to the Rose office so he couldn't say more right then, so Ore let it go at that.

Rei led them to the fireplace where they could warm up. "Welcome home," Aiden said kindly as they passed him.

"Thank you, Aiden," Mizi answered him. "It's good to be home where it's warm and we can not care about the weather so much." Aiden smiled, understanding.

Brianna wasn't in the room but Mizi greeted Brian and Ore took the time to greet Flandras. "It's a small group, isn't it?" he asked, then turned a little more and feigned surprise. "Oh, you two *are* here. I wondered if you'd been given vacation, too."

Andrew and Mina both put on bland faces. "And shall I take the next opportunity like that to knife you, to remind you to see what you need to be seeing?" Mina asked dryly.

Ore raised a hand. "Ah, no, that's okay. Besides, you can't hide when you're even thinking of pulling your knife." Her knife was out faster than he expected, but even so he wasn't where it was. His eyes were wider than they'd been in a long time, but it was Andrew's surprised, then scolded look that made him more surprised. "Oh, an object lesson for Andrew is it? What happened while we were gone, then?"

Mina's slightly surprised look at the question made Ore smile at her. "You did very well Miss Mina. There wasn't any warning at all. It's that Mister Andrew can't hide, as you already know."

"How did you even dodge it then?" Mina asked, put out that he'd done it.

"Because I'm always aware of such things coming my way," Ore answered, his own look going to Mizi who slumped, also scolded. His hand was on Mina's knife hand next. Her wrist immediately relaxed and Ore's eyes went back to Mina's blue–green eyes. He only looked into them. When she relented he scolded quietly, "Don't tease or test when Mistress is still trying to learn that attention is more important than trust or not trust."

Mina put her knife away and bowed to the somewhat stricken Mizi. "I'm sorry, Mizi. It's that I'm trying to teach a similar lesson to Andrew. He'll die to the unseen knife because of his lack of attention."

"Oh, that's what it is," Ore mused to himself as Mizi tried to recover from the surprising exchange. He looked Andrew in the eyes to see that he was working hard to learn it humbly. He shrugged and turned away. "Well, he'll get it soon enough. He's working hard already." He allowed Henry to take his cloak and handed over his winter accessories, too, then bowed to Rei. "I'm ready to give my report, then." He noticed Rei's eyes had to return to him from looking beyond him. The only person that direction was Brian. Ore sighed sadly to himself. If they'd been able to give another person an object lesson, too, then perhaps it was okay. He'd been put behind Mizi for that very reason.

Rei handed his cloak over to Mina and Andrew took Mizi's. As the guards walked over to the pegs on the wall Rei said, "Let's hear it then." Ore gave as complete a report as usual. Rei didn't let Mizi go, making her hear it with him. Ore approved that he was training Mizi in this way, having seen it now a few times in the castle. She learned best by observing before practicing. Ore left out the secret bits, only using couched terms where necessary and ending with, "I'll put the details in my report as usual." Mizi blinked at him and he smiled back at her. "Master likes to know what my opinions on the matters were, not just what was said. Since that would make the spoken report five times as long, I get to have a weary hand at the end instead." She smiled a laughing smile and he returned it to her.

It took a bit for Rei to come back from mentally reviewing it all and ask his questions. He also ended with, "I'll send questions back after I review your very long written report."

"Ah, Master's learned to tease so quickly now, instead of waiting for three hours first," Ore praised him. Rei glared at him and Ore was able to relax. "So, what is it I need to look at before I can go? Ilena hasn't talked to me in four days, so I'd like to go as soon as possible to make sure I still have a wife."

"That's rather surprising," Rei lifted an eyebrow at him.

"I've been trying to reassure him she's just very busy, like Miss Leah's been telling him," Mizi explained, "but after the heavy snows, four days is already too long."

Rei studied Ore for a bit, then said, "Well, it would be, when it's also been the two weeks."

"Indeed, Master," Ore said firmly.

Rei turned and pointed to Ore's desk. On it was a folder bound with a gold cord. Ore froze in shock, his eyes locked onto it. He finally drew in a breath and said, "Well, I guess Master *would* want me to read that before I leave. That *would* be very suspenseful." He turned to Rei with a furrowed brow. "Would he have had Uncle read mine before sending it?"

Rei was thoughtful. "Well, I don't know, but I'd think so?" He mused on that, then said definitively, "Yes. Michael would be even more worried that you'd show up to kill Sasou than me if it was written wrongly, particularly after the last one." He looked to see if Ore understood.

Ore blinked, remembering back and then agreed. "With both of us asking Ilena to scold him for that one and Uncle apologizing for it, he probably required it." Ore walked over to his desk and picked up the folder, noting he had a good–sized stack again now. He might want to postpone going to Falcon's Hollow anyway just to get his report to Rei finished and turned in. The rest of that stack was going to take a while and he didn't want to take work with him to Falcon's Hollow.

Rei clearing his throat made Ore have to focus on the folder in his hand again. He sighed and untied it, letting the ribbon slip to the top of his desk. He opened the folder and read the letter inside of it, going rather chilly again as he did so, as if he were standing outside again after an eight hour ride in the snows.

Ore, Since Sasou never was that formal nor informal with him he wasn't quite sure how to take that. He wasn't sure Sasou ever treated anyone as an equal, yet that was a very "equal" beginning.

I'm sorry I likely won't be able to keep my promise to you. This is your official notification that I'll be giving Kouzanshi to you and Ilena. You've both learned how to take care of it well enough. Be thinking of how you want to handle adding that to your list of duties. We'll talk about options when you all come in the summer.

Let Rei read this when you're done so he knows.

Sasou

Ore looked up at Rei, stricken and really not knowing how to handle the news. "Master, my own hubris has come to haunt me. And Ilena's to her, too." He stiffly handed the letter over.

Rei read it, then slumped. He turned away and motioned Ore should follow him to his desk. He didn't let go of Mizi's hand.

Rei set Sasou's letter on the desk and pulled a piece of paper over and wrote on it. "*There's another letter for you to read, in my rooms. No hurry. I'll get it to you when you're both back here.*"

Ore looked at the letter from Sasou again. He pointed to the last short paragraph and then the first sentence of Rei's. "Those go together, yes?" It looked to him like another example of how they wrote to let each other know who had more information to add.

"Yes," Rei answered. He pointed to the salutations at the beginning and end. "These also. This is 'just him'." He looked sharply into Ore's eyes. Ore went sober, then nodded. He understood. Sasou would also charge titles when he addressed people to give the messages he wanted to send. That helped him to understand that better. He reread the letter and the whole of it was written that way.

He sighed a little, not really wanting that responsibility, yet at the same time knowing in the prideful part of his soul that he and Ilena did already do a much better job in that role than Zade did. "I guess it's good I said my farewell to Lord Yosuko while I was there. The commander did say Zade wasn't going to like me the next time we met. I'm not sure he knew about this order, though. He was thinking of my newest station earned last year." He looked up at Rei with a dry smile. "Do you think he'd trade me Marquis for Grand Duke?"

Rei was aghast, then shook his head at Ore. "While that might be a difficult hat for you to wear, you're the better one for it, and you know it."

Ore pursed his lips a little at Rei, then reached out to pick up the letter. "Even though he *says* he's sorry, he's already promised to leave it alone."

Rei pointed to the words "likely" and "options" before Ore could lift the letter from the desk. "That's the clues he wants to do his best. Talk to Ilena about it first." Motioning for Ore to go ahead and pick up the letter, Rei added quietly, "Don't lose that."

Ore gave him a nod and folded it, putting it inside his jacket. He turned and walked away from Rei's desk, letting Rei take care of the secret message. It was going to take him some time to settle to this one, too. He did hope Ilena had a plan that would let them escape the one more heavy hat. He was sure even she was done being "gifted" them. He decided to lose himself in his report for a bit. Then he was definitely running away to Falcon's Hollow where he could be just Count Ore for a few days.

ATTACK ON REI

An assassination attempt against Rei has Ore in a panic.
(Main event occurred 3-5 Autumn One 543.)

Attack on Rei

Mina opened the letter addressed to her. Such things were rare, not invited, nor wanted. It was more than faintly perfumed and she wondered who was trying to hide a poison under the smell. The words turned her stomach as much as the scent did. "No. I'm not interested at all," she muttered under her breath. She wanted to yell it at the man who'd sent it, then burn it to ashes in front of him. Sadly he wasn't where she could do that and she wasn't about to continue to carry it on her person.

Her pen wrote in strong strokes that would be considered masculine writing by anyone of the courts. She didn't care. That's why she'd practiced the style. The rejection wasn't coated very much by court speech. Only just enough to not bring war on her father and House, and hopefully not on to Rei by association. A second letter was next, this one addressed to her father directly to warn him another letter of request had come to her and from whom. While he was willing to let her be in charge of her future to a great degree, they had this agreement: if anyone sent letters of interest to either one of them, they let the other know. That way they'd know who to stand united against. Or it let Mina know if her father needed the heavier hand of Rei behind him because the House making the request was too strong for him to stand alone against.

Mina's nose wrinkled up as she dropped the letter of request on Rei's desk so he'd know, too. She left it there and headed for the door and the paiges. "See these are delivered expeditiously." It was hard to be the only heir to Yosai Earldom some days. Far too many men with fluff for brains or greedy designs seemed to think they could just take it and her without complaints or consideration of what she, her father, and Rei wanted. She was already Rei's. If they really wanted to woo her, they had to talk to the Prince first. It was very frustrating that they only saw a twenty–two-year-old unmarried heiress to an earldom and thought she'd have even less brains than they did.

On her way back to her desk in Ichijou castle, Rei raised his hand to her, making her pause. "This one might be harder," he said quietly. "I'm passing it up to Sasou."

Mina froze and blinked at him. "Well, I've already refused."

"Of course you have," Rei answered dryly. "They'll send me one next, I'm sure, which is why I'll be talking to Sasou about it." He handed her a folder with a significant look.

Mina sighed and took it back out to the paiges. "See this gets to King Sasou. It's from Rei." That would get it there the fastest. She didn't really want the king involved, but that was Rei's call. She sent another one to her father the next day after Rei told her what Sasou had told him. Earl Durand would need that information to defend himself, too. She wasn't quite sure why the Touka brothers wanted her so badly, but she was very grateful that they were willing to protect her from the idiots of the nation.

-o-o-o-

"Rei, you'll be leaving in five days for Suiran. It's time for you to learn what the garrisons know about the lords of the Region and let the commanders learn who you are." Sasou's expression was the bland that said nothing, but Mina thought he was perhaps a little colder than normal.

She wouldn't be surprised if it was because of the subject matter. The Suiran lords were stubborn, old fashioned, and hard to move for anything save their own selfish desires. Save a rare few like her own father who was somewhat laize fair and who'd rather work with Touka to make his own life easier. She'd understood better why he worked with them once she'd started following Rei. The Toukas she could see did want the nation to move forward smoothly and be in peace. If one worked with them things *were* easier. Why fight that?

They were in the small throne room Sasou met Rei in when he had official things to say to him. It was almost more an office but it wasn't the King's office and usually had few to no guards in it save when Sasou allowed Andrew and Mina to enter it — which he had this day.

Mina was surprised when Sasou's eyes glanced at her. "You'll likely have the opportunity to run into some of House Tercel while you're there. Plan accordingly." Mina's lips pursed as tightly as Rei's did. The cold look in Sasou's eyes matched them. He handed over a folder containing a sheaf of papers. "Here's the itinerary." Rei took the folder and Sasou relaxed slightly. "Don't play overly long, but do find time to relax a bit." He waved them out, his words having surprised Rei. Rei bowed properly, Andrew and Mina also doing the same, and they were leaving the throne room.

Rei's tight back relaxed a bit to be out of his brother's presence, as he always did, but his expression was full of the curiosity the final comment had brought up. He didn't bother waiting to reach his own office before opening up the folder. Mina glanced at Andrew. Andrew agreed with her. He took Rei's elbow and they walked him to a quiet place in the castle, not too far distant, where he wouldn't be disturbed as long as they scowled people off.

The slap of the folder closing meant they were walking again. Rei's strides were long enough to reach the office quickly. As soon as the door was closed behind them, he turned to face them. "He's giving me a *three day* vacation in Kouzanshi when we get there." His scowl was the opposite it could have been, but he wasn't wrong. Three days wasn't really much time at all.

"Well, it's at least some time," Andrew tried to mollify him.

Rei shrugged, then turned for his desk. "Write a letter to Ore at the garrison and tell him to hold any further letters until we get there and how long we'll be there." He paused as Andrew went to his desk to pull out paper and pick up his pen. Rei added a few more orders, then sat down to his desk. Mina sat down to her own work while Rei reviewed a specific page in the folder one more time.

"Mina," her head rose to look at him, "House Tercel is in the center of the Region. Would they come find me on the south end or north end?"

Mina tapped her pen on her finger as she thought about that. "They're also closer to the east side and Father. It wouldn't be surprising for them to confront you on the north side so they could confront Father at or near the same time."

Rei gave a satisfied nod to that. "After Kouzanshi, then." He sighed and put the folder on the corner of his desk. "After you've sent the letter, Andrew, come review it." Andrew gave a distracted nod, but he was done with both tasks soon after.

Mina sighed to herself. "I'm sorry, Rei."

Rei looked up at her in surprise, then shrugged. "As I said, they were going to be difficult. A confrontation is inevitable I suspect."

"What's it about?" Andrew asked, looking between the two of them.

Mina's nose wrinkled. "They want Yosai and I told them no. Father's told them no, Rei's told them no, and I suspect King Sasou has as well, given he wasn't happy today."

Andrew slumped a little. "Ah. No, that won't be good, will it?" They all took the time while getting ready for the trip to think about options, then discussed them on the first part of the tip to Suiran up West Road until Rei couldn't stomach thinking about it anymore. Andrew and Mina would rather he think about the vacation he'd be having with Mizi and Ore anyway. He really did need the opportunity to see them and relax even a little. He'd been missing them very much for the past year.

-o-o-o-

The night before they left Ichijou a paige arrived at Rei's quarters, summoning him to Sasou's presence. This time it was to his private office at his own quarters. One of Sasou's guards walked him there since his own guards were in their quarters already. Rei worked hard to not be overly stiff, but he'd already learned that from years before. He really hated being called personally into either his brother or his mother's presence. They teased horribly, and had such high expectations of him that he felt he'd never meet. It was so hard to face them with any sense of personal worth at all. His shield of firm coolness was all he had to keep himself propped up when he was with them. And this time he didn't even have his guards to support him. He wondered what it was Sasou wanted to say to him privately.

The guard knocked once on the door then opened it after he was called to. "Prince Rei, as ordered, Sire." The guard had only stuck his head in. He opened it wide enough for Rei to walk in, then closed it behind him.

Sasou waved his hand to the chair set near his. They were both plush and covered in pale gold velvet brocaded in brilliant blue. Rei raised his eyebrow but Sasou only looked at him with an expression of neutral expectation of being obeyed. Rei sighed to himself and sat gingerly on the edge of the seat. Sasou lifted the carafe of wine on the small round table between them and poured a small amount into the glass on Rei's side of the table, then topped off his own glass.

Rei gave Sasou a look of *must I really?* Sasou gave him a small smile back and lifted his own cup. "Join me a bit, but I need your attention so I won't make you drink too much tonight." Rei was surprised by the admission, but could live with that much. He lifted the cup and sipped at it. Not surprisingly it was his brother's favorite slightly dry white wine he preferred in the evenings. It wasn't Rei's favorite, but he'd learned to drink it sufficiently by now for this sort of evening and the "drinking training" nights Sasou teased him with when he was made to drink to drunkenness in an attempt to get him to learn to hold his alcohol. Those weren't nights he appreciated very much.

He set the cup back down and asked, "What do you want me to learn tonight then?"

Sasou smiled into his cup, then set it down to look into Rei's eyes. "Tonight I want to teach you about landed lords. The ones in Suiran are the ones you'll get your practice on. This trip is just the beginning of the practicals."

Rei's eyebrows both rose. He settled back in the chair and gave a nod. This would take a while, most likely.

-o-o-o-

The trip around to all of the garrisons of Suiran was quite long, actually. Rei, Andrew, and Mina had been away from Ichijou for three weeks by the time they got to visit with Mizi and Ore in Kouzanshi. The visit of three days in comparison felt rushed, for all it was good to see them again. Only the fact that they still had another sixty days to get back to Ichijou on this long trip made it so that Rei was willing to move on. Every extra day he took was that much longer he wasn't at Ichijou getting his work done there. Not that this wasn't important. It was, but he really didn't want to be away for so long. And he wanted to be out of Suiran before winter.

Eighteen days from leaving Kouzanshi Rei should be in Nijou to visit with his mother, another thing to be both glad for and wish he could skip at the same time. Anywhere in that time would be when House Tercel might act against him, or at least show up to complain at him in person. He was hoping for nothing worse than the latter. Sasou had told Rei he'd be staying at only garrisons in order to keep him protected. Thus it wasn't a surprise when Rei arrived at one of the central garrisons on North Road to find a request from House Tercel there that he meet with them.

What became a surprise was what happened when Rei arrived to talk to the commander in his office. The second son of Tercel was already there before him. Standing before the garrison commander the son of Tercel handed over "evidence" that Andrew had been treasonous against Touka and demanded that Andrew be stripped of his weapons and rank and be placed into prison. Over Rei's protestations, the commander did as Tercel demanded, for "the sake of Prince Rei's safety". He said that he'd send the evidence to Sasou in Ichijou for corroboration. When they'd heard what the King would do, then Rei, Andrew, and Mina could continue on. Of course, Rei was free to leave Andrew in the prison there until they heard from Ichijou and the matter was resolved.

Rei was absolutely incensed. The time it would take for the messages to travel was over two weeks. So much could happen in that time, and it would add time to his own travel schedule. He demanded that the report be sent to Nijou instead and was refused for reasons he found unacceptable. Instead he was told to write up a report countering the Tercel's accusations that would be sent with Andrew's testimony the next morning.

It didn't help that the next morning when they handed over the report, the second son of Tercel insidiously insinuated that Mina might have aided Andrew in his traitorous acts. Rei put his foot down then, refusing to have both of his royal guards taken from him. As a compromise, the commander "merely" took away Mina's sword, leaving her with her knife and allowing her to stay by Rei's side, agreeing that to have both royal guards gone might be a bit much for the First Prince.

Having argued all he could, Rei finally left the commander's office, fuming and needing to cool off. He and Mina walked the halls until they ran into the young Tercel and his personal guards. Already angry, they were cool to the young man. He didn't help his case by bringing up Yosai and "the blindness of the Durands to the importance of the alliance between the Houses". Mina putting her hand on her knife hilt to get him to shut up and leave Rei alone became the reason for the Tercel guards to have their swords out and pointed at the two of them. That was sufficient legal reason for Mina to actually pull her blade in the defense of her liege.

Rei's heart fell as it became apparent that his own sword would also have to defend the two of them. Her knife was too short and put her into harm's way. He couldn't live with that. His heart cried as his hand pulled his sword out of its sheath. It hurt enough to have his protection and aide in the prison. He hadn't been expecting a full treasonous plot with his own assassination as the goal. He should have known, though. When Sasou said things like, "be prepared," he was never talking about small things. This lesson was one that Rei really could have done without. He hoped he survived it.

-o-o-o-

The tapping knock on Ore's Kouzanshi garrison bedroom window sometime in the very early hours of the night had him awake immediately. It was nightwalker coded for emergency. He was out of bed and slipping the window open, a throwing knife in the palm of his hand. The nightwalker on the other side of the window didn't enter it. He only whispered in the nightwalker's carrying way, "Master Rei's in trouble. Mister Andrew's been framed and imprisoned. Miss Mina's the object, but assassination's the goal."

"Where?" Ore was suddenly in a great panic. He tried to stay aware and focused until he could hear all the important details. He was told which garrison to go to, grateful it wasn't too far for him and Fenrier to get to. "When?" he asked next.

"You might make it in time if you don't stop," he was told. Ore drew in a sharp breath. That would be hard. Fenrier might not make it.

"Can you let the stable know to have Fenrier and a second horse saddled immediately?" he requested.

"Aye," he was answered.

"Ah, anything else I need to know first?"

"House Tercel. Second son's been offered to marry Miss Mina. The father has allies supporting him. Yosai has disapproved and will fall second if the assassination is successful, to force Miss Mina into accepting. There's both loyals and traitors in the garrison. The next garrison over's been called but are moving slow, unsure about the truth of the report."

Ore swore under his breath. "Get someone to explain to Mistress I'm not going to be available for the next week or so, but not so you scare her."

"Yessir," he was answered.

"Off you go." He closed the window and turned to get dressed as fast as he could, not leaving his sword nor Messenger badge behind. He didn't know who that informant had been, but he didn't care. It was likely someone from the House of the Queen of Night since that's the sort of thing they knew and watched.

House Tercel had been one of the difficult Houses by the reports he was receiving from the Suiran garrisons he was assigned to communicate with, so it also wasn't surprising they'd been named. He was quite sure Mina was already very angry with them for the marriage proposal being sent when she'd been making sure her father wasn't sending out requests. Anyone who thought to tell her what to do was sadly already out of the running from the first letter, he was quite sure.

Ore drew in a deep breath as he reached for his door handle. From this time on, he was triggered for anyone to jump him. He listened closely to the hallway, then opened the door and checked the empty hall before leaving the room. He closed the door and locked it behind him, then was running for the window in the room opposite his that was still empty since Rei had left it ten days before. He was out that window and up to the roof, to jump across to the next building, continuing on the roof highway of the Kouzanshi garrison until he reached the cafeteria.

He raided the kitchen for just enough to eat to not have to stop on the road and for a large waterskin. Then it was the run to the stable. He thanked the waiting stablehand who was holding the reins of the two horses he'd requested. He tied Fenrier to the other one's saddle. He'd run until that one couldn't any longer, then leave it behind at the closest garrison.

The run was forgotten as Ore's panic kept him focused on his goal. At sunrise he paused to relieve himself in the trees by a stream, letting the horses drink only enough while he did the same and ate a small amount of food. Then they were running again. By the time the horse was stumbling they were almost to the garrison before the one Ore was headed for. He switched out for Fenrier and the other horse was able to keep up just enough without its burden to get to the garrison stable.

Ore hurriedly gave orders to the stablehands, then ran to the commander's office. There he showed his Messenger badge and ordered for three squadrons to follow him to the next garrison at an emergency run, that Tercel had become traitor. When he gave his name, the commander sat upright with wide eyes. Ore's name had been on enough correspondence now for the commander to know what Ore's responsibilities were. He promised the men and Ore was gone. He pushed Fenrier as hard as he dared, glad that his horse enjoyed running this hard and always gave him everything it could. He hoped he'd not ruin him but for Rei's sake he would regardless.

-o-o-o-

Ore was glad all outlying garrisons were built the same. He was able to get Fenrier hidden in a stall of the stable and himself to the weapons room without anyone calling him out. He pilfered the sword he recognized, then grabbed a second one, angered even more that both aides had been refused to have them. It only proved the report he'd received.

He was headed to the prison next, on the outside first. He sang one of the sea chanteys he knew Andrew knew from their trip around the Inner Sea with Rei before Ore had come up to be with Mizi in Kouzanshi. He walked the outside until he heard tapping from above, the second story. Ore was up the wall and hanging on to the bars in that window. A few judicious raps on the glass with the pommel of the sword he was holding and it shattered.

"Here, you need this," he handed the sword through the bars.

"Thanks," Andrew said. "I'm not running away, though."

"No, you're rescuing your liege and partner. They've taken her sword as well." Ore passed it through to him. Andrew growled low as he received it and recognized it.

Andrew turned suddenly as there was sound from inside his cell. Ore stayed silent and still, then whispered, "That's the nightwalker's code. They're letting you out so you can find Master. I still need to find him. You were easier and needed those more."

Andrew gave a sharp nod, although his eyes stayed on the door. "He's been in the usual room, as far as I know. And I think Mina's been allowed to stay next to him."

"Gotcha," Ore answered. "See you there." He was gone. Andrew was headed for the door that had been unlocked and left behind so the person who'd done it wouldn't be associated with the release.

Ore made sure that Andrew made it out safely and was hidden just enough, then he was gone over the roofs to the wing Rei was most likely in. He wasn't happy to hear there were already the sounds of sword–fighting there when he was close enough to hear it. He took in the situation from the roof as fast as he could, trying to understand who was someone to not just outright kill since he didn't know the whole situation and killing a son of Tercel might be worse than not.

The ruffian attacking Mina, who only had her knife to defend herself and Rei with, was one that Ore could deal with. He ran a little farther down the roof and threw one of his knives. The man was on the ground and Mina was wide–eyed for just a moment. Then she was headed for Rei's side. Her knife caught the blade going for Rei just in time for Rei to step back out of the way of it, but the blade coming from the other side still needed deflecting. Ore was impressed Rei managed to do it without falling down.

"You can't have Mina, Mister Tercel," Rei said coldly to the man on his left. "I've not released her yet, nor do you have approval from her father."

That was the clue Ore needed, but he had to get to where Mina wasn't in the way. He didn't want her to move since she needed to be there to protect the right side of Rei. He dropped down into a dark corner then ran a little farther so he had a perfect back shot of the man that Rei hadn't talked to. His knife hit the back of that man's neck as Mina's knife clanged against the sword headed for Rei again. On her back–stroke the man was on the ground, out of the fight. Now it was just the son of Tercel who was in Ore's sights.

However, now that he was where he could see into the wing behind Rei and Mina, he could see other liveried men with swords headed to add themselves to the fight. He swore softly and saw Rei stiffen slightly. That was Mina's cue to turn around and hold her knife out in their defense. Of the four men Ore could see, the one in the back was suddenly falling to the ground. He'd been in mostly shadow so the lordling hadn't particularly seen that. But when the third one from the back fell, the lordling noticed. He swung against Rei in more desperation this time.

Ore felt his Shicchi blood boil. The next knife he threw landed in the calf of that same despicable lordling. That wasn't death. Only maiming enough that Rei could get repositioned to the side to keep the two still coming for him and the lordling in his sights. He moved to the opposite side of Mina and there was a new sound briefly. Ore smiled hard.

The skittering of metal on stone stopped at Mina's feet and she had her sword in her left hand immediately. The first man to reach her and Rei stopped a little short, then attacked with determination. Perhaps their requirement to the assassination was greater than that of seeing the lordling got a reluctant wife. Ore didn't care, nor did Mina. She fought fiercely with both the sword and the knife, the double clangs reverberating with Andrew's sword marking the off–beat against the final swordsman. Ore kept his eyes on the whole scene, but mostly the injured Tercel, to make sure he didn't decide to act again. That man's eyes were searching the darkness by the wall where Ore was, wanting to know who'd injured him.

Ore didn't move. There were entrances in the wall behind him and he wanted to surprise anyone who came through them. There was also the roof above that he didn't have eyes to watch until the fighting in front of him was done. He wasn't the only nightwalker in the building, and who knew which side any of them were on, save the one that had let Andrew out. And that one could have done it because they wanted to frame him further.

Mina was backing Rei up, keeping him behind her, even while fighting her opponent. Rei moved with her. Ore watched them, then understood that Mina wanted Rei closer to where Ore was hiding so that his back was covered properly. Ore could get that. It was likely okay, but he still worried about people on the roof. They were far enough from the little lordling that Ore chanced looking up. So far it didn't look like there was anyone waiting up on the roof, but that was often deceiving. When they were just close enough for a thrown weapon to hit Rei, Ore whispered, "Run!"

Rei ran to the wall to stand near him. A blade did clatter to the ground in front of Rei, but he'd moved fast enough to now be where the angle was bad for that to work. Mina pressed forward enough to be out of range of said thrown weapons herself. Andrew was by her side shortly thereafter, his blade being one too many for the man to deal with, although his strength had kept Mina working hard until then.

"Go find the roof," Ore was ordered by Rei. He wasn't too keen to leave his master's side, nor to move and give himself away, but Rei moved just enough to draw the attention of the person on the roof so Ore could return to the shadowed underhang. He slipped out the door there and ran to the back of the building. He was up the wall, then taking out the nightwalker assassin with his feet and fists, not having any mercy. No one from the underworld attacked his lord and lived. He ran around the entirety of the courtyard the three were in, making sure that the whole of the roof was clear. Then he paused. Soldiers were coming for the wing from Rei's back.

Ore ran until he was as close to Rei as he could get and whistled the call of the sea birds. Rei, Andrew, and Mina all backed up until they were under Ore, near the doorway he'd gone through. He whispered, "There are traitors in the soldiers of the garrison as well. The next garrison over is sending men, but they're behind me. Being in siege until they get here is best done in the kitchen where we can each defend a door and still eat until they get here. Let them work out who lives."

"Do they know about Tercel?" Rei asked, his voice sharp from the stress of fighting for his life.

"Yes," Ore answered, "and are loyal or I'll kill that commander."

Pft. Mina couldn't help the reaction from her own stress.

"Glad you know," Andrew said dryly. "Let's go then." The sounds of the feet of the coming soldiers could be heard now through the door on that side, and the young Tercel had turned to watch them come. His hand was pressed tightly against the wound in his calf, still bleeding out but not badly.

Ore guarded the door under him until the three on the ground had fled far enough he could run after them towards the kitchens. When they arrived there it was to find it thankfully empty. They barred all the doors with the heavy work tables. Then Ore waved them down into the food cellars. There he made them all pick up and carry food and wine. When they were laden down, he led them to the back of the cellar and a hidden door there. The others stared at him in shock. He only smiled at them and motioned them through it, holding a torch he'd picked up and lit from a lamp in the cellar. Andrew went first, then Mina. Ore followed Rei, closing up the hidden passageway behind him.

"Welcome," Rei said as they walked down the dark earthen tunnel. "Good to have you by my side just in time. What brings you?"

Ore smiled. "The Queen of Night's House. They've been watching over you and let me know it was leave immediately or lose you. I picked the former."

"When?" Andrew asked.

"Early this morning," Ore answered.

The other three stopped walking and stared at him. He shrugged. "You know Fenrier likes to run. I brought two, though, and left one behind."

"Dead?" Rei raised a disbelieving eyebrow at him.

"No, Master," Ore scolded. "I'd not do that to a horse. He was glad to get to stay at the last garrison, though." Mina snorted a laugh and Andrew shook his head in relieved disbelief. Rei waved at them and they got moving again.

A worry frown was on Rei's face that Ore didn't like seeing there, for all he knew it had more than one good reason to be there. "Master," he called quietly. Rei glanced back at him. "It's okay. If the House of the Queen of Night has been watching this come to a boil, and let it, then they already have enough evidence to clear Mister Andrew's name and for you to send to Queen Mother to see House Tercel removed. We only need to keep you alive and they'll help you with the rest."

Mina and Andrew were listening closely to Ore's reassurances. They glanced back at him, each wearing their own worried expressions. Rei considered Ore's words, then let his shoulders slump a little. "Well, I guess I'll trust that for now," Rei said quietly. Ore put his hand lightly on Rei's shoulder, understanding how hard it was for Rei to have not had Andrew by his side, and to fear he'd not have him again. Rei shivered under Ore's hand and he tightened his grip slightly until Rei's feet moved with a little more confidence again.

-o-o-o-

The tunnel let them out into the woods on the mountain side of the garrison. Ore led them up alongside one of the many small mountain streams. They paused briefly to clean wounds and wash sweat from their faces. When the trees thinned to just underbrush and grasses, Ore turned them away from the stream. Another fifteen minutes of walking and the sun was glinting off of glass.

Ore walked them up to the front door of the small cottage and opened the door, bowing them into the house. "Really, Ore, how did you know about this?" Rei demanded to know.

Ore glanced at Mina who looked away. "There are often watch cabins like this above the garrisons," he said. "I got lucky about the escape tunnel at a different time and was relieved to see this one has one as well." He turned Rei to look back down the mountain. They could see the whole of the garrison below them, people milling around the courtyard they'd fled from and soldiers hunting the grounds between there and the other buildings the direction they'd gone to.

"It looks like they haven't discovered the kitchen blocked off just yet," Ore said mildly. "We'll set a rotational watch from here until the next garrison's soldiers arrive and we see how that plays out. When it's safe enough, we'll go back." His heart yearned for his own safety to come and set things right. While she might, it wouldn't be in person. He stood there watching the garrison, not able to do anything but wish for it anyway with all his being.

Mina came and took his food and wine burdens from him so he could be first watch while she, Rei, and Andrew reunited. He could tell Mina wanted to hold Andrew, to know he was still her partner, as much as Rei wanted to sit very close to Andrew for the same reason. He sighed and turned back to his chosen duty. He understood very well, but he was close enough to Rei from here. It was his wife he wanted, for all she wasn't his. He was very grateful this day that she was watching over him and the people he cared about, even from the distance she was standing at.

He was leaning against the frame of the door when Mina walked up behind him. "Ore," she said quietly. He waited for her to find her words. She didn't often say the meaningful ones so had to work up to them. "Thank you." He turned so his back was against the frame and he could see her and the garrison.

He reached out and lightly placed his hand on the top of her head. "I'm just glad that we were able to get to you in time," he said. "Thank you for working hard so we could." He took his hand back as she looked away.

She frowned a bit then said, "My heart cried for you both when they started the attack. It was relieving to have that answered, even if later than I wanted."

Ore smiled a little. "I'm sure it was far more heart–pounding than you wanted it to be. My heart was pounding from the time the nightwalker tapped on my window. I barely remember the run, my heart was so loud in my ears the whole time. Even I'm very glad I made it in time." He looked at her soberly until she could take in a deep breath and let it out. She gave a nod but he didn't let her retreat just yet. "What did you tell them the first time they demanded you give in and become the son's wife?"

Her features went to her chiseled cold face she showed the court and world. "Not unless I was a dead corpse."

Ore smiled. "Ah, so that's why they were okay with going through you to get to Master." He couldn't keep the laughter out of his voice. "It didn't matter if you lived or died, they'd get what they wanted in the end regardless."

Mina snorted and rolled her eyes. They both knew she'd been more politic than that, and that she and Rei had only survived because they hadn't wanted to hurt her any more than necessary. Still, Ore understood her need to vent. Mina hesitated a little more, then asked, "Is the Queen of Night really going to have the evidence necessary to resolve this? Do you really know her that well?"

Ore nodded, confident. "I was sent to Kouzanshi to learn everything about her and her House for the Marquis. That's been my research. I'm quite sure. If it doesn't happen that way, shall I go scold her for you?"

"Yes," Mina's lips pursed tightly together.

Ore gave her a promise nod. She continued to stare into Ore's eyes until she could believe it enough to turn and gesture to the scene below them with her head. "Where are they at this point?"

Ore looked back down the mountain again. "They've found the kitchen blocked off and are trying to figure out what's next. It looked like the traitorous set had a conference after that. I've not seen them head up this way yet, but," he pointed into the distance towards the west. Mina narrowed her eyes to see the farther part of the countryside. She shifted into a more firm stance as her eyes saw the fast moving horses carrying the soldiers. "I think they'll get to the garrison before more than a small handful can sneak out of the garrison. If we pick them off in the forest when they get closer, thinking we're inside, then no one can complain that they've run away instead of be imprisoned for being traitors?"

Rei was by their side, looking out at the scene now as well. He nodded. "We can do that," he agreed. "Is it better to stay up here after that or make our way back down then?"

Ore looked back at the garrison. "I'd still rather watch them from here. Some of the traitors will be in the group trying to get into the kitchen, trying to be first in case we didn't know about the tunnel so they can claim we died of wounds before they could get in to save us. I'd like that set taken into custody before we show back up." He looked up at the sky, then said, "And I'd prefer to have someone I trust give us the sign it's safe to go back before we do. I don't know if we'll get that sign, though. We may have to guess based on what we see them do."

"Do we *have* to go back?" Mina asked sourly.

"Well, yes," Ore said as Rei also answered in the affirmative. "We can't clear anyone's name if we don't." He looked at the three others gathered at the door with a twinkle in his eyes. "Although, we could just show up at Nijou and make a fuss, making them come there to defend themselves after the fact. If the House does them in on the way to the castle, I won't complain."

"Ore," Rei was exasperated. "Not like they need to get their hands that dirty. How would that be any proof at all of the traitorous deeds of the Tercels?"

"Our word against theirs, and they can't defend themselves to say it was a lie?" Ore answered, but he was still teasing. He relented at Rei's sigh at him, letting Rei decide what he wanted to do. The Queen Mother wouldn't be merciful to anyone that threatened her son this much, and he'd be willing to be her blade for the same reason. He didn't think Rei would let him go any farther east than this, though. He was still to be with Mizi for now.

-o-o-o-

Ore stayed close to Rei's side once they were back in the garrison again, not trusting anyone and needing to know that if his master was attacked again, his own person could be there first. He hadn't been wrong about the House of the Queen of Night. As soon as things calmed down, Rei was invited into an office. There, one of the squadron heads from the next garrison west was waiting with two others. One was a junior staff member from the garrison they were in and the other was a servant of the Tercels. They told Rei everything he needed to know. While he worked on a summary report to send to his mother and brother, the two witnesses, Ore, and Mina worked on writing down their witnesses to send with it.

Andrew was released by the squadron head and the garrison commander was put in his cell instead, making both Ore and Mina happily vindicated. The squadron head requested that Andrew also write his defense. Having his written statement might help him stay by Rei's side instead of being called early to Nijou for the hearing. Once Andrew's statement was written, the partners stayed close by each other on the wall in the office. It still took them half of the afternoon to finally relax enough to pay more attention to anything other than each other. Ore understood.

-o-o-o-

It was early the next morning when a junior guard came into the office and gave a report to the acting commander. Rei was staying in the office generally when he was awake because it was one of the few places he felt safe — as long as it was the trustworthy person using it. "The medics have arrived from Kouzanshi to see to the wounded. I've taken them directly to the infirmary first. Do you want one escorted to the prison to see to the son of Lord Tercel?"

The commander pursed his lips, but Rei rose to his feet first. "He should be tended to by them, yes, but I'll go." Ore's eyes widened, but he couldn't be surprised too much. Rei was like that. Rei did turn back to Andrew and Mina, though. "You don't have to come. Ore will be enough."

Andrew looked into Mina's eyes. Ore could tell she'd say not to go just because she didn't want to have to see the bastard, but she let Andrew decide. Andrew was the kind to silently face his false accuser without fear or accusation, but he studied Rei first. "Do you want to see what he'll say?" he asked quietly. Rei hesitated, then gave a nod. Ore blinked. He was rather sure that was learned from the time he'd been the one in prison and refused to speak with the aides present.

Andrew and Mina followed them out of the office and to the prison, but stayed outside that hallway door, waiting for them there. Ore followed Rei into the hallway but stayed the silent shadow, working hard to not be menacing. The prince talked to the lordling but was in the main rebuffed. He'd still pay the price to follow in his father's footsteps. Ore knew Rei was saddened by the decision but he wouldn't force the young man.

The door clicked open and allowed two persons into the hall. Ore turned to look and froze. The green eyes looking into his were just as surprised to see him, although Mizi obviously knew Rei was in the hallway since Andrew had let her into it. "Ah, Ore?!"

Ore bowed, his hand over his heart. "Mistress. I was called for."

"And are you alright?"

"Yes," he answered. "I arrived just in time to keep all of us so."

Mizi relaxed. "That's good," she said. Her eyes turned to look at Rei, who was staring at her in shock. "And you?"

"Fine," Rei answered rather automatically. "A few scratches, and a heart that panicked a bit, but otherwise I'm okay."

"That's good," Mizi answered then moved towards the cell Rei was standing in front of, her medical kit clutched tightly in her hand. The junior guard followed her in, a key in hand.

The young Tercel glared at Rei from the floor where he was sitting. Rei just looked mildly back. Mizi looked through the bars when she reached the cell. "I'm a healer from Kouzanshi," Mizi introduced herself. "We were asked to come tend to the wounded here. That looks painful. I'd like to come in and make sure it won't become worse with infection, if you'll allow it."

The young man scowled. "And what will I have to give up to see it tended to?"

"Ah...," Mizi blinked, then looked at Rei.

Rei blinked back at her, then answered the young man, "Nothing, save a little pride, perhaps?" He stepped out of the way and waved Ore over. The guard unlocked the door but the little Tercel looked at them even more suspiciously as Ore arrived close to the group and put his hand lightly on Mizi's shoulder to make her wait a bit.

Mizi looked up at him in surprise. Then she understood. "Oh." She looked at the young man. "Ore's been my guard for a while now. He'll feel better if he can watch at least, since I guess they don't trust you yet. I promise, I'll just tend to the wound and leave."

The young lord gave her an odd look, but finally nodded at her. The look he gave Ore said that if he did anything untrustworthy he'd see him in hell. Ore ignored it. He entered the cell first, then stood where he could get to the young man if he tried anything. They all watched while Mizi did her usual industrious but fine job of tending to the wound Ore had given him in his calf. It had been cleaned and bound sufficiently before, but Mizi pulled out the herbs it would need to heal properly and ground them. Ore itched to help her a little bit, but refused as he was the guard for real this time.

When the wound was bound again and they were out of the cell, to the relief of both Ore and Rei, Mizi turned to the soldier who was locking it again. "I'll be here for about five days, based on how many are wounded.

I'd like to come and tend to that twice a day while I'm here. After that, it should heal sufficiently on it's own if it stays uninfected." The soldier gave her a nod.

She turned to the young Tercel. "You should start flexing it gently tomorrow, but not today yet, to keep the muscle and skin properly flexible. The day after that you can try standing gently on it, but walking may have to be with crutches for a while. Don't overstress it, but also don't be too gentle with it or you'll limp the rest of your life. Rest when it just starts to ache. Warm cloths will help the aching."

Mizi bowed to Rei. "I'll return to the infirmary now. Ryan's there also." Rei let her go with the soldier and surprisingly didn't send Ore with her, but Ore was in the hallway to watch over Rei this time.

When they finally walked out of the hallway, they kept going, picking up Andrew and Mina. Once they were out of the prison, Andrew said, "That was surprising, wasn't it?" Ore and Rei both agreed.

It was no surprise that Rei took them to the infirmary next. His face fell when he saw just how many injuries were there. He walked through the injured, talking to those who didn't look at him with expressions of anger or coolness. A number of those he talked to were very apologetic that they'd allowed him to be attacked in their garrison. Given they could be punished for it by his mother, it wasn't a surprising thing for them to worry over, but Ore noticed that many of them were sad, rather than afraid.

They heard a laugh from Mizi over where she was working with a patient. The patient was laughing with her, joking with her. Rei smiled. "Even the soldiers want to see her smile," Ore said quietly. Rei agreed with some satisfaction.

He stayed in the room talking to soldiers until Mizi and Ryan had finished visiting with all of the injured. Then he took them aside, into the alcove where the medics would write up reports at the table there. "When you've written up your medical reports, I'd like to review them. I'd like to write up commendations for those who stood in my defense and understand what happened better."

"Of course, Rei," Mizi answered immediately. "I'll see you get a copy of them. Do you want to review their initial records, too?"

"Yes, please," Rei asked humbly. "When can I come back to do that?"

She looked at Ryan, then asked, "Maybe in," she glanced over her shoulder at the filled room behind her, "a couple of hours?"

Rei smiled. "I'll come interrupt you and remind you that you also need to eat lunch, then."

Mizi giggled and Ryan looked scolded already. Ore smiled. "That would be necessary generally, yes," he agreed.

Rei hesitated, then asked, "How were you informed to come?"

Mizi frowned. "Shiotsu had a visitor come that was very anxious. He immediately assigned Ryan and I to come as fast as we could. We've brought two others, but they're in the kitchen, working on the tinctures the wounded will need to take daily. The garrison medic is with them helping there since that's an even larger job that what we're doing here. He'll need a few assistants when we go, though, so if a couple who don't have other pressing work to do could be assigned to come help us while we're here, they might be able to keep up with all the work of the final recovery."

"I'll pass on the request," Rei promised.

When he left, he told Ore to stay and watch over Mizi, using his eyes to indicate he didn't trust the ones still in the room that technically should also be in the prison. Ore followed him out the door, closing it behind them. Rei looked at him quizzically. "Master, while I agree with you, that the untrustworthy in the room should be watched, I don't think it should be me."

Rei glared at him a bit, but Ore shook his head. "If the substitute commander hasn't removed them already to the prison then there isn't enough evidence to convict them. I'll come watch over Mistress in the evening after dinner, to remind her to go to bed instead of work herself to death. Have the junior staff member that's part of the House of the Queen of Night select soldiers to watch over the room during the day. They'll collect the final evidence and keep Mistress safe."

Rei considered it, then asked a different question. "Do you think it was a member of that House that let Shiotsu know to send them?"

"I do," Ore answered. "And likely at the same time as they were telling me. It's quite likely Mistress hasn't slept for two nights already. Her hands were unsteady by the final patients and likely her report will be written sloppily and she'll sleep on her food at dinner."

He gave Rei a significant look. "It would be good if Master could convince her to go on a brief walk after dinner to help her fall asleep on his shoulder. Your arm around her will help her finally understand you and we are safe and she can rest properly, without fear and worry." Rei's eyes went wide. Ore soberly added, "Likely it was as much a shock to see Andrew and Mina in the prison and the two of us inside as it was for us to see her. They didn't tell her we'd be here. She's been struggling since then, I think. It was good the soldiers saw it enough to help her laugh."

Rei slumped in understanding. Ore rather thought he'd need it as well, to touch Mizi enough to let out his own fear and stress from the event, to reassure himself he was still alive and well. "Go stay with her until we can get other soldiers in there to watch the room. It might be until dinner today, since the temporary commander's still working on the duty roster generally, trying to work out who's left that's useable." His blue eyes came to look Ore in the eye. "We'll come for the three of you to eat both lunch and dinner together. Don't let her make excuses to stay."

Ore smiled. "I won't. I've learned very well in the last year how get her to move, particularly when she's so tired and can't get her arguments to keep up with mine." Rei chuckled and Ore felt a little better. He gave Andrew and Mina looks that scolded them silently to pay attention and keep Rei safe. They gave him promise nods and he returned to the infirmary to stand quietly in a space where he could keep an eye on them all and an ear on the space outside of it in case he should be called to Rei's side again.

-o-o-o-

When Rei, Andrew, and Mina returned to the infirmary, Ore hadn't been wrong. Mizi had been sleeping on the bench in the alcove for twenty minutes by then, Ryan for a half–hour on the other one. Ore put his finger to his lips as Rei looked with compassion at the two. "Should we not wake them for lunch?"

Ore shook his head. "Go review what you want to see, then wake them up. They'll do better for having had the short nap, but need the better rest of sleeping in beds tonight after a good warm meal fills their bellies.

Mina glared at Ore. "And will you finally sleep tonight, too?"

Ore looked at her wide–eyed. Rei looked at him suspiciously. "Did you also stay up all night to keep watch over me?"

Ore shrugged, not liking being called out by Mina. "Not like I ever sleep much anyway." In the face of three scowls, he relented. "I'll sleep tonight... in Master's room."

Rei's scowl didn't change, but Andrew and Mina were almost in concert agreement with Ore this time. They weren't ready for him to be so unprotected in this place either. Ore's eyes pinned them both. "And I'm not ready yet for you two to not be protecting each other either. You both can't stand outside Master's door tonight. Go requisition three double rooms. They can think Miss Mina will stay with Mistress and Mister Andrew with Ryan."

Rei took a minute to work that out. With a bit of a confused wrinkle on his brow he asked, "You'd put Mizi and Ryan together in a room?"

Ore shrugged. "They won't even notice until morning and then I can tell them I made them go to sleep. It happens often when they get focused and fall asleep in the department without even going home first."

"Ore!" Rei scolded. "You let them sleep on the floor there?"

Ore laughed at him. "You missed seeing all the cushioned chairs and infirmary beds, Master. When the researchers can't even leave the work for being so focused, they'll sleep anywhere once they reach 'working while sleeping'. Mistress has relaxed quite a lot since coming to Kouzanshi. They'll be glad they woke up in beds at all this time, tomorrow. The next night it can be a girl's room and a boy's room." Rei relented and sent Andrew and Mina back to make the room changes.

Ore watched over the room a little longer, until Rei was done with reading through the medical records. Ore noted he wrote down notes for each person. When that work was done, the paper was folded and put into Rei's jacket. He rose and went to Mizi. Lightly his finger brushed the hair out of her face. The look he gave her was one Ore was intimately familiar with. The pained desire made Ore look away. He fought with jealousy for a bit. At least Rei could touch and be with his beloved for even this brief time.

The memory of warm arms around his wounded but bound chest and tearful pleas to stay alive returned to him. He closed his eyes and remembered that warmth. She'd come and saved him at his most fearful point of living or death. His hand lightly touched the place of the scar as Rei's voice softly called Mizi to wakefulness. Ilena's voice would call to him when it was time, when they could also be together again without fear.

"Ore?" the soft voice of his master at his elbow startled Ore. He turned to look into the blue eyes. "I'm letting her wake Ryan," Rei explained then asked, "Are you okay?"

"I guess I'm tired, too," he admitted, not willing to admit to the other.

"I guess I might have to make you take a nap next, then," Rei said dryly. Ore wasn't interested but didn't answer.

That evening, when Rei collected Mizi and Ryan again for dinner, they all walked tiredly to the cafeteria. They collected their food with thanks to the chefs. Mizi and Ryan led them to sit with the other medics from Kouzanshi so they could share reports of their day. Rei let them know that two assistants would arrive in the infirmary in the morning and two in the kitchen so they could be trained so that the one garrison medic wouldn't have to be in two places at once. That relieved all of the Kouzanshi medics.

"Ah!" Mizi sat upright. "What about tonight?"

Rei put his hand firmly on her forearm and just as firmly said, "Soldiers have been assigned for the night shift already as well. If there's an emergency they'll call for one of you, but the injured are already past the point of most danger, by your own report, so you'll all sleep tonight." He glared at her until she relented humbly, then he glared at the rest of the medics. They gave him nods, grateful for the order to rest.

After dinner Andrew and Mina led them to where their rooms were for the night. Rei was relieved that the other two medics were also a female and male pairing so Ryan and Mizi could properly room with a member of the same gender. Rei still asked for time with Mizi, apologizing for keeping her awake longer.

She acquiesced and went to the quiet kitchen garden with him. Ore, Andrew, and Mina stayed far enough away to let them have privacy while keeping the area protected. Ore listened to the sounds of them quietly talking.

He lifted his face to the sky, grateful that he could be alive with them at this time. Hearing Mizi laugh gently helped his heart to not be so heavy as well.

-o-o-o-

"Don't let that happen again, Master," Ore said as seriously as he ever got. "I don't think I can get to you in time again, given you're going farther from me than even here."

Rei drew in a breath and gave a nod. "That's the only one Sasou warned me about, but we won't let our guard down." Mina and Andrew firmly agreed. While they had a lot to learn about what to do to know ahead of time something like this was going to happen and what to do to prevent it, they were determined to make sure they learned it as fast as possible.

It was five days later. Mizi and Ryan had declared the wounded past the time they needed to stay. Rei had used the excuse of interrogating soldiers and monitoring the investigation to stay with her, but he'd already stayed too long. The guards understood why he'd done it, though.

Mizi looked with some worry at Rei. He put his hand on top of her head. "Thank you for coming to help the soldiers. Be safe." Mizi curtsied to him, but then caught his hand as it fell to his side. She squeezed it and he returned the same, then reluctantly let her go. She climbed into the carriage, the last of the four medics to enter it, and the footman closed the door.

Rei glared at Ore, sitting on Fenrier, not able to say what he really wanted to say, nor do what he really wanted to do. Ore gave him a jaunty salute to jolly Rei out of it, going back to sober as he looked Mina then Andrew in the eyes. "Call for any of the House of the Queen of Night if something like this happens again. I don't think it should, given what I know, but I don't know everything." They gave him nods, then he and the carriage were leaving the garrison.

Rei sighed after them, then turned for his own horse, climbing on the white gelding. "Let's go. I'm sure I'll have lots of defending of all three of us to do to Mother when we get to Nijou in nine days. And not just for being late." None of them were looking forward to that. He frowned for the next several hundred feet, then scowled. "I think I'll scold her right back and complain that neither of them have taught us what to do when things like that happen. There were obviously things we could have done beforehand to protect us all better, but I can't even think of what they are!" He pouted for the first half of the morning.

When he'd recovered enough, Mina rode up next to him and looked him in the eye soberly. Once again she said, "I'm sorry, Rei."

Rei looked her in the eyes just as soberly, then finally shook his head. "They wanted more than Yosai, Mina. From the beginning they'd planned on making it my assassination. It's already well known I won't give you up yet and you won't take a husband. I gave it to Sasou because of Ore's reports to me from the information he was getting from the House of the Queen of Night." He scowled a little again. "I'm not happy he sent me up to trip the trap without teaching us what to do first. That will be my first scold to him when we get back." He went back to introspective. That was better than where he'd been before, so Mina fell back to her position half-way back from his front and across from Andrew.

Andrew gave her a soft knowing look. She hurt for him almost more. Sasou was likely to punish him most for not being the one to teach Rei what Rei wanted to know. Andrew fell back just a little so Mina fell back to walk her horse next to him. They leaned towards each other and Andrew whispered in her ear, "The King wanted him to learn this lesson. It was very hard to let it happen." They sat back up and Mina stared at him in shock. Andrew wasn't happy at all.

"*You knew?*" she mouthed at him. Andrew gave one small nod. Mina slumped then put her hand on his knee for a moment. That had to be the hardest position to be in of all, to watch your partner and charge both be put at real risk to their lives and hope that whatever promise of rescue had been given would really happen. Particularly when very little was known about the Queen of Night, her House, and the King didn't and couldn't direct them. If that had been a test of the House, they'd passed it, but Mina wasn't going to forgive Sasou for a while, either. That had nearly gone too far. She'd almost not kept Rei defended twice. Only Ore's knives had saved them at all. She shivered then moved back up to her position. That lesson would never be forgotten by any of them, ever.

www.ingramcontent.com/pod-product-compliance
Lightning Source LLC
Chambersburg PA
CBHW060901210726
48293CB00006B/1906